John Milton
The first four stories

One Thousand Yards
The Cleaner
Saint Death
The Driver

Mark Dawson

AN UNPUTDOWNABLE ebook.
First published in Great Britain in 2013 by UNPUTDOWNABLE LIMITED
Ebook first published in 2013 by UNPUTDOWNABLE LIMITED
This book published in 2017 by UNPUTDOWNABLE LIMITED
Copyright © UNPUTDOWNABLE LIMITED 2013-2017

Formatting by Polgarus Studio

To Mrs D, FD and SD.

One Thousand Yards

A John Milton Novella

Mark Dawson

THREE HOURS *into the flight and he realised he was about to have the dream again. The cabin was quiet: meals cleared, drinks served, lights dimmed. Just the steady drone of the engines. The other passengers were relaxing, some of them beginning to sleep. He reached for his gin and put it to his lips. His hand shook; the ice cubes rattled against the side of the glass.*

It did not come often now. He had made it that way, with the force of his will, yet on those occasions when the dream did overcome him, it came with all its old strength and vigour. He knew the signs: that familiar feeling of being hollowed out, an empty vessel into which it would pour. Fatigue weakened his defences, and he had not slept for two days. He squeezed his eyes shut and gripped the armrests so tightly that his knuckles whitened. His shoulders locked, and the muscles behind his knees and in his calves tightened. He sagged back into the seat, trying to breathe normally but knowing that he was gulping each breath. He was helpless, impotent, and paralysed.

Trapped.

He squeezed his eyes tighter, so hard that tiny pinprick explosions of red and yellow light cascaded against his lids. The dream raced towards him like the pitch- black mouth of a tunnel, inexorable and unavoidable, and suddenly he was plunged into it. It was as vivid as reality. As it started to unspool, like a familiar film he tried to hide away in a dusty box, his rational mind was able to observe and assess it, to compare it with the past, and to acknowledge that he was far from cured.

The desert.
The village.
The madrasa.
The children.
The cheap plastic football swerving in the wind.
The young boy.
The plane coming in fast and low; the roar of its engines echoing through the valley.

From: <redacted>
To: <redacted>
Date: Monday, February 14, 5.55 P.M.
Subject: DPRK

Dear Foreign Secretary,

The P.M. asked for further information on last month's attacks. I therefore attach a report originated by STRATFOR, which apparently confirms what we suspected to be true. I note that our American friends have reached the same conclusion, and that they share our frustration at the impunity with which the DPRK is acting in this regard. They concur with us that the time has come to let them know that there is a red line beyond which they must not cross, and that consequences will flow if they do. I know that the ambassador has reported these sentiments to you.

If there is any follow-up once the P.M. has considered this intelligence, please do, as ever, let me know.

Sincerely,

M.

>>> BEGINS

* * * EYES ONLY * * *

PUBLICATION: analysis/background
ATTRIBUTION: STRATFOR
SOURCE DESCRIPTION: North Korean diplomat
SOURCE Reliability: B
ITEM CREDIBILITY: 2
DISTRIBUTION: Alpha
SOURCE HANDLER: Reva

DPRK sources suggest last month's massive cyber-attack on banks and media companies throughout SK and the West was planned and executed in Pyongyang. SK Banks, including Shinhan, NongHyup and Jeju, together with TV broadcasters KBS, MBC and YTN were all taken offline as code affected circa 48k PCs on their networks. Evidence indicates the attack originated with DPRK's General Reconnaissance Bureau/Military Intelligence Division. The attack spread "wiper" malware—named Jokra—that deleted the master boot records from PCs and attempted to delete volumes from Unix/Linux servers. This resembles previous DPRK hacking patterns. S.K. Ministry of Science, Information, Computer Technology and Future Planning (MSICTFP) confirms validity of evidence and hypothesis.

ENDS <<<

From: <redacted>
To: <redacted>
Date: Tuesday, February 15, 4.25 P.M.
Subject: DPRK

My dear M.,

The P.M. thanks you for your prompt response to his query. He has discussed the issue at high level (including, I believe, with POTUS), and given the excellent assets that you have secured within the DPRK, approval has been given for you to investigate whether there is something that we might do to give them a bloody nose. This latest attack follows the endless posturing with their missiles and the attacks on S.K. assets, and as I indicated in my previous email, it has long since reached the point where something must be done. US assistance is available if you deem it necessary, but knowing you as I do, I suspect that you will want to make a demonstration of our effectiveness when working alone. (I can also report the P.M.'s support for that sentiment.)

I wonder whether this might be something for our mutual friend? This is, of course, eyes only.

My regards to you and your wife,

Morgan

From: <redacted>
To: <redacted>
Date: Tuesday, February 15, 4.50 P.M.
Subject: FWD: DPRK

Dear Control,

I forward the email that I received from the Foreign Secretary yesterday. We have a cell of three indigenous agents active within the DPRK, and while we have no reason to believe that the Politburo is aware of their existence, they are not equipped with either the training or the materiél to mount the kind of operation (which you might charitably describe as audacious) that is currently on the table. Group Fifteen, on the other hand, does not have those problems. You have been tasked with considering whether it is practical to work with our assets in the DPRK in this regard, possibly involving an agent from the Group. How practical would it be for you to insert one?

Regards, etc.,

M.

From: \<redacted>
To: \<redacted>
Date: Wednesday, February 16, 3.42 P.M.
Subject: DPRK

Dear M.,

I have given consideration to your request. It can be done, and I attach a way in which it might be carried out. You are right to describe it as audacious; as you well know, the DPRK is the most difficult state on Earth within which an enemy operative may operate. I am confident, however, that this plan will deliver an agent into the country, and once there, the man I have in mind will have a fighting chance of giving the generals the black eye the P.M. intends.

I wait for confirmation that the course that we have suggested has been approved.

Best regards,

Control

\<attachment redacted>

From: \<redacted>
To: \<redacted>
Date: Friday, February 18, 3.42 P.M.
Subject: DPRK

Dear Control,

We have confirmation from both the P.M. and Washington. The plan that you outline (including assistance from assets in the south of the PRC) is approved. Of course, the existence of this plan—and of your operative, should he be compromised—will be denied should it ever come to light. Standard operating procedure in that regard.

You are on your own: there will be no further correspondence on this matter.

Good hunting.

Regards,

M.

Chapter One

"SIR—are you all right?"

John Milton heard the woman's voice and prised open his eyes. He was feverish with sweat.

A pretty stewardess in a red Air China uniform was peering down at him, concern on her face.

"Sir?"

Milton looked to his right. The passenger on the other side of the aisle was looking at him anxiously. "Sorry—"

"Is everything all right, sir?"

"Yes." He wiped the sweat from his eyes with the back of his hand. "It's fine. I'm a bad flyer. Must've been the sleeping pills. Really, I'm fine."

He took out a handkerchief and wiped his forehead dry. His breathing returned to normal, and his muscles loosened and relaxed. "Where are we?"

"We've landed," she said, with a sunny, surprised smile.

"Already?"

"Welcome to Pyongyang."

Milton sat quietly for a moment, letting consciousness slowly return. How long had he been out? He remembered eating the tasteless meal, then a drink as he watched them cut across the clouds, and then … and then, he couldn't remember. An hour? Two hours? He had thought that he had mastered the blackouts, that he had forced them away, but this was the third time in a week. There had been one in London and then another in his hotel room in Beijing. He couldn't ignore it any longer. They were getting worse, and for a man in his particular line of work, that was a very bad thing indeed.

He concentrated on putting his worries aside. This was no time to be weak. He waited patiently for the queue of passengers to disperse, and then, after grabbing his carry-on luggage from the overhead locker, he disembarked, a little unsteadily, descending the flight of stairs fixed to the back of a pickup truck that had been parked up against the fuselage of the Air China 737.

He stepped down onto the tarmac of Pyongyang Sunan International Airport.

It was an unseasonably cold spring afternoon, and the wind carried in great gusts of icy rain. There was no bus to transfer them to the terminal, and the walk was unpleasant. Milton was hatless, holding a copy of the Chicago *Herald-Tribune* over his head, the other gripping the handle of his bag. The newspaper was quickly sodden. He set his jaw to the cutting wind; there was nothing to be done to prevent it whipping between the folds of his jacket, and it did not take long for him to feel cold to the bone.

Welcome to North Korea, he thought. *How I've missed you.*

Chapter Two

HE KNEW that he would be photographed as he crossed the tarmac, and he was. There was an office with wide windows overlooking the taxiway. It was occupied by the Ministry for the Protection of State Security, a sprawling organisation which had been modelled upon—and developed with the willing assistance of—the Soviet KGB. The operative in position today toted a Canon digital camera with a powerful telephoto lens. His duty was to capture pictures of every passenger who disembarked from a foreign flight.

Milton's photo was already being uploaded to the Directorate as he passed through the double doors into the arrivals lounge. To describe the facility as "international" was to be generous: apart from the flights to and from Beijing, the national carrier—Air Koryo—was responsible for the only other flights. Milton glanced up at the departures board and saw international flights to Bangkok, Khabarovsk, Kuala Lumpur, Moscow, Shanghai and Vladivostok. Indeed, "lounge" was also somewhat of a misnomer: the wide space was equipped with a handful of hard metal benches, its whole purpose to funnel travellers towards the customs and security officials with the minimum of fuss. It was the absences that really struck home: no advertising of any sort, no planes coming and going, no duty-free.

The lounge was not much warmer than its exterior, but Milton took the opportunity to unbutton his overcoat and wipe some of the water from his face. His fellow travellers obediently took their place in line and waited to be called forwards to the kiosks. Milton cast his eye over them once again. There was a group of four European tourists and a number of Koreans returning home. Most were Chinese businessmen, sanctions-busters arranging deals to bring luxury goods into the country for the benefit of the ruling elite. That was what Milton was here to do, too; at least that was what he wanted them to think.

The queue shuffled forwards. The Chinese were processed quickly and with good manners. The Europeans took a little longer. Milton took out his smartphone and thumbed it to life. It picked up the Koryolink telephony network, but there was no mobile internet, and there would be none for so long as he was in the country. He switched it off and put it back into his pocket.

Eventually, he was beckoned forwards by a curt and officious-looking man.

"Your bag," the man said, nodding his chin at the X-ray machine.

Milton laid it on the belt.

"Coat, belt and shoes."

Milton managed to smile as he did what he was instructed; it was the patient and forbearing smile of a man who was used to these ministrations. His name, for the purposes of this trip, was Peter McEwan. The bag slid through the machine, pausing within it as an official studied the monitor that was displaying the X-ray. Milton knew that what he saw, or did not see, in the image would have no bearing on what happened next, and in that, he was right. There were three other officials standing at the end of the belt. Milton knew that they were from the MPSS, and he was not surprised when one of them stepped forwards to haul his case from the belt.

"Your passport, please," said the immigration official.

"Certainly." Milton handed the passport to him as he watched the MPSS man open the case and start to remove the contents.

The man thumbed through the pages. "Mr McEwan."

"That's right."

"You are well travelled."

The passport was stamped with two dozen different destinations: South American banana republics, tinpot African dictatorships, trips to Russia and China. There were a dozen trips to the DPRK, all in the last six months.

"I'm a businessman," Milton replied, trying to find the easy confidence that he imagined would be McEwan's stock-in-trade. He pointed at the MPSS man who was rifling through his things. "I don't understand. What's he doing? My papers are all in order, aren't they? I have a visa from the Ministry of Trade."

The official did not answer him. He handed the passport back to the security officer, who made a similar show of its careful study. Milton smiled again with good-natured patience, but the other passengers had already been cleared to proceed, and the last of them were disappearing towards the exit. He had been in these situations many times before, but there were not many places in the world that were like this. Despite the reassurance of his experience and training, it was difficult not to feel exposed. He felt an empty sensation in his stomach. The remnants of the dream made it worse.

The MPSS man beckoned him to approach. He had the deep pits of acne scars across his face, and he wore a cheap suit that was too big for his slight frame. Milton could tell his type from the way he bore himself: he knew that he wielded a small amount of power, and he was pleased that it gave him the ability to tell arrogant Europeans what to do.

"Mr McEwan."

"Yes, sir."

"What is the purpose of your visit to the DPRK?"

"I was telling your colleague over there—I'm a businessman."

"And what is your business?"

"I sell cars."

He sneered a little. "Why would my country need your Western cars?"

"These are luxury cars."

"You think we cannot make such cars?"

"You don't have any like these."

"I doubt that very much. Why are you here today?"

Milton sighed, a show of the mildest irritation. "A consignment is presently making its way south from China. Eight cars on a trailer. They crossed the border at Sinuiju yesterday. I'm here to make sure that the cars reach the correct customers. What's this all about, sir? It isn't as if I've never been to Pyongyang before."

"This is very true," the man said, his eyes on the passport as he flicked through its pages. "You are a frequent visitor. Very unusual for a European."

"Yes, I've been here several times."

"And you are English, yes?"

Milton manufactured a little impatience. "Yes, as you can see. What's your point?"

"You are sweating, Mr McEwan. You look unwell."

"I'm a bad flyer. I took some pills to help me sleep—I don't think they agreed with me."

"No, you are defensive, too. Why is this?"

"Because my business here is important, and this delay will affect my schedule if it goes on much longer." He paused and then added, "I'm sorry, but my customers do not take kindly to being inconvenienced. Party officials, you understand? The longer I'm wasting my time with you, the less time I have to distribute my cars to the members of the Politburo who have purchased them. And I don't know about you, sir, but I would rather not keep those men waiting."

The threat was obvious. The man considered it, and after another lengthy pause obviously designed to make Milton feel uncomfortable, he relented.

"You are free to proceed, Mr McEwan. Please enjoy your visit to our country."

The passport was returned to him, but his luggage, he noted, was not repacked. Just a petulant reminder that these men had power, he knew, and nothing that need concern him. He folded his clothes and placed them neatly back into the case. He gripped the handle and pulled the case from the desk. He smiled with polite solicitude at the man and wheeled the case away, making his way to the main concourse, where he knew he would be able to pick up a taxi. He did not need to look back to know that the MPSS officials would be watching, and neither did he need to see the additional man with the camera to know that even more pictures were being taken.

A report would be filed and passed up to the relevant department: the Englishman Peter McEwan had entered the country at ten minutes past five in the afternoon; he was in the export business, defying the United Nations' sanctions to deliver high-performance luxury cars to party officials; he was a frequent visitor; and while that did not mean that he would be allowed to go about his business unchaperoned, it did not warrant the perpetual minder that would have been necessary if he were a tourist or someone of whom there was no official history.

Milton wheeled his suitcase out of the terminal and into the bitter cold. What little warmth he had been able to recover as he had been interrogated was soon a distant memory.

Chapter Three

MAJOR KIM Shin-Jo replaced the receiver of the telephone that linked him with the officers in the airport. He double-clicked on the file that had just been emailed to him, and a series of .jpg files were unpacked. He selected one and opened it: a picture of a man filled the screen. He was at the security checkpoint, the X-ray machine visible over his right shoulder. He looked a little over average height for a Westerner—six foot perhaps—and Kim would have estimated his age at somewhere in his late thirties. His hair was black, and his eyes were blue. He was wearing jeans and a turtleneck jumper, a jacket folded over his right arm. European. A patient expression. It was just one of dozens of photographs that had been taken. Kim had privates all across the airport: there was the man who scanned the runway, another two in the concourse, another in the exit lounge. They were his eyes and ears.

Kim was assistant security chief at the Pyongyang Sunan International Airport, responsible for a team of thirty officers. They were placed within the 7th Department of the 2nd Chief Directorate, the section of the Ministry of State Security responsible for operations against tourists.

Kim was not having a good day. Not good at all. He was on edge, a nervousness that it seemed he shared with the entire department. The final preparations to ensure the security of the grand parade were underway, an enormous amount of work that needed to be done and barely enough time to do it all in. The 7th Department was responsible for ensuring that all foreign visitors inside the borders of the DPRK were double and then triple checked. No one thought it was likely that the imperialists or their puppets from the south would attempt an operation on the centenary of the Great Leader's birthday, but the *dictat* from the top was absolutely clear: no chances were to be taken. The eyes of the world would be watching, and national prestige was at stake. Kim had spoken with the colonel as he came on shift this morning, and the man had been absolutely clear. The consequences for failure—any failure, no matter how seemingly insignificant—had been made starkly obvious: there would be a quick trial and then a lifetime spent in the gulag.

Kim had visited the gulag. He had sent enemies of the state there.

The prospect of a one-way trip was more than enough to focus the mind.

Kim printed the picture out, placed it on his desk and studied it again. He clicked across to the database and pulled the man's file. Peter McEwan. There was something about him that made him nervous, but he could not decide what it was. The patient expression, perhaps? He had just been detained, the other passengers were already gone, yet he appeared equable.

Kim could see that McEwan was a frequent visitor to the DPRK. Six visits, all to Pyongyang. Perhaps he had been stopped before or had come to accept the likelihood that it would happen.

And yet, that did not quite ring true.

Intelligence did not suggest anything was afoot. He should have been able to relax. He had received the current circular from the Directorate, and there was no unusual activity reported. And yet...

And yet.

He picked up the telephone and placed a call to the 7th Department HQ. His deputy, Yun Jong-Su, answered. "Comrade Major," he said.

"I have a visitor that I would like you to check, Captain," Kim said. "His name is Peter McEwan. English. I will send you his details now."

"What am I looking for?"

"I do not know. He arrived in the country this afternoon. His file says he has been here several times before, mostly in the last few months. A businessman. Importing luxury cars for the leadership. Everything appears to be in order, yet there is something about this man that makes me feel nervous. Check his file carefully. If anything is amiss—anything, Yun—then you must contact me at once."

"Certainly, Comrade Major."

"Do not let me down."

Kim replaced the receiver and found that he had gritted his teeth. Today was his final day in the job before the promotion he had been chasing for so many months. No more airport, no more interminable studying of the same blank faces, all those same oafish Westerners arriving into the Fatherland with their wide eyes and open mouths. He was being transferred to the State Security Department with responsibility for monitoring political dissidents.

It was a prestigious posting and one he had been honoured to accept.

He was almost there. He just had to negotiate this one final day.

Chapter Four

MILTON HAD to wait five minutes for a taxi. Eventually, one turned up: an old Yugo, battered and dented, probably a hangover from the days when the Russians propped up the North Korean economy. "The Yanggakdo Hotel, please," he said once his luggage was deposited in the back.

The car pulled away, and as they paused to turn onto the deserted highway that would lead into the heart of the capital, Milton allowed himself a brief backwards glance. Two tail cars were behind them.

That was good. He wanted them to follow him.

The main route into the city was known simply as Road Number 1. It was so broad it could easily have accommodated six lanes of traffic, but the restrictions on private ownership of cars meant that there was never anything in the way of congestion.

The landscape was barren and sparse, wide expanses of dusty flatlands with the occasional ramshackle habitation becoming more frequent as they passed into the outskirts of the city. As the taxi travelled into the capital proper, there came the large plane and acacia trees, the lower part of the trunks painted white. Milton had overheard locals discussing the reason for this during a previous visit: it was, variously, to keep away insects, protect the tree from harsh temperatures or, most likely, to denote that the tree was government property and must not be chopped for firewood.

Many of the locals chose to walk in the road since the traffic was so sparse. There were no traffic lights, with uniformed police monitoring the few cars and lorries with the aid of glowing batons. All things considered, downtown Pyongyang provided a reasonably positive first impression.

He still felt off-balance. The dream had passed, leaving tiny gossamer webs of memory that reminded him that he had had it. One thing was for sure: it was bad timing. He would have been nervous without it. This kind of deception was not unusual for a man in his line of work, but there were very few places where the consequences of discovery would be as severe as in the DPRK. There would be no official protest, no consular activity to get him back. As far as the Group was concerned, as soon as he was in the field, he was a totally deniable asset. That rule was rigid; men and women had been lost before, swallowed up into the penal bureaucracies of some of the world's most inhospitable states, never to be seen or heard from again. The prospect of a life spent in a North Korean gaol was not a pleasant one. Nervousness, even for an operative as experienced as Milton, was not an unreasonable response in the circumstances.

The nerves would return again, but he had passed his first inspection. It was important that he attract attention, and Peter McEwan was precisely the sort of man to do that. Milton had read his file cover-to-cover. He was a wanted man in several countries. Flouting international sanctions was just one of the crimes of which he was guilty. His main income was derived from smuggling, and to that end, he had extensive links with criminal concerns all around the world from the Ndrangheta in Sicily to the Los Zetas cartel in Northern Mexico. Drugs, luxury items, arms, counterfeit currency, even people—McEwan was not burdened by conscience, and there was very little that he was not prepared to trade. The man had been chosen because of his reputation and because he was known to the MPSS officials, but the benefit of his notoriety also carried its own burden: Milton had to play a part already known to his watchers. He had to hit all the minute beats of a man for whom there was already a voluminous file somewhere deep in the secret police's vast bureaucracy.

There were imperfections in the plan, of course. If they compared the photographs of Milton with that of McEwan, the deception would not hold for long. Milton had altered his appearance as far as was possible in order to mimic McEwan—the expensive glasses, the slicked-back hair, five days' worth of stubble, the way he walked and held himself—but none of it would hold up under proper scrutiny. It was an approximation, barely more than a sketch, and just as he had made an attempt to capture the man's oleaginous manner, that overbearing arrogance and the air of seediness that accompanied him like a bad smell, any kind of inquisition would strip the falsehoods away just like sunlight burning through early morning mist.

British intelligence had its eye on plenty of men and women like McEwan, individual operators who plied their trade in some of the world's most unpleasant places. Whenever unobtrusive access for a cleaner was required— as now—then the Group would lay its finger on the person who would best allow an agent a means of ingress. The mark would be removed from circulation and replaced. It was a simple ruse, and the moral turpitude of those who made it possible meant that the human cost was more easily ignored. Milton's conscience was not troubled by the cost of his deception.

Outside the window, Pyongyang rolled by. Parts of it were even pretty, with all the blossoms and the flowers. They passed the Revolutionary Martyrs' Cemetery and the Schoolchildren's Palace. They followed the road as it bisected a large public square, where hundreds of Young Pioneers, soldiers and paramilitaries were practicing for the parade, a spectacle of robotic choreography perfected by hundreds of hours of drill. From the sides of buildings and on enormous billboards were the faces of the Great and Dear Leaders: Generalissimo Kim Il-sung and his son, Kim Jong-il, both of them dead and gone but impossible to forget.

The newest pictures were of the young and untested Kim Jong-un, the scion of the line.

Milton had read all of the ridiculous rhetoric that had flowed from the DPRK since Kim had succeeded his father. "Seas of fire." "Merciless vengeance." It was bluster and braggadocio for the most part, but the Koreans had nuclear weapons to back up their threats, and now the country was developing other, more insidious, ways to hurt the West. Milton did not know, nor did he need to know, the political calculus that had led to his being there, sitting in a taxi as it delivered him to the heart of Pyongyang. But as he looked at a row of fresh portraits of Kim Jong-un, Milton knew that the games of brinksmanship that the North had perfected had been played out for too long.

No, Milton did not need to know why the message had suddenly become necessary, only that it was.

He was just the postman.

His job was to deliver it.

Chapter Five

THE HOTEL Yanggakdo, a thousand-room monster that was reserved for foreign guests, sat on the prow of an island in the Taedong River. Westerners called it the Alcatraz of Fun for its revolving restaurant on the roof and its basement of decadent delights: a casino, a swimming pool, a bowling alley and karaoke bars. Milton wheeled his luggage into the reception and checked in. One of the black tail cars had parked near the entrance. Milton noticed that the dark-suited man in the passenger seat had disembarked and followed him into the lobby.

While he waited for his room to be assigned, he made a lazy scan of the foyer. Two others were waiting for him: a man reading his newspaper as his shoes were buffed by a shoe-shine boy and, at the bar, a man who was drinking a cup of tea. The operatives were relaxed and easy, yet they were not experienced enough to hide their purpose from someone like him. If, and when, he left the Yanggakdo, one or both of those men would follow. There would be a car outside, ready to tail him should he avail himself of a taxi. The polite, smiling receptionist would also be in the employ of the secret police, as would be the bellhop who helped him with his luggage. The cleaners, the waiting staff who delivered room service, all would report back to the Directorate of the MPSS that had been assigned the file for Mr Peter Douglas McEwan, the known smuggler from Great Britain.

The room was clean and tidy, pleasant enough. Double-glazed windows behind thin net curtains offered a wide view of downtown Pyongyang. Milton sat back on the bed and took off his shoes. The TV in his room was switched on, looping a series of important events: "Kim Jong-un provides field guidance at the Pyongyang Hosiery Factory," said one report. The next showed the young leader astride a large chestnut horse, inspecting troop movements near the demilitarized zone. Milton took up the remote control and switched through the channels: the BBC, CNN, an anonymous football match with teams that he did not recognise. The room would be rife with bugs, but Milton made no effort to find them, nor even to adapt his behaviour to take them into account. He wouldn't have been able to neutralise them even if he had been able to find them. And he had no way of knowing whether the mirror that faced the bed was two-way.

None of it mattered.

He wanted them to watch.

He took off his shirt and went through to the bathroom to wash his face. The light fell over the tattoo across his shoulders and back, the angel wings tipped with razor claws. He dunked his head in the sink, scrubbing the cold water into his pores, trying to excise the last somnambulant effects of the dream.

He picked up the telephone and dialled a Chinese number. He held a brief conversation with the man at the other end of the line, checking that the transporter with the eight luxury cars had crossed the border successfully. It had, and it was due to arrive in the city tonight, around nine, right on schedule.

He made himself a gin and tonic from the minibar. Cheap Chinese gin, tonic that barely retained any fizz. He took the drink to the window and looked down from the thirteenth floor. The roads were virtually empty. The sky, usually so full of the vapour trails from passing jets, was clear. He stared for a long time. Moranbong Park was half a mile away, and Milton remembered it from his last trip: its host of pagodas, clouds of blossom and the people spreading picnics, drinking rice liquor and singing sentimental folk songs. Red flags fluttered at road junctions. Statues of the Kims could be seen in public places, arms raised aloft in victory that was so pyrrhic as to be a horrible joke. The enormous, clawed finger of the Ryugyong Hotel, designed as the tallest in the world when construction started twenty years earlier, still stood unfinished. An attempt to trump the upstart South, it stood instead as a permanent reminder of the North's failure.

He allowed his thoughts to wander a little. He had an appointment to keep. Two people that he did not know would be waiting for him in the park. His instructions were to leave the hotel after dinner. He was not, under any circumstances, to lose his tail. All he had to do was to be certain to arrive at eight.

Chapter Six

JOHN MILTON took a single table in the restaurant and ate *pansanggi*, a collection of small dishes including grilled beef, brined fish and boiled cabbage. He ate at a leisurely pace, flicking through a translated copy of the *Workers' Newspaper* that he had collected from a rack in the lobby. There were no obvious signs of surveillance, but Milton was sure that the staff were keeping an eye on him. He thanked his waitress and left a ten-euro note as a tip, collecting his overcoat and walking brusquely across the foyer and straight for the exit. He knew that he would leave confusion in his wake; foreigners were not generally allowed to wander the streets without a chaperone. He emerged into the chill air and set off quickly at a fast walk.

It was busy outside: workers went on and off shift at the hotel, factory hands hurried for the busses that would take them to their flats on the outskirts of the city, a few cars and lorries made their way along the roads. Milton did not look back, but he knew that he would immediately be followed. He looked in the window of a small department store and saw one man hurrying after him determinedly. He did not see the large black Mercedes detach itself from the hotel's parking lot, but he heard its engine as it accelerated and overtook him. He turned to see the man in the passenger seat staring at him through the window of the car, and for a moment, he had the grim premonition that he was about to be detained. He had considered the possibility and had decided that he would run, but the chances of successfully making his appointment would be remote. Most likely he would be captured and swallowed up into the vast bureaucracy of the intelligence service, eventually emerging into a gulag—a kaolin mine, a re-education camp—from where he would never escape.

He crossed the road at the entrance to the park, his muscles twitching and his gut watery with nerves, but the order for him to stop did not come.

The park contained many significant monuments, including the Pyongyang Arch of Triumph, where he was to make his rendezvous. The broad avenues were sparsely populated, the occasional jogger passing by or couples strolling towards him, arm-in-arm, idling the evening away. Milton had no need to check his tail. He knew they were there and that they would stay with him for as long as he let them. There would be a panic if they were to lose him, and that was something he could not afford. He needed them there to see the show that they were going to put on for them. If they lost him and flooded the area with agents until they found him again, the plan would not work.

He maintained a careful balance of speed: fast enough to stay ahead of them, yet not so fast that they might panic. He wanted them to think he was a tourist taking in the sights.

He glanced at his watch: seven thirty.

He concentrated on maintaining his sense of calm, but it became harder and harder to do that. He was alone in a hostile country, travelling under a flimsy pretence. He was fooling himself if he thought this was easy, as simple as his last job in Manila or the one before that in South Africa. The wind had dropped a little, and he could hear the men on his tail now, footsteps striking the pavement, unhurried and assured. How far were they behind him? He dared not look. He was frightened. He thrust a hand into his trouser pocket and rubbed a coin between his thumb and forefinger, turning it over so that he could feel the striated edge.

A road crossed the park, and as Milton traversed it, he saw the Mercedes again. It slowed to a halt, drawing in at the kerb, the tinted windscreen revealing nothing. He looked at his watch. Five minutes to eight. He heard footsteps quickening a little behind him. Two pairs. Were they going to take him now?

Finally, he reached the Arch. It was tall, sixty metres at its apex, a larger facsimile of the Arch in Paris. The white granite blocks looked ghostly in the moonlight. A second road, reserved for park officials, was nearby, and parked along it was a Volvo 144. Four vaulted gateways were decorated with azaleas carved into their girth, and it was from the western-facing one that Milton saw the two figures emerge.

A man and a woman.

They moved towards him.

The woman moved ahead and spoke in quiet, accented English. "Mr McEwan?"

"Yes."

"How many followed you?"

"Two on foot. Another couple, at least, by car."

"Where is the car?"

"It was parked by the road. The men on foot—what are they doing?"

"Waiting," the woman replied.

The second man spoke in urgent Korean.

"There's another," the woman said. "Three now. They're coming. We must be quick. Are you ready, sir?"

Milton nodded.

The man made to strike him on the head with a billy club. The blow missed, although it would not have been obvious from a distance and in the deepening gloom. Milton made a show of falling forwards, the man grabbing him beneath the arms and dragging him towards the Volvo. The rear door opened, and he flung him inside.

Chapter Seven

MILTON ALLOWED himself to be half-pushed, half-pulled inside the car and pressed himself down against the seat. The English-speaking woman got in beside him, her companion going around to the passenger seat.

The tyres squealed as the Volvo pulled away.

"Stay down, please," she said.

Milton did as he was told.

"Your papers."

Milton reached into his pocket and handed over his passport and his visa.

The car accelerated, speeding away from a sudden shrill blast of whistles as the three MPSS officers sounded the alert. The blacked-out Mercedes quickly reversed, bumping across the rough ground as it sought the service road. The Volvo had a head start, and the driver quickly took advantage, swinging off the road and barrelling at high speed along the broad path that cut between two neighbouring stands of trees. Joggers stood and gaped as they roared by, the Mercedes giving pursuit but already five hundred yards behind them.

The driver spun the wheel to bring them back onto a main road and took a hard left until they reached a built-up area of the capital again. He slowed, slotting them behind a truck carrying a consignment of watermelons beneath an unsecured tarpaulin that flapped in the wind.

The woman paused to look out of the rear window. Satisfied, she turned back to Milton. "My name is Su-Yung Jong-nam. I will be with you until you have completed your objective."

"The man in the front?"

"My brother, Kun. If you need anything, you must ask me. For now, our objective is to get you away from here."

The driver took a sharp right into a quiet alleyway and parked. It was quiet for a moment, just the restive background sounds of the city as they collected themselves. Su-Yung did not wait for long. She reached into her bag and withdrew a package of documents, including a German passport. She pressed them into Milton's hands.

"Study these. Your name is now Alexander Witzel. You are a German tourist staying at the Pothonggang Hotel. They are looking for an Englishman, remember, not a German. They said you speak the language."

"I do."

Milton checked through the papers. The passport was an impressive fake, bearing his own photograph on the second page. *Another new identity*, he thought, a little wryly. He had lost count of them all by now.

"Is it in order?"

"It's very good," Milton said.

"I am pleased."

"What happened to McEwan? The real one?"

"He was shot. The authorities will find his body in the car once it has been set alight. His passport will be on his person. They will not be able to identify him from his likeness, but they will be able to confirm that it is him from his fingerprints or his teeth."

"How will they have access to that?"

"Mr Milton, my country might be backwards in almost everything else, but one thing that it is extremely good at is discovering information. Mr McEwan has a criminal record in your country. Finding that is a matter of child's play for the Ministry of Information." She shook her head in what might have passed for an expression of grimly patriotic satisfaction. "The police will believe that he is dead, the victim of a smuggling deal that has gone wrong. They will be distracted by a murder hunt, and you will be free to go about your business."

Kun interrupted his sister in hurried, tense Korean.

"My brother is concerned that we are taking too long. We must go, Mr Milton. Are you ready?"

"Yes."

"Then follow me, please."

They walked quickly onto the main street, Milton allowing Su-Yung to extend a lead of ten metres. They reached the entrance to Ragwon Metro Station. It was a squat, curved building with a large clock fixed to the roof above the entrance. A clutch of schoolchildren—dressed in identical white blouses, blue socks and red neckerchiefs—gambolled down the steps and onto the wide forecourt beyond. Su-Yung disappeared into the crowd, and Milton caught his breath for a moment. He was tall enough to see over the people in his way, and he quickly spotted her again. He hurried inside; he had an impression of ornamental decoration, a mixture of Soviet functionalism and oriental opulence, before he was borne forwards onto the escalator that would take them down to the tracks. Milton concentrated on looking as inconspicuous as he could, his eyes glancing across the brightly lit, sombre marble walls as they were ferried downwards. It was as striking as he remembered; only the Moscow Metro came close. With its grandiose architecture, austere cleanliness and cool atmosphere, Ragwon reminded Milton of a museum.

The platform was crowded. Milton stood away from Su-Yung, not even looking in her direction. A mural was painted on the wall, Kim Il-sung holding a book aloft and flanked by two rifle-wielding soldiers, a demure housewife and a worker. The national flag billowed behind them.

The red-and-green-painted train arrived, and they both climbed aboard.

Milton gazed around at the faces in the compartment. It could have been a tube train anywhere in the world. The people wore the same closed expressions, avoiding eye contact as if they were in London or New York. Framed portraits of the Great Leader and the Dear Leader were fixed to both ends of the carriage. The train hushed into another brightly lit strip of platform, and Milton saw the name slide past his gaze: Samhung. They were heading west, away from the centre of the capital.

The woman who had been to his left disembarked, and Su-Yung slid across until she was alongside him. Milton waited for the female guard to raise her signal.

"Did you see anyone?"

"No," Su-Yung said. "I do not believe that we were followed. But we must be careful—the police are everywhere."

"Where are we going?"

"Away from here," she said as the train crept forwards into the tunnel. "You must trust me."

Chapter Eight

MAJOR KIM SHIN-JO was concerned. Alone in his office at the airport, he placed the picture taken at the airport of Peter McEwan face up on the desk in front of him and then slid it eight inches to the left. In its place, he laid out the picture from McEwan's file that Captain Yun Jong-Su had emailed him. There were some similarities between the two pictures—hair and eye colouration, the height was similar, both wore glasses—but that was as far as it went. Yun was sure: the Peter McEwan who had arrived at Pyongyang Airport that afternoon was not the same as the man who had visited six times previously.

Whoever this new man was, he was not who he professed to be.

Kim was prey to the usual lurid terrors that he knew would befall him if he failed the state. The price of failure was well known and not open to negotiation: total humiliation followed by exile if he was lucky. Execution was possible, depending upon the consequences of the failure. If he had been responsible for allowing an enemy spy into the Fatherland, and if that enemy spy was responsible for some grand, awful statement against the Revolution, perhaps during tomorrow's grand parade…

Kim willed himself to remain calm as he picked up the telephone and called his man at the hotel.

"Comrade Major, I was about to call you. The Englishman has left the hotel."

Kim felt a tiny flutter of panic. "What?"

"Ten minutes ago."

"Was he followed?"

"Two men on foot and two by car."

"Why? Did anything happen?"

"He ate his dinner."

"Alone?"

"Yes, sir."

"Was he contacted?"

"Not in his room. He did very little: he had a drink, relaxed on the bed, looked out of the window. Nothing I would consider to be unusual."

"Radio the men now. He is to be arrested. At once."

"Yes, Comrade Major."

Kim replaced the receiver. He prayed it was not too late.

Chapter Nine

THE TRAIN stopped at Pongwha Station. Milton checked the platform and saw nothing. As the doors whispered shut and the train pulled away again, Su-Yung tapped him discreetly on the leg. Milton followed the direction of her gaze. Outside, two men in military uniform were questioning the passengers who were queuing to exit the platform. They were throwing out a dragnet for him.

The final stop on the Chollima line was Puhung. It was the most impressive station yet: chandeliers were spaced at regular intervals along the high, vaulted ceiling, and marble floors seemed to have been polished to an even higher sheen than before. The train pushed up against the buffers, and the doors opened. Milton followed Su-Yung as she disembarked and then quickly scanned the platform: there was no sign of the police. Another large mural of Kim Il-Sung looked down on them.

They followed the crowd to the exit and waited to board the escalator. The station was over one hundred feet below the surface, and their slow ascent took five minutes. Revolutionary music was piped through an array of tinny speakers. There were no hoardings, no displays, no advertisements for new theatre productions or alcohol or upcoming films, only frescoes of the great victories of the Korean people since the Day of Liberation, in the bold, awkward, cartoon style of Soviet realism.

Milton caught himself as four men, two from the military and two from the police, descended quickly on the opposite escalator. Su-Yung did not turn, but Milton noticed as she gave a single, short nod.

Yes, she was saying, *this might be challenging yet.*

She was right. The exit to the street was guarded by four soldiers. A folding table had been arranged to block the way out, and two officials sat at either end, the queue splitting so that they could take half each. The soldiers filling the gaps on either side all carried side arms. A queue had already formed as people waited their turn to hand over their credentials.

Su-Yung was buffeted towards the official sitting on the left of the table, and Milton found himself nudged to the right. He watched the officials run through a practiced routine: they inspected papers and registration cards, comparing the photographs with the faces of their owners. Milton reached into his pocket for his new documents. He inspected them again, idly scanning them in the fashion of someone who finds queuing the most tedious thing imaginable.

If they had discovered his deception, and if they had circulated copies of the photographs that would have been taken of him at the airport...

He reached the front of the queue. The official was stern-faced, with alabaster skin, small dark nuggets for eyes and a sharply hooked nose. He took Milton's papers and scoured them, looking up to gaze into his face and then back down again.

"You are a long way from Germany, Mr Witzel."

"Yes," Milton said affably.

"What is the purpose of your visit to the DPRK?"

"Just to enjoy your excellent country."

"I see." He looked down at the coupon that recorded where he was staying. "And how do you find the Pothonggang?"

"Comfortable."

"Not to your usual standards, though, I'm sure."

Was he making a joke? Milton couldn't tell. "It is very pleasant."

"You will excuse me for a moment, Mr Witzel. I will speak to the hotel to ensure that what you have told me is true. Please wait to the side."

The man stepped away from the table, replaced with seamless efficiency by another official, this one crop-haired and severe, who had been waiting outside.

Milton leant against the wall. He swallowed hard. He turned his eyes to the barrier and watched as Su-Yung took her papers and passed out of the entrance to the station. She did not look back and was quickly out of sight. Milton felt his stomach turn again. When he made a plan, he tested everything to destruction, but here, he was not in control of the situation. His cover was only as strong as its weakest link, and if an Alexander Witzel of Germany had not checked into the Pothonggang, then he would be exposed. There would be nothing for it but to take his chances and run. The four soldiers looked as if they knew how to handle their weapons; he thought he would be able to disable two of them quickly enough, but the other two would be a problem. As the official took out his mobile telephone and dialled the number of the hotel, Milton was reminded of the odds against him.

He was practically alone against the most ruthless and thorough security service the world had seen since the salad days of the Komitet Gosudarstvennoy Bezopasnosti.

The man spoke for a moment in Korean. Milton caught the name 'Witzel' and a word he took to mean 'German,' but apart from that, the language was incomprehensible. He noticed that the official had a holstered pistol fixed to his belt and automatically began to sketch out an alternative plan: the man was of a typically slight Korean build, and it would be a simple matter to put an arm around his neck and draw him in close, using his body as a shield, the other hand liberating him of the firearm. It might increase his odds, if only a little.

The officer smiled at him for the briefest moment. He handed back the passport, the papers tucked into the front cover. "Thank you for your patience, Mr Witzel."

"Everything is in order?"

"Indeed, yes."

"What is this about?"

"We fear a man has been kidnapped—a European man—and it would be remiss of us if we did not do everything in our power to try to locate him. Again, my apologies for the inconvenience."

"It's not a problem at all," Milton said. "I hope you find your man."

Milton passed through the exit and outside. He looked around him and saw Su-Yung appear from the shadows. She nodded, just the single time once again, and set off. Milton fussed with a shoelace that did not need tying so that Su-Yung could have a small head start, and then followed.

Chapter Ten

THE CAR had been a Volvo, a 144. Major Kim Shin-Jo recognised the badge despite the damage that the fire had done to it. The car was blackened with ash and soot, the metal buckled in places. They had needed to pry the boot open with a crowbar. Kim and his deputy, Captain Yun Jong-Su, stood at the rear of the car, peering through the acrid black smoke at the body curled up in the narrow space.

"Get him out," Kim said to the two privates who had found the car.

"Should we not wait for the forensic department?"

"It will serve no purpose. This man is Peter McEwan. He is an English businessman. This"—he indicated the smoking wreck with an irritated flick of his wrist—"has been arranged for our benefit. Our enemies would like us to believe that Mr McEwan went out for a walk after dinner at his hotel this evening, was kidnapped in Moranbong Park and then met his fate. None of that is true." He turned away from the car before either of the baffled privates could ask him what he meant. When he was out of earshot, he turned to Yun and said, quietly, "You agree, Captain?"

"You are undoubtedly correct, Comrade Major. The question is not who this is, but where the person who was pretending to be McEwan is now."

"And more to the point, what he intends to do now that he has eluded our surveillance. This was not a simple thing to arrange. There must be more to it than this."

"You think it is something for the parade?"

"For our sake, I hope not."

They walked towards Kim's state-issued car.

Kim reached inside and took out the best photograph of the imposter from the airport. "Who is he?"

"We do not know, Comrade Major."

"We have had this photograph for hours! Why is it taking so long?"

"We are checking. The Computer and Records Directorate is giving it priority." He paused. "What do we do while we wait for them?"

"McEwan said that he was arranging a delivery of luxury cars. Thankfully, that was not a lie. There is an authorisation at the Ministry of Trade for such a delivery; I have checked. The cargo originated in Dandong and crossed the border yesterday evening. It is due to arrive in the capital tonight. We must assume that anyone involved with it is complicit."

"Where is the cargo now?"

"That is what we must find out."

Yun paused, a little awkwardly. "Do we mention this to the lieutenant colonel?"

Kim had already considered that. He had a hundred men at his disposal: one hundred good men, excellently trained, diligent and loyal to the Fatherland. That might be enough to see off this threat, but the chances of success would increase with more men. That was his problem: if he wanted help, he would have to speak to his superior to get it, and that would mean admitting that mistakes had been made under his supervision.

He would wait. There was no need to panic. They could find this man without causing undue alarm. "I think we can manage this ourselves, Captain. Do you agree?"

Yun seemed relieved at that. The consequences of failure would extend to him, too. "I do, Comrade Major," he said.

Neither man needed to speak the obvious: they were already in a situation of the utmost gravity. If they could find the imposter themselves, then so be it. They could keep it between themselves, and no one else need know. But if they failed and something happened and it was discovered that they had not requested assistance, then that would be the end of them both.

Chapter Eleven

SU-YUNG'S BROTHER, Kun, picked them up once they were a safe distance from Puhung station. It was not the Volvo this time; that car had just been torched with the body of Peter McEwan shut inside the trunk. This car was an old Ford, exported from the South during one of the irregular *détentes* that occasionally thawed relations between the warring neighbours.

Kun took them to a house on the edge of the city. Inside Pyongyang, housing was restricted to one-room "pigeon coops," but there was a little more space the further out you travelled. This accommodation was simple, utilitarian, and monochromatic, built from cement block and limestone. It was a single-storey row of one-room homes stuck together like the little boxes that make up the chambers of a harmonica. The only real colour was the stark red lettering of the huge propaganda sign directly opposite, its boldly vivid message standing out amid all the grey: WE WILL DO AS THE PARTY TELLS US.

Kun did not get out of the car with them.

"Where is he going?" Milton asked his sister.

"The freight is expected tonight. He will make sure it arrives as it should."

Milton watched as the Ford drove away into the jaded neighbourhood and then followed Su-Yung inside. The entrance led directly into a small kitchen that doubled as a furnace room. A large bucket that was a quarter-full of coal sat next to the hearth. The fire it produced was used both to cook and to heat the home. A sliding door separated the kitchen from the main room, where two sleeping mats had been unrolled.

"We will stay here," she told him.

"Is this where you live?"

"No—not here. I have an apartment in the city, much smaller than this. This belongs to a friend of our cause. He is visiting his family in Chongjin tonight. We will not be disturbed. You must be hungry—would you like something to eat?"

Milton said that he would, and Su-Yung disappeared into the kitchen. The electricity was off, so the room was lit by a single paraffin lamp. He looked around: the sleeping mats were made of a thin vinyl that did not promise a particularly comfortable night's sleep, a little heat radiated upwards from an underfloor system that was, he guessed, powered by the furnace, and a few cardboard boxes held clothes and a few cheap objects. It was austere.

He sat on the floor and measured himself: the dream had passed properly now, although he still felt a little weak. That was not unusual. Each episode drained him so completely that it often took a day or two for him to recover fully, and it seemed to be getting worse. He worried that it would affect what he had to do tomorrow—he would need a surgeon's steady hand to achieve his aim—but then he did his best to put the concern aside; worrying about it now would serve no purpose, save rob him of the sleep he knew he needed.

Su-Yung returned with a bowl of broth with a long-handled spoon and a steaming teacup that gave off a rich, acrid tang. "*Sul lang tang*," she announced, handing Milton the bowl.

"What's that?"

"Beef soup. It is a traditional Korean dish. The tea is *nokcha*. Green tea. For years we have imported it from the Chinese, but my countrymen have recently been successful in cultivating the tea plants themselves. A better achievement than all of the Dear Leader's work with nuclear bombs, if you ask me."

They drank the tea quietly, watching the darkness of the night through the open window, the ghostly shape of the city's few skyscrapers forming a dim, irregular skyline in the distance. Milton found that he was developing a fondness for the quietly dignified girl. She, too, was taking a big risk—a much bigger risk, indeed, since she would not be leaving the country once the objective was achieved. Milton knew that there would be loose ends that would eventually lead the authorities back to her: CCTV footage, witness statements, those conspirators who found their tongues loosened in the basement of the building where the secret police carried out their interrogations. When that happened, the results would not be good for her or her brother.

"Why are you doing this?" he asked. "You and Kun?"

Su-Yung paused, looking for the right words. "My country is sick, Mr Milton. It has been sick for many years. People are starving while the Kims and their cronies spend lavishly on themselves. These cars that are being brought into the country, for example—whole families could be fed for months with the proceeds of just one of them. Years. Something must be done."

"But why you?"

Su-Yung stared into her tea. "Why not me?" She paused, giving thought to what to say next. "My father was from the South. He was captured during the war and held here as a prisoner. When the fighting ended, many of the prisoners were exchanged, but the North did not return all of the men that it had taken. My father was one of the unlucky ones." She paused to take a sip of her tea. "North Korean society is very carefully arranged. Everyone has *songbun*—in your country, you might refer to it as reputation or standing. In Korea, it is something that stays with a family forever. It is hereditary. It is why my brother is a janitor and I work in a factory. We will never be able to aspire to anything better. Neither of us could join the Party, even if we wanted to. Our families are always last in line for food. I have a daughter;

she is eleven years old and a wonderful pianist. The music she plays—" She stopped for a moment, wistful. "It is beautiful, Mr Milton, but it makes no difference how good she is. She will never be able to go to music college to study. How is that fair? She is punished for the so-called sins of her grandfather."

"What happened to him?"

"They put him to work in an iron-ore mine. He was a quiet man, who never spoke out of turn. He did not drink for fear that the alcohol would lower his guard and he would say something that he would regret. If your *songbun* is low, you are not given the benefit of the doubt if someone makes an accusation against you. One day, while he was in the mine, he had a disagreement with his foreman. The area in which they were working was unsafe—miners die all the time here—and he refused to lead his men any further until it was properly reinforced. The foreman reported this to the Party. He said that he was disobedient and insubordinate and that he had spoken sarcastically of the Great Leader. I do not believe that this could possibly have been true, but in matters such as these, truth is not important. Two nights later, an army truck appeared outside our little home, and my father was taken away. We think they took him to one of the work camps in the north of the country, but we cannot be sure. It is possible that they shot him. We never saw him again."

The line of Su-Yung's jaw set hard as she clenched her teeth, and for a moment, a fire that Milton had not seen before flashed in her eyes. "That, Mr Milton, is why I am doing what I am doing. Someone has to take a stand against these people, and as I say, it might as well be me." She finished the cup of tea, and as she replaced the cup in the saucer, her cheery demeanour returned. "Now," she said, pointing at the bowl of soup, "you must eat. It is unlikely you will have another opportunity to fill your stomach until much later."

Milton ate. The soup was delicious, substantial and spiced with just the right amount of chilli. He finished the plate quickly and did not object when Su-Yung offered him a second helping. When he was finished with that and the plates had been cleared away, Su-Yung sat down again and handed him another new set of papers. This passport was English, with a sheaf of documents wedged between the covers.

"You are now Mr Michael Callow. You are forty-two years old and a successful businessman. You deal in the buying and selling of crude petroleum, and you have been in the DPRK for a week, negotiating the terms of a contract to supply ten thousand barrels to the Unggi refinery. You have decided to stay an additional few days to watch the parade."

"And you?"

"Tourists are not allowed outside their hotels without a minder. If necessary, I will be yours."

Milton opened the passport and studied the photograph. Callow had blond hair.

"Ah, yes," Su-Yung said with a smile. "I am sorry about that. You will need this." She handed Milton a bottle of hair dye and pointed to the back of the room. "There is a small bathroom over there."

Chapter Twelve

THE TRANSPORTER was a big eighteen-wheeler, with a fully hydraulic trailer that could accommodate eight cars. The driver, a taciturn Chinese from the border town of Dandong, had no idea that the expensive load he had driven into the North was not solely for the enjoyment of the country's elite. The cars had been given a cursory search by the customs officials as he waited to cross into the country, and if—in the admittedly unlikely event—they had discovered the real purpose of the consignment, then it would have been very unlikely that he would ever have left the country again.

He had driven on, ten hours straight. Commercial satellite navigation was pointless in North Korea, so he had relied upon a dated road atlas to navigate the route to Pyongyang. His destination was a goods yard to the west of the city, and he had arrived, more or less on time, the day after Milton's own arrival. A man at the yard had signed the paperwork to acknowledge that the delivery had been made, and then, with extravagant care, the cars had been unloaded one after the other. It was approaching midnight when the driver was finished, the task made more difficult by the brownout that extinguished the overhead floodlights halfway through the job. The driver had got back into his cab and set back off towards the border. Like most of his friends, he hated the North. They all thought that it was a backwards country, a little hole governed by the latest madman in a family full of madmen, altogether more trouble than it was worth. The sooner he set off, the sooner he would be home. He planned to get halfway to the border, where he would sleep in his cab at the side of the road.

Kun picked up Su-Yung and Milton at five in the morning and drove them to the yard. He unlocked the wire mesh gate for them and then disappeared; Su-Yung explained that he was going to arrange new transport for them for when the operation had been completed.

They found the cars parked neatly inside a closed warehouse. They were a very fine collection: a Lexus, two Bentleys, two Mercedes, an Audi, a Ferrari and a Porsche. He found himself nodding his approval: Peter McEwan certainly knew his business. He had arranged the better part of two million pounds' worth of high-performance automotive engineering. He did not know that British intelligence had been monitoring his communications for weeks and, once they realised he was transporting cargo that suited their particular purposes, the operation had been given the green light to proceed.

A consequence of that had been his murder.

"Which car is it?" Su-Yung said.

"The Enzo, I'm afraid," Milton said.

"The Enzo?"

"The red one," he said. The Ferrari was a beautiful, gorgeous machine; it was a shame to have to defile it. He opened the door and ran the palm of his hand across the smoothly carpeted floor behind the front seats. He took a knife and positioned it carefully, pushing the tip until it pierced the fabric and then slicing it open. He reached inside and tore the carpet away, revealing a compartment that had been fitted beneath the cabin. It was ten inches wide and reached from the back to the front, extending all the way beneath the seats.

"Here," he said to Su-Yung. "Give me a hand."

He reached down and withdrew the items that had been hidden inside the compartment: the rifle, an M-4 carbine, a Sig Sauer 9mm, half a dozen fragmentation grenades, a pair of high-powered Zeiss Classic 60mm binoculars and a miniature tracking device.

The rifle was the most important; he picked it up and examined it carefully. A Barrett M82, recoil-operated, semi-automatic, finished with an American walnut stock and a heavy premium barrel. The weapon system that the American snipers preferred, Milton had become accustomed to it during his time with them in the sandpit. The gun had been broken down into pieces, and Milton quickly reassembled it, checking that it had not been damaged in transit. It had not. The Group's quartermaster had arranged the weapon for him to his specific order, and he had reacquainted himself with it on the long ranges on Salisbury Plain. It was an impressive piece of machinery, every bit as well-crafted as the car in which it had been hidden.

"Is it satisfactory?" Su-Yung asked anxiously.

"Yes."

Milton opened the magazine and checked the big bullets. Its ten-shot box magazine was chambered for .50 calibre ammunition, and it was loaded with Raufoss Mk 211 anti-matériel projectiles, his favourite cartridge for this purpose. Each bullet was almost as long as his hand, jacketed in copper with an armour-piercing tungsten core that carried explosive and incendiary components. The ammunition was designed to take out light armour at distance. There had been some suggestion that it should be banned against human targets, but Milton had no view about that; all he knew was that it was excellent at long range and that it made an almighty mess when it hit something soft.

Su-Yung watched him slot the magazine into the breech. "This operation," she said, "we would do it ourselves, but it would be too difficult. The task you have set yourself is not an easy thing, Mr Milton. The distance will be very great. Perhaps half a mile."

Milton slotted the sniper scope to the top of the rifle. It had a 30mm tube, external windage and elevation turrets, parallax adjustment and a fast-focus eyepiece with a bullet-drop compensating reticule. "It won't be a problem," Milton replied, raising the rifle and peering into the scope. "With this, it'll be like they're just in the next room."

Chapter Thirteen

"AND YOU have learned nothing from him, Yun? Still nothing?"

The earlier confidence that Kim had tried to invest in his voice was gone. A distant memory. Now his tone was impatient and ragged with fear.

The truck driver had been very helpful; his assistance was about the only thing that had gone in their favour since this whole mess had unfolded. He had provided a likeness for the man that he had seen at the yard, and this had been cross-checked with the Department's files on suspected dissidents and traitors. The exercise had turned up three possible matches. Each of these three men had been detained and delivered to the basement, where, after a little light persuasion—merely an *hors d'oeuvre* for what was to follow—it had quickly been determined that, of the three, the man they wanted was the second they had collected: Kun Jong-nam, a janitor from Sunan-guyok.

"He is stubborn, Comrade Major."

"I don't care how stubborn he is! We must have what he knows!"

Kim was angry. The interrogation had been unsuccessful. His preferred technique was more considered, a slow escalation that would give the subject plenty of time to consider how much worse things would get for him if he did not divulge the information that the state required. There had been no time for such niceties today. Two of his more brutal privates had tied the man to a chair and beaten him black and blue for fifteen minutes, and when that had not been successful, they had pulled out his fingernails with pliers. Yet, even relying on techniques that Kim found distasteful, they had learned precious little. Kun had revealed that he had been working with his sister, Su-Yung Jong-nam, and that they had collected a Westerner from Moranbong Park. He said that they had pretended to abduct the man, and that, an hour or two later, he had murdered another Westerner—he did not know his name, either—and placed his body in the trunk of the car that they had been using. The car was then torched. Kun said he knew no more than that: he did not know the identity of either Westerner, he did not know the purpose of the shipment of luxury cars, and more specifically, he did not know what was planned.

Kim could not say if that was the extent of the man's knowledge, but he was in no mood to believe that Yun had tried as hard as he could, pushed as hard as he might, without killing the man. If Kun possessed the information that he sought, he would get it out of him. It did not matter if the man died in the process.

He led the way back to the basement. Kun Jong-nam's arms were secured with straps that had been fastened to the chair. The man's face was livid with the reds and purples of incipient bruises, a lurid reminder of what they had already done to him in the short time he had been in custody. Worse was to come, but Kim felt no flickering of conscience, no regret. The man had brought it upon himself. This was the price of disloyalty, and it was to be paid in full.

When beatings with rubber hoses and bamboo poles did not succeed, or when time was pressing, as now, they fell back on narcotic shortcuts. The doctor approached with his syringe, selected a plump vein on the man's wrist, pushed the needle into it and then depressed the plunger. The Pentothal disappeared into his arm; the effects were evident within seconds. The doctor pushed back the man's eyelid and shone a torch into his eye. "He's ready now."

Kim knelt down beside the chair. "Kun, can you hear me?"

"Yes." His voice was slurred, as if he had enjoyed one too many glasses of *munbaeju*.

"My name is Major Kim Shin-Jo. I work with the Ministry of State Security. Do you understand what that means?"

A slurred response: "Yes."

"My colleague tells me that you have been involved with bringing a foreigner into our country. An Englishman. Is that correct?"

"Yes."

"I need your help, Kun. It is very important that I find this Englishman quickly. Do you know where I can find him?"

The man's face crumpled with the effort of denying the drug. "No," he forced out.

"Kun—think very carefully. It will be better for you and your family if you tell me the truth. You understand that this is very serious indeed? You have a sister, I believe? If something happens, she will be shot. You know this?"

"Yes."

"So where can I find the Englishman?"

"I—don't—know."

"Is your sister with him?"

"No." He stammered it, working too hard against the drug, and Kim knew he was lying.

He stepped back and nodded to the doctor.

"I have given him a heavy dose," the man said. "Any more would be dangerous."

"This is not the time for qualms," he snapped. "Do I need to find a replacement?"

"No, Comrade Major."

"Then do it."

Another syringe was emptied into the man's vein. His eyes rolled into his head, and he grinned stupidly before his features slackened and fell loose. His head hung limply between his shoulders.

Kim crouched close so that his mouth was next to the man's ear. "Kun. You must speak honestly. The Englishman you helped into the country—what is he intending to do?"

There was another moment of struggle that played out vividly across the man's helpless face.

"Kun. You must tell me. What is he planning to do? Is it the parade?"

His voice was subdued. "No."

"Then what is it?"

"The—" He fought against the completion of the sentence. "The—"

"Damn it, Kun, what is it?"

"I—don't—know."

Kim stood suddenly, wheeling away from the pathetic spectacle.

"Comrade Major?" Yun said.

"The same again."

"But the doctor—"

"I don't care what he said. This fool is dead whatever happens. If we do not find out what he knows, we will be dead too. See that it is done."

Chapter Fourteen

SU-YUNG TOOK her foot off the brake and crawled ahead. Milton was in the back of the van, watching through the window as they made their way downtown. A line of sickly looking trees had been planted to separate the road from the pavement, and behind them was a terrace of utilitarian buildings, constructed from poured concrete, blocky and depressingly ugly. It reminded Milton of the worst aspects of the Soviet outposts he had visited. Trams and trolleybusses rattled along the inside lane, trucks and the few private cars overtaking them.

Su-Yung spoke without taking her eyes from the road. "How much do you know about what is happening today?"

"Just that there is a parade."

"It is not just *any* parade, Mr Milton. It is the centenary of our esteemed Great Leader's birthday." She made no effort to hide her sarcasm. "The event is being broadcast all around the country. The Workers' Party are even handing out celebratory food rations. Cooking oil, I believe." She snorted derisively.

"How many people will be here?"

"Many thousands. It will be an excellent diversion. The regime will focus its attention on Kumsusan Palace. It is unlikely we will be seen before—well, before you have done what you came here to do."

She drove carefully, slowing when the road narrowed and the sidewalks widened where the meagre shopping district started. There were large state-run stores on either side, but none of them had anything in their windows. Cast-iron flagpoles were placed at every junction, red flags whipping in the light breeze. The roads were swept clean, but everything was so sterile: there were no advertisements of any sort, no graffiti, no life.

There were signs of construction all about, most of it stalled after the foreign money that had been funding it had all dried up. Ahead of them, the road terminated at the huge plaza that surrounded the palace where the parade was to be held. On their right was the Grand People's Study House, the building that passed for the city's main library. On the left, the Ryugyong, the unfinished hotel that was to have been the world's tallest. Ahead of that, across the broad space of the square and perhaps a thousand yards distant, the concrete tower occupied by the military and the secret police.

The Ryugyong was enormous, a giant skeleton of a building that towered over the glittery squalor of Pyongyang like a wireframe spaceship. Su-Yung turned off the road and descended a ramp into the vast maw of its underground car park. The garage was deserted.

"Here we are," she said. "The Chinese were paying for this, but then they decided that they did not need it after all. Then the Germans were interested until Kim frightened them away. It will never be finished now. You have a word for it in English." She paused, searching her vocabulary. "Hubris—that is it. It is a monument to the hubris of the Kims. No one comes here any longer. We will not be disturbed."

Su-Yung headed for the rear corner of the car park and reversed next to an open doorway, where a rough service staircase headed up. She killed the engine. Milton pulled the handle on the sliding side door and pulled it back on its rusty runners. He leaned inside and collected the rifle. He left the other weapons that he had taken from the cars—the gas-operated M-4 carbine, the 9mm, the grenades—in the back to be collected on the way out. The M82 was wrapped in an oily blanket.

Su-Yung went over to check the staircase. She signalled that the way was clear.

Milton followed. The stairwell had not yet been finished with a handrail, and it was unguarded on the left-hand side, the drop lengthening as they ascended further and further until it was hundreds of feet deep. Open walls offered views into the guts of the building: they passed through what was intended to be the cavernous reception, then the dining floor, huge open spaces with their expanses of aging concrete and rusting iron railings presenting something of the post-apocalyptic. Scaffolding wound its way up the inside of the vast heart of the pyramid, hundreds of feet of it. They climbed for five minutes, eventually reaching the eighteenth floor. Su-Yung stepped onto the landing. A corridor led in both directions, left and right. Everything was unfinished: the concrete had been towelled smooth, but there were no carpets, no panelling on the walls; there were empty piles of canvas cement sacks; doors were just open spaces; wiring spilled out of the walls; a line of bare light bulbs stretched away down the corridor with no power to light them; a wheelbarrow was turned onto its side; and a cement mixer stood silently. It was ghostly. Their footsteps disturbed a grey cement dust, so fine that Milton could feel it tickling the back of his throat with every breath.

Su-Yung led the way to a series of rooms that were intended to be an executive suite. There was a large bathroom with plumbing for a toilet, shower and bath, a bedroom and a huge sitting room on two levels. None of the finishes had been applied, and there was no furniture of any sort. It was just a large concrete box, ugly and unloved. The windows had not been glazed, the big floor-to-ceiling apertures spread with plastic sheeting. The sunlight was muted, stained blue as it passed through the translucent material.

Milton unwrapped the rifle and carried it with him to the window. It had no sill, a thin groove all the way around the aperture where the pane of glass would eventually be fitted. The two plastic sheets met in the middle, like makeshift curtains. Milton dropped to one knee and carefully loosened the ties that held the sheets together. He lowered himself until he was prone, relaxing the muscles of his legs and torso so that he was completely flat to the surface. He rested his left elbow on the concrete and carefully brought the rifle around. He unfolded a bipod and screwed it into its housing, pushing it forwards so that the forestock just dipped out of the window. He breathed in, a good, long breath. He held it for five seconds and then breathed out. He waited for the moment of calm to descend, that familiar moment where he almost felt out of his own body. It was a gift, and it had always served him well. It came from deep inside him, a place where stress—and the dream— had never been able to reach. They had made jokes about it in the sandpit, the way he would just zone out, reducing everything to a simple trinity: target, sniper, gun.

He breathed in, held it again, and then breathed out.

He opened the sheeting a little, put the binoculars to his eyes and peered out. He was facing due north. He estimated that he was four hundred feet above street level. This was the tallest building in Pyongyang, and his line of sight was clear and unobstructed. Spread out ahead of him was the broad plaza that fronted the Kumsusan Palace. The palace was a sprawling complex of buildings decorated in the oriental style and of immense scale. A gigantic fifty-foot banner depicting a stylised version of the North Korean flag was fixed to the roof of the palace, and below that, two huge portraits of Kim Jong-il and Kim Il-sung had been hung. A thousand yards away, across the square and behind the palace, was the new office block that he had seen from the street. It had been built ten years ago when Chinese money was still flowing into the country and there were plans for businesses to move in. Times had changed, and it had still not been rented. In an attempt to preserve some kind of dignity, the North had filled it with government offices.

The National Defence Commission.

The Ministry of People's Armed Forces.

The State Security Department.

He guessed it was three hundred feet tall. Tall enough, anyway, from his position.

Milton focussed the binoculars and examined the building. The interior was honeycombed with cubicles, individual monitors glowing at every desk. For a country with such an unreliable electricity supply, an exception had clearly been made for this particular building. Milton knew the reason why: this was also the headquarters of the Reconnaissance General Bureau. The organisation was divided into six bureaus: Operations, Reconnaissance, Foreign Intelligence, Inter-Korean Dialogue, Technical, and Rear Services. Technical was the organisation responsible for signals intelligence, electronic warfare and informations warfare.

Western analysts described its work as cyberterrorism.

It was beginning to make a serious nuisance of itself.

Milton checked his watch: thirteen minutes to seven. He settled, relaxing his muscles against the cold solidity of the concrete floor. In moments, the cold had passed through his clothes and had begun to seep into his body. He concentrated on ignoring it. His pelvis began to ache, a reminder of a wounding from his first tour in Iraq, but he instructed his brain to set it aside. It was a ghost wound, years old, irrelevant.

MI5 only knew that the meeting was scheduled for today, not when it was due to start.

He could be waiting here all day.

Chapter Fifteen

KIM LOOKED at his watch: nearly half past eleven. He paced the observation room, the large two-way mirror looking into the interrogation suite where Yun was continuing to supervise their efforts with the traitor. There was nothing else he could do, except what he was engaged in at the moment: futile recriminations coupled with the more practical step of contacting his deputies at Kumsusan Palace and ordering them to redouble their efforts to find the Englishman.

The prospect of failure and disgrace was very real now. The parade was about to start, and whatever Kun said, it had to be the target. A bomb? A sniper? Perhaps there were more of them than just the Englishman. And what could he do? There were already tens of thousands of people there, a crowd so dense that it would be perfect for one man to hide within. Kim certainly couldn't ask for the parade to be stopped. He had nothing to suggest that was necessary, nothing except the dull, sickening ache in the pit of his gut.

The doctor's drugs had ruined the man's mind now, flipping him into a deep unconsciousness from which he emerged only now and again, generally babbling incoherently. Yet they persevered, Yun asking the same questions over and over and over again.

Who is the agent?

What was smuggled into the country?

What is his target?

And still nothing! Kim felt the bitter, selfish anger of a man who sees a bounty turn to ashes in his hands. His promotion, his position in the ministry, in the Party, his whole life—his foolishness had put everything at stake. He had chided himself for allowing the man to pass into the country in the first place, but until now, he had never failed to believe that he would be able to find him and end the threat that he posed. Each answer, each potential source of knowledge, had crumbled between his fingers. He felt trapped.

Yun suddenly shot to his feet and dashed to the intercom. He thumbed the channel open. "Comrade Major, I have it."

"What is it?" he practically yelped, his heart catching.

"He does not know the man's name, nor does he know what was brought into the country, but he says that he knows what it is that they intend to attack."

"What is it, man? Speak!"

"Not the parade. There's a meeting of the Reconnaissance General Bureau. It is that."

Chapter Sixteen

MIDDAY. Milton was in his fifth hour of lying in wait. He had watched the city come alive, watched the crowds file into the huge square half a mile away. Now, it was packed. Thousands of spectators, people who had been bussed into the capital from the surrounding towns and cities, many of them travelling overnight. They were arranged into neat squares, each square holding hundreds of people, and they were dressed in colourful clothes, bright reds and yellows. The members of each square had been given a colourful banner to wave; some had red, others blue or white. When viewed from above, the national flag was depicted.

The sound of marching bands filled the air, loud even at this distance. Tens of thousands of troops marched alongside the palace, some carrying colourful standards, others armed with rifles and rocket-propelled grenades. They stepped in formation, their legs held straight and lifted high, their arms synchronised in perfect time. Fifty Russian tanks followed the troops and then came the launchers: FROG-7 artillery rockets, Scuds, Hwasong short-range missiles, then Rodong and Taepodong medium-range missiles. Finally, Milton saw the largest missile of all, borne on a six-wheel launcher. It had been painted in camouflage greens and browns, and bannered with messages threatening to destroy the United States and its military. It was the Musudan BM-25, the untested missile that they boasted could reach Alaska.

Large bleachers had been built on the tiered steps of the palace. They were packed with dignitaries: officials from the Workers' Party, members of the intelligence services, high-ranking members of the military. Milton adjusted the rifle's range to ten plus two: one thousand yards plus two minutes of angle. He moved the gun in tiny increments, left to right, staring down the scope at general after general after general.

Then he stopped.

A short, rather chubby figure was suspended between the crosshairs. He wore the usual black Mao suit with a small red pin on the lapel. The pin was the emblem of the North Korean Workers' Party. His face was soft, almost malformed, with small black eyes, fat cheeks and thin, bloodless lips. His skin was unnaturally pallid and his hair was jet black, almost certainly coloured, the sides shorn very close to the scalp. He looked out of place, a spoilt boy in a man's body. He was looking out over the marching soldiers, his right hand brought up just above the level of his eyebrows in an awkward salute. He nodded every once in a while, but he did not smile.

He looked a little like his father.

Milton slipped the index finger of his right hand through the guard and felt the trigger nestle between the second and third joints. He applied a tiny amount of pressure and felt it depress against its oiled springs; just a tiny amount more would be enough to send one of the ten big projectiles in the magazine on its way.

The shot was there for him to take, but his orders were clear.

Milton was just the cleaner.

He was the operative who put the orders of others into practice, and it was not his place to doubt them.

He moved the sniper scope up so that it was aimed at the army building five hundred yards beyond the palace. One thousand yards from his position. He moved it across, methodically, left to right, until he found the room he wanted. A large conference space, a lectern set up at the front before a dozen rows of folding chairs. A projector hung from the ceiling, shining the flag of the DPRK against the white wall that faced it. A table against the furthest wall held pots of tea and coffee. People were slowly assembling. Milton estimated forty, although there were chairs for twice that many and they were still coming.

Today was a banner day for the Technical Bureau of the RGB. Three weeks ago, a cyberbomb created by its talented programmers had been unleashed onto the Internet. The conference had been arranged to discuss why and how the operation had been such a success. They wanted to learn from it so that future attacks could be made even more effective. It had been so successful that great prestige had attached to the RGB, and now officials from across the National Defence Commission wanted to be associated with it. Some would no doubt seek to claim credit after the event.

The list of officials attending was impressive.

Two of the four vice-chairmen of the NDC.

The director of the RGB.

The assistant directors of each of the RGB bureaus.

No doubt the plan was to take them down to the palace for the conclusion of the parade.

Some of them would not be able to keep that appointment.

He waited, keeping still, breathing low, clearing his mind. He tuned out every possible distraction: the night from the morning, the dust in his lungs, his surroundings. He was aware that Su-Yung was waiting behind him, but she, too, soon faded away into nothing.

It was just him, his rifle, his targets.

He concentrated on that.

Him, his rifle, his targets.

Nothing else mattered.

Time.

The attendees started to take their seats.

Milton nudged the rifle half an inch to the left and acquired his first target.

He flipped the kill switch, making the rifle live.
Breathe in, hold it.
Wait.
Wait.
Wait.
Now.
He pulled the trigger.

Chapter Seventeen

KIM RUSHED between the opening doors of the elevator car and, shouldering aside the attendants who were guarding the door, tumbled into the offices of the Reconnaissance General Bureau. Yun had telephoned ahead with news of the threat, but, as he had breathlessly relayed to Kim as the major sped across the city, the security officers had dismissed his fears with supercilious disdain. There was, they said, nothing that a single man could do to threaten the leadership of the People's Army. To suggest otherwise was ridiculous. The building's security had never been breached and was considered to be impregnable, but to humour him, it would be checked. In the absence of better evidence of the threat—the narcotic ramblings of a man whose mind had been broken were not sufficient—the meeting could not possibly be cancelled. Kim knew why: no one would want to admit to the generals that there was the possibility that they might be fallible.

He ran to the conference room where the meeting was to be held, angrily presented his credentials for inspection and went inside. Proceedings had already commenced. The opening address was being given by Lieutenant General Kim Yong-chol, one of the vice-chairmen. He was praising the computer programmers who had executed such an audacious attack on the Imperialists and their southern lackeys. They were, he opined, in the vanguard of a new kind of war, the kind of war that would send the enemies of the Fatherland back to the dark ages. The usual nonsense, but this audience was primed for it. The room was large, and Kim had entered at the rear, the disturbance kept to a minimum. He took it all in quickly: there was no sign of the Englishman, not that he expected to find any. It was a bomb, surely. He had smuggled a bomb into the country, hidden it here and rigged it to explode. He was going to take out as many of the generals as he could.

"Excuse me!" he shouted. "Comrades! My name is Kim Shin-Jo. I am a major in the Ministry of State Security. I must ask you—"

His eye caught something out of the window, and the words caught in his throat: he didn't know what it was. A flash of light? The quickest glint of something? A reflection? He glanced across the cityscape to the half-finished Ryugyong Hotel, the only building in the city that was taller than this one. It was half a mile away. Time slowed down. He saw it again, definitely coming from the hotel, that huge tapered arrow pointing straight up into the lowering sky.

People had turned to look at him.

He saw another tiny bloom of light, a different kind of flash against the dark concrete of the hotel's bare skeleton, and then heard a strange sound, a pop that was similar and yet dissimilar to the sound that the seal on a jar of coffee makes as it is pierced. His warning went unsaid as the general toppled backwards, breaking his fall on the edge of the lectern for a moment, but then sliding to the right as his body lost purchase and completed its journey with a graceless thud to the stage. The disbelief came first—the whole room experienced it—and then the thought that the general must have fainted before Kim realised, with shocking and awful clarity, that the odd noise he had heard before was the sound of something shearing through glass, a noise announcing that a spiderweb of fracture, delicate strands radiating from a central point, had suddenly been flung across the large window a dozen feet from the general at his lectern, and that at its centre a small, round hole had been drilled in the glass, which, though badly damaged, held. It took a second more for the pulverised remains of the man's head to start leaking blood, the dark bloom spreading from his body, a crimson corona, at which point the human fear of blood—primal, automatic—asserted itself. Screams and panic and rushing for the exits and diving for cover but, by that time, two more bullets were already on their way downrange.

The weakened window bulged once, twice, and collapsed in a million pieces of broken glass that shone like diamonds.

The Englishman was disastrously, cataclysmically accurate. He was aiming for headshots and hit both perfectly, blowing each one all over the insides of the conference room. He hit the director of the RGB an inch above the right temple, the bullet pulverising his skull into fragments that sprayed across the room (those nearby would be tweezering fragments from their flesh for days afterwards). The man slumped forward until his chest fell between his knees and, thereby unbalanced, his body rolled forward off the chair and to the ground. His comrade, yet another general, swivelled his head at the sudden commotion and experienced a moment's worth of complete horror to see his colleague without a head before the third bullet hit him between the eyes, dead centre above the line of his nose. The fifty-calibre projectile ploughed straight through skull and brain matter, exiting with horrendous gushers of blood, brain, and bone fragments. Both bullets slammed into the thin partition walls, passed through the next two offices and, eventually, their momentum sufficiently impeded, exploded in a shower of zirconium sparks that immediately started hungry fires.

Kim found that he was on the floor. People were rushing around him, jostling him, treading on his hands. He clambered upright. The chief of the General Staff collided with him.

The man flung him aside. "Get out of the way, you fool!"

The fourth bullet struck the general on the right side of his face, digging its way through flesh and bone and teeth enamel, ploughing through the rear of the throat and into the bone of his shoulder, atomizing it into thin pink mist on the exit. His knees locked, even against the sudden and awful collapse of his weight, so instead of tumbling he pivoted and was almost lowered downwards, dropping into a chair as if it was his favourite armchair at the end of a difficult day.

The bullets flew with delayed supersonic bangs that rang out only as the audience was beginning to realise what was happening to them.

The fifth shot was already on its way by then.

It struck a general who had been sitting in the first row, also in the head.

The result was identical.

The conference room erupted in panic—pure pandemonium—but there was nowhere for any of them to go. Every seat had been filled, and as the attendees tried to make for the passages at the end of the rows, they tripped over the chairs and each other. A scrum developed at the door. Kim dropped to the ground and wrapped his arms over his head. There was nothing he could do until the Englishman grew tired of his sport, shooting fish in a barrel.

Chapter Eighteen

SOMEONE HAD overturned the table with the urns of coffee and tea. Milton watched through the scope as his fifth and final target sheltered behind it. He fired. An inch of plywood was like a skin of tissue to a fifty-calibre bullet travelling at 2,700 feet per second. Another huge bloom of blood splashed out onto the beige-coloured wall.

Milton stopped shooting.

His ears were ringing.

"Is it done?" Su-Yung said.

The next sound he heard, unmistakeably, even at this distance, was the muffled sound of screaming.

"It's done."

The unfinished room was full of the smell of burnt powder. Milton pushed himself backward on his toes and his forearms, moving away from the window. He swept the six spent shell cases into a pile. He scooped them into his hands and dropped them into his pocket. They were hot to the touch.

"How many?"

"Five," Milton said.

"But you only shot six times. You hit five?"

Milton nodded.

"Extraordinary."

Milton indicated the rifle. "I just point and shoot."

"That is a painful lesson for them to learn. And in their own building."

Milton said nothing.

"We must go," Su-Yung said. "They will close down the area. We must not be here when that happens. Your cover will not stand up to scrutiny."

Milton came to his knees and stood up. He closed the plastic sheeting again, feeding the ties through the corresponding eyelets and tightening them. There was no sign that he had ever even been here. He wrapped the rifle in the blanket again, and they made their way back down the stairwell. The garage was still deserted, gloomy and silent, although the sound of sirens was audible from outside. Su-Yung went to the van, but when she turned back to Milton, she looked concerned.

"What is it?"

"Kun was supposed to meet us here. He was going to drive you out of the city."

"He's been delayed?"

"No, he would not allow that to happen. My brother is a very dependable man. I am afraid that he must have been arrested." She frowned, composing herself, and then set her face with a stern expression. "It is no matter. I know where you need to go. I will drive you." She opened the door and pulled herself inside. "Quickly. We cannot wait."

Milton tossed the rifle inside and got in after it, sliding the side door closed. Su-Yung reversed and, driving with particular care, drove them up the ramp and out onto the street. Milton risked a glance out of the window: the crowd from the square was beginning to disperse, hundreds of people choking the pavements, some of them walking in the road. There was no sign that anything was amiss. The noise of his six shots would have been absorbed by the clamour of the parade. Milton doubted that these people would ever know what had just taken place three hundred feet above their heads; the regime would suppress the news, replacement generals would be promoted to fill the spots vacated by the dead, and little would change. But those men would know, now, that they were not safe, not even in the redoubt of their own capital.

Milton sat quietly in the back, shielded from observation. He knew that if they were stopped, it would be almost certain that he would be seen, and if that happened, there would be more bloodshed. He laid down the sniper rifle and collected the M-4 instead. He popped the magazine free and checked the load. He slid it back into the port and punched it home with the heel of his hand. Then, he took the tracking device from his pocket. It was small, about half the size of a smartphone, and would transmit his location and receive the location of his destination via the American military's GPS satellite network. It was accurate to a metre, and the battery was good for a week. That ought to be long enough. He thumbed the switch, and a red light glowed to signify that the unit was active.

Su-Yung drove on.

Chapter Nineteen

MILTON KILLED the engine of the boat and let it drift. He was two miles off the eastern coast, drifting through a thick blanket of sea mist. He had initially thought that the weather had been kind, shielding him from view as he put out from the tiny inlet near to Jungsan in Pyongyang Province. On two occasions he had heard the engines of old Russian-built MiGs overhead, and both times the jets had curved away with no indication that he had been seen. Now, though, the fog was less helpful. It blinded him, too, and he needed to see where he was going so that he could make his rendezvous.

It had taken him and Su-Yung two days to reach the coast. The first day was the worst, crawling through the city until they found quieter roads where they could travel more quickly without causing suspicion. They found a deserted barn near Taedong and sheltered there until darkness had fallen, and then set off again. They travelled only at night, driving carefully, the van's lights off, the M-4 laid out across his lap and the 9mm thrust into the waistband of his jeans. There had been several moments where he had been sure they were about to be discovered. The worst was the army jeep that had bounded along the main road just as they had turned off it. The driver had stopped at the beginning of the bridge that spanned the creek they had just crossed, the spotter in the back scanning the landscape with a pair of infra-red binoculars. A big .30 calibre machine gun was mounted on the back of the jeep; if they saw them, he knew that that monster would chew them up. Su-Yung and Milton were quiet, hardly breathing, but the soldiers did not see them. They moved away after a long five minutes, and they did not come across them again.

The next night they reached Jungsan. It was a small fishing village, and they had found the boat that Kun had arranged for him without difficulty. Su-Yung waited at the jetty as he embarked, transferring his weapons into the wheelhouse. Her face was blank, austere, and he knew that she was thinking of her brother. She waved him off as he started the engine and put out to sea. Milton had tried to persuade her to head north, to China, but it was a pointless exercise. She had decided to go back to the city to look for Kun. She was determined, and she would not give him up.

Milton relied on the tracking beacon to guide him to the exfiltration point. It had been silent for the first few hours, but then it had started to chirp. It sounded regularly now, a low buzz every few seconds. He knew he was close, but he couldn't see where he was supposed to be going.

He thought, then, that he saw a hulking shape to port, but the mist rolled in even thicker, and he doubted himself. The temperature was icy, and the journey had chilled him to the bone, his teeth chattering helplessly. He cocked his head, listening. All he could hear was the slow lap of the water against the prow of the boat, the buzzing of the beacon and, he fancied, the mournful boom of a foghorn in the direction of the shore.

A voice away to his right. He held his breath, listening hard. The voice came again, distorted in the mist, and he pulled on the oars, nudging the skiff around in the direction that he guessed it was coming from. He saw a dull glow, a bloom of fuzzy light a hundred yards to his right. He pulled on the right oar, turning the skiff again, and made for it. He heard his own name being called, loudly, and then the wind picked up, a gust of ten or twelve knots, the sounds blown away. He pulled the oars harder, increasing his speed. The fulgid glow was extinguished and quickly replaced by a powerful spotlight.

"I'm here," he yelled out, his voice weak and unreal. "Over here!"

A long, low shape, the deepest black and enormously large, formed itself from out of the mist ahead of him. He saw the raised conning tower and the sleekly curved sides of the hull where they met the crashing waves. As he grew closer, he could discern the shape of the ship: a long, fattened cigar, three hundred feet from port to stern. HMS *Ambush* had been positioned off the coast for a week, waiting for its twin optronic masts to detect the telltale signal of his tracker. The skiff bumped up against the side of the submarine, and a rope was tossed down. Milton fished it out of the icy sea, fastened it to the gunwale and pulled himself up. He grabbed the mittened hand that reached down for him. He could see the gold leafing on the peak of a Navy cap beneath the fur trimming of a parka hood.

"Good evening, sir," the man called as Milton clambered aboard the hull. "How was your trip?"

"I've had better. What's the news?"

"It'd be fair to say you've created quite a stir."

Milton negotiated the hatch and followed the officer down into the guts of the submarine. The steady pulse of the engines started, the anchor chain roared back into the aft main ballast tank, and the *Ambush* started to submerge beneath the waters of the quiet bay.

The Cleaner

A John Milton Novel

Mark Dawson

"We deal in lead, friend."
Vin, 'The Magnificent Seven'

PROLOGUE

THE ROAD THROUGH THE FOREST was tranquil, the gentle quiet embroidered by the gurgling of a mountain rill and the chirruping of the birds in the canopy of trees overhead. The *route forestière de la Combe d'Ire* was potholed and narrow, often passable by just one car at a time. Evergreen pine forests clustered tightly on either side, pressing a damp gloom onto the road that was dispelled by warm sunlight wherever the trees had been chopped back. The misty slopes of the massif of the Montagne de Charbon stretched above the treeline, ribs of rock and stone running down through the vegetation. The road followed a careful route up the flank of the mountain, turning sharply to the left and right and sometimes switching back on itself as it traced the safest path upwards. The road crossed and recrossed the stream, and the humpback bridge here was constructed from ancient red bricks, held together as much by the damp lichen that clung to it as by its disintegrating putty. The bridge was next to a small enclosure signed as a car park, although that was putting it at its highest; it was little more than a lay-by hewn from the hillside, a clearing barely large enough to fit four cars side by side. Forestry reserve notices warned of "wild animals" and "hunters."

It was a quiet and isolated spot, the outside world excluded almost as if by the closing of a door.

Milton had parked his Renault there, nudged against the shoulder of the mountain. It was a nondescript hire car; he had chosen it because it was unremarkable. He had reversed into the space, leaving the engine running as he stepped out and made his way around to the boot. He unlocked and opened it and looked down at the bundle nestled in the car's small storage space. He unfolded the edges of the blanket to uncover the assault rifle that had been left at the dead drop the previous night. It was an HK53 carbine with integrated suppressor, the rifle that the SAS often used when stealth was as important as stopping power. Milton lifted the rifle from the boot and pressed a fresh twenty-five-round magazine into the breech. He opened the collapsible stock and took aim, pointing down the middle of the road. Satisfied that the weapon was functioning correctly, he made his way towards the bridge and rested it in the undergrowth, out of sight.

Milton had scouted the area and knew it well. To the north, the road eventually led to Saint-Jorioz, a medium-sized tourist resort that gathered along the shore of Lake Annecy. The descent to the south led to the small village of Chevaline. The village made its living from farming, but that was supplemented by renting the picturesque chalet farmhouses to the tourists who came for cycling and hiking. Milton had stayed in just such a chalet for the past three days. He had spent his time scouting the area, departing on his bike early in the morning and returning late at night. He had kept a low profile, staying in the chalet apart from those trips out.

Milton heard the engine of the BMW long before he saw it. He collected the rifle and slipped behind the trunk of an oak, hiding himself from the road but still able to observe it. The wine-coloured estate car was in second gear, struggling a little with the steep camber of the road. It emerged from the sharp right-hand turn, its lights illuminating a path through the gloom.

The car slowed and turned in towards the Renault. Milton held his breath, his pulse ticking up, and slipped his index finger through the trigger guard of the rifle. The driver parked alongside and switched off the engine. Milton could hear music from the interior of the car. The passenger-side door opened, and the muffled music became clearer: French pop, disposable and inoffensive. The passenger bent down and spoke sharply into the car, and the music was silenced. For a moment all Milton could hear was the crunch of the man's shoes on the gravel, the rushing of the water, and the wind in the leaves. He tightened his grip on the rifle and concentrated on keeping his breathing even and regular.

The driver's side door opened, and a tall, dark-skinned woman stepped outside.

Milton recognised both of them. The passenger was Yehya al Moussa. The driver was Sameera Najeeb.

He stepped out from behind the trunk and brought the HK53 to bear. He flicked the selector to automatic and fired off a volley of shots. The bullets struck Najeeb in the gut, perforating her liver and lungs. She put her hand to her breast, confusion spreading across her face, and then pivoted and fell back against the side of the car. Najeeb shrieked, moving quickly, ducking down beneath the line contour of the car. Milton took two smooth sidesteps to his right to open up the angle again and squeezed off another burst. The scientist was trying to get back into the car; the bullets tattooed his body in a line from throat to crotch.

The fusillade sounded around the trees for a moment. Frightened birds exploded into the air on wingbeats that sounded like claps. The echo of the reports died and faded away, and then, short moments after the brutal outburst of violence, all was quiet again: the wind rustled through the trees, the water chimed beneath the bridge, a nightingale called from high above.

Milton paused. There was another sound.

A second car approaching.

Hiding would have been pointless; the bloody tableau would give him away. The car emerged from the mouth of the forest. It was a Renault Mégane painted blue with white and red chevrons screen-printed across the bonnet. The policeman in the front of the car must have seen him immediately. The Mégane came to a sudden stop fifty feet away.

Milton ejected the magazine and slapped in a replacement.

The officer opened the door and stepped out of the car, his hand on the butt of his holstered pistol. "*Arrêt!*" he called out.

Milton did not pause to think. His reaction was hard-wired, a response that had been drilled into him across ten years so that now it was automatic, an expression of muscle memory without conscience, sudden and terribly deadly. He swung the rifle around and squeezed the trigger for a longer burst. The car was peppered with bullets, half a dozen slamming into the radiator and bonnet, another handful into the windscreen. The officer was struck in the face and chest, stumbling backwards and then dropping onto his back, where he lay for a moment, twitching horribly. Milton walked towards him, the gun cradled low, and put a final bullet into his head. Finally, the man lay still.

Peacefulness returned, ornamented now by the sound of the shards of glass that fell to shatter on the road from the breached windscreen.

Milton crossed the road to the Renault. He opened the boot and wrapped the rifle in its blanket, then stowed it away carefully beneath the spare wheel in the false floor. He pulled on a pair of latex gloves and collected the ejected shell casings from the rifle. There were forty of them, and they were still hot to the touch. He dropped them into a small evidence bag. He crouched by Najeeb's body and frisked her quickly and efficiently. He found her smartphone and a USB stick and bagged them both.

He went around to the other side of the car and lowered himself to examine al Moussa. The door was open, and as he raised his gaze from the body to peer inside, he saw a small, pale face staring back out at him. Milton did not rush. There was no need. The face belonged to a young boy, perhaps five or six years old. His skin and his hair were dark, and his features recalled those of his parents. He was cowering in the foot space, a streak of blood across his forehead as if it was paint that had been thrown over him. It was not his blood: it was blowback from his father.

Milton reached for the Sig Sauer he carried in his shoulder holster, his fingers brushing against the butt. The boy held his eyes. His face was white and quivering with fright, but he did not look away. He was brave. Milton felt a swell of vomit in his throat as his memory cast him back twenty years and a thousand miles away. He remembered another young boy, a similar age, the face peaceful despite the obscenity of his death.

He lowered his hand from the Sig and stepped back. He gently pulled the man's body onto the muddy surface of the lay-by and went back to the car.

"Stay there," he told the boy. "Help is coming."

He closed the door. He checked that he had removed the evidence of his presence and, satisfied, got into the Renault, put it into gear and drove away.

He turned to the north, upwards, and drove towards the lake.

PART ONE

The Cleaner

The man was on the bed, his hands clenched into claws over his heart and his teeth grinding over and over again. His eyelids flickered, and sometimes he moaned, strangled words that would have made no sense if anyone had been there to hear them. His body was rigid with tension, sweat drenching his body and the sheets. The dream came more often now, sometimes every night, always the same. He was lying prone, flat in the cushioned warmth of sand dunes. The sun was directly above him, a midday sun that pounded the desert with a brutal heat that made the air shimmer, the mountains in the distance swaying as if viewed through the water of a fish tank. The landscape was arid, long swathes of dead sand that stretched for as far as the eye could see. The only vegetation was close to the banks of the slow-moving river that eventually found its way into the Tigris. A single ribbon of asphalt was the only road for miles around, deep drifts of sand blown across it.

Chapter One

CONTROL SQUINTED through the windscreen of the XJS as he pulled into the empty fast lane and accelerated past a lumbering articulated lorry. The sky had been a bloody crimson last night, and when the sun returned in the morning, it had risen into a clear, untrammelled blue sky. There was heat and light in those early rays, and he angled the blind to shade his eyes. The radio was tuned to the *Today* programme and the forecaster predicted a week of searing heat. The seven o'clock news followed the weather—the lead item was the shooting of two tourists and a policeman in the French Alps. The victims had been identified, but as yet, a motive for the killing had not been found. It was "senseless," a French policeman concluded.

That, Control thought, was not true. It was far from senseless. The operation had been the result of long and meticulous planning, six months spent cultivating the targets and gaining their trust and then weeks setting up the meeting. The objective had been successfully achieved, but it had not been clean. There were two errors that would need careful handling, errors that raised doubts over the performance of the man who had carried out the operation.

The fact that it was Number One was troubling.

It had been Control's operation. He knew the targets intimately. Yehya al Moussa had been an atomic research scientist. Sameera Najeeb was an expert in microwave technology. They were married, and until recently, both had been in the employ of the Iraq Atomic Energy Agency. Following the fall of Saddam, they had been recruited by the Iranians, and with their help, the Ahmandinejad regime had made progress towards its goal of becoming a nuclear power. A decision had been made, somewhere in MI5, that the couple was too dangerous to live. That decision had been rubber-stamped in another anonymous grey office in Whitehall, and their files had been marked with red and passed to Group Fifteen to be actioned. It was important, and because of that, Control had selected Number One for the assignment.

As he turned the Jaguar off the motorway at the exit for Central London, Control reviewed his preparation. The two had come to France under the pretext of a long-deserved holiday. The real reason, however, and the reason for their diversion into the Alpine countryside, was to meet an employee of Cezus, a subsidiary of Areva, the global leader in the market for zirconium. That metal was used, among other things, for nuclear fuel cladding. Iran needed zirconium for its reactors, and al Moussa and Najeeb had been led to believe that their contact could supply as much as they needed. But there had been no employee. There was no zirconium. There was to be no meeting, at least not the rendezvous that they had been expecting.

Control tapped out a rhythm on the steering wheel as he passed into London. No, he thought, the preparation had been faultless. The problems were all of Milton's making. The dead *gendarme* would give the French police a strong personal motive to locate the killer; one of their own had been murdered. It would make them more tenacious and less likely to shelve the investigation when the trail went cold, as Control knew that it would. That was bad, but even worse was the boy. A child, orphaned by the killer, cowering in the car as he watched his parents' murders. That was dynamite, the hook upon which the press would be able to hang all of their reporting. It ensured the story would run and run.

Control slowed and turned the Jaguar into the underground car park beneath a small building huddled on the north bank of the Thames. It was a sixties build, constructed from brick and concrete without style or grace. Five floors, anonymous. The car idled as the garage door rolled up with a tired metallic creak. The sign painted onto the door read GLOBAL LOGISTICS.

He drove inside, pulled up next to the secure elevator, and got out of the car. The lift arrived, and he embarked, pressing the button for the third floor. The lift eased to a halt, the doors sighed open, and he stepped out into the bustling open-plan space beyond. Analysts stared at monitors and tapped at keyboards, printers chattered, and telephones chimed incessantly. Control passed through the chaotic space to a corridor lined with thick carpet, following it around to the right so that the clamour behind him faded to a gentle hum of activity. A number of green baize doors faced the corridor, and he picked the one at the end, pushing it open and walking through.

David Tanner, his private secretary, looked up from his computer. "Morning, sir," he said. Tanner was ex-army, infantry, like Control and all of the other operatives who worked for him. Tanner's career had been forestalled by an IED on the road outside Kabul. It had cost him his right leg below the knee and the posting to the SAS that he had craved. He was a good man, easy-going and pleasant to share a drink with, and he guarded access to his commanding officer with fierce dedication.

"Morning, Captain," he said. "What does the morning look like?"

"You're speaking to the director at midday. Wants an update on the French situation."

"I'm sure she does. And Number One?"

"Waiting for you inside, sir."

"Very good."

He went through into the office. It was a large room that offered an expansive view of the river. There was a central table with a bowl of flowers, and two comfortable club chairs on either side of the fire. There were no filing cabinets, and nothing that looked official.

Milton was standing at the wide window at the other end of the room, smoking a cigarette and looking down on the broad sweep of the Thames. Control paused by the door and regarded him; he was dressed in a plain dark suit that looked rather cheap, a white shirt and a black tie.

"Good morning, Number One," he said.

"Morning, sir."

"Take a seat."

He watched as Milton sat down. His eyes were implacable. He looked a little shabby, a little worn around the edges. Control recalled him when he joined the service. He had sported Savile Row suits, shirts from Turnbull & Asser, and was perfectly groomed at all times. He did not seem to care for any of that any longer. Control didn't care what his agents looked like, so long as they were good at their job, and Milton was his best; that was why this latest misadventure was so troubling.

There came a knock at the door. Tanner entered bearing a tray with a pot of tea and two bone-china cups. He set the tray down on the sideboard, and after confirming that there was nothing else that Control needed, he left them alone.

Control got up and poured the tea, watching Milton as he did so. One did not apply for a job like his, one was chosen, and as was his habit with all the operatives who worked for him, Control had selected him himself and then supervised the year of rigorous training that smoothed away his rough edges and prepared him for his new role. There had been moments when Milton had doubted his own suitability for the position, and Control had not so much as assuaged the doubts as chided him for even entertaining the possibility that his judgment might have been awry. He prided himself on being an excellent judge of character, and he had known that Milton would be the perfect field agent. He had been proved right. Milton had started his career as Number Twelve, as was customary. And now, ten years later, all his predecessors were gone, and he was Number One.

Milton was tense. He gripped the armrest of the chair so tightly that his knuckles whitened. He had not shaved that morning, the strong line of his jaw darkly stubbled. "The boy?" he said.

"Traumatised but otherwise fine, from what we can gather. As you would expect. The French have him in care. We don't think they've spoken to him yet. Did he see you?"

"Yes."

"That could be awkward."

Milton ignored him. "Did you know?"

"Know what?"

"That he'd be there."

"We knew he was in France. We didn't think they would bring him to the meeting."

"And you didn't think to tell me that they might?"

"Remember who you're talking to," Control said angrily. "Would it have made a difference?"

Milton's cold stare burned into him.

"There's no point in pretending otherwise—the boy is a problem. The damned policeman, too. It would've been tidy without them, but now, well, they're both loose ends. They make things more complicated. You'd better tell me what happened."

"There's not much to say. I followed the plan to the letter. The weapon was where it was supposed to be. I arrived before the targets. They were there on time. I eliminated both. As I was tidying up, the gendarme arrived. So I shot him."

"The rules of engagement were clear."

"Indeed, sir. No witnesses. I don't believe I had a choice."

"You didn't. I'm not questioning that."

"But you're questioning something?" Milton said.

Again, his tone was harsh. Control ignored it. "You said it yourself. No witnesses."

"The boy? Why I didn't shoot him?"

"It might be distasteful, but you know how clear we are about how we conduct ourselves on operations." Control was tense. The conversation was not developing as he had anticipated, and he was not in the business of being surprised. There was a whiteness around the edges of Milton's lips. The blue eyes still stared blankly, almost unseeingly.

"I've seen a lot of dead bodies since I've been working for you, sir."

Control replied with as much patience as he could manage. "Of course you have, Milton. You're an assassin. Dead bodies are your stock-in-trade."

He might not even have heard him. "I can't keep pretending to myself anymore. We make decisions about who lives and who dies, but it's not always black and white when you're in the middle of it. As you say, the rules of engagement were clear. I should have shot him. Ten years ago, when I signed up for this"—the word carried a light dusting of contempt—"I probably would have shot him. Like a good soldier."

"But you didn't."

"I couldn't."

"Why are you telling me this?"

"Ten years is a long time for this kind of work, sir. Longer than anyone else. And I haven't been happy lately. I don't think I've ever really been happy."

"I don't expect you to be happy."

Milton had become agitated and pressed on. "I've got blood on my hands. I used to tell myself the same things to justify it, but they don't work anymore. That policeman didn't deserve to die. The boy didn't deserve to lose his parents. We made a widow and an orphan because of a lie. And I'm not doing it any longer, sir. I'm finished."

Control spoke carefully. "Are you trying to resign?"

"You can call it whatever you like. My mind is made up."

Control rose. He needed a moment to tamp down his temper. This was perilously close to insubordination, and rather than lash out, he went across to the mantelpiece and adjusted the photograph of his family. He spoke carefully: "What's the Group for, Milton?"

"Framing. Extortion. Elimination."

"Jobs that are too dirty for Her Majesty's security services to touch."

"Quite so, sir."

"And your job?"

"Cleaner."

"Which means?"

"'From time to time Her Majesty's government needs to remove people whose continued existence poses a risk to the effective conduct of public order. The government requires particularly skilled professionals who are prepared to work on a non-attributable basis to deal with these problems.' Cleaners."

He smiled without humour. That was the job description he had used when he recruited him all those years ago. All those neutral euphemisms, all designed to make the job easier to palate. "It takes a special kind of man to do that kind of work. There are so few of you—and, unfortunately, that makes you rather difficult to replace." He paused. "Do you know how many people you've eliminated for me?"

Milton replied without even thinking. "One hundred and thirty-six."

"You're my best cleaner."

"Once, perhaps. Not anymore. I can't ignore it any longer. I can't keep my mouth shut just to avoid being unprofessional. I'm lying to myself. We have to face facts, sir. Dress it up however you like—neutralisation, elimination—but those are just euphemisms for what it is I really do. I'm paid to murder people."

Control was not getting through to him. "Murder?" he exclaimed. "What are you talking about, man? Don't be so soft. You want to moralise? You know what would happen if the Iranians get the bomb. There'll be a war. A proper war that will make Iraq look like a walk in the bloody park. Thousands of people will die. Hundreds of thousands. Removing those two made that prospect a little less likely. And they knew the risk they were taking. You can call it murder if you like, but they were not innocents. They were combatants."

"And the policeman? The boy?"

"Unfortunate, but necessary."

"Collateral damage?"

Control felt he was being goaded. He took a breath and replied with a taut, "Indeed."

Milton folded his arms. "I'm sorry, sir. I'm done with you. I'm finished."

Control walked up to Milton, circled him close, noticed the tension in the shoulders and the clenched fists. "No one is ever really finished with me. You can't resign. You can't retire. You're a murderer, as you say. It's all you know. After all, what can you chaps do after you leave me? Your talents are so specialised. You use a gun. You use your fists. You use a knife. What else could you do? Work with children? In an office? No. You're unskilled labour, man. This is what you are."

"Then find yourself another labourer."

He banged a fist on the mantelpiece in frustration. "You work for me for as long as I bloody well want you to or I'll have you destroyed."

Milton rose to face him. His stature was imposing, and his eyes were chilling. They had regained their clarity and icy focus. They were the eyes of a killer, and he fixed him in a pitiless gaze. "I think we're finished, sir, aren't we? We're not going to agree with each other."

"Is that your final word?"

"It is."

Control put his desk between them and sat down. "You're making a terrible mistake. You're on suspension. Unpaid. I'll review your file, but there will be discipline. Take the time to consider your position. It isn't too late to repair the damage this foolish stand has caused you."

"Very good, sir." Milton straightened his tie.

"You're dismissed."

"Good day, sir."

Chapter Two

MILTON FOUND A BAR. His anonymous, empty hotel room did not appeal to him. The confrontation with Control had unsettled him; his hands were shaking from anger and fear.

There was a place with a wide picture window that faced the river. He found a table that looked out onto the open water, the buildings on the opposite bank, the pleasure craft and barges churning through the surf and, above, the blazing sun in a perfectly clear sky. He wanted a large whiskey, to feel the alcohol, his head beginning to spin just a little. He knew one way to stop thinking—about everything—could be found in the bottom of his glass, but he managed to resist the urge. It was short-term relief with long-term consequences. He focussed on the number that he kept in his head—691—and ordered an orange juice instead. He sat brooding, turning the glass between his fingers, watching the boats.

There was a television above the bar. The volume was turned down with subtitles running along the bottom of the screen. The channel had been set to one of the twenty-four-hour news programmes, and an interview with a minister on Parliament Green was abruptly replaced by an overhead helicopter shot of a wooded mountain landscape. A caption flashed that it was near Lake Annecy, France. The camera jerked and zoomed until the screen was filled with a shot of a wine-coloured BMW. It was parked in a small clearing. The camera zoomed out, and a second car, blue with white-and-red chevrons, could be seen. Bloodstains were visible on the muddy ground around the cars. The captions along the bottom of the screen said "massacre," and "outrage."

The bartender shook his head. "Did you see that?"

Milton grunted.

"You know they found a boy in the car?"

Milton said nothing.

"I don't know how someone could do that—murder a family on a holiday. How cold-blooded is that? You ask me, that little boy was lucky. If whoever it was had found him, I reckon he would've been shot, too."

The news report switched to another story, but it was no good. Milton finished the juice and stood. He needed to leave.

Chapter Three

THE PLATFORM for the Underground was busy. A group of young foreign travellers who didn't know any better had congregated near the slope that led up to the surface, blocking the way with their suitcases and chattering excitedly in Portuguese. Their luggage was plastered with stickers that proclaimed their previous destinations. Brazilians, he guessed. Students. Milton picked his way through them so he could wait at the quieter, less populated end of the platform. There was a lone traveller there, standing right up at the edge. She was black, in her early thirties, and wearing the uniform of one of the fast-food chains that served the area around the station. She looked tired, and Milton saw that she was crying, her bottom lip quivering and tears rolling down her cheeks. Milton was not good with empathy, and he would not have known where to start were he to try to comfort her, but he had no interest in that. Not today. He had too much on his mind. He moved along.

He felt awful again. His mood had worsened. He felt light-headed and slumped down onto an empty bench. He started to sweat, his hands first, then his back, salty beads rolling down from his scalp into his eyes and mouth.

He recalled the overhead shot of the forest from the television helicopter. There had been three pegs on the ground, marking the spots where the bodies had been found. He knew he should stop, think of something else, but he couldn't, and soon he recalled the nightmare again, the flashes from years before: the flattened village, the blood splashed over the arid ground, the body of the boy, the peppery smell of high explosives and cloying death. He floated away from that, running onto all the other things he had done and seen in the service of Queen and country: dingy rooms and darkened streets, one hundred and thirty-six victims laid out in evidence of the terrible things he had done. A shot to the head from a sniper rifle, a knife to the heart, a garrotte around the throat pulled tight until the hacking breaths became wheezes that became silent, a body desperately jerking, then falling still. One hundred and thirty-six men and women faced him, accused him, their blood on his hands.

A loud scream yanked him around.

The students were staring down the platform at him. He took it all in, the details. Was it him they were pointing at? No. They were pointing away from him. The woman wasn't there. Another scream and one of the students pointed down onto the track. Milton stumbled to his feet and saw her deliberately laid across the rails. It was an incongruous sight. At first he thought she must have been trying to collect something that she had dropped, but then he realised that she had laid herself out in that fashion for a purpose. He spun around; the glowing digital sign said the next train was approaching, and then Milton heard it, the low rumble as the carriages rolled around the final bend in the tunnel. There wasn't any time to consider what to do. There was an emergency button on the wall fifty feet away, but he knew he wouldn't be able to reach it in time, and even if he did, he doubted the train would be able to stop.

He jumped down from the platform onto the sleepers.

He stepped over the live rail.

The train drew nearer, a blast of warm air pouring out of the mouth of the tunnel.

Milton knelt down by the woman.

"No," she said. "Leave me alone."

He slipped one hand beneath her back and the other beneath her knees. She was slight, and he lifted her easily. The train turned the final bend, its headlights shining brightly. Its horn sounded, shrill and sudden, and Milton knew it was going to be touch and go. He stepped over the live rail again and threw the woman up onto the platform. The train's brakes bit, the locked wheels sliding across the metal with a hideous shriek, as Milton planted his hands on the lip of the platform and vaulted up, rolling away just as the engine groaned by, missing him by fractions.

He rolled over, onto his back, and stared up at the curved ceiling. His breath rushed in and out.

The train had stopped halfway into the station. The driver opened the door and sprinted down the platform towards him. "Are you all right, mate?"

"Fine. Check her."

He closed his eyes and forced his breathing to return to a regular pattern. In and out, in and out.

"I thought you was a goner," the driver said. "I thought I was gonna hit you both. What happened?"

Milton didn't answer. The students had made their way down the platform, and the driver turned his attention to them. They reported what they had seen in singsong, broken English: how the woman had lowered herself from the platform and laid herself out across the rails, how Milton had gone down after her and pulled her away from danger.

"You're a bloody hero, mate," the driver said.

Milton closed his eyes again.

A hero?

He would have laughed if that wasn't so ridiculous. It was a bad joke.

Chapter Four

AN AMBULANCE arrived soon afterwards. Milton sat next to the woman on the bench as she was attended to by the paramedics. She had cried hysterically for five minutes, but she quickly stopped, and by the time the paramedics had arrived, she was silent and unmoving, staring fixedly at the large posters for exotic holidays and duty-free goods that were plastered across the curved wall on the other side of the tracks.

One of the paramedics had taken the woman's purse from her bag. "Is your name Sharon, love?" he asked. She said nothing. "Come on, love, you have to talk to us."

She remained silent.

"We're going to have to take her in," the paramedic said. "I think she's in shock."

"I'll come, too," Milton said.

"Are you a friend?"

Leaving her now would be abandoning her. He had started to help, and he wanted to finish the job. He would leave once her family had arrived.

"Yes," he said.

"Come on, sweetheart. Let's get you checked out properly."

Milton followed behind the ambulance as they took the woman to the Royal Free Hospital. They wheeled her into a quiet room and made her a cup of warm tea, full of sugar. "We're just waiting for the doctor," they said to her. "Get that down you; it'll make all the difference."

"Thank you," she murmured.

The paramedic turned to Milton. "Are you all right to stay with her? He's on his way, but it might be twenty minutes."

"Yes," Milton said. "Of course."

He took the seat next to the bed and watched the girl. She had closed her eyes, and after a few minutes, Milton realised that she had drifted into a shallow sleep. Her chest rose and fell with each gentle breath. Milton regarded her. Her hair was of the deepest black, worn cut square and low on the nape of her neck, fanned out on the white hospital linen to frame a sweet almond-shaped face. Her eyes were wide under finely drawn eyebrows, slightly up tilted at the corners. Her skin was a perfect chocolate-brown and bore no trace of makeup save a light lipstick on her wide and sensual mouth. Her bare arms were slender, and her hands, folded beneath her breasts, were small and delicate. Her fingernails were chewed down, the red varnish chipped. There was no ring on her finger. The restaurant uniform was a utilitarian grey, lasciviously tight across her breasts. The trousers flowed down from a narrow, but not thin, waist. Her shoes were square-toed and of plain black leather. She was very pretty.

Milton let her rest.

Chapter Five

SHE AWOKE a full two hours later. At first her pretty face maintained the serenity of sleep, but that did not last for very long; confusion clouded across it and then, suddenly, came a terrible look of panic. She struggled upright and swung her feet off the bed and onto the floor.

"It's all right," Milton said. "You're in hospital. You've been asleep."

"What time is it?"

"Six."

"Jesus," she said. "I'm so late. My boy—I need to be home." She looked around, panicked. "Where are we?"

"Hospital."

"No," she said, pushing herself onto her feet. "I have to be home. My boy will be there. He won't know where I am; he won't have had his tea. No one's looking after him."

"The doctor's been. He wanted to speak to you. He's coming back when you're awake."

"I can't. And I'm fine, besides. I know it was a stupid thing to do. I'm not about to do it again. I don't want to die. I can't. He needs me." She looked into his face. Her expression was earnest and honest. "They can't keep me in here, can they?"

"I don't think so."

She collected her bag from the chair and started for the door.

"How are you going to get home?" Milton asked her.

"I don't know. Where is this?"

"The Royal Free."

"Hampstead? I'll get the train."

"Let me drive you."

"You don't have to do that. I live in Dalston. That must be miles out of your way."

"No, that's fine. I live just round the corner—Islington." It was a lie. "It's not a problem."

The medical staff were uncomfortable about their patient discharging herself, but there was nothing that they could do to stop her. She was not injured, she appeared to be rational, and she was not alone. Milton answered their reflexive concern with a tone of quiet authority that was difficult to oppose. She signed her discharge papers, politely thanked the staff for their care, and followed Milton outside.

Milton had parked in the nearby NCP building. He swept the detritus from the passenger seat, opened the door, waited until she was comfortable, and then set off, cutting onto the Embankment. He glanced at her through the corner of his eye; she was staring fixedly out of the window, watching the river. It didn't look as if she wanted to talk. Fair enough. He switched on the CD player and skipped through the discs until he found the one he wanted to listen to, a Bob Dylan compilation. Dylan's reedy voice filled the car as Milton accelerated away from a set of traffic lights.

"Thanks for this," Sharon said suddenly. "I'm very grateful."

"It's not a problem."

"My boy should be home. He'll be wanting his tea."

"What's his name?"

"Elijah."

"That's a nice name."

"His father liked it. He was into his Bible."

"How old is he?"

"Fifteen. What about you? Do you have any kids?"

"No," Milton said. "It's just me."

He pulled out and overtook a slow-moving lorry, and she was silent for a moment.

"It's because of him," she said suddenly. "This morning—all that. I know it's stupid, but I didn't know what else to do. I still don't, not really. I'm at the end of my tether."

"What's happened?"

She didn't seem to hear that. "I don't have anyone else. If I lose him, there's no point in carrying on."

"Why don't you tell me about it?"

She looked out of the window, biting her lip.

"How have you lost him?"

She clenched her jaw. Milton shrugged and reached for the radio.

She spoke hurriedly. "There's a gang on the Estate where we live, these young lads. Local boys. They terrify everyone. They do what they want—cause trouble, steal things, deal their drugs. No one dares do anything against them."

"The police?"

She laughed bitterly. "No use to no one. They won't even come into the Estate unless there's half a dozen of them. It'll calm down a bit while they're around, but as soon as they go again, it's as if they were never even there."

"What do they have to do with Elijah?"

"He's got in with them. He's just a little boy, and I'm supposed to look after him, but there's nothing I can do. They've taken him away from me. He stays out late, he doesn't listen to me anymore, he won't do as he's told. I've always tried to give him a little freedom, not be one of those rowdy Jamaican mothers where the kids can't ever do anything right, but maybe now I think I ought to have been stricter. Last night was as bad as it's ever been. I know he's been sneaking out late at night to be with them. Normally he goes out of his bedroom window, so I put a lock on it. He comes into the front room, and I tell him he needs to get back to bed. He just gives me this look, and he says I can't tell him what to do anymore. I tell him I'm his mother and he has to listen to me for as long as he's under my roof. That's reasonable, isn't it?"

"Very."

"So he says that maybe he won't be under my roof for much longer, that he'll get his own money and find somewhere for himself. Where's a fifteen-year-old boy going to get the money for rent unless it's from thieving or selling drugs? He goes for the door, but he's got to come by me first, so I get up and stop him. He tells me to get out of the way, and when I won't, he says he hates me, says how it's my fault his father isn't around, and when I try to get him to calm down, he just pushes me aside, opens the door and goes. He's a big boy for his age, taller than I am already, and he's strong. If he won't do as he's told, what can I do to stop him? He didn't get back in until three in the morning, and when I woke up to go to work, he was still asleep. "

"Have you thought about moving away?"

She laughed humourlessly again. "Do you know how hard that is? We were in a hostel before. I used to live up in Manchester until my husband started knocking me about. There was this place for battered women; we ended up there when we got into London. I'm not knocking it, but it was full up. It was no place to bring up my boy. I was on at the Social for months before they gave us our flat. You have no idea the trouble it'd be to get them to move us somewhere else. No. We're stuck there."

She paused, staring out at the cars again.

"Ever since we've been in the Estate we've had problems. I worry about Elijah every single day. Every single day I worry about him. Every day I worry."

Milton had started to wonder whether there might be a way that he could help.

"I'm sorry," she said. "Here I am telling you all my troubles and I don't even know your name."

Milton almost reflexively retreated to his training and his long list of false identities, but he stopped himself. What was the point? He had no stomach for any of that any longer. A foundation of lies would not be a good place to start if he wanted to help this woman. "I'm John," he said. "John Milton."

He approached the junction for Whitechapel Road and turned off.

"I'm sorry for going on. I'm sure you've got your own problems. You don't need to hear mine."

"I'd like to help."

"That's nice of you, but I don't see how you could."

"Perhaps I could talk to him?"

"You're not police, are you?"

"No."

"Or the Social?"

"No."

"I don't want to be rude, Mr. Milton, but you don't know Elijah. He's headstrong. Why would he care what you said?"

He slowed down as they approached a queue of slower-moving traffic. "I can be persuasive."

Chapter Six

CONTROL HAD REQUESTED Milton's file from the archive, and after it had been delivered, he shut himself away in his office with a pot of tea and a cigar and spread the papers around him. It was late when he started, the sun long since set and the lights of the office blocks on the opposite side of the Thames glittering in the dark waters of the river. He lit the cigar and began his search through the documents for a clue that might explain his sudden, and uncharacteristic, decision. Their conversation had unsettled him. Milton had always been his best cleaner. His professionalism had always been complete. He maintained a vigorous regimen that meant that he was as fit as men half his age. His body was not the problem. If it was, he mused ruefully, this would have been easier to fix. The problem was with his mind, and that presented a more particular issue. Control prided himself on knowing the men and women who worked for him, and Milton's attitude had taken him by surprise. It introduced an element of doubt into his thinking, and doubt, to a man as ordered and logical as Control, was not tolerable.

He held the smoke in his mouth. Milton's dedication and professionalism had never wavered, not for a moment, and he had completed an exemplary series of assignments that could have formed the basis for an instruction manual for the successful modern operative. He was the Group's most ruthless and efficient assassin. He had always treated his vocation as something of an art form, drawing satisfaction from the knowledge of a job well done. Control knew from long and vexatious experience that such an attitude was a rarity these days. Real artisans—real *craftsmen*—were difficult to find, and when you had one, you nurtured him. The other men and women at his disposal tended towards the blunt. They were automatons that he pointed at targets, then watched and waited as they did their job. Their methods were effective but crass: a shower of bullets from a slow-moving car, a landmine detonated by mobile phone, random expressions of uncontrolled violence. It was quick and dirty, flippant and trite, a summation of all that Control despised about modern intelligence. There was no artistry left, no pride taken in the job, no assiduity, no careful deliberation. No real nerve. Milton reminded Control of the men and women he had worked with when he was a field agent himself, posted at Station M in the middle of the Cold War. They had been exact and careful, their assignments comprising long periods of planning that ended with sudden, controlled, contained violence.

Control turned through the pages and found nothing. Perhaps the answer was to be found in his history. He took another report from its storage crate and dropped it on his desk. It was as thick as a telephone directory.

In order for a new agent to be admitted to the Group, a raft of assessments were required to be carried out. The slightest impropriety—financial, personal, virtually anything—would lead to a black mark, and that would be that, the proposal would be quietly dropped and the prospective agent would never even know that they had been under consideration. Milton had been no different. MI5 were tasked with the compilation of the reports, and they had done a particularly thorough job with him. They had investigated his childhood, his education, his career in the army and his personal life.

John Milton was born in 1968. He had no brothers or sisters. His father, James Milton, had worked as a petrochemical engineer and led his family on a peripatetic existence, moving every few years as he followed work around the world. Much of Milton's early childhood was spent in the Gulf, with several years in Saudi Arabia, six months in Iran during the fall of the Shah, then Egypt, Dubai and Oman. There had been a posting to the United States and then, finally, the directorship of a medium-sized gas exploration company in London. The young Milton picked up a smattering of Arabic and an ability to assimilate himself into different cultures; both talents had proven valuable in his later career.

His life had changed irrevocably in 1980. His mother and father were killed in a crash on a German autobahn, and John had been sent to live with his aunt and uncle in Kent. A substantial amount of money was bequeathed to him in trust, and it was put to good use. He was provided with a first-class private education, and after passing the rigorous entrance examination, he was sent up to Eton for the autumn term in 1981. His career there was not successful, and thanks to an incident that MI5 had not been able to confirm (although they suspected it involved gambling), Milton was expelled. There was a period of home tutoring before he was accepted at his father's old school. He stayed there until he was sixteen and then took a place at Cambridge to read law.

He was involved in the OTC, and it had been no surprise to anyone when he ignored the offer of a pupilage at the Bar to enlist in the army. After spending eight years with the Royal Green Jackets, he decided to attempt SAS selection. The process was renowned for being brutally difficult, but he passed, easily. While serving with Air Troop, B Squadron, 22 SAS, Milton worked on both covert and overt operations worldwide, including counterterrorism and drug operations in the Middle East and Far East, South and Central America, and Northern Ireland. Control decided that he was the perfect replacement for Number Seven, who had been killed while on operations in China. He made the pitch himself. It was a persuasive offer, and Milton had accepted immediately.

Control put the history aside and turned back to contemporary papers. Milton's recent yearly assessment had seen a significant dip in results, and as he turned back through the years, he noticed a trend that had remained hidden until then. The assessments were intense and combined a rigorous physical examination, marksmanship tests and a psychological evaluation. Milton's performance in all three elements had been in decline over the last three years. The drop was steepest this year, but it was not isolated. He chided himself for missing it. His continued success in the field had blinded him. He was so good at his job that the suggestion that he might not have been infallible was ridiculous. Now, as he examined his file with the benefit of hindsight, he saw that he had missed a series of indicators.

His physical examinations returned strong results. He was fit, with the cardiovascular profile of a man fifteen years younger. He made it his habit to run a marathon every year, and the times had been noted and added to the file; he had never finished the course in more than three and a half hours. Nevertheless, he had suffered a series of injuries in the field that had exerted a toll on his body. Since joining Group Fifteen he had been shot twice, stabbed in the leg and shoulder, and had broken more than a dozen bones. He reported the usual aches and pains, but the physician suggested that he was being stoic for the benefit of the examination and that it was likely that he was in mild to moderate pain most of the time. Blood tests detected the beginning of mild arthritis in his joints, a condition for which there was a familial history. He took a cocktail of drugs: gabapentin for his nerve damage and oxycodone for general pain relief.

Control relit his cigar and picked up his psychological assessment. He stood to stretch his legs and read the report next to the window. As he skimmed through the pages, he realised that missing the warning signs contained within had been his most egregious error. The psychiatrist noted that Milton had complained of sleeplessness and that he had been prescribed promathazine to combat it. There had been a discussion about reasons behind the problem, but Milton had become agitated and then angry, refusing to accept that it was anything other than an inability to quieten a busy mind. The psychiatrist suggested that Milton's naturally melancholic temperament indicated mild depression and that he seemed to have become introspective and doubting. The report concluded with the recommendation that he be monitored on a more regular basis. Control had ignored it.

Damn it.

Milton was a valuable asset, and he had wilfully ignored the warning signs. He did not want to admit that there might be a problem, and his inaction had allowed it to metastasise.

He put the files back into the storage crate and lit a second cigar. There came a knock at the door.

"Come in," he called.

Christopher Callan came into the office. He was Number Twelve: the most recent recruit to the Group. He had been transferred from the Special Boat Service after a career every bit as glittering as Milton's had been. He was tall and slender and impeccably dressed. His jacket was two-buttoned, cut from nine-ounce cloth. The pockets were straight, and the lining was simple and understated. There was a telltale faint bulge beneath his left armpit, where he wore his shoulder holster. He did not wear a tie. The trousers were classically cut, falling down to the back of his shoe. He was strikingly handsome although his head was round and small, supported by a muscular neck. His scalp was covered with tight blond curls that were almost white, reminding Control of the classical hair of the statues of da Vinci. His skin was a pristine white, and his grooming immaculate. There was a cruelty to his thin-lipped mouth, and the implacability that veiled those pale blue eyes seemed to infect the whole face.

"You wanted to see me, sir?" he said.

"Yes, Callan. Take a seat." He inhaled deeply, taking the smoke all the way back into his throat, then blowing it out. "We've got a bit of a problem. It's one of the other agents—do you know Number One?"

"Only by reputation."

"You've never worked with him, though?"

"No, sir. Why?"

"Afraid he's started to behave a little erratically. I want you to find out everything you can about him—where he's living, what he does with his time, who he's seeing. Everything you can."

"Yes, sir. Anything else?"

"No. Start immediately, please."

"Of course." Callan stood and straightened his jacket. "Number One was in France, sir? The Iranian scientists?"

"That's right."

Callan nodded thoughtfully. "That was unfortunate."

Control looked at him and knew that he would have followed the rules of engagement to the letter. He would not have left any witnesses. He had the same single-minded ruthlessness as Milton when he joined. He had made a reputation for it in the SBS; that was the characteristic that had appealed to Control when he had recruited him.

"Daily reports, please, Number Twelve. Get started at once. You're dismissed."

He turned to face the window again, the door closing softly behind him. He gazed through the cloud of cigar smoke, through his pensive reflection and out into the darkness beyond. Traffic streamed along Millbank on the other side of the river, tail lights leaving a red smear across the tarmac.

He thought of Milton.

Control was a craftsman, too. His agents were his tools. Sometimes, when they got old and unreliable, when their edge grew rusty and could no longer be whetted, they had to be replaced.

Perhaps it was time.

He wondered if that was what he would have to do.

Chapter Seven

ELIJAH WARRINER was frightened as he waited for the train to pull into the station. They were at Homerton, sitting on one of the metal benches, the red paint peeling away to reveal the scabrous rust beneath, the air heavy with the scent of stale urine and the sweet tang of the joint that was being passed around. Elijah stared across the track at the side of a warehouse marked with the tag that indicated that this was their territory: LFB, in ten-foot-high neon yellow and green letters, the black outline running where rain had mixed with it before it had dried.

LFB.

The London Fields Boys.

They ran things around here.

There were six of them on the platform. Pops, the oldest and the biggest, was in charge of the little crew. The other boys were arrayed around him on the platform: Little Mark was smoking a joint with his back to the wall; Pinky had his headphones pressed against his head, the low drone of the new Plan B record leaking out; Kidz and Chips were eyeing up the girls from the Gascoyne Estate, who were also waiting for the train. They were all dressed in the same way: a baseball cap, a hooded top, low-slung jeans and brand new pairs of Nikes or Reeboks. Some of them had their hoods pulled up, resting against the brim of their caps and casting their faces in dark shadow. They all wore bandanas tied around their necks.

It was just before half past five, and rush hour was just beginning.

Pops put his around Elijah's shoulders and squeezed him hard, using his other hand to scrub at his head. "JaJa, chill," he said. "Nothing to worry about."

Elijah managed to smile. Pops was wearing the same uniform as all the others, but he had a pair of diamond earrings, a chunky ring on each hand and a heavy golden chain around his neck. They denoted his position as an Elder, and, of course, the fact that he had more money than the rest of them. Elijah watched as Pops took out his bag of weed and his packet of papers. "My grandma taught me to build zoots, get me?" Pops spread a copy of the Metro across his lap and arranged his things: the bag of weed, his papers, his lighter. "This is penging high-grade," he said, indicating the transparent bag and its green-brown contents. He unsealed it and tipped out a small pile. "You need to get yourself in the right state of mind before something like this. Can't do no better than a good zoot, know what I'm saying?"

Elijah nodded.

"You blazed before?"

"Course," Elijah said, trying to be disdainful. He had already been smoking for six months, ever since he had started hanging out with the young LFBs on the gangways and stairwells of Blissett House. That had frightened him, too, at first, and he had found that the first few drags made him retch, his eyes watering. But it was no big thing, though, and he had quickly got used to it. There was always a zoot being passed around, and he always made sure he had some.

Pops laughed at his indignant response. "Trust me, young 'un, you ain't blazed nothing like this." He opened a paper and filled it with a thick line of weed. He inserted a roach, brought the packet to his lips, licked the gummed end and sealed it. He lit the end and took a long drag, smacking his lips in appreciation. He toked again and passed the joint to Elijah. "Go on, younger, get some."

Elijah took the joint and, aware that Pops and the others were watching him, made sure that he didn't show any nerves as he put it between his lips and sucked down deep. The smoke was acrid and strong, and he spluttered helplessly. The other boys hooted at his discomfort.

"Look at the little joker," Pinky exclaimed. "He's gonna die from all that coughing."

"Hush your gums," Pops chided. "Let him enjoy himself. What you think, younger?"

"Buzzin'," Elijah managed.

"Yeah, man—buzzin'. You know what makes it so fine?"

Elijah shook his head, still dizzy.

"Piss. The growers piss on the dirt. Makes it more potent, gives the skunk a kick."

Elijah spluttered in disgust and almost retched again.

Pops grinned at him as the train rolled towards them. "Get yourself together, younger. Here it comes. This is it. You wanna be with us, you gotta do this. Everyone has to if they want to be mandem. You ready?"

"Yeah."

Elijah felt a sudden blast of light-headedness. It added to his feeling of fright, and he suddenly felt sick. He turned away from Pops, bent double, and vomited the fried chicken he had eaten ten minutes earlier, half-digested slops splashing between his legs, splattering against the new trainers he had robbed from the shop in Mare Street the previous day.

The others hollered.

"He's sicked up all over his creps!" Chips exclaimed.

"Come on," Pops said. "Get yourself together. Train's here."

The line was one of the main routes into Olympic Park, and the trains had all been cleaned up for the Games. The doors opened, and commuters working at the big new shopping centre, many still wearing their corporate uniforms, spilled out onto the platform. Pops pulled up his bandana and shrugged his hood up and over his cap until all of his face was obscured, save his eyes. The others did the same and, his hands shaking, so did Elijah. Pops was behind Elijah, and he pushed him into the crowded carriage, the others following behind.

Elijah had seen a train get steamed before, and he knew what to expect. Pushing him further into the carriage, Pops and the others started to hoot and holler, surging down the aisle between the seats. The noise was disorientating and frightening, and none of the passengers seemed able to react. Pops barged into the space between two benches that faced each other and ripped the mobile phone from the hand of a man in a suit. The others did the same, taking phones and tablets, dipping purses from handbags, removing wallets from the inside pockets of jackets and coats, yanking necklaces until they snapped and came free. Elijah followed behind Pops, and as they went from passenger to passenger, he took the items that Pops handed back to him and dropped them into his rucksack. His fright melted away as the adrenaline burned through his body at the thrill of what they were doing, robbing and stealing, and no one was doing a damned thing to stop them.

A young man in a suit stared at them as they advanced along the carriage. He had a Blackberry in his hand.

"What you looking at?" Pops said. "You wanna get slapped up?"

The man didn't reply.

"You wanna get shanked?" Chips reached into his pocket and took out a knife with a six-inch blade.

Still the man was silent. Elijah looked at him and recognised the fear in his eyes. He wasn't defying them; he was just too scared to do anything.

"Jack him, younger," Pops said to Elijah, shoving him forwards.

Elijah stepped up to him. "Give me the phone."

The man didn't resist and held it up for Elijah to take. He put it in his rucksack with all the rest. He looked down at the man, into his eyes, and made a quick, sudden movement towards him. The man flinched, expecting a blow that didn't come. Elijah had never caused that kind of reaction before. He had always been the smallest or the youngest, the butt of the joke. Just being with the LFB made all this difference. People took him seriously. He laughed, not out of malice, but out of disbelief.

Little Mark was standing in the doorway, wedging the door and preventing the train from departing. "Boi-dem!" he yelled.

It had only taken them a few seconds to work their way through the carriage although it had felt like much longer. Pops pushed Elijah ahead of him as the boys surged on, the commuters parting as they piled out of the carriage. Outside, on the platform, Elijah could hear the sound of sirens from the street below. Little Mark dropped down onto the tracks and crossed over the rails to the other side, the others following after him. Elijah clambered back onto the platform, vaulted the wooden fence, and scrambled down the loosely packed earth of the embankment, sprinting down Berger Road and turning onto Wick Road, then across that and into the Estate. They had grown up with the alleys and passageways and knew them all instinctively. The police would have no chance if they tried to follow them.

Elijah jogged in the middle of the group, his rucksack jangling and heavy with their loot. The trepidation had disappeared, its place taken by a pulsing excitement at the audacity of what they had done. They had stormed that train, and the people inside had been scared of them. They had sat there with their posh suits and expensive gadgets and no one had done anything. Elijah was used to being told what to do—his parents, teachers, the police—and this had been a complete reversal. He remembered the look on the face of the man with the BlackBerry. He was a grown man, a professional man, with expensive clothes and things, the kind of man who probably had an expensive flat in Dalston or Hackney or Bethnal Green because those places were cool, and he had been frightened of him. Scared.

Elijah had never experienced what it was like to be feared before.

Chapter Eight

MILTON DROVE THEM into Hackney. The road was lined on both sides by shops owned by Turks, Albanians and Asians—all trying to sell cheap goods to people who couldn't afford them—past fried chicken shops, garages, past a tube station, across a bridge over the A12 with cars rushing by below, past pound shops and cafés, a branch of CashConverter, a scruffy pub. The faces of the people who walked the road bore the marks of failure.

Sharon directed him to take a left turn off the main road, and they drove into an Estate. They drove slowly past a single convenience store, the windows barred and a Plexiglas screen protecting the owner from his patrons. Three huge tower blocks dominated the area, each of them named after local politicians from another time, an optimistic time when the buildings would have appeared bright, new and hopeful. That day had passed. They were monstrously big, almost too large to take in with a single glance. They drove around Carson House, the tower marked for demolition, its windows and doors sealed tight by bright orange metal covers. There was a playground in front of it, hooded kids sitting on the swings and slides, red-tipped cigarettes flaring in the hot dusky light.

Sharon directed Milton to Blissett House, and as he rolled the car into a forecourt occupied by battered wrecks and burnt-out hulks, the decay became too obvious to miss. Window frames were rotting, paint peeling like leprous scabs. Concrete had crumbled like meringue, the steel wires that lent support to the structure poking out like the ribs of a decaying carcass. Milton looked around. Blissett House looked like it had been built in the fifties. It would have seemed futuristic then, a brand-new way of living that had risen from the grotty terraces that had been cleared away, the council finishing the job that the Germans had started. It was twenty storeys high, each floor accessed by way of an external balcony that looped around a central shaft. There was a pervading sense of menace, a heavy dread that settled over everything like smog. The doors and windows were all barred. Graffitti'd tags were everywhere. One of the garages on the first-floor level had been burned out, the metal door half ripped off and hanging askance. An Audi with blacked-out windows was parked in the middle of the wide forecourt, the door open and a man lounging in the driver's seat, his legs extending out. The baleful rhythmic thump from a new dubstep track shuddered from the bass bins in the back of the car.

Milton pointed his key at his Volvo and thumbed the lock. It seemed a pointless affectation, and the car looked vulnerable as they walked away from it. He was grateful, for once, for the state of it. With the exhaust lashed to the chassis with wire and the wing folded inwards from the last time he had pranged it, it was nothing to look at. It was, he hoped, hardly worth taking, or else he was going to have a long walk home.

He followed Sharon towards the building. The man in the Audi stared at him through a blue-tinged cloud of dope smoke, his eyes lazy but menacing. Milton held his stare as he crossed his line of vision. The man's hair was arranged in long dreads, and gold necklaces were festooned around his neck. As their eyes met, the man nonchalantly flicked away the joint he had finished and tugged up his T-shirt to show the butt of the revolver shoved into the waistband of his jeans. Milton looked away. He didn't care that the man would consider that a small victory. There was nothing to be gained from causing trouble.

Sharon led the way to the lobby. "The lifts don't work," she apologised, gesturing to the signs pasted onto the closed doors. "Hope you don't mind a little climb. We're on the sixth floor."

The stairwells were dank and dark and smelled of urine. Rubbish had been allowed to gather on the floor, and a pile of ashes marked the site of a recent fire. A youngster with his hood pulled up over his head shuffled over.

"You after something?"

Sharon stepped up to him. "Leave off, Dwayne."

"Where's JaJa?" he asked her.

"Don't you be worrying about him," she said.

"You tell him I want to see him."

"What for?"

"Just tell him, you dumb sket."

Milton stepped between them.

The boy was big for his age, only a couple of inches shorter than he was, and his shoulders were heavy with muscle. He squared up and faced him. "Yeah? What you want, big man?"

"I want you to show a little respect."

"Who are you? Her new boyfriend? She's grimey, man. Grimey. I seen half a dozen brothers going in and out of her place last week. She's easy, bro—don't think you're nothing special."

The boy was making a point; he didn't know what Milton's relationship with Sharon was, and he didn't care. He was daring Milton to do something. There didn't seem to be any point in talking to him. Milton slapped him with the back of his hand, catching him by surprise and spinning him against the wall. He followed up quickly, taking the boy's right arm and yanking it, hard, all the way up behind his back. The boy squealed in pain as Milton folded his fingers back, guiding him around so that he faced Sharon.

"Apologise," he said.

"Mr Milton," Sharon said hesitantly.

"Apologise," Milton ordered again.

The boy gritted his teeth, and Milton pulled his fingers back another inch. "Sorry," he said. "Sorry. Please, mister—you're breaking my fingers."

Milton turned him around so that he was facing the open door and propelled him out of it. He landed on his stomach, scraping his face against the rough tarmac. The man in the tricked-out car looked over, lazy interest flickering across his face.

"You didn't need to do that," Sharon said. "It's best just to ignore them."

"Good manners don't cost anything. Come on—let's get inside. I bet you could do with a cup of tea."

They climbed the stairs to the sixth floor and followed the open walkway to the end of the block. A couple of youngsters were leaning against the balcony, looking out over the Estate below and, beyond that, the streets and houses that made up this part of Hackney. Milton recognised from experience that they had been stationed as lookouts, and that, from their perch, they would be able to see the approach of rival gang bangers or police. They would call down to the older boys selling their products on the walkways below. The dealers would vanish if it was the police or call for muscle if it was a rival crew. Milton said nothing. The boys glared at them as they approached.

Flat 609 was at the end of the block, where the walkway abutted the graffiti-marked wall. The door was protected by a metal gate and the windows were behind similar grilles. Sharon unlocked the gate and then the heavy door and went inside. Milton followed, instinctively assessing the interior. The front door opened into a tiny square hallway, one of the walls festooned with coats on a row of hooks and a dozen pairs of shoes stacked haphazardly beneath it. Post had been allowed to gather beneath the letter box, and Milton could see that most were bills, several of them showing the red ink that marked them as final demands. The hallway had three doors. Sharon opened the one to the lounge, and Milton followed her inside.

It was a large room furnished with an old sofa, a square table with four chairs and a large flat-screen television. Videogames were scattered on the floor.

"How many children do you have?" Milton asked.

"Two. My oldest, Jules, fell in with the wrong sort. He has a problem with drugs—we only ever see him when he wants money. It's just me and Elijah most of the time."

Milton was a good listener, and Sharon started to feel better. Just talking to him helped. Perhaps he was right and there was something he could do. It wasn't as if she had had any other offers of help. The Social was useless, and the last thing she wanted to do was get the police involved. They wouldn't be sympathetic, and Elijah would end up with a record or something, and that would be the end of that as far as his future was concerned.

"Why don't you sit down?" Milton suggested. "I'm guessing this is the kitchen?"

She nodded.

"So go on, sit down and relax. I'll make you a cup of tea while we wait for your son."

Chapter Nine

WHEN ELIJAH opened the door to their flat, there was a white man he had never seen before sitting in the front room. He was tall, with strong-looking shoulders and large hands, and plain to look at in a loose-fitting suit and scuffed leather shoes. The scar across his face was a little frightening. He was in the armchair Elijah used when he was on his PlayStation, drinking a cup of tea. Elijah's first thought was that he was police, a detective, and he suddenly felt horribly exposed. Pops had told him to take the gear they had tiefed from the people on the train and keep it safe while he arranged for someone to buy it from them. It swung from his shoulder, clanking and clicking.

His mother was sitting opposite the man. She got up as he came in through the door.

"Where've you been?" she said. "You're late."

"Out," he replied sullenly. The man put down his cup of tea and pulled himself out of the armchair. "Who are you?"

"This is Mr Milton."

"I was talking to him." Elijah looked up at the man. There was a flintiness in his icy blue eyes. Elijah tried to stare him out, but although the man was smiling at him, his eyes were cold and hard and unnerving. He made Elijah anxious.

He held out a hand. "You can call me John," he said.

"Yeah, whatever." The heavy rucksack slipped down his shoulder, rattling noisily. He shrugged it back into place and stepped around the man to go to his room.

Sharon got to her feet and stepped in between him and his door. "What's in the bag, Elijah?"

"Nothing. Just my stuff."

"Then you won't mind me having a look, will you?"

She took the bag from him, unzipped it and, one by one, pulled out the mobile phones, watches, wallets and two tablet computers. Silently, she lined them up on the dining table and then, when she was done, turned to face him with a frightened expression on her face. "How did you get this?"

"Looking after it for a friend."

"Did you steal it?"

"Course not," he said, but he knew he sounded unconvincing. He was aware of the big man in the room with them. "Who are you?" he asked again. "Police? Social?"

"I'm a friend of your mother. She's worried about you."

"She needn't be. I'm fine."

Sharon held up an expensive-looking watch. "This is all tiefed, isn't it?"

"I told you, I'm just looking after it."

"Then you can take it straight back to him. I don't want it in the house."

"Why don't you just mind your business?" He dropped everything back into the rucksack and slung it across his shoulder.

"Who is it?" she said as he turned for the door.

"You don't know him."

"Show your mother some respect," Milton said. "She doesn't deserve you speaking to her like that."

"Who are you to go telling me what to do?" he exploded. "I ain't never seen you before. Don't think you're anything special, neither. None of her boyfriends last long. They all get bored eventually, and we don't never see them no more. I don't know who you are, and I'm not going to bother to find out. I won't ever see you again."

"Elijah!"

Milton didn't know how to respond to that, and he stepped aside as Elijah made for the door. Sharon looked on haplessly as her son opened it, stepped out onto the landing, and slammed it behind him.

Chapter Ten

ELIJAH PASSED through the straggled group of customers that had gathered outside the entrance to Blissett House. The boys called them "cats" and took them for all they were worth. They passed out their bags of weed and heroin, their rocks of crack, snatching their money and sending them on their way. They didn't get very far. One of the empty flats had been turned into a crack house, and they scurried into it. When they shuffled out again, hours later, they were vacant and etiolated, halfway human, dead-eyed zombies, already desperately working out where they would find the money for their next fix.

Elijah made his way through the Estate to the abandoned flat that the LFB had claimed for themselves. A family had been evicted for non-payment of rent, and now the older boys had taken it over, gathering there to drink, smoke and be with their girls. Elijah had never been inside the flat before, but he didn't know where else he could take the rucksack and the things that they had stolen.

He was furious. Who was that man to tell him what to do? He didn't look like any of his mother's boyfriends—he was white, for a start—but he had no reason to come and stick his nose into his business. He told himself that he wouldn't see the man again, that he'd get bored, just like they always did, and it would be him who told his mother that it didn't matter, that he would look after her. He had been the man in the house ever since his older brother had vanished. He had been grown up about it all. He'd had to; there wasn't anyone else.

The flat was in the block opposite Blissett House. Elijah idled on the walkway, trying to muster the courage to turn the corner and approach the doorway. It was on the eleventh floor and offered a panoramic view of the area. He looked beyond the Estate, across the hotchpotch of neater housing that had replaced two other blocks that had been pulled down five years ago, past the busy ribbon of Mare Street and across East London to glittering Olympic Park beyond. He rested his elbows on the balcony and gazed down at their flat. His bedroom had a window that looked out onto the walkway. He remembered lying in bed at night and listening as the older boys gathered outside, the lookouts that were posted to watch for the police or other boys. They would talk about money, about the things they would buy, about girls. They talked for hours until the sweet smell of weed wafted in through the open window and filled the room. Elijah's mother would occasionally hustle outside, shooing them away, but they always came back, and over time, she gave up.

It was intoxicating. The boys seemed special to Elijah. They were cool. They were older, they had money, they weren't afraid of girls. They talked about dealing drugs and tiefing, the kind of things that Elijah's favourite rappers rapped about. It was a lifestyle that was glamorous beyond the day-to-day drudgery of school and then helping his mother with the flat. It didn't seem wrong to want a little bit of it for himself.

The boys knew Elijah could hear them, and eventually, they started to include him in their conversations. It wasn't long until he opened the window all the way and started talking to them. He asked how he could get his own money. They told him to stand watch for them, and he did. When they came back, they gave him a brand-new PSP. The week after that they gave him money. He had never seen a fifty-pound note before, but they pressed one into his hand. They started to talk to him more often. They offered him his first joint. He spluttered helplessly as he tried to smoke it, and they laughed at him as he desperately tried to look cool.

It wasn't long before they gave him the chance to make more money. He was small, with tiny arms that could fit through car windows that had been left open. He would open the locks from the inside, and the boys would tear out the car stereos and steal anything else that had been left behind: GPS devices, handbags. They would steal six or seven a night, and Elijah would be given fifty pounds. He put the cash in a shoebox that he hid under his bed. His mother never asked where he got the money for his new clothes. Elijah knew that she wasn't stupid. She just didn't want to hear him say it.

He watched as the door opened and the white man stepped outside. Elijah watched him make his way along the walkway and, after descending the stairs, emerge out onto the forecourt. He walked towards a beaten-up old car, pausing at the door and then crouching down at the front wheel. Elijah could tell from the way the car slumped to the side that the tyre had been slashed. He grinned as the man took off his jacket, removed a spare from the boot and started to go about changing it.

A couple of the older boys were smoking joints on the walkway.

"Alright, younger?" The boy's real name was Dylan, but they called him Fat Boy on account of how big he had been as a young teenager. He had grown out of that now; he was nineteen, six foot tall and full of muscle.

"Is Pops here?"

"He's inside. What do you want?"

"I need to see him."

"Alright, bruv. He's in the back. Knock when you get in."

The flat had been taken over by the LFB. They had sprayed their tag on every spare wall, and a huge, colourful version filled the wall in the lounge. Boys from the Estate lounged around, some playing FIFA on a stolen flat-screen television. Others were listening to the new album from Wretch, arguing that it was better or worse than the new tracks from Newham

Generals or Professor Green. Trash was shoved into the corners: empty paper bags from McDonald's, chicken bones that had been sucked clean, empty cigarette packets, cigarette papers. Everyone was toking, and Elijah quickly felt dizzy from the dope smoke that rolled slowly through the room. A couple of the boys looked up, clocked him, ignored him again. No one acknowledged him. The room was hectic and confusing with noise. Elijah felt young and vulnerable but dared not show it.

"Look who it is!" whooped Little Mark.

"Baby JaJa," Pinky sneered. "It's late, younger, shouldn't you be tucked up in bed?"

"Leave him alone," Kidz chided.

Elijah reluctantly made his way across the room to them. Little Mark's real name was Edwin, and he lived in a flat on the seventh floor of Blissett House with his dad. Elijah did not know Kidz's real name, only that he lived in Regis House and had a reputation as the most prolific mugger in the crew. Pinky's real name was Shaquille, he was usually quiet and surly and had a nasty reputation. Elijah tried to keep his distance whenever he was around.

"What you doing here?" Kidz said as he came alongside them.

"Came to see Pops," he said.

Pinky nodded to the rucksack across his shoulder. "Afraid your mum finds out what you've got in there?"

"I ain't afraid," Elijah said.

"That's from earlier, right? The gear from the train?"

"Yes."

"What you bring it with you for, then? You stupid or something?"

"I ain't stupid, either."

"Look pretty stupid from where I'm sitting."

Kidz smiled at him indulgently. "How you going to explain it if you get pulled by the feds?"

Elijah felt himself blush.

"Told you he was stupid," Pinky said. "A stupid little kid. He ain't right for LFB."

"Lucky for him that's not for you to decide, then, innit? Ignore him, young 'un. Pops is in the back. Go on through."

Elijah made his way through the room. The layout of the flat was identical to his own, and he guessed that Pops was in the main bedroom. He knocked on the door. A voice called that he could come in.

The room was dark. Pops was standing next to the open window, blowing smoke into the dusky light beyond. He had removed his shirt, and his muscular torso glistened with a light film of sweat. He had a tattoo of a dragon across his shoulders and, on his bicep, the letters L, F and B. His heavy gold chain glittered against the darkness of his skin. A white woman sat on the edge of the mattress they had put in the room. She straightened her skirt as she got to her feet. She was older than Pops, looked like she was in her thirties, and dressed like the office workers from the city who had seeped into the smarter parts of the borough. Elijah had heard about her; the rumour was that she was something in the city and that she had a taste for the crack.

Pops crossed the room and kissed her gently on the cheek. "I'll see you tonight," he said. She ran her palm across his cheek, collected her jacket, and left the room.

Pops found his T-shirt and pulled it over his head. Elijah caught himself wondering how old he was. His brown skin was unmarked, his eyes bright and intense. Elijah guessed he was eighteen or nineteen, but he had a hardness about him that made him seem older. It was a forced maturity, a product of the road, of the things he had seen and done. It had flayed the innocence out of him. "What's the matter, younger?"

"My mum caught me with this," he said, shrugging the rucksack from his shoulder and letting it hang before him. "She'll nick it off me if I have it in the house."

Pops laughed. "Don't fret about it, younger. We'll look after it here." He took the bag and tossed it onto the mattress. "Fucking day, I'm all done in." He took a bag of weed from his pocket and found a packet of rolling papers on the windowsill. "You want a smoke?"

Elijah had never been alone with Pops before. He was talking to him, taking him seriously, and it made him feel special. "Go on, then," he said, trying to sound older than he felt.

Pops busied himself with making the spliff. "You have fun this afternoon, blood?"

"Yeah."

"You nervous?"

Elijah took the joint and put it to his lips as Pops sparked it for him. "A bit."

"That's okay," he said. "S'alright to be nervous. Nerves mean adrenaline, and adrenaline is good. Keeps you sharp. You were quick when boi-dem came. Away on your toes."

"I've always been good at running," he said.

"That's the thing, younger. That's gonna be useful. You can't never let the feds get hold of you. The thing that keeps me running, even when my lungs are burning like someone's sparked up a spliff in my chest, even when the stubborn side of me wants to turn around and get ignorant, face them like a man, that's when I remember I've already spent way too many nights sitting on a blue rubber mattress in a cell, who knows how many times it's been pissed on, that's when I remember getting caught by boi-dem's a no-no. You can't come back to the manor and big up your chest about getting shift by boi-dem. Bad bwoys ain't supposed to get caught, JaJa. Especially not black boys." He grinned at him. "It's all good. You did good."

Elijah felt a blast of pride that made his heart skip. No one had said anything like that to him before. His teachers thought he was a waste of space, he didn't have a dad, and his mum was always nagging. He drew in on the joint, coughing as the smoke hit his lungs.

"We ain't really talked before, have we?"

Elijah shrugged. "Not much."

"What you going to do with your life, little man?"

The question caught him off guard. "Dunno," he said.

"You got no plans? No dreams?"

"Dunno. Maybe football. I'm not bad. Maybe that."

"'Maybe football,'" Pops repeated, smiling, taking the joint as Elijah passed it back to him.

"I'm okay at it," Elijah said defensively, wondering if he was being gently mocked. "I'm pretty fast."

"I'll say you are," Pops said, taking a long toke on the joint. "You like the Usain Bolt of Hackney."

Pops dropped down on the mattress. He patted the space next to him, and Elijah sat too. It might have been the weed, but he felt himself start to relax.

"Listen, younger, I'm going to tell you something. You won't think it's cool, but I know what I'm talking about, and you'd do yourself a favour to listen, alright?" He settled back so that he was leaning against the wall. "It's good to have dreams, but a man needs a plan, too. Maybe you are decent at football, maybe you are good enough to make it, but how many kids do you know from these ends who've done it? Maybe you can think of one, but I don't know any. Football is a dream, right, and, like I say, it's good to have dreams, but a man's got to have a plan, too. A realistic one, just in case his dreams don't pay off. You know what I'm saying?"

"What about the street?"

"Seriously, younger? The street can be a laugh, you don't get too deep into it, but the street ain't no plan."

"You're doing it."

"Only for now. It's not a long-term thing."

"I know people who do alright."

"The kids shotting drugs?"

"Nah, that's just baby steps, I mean the ones above them."

"Listen to me, Elijah—there ain't no future on the street. Some brothers do make it through. I know some who started off as youngers, like you, younger than you, then they work their way up with shotting and tiefing until they become Elders, and then some of them keep out of trouble long enough and get made Faces. But, you look, every year, some of them get taken out. Some get lifted by the feds, others ain't so lucky, and those ones get shot and end up in the ground. Like Darwin, innit? Survival of the fittest. You want, we could have a little experiment—we could start with a hundred young boys, kids your age, and I reckon if we came back five years later to see how they be getting on, maybe one or two of them would still be making their way from the street. The others are out, one way or another. Banged up or brown bread. I don't know what you're like when it comes to numbers, but me, it's like how you are at football—I ain't too bad at all. I'm telling you, younger, one hundred to one or two ain't odds I'm that excited about."

"What about today? You were out with us."

"I know—you think I sound like a hypocrite, and that's fair enough. Maybe I am. But I ain't saying stealing stuff is bad. It ain't right that some people have everything they want and others—people like us—it ain't right that we don't have shit. That stuff we nicked today, them people was all insured. We gave them a scare, but they didn't actually lose nothing. They'll get it all back, all shiny and new. We deserve a nice phone, a camera, an iPod, whatever, and we ain't going to get it unless we take it. I reckon that's fair enough. I reckon that makes it alright to do what we did. But it ain't got a future. You do it ten times, twenty times maybe if you get lucky, eventually you're going to get nicked. Someone gets pulled and grasses you up. Your face gets on CCTV. The feds have got to do something about it in the end. See, what we did this afternoon is short-term. If you want to have those things properly, without fear that they're going to get taken away from you and you're going to get banged up, then there ain't nothing else for it—you got to play the game by their rules."

"How?"

"You got to study. You got to get your exams. You probably think I'm high saying that"—he nodded at the joint, smiled, and then handed it across—"but think about it a little, and you know I'm talking sense. I didn't pay no attention at school. I was a disaster, couldn't stand it so I hardly went at all, and I couldn't wait until I was old enough so that I didn't have to no more. I'm older now, I've got more experience, and I'm telling you that all that stuff they say about studying is true. If I'd paid attention more, did better, what I'm trying to do with myself now would've been a million times easier."

Elijah was confused. "What are you doing?"

"So I said I was okay with numbers? Always have been, just something I've got a talent for. I'm going to night school to get my A-level. Maths. You know my woman? You know what she does?"

Elijah had heard. "Something in the city?"

He nodded. "Accountant. She says if I can get my exams, she can get me a job with her firm. Nothing special, not to start with, post room or some shit like that, but it's a foot in the door. A chance to show them what I can do. After that—who knows? But I'll tell you this for nothing, younger, I ain't going to be doing what we did this afternoon for much longer."

Elijah sucked on the joint again, stifling the unavoidable cough. The conversation had taken him by surprise. He had always looked up to Pops, thought that he was cool, and he was the last person he would have expected to tell him to stay in school and work hard.

"You did good today. Like I said, you got potential. I saw it in you right away. That wasn't easy, I remember my first time, I was sick as a dog, they had to push me onto the bus, and then I was completely useless. None of that with you, was there? You got balls. That's great. But just think about what I've said, alright? There's no future there for you. For any of us."

They smoked the rest of the joint together before Pops got up. "I got to breeze. Got school. My exams are in a month, and we're revising. Equations and all that shit. Don't want to be late."

The night was warm and close, and the walkway was empty as they both stepped outside. Pops bumped fists with him and descended the stairs. Elijah rested his elbows on the balustrade, looking across to Blissett House and his mother's flat, then down into the yard as Pops emerged, walking confidently and with purpose, acknowledging the monosyllabic greetings from the strung-out cats and the boys from the gang who sold them their gear. Pops was liked. Respected. Elijah nodded to himself.

He fancied some of that himself.

PART TWO

Murder Mile

He wiped the sweat from his face and put the scope of his rifle to his eye, gazing down onto the plains below. The village was five hundred yards away, clustered around the river. Two dozen huts, the villagers making their living from the herd of goats that grazed on the scrappy pasture to the north and west. It was a small habitation gathered around a madrasa; children played in the dusty yard outside, kicking a ball, a couple of them wearing the shirts of teams he recognised. He took a breath and held it, the rifle held steady, the stock pressed into the space between his shoulder and neck. He nudged the rifle left to right, examining each hut individually. Nothing was out of place: the women were working at home while the men tended the animals in the pasture. He moved the scope right to left until the missile launcher was centred in the crosshairs. A Scud launcher, an old R-11, Russian made. He squinted down the sight, placing each member of the crew. Three men, Republican Guard. He centred each man in the crosshairs, his finger held loosely through the trigger guard, the tip trailing against the edge of the trigger. He nudged the scope away again so that he could focus on the madrasa: five children in the yard, their cheap plastic ball jerking in the wind as they kicked it against the wall of the hut. They were happy. The launcher meant nothing to them, nothing compared to their game and the fun they could have together. He heard their laughter delivered to him by a welcome breath of air.

Chapter Eleven

JOHN MILTON AWOKE at six the next morning. He had slept badly, the damned nightmare waking him in the middle of his deepest sleep and never really leaving after that, the ghostly after-effects playing across his mind. He reached out to silence his alarm and allowed himself the rare luxury of coming around slowly. His thoughts turned to the previous evening, to Sharon and Elijah. He recognised elements of his own personality in the boy: the stubbornness and the inclination to resist authority. If they lived under different circumstances, it would have done no harm for the boy to test her limits. It was natural, and he would have returned to her in time. Their circumstances did not allow him that freedom, though. Milton could see how the attraction of the gang would be difficult for him to resist. If he allowed himself to be drawn into their orbit, he risked terrible damage to his prospects: a criminal record if he was lucky, or if he wasn't, something much worse.

Milton did not own or rent a property. It was unusual for him to be in the country for long periods, and he did not see the point of it. He preferred to be unencumbered, flexible enough to be able to move quickly whenever required. His practice was to stay in hotels, so he had booked a room in an American chain, an anonymous space that could have been anywhere in the world. The hotel was on the South Bank of the Thames, next to Westminster Bridge, and when he pulled the curtains aside, he was presented with a view of the pigeons and air-conditioning units on the roof of the adjacent building and, beyond that, the tower of the Houses of Parliament. The sky above was cerulean blue, and once again, the sun was already blazing. It was going to be another hot day.

He showered and shaved, standing before the mirror with a towel around his waist. He was six foot tall and around thirteen stone, with an almost wiry solidity about him. His eyes were on the grey side of blue, his mouth had a cruel twist to it, there was a long horizontal scar from his cheek to the start of his nose, and his hair was long and a little unkempt, a frond falling over his forehead in a wandering comma. There was a large tattoo of angel wings spread across his shoulders, claws at the tips and rows of etched feathers descending down his back until they disappeared beneath the towel; it was the souvenir of a night in Guatemala, out of his mind on Quetzalteca Especial and mescaline.

Milton dressed and went down to the restaurant for breakfast. He found a table to himself and filled his plate with scrambled eggs from the buffet. He drank a glass of freshly squeezed orange juice, poured a cup of strong coffee, and flicked through the pages of the *Times*. The front page was dominated by the news of the killing in France. The *gendarmerie* were waiting to speak to the boy. It was hoped that he would be able to tell them what had happened and, perhaps, identify the man who had killed his parents.

Milton folded the paper and put it to one side.

He returned to his room and packed. He had very little in the way of possessions, but what he did own was classic and timeless: a wide, flat gun-metal cigarette case; a black oxidized Ronson lighter; a Rolex Oyster Perpetual watch. There was little else. He smoked a cigarette out of the window as he transferred his clothes from the wardrobe to his suitcase, put on a pair of Levis and a shirt, slipped his wallet and phone into his pocket, and took the lift down to reception.

"I'd like to check out, please," he told the receptionist.

She keyed his details into her computer. "Certainly, Mr. Anderson. How was your stay with us?"

"Very pleasant."

He settled the bill in cash, collected the Volvo from the underground car park, and drove back to Hackney.

He drove through the Square Mile, its clean streets, well-shod denizens, steepling towers and minarets a gleaming testament to capitalism. He continued past Liverpool Street, through trendy Shoreditch, and then passed into the hinterland beyond. Milton had noticed the arcade of shops as he had driven home last night. There was an estate agent's between a fried chicken takeaway and a minicab office. He parked and walked along the arcade, pausing to look at the properties advertised in the window. He went inside, and a man in a cheap, shiny suit asked him if he could be of help.

"I'm looking for a place to rent."

"Furnished or unfurnished?"

"Furnished."

"Anywhere in particular? We've got a nice place in a school conversion near to the station."

"Somewhere close to Blissett House."

The man looked at him as if he was mad. "That's not the best area. It's rough."

"That's all right."

"Do you work in the city?"

"No, I'm a writer," he said, using the cover story he had prepared as he had travelled across London. "I'm researching a book on police corruption. I need to be in the middle of things. I don't care if it's rough. It's better if it's authentic. Do you have anything?"

The man flicked through his folder of particulars, evidently keen not to look a gift horse in the mouth. "We just had a place come up on Grove Road. Terraced house, two bedrooms. I wouldn't say it's anything special, but it's cheap, and it's on the edge of the Estate. Best I can do, I'm afraid. Most stock in the blocks themselves are kept back for council tenants."

"Can you show me?"

"Of course."

The maisonette was close to the office, and since it was a bright, warm day, they walked. The hulk of Blissett House loomed over them as they passed beneath the railway line and into an Estate that had been cleared, the brutalist blocks replaced by neat and tidy semi-detached houses. They were painted a uniform pale orange, and each had its own little scrap of garden behind a metal fence. Some houses were occupied by their owners and marked by careful maintenance. Others were rented, distinguished by overgrown lawns that stank of dog excrement, boarded windows and wheelie bins that overflowed with trash. They continued on, picking up Grove Road.

The house that the agent led them to was the last in a terrace that was in a poor state of repair. It was a tiny sliver of a house, only as wide as a single window and the front door. Solid metal security gates had been fitted to the doors and windows, graffiti had been sprayed on the walls, and the remains of a washing machine had been dumped and left to rust in the street right next to the kerb. The agent unlocked the security door and yanked it aside. The property was spartan: a small lounge, kitchen and bathroom on the ground floor and two bedrooms above. The furniture was cheap and insubstantial. The rooms smelt of fried food and stale urine.

"It's a little basic," the agent said, not even bothering to try to pretend otherwise. "I'm sorry. We have other places, though. I've got the key for another one, much nicer, ten minutes away."

"This'll do," Milton said. "I'll take it."

Chapter Twelve

IT TOOK HALF AN HOUR back at the office for the formalities of the lease to be taken care of. Milton paid the deposit and the advance rent in cash. There were no references or credit checks required, which was just as well, since a search of Milton's details would not have returned any results. The agent asked him whether he was sure that the house was what he wanted, and, again, offered a handful of alternatives that he thought would be more appropriate. Milton politely declined the offer, thanked him for his help, took the keys, and left the office.

There was a small mini-market serving the area. It was sparsely stocked, a few bags of crisps and boxes of cereal displayed under harsh strip lights that spat and fizzed. Alcohol and cigarettes, however, were well provided for, secured behind the Perspex screen from behind which the owner surveyed his business with suspicious eyes. Milton nodded to the man as he made his way inside and received nothing but a wary tip of the head in return. He made his way through the shop, picking out cleaning products, a carton of orange juice and a bag of ice. He took his goods to the owner and arranged them on the lip of counter ahead of the screen. As the man rang his purchases up, Milton looked behind him to shelves that were loaded with alcohol: gin, vodka, whiskey.

The owner caught his glance. "You want?"

He paused and almost wavered. 692 days, he reminded himself. 692 going on 693.

He needed a meeting badly.

"No, just those, please."

Milton paid and returned to the maisonette. He unlocked the doors and scraped the security door against the concrete lintel as he yanked it aside. It didn't take long to establish himself. He unpacked in the larger of the two bedrooms, hanging the clothes in a wardrobe made of flimsy sheets of MDF. He spread his sleeping bag out across the lumpy mattress, went downstairs to the kitchen, and took out the mop and bucket he found in a small cupboard. He filled the bucket with hot water, added detergent, and started to attack the layers of grease that had stratified across the cheap linoleum floor.

It took Milton six hours to clean the house, and even then, he had only really scratched the surface. The kitchen was presentable: the floor was clean, the fridge and oven had been scoured to remove the encrusted stains; the utensils, crockery and surfaces were scrubbed until the long-neglected dirt had been ameliorated. There were mouse droppings scattered all about, but save clearing them away, there was nothing that Milton could do about that. He moved on to the bathroom, spending an hour scrubbing the toilet, the sink and the bath, and washing the floor. When he was finally finished, he undressed and stood beneath the shower, washing in its meagre stream of warm water until he felt clean. He put on a fresh T-shirt and jeans, took his leather jacket from where he had hung it over the banister, went outside and locked the door behind him. He set off for the main road.

He took out his phone and opened the bookmarked page on his internet browser. He double-tapped an icon, and his mapping application opened. His destination was a three-mile walk away. He had an hour before the meeting, and it was a hot evening. He decided that rather than take the bus, he would walk.

St Mary Magdalene church was on the left-hand side of the road, set back behind a low brick wall, well-trimmed topiary and a narrow fringe of grass studded with lichen-covered gravestones from a hundred years ago. A sign had been tied to the railings: two capital As set inside a blue triangle that was itself set within a blue circle. An arrow pointed towards the church. Milton felt a disconcerting moment of doubt and paused by the gate to adjust the lace of his shoe. He looked up and down the street, satisfying himself that he was not observed. He knew the consequences for being seen in a place like this would be draconian and swift; suspension would be immediate, the termination of his employment would follow soon after, and there was the likelihood of prosecution. He was ready to leave the service, but on his own terms and not like that.

He passed through the open gate and followed a gravel path around the side of the building, descended a flight of stairs, and entered the basement through an open door. The room inside was busy with people and full of the noise of conversation. A folding table had been set up and arranged with a vat of hot water, two rows of mismatched mugs, a plastic cup full of plastic spoons, jars of coffee and an open box of tea bags, a large two-pint container of milk, a bowl of sugar and a plate of digestive biscuits. The man behind the table was black and heavyset, with a well-trimmed salt-and-pepper beard and hair cropped close to his scalp. His arms bulged with muscle, and his shirt was tight around his chest and shoulders.

Milton approached the table.

"Can I get you a drink?" the man said.

"Coffee, please."

The man smiled, took one of the mugs, and added two spoonfuls of coffee granules. "Haven't seen you before."

"My first time."

The man poured hot water into the mug. "Your first meeting here, or your first ever?"

"First time here."

"All right then," the man said. A silence extended, but before it could become uncomfortable, the man filled it. "I'm Rutherford," he said. "Dennis Rutherford, but everyone just calls me Rutherford."

"John."

"Nice to meet you, John." He handed him the mug. "Help yourself to biscuits. The meeting's about to get started. It's busy tonight—go in and get a seat if I were you."

Milton did. The adjacent room was larger, with a low, sloping ceiling and small windows that were cut into the thick brick walls that served as foundations for the church above. A table had been arranged at one end with two chairs behind it, and the rest of the space was filled with folding chairs. A candle had been lit on the table, and tea lights had been arranged on windowsills and against the wall. The effect was warm, intimate and atmospheric. Posters had been stuck to the walls. One was designed like a scroll, with twelve separate points set out along it. It was headed THE TWELVE STEPS TO RECOVERY.

Milton took a seat near the back and sipped the cheap coffee as the chairs around him started to fill.

A middle-aged man wearing a black polo-neck top and jeans sat at one of the chairs behind the table at the front of the room. He banged a spoon against the rim of his mug, and the quiet hush of conversation faded away. "Thank you," the man said. "Good to see so many of you—I'm glad you could come. Let's get started. My name is Alan, and I'm an alcoholic."

Milton sat quietly at the back of the room. Alan was the chairman, and he had invited another speaker to address the group. The second man said that he was a lawyer, from the city, and he told his story. It was the usual thing: a man who appeared to be successful was hiding a barrage of insecurities behind addictions to work and drink, a tactic that had worked for years but now was coming at too high a price: family, relationships, his health. The message was clichéd—Milton had heard it all before, a thousand times before—yet the passion with which the man spoke was infectious. Milton listened avidly, and when he looked at his watch at the end of the man's address, half an hour had passed.

The floor was opened after that, and the audience contributed with observations of their own. Milton felt the urge to raise his hand and speak, but he had no idea how best to start his story. He never did. Even if had been able to tell it, he would not have known where to start. There was so much that he would not have been able to relate. He felt the usual relief to be there, the same sense of peace that he always felt, but it was something else entirely to put those thoughts into words. How would the others feel about his history? The things that he had done? It made him feel secretive, especially compared to the searing honesty of those around him. They talked openly and passionately, several of them struggling through tears of anger and sadness. Despite the sure knowledge that he belonged there with them, his inability to take part made him feel like a fraud.

Chapter Thirteen

AT THE END of the meeting a group gathered to talk and smoke cigarettes outside. They smiled at Milton as he climbed the steps from the basement. He knew that their smiles were meant as encouragement for him to stop and speak. They meant well, of course they did, but it was pointless; he couldn't possibly. He smiled back at them but didn't stop. He had no idea what he would say. Far better to make a quick exit.

"Hey, man—hey, hey, hold up."

Milton was at the gate, ready to turn onto the street to start the walk home. He paused and turned back. The man who had been serving the coffee, Rutherford, was jogging across in his direction. Milton took a moment to consider him again. He was big, over six foot tall and solid with it, several stones heavier than he was. He loped across the churchyard, moving with an easy spring that suggested plenty of strength in his legs.

"You don't hang about," he said as he reached him. "There's a café down the road. People stop for coffee or a bite to eat, have a chat. You should come."

Milton smiled. "Not for me. But thanks."

"You didn't speak in the meeting. There's no point just sitting there, man. You got to get stuck in."

"Listening's good enough."

"Not if you want to really make a difference. I had that problem myself, back when I first started coming. Thought it was crazy, no one was gonna want to listen to my shit. But I got over it in the end. Eventually, the way I saw it, coming along and not doing anything was a waste of my time. That's why I do the coffees—start small, right, and take it from there? You got to get involved." Rutherford spoke slowly and deliberately, as if measuring each word. The effect was to imbue each with a persuasive weight. He was an impressive man.

"I suppose so."

"Which way you headed, man? Back to Hackney?"

"Yes."

"Me too. Come on—you don't mind, we can walk together."

"You don't want to go to the café?"

"Nah, won't make no difference if I miss it tonight. I'm up at six tomorrow; I should probably get an early night."

Milton would have preferred to walk alone, but there was something infectious in Rutherford's bearing that stalled his objections, and besides, it didn't look like he was going to take no for an answer. They set off together, making their way along Holloway Road towards Highbury Corner.

He started speaking. "What's your story, then?"

Milton took a breath. "The same as most people, I suppose. I was drinking too much, and I needed help to stop. How about you?"

"Same deal, man. I was in the Forces. Fifteen years. Saw some stuff I never want to see again. I only stopped feeling guilty about it when I was drunk." He turned to look at him. "Don't mind me being presumptuous, John, but you're a soldier too, right?"

"Is it that obvious?"

"You know what it's like—we got that look. Where did you serve? The Sandpit?"

"For a while."

"Ireland?"

"Yes."

"I been all over the place too, man. 'See the world,' that's what they told me when they were trying to get me to sign up, like it's some glamorous holiday. It was fun for a while, but then I saw what it was really all about. By the time I got wise to it, I was a raging drunk."

"What happened?"

"Look, I ain't saying I'm not grateful for what the army did for me. When I was a younger man, ten years ago, I got into all sorts of mess that I didn't want to be getting involved in. Trouble, man, all kinds of trouble. Got myself in with a bad crowd from around here. Ended up doing plenty of things I regret. Drink and drugs—you know what it's like. I got friends from around that time, plenty of them got banged up, and a couple of them are dead. Could've easily been me. The army was a way to get away from all that." He spoke fluently, settling comfortably into a story that he had clearly told many times before, probably at the meetings. "And it worked, least for a time. Took me away from here, broadened my horizons, gave me structure and discipline in my life. And those things are good things, things I needed. But they come at a price, right? The things I saw while I was out there doing my thing—" He paused. "Well, shit, it got so bad by the end that I could only live with myself with a drink inside me. You know what I mean?"

He was full of heat and passion. Milton said that he understood.

"I don't take this life lightly, John. The way I see it, the Fellowship has given me a blessing. The gift of knowledge. I can see what's wrong with how things are. I know the things that work and the things that don't. Drink and drugs—they don't. Not many people get given a chance to make a difference, but I did. And, one day at a time, I ain't going to throw it away."

They passed into the busy confluence of traffic and pedestrians circulating around the roundabout at Highbury Corner and moved onto Dalston Lane. Youngsters gathered outside the tube, ready to filter towards the pubs and bars of Islington High Street. Touts offered cheap rides, immigrants pushed burgers and hot dogs, drunken lads spilled out of the pub next to the station.

"How?" Milton asked him.

"How what, man?"

"How are you going to make a difference?"

"Boxing. I used to be a tasty heavyweight when I was a lad. I got to be big early, big and strong, and I had a right hand you didn't want to get hit by. If I'd stayed with it, who knows? I wouldn't have got into the trouble I did, that's for sure. I wouldn't have gotten into the army, and I reckon I was probably good enough to make a decent career out of it. I'm too old and out of shape for that now, but I've still got it all up in here." He tapped a finger to his temple. "So I've set up a club for youngsters, see? Amateurs, girls and boys, all ages. They ain't got nothing to do around here, nothing except run with the gangs and get into mischief, and I know better than most where that road leads. You're a younger born here, you run with one of them gangs, there are two places for you to go: prison or the crematorium. The military is one way out, but I can't recommend that no more. So I try to give them another way. Something else to do, some structure, some discipline, and you hope that's enough. It can be the difference. And the way I see it, if I help a handful of them get away from temptation, that's good enough. That's my job done."

"I used to box," Milton said, smiling for the first time. "A long time ago."

Rutherford looked him up and down: tall, lean and hard. "You've got the look for it," he said. "Cruiserweight?"

"Maybe these days." Milton smiled. "Middleweight back then. Where's the club?"

"Church hall on Grove Road, near the park. Monday, Wednesday and Friday nights and all day Saturdays. Got about twenty regulars now." His eyes flashed with passion. "Got some kids who are on the fringes of the gangs. Some of them have potential. This one girl, man, you wouldn't believe how hard she can hit. Like a piledriver, knocked this lad who was giving her lip into the middle of next week. He never gave her lip after that." He grinned at the memory of it.

They reached Milton's turning. "This is me," he said.

Rutherford cocked an eyebrow in surprise. "You living in the Estate?"

"Yes."

Rutherford sucked his teeth.

"Not good?"

"You're in the worst bit of Hackney, and Hackney's different. You talk about Waltham Forest, you talk about Camden, Southwark, Lambeth, all the rest—sure, they got bad people there. Plenty of serious players. But here? Man, Hackney's different. You understand? The boys here are more serious than anywhere else. Everyone is banging. I mean, *everyone*. You can't even compare what it's like here with them other places. You best be careful, you hear? Don't matter how big you are; they won't care about that. They got a knife or a shooter and they think you're worth rolling, I'm telling you, man, it don't matter how mean you look, they'll do it."

"Nice to meet you, Rutherford."

"You too, John. You take it easy. Maybe I'll see you at the meeting next week?"

"Maybe."

"And say something next time, all right? You look like you got plenty on your mind. You'll be surprised the difference it makes."

Milton watched as the big man walked away from him. He turned off the main road and headed into the Estate, stopping at the mini-market to buy another bag of ice. He ignored the sullen aggression of the teenagers who were gathered outside the shop, the silence as he passed through them and then the hoots of derision, the calls of "lighty!" and "batty boy" as he set off again. Most of them were young, barely in their teens. Milton didn't give them a second look.

It was half-ten by the time he returned to the maisonette. He took the carton of orange juice and poured into one of the newly cleaned glasses. He opened the bag of ice and dropped in three chunks, putting the rest in the freezer. He took off his clothes and put his gun and holster under a pillow. He swilled the juice around to cool. He pulled a chair up to the window, then went and sat down, letting the hot air, the compound smell of baked asphalt and fried food, breathe over his body. He sipped the cool drink, feeling the tang against the back of his throat, felt it slide cold down his throat and into his stomach.

He filled up his glass again, this time with more ice, and sat back down. The bedroom overlooked the front of the house. He looked out onto the street and, beyond that, the looming mass of Blissett House. A group of young boys had gathered at the junction of the road, the glowing red tips of their cigarettes and joints flaring as they inhaled.

Milton felt restless. He went over and took his gun from beneath the pillow, slipped out the magazine, and pumped the single round onto the bed. He tested the spring of the magazine and of the breech and drew a quick bead on various objects round the room. His aim was off, just a little, but detectable nonetheless. It was the tiny tremor in his hand. He had noticed it in France, and it seemed to be getting worse. He snapped the magazine back. He pumped a round into the breech and replaced the gun under the pillow.

He watched the kids outside for another five minutes, the sound of their raucous laughter carrying all the way back to the open window. Then, tired, he closed the curtains, finished undressing, and went to bed.

Chapter Fourteen

ELIJAH WATCHED the Vietnamese hassling the shoppers as they came out of Tesco. They were in the car park, far enough away from the entrance to go unnoticed by the security guards. They stepped up to the shoppers with their trolleys full of groceries and held open the satchels that they wore around their shoulders. There were four of them, two men and two women, all of them slim and dark-haired. The satchels were full of pirated DVDs. They were given the brush-off most of the time, but occasionally, someone would stop, rifle through the bags, and hand over a ten-pound note in exchange for a couple of them.

"You ready, younger?" said Pops.

"Yeah," Elijah said. "Ready."

"Off you go, then."

He did exactly as Pops had instructed him. One of the Vietnamese women was distracted by Little Mark, who pretended to be interested in her DVDs. She kept her money in a small shoulder bag that she allowed to hang loosely across her arm. Elijah ran up to her, and her attention diverted, he yanked on the bag as hard as he could. Her arm straightened as he tugged the bag down, her fingers catching it. A second, harder tug broke her grip, and he was away. He sprinted back again, the other boys following after him in close formation. The two men started in pursuit, vaulting the wall that separated the car park from the pavement and the bus stop beyond, but it didn't take long for them to abandon the chase. They were outnumbered and being led into unfriendly territory. They knew that the money wasn't worth the risk.

The boys ran down Morning Lane, whooping and hollering, eventually taking a sharp left along the cycle path that ran underneath the East London Line. They sprinted up the shallow incline on the other side of the tunnel and slowed to a jog. Once they were in the Estate, they found a low wall and sat down along it.

Pops held up his fist, and Elijah bumped it with his. He beamed with pride. He knew he ought to keep his cool, hide away the excitement and happiness that he felt, but he couldn't help it. He didn't care how foolish it made him look.

"How much you get?"

Elijah took the notes from his pocket and fanned through them. "Two hundred," he reported.

"Not bad." Pops reached across and took the notes. He counted out fifty and gave it back to Elijah. "Go on, younger, put that towards some new Jordans. You done good."

Little Mark went into the minimart nearby and returned with a large bottle of cider and a bagful of chocolate. The cider was passed around, each boy taking a long swig of it. Elijah joined in when the plastic bottle reached him, the sickly sweet liquid tasting good as he tipped it down his throat.

"What did you get?" Kidz asked.

Little Mark opened the bag and emptied out the contents. He laid the bars out on the wall. "Twix, KitKat, Mars, Yorkie."

"Too pikey."

"Maltesers. Milky Way."

"Too gay."

"Got them for you, innit? Galaxy, Caramel—that's it. You want something else, go get it yourself."

Pops tossed the chocolate around, and they devoured it.

"I gotta jet," Pops said eventually, folding the wad of notes and sliding them into his pocket. "My woman wants to see me. I'll see you boys tomorrow, a'ight?"

"Hold up," Little Mark said. "I'm going your way."

"Me, too," Kidz said.

Elijah was left with Pinky. He wanted to go with the others, but Pinky got up and stretched. "Come on," he said. "I'll walk back with you."

They set off together, making their way through the Estate and cutting across a scrubby patch of grass. Pinky was a little older and a little taller than Elijah. His face was sharply featured, with a hook nose and prominent cheekbones. He was normally boisterous and brash, full of spiteful remarks, yet now he was quiet and brooding. Elijah quickly felt uncomfortable and wondered if there was a way he could disentangle himself without causing offence. They made their way through the Estate to a children's playground. The surface was soft and springy beneath their trainers, but the equipment had all been vandalised. The swings had been looped over the frames so that they hung high up, uselessly, and the roundabout had been pulled from its fixings. Vials of crack were crushed underfoot, shards that glittered like diamonds amid the dog mess, discarded newspaper and fast-food wrappers.

"Let's sit down here for a minute," Pinky said, pointing to a bench at the edge of the playground. "Something I want to talk to you about."

Elijah's nerves settled like a fist in his stomach. "I got to get back to my mums."

"You don't want a quick smoke?" Pinky reached into his jacket and grinned as he opened his hand; he had a small bag of weed and a packet of Rizlas. "Sit yourself down. I wanna get high. Won't take long."

Elijah did as he was told and sat.

Pinky was quiet as he held the cigarette paper open on his lap and tipped a line of marijuana along the fold. He rolled the joint with dexterous fingers, sealed it, and put it to his lips. He put flame to the end and sucked down greedily. He did not give the joint to Elijah.

"You quietened down now, little man," he said.

"Yeah?" Elijah said uncertainly.

"You don't wanna get too excited."

"What do you mean?"

"That big smile you had on your face back then. Like you'd won the fucking lottery. Robbing those nips ain't nothing. Rolling that train weren't, either. You ain't done shit yet."

Elijah was ready to fire back some lip, but he saw the look in the boy's face and decided against it. He knew banter, and this was something different; hostility sparked in his dark eyes, and he could see it would take very little for the sparks to catch and grow into something worse.

"You don't know me, do you?"

"What you mean?"

"You don't know who I am."

"Course I do."

"So?"

"You're Pinky," he said with sudden uncertainty.

"That's right. But you don't know me, do you? Not really know me."

"I guess not."

"You know my brother? Dwayne? You heard of him?"

"No."

The joint had gone out. Pinky lit it again. "Let me tell you a story. Five years ago, my brother was in the LFB, like me. They called him High Top. Your brother, Jules, he was in, too. The two of them was close, close as you can be, looked out for each other, same way that we look out for each other, innit?" He put the joint to his lips and drew down on it hard.

"There was this one time, right, there was a beef between this crew from Tottenham and the LFB. So they went over there, caused trouble, battered a couple of their boys. Tottenham came over these ends to retaliate, and they found your brother and my brother smoking in the park. Like we are right now. They got the jump on them. They was all tooled up, and our brothers didn't have nothing. Rather than stay and get stuck in, your fassy brother breezed. Straight out of the park, didn't look back, forgot all about my brother. And he wasn't so lucky. The Tottenham boys had knives and cleavers, and they wanted to make an example out of him. They cut my brother up, bruv. Sliced him—his face, across his back, his legs, all over. Ended up stabbing him in the gut. He was in hospital for two weeks while they stitched him together again. His guts—they was all fucked up. He weren't never the same again. He has to shit into a bag now, and it ain't never going to get better. Turned him into a shadow of himself."

"Fuck that," Elijah managed to say. "My brother would never have done that."

"Yeah? Really? Your brother, what's he doing now?"

"We don't see him no more."

"Don't go on like you don't know. I seen him—he's a fuckin' addict. He was a coward then, and now he's a fuckin' junkie."

Elijah got up from the bench.

"Give me that money," Pinky said.

Elijah shook his head. "No. Pops gave it to me. I earned it. It's mine."

"You wanna fall out with me, little man?"

"No—"

Pinky grabbed him by the lapels of his coat and shoved him to the ground. He fell atop him, pressing his right arm across his throat, pinning him down, and reached inside of his jacket with his left hand. He found the notes and pocketed them.

"Remember your place," he said. "You ain't nothing to me. You think you a gangster, but you ain't shit. Give me lip like that again and I'll shank you." He took out a butterfly knife, shook it open, and held the blade against Elijah's cheek. "One jerk of my hand now, bruv, and you marked for life. Know what it'll say?"

"No," Elijah said, his voice shaking.

"Pinky's bitch."

Elijah lay still as Pinky drew the cold blade slowly down his face. Pinky took a bunched handful of his jacket and pulled his head up and then, with a pivot, slammed him down again. The surface was soft but, even so, the sudden impact was dizzying. Pinky got up and backed away. He pointed at Elijah's head and laughed. Elijah felt a dampness against the back of his crown and in the nape of his neck. He reached around, gingerly, expecting to find his own blood. He did not. Pinky had pushed him back into dog mess. The shit was in his hair and against his skin, sliding down beneath the collar of his jacket.

"Later, little man." Pinky laughed at him. He left Elijah on the ground.

He bit his lip until the older boy was out of sight, and then, alone, he allowed himself to cry.

Chapter Fifteen

MILTON WAITED until the sun had sunk below the adjacent houses before he went out to scout the area. It was a humid, close evening. The stifling heat of the day had soaked into the Estate, and now it was slowly seeping out. Televisions flickered in the front rooms of the houses on his street, most of the neighbours leaving their windows uncovered. Arguments played out of open doors. The atmosphere sparked with the dull electric throb of tension, of barely suppressed aggression and incipient violence.

The area seemed to come alive at night. There were people everywhere. Youngsters gathered on street corners and on weed-strewn playgrounds. Others listlessly tossed basketballs across a pockmarked court while they were watched by girls who laced their painted nails through the wire-mesh fence. A lithe youngster faked out his doughty guard and made a stylish lay-up, the move drawing whoops from the spectators. Music played from the open windows of cars and houses. Graffiti was everywhere, one crude mural showing groups of children with guns killing one another. Milton carried on, further along the road. A railway bridge that bore the track into Liverpool Street cast the arcade of shops below into a pool of murky gloom. A man smoking Turkish cigarettes levered rolls of carpet back into his shop, drivers gathered around a minicab office, the sound of clashing metal from the open windows of a gym with a crude stencil of Charles Atlas on the glass. The arcade carried the sickly smell of kebab meat, fried chicken, and dope.

Milton took it all in, remembering the layout of the streets and the alleyways that linked them. Two streets to the east and he was in an area that bore the unmistakeable marks of gentrification: a gourmet restaurant, a chichi coffee shop that would be full of prams in the daytime, a happening pub full of hipsters in drainpipe jeans and fifties frocks, an elegant Victorian terrace in perfect repair, beautifully tended front gardens behind painted iron fences. Two streets west and he was back in the guts of the Estate, the ten-storey slabs of housing blocks with the nauseatingly bright orange balconies festooned with satellite dishes.

Milton crossed into Victoria Park, a wide-open space fringed by fume-choked fir trees. A series of paved paths cut through the park, intermittent and unreliable streetlamps providing discreet pools of light that made the darkness in between even deeper and more threatening. The area's reputation kept it quiet at night save for drunken city boys who used it as a shortcut, easy pickings for the gangs that roamed across it looking for prey.

Milton passed through the gate and walked towards the centre. A group of youngsters had congregated around one of the park benches. One of their number was showing off on his BMX, bouncing off the front wheel as the others laughed at his skill. Milton assessed them coolly. There were eight of them, mid-teens, all dressed in the uniform: caps beneath hoodies, baggy jeans and bright white trainers.

He kept walking. As he drew closer, he heard the sound of music being played through the reedy speaker of a mobile phone. It had a fast, thumping beat and aggressive lyrics. The rapper was talking about beefs and pieces and merking anyone who got in his way.

One of the group sauntered out from the pack and blocked his path.

"What you want, chichi man?" The boy showed no fear. His insolence was practiced and drew hollers of pleasure from the audience.

"I'm a journalist," he said.

"You BBC? You on the television? Can you get me on the TV?"

"No, I'm working on a book."

Laughter rang out. "No one reads books, bro."

"It's about police corruption. You know anything about that?"

Milton watched the boy. He was a child, surely no older than fifteen. There was a disturbing aspect to his face, a lack of expression with his eyes constantly flickering to the left and right. Milton had seen that appearance before; soldiers from warzones looked that way, a pathological watchfulness to ward against the threat of sudden attack. Milton knew enough about psychology to know that kind of perpetual vigilance was unhealthy. He knew soldiers who had been constantly on the alert for danger, who equated any show of emotion with violence, and from whom all feeling had been smelted. They became machines.

"The pigs are all bent, man," the boy told him. "You might as well write about the sky being blue or water being wet. You ain't teaching no one nothing round these ends. No one's gonna read that."

"Do you know Elijah Warriner?"

"What's he got to do with the feds?"

"I want to talk to him. I heard he's around here sometimes. Is he a friend of yours?"

"That little mong ain't my friend, and there's no point talking to him. He don't know fuck all. You want, though, we could have a conversation? You and me?"

Milton noticed one of the boys in the group take his phone from his pocket and start to tap out a message. "Fine," he said. "What would you like to talk about?"

"Wanna know about violence? I shanked a guy last week. Want to know about that?"

"Not really."

"I could shank you, too. I got a knife, right here in my pocket." He sauntered forwards, towards Milton, still showing no sign of how outsized he was. He patted the bulge in his hip pocket. "Six-inch blade, lighty. I could walk up to you right now, like this, take the knife, shank you right in the guts." He made a fist and jabbed it towards Milton's stomach. "Bang, you'd be done for, blood. Finished. I could make you bleed, big man, right in the middle of the park. Ain't no one gonna come and help you out here, neither. What you think of that?"

Milton said nothing.

"Man got shook!" one of the others shouted out. "Pinky shook the big man."

Milton looked down at the boy. He was tall and thin and wiry, couldn't have been more than nine stone soaking wet. Calling his bluff would provoke the escalation he seemed to want, and there was no point in doing that. He wanted them to think he was a journalist, harmless, a little frightened and out of his depth. The hooting and hollering around them continued, but the atmosphere had become charged.

"I might shank you the moment you turn your back."

Milton noticed a group of boys cycling across to them from the edge of the park.

"Don't turn your back on me, big man. You don't mean nothing to me. I might do it just for a laugh."

The group on the bikes reached them. There were half a dozen of them. Milton recognised Elijah at the back. The biggest boy—Milton guessed he was seventeen or eighteen—propped his bike against the bench and strutted over to them.

The boy walked across to the group. "Alright, Pinky?" he said to the youngster who had threatened him. "What's the beef?"

"Nah," the boy said. "Ain't no beef."

Milton ignored him and addressed the newcomer. "Are you in charge?"

"You could say that."

Milton pointed over at Elijah. "I want to talk to him."

"You know this man, Elijah?"

A look of suspicion had fallen across his face. "Yeah," he said warily. "He was with my mums."

"And do you want to talk to him?"

Elijah shook his head.

"Sorry, bro. He don't want to talk to you."

"He say he a *writer*," one of the boys reported, loading the last word with scorn.

"That right?"

"That's right. A journalist."

"Bullshit. You ain't a journalist, mate. If you're a journalist, then I'm going to win the fucking X Factor. You must think I was born yesterday. What are you? Social?"

"He's po-po!" one of the other boys cried out. "Look at him."

"He ain't a fed. Feds don't come into the park unless they've got backup."

The atmosphere was becoming fevered. Milton could see that it had the potential to turn quickly, and dangerously. He concentrated on the older boy. "What's your name?"

"You don't need to know my name."

"I don't want any trouble."

"Then you don't wanna come walking through our ends late at night, do you, bruv?"

"I'm not police. I'm not Social. You don't have anything to worry about."

The boy laughed scornfully. "Do I look worried?"

"No, you don't," Milton said. He raised his voice so that the others could hear him. "Tell Elijah that I want to talk to him. I'm going to have my breakfast in the café on Dalston Lane every morning from now on. Nine o'clock. Tell him I'll buy him breakfast, too. Whatever he wants. And if he doesn't want to meet me, he can call me here instead." Milton reached into his pocket and took out a card with the number of his mobile printed across it. He gave it to the older boy, staring calmly into his face. A moment of doubt passed across the boy's face, Milton's sudden equanimity shaking his confidence. He took the card between thumb and forefinger.

"Thank you," Milton said.

Milton turned his back on the group and set off. He felt vulnerable, but he made a point of not looking back. He felt an itching sensation between his shoulder blades, and as he walked, an empty Coke can bounced off his shoulder and clattered to the pavement. They whooped at their insolent bravado and called out after him, but he didn't respond. He kept walking until he reached the gate next to the lido. He stopped and looked back. The boys were still gathered in the centre of the park. No one had followed.

He was satisfied that the house had not been disturbed while he was away, and allowing himself to relax, he took off his shirt and stood bare-chested at the open window. He snapped open the jaws of his lighter, put flame to a cigarette, and stared into the hot, humid night. The atmosphere was feverish, as taut as a bowstring. He took a deep lungful of smoke and expelled it between his teeth with a faint hiss. He could hear the sound of children on the street, the buzz of televisions, a siren fading in and out of London's constant metropolitan hum.

What on earth was he doing here?

Milton blew more smoke into the darkness and tossed the spent dog-end into the garden below.

He undressed and got into bed. The mattress was lumpy and uncomfortable, but he had slept on much worse. He reached one hand up beneath the pillow, his palm resting on the cold steel butt of the Sig Sauer. He calmed his thoughts and went to sleep.

Chapter Sixteen

JOHN MILTON had a strict morning regime, and he saw no reason to vary it. He pulled on a vest and a pair of shorts, slipped his feet into his running shoes, and went out for his usual run. It was just after seven, but the sun was already warm. The sky was a perfect blue, deep and dark, and Milton could see that it was going to be another blazing day.

His head had been a little foggy, but the exercise quickly woke him. He ran through the Estate and into Victoria Park, following the same route that he had taken before. The park was quiet now, and the undercurrent of incipient violence was missing. The baleful groups of boys had been replaced by people walking their dogs, and joggers and cyclists passing through the park on their way to work. Milton did two laps around the perimeter, settling into his usual loping stride, and by the time he peeled back onto the road and headed back towards the house, he was damp with sweat.

He followed a different route back through the Estate and came across an old chapel that had evidently found itself an alternative use. A sign above advertised it as Dalston Boxing Club, and posters encouraged local youngsters to join.

He ran back to the house, stripped off his sodden clothes, tentatively stepped into the grimy bath tub, and turned the taps until enough warm water dribbled out of the shower head to make for a serviceable shower. He let the water strike his broad shoulders and run down his back and chest, soothing the aches and pains that were always worse in the morning. He closed his eyes and focussed his attention on the tender spots on his body: the dull throb in his clavicle from a bullet's entry wound five years ago, the ache in the leg he had broken, the shooting pain in his shoulder from an assassin's knife. He was not as supple as he had once been, he thought ruefully. There were the undeniable signs of growing old. The toll exacted by his profession was visible, too, in the latticework of scar tissue that had been carved across his skin. The most recent damage had been caused by a kitchen knife that had scraped its point across his right bicep. It had been wielded by a bomb-maker in Helmand, a tailor who assembled suicide vests in a room at the back of his shop.

He stood beneath the water and composed his thoughts, spending ten minutes examining the details of the situation in which he had placed himself. He considered all the various circumstances that he would have to marshal in order to help Sharon and her son.

He dressed in casual clothes, left the house, and made his way back to the boxing club. The door was open, and the repeated, weighty impacts of someone working on a heavy bag were audible from inside. He went inside. The chapel's pews had been removed, and the interior was dominated by two empty boxing rings that were crammed up against each other, barely fitting in the space. They were old and tatty, the ropes sagging and the canvas torn and stained. Several heavy bags and speed bags had been suspended from the lower ceiling at the edge of the room. A large black man was facing away from him and hadn't noticed his arrival. Milton watched quietly as the man delivered powerful hooks into the sand-filled canvas bag, propelling it left and right and rattling the chain from which it had been hung. The muscles of his shoulders and back bulged from beneath the sweat-drenched fabric of a plain T-shirt, his black skin glistening, contrasting with the icy white cotton.

Milton waited for him to pause and took the opportunity to clear his throat. "Rutherford?"

He turned, and his face broke into a wide, expressive smile. "Hey! It's the quiet man."

"How are you?"

"Very good. It's John, right?"

"Yes, that's right. Sorry to disturb you. Could I have a word?"

Rutherford nodded. He reached down for a towel and a plastic water bottle and went over to a pew that had been pushed against the wall at the side of the room. He scrubbed his face with the towel and then drank deeply from the bottle.

"This is impressive," Milton said.

"Thanks. It's hard work, but we're doing good. Been here a year this weekend. Don't know how much longer we'll be around, though. Ain't got much more money. The council do us a decent price on the rent, but they're not giving it away, and I can't charge the kids much more than I'm charging at the moment. Something has to happen, or we won't be here next time this year."

"Can anyone join?"

"If they're prepared to behave and work hard. You got someone in mind?"

"I might have."

The man took another swig from his bottle. "Who is it?"

"He's the son of a friend. He's going off the rails a little. He needs some discipline."

"He wouldn't be the first boy like that I've had through those doors. We've got plenty of youngers who used to run in the gangs." The man spoke simply and inexpressively, but his words were freighted with quiet dignity and an unmistakeable authenticity. Milton couldn't help but be impressed by him. "Which gang is it?"

"I'm not sure. I met some of them in the park last night."

"That'll be the LFB, then. London Fields Boys."

"What are they like?"

"Been around for a long time—they were running around these ends before I went away, so plenty of years now. I remember we had a beef with them on more than one occasion—big fight in the park this one time, we uprooted all these fence posts and chased 'em off. The members change all the time, but they've always had a bad reputation. How deep's your boy involved?"

"Not very, I think. He's young."

"If you've caught him early, we'll have a better chance of straightening him out."

"So you take new members?"

"Always looking for them. Bring your lad along. We'll see what we can do."

"Going to the meeting on Tuesday night?"

"Perhaps," he said.

"Might see you then."

Milton made his way back to the main road.

He went into the café and took a seat.

"Scrambled eggs with cream, two rashers of bacon, and a glass of orange juice," he said when the girl came to take his order. He was hungry.

He checked his watch. It was a little after eight. The food arrived, and he set about it. When he was finished, it was a quarter past. He opened the newspaper on the table and read it. There was a short story about the killings in France, but no new details. He skipped ahead, turning the pages and reading until half past eight, and then nine. There was no sign of Elijah. Fair enough, he thought, as he went to settle his bill. He hadn't expected it to be easy. Getting through to the boy was going to take some time.

Chapter Seventeen

LITTLE MARK, Kidz and Elijah had met for lunch at the fast-food place nearest to the gates of the school. Elijah had hurried out from double science when he received the text from Pops earlier that morning. He was wearing the white shirt, green blazer and black trousers that made up his uniform, and he felt stupid as he jogged the last few yards down the road to the arcade. Little Mark was wearing his usual low-slung jeans and windcheater, and Kidz was wearing cargo pants and a hoodie.

"You look nice." They laughed at him as he drew alongside.

"I know," Elijah said ruefully. "I look stupid."

"You still going to school?"

"Yeah," Elijah said. "So?"

"Not saying nothing," Kidz said, stifling a laugh.

"I don't go all the time," he lied.

"What you doing out here anyway? Thought you'd be in the canteen with all the other little squares?"

"Got a text from Pops. He told me to be here."

Other kids from school started to arrive. The canteen was only ever half full; everyone preferred to come down here for fried chicken and pizza.

"Had an argument with my mums this morning," Little Mark said.

"Let me guess—you ate everything in the house?"

Little Mark grinned. "Nah, bro, I slept right through my alarm."

"Probably ate that, too."

"I'm in bed, right, and it's eight or something, and my mums is shouting at me to get up, says I'm gonna miss school, and this is the first time I realise, right, she still thinks I *go* to school. I ain't been for six months."

"Shows how much she pays attention to you, bro. That's child abuse, innit? That's neglect. You ought give that Childline a call."

The happy laughter paused as they heard the rumbling *thump thump thump* of the bass. It was audible long before they even saw the car, but then the black BMW turned the corner, rolled up to the side of the road, and parked.

"Shit, bruv," Little Mark said. "You know who that is?"

"What's he doing here?" Kidz said, unable to hide the quiver of nervousness in his voice.

"Who?" Elijah asked.

"You don't know shit," Kidz said sarcastically. "That's Bizness's car. You never seen him before?"

Elijah did not answer. He hadn't, but he didn't want to admit that in front of the others. He had the new BRAPPPPP! record, and their poster was on the wall of his bedroom, but that all seemed childish now.

The BMW kept its engine running. It was fitted with a powerful sound system, and heavy bass throbbed from the bass bins that had been installed where the boot had been. Elijah looked at the car with wide eyes. He knew it would have cost fifty or sixty thousand, and that was without the cost of the custom paint job, the wheel trims, the sound system and all the other accessories.

The front door of the BMW opened, and a man slid out from the driver's seat. Elijah recognised him immediately. Risky Bizness was tall and slender, a good deal over six feet, his already impressive height accentuated by an unruly afro that added another three or four inches. His face was striking rather than handsome: his nose was crooked, his forehead a little too large, his skin marked with acne scars. His eyebrows, straight and manicured, sat above cold and impenetrable black eyes. He was wearing a thin designer windcheater, black fingerless gloves, and his white Nike hi-tops were pristine. He wore two chunky gold rings on his fingers, diamond earrings through the lobes of both ears, and a heavy gold chain swung low around his neck.

"A'ight, youngers," he said.

"A'ight, Bizness?" Kidz said.

"Which one of you is JaJa?"

Elijah felt his stomach flip. "I am."

Bizness smiled at him, baring three gold teeth. "Don't worry, younger. I ain't gonna bite. I got something I want you to do for me. Get in the car. Won't take a minute."

Kidz and Little Mark gawped at that, but Elijah did as he was told. The interior of the car was finished in leather, and the bass was so loud it throbbed through his kidneys. Bizness got into the car next to him and closed the door. He leant forwards and counterclockwised the volume so he could speak more easily.

"One of my boys has clocked you, younger. Says you got a lot of fight in you. That right?"

"I don't know," he said, trying to stop his voice from trembling.

"He says you do. You hang with Pops's little crew, right?"

"Yeah," Elijah said, tripping over the word a little.

"Don't be so nervous—there ain't no need to be scared of me."

"I ain't scared."

"That's good." Bizness grinned, gold teeth glinting in his mouth. "Good to see a younger with a bit about himself. Says to me that that younger could make something of himself, get a bit of a reputation. Reminds me what I used to be like when I was green, like you, before all this." He brushed his fingers down his clothes and then extended them to encompass the car. "Get me?"

"Yes."

"So a friend of a friend says to me he's heard of a younger who's just starting running with Pops's crew, that he's got some backbone. Sound like anyone you know?"

"I guess."

Bizness snorted. "You guess." He looked him up and down. "You're big for your age."

"Big enough," he said defensively.

"That's right, bruv. Big enough. I like it. It ain't the size of the dog in the fight, it's the size of the fight in the dog, that right? You got some balls, younger. I like that. How old are you?"

"Fifteen."

"Fifteen. Just getting started in the world. Getting a name for yourself. Getting some *respect*. That's what you want, right?"

"Yeah," he said.

"Yeah. You're at what I'd call a crossroads, right—it's like *Star Wars*. You watched that, right, that last film?"

"Course," he replied indignantly.

"And it's shit, right, for the most part, except there's that one bit that makes sense, you know where Anakin has that choice where he can either go the good way or the bad way? The light or the dark? He thinks like he's got a choice, but he ain't got no choice at all, not really. It's an illusion. The dark side has him by the balls, and it ain't never going to let him go. Destiny, all that shit, you know what I mean? That's where you are, blood. Your teachers, the police, the Social, your mums—they'll all say you got a choice, you can choose to try hard at school, get your exams, get a job, except that's all bullshit. Bullshit. Brothers like us, we ain't never going to get given nothing in this world. Trouble is, a black man loves his new trainers too much. Right? And if we want to get the stuff we like, we gonna have to take it. Right?"

"Yeah." Elijah laughed nervously. Bizness was charismatic and funny, but there was a tightness about him that made it impossible to relax. Elijah got the impression that everything would be fine as long as he agreed with him. He was sure that arguing would be a bad idea.

"So we agree that getting busy on the street is the only way for you to get along in this world. It ain't easy, though, not on your own. Lots of brothers all got the same idea. You want to be successful, you want the kids you hang around with to take you seriously, you need to build up your rep. I can help you with that. You start hanging out with me, your little friends all find out you're in my crew, how quickly do you think that's going to happen?"

Elijah could hardly keep the smile from his face. "Quick."

"No, not quick, blood—instantaneously." Bizness clicked his fingers. "Just like that. So when I heard there was this new younger on the street, already making a name for himself, getting some respect, I say to myself, that's the kind of little brother I used to be like, maybe there's something I can do to help get him started in life. I'll do it for you, I guarantee it, but first I need you to prove to me that you're up to it."

"I'm up to it," Elijah insisted. "What is it? What do I have to do?"

"Nothing too bad, I just got something I need taking care of for a little while. You reckon that's the sort of thing you could do for me?"

"Course," Elijah said.

Bizness took a Tesco carrier bag and dropped it into Elijah's lap. It was heavy, solid. It felt metallic.

"Take this home and keep it safe. Somewhere your mums won't find it. You got a place like that?"

Elijah thought of his comic box. "Yeah," he said, "she don't never come into my room anyway. I can keep it safe."

"Nice."

"What is it?"

Bizness grinned at him. "You know already, right?"

"No," he said, although he thought that perhaps he did.

"There's no point me telling you not to look. I know you will as soon as I'm gone. Go on, then—open it."

Elijah opened the mouth of the bag and took out the newspaper package inside. He unfolded it carefully, gently, as if afraid that a clumsy move might cause an explosion. The gun sat in the middle of the splayed newspaper, nestling amongst the newsprint like a fat, malignant tumour. He tentatively stretched out his fingers and traced them down the barrel, the trigger guard, and then down the butt with its stippled grip. His only knowledge of guns was from his PlayStation, and this looked nothing like the sleek modern weapons you got to use in *Special Ops*. This looked older, like it might be some sort of antique, something from that *Call of Duty* where you were in the war against the Nazis. The barrel was long and thin, with a raised sight at the end. The middle part was round and bulbous, and when Elijah pushed against it, he found that it was hinged and snapped down to reveal six chambers honeycombed inside. A handful of loose bullets gathered in the creases of the newspaper.

"What is it, an antique or something?"

"Don't matter how old it is, bruv. A gun's a gun at the end of the day. You get shot, you still gonna die. Go on, it's not loaded—cock it. You know how to do that?"

The hammer was stiff, and he had to pull hard with both thumbs to bring it back. He pulled the trigger. The hammer struck down with a solid click, and the barrel rotated. The gun suddenly seemed more than just an abstract idea, it seemed real and dangerous, and Elijah was frightened.

"You keep that safe for me, bruv, and be ready—when I call you, you better be there, no hanging around, thirty minutes tops. Alright?"

"Alright," he said.

"A'ight. I was right about you—someone I can rely on. Yeah. A'ight, out you get, younger. I got to get out of here. Supposed to be seeing my manager, you know what I mean? New record out tomorrow."

He held out his closed fist for Elijah to bump. Elijah did, everything suddenly seeming surreal. He stepped outside, holding the carrier bag tightly; it was heavy, and the solid weight within bumped up against his thigh. The bass in the BMW cranked back up, and the engine revved loudly.

Kidz and Little Mark were sitting on a wall, waiting for him. They both wore envious expressions, wide-eyed and open-mouthed.

"What did he want?" Kidz said.

Bizness sounded the horn twice, let off the handbrake, and fishtailed away from the kerb, wheelspinning until the rubber bit on the tarmac.

"Just a chat," Elijah said.

"What's that?" Little Mark said, pointing at the bag.

He clasped the bag tightly. "Nothing."

Chapter Eighteen

MILTON WAS IN THE CAFÉ AGAIN at nine o'clock. The proprietor recognised him. "Scrambled eggs with cream, two rashers of bacon and a glass of orange juice?"

Milton nodded with a smile and took the same table as before. He unfolded his copy of the *Times* and turned the pages as he waited. He turned the page to an article on a shooting in Brixton. A young boy, reported to be sixteen years old, had been shot and killed by another boy. He had passed through the territory of a rival gang to see a girl. The story was backed with a comment, the reporter recounting the deaths in what they were calling the Postcode War. Thirty young boys, almost all of them black, killed this year, and it was only halfway through August. Most of them shot or stabbed, one bludgeoned to death with a pipe.

The proprietor brought over his breakfast. "Terrible," he said, nodding at the open newspaper. He was a Greek, his face grizzled with heavy stubble. He had sad eyes. "When I was growing up, you had an argument with someone you knew and the worse thing that'd happen is you end up having a punch-up, get a black eye or a bloody nose. These days, with them all tooled up like they are, all those guns and knives, you're lucky if you just end up in hospital. And the only thing most of the victims had done wrong was going out of one area and into another."

"How many of them were from around here?"

"Three. One of them was just down the road. They shot him. Tried to get into the hardware shop, but they finished him off before he could."

"The police?"

He laughed bitterly. "They ain't got a clue half the time." He sneered at the thought of it. "Don't get me started on them; your breakfast will be cold by the time I've finished. You enjoy it, all right? There's more tea if you want it."

Milton saw Elijah Warriner standing in the doorway. He was unmistakeably nervous, and Milton thought he might be about to turn and leave. He smiled and waved at the boy, gesturing that he should come inside. Elijah took a look up and down the street and, satisfied, came inside. He was wearing brand-new trainers. Despite the heat he was wearing a bright orange puffa jacket that was obviously expensive. He had a Dallas Cowboys shirt beneath the jacket, and beneath that, Milton could see a thick gold chain.

"Sit down," Milton told him, and after another reluctant pause, he did. "I'm glad you came."

"Yeah," Elijah grunted.

"What do you fancy?"

The boy said nothing. His eyes darted around the café. A diamond stud shone against the dark skin of his ear. The jewellery looked obscene on such a young child. Milton noticed that he had chosen a chair that faced away from the window. He did not want to be seen.

"Breakfast?"

"Ain't hungry."

"Well, I am. I'll get some extra chips in case you change your mind."

Elijah slouched back in the chair, trying hard to appear nonchalant. Milton loaded his fork with eggs and put it into his mouth, watching the boy. He made sure he appeared relaxed and said nothing, leaving it for Elijah to speak first. The boy turned the newspaper around and read the short article on the murdered boy. He finished it and shook his head derisively. "Them boys in Brixton ain't shit. They come up these ends and we'd send 'em back to their mammas."

"What's your gang?"

"LFB," Elijah replied proudly.

"London Fields Boys?"

"S'right."

"I've seen the graffiti on the walls."

"Yeah, all this round here, this is our ends."

"Don't think I've seen you in the papers."

"We are—I mean, we have been."

"Perhaps you're not bad enough."

"What you mean?"

"You need a reputation, don't you?"

"We're plenty bad enough."

"But it looks like you have to kill someone to get into the papers."

"You don't think we've merked anyone?"

"I don't know. Some of the boys you've been hanging out with—maybe they have. But I know you haven't."

"Fuck you know?"

Milton put his knife and fork down and carefully wiped his mouth. He pressed his finger against the photograph of the dead boy. "Do you really think you could do that? You think you could go up to another boy, take out a gun, and pull the trigger?"

Elijah tried to hold his gaze but could not. He looked down at the table.

Milton shook his head. "You don't have it in you. You don't have it in you for your own conscience to haunt you for the rest of your whole life, telling you you've robbed a wife of her husband, children of their father, brothers, friends, everyone. Look at me—I know if a man has it in him. Do you have it in you?"

Elijah stood up. "I didn't come here to get lectured."

"I'm trying to put things into perspective."

"Don't need that," he said, making a dismissive gesture with the back of his hand.

"It's not a bad thing. Why would anyone choose to be like that?"

"You ain't got any idea what you're on about."

"Sit down, Elijah."

His words had no effect. "'Sit down, Elijah?' Who'd you think you are? You don't know shit about me. You don't know shit about anything—about these ends, what it's like to be here, what we do. You obviously think you do, but you don't."

"I'm sorry. Sit down. Let's talk."

He was angry now, and Milton could see he wouldn't be able to calm him down. "I don't know what I was thinking, coming here to see you. You can't help me. You got no idea. I must have been out of my mind."

He turned and left, the door clattering behind him. Milton rose and followed him into the street. Elijah was heading back towards the Estate, his hood pulled up and his shoulders hunched forwards. Milton was about to set off after him before he thought better of it. He went back inside and sat down again before what was left of his breakfast. He cursed himself. What had he been thinking? He had let his temper get the better of him, and now he had lost his opportunity to get through to the boy. He was stubborn and headstrong, and the direct approach was not going to be successful. He would have to try another way.

Chapter Nineteen

POPS AND LAURA had gone to the Nandos on Bethnal Green Road for dinner and then had taken the bus down towards the cinema in Shoreditch. It had been a good evening. Pops was off the Estate, and there was no need for him to impress anyone, or uphold his rep, or put anyone else down. He had an act, and he played it well: hard, impassive, sarcastic. To reveal otherwise would be dangerous, a sign of weakness. He remembered, with vivid clarity, the documentaries his biology teacher had shown them in middle school when she wanted to go off and smoke a fag in the playground. There had been one about the lions in Africa, the Serengeti or whatever the fuck place it was, and it had stuck in his head ever since. Leadership was all about image. The top lion needed to show the others in the pride that he wasn't to be messed with. If he showed weakness, they'd be on him. They'd fuck him up. Pops knew that there were other Elders in the LFB who would fuck him up, too, if he gave them reason.

It was different with Laura. He could relax and be himself. It was always like that with her. She loved her crack, but Pops knew she was into him for much more than just getting lickey. She was older than him, ten years older, and she had that sense of confidence that older women had. She wasn't like the skanky goonettes on the Estate, always mouthing off, screeching and pouting and giving attitude. They were just girls where Laura was a woman. She was cool. And, man, was she fine.

The film had been running for thirty minutes when the call came. Pops felt his phone vibrating in his pocket, and he took it out to check the caller ID: it was Bizness. His stomach plummeted, and his chest felt tight. He did not want to answer it, but he knew that there was no choice, not where Bizness was concerned. He had stabbed a boy before who had ignored his calls. He said it was a mark of disrespect. Respect was the most important thing in Bizness's life, or at least that was what he said.

He took the call, pressing the phone against his ear. "Bizness," he said quietly.

He could hear the sound of loud music in the background. "Where are you, man?"

"Watching a movie."

"Nah, bruv, don't be chatting breeze—what, you forgot the party tonight?"

Pops gritted his teeth. He hadn't forgotten, far from it. He knew about the new record, and the party to celebrate its launch, and he had decided to ignore it. He had been to the party that launched the collective's first record, eighteen months ago, and he had not enjoyed himself. The atmosphere was aggressive, feral, and there had been several beefs that had the potential to turn even more unpleasant than they already were. The relationships within the group were built on uncertain foundations. All the talk of being brothers was fine, but talk was just talk, and there was a swirl of jealousy beneath the surface that was always ready to erupt. Pops knew all of the crew, some better than others, and juggling loyalties between them was more effort than it was worth.

Bizness was currently at the top of the tree, and it had been that way for the last six months. He had replaced Lambie once he had been done for possession of a firearm and sent down for four years. There were always pretenders to his crown, and his treatment of them was always the same: constant dissing that turned violent when the dissing didn't work. Beatings, then stabbings if the beatings didn't work, and at least two shootings that he knew about. One of those shootings he knew about from close personal experience, close enough for the poor bastard's blood to land all over his jacket.

Pops didn't need that kind of aggravation in his life tonight.

"You coming, then?" Bizness pressed.

There were a couple in the seats in front of him, and the man turned around and glared at him, trying to act big in front of his woman. Pops felt his anger flare. He jerked his head up, his eyebrows cocked, and the man turned away.

"Nah, I don't know, man."

"I ain't asking," Bizness said. "I'm telling."

Pops sighed. There was no point in resisting. "Alright," he said.

"You with your gash?"

Pops looked over at Laura. She was watching the film, the light from the screen flickering against her pale skin. "Yeah."

"Bring her with you, a'ight? And bring that younger. What's his name, JaJa? Pick him up, and tell him I need that package he's holding for me. There's gonna be hype tonight, I'm hearing things. I wanna make sure I don't get caught with my dick out. Bring your piece, too."

And with that, Bizness ended the call.

Pops stared at the screen as it slowly faded to black. The first act of the film came to a crashing conclusion, yet he didn't really notice it. He was thinking of Bizness and whether there was any way they could show their faces at the party and then leave. He was unable to think of anything. Bizness would just see that as a diss, probably worse than not going at all, and he'd be in the shit.

He tried to put it into perspective. Maybe he was being ungrateful. He felt the thick wad of ten-pound notes in his pocket, the cold links of his gold chain resting against his skin, the heavy weight of the rings on his fingers.

None of that came for free. You had to do things you would rather not do. That was how you got all the nice stuff you wanted. That was just the way it was.

"Come on," he whispered over to Laura.

"What?"

"We gotta split. There's a party; we got to go to it."

"Can't we go afterwards? This is good."

"Gotta go now, baby," he said, taking her by the arm and drawing her down into the aisle. He held his phone in his other hand, and using his thumb, he scrolled through his contacts until he found Elijah's number.

Chapter Twenty

THE PARTY was in Chimes nightclub on Lower Clapton Road. Pops parked next to the beaten-up Georgian houses on Clapton Square, and they walked the rest of the way, past the discount stores and kaleidoscopic ethnic restaurants, past the police posters pasted onto the lamp posts exhorting locals to "Nail the Killers in Hackney." The club was on the edge of the major roundabout that funnelled traffic between the City and the East End, and marked the beginning of Murder Mile, the long stretch of road that had become inextricably linked with gun crime over the past few years.

The club was in a large and dilapidated old building facing the minarets of an enormous mosque. It was a hot and enclosed series of rooms, and condensation dripped from the patched and sagging ceilings overhead. The largest room had been equipped with a powerful sound system, and Elijah had been able to hear the rumble of the bass from where Pops parked his car. Lights rotated and spun, lasers streaked through the damp air, strobes flickered with skittish energy. The rooms were crammed with revellers: girls in tight-fitting tops and short skirts, men gathered in surly groups at the edges of the room, drinking and smoking and aiming murderous glances at rivals. A tight wire of aggression passed through the room, thrumming with tension, ready to snap. The bass line thumped out a four-four beat, repetitive and brutal, and the noise of a hundred shouted conversations filled the spaces between as an incomprehensible buzz.

Elijah caught himself gaping. He had never been to anything like this before, and he could hardly believe he was here. All the members of BRAPPPP! were present, the whole collective, two dozen of them, each bringing their own entourage of friends and hangers-on. He recognised them from the poster in his room and the videos he had watched on YouTube. The new record had been played earlier, and now the DJ was mixing old-school Dr Dre and Snoop Dogg. Pops was alongside him, his face bleak, his hand placed possessively against the small of his girl's back.

Bizness appeared from out of the crowd, noticed them, and made his way across. He moved with exaggerated confidence, rolling his hips and shoulders, and his face was coldly impassive. He responded to the greetings from those he passed with small dips of his head or, for closer friends, a fist bump. "A'ight," he said as he reached their group. He regarded them one at a time, his face unmoving until his gaze rested on Laura. The blank aggression lifted, and he parted his wide lips, revealing his brilliantly white teeth with the three gold caps. "Alright, darling," he said, ignoring Pops altogether. "Remember me?"

"Of course," Laura said, her eyes glittering.

"You heard the new record yet?"

"Yeah."

"You like it?"

"Course."

"That's what I like to hear. You looking *fine* tonight, darling. You totally bare choong."

She did not reply, but her helpless smile said enough. Pops noticed it, and a tremor of irritation quivered across his face.

Bizness ignored Pops and the others and turned to Elijah. "Come with me, younger," he said, and without waiting for a response, he led the way through the crowd. A tall, heavyset man wearing an earpiece was stationed at a door next to the bar, and as Bizness approached, he gave a stiff nod and stepped aside. The room beyond was small and dark, with sofas against the walls and drapes obscuring the light from the street outside. There were three others in the room, arching their backs over a long table that was festooned with two dozen lines of cocaine, arranged in parallel, each four inches long. Elijah recognised the others as members of BRAPPPP!: MC Mafia—the rapper who sounded a little like Snoop—Icarus and Bredren.

Bizness walked across to the table and took out a rolled-up twenty-pound note. He lowered his face to the nearest line, and with the note pressed tightly into his nostril, he snorted hard. Half of the line disappeared. He swapped the note into his other nostril and snorted again, finishing the line. He pressed his finger to one nostril and then the other, snorting hard again, and then rubbed a finger vigorously across his gums. With an appreciative smack of his lips, he offered the note to Elijah. "Want one?"

Elijah had never taken cocaine before, and he was scared, but he felt unable to refuse. Bizness and the others were watching them. Bizness's face was inscrutable, and he did not want him to think he was a little boy. He shrugged, doing his best to feign nonchalance, dipped his head to the table, and snorted the powder. He managed a quarter of the line, the powder tickling his nose and throat. The sneeze came before he had moved his head, and it blew the rest of the line away, a little cloud of white that bloomed across the table, the powder getting into his eyes and his mouth.

Bizness laughed at his incompetence. "You ain't done that before, have you, bruv?"

"Course I have," he said, blushing hard.

"Sure."

The word was drawn out, freighted with sarcasm, and Elijah cursed himself for being so green. They would think he was a baby, and that was no good. He would show them otherwise. He stood back from the table and shrugged his rucksack off his shoulder. He unzipped it, reached inside, and drew out the bundle wrapped with newspaper. "I brought it," he said, holding it in both hands, offering it to Bizness.

"I don't need it," he said.

"What?"

"You do."

"What?"

"Check me, younger," he said. His voice was blank, emotionless. "You like what you see here out there tonight? You were having a good look around, weren't you? I saw. You see what we got? I ain't talking about the little things. Someone like Pops, he thinks it's all about getting himself new clothes, new trainers, a good-looking gyaldem, saving up for a nice car. I ain't dissing him, each to his own and that, but he's got a severe case of what I call limited horizons. He ain't going nowhere. He's at his peak right now, that's it for him. You youngers look up to brothers like that, some of you might even get to his level, but others, the ones with ambition, that ain't never going to be good enough. The ones who are going somewhere *know* they can do better. You get me, bruv?"

Elijah nodded. Bizness's breath was heavy with the smell of booze and dope.

"I'm gonna give you a demonstration of what I mean later tonight. That bitch of his, the white girl, I know you saw the way she clocked me earlier. You see, younger—who you reckon she's going home with later? That girl's getting proper merked, and it won't have nothing to do with him."

The other men in the room laughed at that, a harsh and cruel sound. Elijah swallowed hard.

Bizness reached out a clammy hand and curled it around the back of Elijah's head. He crouched down so that they were on the same level and drew Elijah's face closer to his own. The smell of his aftershave was sickly, and as he looked into the man's face, he saw that his eyes were cold, the pupils shrunk down to pinpricks, the muscles in his cheeks and at the corners of his mouth jerking and twitching from the cocaine. "It's about power, younger. Everything else follows after it. You get me?"

"Yes."

"You want to be with us, don't you? BRAPPPP!, right, we're like brothers. We'd do anything for each other. But you wanna get in with us, be one of us like that, you got to show us you got what it takes. And I ain't talking about robbing no shop or turning over some sad mug for his iPhone. That shit's for babies. You want to get in with the real gangsters, you got to do gangster shit."

Bizness had not removed his hand from Elijah's neck. Their faces were no more than six inches apart, and his eyes bored straight into Elijah's like lasers. "Younger," he said, "I got a problem, and you're gonna help me sort it. I heard a rumour that this joker I know is coming to the party tonight. You know Wiley T?"

Elijah did. He was a young rapper who was starting to build a reputation for himself. He came from Camden, where he had shot videos of him rapping on the street. He had uploaded them to YouTube, and they had gone viral. Elijah had heard that he had been offered a record contract because of those videos. Everyone was talking about it at school, discussing it jealously, coveting his good fortune, agreeing it was proof that it could be a way out of the ghetto. A long shot, but a shot nonetheless.

"I invited him," Bizness explained. "He thinks we're gonna shake hands and make up, but we ain't. He's been dropping bars on YouTube about me. You probably heard them?"

Elijah nodded, and without thinking what he was doing, he started to intone—"'You walk around showing your body 'cause it sells / plus to avoid the fact that you ain't got skills / mad at me 'cause I kick that shit real niggaz feel…'" He realised what he was saying before the pay-off and caught himself, saying that he didn't know the rest.

"'While 99% of your fans wear high heels,'" Bizness finished with a dry laugh with no humour in it. "Ain't a bad little diss, but bitch must've forgotten there's got to be a comeback when you drop words on me, and you better know it ain't going to be in something I put up on fucking YouTube for a laugh with my mates. He thinks he's a thug, but he ain't. He's a little joker, a little pussy, and he needs to get dooked."

Elijah's hands had started to shake. The direction the conversation was taking was frightening him, and he knew he was about to be asked to do something that he really did not want to do. Bizness unwrapped the gun from its newspaper wrapper and checked that it was loaded. "You ever shot a gun before, bruv?"

"No," Elijah managed to say.

Bizness extended his arm and pointed the gun at MC Mafia. He drew Elijah closer to him so that their heads touched. "It ain't no thing. You take the piece and aim it. That's right—look right down the sight."

"Come on, Bizness," Mafia said. "Aim that shit some other place. That ain't cool."

"Put your finger on the trigger, and give it a squeeze. It'll give you a little kick, so make sure you get in nice and close to the brother you want to shoot. You get in close, you won't miss. Easy, bruv."

He aimed away. Mafia exhaled and cracked a joke, but he could not completely hide his fear. Bizness was mental; they all knew it. Unpredictable and dangerous.

Bizness placed the gun carefully in Elijah's hands. "I want you to keep this. Keep your eyes on me tonight, a'ight? When he gets here, I'm gonna go up to him and give him a hug, like we're best friends. That's your signal. Soon as I do that, you gonna go up to him real close and put all six rounds into him. Pull the trigger until it don't fire no more. Blam, blam, blam, blam, blam, blam. You my little mash man, JaJa. We gonna make a little soldier out of you tonight, you see."

Chapter Twenty-One

RUTHERFORD PAID the barman, collected the two pints of orange juice and lemonade from the bar, and headed back outside. It was a warm evening, and he and Rutherford had found a table in the beer garden of the pub that faced onto Victoria Park. It was busy: Tuesday was quiz night, and the pub was full with teams spread out around the tables. The garden was busy, too, most of the tables occupied and with a steady stream of passers-by making their way to and from the row of chichi boutiques that had gathered along the main road. Rutherford remembered when this area had been one of the worst parts of the East End, battered and drab and the kind of place where you could get rolled just as easily as crossing the road. Now, though? The money from the city had taken over: all the old warehouses had been turned into arty studios, the terraces had been turned into apartments, and the shops were filled with butchers where you could pay a fiver for a burger made of buffalo, fancy restaurants and furniture shops. They said it was progress, and things were better now. Rutherford didn't miss the aggravation, but he did miss the soul of the place; it was as if its heart had been ripped out.

The meeting had been held in the Methodist Hall around the corner. Once again, Milton had sat quietly, keeping his own counsel. Rutherford was on the opposite side of the circle of chairs and had watched him. His face had been impassive throughout; if he had felt any response to the discussion, then he had hidden it very well. When the meeting had finished, Rutherford had suggested they go to the pub for a drink. He had not expected Milton to agree, but he had.

Rutherford set the pints down on the table and sat down. "Cheers," he said as they touched glasses.

Milton took a long draught. "So how long were you in for?" he asked him.

"The army? Sixteen years."

He clucked his tongue. "That's a long stint. Where?"

"All the usual places: Kosovo, Iraq, Afghanistan. Lots of fun."

"I can imagine. Doing what?"

"Royal Engineers. Bomb disposal. I've always been decent enough at breaking things down and putting them back together again; it was a pretty obvious move for me once I'd got my feet wet for a couple of years. I was one of the lads they sent to defuse them for the first five years, and then when the brass thought I had enough common sense about me, they bumped me up to major and put me onto investigations—we'd get sent in when one of them went off to try to work out what it was that had caused it: pressure plate, remote detonation or something new. By the time I'd had enough, it was getting silly—the Muj started planting second and third devices in the same place to try to catch us out. A mate of mine I'd been with almost from the start lost both his legs like that. Stepped on a plate next to where they'd blown up another one fifteen minutes earlier. I was right behind him when it happened, first person there to help while they sent for the medics. I didn't need much encouragement to get out after seeing that." He looked over the rim of his pint at Milton. "What about you? What did you do? From the looks of it, I'm guessing ex-Special Forces." When Milton said nothing, Rutherford shrugged. "Well, that's your business."

He noticed that Milton's hand was shaking a little; drops fell over the lip of the glass and dribbled down the glass.

"SAS," he said eventually. "Is it that obvious?"

"Oh, I don't know—you stay in long enough and you get to know the signs."

"I was hoping it'd wash off eventually." He laughed mirthlessly. "I haven't been a soldier for years."

"Why'd you get out?"

"We've all got our own stories," he said. A jet from the city airport arced away to the south. A bloated pigeon alighted on the table opposite and was shooed off again.

Rutherford could see that Milton had no interest in talking about whatever it was that had happened to him. "What have you been doing since?"

"Some things I can't talk about," he said, with a shake of his head. They had both finished their drinks. Milton stood. "How about a coffee? We can work out how I can help you with the club."

Rutherford watched him negotiate the crowd gathered at the door. He knew that there was a lot that Milton wasn't telling him, and he guessed— well, it was pretty obvious, really—that he was still involved in soldiering in some capacity or another. The reticence was not what he would have expected of a grunt who was selling his experience as a mercenary; for his money, the discretion made it more likely that he was involved in something like intelligence. The conclusion led to more questions than it answered: what, for example, was an intelligence agent doing getting involved with a little hoodrat from Hackney? A spook? What sense did that make?

Rutherford had no idea how to even begin answering that one.

Milton returned with two cappuccinos.

"So," he said, "the boxing club. You're struggling. How can I help?"

"I can always do with more hands," Rutherford said thoughtfully. "There's a list of what's wrong with that place that's as long as my arm, man. The roof leaks, the wiring's all over the place, the walls need painting, the canvasses are torn and stained with God only knows what—there's only so much that I can do on my own, you know, with the club to run. If you're serious—?"

"I am."

"—then I'd say thank you very much. That would make a big difference."

"Fine. How about tomorrow morning? See what I can do?"

Rutherford raised his cup. "You bringing that younger you mentioned?"

"I'm working on that," Milton said.

Chapter Twenty-Two

CHRISTOPHER CALLAN, Number Twelve, drove across town to Hackney, following his satnav to Victoria Park. It was a hot, sticky night, and he drove with the windows open, the warm breeze blowing onto his face. He looked around distastefully. It was a mongrel area: million-pound houses cheek by jowl with slumlike high-rises. He reversed into a parking space in one of the better streets, locked the car, and set off the rest of the way on foot. His destination was marked on his phone's map, and he followed it across the southern end of the park, alongside a wide boating lake with a fountain throwing water into the air and Polish immigrants fishing for their dinners from the banks. Finally, he turned onto Grove Road.

Milton had used his phone earlier, and HQ had located the signal, triangulating it to the terrace that Callan was approaching. He picked his way along the untidy road until he reached the address, passing by on the other side before turning and passing back again. That side of the road was comprised of cheap terraced housing that might, once, have been pleasant. It was far from pleasant today, with the occasional property that had been well maintained standing out amidst the pitiful neglect of its neighbours.

Callan wondered what Milton was doing in a place like this. He slowed as he came up beside number eleven, taking everything in: the rotting washing machine in the gutter; the broken staves of the fencing across the road, lashed around with chicken wire; the bars on the doors and ground-floor windows. The windows of the house were open, and the curtains were drawn, the puce-coloured fabric puffing in and out of the opening, ruffled by the sweaty breeze. A lamp was on inside, the light flickering on and off as the curtains swayed. Callan couldn't tell if anyone was home.

A Volvo was parked by the side of the road. Callan recognised it from Milton's file. The car looked at home among the battered heaps that filled the parking spaces around it. He slowed as he passed the Volvo and, moving quickly and smoothly, dipped down and slapped a magnetic transmitter inside the wheel arch.

Callan did not want to tarry. He had no desire to draw attention to himself. He didn't think that he had ever met Milton before, but he could not completely discount the possibility that he might somehow have known him. No point in taking chances.

He reached the end of the road, paused for a final look back again, and set off for the main road. He took out his phone and dialled.

"Callan," said Control.

"Hello, sir. Can you talk?"

"Are you there?"

"I'm just leaving now. Awful place. Small house in a terrace. Looks like council housing. It's a sink Estate, not a good area, kids out on the street corners, pit bulls, messy, rubbish left out to rot in the gardens—you can picture the scene, I'm sure. God only knows what he's doing here."

"You've no idea?"

"None at all."

"What about the house—did you look inside?"

"Couldn't. I couldn't be sure he wasn't at home. I didn't try to get any closer than the street. I can come back for that."

As he walked back along the fringes of the Estate, he noticed that he was being followed. Two older teenagers on BMXs were lazily trailing him, kicking the bikes along on the other side of the road.

"What about his car?"

"You can tell Tech that the tracker has been fixed."

Callan took a right turn off the main road and watched as the two boys bounced down off the kerb and crossed against the flow of the traffic. The two started to close the distance between them.

"Sorry, sir. I'll have to call you back."

He pressed the toggle on the headphones to end the call. The road turned sharply to the left, and Callan stopped to wait for the boys. They rolled up to him. They both wore baseball caps pulled down low with their hoods tugged up so that the fabric sat on the brim. The bottom half of their faces were covered with purple bandanas. Only their eyes were visible. It was impossible to guess their age, but they were both large and rangy, their bikes almost comically small for them.

"Got the time, bruv?" the first boy said with insouciant aggression, putting his foot down and stopping. If he replied to the request, no doubt the next step would have been for him to have been relieved of his watch, together with his phone and wallet.

"Time you got off home, I reckon."

The boy rolled a little closer. "You want to watch who you're giving lip to, lighty. You could end up in a lot of mess." The second boy got off his bike and walked forwards. He hawked up a ball of phlegm and spat it at Callan's feet. "Give me your phone."

Callan felt his skin prickle and his muscles tightening. The sensation was familiar to him. The surge of adrenaline. Fight or flight. It was rarely flight with him. "I don't want any trouble," he said meekly.

The second boy took his hand out of the pocket of his jacket. He was holding a kitchen knife in his fist. "Give me your phone and your cash, a'ight, else you're gonna get jooked."

The boy came closer, and Callan let him. When he was within arm's reach, he lashed out suddenly with his right hand, the fingers held out straight, the thumb bracing them from beneath. The strike landed perfectly, and forcefully, Callan's hard fingertips jabbing into the boy's throat, right into the larynx. He dropped the knife and clutched his throat as he staggered back, choking, temporarily unable to draw breath. The first boy tried to hike up his jacket so that he could get to the knife he was carrying in his belt, but he was impeded by his bike and was far too slow. Callan closed the distance between them with a quick hop and, bending his arm, struck the boy in the face with the point of his right elbow. The pedals tripped the boy as he staggered away, and he fell onto his back, blood already running from his broken nose. The boy Callan had struck in the throat was still gasping for breath, and Callan almost lazily cast him to the ground, sweeping his legs out from beneath him. He crouched down and grabbed the boy by the scruff of his collar. He raised his head six inches from the pavement and then crashed it backwards, slamming his crown against the edge of the kerb, fracturing his skull and knocking him out.

Callan stood, brushed himself down, and set off again.

Chapter Twenty-Three

ELIJAH RETURNED to Pops and his woman after Bizness had finished talking to him. Pops looked surly, brooding over his JD and casting careful glances out across the room to where Bizness and MC Mafia were talking with two good-looking girls dressed in crop tops and obscenely short skirts. Elijah watched them too, unable to concentrate. He felt a dizzying mixture of emotions: fear, that he had been asked to do something that he did not want to do, but also pride. He knew it was foolish to feel that way, but he could not deny it. Where were his friends tonight? Where were Little Mark and Kidz, Pinky and the others? They weren't here. Bizness had chosen *him* for the task. Surely that must mean something. He trusted him. He could not help visualising a future in which he was a member of BRAPPPP!, too. The newest member. The youngest. The one with the reputation, the one no one would doubt. He thought of the lifestyle, the money. He would drag his family up with him, away from the Estate. His mum wouldn't need to work three jobs to make ends meet. They would buy a little house, with a little garden. Perhaps he could help Jules, too. Rehab or something. Things would be better than they were now.

He knew the price for all of this, but he tried not to think about it.

If he did, he would run.

A stir of interest rippled through the crowd as a small group of boys passed in through the entrance to the club. There were four of them, and at their head, Elijah recognised Wiley T. He knew that he was only two years older than him; he was a mixture of youth and experience. His face was fresh, and he still walked with a lazy adolescent lope, but his body language was confident. He punctuated his sentences with exaggerated gestures designed to draw attention to himself, and he smiled widely at a nearby group of girls, a confidence that Elijah could not begin to hope to emulate. Elijah knew enough about him from his YouTube profile. He was a street boy, like him, and their education was the same. He recognised the flicker of furtive watchfulness in his eyes. Boy was older than his years.

Elijah felt a nugget of ice in his gullet as Bizness approached Wiley and offered his hand. The younger man sneered and did not take it. Bizness moved forwards in an attempt to draw Wiley into an embrace, but he stepped away, a derisive expression on his face. He said something, and then, as Bizness backed away, he threw a punch that rattled against his jaw. The fight that followed flared quickly and viciously, with members of both entourages folding into one another, fists flying.

Elijah watched from the other side of the room. His rucksack was at his feet, the zip half undone, and as he looked down into it, the dull metal of the gun sparkled in the light from a glitterball overhead. Bizness separated himself from the melee and glared at Elijah, his face twisted with fury. He mouthed one word: "Now." Elijah felt his life folding down into that one small, awful point. It was over for him. He picked up his bag and lifted it to his waist, just high enough that he could reach his right hand inside for the gun. His fingers brushed the metal, encircled it so that the cold was pressed into his palm and his finger found the trigger guard and, within it, the subtle give of the trigger.

The noise of the party seemed to muffle and fade as Elijah started across the room.

Everything slowed to a crawl.

He glanced into the faces of the people around him, but nothing registered.

He felt completely alone.

He closed the distance to the brawl. He squeezed the gun into his palm and started to bring it up to the open mouth of the bag.

Pops took him by the arm and pulled him aside. "Don't be an idiot."

Elijah looked up at him dumbly.

"Be clever, younger. Do that and your life is finished. You think the feds won't find out? You think he won't rat you out to save his own skin?"

Elijah was unable to speak.

"Go home, JaJa. Go on, fuck off, fuck off now, take that bag with you, drop it in the canal, and don't ever tell no one a word about it."

On the other side of the club, the fight was getting worse. A dozen men were brawling now, and as Elijah watched, one of them fell to the ground. Bizness was onto him quickly, kicking him again and again in the head. Pops gently turned him towards the exit and pushed him on his way.

Elijah kept going. He did not look back.

Chapter Twenty-Four

POPS SAT in the front of his car, his forehead resting against the steering wheel. He had driven aimlessly for an hour, trying to arrange his thoughts into some sort of order, and had eventually found his way to Meynell Street, the sickle-shaped road that hugged the edge of Well Street Common. It was a middle-class area with big, wide houses that cost the better part of half a million pounds each. The boys rarely came up here. It wasn't worth the risk. It was a good distance from the Estate, and they knew that if they started causing trouble, the police would respond quickly, and in numbers. Far better to stay in their ends, on the streets that they knew, and where their victims were not deemed important enough to demand the same protection.

He looked out over the small park, pools of lamplight cast down at the junctions of the pathways that cut across it. He had switched off the car's engine, but the dashboard was still lit, casting queasy green light up onto his face, illuminating his reflection on the inside of the windshield. He examined himself and thought, again, that he looked older than he was. His skin looked almost grey in the artificial light, and his eyes were black and empty, denuded of life, of their sparkle. Pops was nineteen, but he felt older. He had seen things that he could not forget, no matter how hard he tried. He gave it big with the others because there was nothing else he could do. You showed weakness, you got eaten; that was the way it was. The rules of the jungle, he thought again. Just like the Serengeti.

But Pops was different. He was smart. He had a plan, and he would leave on his terms when he was ready. He was careful with his money, saving every month, and he wanted twenty grand in his account before he called it a day. He had been a decent student at school before he had been sucked down into the LFB, and he wanted to finish his education. And then, who knows, maybe he would go to college. You needed paper for that. Until then, until he had enough, there was no choice but to keep up his front. If he let down his guard, even for a minute, there were plenty of youngers who would seize their chance. There would be beef, there would be hype, and it would end up badly for all of them.

His mind flicked back to the end of the party. The fight had ended almost as quickly as it had begun, yet it had curdled the mood, like poison dripped into an open wound. Wiley and his boys had taken a terrible beating, with one young boy left unconscious on the floor, his face kicked into a mess of blood and mucus. Pops watched as his body jerked and twitched and knew that he needed a doctor, and quickly. He quietly went into the toilets and called 999, leaving an anonymous message that an ambulance was required.

By the time he returned outside, the lights had been turned on, and people were starting to go. He had heard police sirens in the near distance, too. Definitely time to leave.

He looked over at the passenger seat. Laura's handbag was resting against the cushion. Pops had bought her the bag for Christmas after she mentioned that she liked the designer. It had cost plenty, but she was worth it. He had searched the club for her, but she had already gone. He didn't know where she was now, but he knew she was with Bizness. He had known that he wanted her. He made no secret of it, joking with Pops about the fact that one day he'd just take her and that there was nothing he would be able to do about it. Pops would laugh it off most of the time, making sure that he kept his seething anger to himself. As long as he kept her away from him, everything would be all right. But that had not been possible tonight. Bizness had suggested before the fight that the party would eventually relocate to his studio and that she should come. The invitation had not been extended to Pops. She had been drunk and high, and she knew that Bizness was offering her more of the same. He had lost her. He had always known it would happen, eventually, and now it had. He had gone to his car and driven away.

He looked out into the darkness, staring through his own reflection as the light of a bicycle bounced up and down, a rider passing across the park. He thought of JaJa and how close the boy had come to ruining his life. The party had made his mind up for him. Bizness was a bad man, he was out of control, and Pops knew it was insanity to think otherwise. He did not care about anyone other than himself. JaJa, young and pliable and vulnerable, the boy was just a tool to him, a means to an end. He would have used him to dook Wiley, and then, when the feds came knocking, he would give him up.

Yes, Bizness was out of control, and he had to do something.

He reached into his pocket for his wallet. Inside, hidden beneath his credit cards, was the business card that the man in the park had given him. There was something about him that stuck in his head. Pops could not put his finger on it, but there was something that said he might be able to help. He had not been able to throw the card away, and while the others had sent him off with a barrage of abuse, he had quietly slipped it into his pocket.

He took out his phone and switched it on, the display coming to life. He carefully entered the man's number. The call connected but, after ringing three times, went to voicemail. Pops listened to the bland message, then the beep, and ended the call without speaking. What was he doing? He knew nothing about this man. How could he trust him? What was he going to say?

He put the phone away, started the engine, reversed the car, and rolled slowly back towards the Estate.

Chapter Twenty-Five

MILTON WAS NOT ALONE in the waiting room. A portly middle-aged woman was slumped into one of the plastic seats, her expression bearing the marks of frustration, helplessness and anger. Her eyes followed Milton as he sat down on one of the chairs opposite her, but she didn't speak. The police station smelt the same as all the others he had visited, all around the world: the same mixture of scrubbing soap, disinfectant and body odour. It had the same weary atmosphere, the sense of a heavy relentlessness.

He gazed at the posters tacked onto a corkboard that hung from the wall; young black men staring into police cameras with expressions of dull, lazy violence. The crimes they were alleged to have committed were depressingly similar: an assault with a knife, an armed robbery at a betting shop, a shooting. There were two murders with the same police task force—Trident—dealing with them both. Black on black. A poster showed a young boy staring out from behind a lattice of bars, the message warning that this was the inevitable destination for those who got caught up with gangs. The boy in the poster was young, in his middle teens. The same age as Elijah. He looked small, vulnerable and helpless.

Milton looked at the clock on the wall for the hundredth time: it was five minutes past three in the morning.

"Who you here for?" the woman said.

"The son of a friend," Milton said.

"What've they got him in for?"

"I'm not sure."

"Won't matter," she declaimed. "Won't matter if he did it or not, neither. They need to get something cleared up, they'll say he did it, and that'll be that. Look at my boy. He ain't perfect, God knows he ain't, but he didn't do half the things they said he's done. It's because he's black, from the wrong ends, in the wrong place at the wrong time. The police are racist pigs."

Milton said nothing. He was not disposed to have a conversation with her, and after a long moment of silence, she realised that. She clucked her tongue against her teeth, shook her head, and went back to staring dully at the posters on the wall.

Sharon had called Milton just after midnight. She explained that the police had visited the flat and arrested Elijah. She had heard him coming back late. She only had vague details: the police had said something about a fight at a club, a man beaten halfway to death. Elijah was supposed to have been identified as a witness. Sharon didn't know what to do and sounded at the end of her tether. Milton had said he would deal with it.

"Is anyone here for Elijah Warriner?"

The policeman was middle-aged, a little overweight, and with wispy fronds of white hair arranged around a bald crown. He looked tired.

"I am," Milton said.

The officer opened the door and indicated inside. "Would you step in here for a moment, sir."

"What about my boy?" the woman squawked. "You've had him in there for hours."

The sergeant regarded her with a tired shrug. "They're just finishing up with him, Brenda."

"You charging him?"

"He said he did it."

"Bail?"

"I expect so. Just wait there; we'll get to you as soon as we can." He turned back to Milton. "Sir?"

Milton did as he was asked. The room beyond was small, with a table and two plastic chairs. The surface of the table had been scarified with carved graffiti, the letters LFB repeated several times. The policeman shut the door and indicated that Milton should sit. He did, the policeman taking the other chair.

"Who are you?" the policeman asked him.

"I'm a friend of Elijah's mother. And you?"

"Detective Sergeant Shaw."

"What are you holding him for?"

"There was a serious assault at a party yesterday evening. A lad from Camden was beaten. GBH, pretty serious. Elijah was there when it happened."

"Is he a suspect?"

"I don't know yet. Probably not. But he was definitely a witness. He admitted he was there. Save that, he won't talk. Not that I'm surprised; they never do." He sighed and took a packet of cigarettes from his pocket. There were no-smoking signs on the wall, but he ignored them, taking a cigarette and lighting it. He offered one to Milton, who declined. Shaw drew deeply on the cigarette, taking the smoke into his lungs and then exhaling it in a second, longer sigh.

"Look—Mr Milton—I'm not sure what's going to happen to him, but let me make a prediction. Elijah's in a dangerous position. Chances are, he's going to get away with whatever happened this time. But that doesn't mean he's going to be all right. He's not right in the gang yet, but he's on the edge. It won't take much to tip him over, and if that happens, he'll definitely be back here again, and then he'll get nicked. He might get community service for whatever he ends up doing, but that won't straighten him out. The time after that he'll get prison. And that's if he's lucky to live that long. Plenty of them don't. I've seen it dozens of times."

"These other lads he's been messing around with—the gang? Who are they?"

"The London Fields Boys?"

"I don't know very much about them."

"Let me give you a little history, Mr Milton. I've been a policeman around here for the best part of twenty years. That's a long time to work in one place, but it means I've got a better idea of this borough than most. I'll be honest with you—Hackney's never been a particularly nice manor. It's always been poor, there've never been enough jobs to go around, and there's never been enough for kids to do. You take a situation like that, it's normal that you're going to get a problem with crime. It's not the easiest place in the world to be a copper, but for most of those years, it's been manageable. You'd get the odd blagging, drunken lads getting into scraps after too many bevvies on a Friday night, chaps going home after the pub and slapping their women around. You'd always have a GBH on the go, and there'd be the odd murder now and again. Not the best place in the world, lots of problems, but by and large, we kept a lid on it.

"Now, you look at the last five years, and things have changed so much I hardly recognise it sometimes. We've always had gangs of young lads, and they've always gotten into scrapes. Petty stuff—fights, nicking things, just making a nuisance of themselves. But then they all started getting tooled up. They're all carrying knives. Some of them have guns. You add that to the mix, then you have a gang from another borough coming in here looking for trouble, things get serious very quickly. When I was a lad, we used to play at cops and robbers. These days, they're not playing. They're all tooled up, one way or another, and it's not all for show. The guns are real, and they don't care if they use them or not. I don't know if he'll listen to you more than he's listened to me, but you've got to get some sense into him. If you don't..." He let the words drift away before picking it up again. "If you don't, Mr Milton, then he's not going to have very much of a life."

Chapter Twenty-Six

MILTON WALKED out of the police station with Elijah behind him. He looked out into the street. It was a hot night, broiling, and even though it was coming around to four in the morning, there were still people about. The atmosphere was drunken and aggressive. Men looked at them as they passed, assuming that a white man on the steps of a police station must be a detective. There was contempt in their faces, violence behind their sleepy, hooded eyes. Milton had called a taxi while he was waiting for Elijah to be processed, and it was waiting for them by the kerb. He opened the rear door for Elijah and then slid in next to him. He gave the driver the address for Blissett House and settled back as they pulled into traffic.

He looked across at the boy. He had the downy moustache and acne of a teenager, but there was a hardness in his face. His eyes were fixed straight ahead, and his face was set, trying to appear impassive, but his hands betrayed him; they fluttered in his lap, picking at his nails and at swatches of dead skin.

"You know you're in trouble, Elijah."

He did not reply, but the fidgeting got worse.

"Let me help you."

When he finally spoke, it was quiet and quick, as if he did not want the taxi driver to overhear him. "You ain't police?"

"No."

"You swear it?"

"I'm not the police. You can trust me, and I want to help. What's the problem?"

Still he was not convinced. "Why you want to help us? What's in it for you?"

"It's a long story."

"I ain't saying nothing unless you tell me why."

Milton thought for a moment about what to say. "I've done some things in my life that I'm not proud of," he said carefully. "I'm trying to make up for them. That good enough for you?"

"What kind of things?"

"Bad things," Milton said. "That's enough for now. This is about you, not me."

Elijah looked down at his lap. Eventually, the residual fear of his situation defeated his bravado, the reluctance to admit that he needed help, and the fear of what might happen to him if the others discovered that he had spoken out of turn. "Alright," he said. "Last night. I was there. I saw what happened."

Milton told him to explain. Elijah spoke quietly and quickly.

"Who had the gun?"

"Me. Bizness gave it to me last week, told me to keep it for him until he needed it. You need heat, right, with our rep? You get a beef, like we had with Wiley and his crew, you don't have a blammer, you done for. Finished."

"Who's Wiley?"

"This rapper. He's been dissing Bizness. He had to make an example, man. Can't have that kind of nonsense going on, YouTube and everything. Bad for business. Bad for your rep."

"You gave the gun to him?"

"Nah, man. I had it. He wanted me to do it myself."

"And?"

"I didn't know what to do. I started walking over towards where this fight had started, Bizness and Wiley were going at it, I put my hand in my bag, the gun was there, and then the next thing I know Pops has come over to me, grabbed my arm, and told me to breeze. I did—went straight home."

"Did you tell the police you had the gun?"

He looked indignant. "I didn't tell them shit."

That was good, Milton thought. The boy was hanging on by his fingertips, but he still had a future. "This Bizness. Who is he?"

Elijah looked at him with a moment's incredulity before remembering that Milton was older, and naïve, and that there was no reason why he would have heard of him. "Risky Bizness. He runs things around here. He's been in the LFB for years, since he was a younger, like me. He's one of the real OGs."

"One of the what?"

"Original Gangsters, man. He's got himself involved with everything— the shotters sell the gear and pass the paper up to the Elders, and the Elders pass it up to the Faces like Bizness. He makes mad Ps. He built himself a record studio out of it, and now he's got himself a record deal. He's famous on top of everything. He's a legend, innit?"

"What's his real name?"

Elijah shrugged. "Dunno. I've never heard no one call him anything but Bizness."

The taxi turned into the road that led towards Blissett House. Milton told the driver to pull over. He guessed that Elijah would prefer not to be seen getting out of a cab with him, and he saw, from the look of relief on his face, that he had been right.

"All right, Elijah," he said. "This is what I want you to do. Go home to your mother. She's beside herself with worry. Get to bed. Don't answer your phone, particularly if it's Bizness or any of the other boys in the gang. You need a little space between you and them at the moment. Do you hear me?"

"Yes," he said. "What about the police?"

"I think that will be all right. I've given them my number. If anything comes up, they'll call me, and we can take it from there. Now then—what did you do with the gun?"

"Dropped it in the canal."

"Do you promise?"

"Yeah," he said. "I don't want nothing to do with it."

"That's good." He reached over and opened the door. "Go on, then. We'll let this blow over."

"And then?"

"I've got something for you I think you might enjoy. Meet me in the café in the morning. Nine o'clock. Bring your sports kit from school."

"Nine? That's, like, just five hours. When am I gonna get some sleep?"

"You can sleep afterwards. Nine o' clock, Elijah. I've got something for you to do that you're going to be good at."

PART THREE

Strapped

Laughter, and then something else. A low drone. His stomach knotted. No. The plane was still a dot on the horizon, but it was closing quickly. Beneath the radar. A Warthog, onion-shaped bombs hanging beneath its wings. He threw his rifle aside and scrambled down the escarpment, the loose sand sliding down with him, his boots struggling for purchase, failing, and he was tumbling down the last few metres, landing at the bottom with a heavy thump that drove the air from his lungs. He got to his knees and then to his feet, his boots skidding off the dirt and scrub as he pushed off, his arm sinking down to the wrist as he tried to keep upright.

He ran towards the village. Five hundred yards, four hundred. The sound of the Warthog's engines was louder now; it was coming in low, a thousand feet up, not rushing, the pilot taking his time. Three hundred. He ran, boots sinking up to the laces with each step, thighs pumping until they burned. He gasped in and out, his lungs so full of the scorched air that he felt like they were alight. Two hundred. He was close enough to yell out now, and he did, screaming that they had to take cover, that they had to get inside. One hundred, and he was close enough to see the faces of the children outside the madrasa. The cheap plastic ball had sailed in his direction, and he could see the confusion and fear in the face of the boy who had been sent to fetch it. Five years old? Surely no older. He yelled at him to get down, but it was too late, it had always been too late. It would not have mattered if he had been able to get to them sooner; the decision had already been taken.

The Warthog's engines boomed. The boy turned away from him to face it. The ball rolled away on the breeze. A blinding flash of white light. The deafening crack of a terrible explosion. He was picked up and thrown back twenty feet in the direction that he had come. A second and third explosion seemed to bend the world off its axis, the noise blending from a roar into a continuous, high-pitched whine. He lay staring up into the sun while the air around him seemed to vibrate as if someone had smashed a cello with a sledgehammer. He rolled over and pushed his head up, working his arm around until he could prop himself against his elbow. Above, slowly unfurling, was a dark cloud of black smoke that rose and shifted until it had obscured the sun. He smelt burning flesh and the unmistakeable acrid tang of high explosive.

His hearing resolved as the Warthog swooped over and away. He pushed himself up until he was on his knees. A huge crater was in the centre of the village. The launcher was gone. The madrasa was gone. The children were gone, too, or so he would have thought until his eyes tracked around to the right and he saw red splashes of colour on the ground and glistening red ribbons of flesh suspended from the bare branches of a nearby tree.

Fifty feet away, in the open desert, the plastic ball rolled with the wind.

Chapter Twenty-Seven

THE NIGHTMARE was as bad as Milton could remember it. When he awoke, the sheets were a bunched-up pile on the floor, soaked through with sweat. His brain was fogged and unclear. He rose and went for his usual run, the best way he knew to chase it away. The streets were quiet, and the park was empty. He ran two laps, following the line of trees, pushing himself harder on the second so that by the time he returned to the road, he was sweating and breathing heavily. He chose a return route that took him past the boxing club. The door was open, the slapping of a skipping rope audible from inside. He didn't stop and returned to the house, where he showered and dressed. He stood before the mirror again and checked that the outline of his pistol was not obvious against the cut of his jacket. He locked the door and went to the café for his breakfast. Elijah was already waiting for him. The boy was sitting in a booth.

"This better be good," he said, a little surly.

"Get any sleep?"

"Nah, not much. I'm knackered."

"Where's your kit?"

Elijah nodded at the black Nike sports bag resting on the chair next to him.

"Good lad. You hungry?"

"A bit," he conceded.

"All right, then. You'll need to eat. You're going to be working hard this morning."

"What are we doing?"

"You'll see," Milton said. The proprietor came over to take their order. Milton ordered two plates of scrambled eggs and bacon, a portion of chips and two glasses of orange juice.

"Is your mother all right?"

"What you mean—about me getting nicked? Yeah, she's alright."

"She worries about you, you know."

"I know," Elijah said. "I don't mean to upset her."

"I know you don't." The boy seemed more disposed to speak this morning, and Milton decided to take advantage of the boy's mood. "How are things at home?"

"How you mean?"

"How does your mum manage?"

"What you think it's like? We got no Dad, Mum works three jobs, and there's still hardly enough money coming in to feed us, buy clothes. Me and my brother—you get into a situation like that and you do what you got to do, innit? My mum knows what I've been doing—she just don't wanna ask."

"Would you have listened to her?"

The food arrived before he could answer. The proprietor handed them each a plate of eggs and bacon and left the chips in the middle of the table. "You know about Jules?" Elijah said when he had left them. "My brother?"

"Not really."

"He's five years older than me. Me and him, we grew up with nothing. You go to school and you're the one with the uniform with the holes in it. I never got no new shirts or trousers or nothing like that—all I got was his hand-me-downs; Mum would find the holes and just keep patching them up. There were patches on the patches eventually. You know how that makes you feel?"

Again, Milton shook his head.

"Makes you feel like a tramp, bruv. The other kids laugh at you like you're some kind of special case." Elijah took a chip, smeared it with ketchup, and put it into his mouth. He chewed, a little nervously, still unsure whether he was doing the right thing in talking to Milton. "Then you see the brothers with their new clothes, parking their flash cars outside their mommas' flats, you see them things, and you know what's possible. They ain't got no patched-up uniforms. Their shoes don't have holes in them. Jules saw it. He was in the LFB before me. He came back with new trainers one day, and I knew. Then he bought himself new clothes for school, more trainers, a phone, nice jewellery. He started to make a name for himself. Kids at school who used to take the piss out of him didn't do that no more. He got some respect.

"One day, he comes back, and he tells me that I have to come down to the road with him. I do like he says, and there it is, he shows me this car he's bought. It ain't nothing special, just this second-hand Nissan, beaten up to shit, but he's bought it with his own money, and it's his. The way I see it, there ain't nothing wrong with that. It don't matter where he's got it from, he's entitled."

"There are other ways to get the things you want," Milton said.

"What? School?" He laughed at that. "You think I can get out of here by getting an education? How many kids in my ends you think get through school with an education?" He spat out the word disdainfully. Just for a moment, his eyes stopped flicking back and forth and he stared straight at Milton. "I ain't gonna get the kind of education that can help me by sitting in the classroom, listening to some teacher going on about history or geography. Teachers don't give a shit about me. Let's say I did pay attention, and I get good grades so I could go to university. You have to pay thousands for that these days—so how do we afford that?" He shook his head with an expression of clear and total certainty. "Education ain't for people like me, not round here. Let me make this simple for you: my... brother... was... my... education. All I saw was guys with their cars and their clothes. His Nissan taught me more than anything I ever learned in school. Exam grades ain't gonna get me any of that. All they'll get me is a job flipping burgers in Maccy D's and that ain't never going to happen. I know what you can get if you play the game."

Milton detected a weak spot and pressed. "Where's Jules now?"

A flicker of discomfort passed across his face. "He was shotting drugs, right—the crack, selling it to the cats—then he started doing it himself. Couldn't deal with it. He got into trouble, didn't kick up the paper like he was supposed to do. He had some beef with the Elders, and he ended up getting a proper beating. Nothing he didn't deserve, mind—there are rules you got to follow, and if you don't, you get what you get. Anyway, one day he never came back home. My mums spoke to him on the phone, and he said he had to get away. I've seen him a few times since—this one time, I was in town, going to buy some new trainers from JJB, and I see him there on Oxford Street, sitting against a shop with a cap on the ground in front of him, begging for change. He's an addict now. It's disgusting. I just kept walking. Didn't say nothing to him. We don't see him no more."

"And you look up to him?"

"Not any more, man, not how he is now. But before that? Yeah—course, he's my brother, course I looked up to him. I seen how he got what he wanted, and I seen how it works better than your schools and books. I just ain't gonna make the same mistakes he did."

Milton paid after they had finished their food, and they set off. The club was a fifteen-minute walk from the main road, and Milton took the opportunity to continue the conversation. Milton sketched in the lines of a meagre, uninspiring life and quickly came to understand how the excitement and the camaraderie of the street had proven to be so attractive to the boy. He inevitably thought of his own peripatetic childhood, dragged around the embassies and consulates of Europe and the Middle East as his father followed a string of different postings. Money had never been a problem for the Miltons, but there were still comparisons to be drawn between Elijah's early years and his own. Loneliness, a lack of roots, no foundations to build on. The army had become Milton's family, and then the Group. But even that had come to an end. Now, he thought, he was on his own again. Perhaps that was for the best. For some people, people like him, perhaps that was the natural way of things.

The doors of the church hall were thrown wide, and the sound of activity was loud, spilling out into the tree-lined street. Milton led the way inside, Elijah trailing a little cautiously behind. There were two dozen boys at the club this morning, spread between the ring and the exercise equipment. Two pairs were squeezed into the ring together, sparring with one another. The heavy bag resounded with the pummelling blows of a big, muscled elder boy, and the speed bag spat out a rat-tat-tat as a wiry, sharp-elbowed girl hit it, her gloved fists rolling with the fast, repetitive rhythm. Others jumped rope or shadow-boxed, and two older boys were busy with rollers on the far side of the room, whitewashing the wall.

"Boxing?" Elijah exclaimed.

"That's right."

"I ain't into this," he said. "You're having a laugh."

Milton turned to him. "Give it a chance," he said. "Just one morning, see how you get on. If you don't like it, you don't ever have to come back. But you might surprise yourself."

Rutherford noticed them and made his way across the room. "This your boy?"

"I ain't his boy," Elijah said dismissively.

"He's not sure this is for him," Milton said, patiently ignoring his truculent attitude.

"Wouldn't be the first lad to say that the first time he comes in here. How old are you, son?"

"Fifteen."

"Big lad for your age. Reckon you might have something about you. I'm Rutherford. Who are you?"

"JaJa."

"All right then, JaJa. Have you got kit?"

Elijah gave a sullen shrug.

"I'll take that as a yes. The changing room is out the back. Get yourself sorted out and get back out here. We'll see what you can do."

Milton was surprised to see that Elijah did as he was told.

"Leave him with me for a couple of hours," Rutherford said. "I think he's going to like this more than he thinks he is."

Chapter Twenty-Eight

MILTON LOOKED at the jobs that needed doing. As Rutherford had suggested, the hall was in a bit of a state. The walls were peeling in places, large swathes of damp bubbling up beneath the paint and patches of dark fungus spreading up from the floor. Some of the floorboards were rotting, one of the toilets had been smashed, and the roof leaked in several places. Buckets had been placed to catch the falling water, and looking up to fix the position on the roof, Milton took the ladder that Rutherford offered, went outside, braced it against the wall, and climbed up to take a better look. Several of the tiles were missing. He climbed back down, went to the small hardware store that served the Estate, and bought a wide plastic sheet, a hammer and a handful of nails. He spent the next hour and a half securing the sheet so that it sheltered the missing tiles. It was only a temporary fix, but it would suffice until he could return with the materials to do the job properly.

When Milton returned to the church hall, he found Elijah sparring inside the ring. The boy was wearing a head guard, vest and shorts, his brand-new Nikes gleaming against the dirty canvas. His opponent looked to be a year or two older and was a touch taller and heavier, yet Elijah was giving him all he could handle. He was light on his feet and skipped in and out of range, absorbing his opponent's slow jabs on his gloves and retaliating with quick punches of his own. Milton had been a decent boxer in the Forces and was confident that he knew how to spot raw talent when he saw it. And Elijah had talent; he was sure about that.

Elijah allowed the bigger boy to come onto him, dropping his head so that it was shielded between his shoulders and forearms. The boy dived forward, Elijah turning at the last moment so that his jab bounced off his right shoulder, leaving his guard open and his chin exposed. Elijah fired in a straight right-hand of his own, his gloved fist crumpling into the boy's headguard with enough force to propel his mouthguard from his mouth. He was stood up by the sudden blow, dazed, and Elijah hit him with a left and another right.

The boy was staggering as Rutherford rang the bell to bring the sparring to an end.

Elijah turned to step through the ropes, but Rutherford sent him back again with a stern word. He went back to his opponent, and they touched gloves. "That's better," Rutherford said as he held the ropes open for the two of them. He sent them both to the changing rooms. He saw Milton and came across to him.

"Sorry about that," Milton said.

"Boy's keen. Needs to learn some discipline, though."

"What do you think?"

"There's potential. He's got an attitude on him, no doubt, but we can work with that."

"You'll have him back, then?"

"For sure. Bring him on Tuesday night; we'll get to setting him up a regular regime, start training him properly."

MILTON OFFERED to buy Elijah dinner wherever he liked. The boy chose the Nando's on Bethnal Green Road and led the way there. They took a bus from Dalston Junction, sitting together on the top deck, Milton with his knees pressed tight against the seat in front and Elijah alongside. The restaurant was busy, but they found a table towards the back. Milton gave Elijah a twenty-pound note and told him to get food for both of them. He returned with a tray laden with chicken, fries and soft drinks. He put the tray on the table, shrugged off his puffa jacket, and pushed a plate across the table.

"What is it?" Milton asked.

"You never eaten in Nando's before?"

"Not that I can remember."

"You got peri peri chicken and fries," he explained. "If you don't like that, there's something wrong with you, innit?"

Milton smiled at the boy's enthusiasm and took a bite out of the chicken. He looked out around the restaurant: there were tables of youngsters, some with their parents, and groups of older adolescents. There was a raucous atmosphere, loud and vibrant. He noticed a young couple with two children, probably no older than six or seven, and for a moment, his mind started to wander. He caught himself. He had moments of wistfulness now and again, but he had abandoned the thought of a family a long time ago. His line of work made that idea impossible, both practically and equitably. He was never in the same place for long enough to put down roots, and even if he did, the risks of his profession would have made it unfair to whoever might have chosen to make her life with him. The state of affairs had been settled for long enough that he had driven daydreams of domesticity from his mind. That kind of life was not for a man like him.

"So where did you learn to fight like that?" he asked him.

He shrugged. "Dunno. The street, I guess. My mums says I got a temper on me. She's probably right. I get into fights all the time."

"A temper's not going to do you any favours. You'll need to keep it under control."

Elijah dismissed the advice with a wave of his drumstick. "I know what it was. When I was younger, primary school, I was out playing football in the park when this bigger boy, Malachi, he comes onto me with his screwface on after I scored a goal against his team. He punched me right in the face, and I didn't do nothing about it. I wasn't crying or nothing, but when I got home, my mum saw that I had a cut on my head, and she was on at me about how I got it. I told her what happened, and she sent me back out again." He swallowed a mouthful and put on an exaggerated impression of his mother's voice. "'Listen good,' she said, 'I'm your mum. I protected you in my womb for nine months. I gave birth to you. I didn't do none of that so other people could just beat on you. Go outside and don't come back in until you've given that boy a good seeing to, and I'm going to be watching you from the balcony.' So I did what she said and sorted him out. I never let anyone push me around after that."

Milton couldn't help laugh, and after a moment, the boy laughed along with him.

"I don't know anything about you, do I?" he said when they had finished.

"What would you like to know?"

The boy was watching him curiously over his jumbo cup of Coke. "What do you do? For a job, I mean?"

"This and that," he said.

"Because we all knew you ain't no journalist."

"No, I'm not. We spoke about this. I'm not—"

"So what is it you do? Come on, man. I've told you plenty about me. Only fair. You want to get to know me properly, how you expect that if you got kinds of secrets and shit I don't know about?"

He said, awkwardly, "It's a little hard to explain."

"Try me."

"I'm a"—he fumbled for the right euphemism—"I'm a problem solver. Occasionally, there are situations that require solutions that are a little out of the ordinary. I'm the one who gets asked to sort them out."

"This ain't one of those situations?"

"I don't understand."

"Me, I mean. This ain't work?"

"No. I told you, it's nothing like that."

"So what, then? What kind of situations?"

"I can't really say anything else."

"So you're saying it's secret?"

"Something like that."

Elijah grinned at him. "Cool. What are you, some kind of secret agent?"

"Hardly."

"Some kind of James Bond shit, right?" He was grinning.

"Come on," Milton said. "Look at me—do I look like James Bond?"

"Nah," he said. "You way too old for that."

Milton smiled as he finished one of his chicken wings.

"So tell me what it is you do."

"Elijah, I can't tell you anything else. Give me a break, all right?"

They ate quietly for a moment. Elijah concentrated on his chicken, dipping it into the sauce, nibbling right up to the bone. He wiped his fingers on a napkin. A thoughtful look passed across his face.

"What is it?"

"Why are you helping me and my mum?"

"Because she needed it. You both did."

"She manages fine," he said, waving the chicken leg dismissively. Milton realised that Sharon had not explained to her son the circumstances of how they had met. That was probably the right thing to do; there was no sense in worrying him, but at the same time, if he knew how desperate he had made her feel, then perhaps he would have corrected his course more readily, without the need for help. It didn't really matter. He was making good progress now, and it was up to Sharon what she told her son. Milton was not about to abuse her trust.

Elijah was still regarding him carefully. Milton realised that the boy was shrewder than he looked. "No other reason?"

"Such as?"

"Such as you want to be with my mum."

Milton shook his head. "No."

"She's had boyfriends," Elijah said discursively. "Not many, but some. None of them were any good. They all give it the talk until they get what they want, but when it comes down to it, when they need to back it up, they're all full of shit. It breaks her up when they leave. It's just me and her most of the time. It's better that way."

"You don't think she's lonely?"

"Not when I'm there."

"She'll find someone eventually."

Elijah wrinkled his nose. "Nah," he said. "She don't need no one else. She's got me."

Milton felt a flicker of encouragement. The boy's attitude was changing, the hardened carapace slowly falling away. He watched him enthusiastically finishing the chicken, the sauce smearing around the corners of his mouth, and for that moment he looked exactly what he was: a fifteen-year-old boy, bravado masking a deep well of insecurity, anxiously trying to find his place in the world. Milton realised that he had started to warm towards him.

Chapter Twenty-Nine

CALLAN WALKED purposefully up the street, the row of terraced houses on his left. He passed the house that Milton had taken and slowed, glancing quickly through the single window. A net curtain obscured the view inside, but it didn't appear that the house was occupied. He continued fifty yards up the road, turned, and paused. Traffic hurried busily along the road. A few youngsters loitered aimlessly in front of the arcade of shops at the distant junction. The blocks of 1950s social housing loomed heavily behind their iron railings and scrappy lawns.

He watched carefully, assessing.

He started back towards the house, reaching into his pocket for his lock picks as he did so. A couple walked towards him, hand in hand, and Callan slowed his pace, timing his approach carefully so that the couple had passed the door to Milton's house before he reached it.

He took out his lock pick and knelt before the door. He slid the pick and a small tension wrench into the lock and lifted the pins one by one until they clicked. It had taken him less than five seconds. He turned the doorknob and passed quickly, and quietly, inside.

He took out his Sig Sauer and held it in both hands, his stance loose and easy. He held his breath and listened. The house was quiet.

He did not know how long he had before Milton returned, so he worked quickly. He pulled a pair of latex gloves onto his hands, and with his gun still held ready before him, he went from room to room.

The house was cheaply furnished and in need of repair and decoration. Milton had brought hardly anything with him. Callan found a rucksack, a handful of clothes hung carefully in a rickety cupboard, some toiletries in the bathroom, but little else. There were pints of milk and orange juice in the fridge and a half-eaten loaf of bread, but nothing else.

The investigation posed more questions than it answered. What was Milton doing here, in a place like this?

He went into the front room and shuffled through the envelopes on the table. They were old bills, addressed to a person whom Callan assumed was the previous occupier. He turned a gas bill over and saw that a note had been scribbled on the back.

SHARON WARRINER
FLAT 609, BLISSETT HOUSE

He took out his phone and took a photograph of the address. He slid the envelope back into the pile and left the room as he had found it.

He holstered the Sig Sauer, opened the door to the street, and stepped outside. The road was clear. He closed the door and stuffed the latex gloves into his pockets. He set off in the direction of the tube station.

Chapter Thirty

ELIJAH HAD BEEN working on the heavy bag and was sweating hard as he sat down on the bench. He took off his gloves and the wraps that had been wound tightly around his fists. His knuckles had cut and blistered during the session, and blood had stained the white fabric. He screwed the bandages into a tight ball and dropped them into the dustbin. The hall was busy. Two boys were sparring in the ring, and another was firing combinations into the pads that one of the men who helped Rutherford was wearing. The man moved them up and down and side to side, changing the target, barking out left and right, the boy doing his best to keep pace. Other boys skipped rope, lifted weights, or shadow-boxed in the space around the ring.

Rutherford came over to him and sat down. "How you feeling, younger?"

"I feel good."

"Looking good, too. That was a good session."

"How did I do?"

"You did good. You got to work on your guard a little. You leave your chin open like that and it don't matter how slippery and quick you are, someone'll eventually get lucky and stitch you, and that'll be that—but we can sort that for you. You got a lot of potential. You work hard at this, who knows?"

"What you mean? I could make something of it?"

"It's too early to say that, younger. But you got potential, like I said." Rutherford paused for a moment, his eyes drifting across the room. "You're running with the LFB, right?"

Elijah said that he was.

"That's right. Your friend told me. You know we don't have none of that in here, right? No colours, no beefs, nothing. You all right with that?"

"Yeah," he said. "It's not like I'm tight with them or anything. It's a recent thing. I know some of the boys, that's it."

"Then we ain't going to have a problem, then. That's good."

"You were involved, weren't you? The streets, I mean?"

"Yeah," Rutherford said. "Long time ago. Is it obvious?"

"I see the way the other boys look at you. It's not hard to guess. Who were you with?"

"LFB."

"What did you do?"

"The usual—rolled people, shotted drugs, tiefed stuff. But my speciality was robbing dealers."

"Seriously?"

"Why not? You know they've got to be carrying plenty of Ps, and if you take it, what they going to do? I know they ain't going to the feds." He sat down on the bench next to Elijah. "Some days," he said, "we'd head down onto the Pembury or into the park and we'd rob the shotters. Same guys, every day. They'd never see us coming. You put them up against the wall, and it's 'give me your money, nigger.' They know I'm strapped; they ain't going to risk getting shot. Day in, day out, gimme the money, your jewellery, your phone—anything they had. Who they gonna tell? If we knew where there was a crack house, we'd go in there and clear the place out too. No one's packing in a crack house, see—no one wants to be caught with drugs and a gun for no reason, so you just stroll in, get your blammer out, and everyone's too wasted too argue. But you got to be strapped. Always knew that—you got to be strapped. You turn up to a place like that with a knife, man, you're gambling with your life. And you got to be strapped all the time, because when you rob another gang's crack house, the cats'll stop going, and that costs money. When the crew ask around, they'll find out who's done what they done, and they're gonna want to take action to make sure it don't happen again."

"Didn't you feel bad?"

"Sometimes, when I was lying in bed thinking about the way my life was going, course I did. But then you think about it some more, and you got money and power, so in the end you persuade yourself there was nothing in it. You tell yourself it's the law of the jungle, the strong against the weak. And I was strong, that's the way I saw it then. But I wasn't strong. I was a bully hiding behind a 2-2, and I was foolish. Young, proud, full of shit and foolish. But the way I saw it, I knew the players we was going after was doing the same shit to other people. It's kind of like—this is the road—this is how it is. If you don't like it, get off the road."

"What happened?"

"In the end?" He shook his head and sucked on his teeth. "In the end, younger, it happened like it was always gonna happen. We rolled a crack house, only this time the Tottenham boys were wise to it. They had a couple of mash men with blammers there themselves, waiting for us. Soon as we got in there, they pulled them out and started shooting the place up. I took out my strap and fired back. Didn't know who I was shooting at. Bad things happened."

"You killed someone?"

"Like I said, bad things happened. I had to get away, so I signed up for the army."

"How old were you?"

He turned the question around. "How old you say you are?"

"Fifteen."

"That's right. I had just five short years on you, younger. I'm thirty-six now. I got out six months ago. I did sixteen years in the army. Two wars. Longer than you been around in this world."

"Shit."

"Yeah, that's right—shit. You see why I do what I do now, JaJa? I know where the road is gonna take youngsters like you if you don't pay attention. There ain't no chance it can go anywhere else. I know I probably sound like it sometimes, but I ain't trying to patronise. I just *know*. You follow the road you're on for too much longer, you'll get in so deep you don't even know how to begin getting out. And then, one day, the road will take you, too. You'll get shot or shanked, or you'll do it to someone else, and the Trident will lock you up. And either way, that'll be it—the end of your life. If I can help a couple of you boys get straight, get off the road, then, the way I look at it, I'm starting to give back a little, pay back the debt I owe."

The door to the street opened, and Pinky came inside. Elijah stiffened.

"You know him?" Rutherford said.

"Yeah. Does he come here, too?"

"Used to, but I haven't seen him for a while. You two get on?"

"Not really."

"No, I bet—he's not an easy one to get along with. He's got a whole lot of troubles." Rutherford got up as Pinky approached them. "Easy, younger," he said. "How's it going? Ain't seen you for a couple of weeks."

"Been busy." The boy said it proudly, and Elijah knew exactly what he meant.

"That right? How much you made this week, playa?"

"Huh?"

"Your Ps. I know you been shotting. I saw you, up on the balcony at Blissett House. How much?"

Pinky stared at Elijah and grinned as he said, "Five-o-o."

Rutherford sucked his teeth. "Five hundred," he said. "Not bad."

"Not bad? Better than you'll make all month."

"Probably right," he conceded with an equable duck of his head. "So let me get that straight... five hundred a week, over a whole year, you keep taking that you're gonna end up with what, twenty-five thousand? What you gonna do with that much money?"

"I'm gonna buy me a big-screen TV, a new laptop, some games, some clothes and shoes, and then I'm gonna save the rest. I got plans, get me?"

"That right?"

"Yeah," he said, a little aggression laced in the reply. "What about it?"

"Where you gonna save it?"

"What you mean? In a bank—where else?"

Rutherford shook his head. "You're sixteen years old. You telling me you're going to walk into the NatWest and give them twenty grand and tell them to stick it in your account? Really? That's your plan?"

"Yeah."

"No, you ain't."

"Fuck you!" he said. "It's my money. Mine. They can't take it off me. No one can."

"You take it into a bank, and I'll tell you exactly what's gonna happen—they'll be onto the feds before you're halfway out the door. Next thing you know you're on the deck eating pavement, and then you'll do time. That's if you last that long. Because what'll most likely happen is some brother will nick it off you. And while they're at it, they'll probably merk you, too. And it's no good being rich when you're dead."

"Fuck you, man," he spat. "Fuck you know?"

Rutherford absorbed his invective and stared back at the boy with a cold hardness in his eyes that Elijah had not seen before. For a moment, it was easy to imagine the intimidating effect he must have had when he was younger. "What do you mean, what the fuck do I know? You know where I've come from. You know what I been, what I've done. I don't have to put up with your shit, either. Go on, you don't want to listen to me, fuck off. Go on. If you want to stay, then stay. I'll tell you how you can make that kind of money, but legit so you *can* put it in a bank account, so no one's gonna take it off you and drop you stone dead."

Pinky squared up, and for a moment, Elijah expected him to fire back with more lip. Rutherford stood before the boy implacably, calm certainty written across his face. He was not going to back down.

"A'ight," Pinky said, and the tension dissipated in a sudden exhale. He forced a grin across his face. "Cotch, man. I'm just creasing you."

"Get your kit on if you want to stay," Rutherford told him sternly. "You've gotten all flabby, all this time you been taking off. You got some catching up to do."

"Funny man." Pinky hiked up his Raiders T-shirt. He was thin and wiry, the muscles standing out on his abdomen in neat, compact lines. "Don't chat grease. Flabby? Look at this—I'm ripped, playa."

"Get yourself in the ring. I got someone who'll see whether you still got what it takes."

"That right? Who's that?"

Rutherford turned to Elijah. "You up, younger. Get new wraps on. The two of you can spar. Three rounds."

Pinky looked at Elijah and laughed. "Him?" he said derisively. "Seriously?"

"Talk's cheap, bruv. You think you can take him? Let's see it in the ring."

"I'm on that," he said, firing out a quick combination, right-left-right. "This little mandem gonna get himself proper sparked."

Pinky went back to the changing room, and when he returned, he had changed into a pair of baggy shorts that emphasised his thin legs. Elijah wrapped his fists again and laced up his gloves. The two boys stepped through the ropes and, at Rutherford's insistence, touched gloves.

Pinky was older than Elijah, but they were similar in physique. He came forward aggressively, fighting behind a low guard and firing out a barrage of wild combinations. He was quick but not particularly powerful or accurate, and Elijah was able to absorb the onslaught without difficulty, taking it on his arms or dodging away. He spent the first round that way, absorbing his attacks and firing back with stiff punches that beat Pinky's absent guard, flashing into his nose or against his chin. Elijah knew that his punches were crisp rather than powerful, but that was all right. He was not trying to hurt Pinky, not yet. Each successful blow riled the older boy, and he came forward with redoubled intent. Elijah let him, dancing away or smothering the blows when he could not, letting Pinky wear himself out.

Rutherford rang the bell as the first two-minute round expired, and the two boys broke to separate corners to take a drink.

"I'm gonna dook you up, younger" Pinky called across the ring, lisping around his mouthguard.

"Didn't do nothing first round," Elijah retorted. "Look at me—I'm hardly even sweating."

The other boys had stopped to watch the action. A couple had wandered across to stand next to Rutherford, and others were idling across to join them.

Rutherford rang the bell.

They set off again. Pinky moved in aggressively, firing out another wild combination, rights and lefts that Elijah disposed of with ease. Rutherford was watching him from the side of the ring, and Elijah decided that it was time to give him his demonstration. He stepped it up a gear. Pinky moved forward again, and Elijah sidestepped his first flurry, firing in a strong right jab that stood him up, a left and a right into the kidneys and then, his guard dropped, a heavy right cross. Pinky fell back, but Elijah did not stop. He followed the boy backwards across the ring, firing hooks into the body. Pinky fell back against the ropes, and Elijah pivoted on his left foot and delivered a right cross with all of his weight behind it. Pinky took the punch square on the jaw and fell onto his back.

Rutherford rang the bell and clambered into the ring. Pinky was on his hands and knees, his mouthguard on the canvas before him, trails of spit draping down to it from his gasping mouth. Rutherford helped him to his feet and held the ropes open for him. He said nothing, barely even looking at Elijah as he slipped down to the floor and went back to the changing rooms. The watching boys were hooting and hollering, impressed with the show that Elijah had put on. One of the older boys declared that Elijah had banged Pinky out. Elijah could not prevent the grin that spread across his face.

Rutherford drew Elijah to one side and helped him to unlace his gloves. "Listen here, younger," he said. "You've got skills. You let him wear himself out there, didn't you?"

Elijah shrugged. "Didn't seem no point to get into it with him. He's bigger than me. Would've been too strong, I come onto him straight up. Seemed like a better idea to let him work himself out, let him get weak, then come in and spark him."

Rutherford smiled as he explained his tactics. "You thought all that out for yourself?"

"I used to play that way on my PlayStation. Ali and Foreman, innit? Rope-a-dope."

"You learned that from a videogame?"

"Yeah," he said.

"Why not?" Rutherford laughed. "Look, little man, I know you're only just starting out, been here just a handful of times and all, but I think you're ready to step it up. We've got a night coming up with a club in Tottenham. It's like we got here; a friend of mine runs it. He's gonna bring his boys down so we can see what's what. He'll have five of his best lads; I'll pick five of mine. I'd like to put you in the team. What you say? Sound like something you might be interested in?"

Elijah's heart filled with pride. No one had ever said he was any good at anything. None of his teachers, none of his friends, not even his mum, not really. "Course," he said. He didn't know what else to say.

Rutherford put one of his big hands on his shoulder. "Good lad. Thought you'd be up for it. It's Thursday night. Speak to the fellow who brought you down. Mr Milton. See if he wants to come?"

Elijah thought of Milton. Would he come if he asked him? Elijah was surprised to find that he half hoped that he would. "A'ight," he said. "I'll tell him about it."

Chapter Thirty-One

MILTON LOOKED at the window of Sharon's flat. It was barred, but somehow, it had still been broken. The window faced into the sitting room, and a wide, jagged hole had been smashed in the centre. The wind had sucked the curtains out, and now they flapped uselessly, snagged on the sharp edges of the glass. Fragments had fallen out onto the walkway, and now they crunched underfoot, like ice.

He had called Sharon half an hour earlier to ask after Elijah. She had been upset, barely able to stifle the sobs, and he came straight across. A brick was lying incongruously on the cushion of the sofa, glass splinters sparkling all around it. Someone had pushed it through the glass.

"Just kids mucking about," Sharon said miserably. "They don't mean anything by it."

"Has it happened before?"

She shrugged, a little awkwardly. "Sometimes."

"You'll need to get it fixed."

"I spoke to the council. They say they can't do it until next week."

"You can't leave it like that until then. Let me take care of it."

"I can't ask you to do that."

"It's not a problem. Simple job. I just need to get some bits and pieces. It'll take me half an hour."

She smiled shyly at him. "On one condition—you let me cook you dinner."

"Deal," Milton said.

Milton sized up the job and then visited the hardware store in the centre of Hackney to collect the equipment and materials that he would need.

A handful of lazy youngsters had gathered by the time he returned, leaning against the balustrade at the end of the balcony. They stared at him with dull aggression as he set his purchases down and removed his jacket. He unscrewed the cage that contained the metal bars and stood it carefully against the wall. He spread an old sheet on the balcony outside the window and knocked out the largest fragments of glass, using a hammer and chisel to remove the smaller pieces. He chipped out the putty from the groove in the frame and plucked out the old glazing sprigs with a pair of pliers. He sanded the rough patches, applied a primer, and then filled in the holes and cracks. He kneaded putty into a thin roll and pressed it into the frame, then carefully lowered the new pane of glass into place, pressing carefully so that the putty squeezed out to form a seal. He added new sprigs to hold the glass in place and pressed more putty into the join between the panel and the frame, trimming away the excess with the edge of his chisel. He heaved the metal cage up to the window and screwed it back into place. Finally, he stepped back against the balustrade and admired his handiwork. The job was well done.

"You wasting your time," one of the kids called over to him. "No one likes her. She ain't from round these ends. She should get the hint, innit, go somewhere else?"

"She's not going anywhere," Milton said.

"It gonna get broke again, soon as you gone."

"Leave her alone. All right?"

"What you gonna do about it, old man?"

All Milton could think about was going over to teach them some manners, but he knew that that would just be for his own gratification. It wouldn't do Sharon any good. He couldn't be with her all the time, and as soon as he was gone, she would be punished. It was better to bite his tongue.

The boys stayed for another ten minutes, hooting at him to try to get a response, but when they realised he was ignoring them, they fired off another volley of abuse and slouched all the way down to the bottom of the stairs. Milton watched them go.

It was a little past seven when he had finished with the window to his satisfaction. He tidied away his tools and went inside. The television in the lounge was tuned to the BBC's news channel. A man in Tottenham had been shot dead by police. The presenter said he was a drug dealer and that the police were reporting that he had been armed. Milton watched it for a moment, not really paying attention, and then found the remote control and switched it off.

Sharon had pulled the table away from the wall and laid it for dinner. She had prepared a traditional Jamaican dish of mutton curry. Milton helped her to clear the table when they had finished. He took out his cigarettes. "Do you mind?" he asked her.

"What are they?" she said, looking at the unfamiliar black, blue and gold packet.

"Arktika. They're Russian."

"I've never seen them before. Where do you get them?"

"Internet," he said. "Every man needs at least one vice."

"Russian fags?"

"I met a man once, a long time ago. He was Russian. We found ourselves in a spot of bother, and these were all we had. Three packets. We made them last four days. I'd developed a bit of a taste for them by the end. Vodka too, but only the good stuff."

He opened the carton and offered it to Sharon. She took a cigarette and allowed Milton to light it for her. He lit his and watched as she took a deep lungful of smoke, letting it escape from between her lips in a long sigh.

"You've been so good to me," she began after a quiet moment. "I don't know why."

Milton inhaled himself, the tobacco crackling as the flame burned higher. "You've had some bad luck," he said. "Things aren't always fair. You work hard with Elijah; you deserve some help. I'm just glad I can do that."

"But why me?"

"Why not you?" he retorted. He let the peacefulness fall between them again, his thoughts gently turning on her question. Why her? Had it just been a case of his being there at just the right time, or was there something else, something about Sharon that drew him toward her? Her vulnerability? Her helplessness? Or had he recognised in her some way to make amends for the things that he had done?

The sons that he had orphaned.

The wives that he had widowed.

He didn't know the answer to that, and he didn't think it would serve to dwell upon it.

He drew down on the cigarette again.

"Can I get you a drink? Don't have any vodka, but I think I have some gin, and some tonic, maybe."

"I don't drink anymore," he said. "A glass of water is fine."

She went through into the kitchen. Milton stood alone in the sitting room and examined it more carefully than he had before. He noticed the small details that Sharon had included in an attempt to make the blandly square box more homely: the embroidered cushions on the sofa, the box of second-hand children's toys pushed against the wall, the Ikea curtains that hid the bars on the windows outside. He went over to the sideboard. Sharon had arranged a collection of framed pictures of her children, the two boys at various stages of their lives. He picked one up and studied it; it was a professional shot, the sort that could be bought cheaply in malls, with Sharon pictured on a chair with the children arranged around her. Milton guessed it was taken four or five years ago. Sharon's hair was cut in a different shape, and her face was absent the perpetual frown of worry that must have sunk across it in the interim. Elijah was a sweet-looking ten-year-old, chubby, beaming a happy smile and without the wariness in his eyes. His older brother, Jules, looked very much like him. He had an open, honest face. He must have been the same age as Elijah was now. There was nothing to suggest a predisposition towards self-destruction, but Milton guessed that he must already have started along the path that would eventually lead him to ruin.

Sharon emerged from the kitchen with two glasses in her hands. "My boys," she said simply. "I failed with Jules. I'm not going to let the same thing happen to Elijah."

"You won't."

She smiled sadly, resting both glasses on the table. Milton watched as a single tear rolled slowly down her cheek, and he went to her, drawing her into his body and holding her there, his right hand reaching around to stroke her hair.

She gently pulled back and looked up into his face. Her eyes were wet and bright. Milton pushed her against the wall and kissed her, hard, on the mouth. She pulled away, and Milton took a step back to give her room. "I'm sorry," he said, but her hands came up, her fingers circling his wrists, and she drew him back towards her until their bodies touched. She moved his hands downwards until they were around her slender waist and angled her head to kiss him, her mouth open hungrily. Milton embraced her passionately, his tongue forcing her teeth apart, her own tongue working shyly at first and then more passionately. Milton pulled her even more tightly into his body, crushing her breasts against his chest. She gasped, disengaging her mouth and pressing her cheek against his, her mouth nuzzling his neck. They stayed like that for a moment, breathing hard, Milton feeling her hard breasts against his sternum, his hands sliding down into the small of her back.

She leant back a little so that she could look up into his face. She gently brushed aside the lock of black hair that had fallen across his damp forehead. Her hand slid into his, their fingers interlacing, and then she pulled him after her, leading the way across the sitting room to the door that led to her bedroom.

Chapter Thirty-Two

ELIJAH AWOKE AT EIGHT, just as usual, and got straight out of bed. His body felt sore from exercise, but it was a good pain, a steady ache that told him he had worked hard. He thought of his muscles, the little tears and rips that would regenerate and thicken, making him stronger. He thought of Pinky and the session in the ring. He had dreamt about that in the night, replaying the two rounds over and over again. It was one of those good dreams where it made him feel happy at the end, not the nightmares that he usually had. He thought of the boys who had been watching. "He banged Pinky out," one of them called, and there had been something different in the way that he looked at him, the way that they all looked at him. He felt a warmth in his chest as he thought about it again.

He took off his shirt, opened his cupboard door, and looked at his torso in the full-length mirror. He was lean and strong, the muscles in his stomach starting to develop, his arms thickening, his shoulders growing heavier. His puppy fat was disappearing. He knew from the few pictures he had found in his mother's room that his father had been a big man, powerfully built, and he had always hoped that he might inherit that from him. He wanted to be like Rutherford. A man that size, who was going to mess around with him?

He found a clean T-shirt and pulled on his jeans. He threw his duvet back across his bed, straightened it out, and went into the sitting room. It was empty. That was strange; his mother was normally up well before him, preparing his breakfast before she went off to work.

"Mums," he called.

There was no reply.

He went into the kitchen and poured himself an orange juice. He went and stood before the door to her bedroom. It was closed.

"Mums," he said again, "I can't find my iPod. You awake?"

He heard the sound of hasty movement from inside and, without thinking, reached for the door handle and opened it. His mother was half out of bed, fastening the belt of her dressing gown around her waist. She was not alone. Milton was sitting in her bed, the covers pulled down to reveal his hard, muscular chest.

Elijah felt his stomach drop away. He felt sick.

"Oh no," he said.

"Elijah," his mother said helplessly.

"What? What's going on?"

"*Elijah.*"

He backed out of the room.

His mother followed him, stammering something about him needing to be calm, about how he shouldn't lose his temper, how he should listen, but he hardly heard her. She came into the sitting room as he scrabbled on the floor for the trainers he had left there after he came in last night. Milton came out of the bedroom, his trousers halfway undone and hastily doing up the buttons of his shirt.

"Come on, Elijah," he said. "Let me talk to you."

"You said you weren't like the others."

"I'm not."

"I thought you wanted to help me?"

"I do."

"No, you don't. You just want her to think you do so you can get with her. What's wrong with me? You must think I'm an idiot. I can't believe I fell for it."

"You're not an idiot, and that's not how it is. I do want to help you. It's very important to me. What happens between me and your mum doesn't make any difference to that."

"You can fool her if you want, but you ain't fooling me, not anymore." He stamped his feet into his trainers and laced them hurriedly.

"Elijah..." Sharon said.

"I'll see you later, Mum."

She called after him as he slammed the door behind him. He stood on the balcony in the fresh morning air. The kids at the end of the balcony sniggered, and as he turned back, he saw why: someone had sprayed graffiti across the front door, and the paint, still wet, said SLUT.

Elijah went across to the boys. Elijah knew them by reputation; they were a year or two older than him. They occasionally passed through the Estate to sell Bizness's gear.

"You think that's funny?" he said.

"Look at the little chichi man," the oldest of the three said. "Hush your gums, younger, you know it's true."

"Wouldn't be so touchy about it if he didn't, would he? Your mum's a grimey skank, bruv, you know she is."

Elijah was blinded by a sudden, unquenchable flash of anger. He flung his arm out in a powerful right cross, catching the boy flush on the chin. He dropped to the concrete, his head bouncing back off the balustrade, and lay still. He turned to face the other two. They gaped, and then, as they saw the ire that had distorted Elijah's face, they both backed away. Elijah's fist burned from the impact, and as he opened and closed his hand, he saw that his knuckles had been painted with the boy's blood.

The door to the flat opened behind him. He turned back to see Milton emerging, barefoot. "Elijah," he called out. "Please—let me talk to you."

He leapt over the boy and made for the stairs, kicking the door open and taking them two at a time. He was crying by the time he reached the bottom; hot, gasping sobs of disappointment and disenchantment and the sure knowledge that any chance he had of striking out on a different path was gone. He could not trust Milton. He had used him, and like a callow little boy, he had given himself away cheaply and unquestioningly. He could not trust him, and there was no one else. He had always known he was alone. This had been just another false hope. He would not fall for it so easily again.

He found his phone in his pocket and swiped through his contacts until he found Bizness's number.

Chapter Thirty-Three

POPS DROVE his car into Dalston and parked next to a Turkish restaurant on Kingsland Road. He killed the engine and sat quietly, watching the pedestrians passing next to him. Bizness had called him thirty minutes earlier and told him to come to his studio. He made no mention of Laura, nor did Pops expect him to. He would feel no guilt for what he had done. The way he would see it, he was entitled to take whatever he wanted. A woman was no different to money, time, or possessions. If Bizness wanted it, then it was his.

Elijah was in the passenger seat. Bizness had told him to collect him and bring him along. Pops tried to engage him in conversation when he picked him up, but the youngster didn't respond. His face was clouded with anger, and he was completely closed off. Something had happened to him; that much was obvious.

"Here we are, younger," he said to him. "I don't know what Bizness wants with you, but be careful, alright?"

Elijah grunted, but other than that, he did not respond.

Pops tried again. "Listen to me, JaJa. You don't have to do nothing you don't want to do. Nothing's changed from before. If you'd gone through with what he wanted, you'd either be dead or in prison now. You hear me?"

Once again, Elijah said nothing. Pops hardly knew the boy, but he had never seen him like this. He looked older, more severe, his lack of emotion even a little frightening. Pops realised with a sudden flash of insight that the boy reminded him of himself, five years earlier. Anger throbbed out of him. He was frightened for him.

Elijah pulled back the handle and pushed the door open. He got out, slammed it behind him, and crossed the pavement to the door of the studio.

"Alright, then," Pops said in his wake. He got out, locked the car, and followed.

The studio was on the first floor of the building, above the restaurant. Pops held his thumb against the buzzer and spoke into the intercom. The lock popped open, and he went inside. Pops knew the history of the place. Bizness had bought the two flats that had been here before and spent fifty thousand knocking them through into one large space. He followed the dingy flight of steps upwards, frayed squares of carpet on the treads and framed posters of BRAPPPP! hung on the walls on either side of him. They were ordered chronologically, and the pictures nearer the ground floor, before the collective discovered that popularity was inextricably tied to notoriety, even seemed a little naïve. The final poster before the door at the top of the stairs was of Bizness standing alone, bare chested, holding a semi-automatic MAC-10 pistol in one hand and smoking a joint with the other. Pops remembered the first time he had seen the poster. He had been awed, then, a black man with power who was unafraid of putting a finger up at society's conventions; now, he found it all predictable and depressing. There was no message there, no purpose. The power was illusory. It was all about the money.

The sound of heavy bass thudded from the room at the top of the stairs. The interior door was open, and Pops pushed it aside. The rooms beyond comprised a small kitchen strewn with takeaway packaging and an area laid out with plush sofas and a low coffee table. At the other side of the building was the studio itself, sealed off behind a glass screen with its recording booth and mixing suite. The rest of the area was busy with people, and the noise was cacophonous; the latest BRAPPPP! record was playing through the studio's PA, the repetitive drone blending with the shouts and whoops of the people in the room, everyone struggling to make themselves heard. Pops recognised several members of the collective and the hangers-on who trailed them wherever they went. Bizness was sitting with his back against the arm of the sofa, his legs stretched out across it, his feet resting in Laura's lap. He was shirtless, exposing the litany of tattoos that stretched across his skin. The word GANGSTER had been tattooed across his stomach in gothic cursive, the letters describing a long, lazy arc above his navel. IN GUNS WE TRUST was written, two words apiece, across the backs of his hands.

Laura looked up as Pops entered, her eyes flickering to his face for a moment. There was barely a moment of recognition before her unfocused gaze washed over him. The muscles in her face were loose, flaccid. He tried to hold her attention, but it was a waste of time. She turned her face to the low table in front of her, where several lines of cocaine had been arranged across the surface. She ignored them, languidly reaching her fingers for the crack pipe that trailed tendrils of smoke up towards the ceiling. She grasped it and put it to her lips, inhaled, and then closed her eyes. Pops's heart sank. She toked, the smoke uncurling from her nostrils and rolling up past her cheeks, obscuring her blank eyes. She ignored him completely. It was as if he wasn't there.

Bizness grinned at them both, displaying his gold teeth. He reached over for a remote control and quietened the music so he could more easily be heard. "Look who it is, my two best bredderz. Big Pops and little JaJa. A'ight, bruv?"

Pops felt his hands curling into fists. "Bizness," he said, forcing himself to smile. He could not stop himself from looking over at Laura again, just for an instant, and Bizness noticed. He said nothing—there was no need for it—but his lips curled up in a derisive grin, the light glittering off the gold caps. Everyone in the room knew what had happened, that Bizness had clicked his fingers and taken her from him, doing it without compunction, like it was no big thing. Not even acknowledging it to his face was the biggest dis of all. It said Bizness didn't care. That Pops's reaction was irrelevant, and that there was nothing he could do about any of it. Pops felt his anger flare, but he forced himself to suppress it. There was no move for him to play. Laura was gone. She was with Bizness now, for however long he wanted her. If he showed his anger, there would be hype, and there could only be one outcome after that.

Bizness turned to Elijah. "And my little soldier, how are you doing, younger?"

"I'm good," Elijah said. He went over to Bizness and held up his closed fist.

Bizness looked around the room, his mouth open in an expression of delighted surprise. "Look at the little hoodrat," he exclaimed.

Elijah ducked his head and shrugged his shoulders.

"He got some serious attitude, innit?" Bizness bumped fists with him. "So what happened to you the other night, soldier?"

"Sorry 'bout that," Elijah said. He angled his face a fraction, enough to turn his gaze onto Pops, and it was clear from his expression that he blamed him for not carrying out his instructions. "The fight—I lost my nerve. Won't happen again."

"That right? You still wanna get involved?"

"Yeah. For definite."

"Because that problem ain't gone away. We made our point, but the little fassy ain't listening. Put up another message for us last night. You see it?"

Elijah shrugged again. There was an open laptop resting on the table. Bizness stretched across and tabbed through the open windows to YouTube. The video he wanted had already been selected, and he dragged the cursor across and set it to play. Pops had seen Wiley T's uploads before, and this met the usual pattern. The boy was rapping on the streets of Camden as a friend filmed him with a handheld camera. The bars he was dropping were all about Bizness and the brawl at the party. Bizness was right: Wiley was not backing down, and if anything, the incident had made him even more brazen. It was an escalation, a direct and unambiguous dis. He questioned Bizness's heritage, his legitimacy and the size of his manhood, all in artfully rhymed couplets. He ended by calling him out for a battle, doubting that the invitation would be taken up. Wiley was good, much better than Bizness, and it was that, Pops knew, rather than the content of his bars that had upset him so badly.

Elijah watched the video, his face darkening. "He's got some front," he said when it came to an end, "don't he?"

"Fucking right he got some front. Everyone knows I'd take him down if we battled, a'ight, so what's the point? Nah, bruv. There ain't nothing else for it—he's got to get merked. Can I count on you, young 'un? You ready to stand up?"

He turned to Pops again, his eyes blazing with purpose. "Yeah," he said. "Man needs to get dooked, innit. Be my pleasure to do it for you."

Bizness laughed harshly, and following their cue, the others in the room quickly followed suit. "Little man found his balls, eh? Good for you—good for you. You still got the piece?"

"In my bedroom."

Bizness extracted himself from the sofa, stretching himself out to his full height. He took a joint from the boy next to him and inhaled deeply. He knelt down, taking Elijah by both shoulders, and breathed the smoke into his face. "We'll make a rude boy out of you, JaJa. A good little soldier."

Chapter Thirty-Four

JOHN MILTON sat in the threadbare armchair in the front room of the house, staring at the stains on the wall and thinking. He had left Blissett House soon after Elijah. Sharon had been upset at the confrontation and, apologising as she did so, told him that it was probably better if he left. She said that what had happened had been a good thing, and that she didn't regret it, but that she had to put her child first. Milton understood. He had not planned for the night to develop as it had, and he had been surprised at his reaction. There was something about her that drew him in, her endearing combination of quiet dignity and vulnerability, perhaps. She was attractive, but he wished he had shown more restraint. Elijah had been making progress, and now he didn't know how much damage had been done.

His mobile was on the table. It started to ring. Milton picked it up and checked the display. He did not recognise the number.

"Yes?" he said.

"Hello?" said the caller.

"Who's this?"

"You the man? The man in the park?"

"Who's this?"

"I met you a week ago. You were looking for Elijah."

"Which one are you?"

"You gave me your number."

Milton remembered the boy: older than the others, bigger, a strange mixture of tranquillity and threat in his expression. "I remember," he said. "What's your name?"

"Call me Pops."

"No—your real name."

There was a pause as the boy weighed up whether he should say. "Aaron," he said eventually.

"All right, then, Aaron. I'm John. How can I help you?"

The boy's voice was tight, tense. "You were looking out for JaJa, weren't you? You wanted to help him."

There was something in the boy's tone that made him fearful. "What about him?"

"He's in trouble. He's in real trouble, man. Serious." There was a pause. "Shit, I'm in trouble too. Both of us."

"You better tell me about it. What's the matter?"

"Just so I know, you ain't a journalist, are you?"

"No."

"And you ain't no police, neither?"

"No."

"What do you do, then, you so sure you can help?"

"I can't tell you that. But all you need to know is that I have a particular set of skills and that if you're in trouble, then I can help you. Beyond that you'll have to trust me." There was a pause on the line, and Milton noticed that he was holding his breath. "Are you still there?"

"Yeah," the boy said. "I'm here."

"It sounds like we need to talk."

"Yeah. Can we meet?"

"Of course."

"Now? I'm in the park, next to the fountains. You around?"

"I can be."

"I'll be here for another thirty minutes, then."

The boy ended the call without saying anything else.

Milton walked the short distance to Victoria Park and made his way to the fountain. It had been another stifling day, and the grass was parched and flattened in squares where picnic blankets had been stretched across it. The night was darkening, the wide expanses gloomy between the amber cones from the occasional streetlamp. A jumbo jet slid across the gloaming, its lights winking red as it curled away to the west. The big Estate buildings on the southern edges of the park hunched over the fringe of trees and railings, twenty-storey blocks of concrete, depressingly stolid, oppressive. It was a changing of the guard: the last joggers, cyclists and dog walkers passed around the outer circle as groups of youngsters gathered on the benches beneath the streetlamps to smoke and joke with one another. Milton noticed all of them, a habitual caution so ingrained that he did not even realise it, but he paid them no heed. He followed the outer circle around from the pub and then took the diagonal path that cut straight to the memorial and the glassy squares of water that attended it. A homeless man sat at one of the benches, massaging the ears of the thin greyhound huddling next to him. There was no one else. Milton walked slowly around the monument, making a show of examining it, before sitting at one of the empty benches to fuss with a lace that did not need tying. The water was still and flat and perfectly reflective, a rind of moon floating in the shallow depth. He set to waiting.

Twenty minutes passed before he looked up to see someone else turn off the outer path and head towards the monument. Despite the late heat, the figure was wearing a bomber jacket over the top of a hoodie, the hood pulled over the head like a cowl. Pristine white trainers almost shone in the gloom.

Milton got up from the bench and idled towards the monument. As the boy got closer, he recognised the face beneath the hood. His skin was black and perfectly smooth, his eyes and teeth shining.

"A'ight," the boy said in a low monotone, angling his head in greeting.

"Hello, Aaron."

"We can head towards the pond, over there. Ain't no one there this time of the day."

They set off side by side. Milton studied the boy through the corner of his eye. He was large, not much shorter than Milton but heavier, and he walked with a roll to his step, his head and shoulders slouched forwards. He dressed like all the others: hooded jacket, low-slung jeans with the crotch somewhere between his knees, the brand-new trainers, pieces of expensive jewellery. It was the uniform of the gang, topped off by the purple bandana knotted around his throat. He wore it all naturally. He was quiet and composed, his eyes on the path. They continued that way for a minute, Milton happy to wait until the boy was ready to speak.

They were approaching the pond when he finally spoke. "JaJa needs help," he said. "He's got in with a bad man. I tried to keep him out of it, but he ain't listening to me anymore. Ain't nothing else I can do for him."

"Is it Bizness?"

"You know him?"

"Elijah spoke to me after he was arrested. I know a little about him. Is he dangerous?"

"What, man, are you fucking high? Is he *dangerous?* Seriously? Bizness's a psycho, innit? He was always bad, but since his ego got to be like it is now, he's turned into a monster."

"What about you?"

"What about me?"

"You said you needed help, too."

He cleared his throat awkwardly. "Bizness's the same age as I am. We were at school together. We used to be tight, but we ain't no more, and he's finished with me. I dunno, the last few weeks it's as if he's been provoking me, starting hype like he wants to get a reaction. I seen it happen before. He don't let anyone get too influential, start taking his thunder, see, and then when they do, when he thinks they might be getting to be a threat"—he clicked his fingers—"then he gets rid of them. One way or another."

"And you're a threat."

"Nah, man. I ain't like that. I want out, but he don't know that."

"So tell him."

He laughed bitterly. "Don't work that way, man. You get in, you're all the way in. You ain't done until he tells you you're done. And there ain't no talking with him."

Milton reflected that he knew what that felt like. He said nothing.

"Look, it ain't about me, not really. I *am* getting out, whether he likes it or not. It's the younger who needs help."

They reached the pond. A sign describing the nearby flora and fauna had been defaced with graffiti—Milton guessed that the 925 was a rival gang tag—and the bracket that should have held the buoyancy aid had been vandalised, snapped wood showing white through the creosote like splintered bone. Pops sat down on the bench and took a joint from his pocket. "I come down here now and again," he said, lighting the joint with his lighter. "I know it sounds pathetic, but I used to be in the Scouts when I was younger. The fucking Scouts. We used to come down here once a year and dredge the whole lot. You wouldn't believe the things people used to dump—washing machines, shopping trolleys, everything covered in sludge and weeds. We always joked we'd pull out a dead body one day. What I know now, I'm half surprised we never did. There are guns and shanks in there. I know *that* for a fact."

The boy offered the joint to Milton. He shook his head. The boy shrugged and smoked hard on it instead.

"So tell me about Elijah."

"You know about what happened at the party?"

"He told me."

"There's a man Bizness wants to have shot. JaJa mention Wiley?"

"A little."

"Bizness's got beef with him. Wants him gone. That was what the club was all about. He wants JaJa to do it. He had the gun that night. I thought I'd got through to him. I sent him home when I saw what was happening. I thought he'd listen to me. Something must've happened since." His voice trailed off. Milton said nothing. "So then I got a call from Bizness yesterday to say I had to pick JaJa up and bring him to his studio. I never seen the younger like that before—he was angry, man, he had this proper screwface on like he was ready to fucking *explode*. Bizness loves that, course, and he asks him whether he's ready to do what he wants him to do with Wiley."

A dog walker skirted the far side of the pond. His dog, a pit bull heavy with a fat collar of muscle, chased the ducks into the water.

"And Elijah said he'd do it?"

Pops nodded.

Milton felt sick in the pit of his stomach. "When?"

"I don't know the details. Bizness won't tell me. I'm not that close to him, and I don't think he trusts me no more, anyway."

"Is there anything else?"

"Can't think of nothing." He paused. "Except—"

"Go on."

The boy clenched his teeth so hard that the strong line of his jaw jutted from his face. "My girl's got involved with him, too. She's vulnerable. Got a weakness for drugs, and he won't look out for her like I did. Last time I saw her, she was smoking crack with him. It'll be skag next. She'll end up on the streets for him, I seen that before, too. Or she'll end up raped or dead."

Milton sat quietly.

"So what are you going to do?"

"I don't know," Milton said.

"You said you could help me, man."

"I will. But you have to work with me."

"How?"

"First things first: you have to speak to the police."

Pops kissed his teeth. "Go to the feds? You know what would happen to me if Bizness found out I'd been grassing? I'd end up in that fucking pond with a bullet between my eyes." Pops stood abruptly. "If that's the best you can do, we're finished. Police aren't going to do nothing until JaJa's got blood on his hands and my girl is fucking dead. I'm wasting my time with this bullshit."

"Grow up, Aaron," Milton said. His voice was emotionless, iron hard and utterly authoritative. "Sit down."

He did as he was told, adding, self-pityingly, "What's the point?"

"Because I'm going to take him out of the picture," Milton said. "Tell them what happened at the club. The boy who got beaten, you saw all that?"

Pops looked down at his feet. "Yeah, man, I saw it."

"That's good," Milton said. "They'll have to take that seriously."

"What you gonna do?"

"I'm going to have a word with Bizness."

He laughed. "A word? No offence, man, but he ain't gonna listen to you."

"He'll listen to me," Milton said. "You'll have to trust me about that."

Milton stood, and they started back towards the main road. "This is what we're going to do—you're going to go to the police and tell them about what happened at the club. Leave Elijah out of it, but tell them everything else."

"It won't do nothing. It'll be my word against theirs."

"Maybe. But it will be a useful distraction."

"And then what?"

"You'll get your friend off balance just as I give him something else to think about. I want him to take me seriously when we speak. I'm going to need some information from you about how his operation is put together—who works for him, how he makes his money, where he keeps it. Can you help me with that?"

"Yeah."

Milton asked a series of questions, and Pops provided awkward, but reasonably comprehensive, answers. Milton memorised the information, filtering it and arranging it as he built a picture of Bizness's business. The man had numerous interests in the local underworld, his malign influence stretching from drugs to prostitution and robbery. His music was clearly lucrative, but it would be as nothing compared to the profit he was turning from his illegal businesses. It was good that he was spread among different businesses and areas. That would mean that there would be plenty of vulnerable spots that Milton would be able to exploit.

"How does he communicate with everyone?"

Pops looked at him derisively. "How'd you think, man? Smoke signals? Homing pigeons? Facebook, BBM, texts. Pay-As-You-Go phones. Nothing he could ever get nailed with by the feds if they got hold of it. If he needs to meet to talk business, he'll get someone else to make the call to set it up and then arrange the meet somewhere, in the open, where it's impossible for the boi-dem to bug him. He's careful, man. Precise. Plans everything like he's in the military or something. Police think their old ways still work, but people— the real players like him—man, they been around long enough to have seen brothers get nicked all sorts of different ways, and they remember all of them. You got to get up early to pull a fast one on him."

They reached the fringe of trees that provided a canopy of leaves over the path at the outer edge of the park. The pub at the junction was growing busier, with loud customers spilling into a beer garden decorated with fairy lights.

"All right," Milton said. "That's enough for now. Go to the police tomorrow. All right?"

"Yeah," Pops said sullenly.

"Don't let me down. It's important."

"A'ight," he conceded. "Tomorrow. When will I know you've done something."

"You'll know."

Chapter Thirty-Five

MILTON TOOK the underground to Oxford Circus and emerged, blinking, into the hard bright light of another stifling summer's day. The temperature had continued its inexorable uptick into the mid-thirties, but now it had become damply humid, a wetness that quickly gathered beneath Milton's armpits and seeped down the middle of his back. The atmosphere lay heavy over the city, a woozy stupor that could only be alleviated with the inevitable thunderstorm that the forecast was predicting for later.

The Sig Sauer in its chamois holster was a heavy, warm lump beneath Milton's shoulder. The air in the tube had been cloying and dense, and Milton was pleased to have left it behind him. The confluence of Regent Street and Oxford Street was a busy scrum of sluggish tourists and frustrated office workers on their lunch breaks. Traffic jammed at the lights, taxi drivers leaning on their horns to chivvy along the busses that tarried to embark passengers. Tempers were stretched as tight as piano wire, arguments flaring and confrontations held just beneath the surface.

Milton's phone vibrated in his pocket.

"Hello?" he said.

"Is that John?"

"Who's this?"

"Rutherford. Is everything all right?"

"I'm a little busy."

"It's Saturday afternoon, I've been expecting your boy to come for training, but there ain't no sign of him. What's happening?"

"There's been a setback," Milton said as he crossed the road at the lights. "I'm taking care of it. I have to go."

Milton ended the call. He turned in the direction of the tall, crenulated finger of Centre Point. HMV was fifty yards along the road, the sound of heavy bass throbbing from the wide-open doorway into the cavernous space beyond. Milton surveyed the interior: racks of music and films; T-shirts; magazines; and, on a stage that had been erected in the middle of the shop, a table and a tall stack of CDs. A long queue of youngsters—mostly young boys, but also a handful of girls—snaked back from the table around the aisles and back almost to the entrance. Behind the table sat six members of BRAPPPP! The collection comprised the better known members of the collective: MC Mafia, Merlin, Icarus, Bredren. The female singer, Loletta, sat in the middle, haughty with her strikingly good looks, a highlight for the hormonal teenage boys who waited to be presented to her.

Milton recognised Bizness from the pictures on his Facebook and Twitter profiles. He was wearing a Chicago Bulls singlet, the top revealing an angular torso: long, skinny arms with the sharp points of his elbows and shoulders. His skin was extensively tattooed, and gold teeth glittered on the rare occasion when he disturbed the studied blankness of his expression to smile. He sat at the head of the table, the last member of the collective to receive the fans, like a king or a mafia don accepting the fealty of his subjects. They came to him, wide-eyed and open-mouthed, their CDs passed along the table with him finally adding his mark and sending them on their way. He spoke with some, bumped fists with others, but all left elated by their encounter with their hero. Milton could see, quite clearly, the power that the man—and the lifestyle he typified—had on them. He was an aspirational figure, living proof that the success he rapped about was possible to have. Milton did not respect him for this, but he recognised it and its influence, and filed it away for future reference.

A large display had been erected at the front of the shop, loaded with the collective's new album and an assortment of other merchandise. Milton took a copy of the record and a T-shirt and joined the end of the queue. It was moving slowly, and Milton guessed it would take half an hour to get to the front. He did not have the patience to wait for that, and taking advantage of the fact that it would have been difficult to imagine anyone less likely to jump the queue, he made his way to the front. "One minute," he said to the two young boys who were about to go forwards. "I just need a quick word with him. Won't hold you up long."

The table was fenced in by crowd-control barriers, and two large bouncers stood guard at the entrance to the enclosure. They glared at him as he passed between them. Milton passed along the table, ignoring the others and making his way directly to Bizness.

He stopped in front of him. "Good afternoon."

Bizness bared his teeth in a feral grin, the golden caps sparkling. "Look at this." He laughed, jutting his chin towards Milton. The others laughed, too. "You in the wrong section, man. Old folks' music is over there."

"No, it's you I want to see."

Bizness threw up his hands and chuckled again. "Fine, bruv, where's your record, then? Give it here. What you want me to say?"

"I'm not here about your music."

"Come on, man, enough of this bullshit. If you ain't got nothing to sign, get the fuck out the way. Lot of brothers and sisters here been queuing hours to see us, you gonna end up causing a motherfucking riot you don't stop slowing the queue down."

"I need to talk to you. And you're going to listen to what I have to say."

"The fuck—?"

Milton ignored him. He stared at Bizness, his eyes icy and unblinking, with no life or empathy in them, until the confusion on the younger man's face faded and a cloud of anger replaced it. "I'm going to ask you nicely for two things," Milton said. "First, a woman named Laura has been associating with you. You are going to stop seeing her. If she comes to visit you, you are going to send her away."

"That's your first thing? A'ight, go on, you're an entertaining fucker. What's the second thing?"

"I know what you're planning for a young lad I know. Elijah Warriner. You call him JaJa. That is not going to happen. You are to stop seeing him, too. If I hear that you've been seen with him, there is going to be trouble. If just one hair on his head is hurt, we're going to have another conversation. But it won't be as civil as this one."

"You hear this motherfucker?" Bizness hooted at the others. They were all watching the exchange. "You asking me nicely, right? You better tell me, old man, just so I know, what you gonna do if I tell you to take your requests and shove them right up your arse? Tell me not-so-nicely? Raise your voice? Get out of here before you make me lose my temper. I ain't got time for this."

The bouncers took a step towards Milton, but Bizness stayed them with an impatient wave of his hand.

Milton did not look at them. He did not move away from the table. "You won't take me seriously now, but I'm going to give you a demonstration tonight of what will happen if you ignore my instructions. Something is going to happen to your interests, and I want you to think of me and what I've told you when you hear about it. Do you understand?"

Bizness surged up from his chair so quickly that it clattered behind him. "Do *I* understand?" Any vestige of his previous joviality was banished now, his eyes blazing with anger. "You come in here, with my bredderz around me, and you start making threats? Shit, man, you the dumbest motherfucker I ever met. I'm going to tell you one more time—get the fuck out of this shop before I throw you out my goddamn self. Do *you* understand?"

Bizness stepped around the table and took a step towards Milton. He did not flinch and, instead, fixed his pitiless stare on Bizness's face. "I've said what I needed to say. I hope you understand. I hope you remember. Do what I've told you, or the next time won't be so pleasant."

Bizness drew his fist back. Milton caught it around his ear before he could throw a punch and dug his thumb and index finger into the pressure point. Bizness yelped at the abrupt stab of white-hot pain and stumbled backwards, bouncing against the trestle table. The pile of posters tipped over, a glossy tide of paper that fanned out across the floor.

"Tonight," Milton said, smiling down at Bizness, a cold smile that was completely without humour. "Pay attention tonight. I want you to think of me."

He made his way to the front of the shop.

PART FOUR

Risky Bizness

Chapter Thirty-Six

MILTON PULLED OVER, extinguished the lights of the car, and switched off the engine. He left the radio on so that he could finish listening to the news. The bulletin reported that a protest outside a police station in Tottenham had deteriorated into a riot. Relatives of a man who had been shot by police two days earlier had gathered to protest his killing. Others had joined in, and the crowd had started to pelt the police with bottles and bricks. There were reports that cars and a double-decker bus had been set alight. Milton drew down on the cigarette he was smoking and blew the smoke out of the window. It was a hot night, close and humid. There was something in the air, a droning buzz of aggression. It wouldn't take much to ignite it.

He switched off the radio, opened the glove compartment, took out his holstered knife, and pulled up the sleeve of his right trouser leg. He wrapped the holster around his calf and fastened the Velcro straps. He checked in his mirrors that the pavement outside was empty, and satisfied that he would not be observed, he took his Sig Sauer from its holster and checked the magazine. It was full. He pumped a bullet into the chamber so that the gun was ready to fire. He slid it back beneath his armpit.

He looked around again. This part of Dalston Lane comprised a Georgian terrace of tall, two-storey houses with Victorian shop fronts that had been built over their front gardens when the railways arrived a hundred years earlier. The houses behind the shops had recently been used for social housing, but as time passed and their tenants were moved into the high-rise blocks that dominated the nearby skyline, they had been allowed to begin their long slide into decrepitude. Those that were left vacant were boarded up. Damaged roofs were left unrepaired. Windows were shattered and left open to the rain. Four houses had been gutted by fire, the exposed bricks crusted black with soot and ash and the timbers exposed like cracked and broken bones. Those buildings had been condemned and demolished, tearing holes in the terrace like the teeth yanked from a cancerous mouth. Boards had been erected around the blackened remnants of the extension, and these had been scarified by graffiti and posters for illegal raves.

The Victorian extensions were occupied by local businesses. The entire house and extension at the corner of the road was a doctor's surgery, with bars on the door and the windows plastered with posters about sexually transmitted diseases and nutrition. Next to that was an Indian restaurant, then a shop selling musical instruments, a Laundromat, a business selling second-hand kitchen equipment, then a newsagent. Adjacent to that a façade announced the Star Bakery, but the shutters had been in place for so long that the rust had fastened the padlocks to their tethers. The property alongside had seen its extension occupied by a squatter. It had been a bicycle shop years before, the block typography of its original frontage still visible despite the etiolation of the weather and the fumes from the busy road. The wide picture windows were obscured by sheets of newspaper and a printed notice that had been glued to the door declared that the squatters enjoyed rights of occupation and could not be evicted without a court order.

Milton scanned it all quickly. The terrace behind the squat was one of Bizness's most profitable crack houses. Pops had told him everything. Heroin and crack were sold around the clock, rain or shine. Most of the customers were poor locals, drawn in from the surrounding Estates, but a significant minority of the customers were white, very often professional and middle class.

Milton got out of the car. He went around to the back, opened the boot, and took out a jerrycan that he had filled with petrol from the garage on Mare Street. There was no sense in making his entry through the front door. It looked as if it was locked, just enough of a delay to allow for escape should the police arrive for a clean-up. Milton had another idea. The terrace was listed, and the plans were available online. He had visited the library and downloaded them, reviewing them before he came out. He knew that there was another way in. He followed the road to the junction, taking a right turn and then, before he reached a tawdry pub, another sharp right. A narrow cul-de-sac led around the back of the terrace. Overflowing dustbins were stacked up against the wall, and detritus had been allowed to gather in the gutter. Each house had a rear entrance, and the one that served the crack house was wide open. Silly boys.

Milton took out his Sig and went inside. The first room used to be a kitchen. Old appliances had been left to rot, with anything that could be easily removed long since sold for scrap. The walls were partially stripped and scabbed with lead paint, and the remnants of a twee wallpaper that depicted an Alpine scene had been left to peel away like patches of dead, flaking skin. Empty cardboard boxes and fast-food wrappers were scattered on the floor. A single man, strung out and emaciated, was slumped against the wall. He was unconscious, and Milton would not have been able to say whether he was dead or alive. He heard low conversation from the front of the house and set off towards it. The junkie's arm swept around sharply and his eyes swam with drunken stupor, but he paid Milton no heed as he passed through the room.

He moved through a hallway with a flight of stairs leading up to the first floor. Patterned linoleum was scattered with drug paraphernalia. A mattress rested upright against the wall. Another junkie was asleep on the floor. Milton tightened the grip on the butt of his pistol as he stepped carefully around him.

The noises were coming from the front extension. Milton paused in the shadows at the doorway to assess his surroundings. The only furniture was a sofa and a huge, monolithic television. It was a big unit with a cathode ray tube, and it had been left on, badly tuned, scenes from a soap occasionally resolving out of the distortion of static. The front door was ahead of him, barricaded with an old sideboard that had been propped against it. Vivid wallpaper with a woodland design had been hung on the wall, the paper stained yellow by months of smoke. There was no ventilation, and the atmosphere was thick and heavy, woozy, a sickly miasma.

There were a dozen people inside the room. Men and women, mostly supine, their heads lolling insensately, unfocussed eyes lazily flicking across the television screen. They were all black, dressed cheaply, feeble and thin. Plastic bottles were arranged in neat rows, each of them full of urine. A collection of shoes, random and unpaired, was pushed into one corner. Empty vials of crack had been ground underfoot, crunching like fresh snow as the addicts shuffled across the room to the two men who were sat on the sofa. They were clear-eyed and moved with crisp purpose as they exchanged vials of crack for their customers' crumpled banknotes. They were younger than their patrons; Milton guessed in their late teens, not long out of school. They were dressed in low-slung jeans, the crotch hanging down between the knees, there were diamond ear studs and golden chains, and both wore the colourful purple bandana of the LFB around their necks. These were the dealers, one step up from the shotters, Bizness's representatives on the street. They sold the drugs and then protected the house so that their customers had somewhere to get high and then buy from them again.

Milton shuddered in revulsion.

He assessed the situation. The junkies were too far gone to pose any kind of problem, and he discounted them. The two dealers looked fit and strong, and there was a kitchen knife resting on the arm of the sofa. That would be a problem if they could get to it before he had disabled them. He could not discount the possibility that they were armed, either.

Milton suddenly decided.

He sprang across the room and lashed out with the barrel of his pistol. He struck the bigger of the two men across the temple, a stunning blow that dropped him to his knees. The second man stretched across the sofa, but Milton had anticipated his move, firing out a kick that struck him in the side of the chest and brought a whistle of pain from him. The man's hand fell short, the knife dislodged from its perch by the attempt. Milton's hands grabbed the man in two places—bunching into his singlet and by waist of his trousers—and he heaved him off the sofa and onto the floor. The sharp edges of crushed vials and syringes bit into his face and throat as he tried to find his feet. Milton followed him to the floor, pinning the point of his knee between his shoulder blades and pressing down. He took the Sig and pressed the barrel into the cornrows on the top of the man's head.

"Pay attention," he said. "I want you to deliver a message to Bizness. Tell him that this is what I said would happen. If he doesn't do what I told him to do, tell him that this will keep happening. One crack house at a time. Do you understand? Nod if you do."

The man jerked his head awkwardly against the floor.

"All right. You're going to get up now, and you are going to clear these people out. Then you grab your friend over there and get him out, too. If you do anything foolish, I'll shoot you. Understand?"

Milton got up and backed away. He took the jerrycan and poured the petrol across the floor, on the sofa, sloshing it across the thick curtains. If the boy needed motivation, Milton's self-evident plan was it. He did as he was told, ushering the crackheads out the back and then returning to collect his friend, propping him up and helping him away.

The room quickly stank of petrol. Milton took out his lighter and thumbed it to flame. He played the lighter over a rag, and blue-white flame consumed it hungrily. Milton dropped it onto the sofa, and with a quiet exhalation, the fabric caught fire. The flame spread quickly over the upholstery, stretching higher and higher until it started to scorch the ceiling. It raced across the floor to the walls, a quiet crackling that quickly became a hungry roar, with black smoke billowing up to the roof and then spewing back down again.

Milton went out into the alley gun-first, only holstering the Sig Sauer when he saw that both boys had fled. He walked briskly, making his way back onto the main road and to his car. He unlocked the door and slipped inside.

Across the street, the squat was burning fiercely.

Chapter Thirty-Seven

CHRISTOPHER CALLAN paused outside Flat 609, and then, satisfied that it was the correct address, he knocked firmly, three times, on the door. He heard sounds of activity inside: the chink of pieces of crockery being knocked together, a door opening on a rusty hinge, and then footsteps approaching. A woman opened the door. Callan guessed that she was in her early thirties. Dark black hair, smooth skin, wide eyes, a slender build. She was wearing the uniform of a fast-food chain.

"Yes?"

Callan smiled. "Excuse me. Sorry for disturbing you. Are you Sharon Warriner?

Her eyes narrowed. "Who's asking?"

"I'm Detective Constable Travis."

Her face fell. "It's Elijah, isn't it?"

"Elijah?"

"My boy—what's he done?"

"No, Mrs Warriner, it's not that. Nothing to do with Elijah. Would it be all right if I came inside for a minute?"

"What's it about?"

She had the usual suspicion of the police, Callan saw. It was to be expected in a place like this. He reached into his jacket pocket and took out the file picture of Milton. "Do you know this man?"

She became confused as she studied the picture. "That's John."

"John Milton?"

"Yes. I don't understand. What's he done?"

"Can I come in, please? Just five minutes."

She reluctantly stood aside and let him through. They passed through the small hallway and into the lounge. It was a large room, the décor a little tatty and tired, an old sofa, a table with four chairs, a flat-screen television, PlayStation games scattered across the floor. Sharon stood stiffly; her suspicion had not been assuaged, Callan could see that, and he was not going to be invited to sit. Fair enough. He wouldn't be long. In some ways, he had already seen enough.

"How do you know Mr Milton?"

"He's a friend."

"How did you meet him?"

She paused, her face washed by a moment of worried memory. "I just did," she said. "What's this about, please?"

"What's he doing here?"

"I told you, he's a friend. He's helping me with my son."

"How?"

"I'm sorry, Detective, but I don't understand how any of that is relevant. What has he done wrong?"

"I'm afraid I can't tell you that. Please—how is he helping you?"

She waved her hand agitatedly. "My boy, Elijah, he can be a bit of a handful. Headstrong, like they all are at his age. Mr Milton is"—she paused, searching for the right word, and then repeated the same one again—"helping me with him, like I said. I don't understand why you're asking me—has he done something wrong? Should I be worried?"

Should she be concerned? Callan suppressed the smirk. She had no idea. None at all. "No," he said, "there's no reason to be concerned. I'm sorry I can't say any more than that."

She made for the door. "Then I'm sorry, Detective, if you can't tell me what Mr Milton has done, then I'm not sure what else I can do to help." She opened the door. "Do you mind? I have to get ready for bed. I start work early in the mornings."

"Of course," Callan said. "Thank you for your help. Sorry again for disturbing you."

He looked around again as he allowed her to shepherd him to the door. Unpaid bills on the floor. Paint peeling from the walls. Bars across the windows. What was Number One doing in a place like this, with a woman like this? He supposed that she was pretty, after a fashion, but that wasn't a good enough reason to explain anything. The only thing that made any sense at all was Control's contention that something had broken inside Number One's head, and that, if it was true, would not be good for him at all. He politely bid the woman good night and walked over to the balcony as she shut the door behind him. He rested his elbows on the balustrade and looked out over the East End. It was a hot night, the air torpid and sluggish. Sirens wailed in the streets nearby, and a group of youngsters had gathered in the open space below, their raucous laughter reaching up to him. Callan did not understand any of it. His task was to gather evidence, not to draw conclusions, yet he could not help but wonder: what on earth had happened to Number One?

Chapter Thirty-Eight

STOKE NEWINGTON POLICE STATION was a modern three-story building with wide windows on the ground floor. They were all lit up, lights burning behind them. Pops walked towards the entrance but did not go in. They had one of those old-fashioned blue lanterns hanging from the wall, and he carried on beneath it and further along the road before he stopped, crossed over, and headed back in the same direction again. He had repeated the pattern for the last half an hour, passing up and down the tree-lined road, thinking about choices and consequences. What he was about to do would change everything for him. There was no point in pretending that it wouldn't, and the gravity of what he was contemplating frightened him. If he did as he had been asked to do, there would be no turning back for him. His life would be yanked off course and sent in a different direction.

There was a Turkish barber shop opposite the station. He sat down, resting his back against the window, and took the half-finished joint from behind his ear. He held it in the flame of his lighter and toked on it until it caught, drawing in a big breath of smoke. He held it in his lungs for a long moment and then blew it away. He needed to settle down, to relax. He drew his legs up to his chest and leant forwards, resting his forehead against his knees. He was hopelessly on edge.

Choices. He stared across the slow-moving traffic to the lit windows of the station. He knew that speaking to the police was a fundamental thing. It would make him a grass. He was at a junction; consequences one way, but consequences the other way, too. He had thought about it for long enough, before he met Elijah, before Bizness turned his back on him, before Laura, before Milton. There were always choices, even when you thought there were none. It had been his choice to join the LFB, to start mugging and steaming, to start selling drugs. There had been different choices at every point, but the problem was that those alternatives were harder or less lucrative or less cool than the life he could have on the street. He had told the youngers that came up that the easy way was the best way, but he had always known that the stories he told them were lies. He had always known. He lied to them and to himself. He had persuaded himself that he was right, but now, well, now there was nothing else for it but to face the truth.

Because the truth of it was that there was always a choice.

The shopkeeper had a small television above the counter, and Pops could hear it through the open door. There was nonsense in Tottenham tonight, brothers getting together and wrecking the place. He could hear the reporter speaking from the scene, the sound of yelling in the background, things getting smashed up. Pops listened absently to it for a moment, not really paying attention, toking on the joint and letting the smoke slowly seep out from his nostrils. He finished it, sucking the flame down to his fingertips, and dropped it to the ground, grinding the roach underfoot.

He crossed the street, pushed open the door, and went inside.

A female officer was on duty.

"How can we help you?" she said.

"I want to talk someone about Israel Brown."

The woman looked at him askance. "Who's that, then?"

"You probably know him as Bizness. The rapper. He beat a boy half to death in Chimes last week. I was there. I saw it all."

Chapter Thirty-Nine

BIZNESS STARED out of the tinted window of the BMW at the burnt-out house. A fire engine was still at the scene, a fireman playing water over the smoking wreckage. The ceiling of the extension had collapsed, and the window had buckled and shattered from the heat, revealing the blackened mess beyond. He didn't own the house, and it wasn't worth shit, anyway, but that was not the point. It was Bizness's property. It served a purpose, and it made him a lot of paper. Now he was going to have to find somewhere else, spread the word, get things going again. It would cost him time and lose him money.

"Mother*fucker*," he said, slamming his fist against the steering wheel.

Mouse was in the passenger seat. "We got a problem, Bizness."

"You think? Shut the fuck up, Mouse. You don't know shit."

Levelz and Tookie, the two boys who had been working the squat, had told him what had happened. The man had attacked the place just after midnight, taking them by surprise. He had beaten them both, passed on his message, cleared the junkies out, and fired the place.

There would be a price to pay for that.

The door behind them opened, and a man slid into the seat. Bizness glanced up in the rear-view mirror. Detective Inspector Wilson glared back into his eyes.

"What's going on, lads? Who did this?"

"Someone who's gonna wish they never got involved with me. You don't need to worry about it."

"Are you sure about that? Because I'm pretty sure that when the fire service confirm that this is arson, there's going to be an investigation."

"Take it easy, a'ight? I know who did it. And I'm gonna sort it."

"You better make sure that you do. You've got to keep a lid on things. Having one of your places go up like it's bonfire night isn't good for my blood pressure. You want to operate around here without any trouble from me, you keep things quiet."

"Nah, man, me operating around here depends on you getting your cut every Friday."

Wilson ignored him and stabbed a finger against the window. "Things like that don't give me much confidence, son. I turn a blind eye to you because I don't have time to start worrying about lads from outside the postcode causing trouble. There are plenty of others who can keep a lid on things if you can't."

"That you making a threat?"

"No, that's me telling you that it's going to cost you ten from now on if you want to stay in business."

"Fuck, man, don't gimme that shit. You're doubling the fee?"

"There a problem with that?"

Bizness gripped the steering wheel hard. "Nah," he said. "Ten's fine."

"There are other benefits to working with me," Wilson said.

"Yeah? Like what?"

"Advanced warnings. You've got more trouble coming your way. Your boy Pops?"

"What about him?"

"He came into the nick last night. Says he's willing to give evidence against you."

"Against me?"

"So he says."

"For what?"

"Beating up that kid in Chimes."

"Man, that was nothing."

"Tell that to the kid's parents. He's still in hospital."

"Pops don't got shit."

"He's saying he was there."

"And he's gonna talk?"

"That's what I heard."

Bizness glowered through the tinted windscreen, watching as the passing cars slowed so that their drivers could gawp at the smoking wreck of the crack house. The problem with the man who did that and now this? Timing was bad. Timing was awful. Bizness nodded grimly. Fair enough, he thought. Timing was awful, but sometimes that's the way it was, the hand you got dealt. They were two small problems, and they could both be sorted. He started to work out angles, tactics.

"You've got to keep on top of things, son," Wilson said. "Do I have a reason to be concerned?"

"No," he said, gritting his teeth. "No reason. It'll all get sorted."

Chapter Forty

PINKY REACHED the door to Bizness's studio and pressed the intercom.

"Yeah?"

"I'm here to see Bizness."

"He ain't in. Go away."

"Don't talk chat, bruv. I saw him come in."

"Piss off, younger."

"Nah, it's about what happened at HMV yesterday. I got some information."

"You can tell me."

"Don't think so," he said. "I'll tell him myself, or I won't bother."

There was a click as the intercom was switched off. Pinky paused, holding his breath. The intercom crackled into life again. "Alright. Come up."

The lock buzzed, and the door clicked open.

Pinky climbed the stairs, the framed BRAPPPP! pictures on the walls on either side of him. He was nervous. Bizness had a reputation, a bad one, everyone knew that, and part of that reputation was that he could be unpredictable. All the stories Pinky had heard about him were at the front of his mind. He wasn't stupid, he knew plenty of them were made up for the sake of his image, but there were others he knew were true, and it was those that he was thinking about now.

He stepped through into the large room at the top of the stairs. Bizness was on the sofa, his feet propped up against the edge of the coffee table. A flat-screen television was fixed to the wall and tuned in to Sky News. Pinky had heard all about the riots that had started in Tottenham last night. He had been excited by it, at the idea of looting all those shops. Now it seemed like the trouble had spread to Enfield and Brixton. Footage from a helicopter showed a police car on fire.

"What's your name, boy?"

"Pinky."

"Alright, Pinky, you better have a good reason for coming up here. I'm a busy man, lot on my plate. I ain't got no time for signing no autographs."

"I'm not here for that," he said.

"Then you better tell me what you are here for."

"I got some information," he said. "That old man who got into it with you at the record signing—I saw it on YouTube."

"What?"

Pinky took out his phone. He had already cued up the video, and now he hit play. The video rolled; someone in the shop had filmed the conversation between Bizness and the old man. The camera was close enough to see the expressions on their faces, the implacability of the man and Bizness's growing anger. Their argument reached its crescendo, and Bizness lost his balance, stumbling backwards and tripping. The sound of laughter came as he sprawled amid the spilled posters and CDs.

"Who the fuck uploaded that?" he spat, grabbing the phone from out of Pinky's hand. There were several pages of comments, most of them jokes at Bizness's expense, and Pinky hoped that he would not read them. He did not; he played the video again and then tossed the phone back, his eyes flaring with anger.

"It's about the man," Pinky said.

Bizness's eyes narrowed, and the animation washed from his face. Pinky realised he would have to tread carefully. "Go on, then—don't just sit there, tell me what you know."

"There's a boy on the Estate, you've been asking him to do stuff for you—JaJa?"

"Yeah. What about him?"

"I was outside his mum's flat the day before yesterday. It was in the morning. Early—we'd been up late, selling shit to the cats, we was just about to call it a night. Anyway, right, I saw Elijah coming out, looking all upset and shit, and then, right after him, out comes that man. It was definitely him, no doubt. He was half-undressed, had his shirt off."

"What you saying? It's Elijah's dad?"

"Nah, his dad's in prison."

"So who is it?"

"Dunno. His mum's a skanky ho—some bloke she picked up, I reckon."

Bizness zoned out as he tried to remember what the man had said to him. "He told me to stay away from the boy," he recalled.

"Him and Pops's bitch," Mouse offered.

"You know anything else?" Bizness asked.

"Nah, that's it. I thought it could be useful so I came over."

"It is useful, younger. I appreciate that, you making the effort. You done good."

"There was another reason for coming," he said. It had gone as well as he could have expected, and now here it was, the opportunity he had been hoping for.

"Go on," Bizness said sceptically.

"I been thinking," Pinky said. "I know you asked JaJa to do some things for you." He left the "things" vague, but he knew all about the incident at the launch party. "Between you and me, boy ain't up to much. He's just a little kid, gets scared about things."

"You ain't that much older yourself, younger."

"Nah, true enough, but me and him ain't got nothing in common. There ain't nothing you could ask me to do for you that I wouldn't get done. You know what I'm saying? You want to ask around, people will tell you. I'm reliable. I don't mess no one about. When I say I'm going to do something, I do it. You don't need to worry about it, it gets sorted, you know what I'm saying?"

"That so?"

"Yeah," he said. "Thing is, I'm looking for a change. I'm ambitious, man, and I'm getting bored hanging around in the same old crew. I want to do mad shit, but Pops don't have his heart in it no more. We just hang around these ends doing the same tired old shit day after day. The way I see it, I could do that kind of stuff with you."

Bizness looked over at Mouse and grinned. "The balls on this one, eh? Reminds me of what I used to be like."

"All you need to do is give me a chance—I promise I won't let you down."

"You don't take no for an answer, do you?"

Pinky shook his head.

"A'ight, I'll tell you what, younger, there is something you could do for me."

"Yeah?"

"Yeah." He reached into his pocket and pulled out a crumpled ten-pound note. "First of all, though, I'm hungry—go down to Maccy D's and get me a Ready Meal, a'ight? Here." He handed him the note as the other boys started to laugh.

Pinky felt the colour running into his cheeks. He pretended he wasn't bothered. "Alright."

"Big Mac and a Coke. And be quick. I ain't eaten all day."

Chapter Forty-One

POPS CAME out of the takeaway with a bucket of fried chicken. The boys were waiting outside, arranged around a bench opposite the parade of shops. Little Mark was cleaning his new Nikes with a piece of tissue; Kidz, Chips and Pinky were hooting at a couple of pretty girls outside the launderette; and JaJa was sitting facing half away from them, a scowl on his face. They were drinking a six-pack of beer that Little Mark had stuffed down the front of his jacket in the mini-market when they went in for chocolate earlier. Pops put the bucket down on the seat and took off the lid. He helped himself to a breast and bit into it. It was crisp, with just the right amount of grease to it. The others helped themselves.

"I'm hungry," Little Mark said.

"You're fat," Chips retorted.

"Piss off," he said, but his eyes shone. Little Mark didn't care if they teased him about his weight. He knew he was fat; he couldn't deny it, and he didn't care. He liked being the centre of attention.

"I'm bored," Chips said.

Kidz looked up. "What we gonna do, then?"

"Dunno."

"Go see a film?"

"Nah. Nothing on. All shit."

"What then?"

Chips raised his voice. "See if those fine girls fancy hanging out?"

The girls heard him, snorted with derision, and disappeared into the launderette.

"Something else, then."

"Dunno."

Pops looked at Elijah. He glared back at him sullenly. His eyes were piercing, and for a moment, he wondered if there could have been any way that he could have found out about his visit to the station. No, he thought after a moment of worried consideration. No, there couldn't be. He had been careful. They would all know eventually, but not yet.

Little Mark spoke through a mouthful of chicken. "We could go and look at that crack house—you seen that shit?"

"That place Bizness had?"

"So they say," Chips said.

"In Dalston?" Kidz asked.

Chips nodded.

"What happened?"

"Burned to the ground," Little Mark replied, fragments of fried chicken spilling out of the corner of his mouth. "Some guy turns up, beats the shit out of the two boys who were there to look after the place, pours petrol around the place, and sets it off." He spread his fingers wide. "Whoosh."

"Who was it?"

"Fuck knows. Some cat, probably, didn't have any money for his fix and went mental or something."

"Whoever that cat is, man, I would not want to be him when Bizness gets hold of him."

"That shit's going to be epic."

"*Medieval.*"

"He should film it, stick it on YouTube. That's viral, innit."

"Stop it happening again."

"Nah," Little Mark decided. "Can't be bothered. Dalston's too far, and I'm still hungry."

"You always hungry, fatman."

"It wasn't no cat who did it," Chips said. "You hear what happened at the BRAPPPP! signing? Some old guy, like in his forties or some shit like that, he turns up in the queue and basically calls Bizness out."

"You see it?"

"Someone put it on YouTube. The old man goes toe-to-toe with him, stone cold, they have words, and he does this ninja death grip on his hand. Bizness ends up on his arse in front of everyone. What I heard, they reckon the guy who did that is the same guy who burned down the crack house."

"He's a dead man," Kidz said.

"You ain't wrong."

Elijah gave out an exasperated sigh.

"You hear about it, JaJa?" Chips said.

"Yeah."

"What you reckon?"

"I reckon none of you know what you're talking about."

Pops watched the five of them, the easy banter that passed between them. Only JaJa was quiet, the rest joshing and ribbing each other without affectation or agenda. They were what they were: young boys caught in the awkward hinterland between being children and men. He felt a moment of mawkishness. He had grown up with them. They were his boys, yet his days as one of them were limited now. When they learned that he was going to give evidence against Bizness, they would shun him as surely as if he had thumbed his nose at them personally. He would be a grass, and there would be beef between them, serious hype, and things could never be the same after that.

"Pops, man," Kidz said as he started on his second breast, grease smeared around his mouth. "What we gonna do?"

His train of thought depressed him. "I don't know," he said, his voice blank. "Do what you want."

"We could steam a bus?"

"Up to you, innit."

"What are you doing?"

"Stuff."

Little Mark looked at his BlackBerry. "Get this," he said. "Just got a message from my boy in Hackney. You know all that rioting and shit in Tottenham?"

"And Brixton."

"Yeah, now it's spreading all over. There's a big crowd getting together on the High Street. Hundred kids already and no sign of boi-dem anywhere. It's kicking off."

"Fuck we waiting here for?" Chips said. "That's what we doing tonight, right? Let's breeze."

They all rose.

"You coming, Pops?" Little Mark asked.

"Nah, bruv. I got things to do."

Pinky stopped and looked at him quizzically. "Where you heading?"

"Homerton."

"Going through the park?"

Pops said he was.

"I'll come with you."

"You're not going with the others?"

"Nah, bruv. I'm not into rioting and shit. Waste of time."

Pops shrugged. He would have preferred to walk to college on his own, but he wasn't ashamed of it any more. Who cared if they knew? And Pinky, more than the rest of them, needed to see that there were other alternatives to the street. Perhaps it would help give him a nudge to do something else. And if it didn't, if he thought worse of him, well, Pops didn't care about that any longer.

"A'ight," he said to the others. "Laters."

They bumped fists, and Pops had another moment of sentimental affection for them all. He quickly recalled some of the things they had done together. Long, hot summer nights, smoking weed in the park, watching the world go by. He smiled at the memories. Another world. It was all finished and gone now.

With Pinky loping along beside him, he set off towards the park.

Chapter Forty-Two

IT WAS SEVEN O'CLOCK and still bright and warm.

"Where you going, then?" Pinky asked him.

"Like I said, I got an appointment."

"Yeah?"

"That's right."

"Who with?"

Pops sighed. "No one, Pinky. I'm going to college."

"Course you are," Pinky replied, managing a wide grin.

"I'm serious."

"Bollocks, man."

"Twice a week. Night classes."

"Serious?"

Pinky was about to laugh again, but he saw that Pops was staring at him darkly and stifled it.

College, he thought. What was the point of that? Studying, books, teachers—he had no interest in any of it. Pinky had always been a little slow in school. It wasn't as if he had never tried. He had given it a go when he was younger, but it didn't seem to matter what he did; the others were always better at reading and numbers and shit, and coming bottom of the class again and again got to him eventually. In the end, he had just stopped bothering. Stopped going. The school did nothing about it, his mums didn't care either way, and no one seemed to miss him. Might as well just be philosophical about it. You couldn't be good at everything. He'd concentrate on the stuff he knew he was good at: robbing, tiefing, shotting, frightening people. Those were his skills. He'd work on them, get better at it. That was where the money was. That was where the power and respect were, too.

"Why's it so funny?" Pops asked him.

"Dunno. It's just—well, it's just not something I can imagine any of the others being interested in, that's all."

Pops snapped, "Because they're not interested means it's a bad idea?"

"Dunno," he said, surprised at the heat in Pops's voice.

"So what's your plan? You must have one. Or you planning on being on the street all your life?"

"Hadn't really thought about it," he said. "It's not so bad, though, is it? I get to hang out with my mates, and I still make more money in a week than my mums does in a month."

Pinky could see that Pops was about to say something else, but he sighed and shook his head instead. "Never mind." He sighed. "You're right. School isn't for everyone."

They walked along the Old Ford Road and crossed at the shops. A police car, its lights flashing and siren wailing, rushed by at high speed. They walked up to the roundabout and crossed there, too, passing through the park gates and heading north. There were fewer people in the park than on the street. Pinky looked around. It was quiet. He felt his fingers start to tremble.

"You can disagree if you want, but if you want to get on in life, you need to have the grades."

"That's what you're doing? Exams and shit?"

"Yes."

"For what?"

"For a job. Work."

Pinky gestured around at the park and the streets beyond. "You don't want to do this no more?"

"Everything comes to an end."

Pinky had looked up to Pops when he started to make his way on the street. He had been a powerful figure, successful and feared, not afraid to get stuck in so that he could get what he wanted. He was what Pinky would have considered a role model. He couldn't believe how wrong he'd been about that. Bizness had shown him. Pops was nothing to look up to. He wanted out. He couldn't hold on to his woman. He was a fassy. A sell-out, a fraud who didn't deserve anyone's respect. Choosing to go back to school was just another example. And if what Bizness had said was true: going to the police? He felt sick when he thought about the way he had aspired to be like him. How could he have got it so wrong? He was nothing to look up to. He was nothing at all.

"Yeah," he said. "I guess."

"What are you going to do with your life?"

"Smoke a lot of weed." He laughed. "Work on my rep, make sure everyone knows who I am."

"Can't do this forever, man."

"Why not?"

"You just can't."

"Nah," Pinky said, suddenly overcome with the urge to put Pops in his place. "You're talking shit, man. Just because you ain't got the stomach for it no more don't mean the rest of us have to feel the same way."

He had never spoken to Pops like that before. A week ago, he would not have had the nerve, but he knew more now. There was no reason to fear him. And he didn't need to listen to his sanctimonious nonsense.

Pops gave a gentle shake of his head but did not rise to it.

They walked on.

Pinky's bag bounced against his hip as he walked. He held it in place with his right hand; it was heavy, and it felt solid.

"Where you going, anyway?" Pops said. "Following me around like a bad smell."

"Just fancied a walk," he said. "Nice night, innit?"

He stopped, letting Pops take several steps forward until he was next to a park bench.

He opened the bag and reached inside. He took out the gun that Bizness had given him. It was a Russian gun, an old Makarov. He had practiced with it in the quieter part of the park, getting used to the weight of it, how it felt in his hand.

"Oi," he said. "Pops."

Pops stopped and turned. "What is it?"

Pinky pulled the gun up and levelled his arm, bracing his shoulder for the recoil.

"This is from Bizness," he said, just as he had been told.

Pops started to say something, but he didn't, his voice just tailing off. Perhaps he was going to explain, to apologize, to beg for his life, but what he must have seen in Pinky's dead eyes made it all useless. Maybe he just accepted it. The gun cracked viciously again and again—four times—and then fell silent. Pops fell back against the bench and sat for a moment, looking up at the darkening sky. His fingers opened in a spasm as he clutched at his chest. Then his head fell sideways and then the right shoulder and finally the whole upper part of his body lurched over the arm of the bench as if he were going to be sick. But there was only a short scrape of his heels on the ground and then no other movement.

Pinky looked around. There was no one near them. He started to giggle, nervous at first and then faster and faster, unable to control it. He tugged his hood down low over his face and set off, crossing the wide-open space at a jog and then cutting through a straggled hedge and into a patch of scrub beyond. He paused there, taking a moment to catch his breath.

His heart was racing. He had done it. He had lost his cherry, killed a man.

Breathing deep and even, but trembling with adrenaline, he clambered over a wall and dropped down onto the pavement beyond. As he set off back towards the Estate, he heard the sound of police sirens in the distance.

Chapter Forty-Three

MILTON SAT in the front room with the pieces of his Sig Sauer arranged on the table before him. He often stripped and cleaned the gun whenever he needed to think; there was something meditative about the process. He removed the magazine and racked the slide, ejecting the chambered round. He disassembled the gun, removing the slide, barrel, recoil spring and receiver, wiping away the dust from the barrel with a bore brush before squeezing tiny drops of oil onto the moving parts. The routine had been driven into him over the course of long years. He had seen men who had been shot after their weapons jammed; two of his own victims had been damned by their bad habits when they might otherwise have held an advantage over him.

He had piggy-backed next door's Wi-Fi and was streaming the radio through his phone. The riots had spread to Hackney now, too, and there were reports of disturbances in Birmingham and Manchester. Milton thought of Elijah and hoped that he was sensible enough to stay out of the way. Aaron had left him a message earlier in the day: he had not noticed any real change in the boy; he was still hanging out with the other boys although he was, Aaron thought, quieter than usual. He said that he seemed to be angry about something but that he had not spoken with him to confirm it. As far as he knew, there had been no new contact with Bizness.

Milton tapped out one of his Russian cigarettes and lit up. He considered Bizness. Last night's message would have been received, and if he had any sense, it would have been listened to. Perhaps he had taken Milton's advice and was going to stay away from Elijah. Perhaps. Milton wet an ear bud with cleaning solvent and inserted it into the breech end of the barrel, working it back and forth and swabbing out the chamber and bore. Perhaps not. No, Bizness was not the kind of man who would back down. He had made his point, but he had anticipated that it would be necessary to underline it. Another demonstration would need to be made. Milton looked over at the scrap of paper on the arm of the sofa. Aaron had provided the address for a second crack house. He planned to take it down tonight.

He heard the boom of heavy bass from a car stereo, gradually increasing as it neared the house. The thudding rattled the windows in their frames. He pulled aside the net curtains to look at where it was coming from. A car with blacked-out windows was moving slowly along the side of the road, and as he watched, the passenger-side window rolled down. The car drew up alongside the house. A figure leant out of the window, bringing up a long assault rifle. With something approaching a mixture of professional curiosity and alarm, Milton recognised the distinctive shape of an AK-47. The car passed into the golden cone of light from a streetlamp, and Milton could see Bizness' face, his features contorted with a grin of excitement that looked feral.

Milton threw himself to the floor as the AK fired. The glass in the window was thrown out by the first few rounds, splashing down around his head and shoulders and shattering against the floorboards. Bullets studded against the thin partition walls, dusty puffs of plaster exhaling from each impact. The mirror above the fireplace was struck, cracking down the middle with each half falling down separately against the mantelpiece. A jagged track was pecked across the ceiling, more plaster shaken out to drift down like the thinnest of snow. The thin door was struck, the cheap MDF torn up and spat out.

Outside, someone screamed. Milton crawled behind the sofa, pressing himself into cover. The table with the pieces of his Sig was out of reach; he dared not make an attempt to retrieve it, and even if he had been able to get it and assemble it, he would have been badly outgunned. The AK had been fitted with a drum, and he knew that it would have around seventy-five rounds if it was full to capacity. At a standard rate of fire the gun would chew through that in fifteen seconds.

As he was considering this, the shooting stopped.

He stayed where he was, waiting. Residual bits of glass fell from the wrecked frame, tinkling as they shattered against the floorboards. Milton's breath was quick. He did not move.

He heard a loud whoop of exultation, a car door opening, and then— panic spilling into his gut—he saw a small metallic object sail through the smashed window, bounce against the wall and fall back, landing on the sofa with a soft thump. A second followed. Milton knew what they were and scrambled up, desperately trying to find purchase for his feet as he threw himself out of the door and into the hall. The first grenade detonated with an ear-splitting bang, ripping the door from its hinges and sending a thousand razor-sharp fragments of shrapnel around the room. The second exploded seconds later. Shards sliced through the partition wall and into the hall, spiking into the masonry like tiny daggers. Milton shielded his head with his hands, pieces of debris bouncing off him.

He heard a car door slam shut, an engine rev loudly, and then the shriek of rubber as tyres bit into the road. He opened the bullet-shredded front door and stepped out onto the street. The BMW was speeding towards Bethnal Green, turning the corner and disappearing from view. Pedestrians on the other side of the road were staring in open-mouthed stupefaction at the scene before them. Residents of the block opposite were hanging out of their windows. The house had been sprayed with bullets. Most had passed through the window, but others had lodged in the brickwork. Dozens of spent cartridges glittered on the road and the pavement, a host of red-hot slugs, many still rolling down towards the gutter.

Milton was not interested in discussing what had happened with the police, and there was no reason for him to stay. He quickly piled his clothes into his bag, collected the pieces of the gun, shut the door, got into his Volvo and set off.

Chapter Forty-Four

MOUSE WAS DRIVING the new whip, the BMW. Bizness was in the passenger seat, and Pinky was in the back. Traffic was crawling along Kingsland Road. There were youngers everywhere, hundreds of them, kids from the gangs with their faces covered and white kids you'd never normally see this deep in the heart of Hackney. As he watched, he saw different kinds of people in the crowd: professionals in suits, older people, plenty of girls, not so much watching the boys as involved up to their necks themselves. Ahead, they saw two boys in tracksuits with hoods pulled up over their caps dragging an industrial bin into the middle of the road. Another boy poured something into the bin and then dropped a flame into it. The fire caught quickly, and in seconds, a powerful blaze was reaching up to the roofs of the three-storey buildings on either side of the road. Opposite them, a single hooded boy stood in the middle of a trashed Foot Locker, empty boxes and single, unpaired trainers strewn all about him. An old man, must have been seventy, grabbed a hat and bolted. A kid came out from the warehouse, balancing eight boxes of shoes. Ahead of them, a people carrier with a disabled badge in the window pulled over, and the grown man waiting for it quickly filled it with protein shakes from Holland & Barrett. Two girls pushed a wheelie bin full of the clothes they had taken from one of the local boutiques. Bizness had been following events on Twitter all afternoon: kids were rioting in Tottenham, Brixton, Enfield, Edmonton, Wood Green, all over London. And the feds were nowhere.

The car came to a halt. "Fucking *look* at this," Mouse exclaimed. "Shit is mental."

Bizness couldn't keep his eyes off the scene before him: a group of boys had gathered along the same side of a Ford Mondeo, heaving it in unison until they had it on two wheels and then, with a final effort, tipped it onto its side. They hooted in satisfaction before moving on to the Vauxhall parked ahead of it. Bizness grinned at it all. "Boi-dem shoot a brother like they did, what they expect? This was always gonna happen. People got no money, got nothing to do. It's been a riot waiting for an excuse for months round here."

He craned his neck around so that he could look into the back at Pinky.

"You done good tonight, younger. Did exactly what I told you. Ain't no way no one's going to be able to tie that back to us, and anyway, it's all gonna get lost in all this nonsense."

"Yeah," Pinky said proudly. "Thanks."

"First time you done that, right?"

"Yeah."

"How was it?"

"Cool," Pinky said. "You should've seen his face when I pulled the gun on him." He giggled. "Looked like he was going to shit his pants. Then"— he made the shape of a gun with his forefingers—"blam, blam, blam, blam."

Bizness looked at him. There was a smile on his face, but there was no emotion in his eyes. They were blank and empty. Boy was a stone-cold killer. It was a little unsettling. He could see he wasn't the smartest kid, and he knew he'd end up getting merked himself eventually, but until that happened, he'd keep him close. People like him, with no empathy, they were hard to find. They were useful, too. There were plenty of people he could do with having out of the way. Wiley T, for a start. Finish the job that JaJa never even started.

"That's sorted out your problem, then?"

The boy craved his approval, like they all did. He laughed derisively. "There ain't no case without Pops. That's finished."

"Won't hurt with the stuff on YouTube, either," Mouse offered.

Bizness felt his mood curdle just a little. He remembered that someone had recorded the old man standing up to him at the record signing, posting the clip online. There had been traffic on his Facebook page, too, and he had been called out for it. Mouse was right: when word got around that he had put out the hit on Pops and that he had shot up the old man's house, things would soon be back the way they were supposed to be again. No one would be stupid enough to stand up to him now. Bizness wasn't the things they were saying. He wasn't a hoodrat. He wasn't a kid you could just scare off. He was a serious player. A gangster with a reputation to defend. An authentic, one hundred percent OG.

"Yeah," he agreed. "That shit's gonna be good for business."

That brought his thinking around. Business. It had been easy to find a replacement for the Dalston Lane crack house that the old man had torched. It wasn't as if Hackney was short of empty properties, and Levelz and Tookie had found a new place ten minutes away. They were already setting up again and putting out the word. Bizness hated crack heads, and he hated crack houses, but they brought in plenty of Ps, and he knew how to make the business work. It was like any business; you just needed to advertise, create a little demand, that was all. In this case you let it be known that there was cheap crack to be had, and then you waited for your punters to come. Easy. It was like spreading shit and waiting for the fungus to grow.

"No way through here," Mouse said. "We gonna have to detour." He edged the Beamer further along the road until they could take a side street. He buried the pedal, and they lurched forwards, wheels squealing as the rubber gripped. Bizness stared out of the window as they passed the rows of terraced houses and then the ugly boxes of the Estate.

Youngers were gathered on the street corners, their eyes following the car. Bizness wondered whether they knew who it belonged to. Some of them did, you could tell from their faces; he loved it when they nudged their friends and told them that it was him, loved the open mouths and their surprise. It made him feel good. He had been one of them, once, stood around on the streets and doing nothing, shotting a little if he could get his hands on any merchandise, getting into beefs with other boys, looking for hype with lads from outside the postcode. He liked to remind himself how far he had come, how far he had left them behind. He was a player now; there was no question about it. He was a Face, and everyone knew it. Some had started calling him the God of Hackney. He liked that. Maybe he'd change his name, release a solo record under that next. The God of Hackney. Had a ring to it, for sure. BRAPPPP! couldn't go on forever, and after all, as far as most people were concerned, he was BRAPPPP!, anyway.

"We picking up JaJa now?" Pinky said.

"Yeah. You know what to say to him?"

"Just what I saw, innit," he said. "Ain't no problem."

The boy was the last loose end he had to snip. He was waiting for them next to the entrance to the lido in London Fields. Mouse had BBMed him earlier and told him to wait for them. He slowed the car to a stop. The boy got in next to Pinky, shut the door, and Mouse accelerated away again.

"A'ight, younger. How you doing?"

"Alright," Elijah said hesitantly.

Bizness was pleased to see that the boy was still nervous around him. That was good.

"What's he doing here?" Elijah said, nodding at Pinky.

"He's in the crew now," Bizness said. "You heard about Pops?"

He looked down at his new trainers pressed close together in the footwell of the car. "Yeah."

"What you hear?"

"He got shot."

"Other people know, too?"

"People are talking about it."

Bizness folded his arms. "He had it coming to him, younger. Mandem was up to no good. First rule—you don't ever, *never*, grass to the feds. You do that, you're worse than a dog. I know you know that, but it pays to keep it at the front of your mind. Pops forgot, see? And so he got what was coming to him. Ain't no reason to feel bad about it."

"You did it?"

"Nah. I made it happen."

"Who, then?"

"You sitting right next to him."

Elijah gaped at Pinky. "Him?"

"Yeah. Boy did good, just what I told him to do. Put four bullets into him. Ice cold. You want to pay attention. You got a lot to learn."

"What do you mean?"

"I ain't forgotten what happened with Wiley T, little man. You still got to make up for that."

Elijah kept his eyes fixed on the floor. Yeah, Bizness thought, boy was real scared, of him and now of Pinky, too. That was just how he wanted it. You could get someone who was scared to do just about whatever you wanted them to do.

He changed the subject. "Reason you're here, I want to talk to you about something. This man, the old fassy who burnt down my property—you know what we did to him today?"

He shook his head.

"There's an AK-47 in the boot. We shot his house up."

"You killed him?"

"Nah—we saw him come out, but he probably got shot, though, either that or the grenades we tossed in through his window would've done him. Messed his place up good. He won't be bothering us no more." He grinned at the thought of it. "It's the same thing as Pops, see? Can't have people questioning me, disrespecting me. You have to make an example out of people like that. You get me?"

Elijah nodded. It was a small, timid gesture.

"So," Bizness went on, "the thing is, I heard something that's troubling me. I heard you know who he is."

"I—"

"Don't mess me around on this, younger. It's important. Pinky?"

"I was outside your mum's flat last week, wasn't I? I saw him coming out. The HMV thing, too, I recognised him from there. I got an eye for faces, know what I mean? It was the same old man, I'm sure of it."

"Come on, then, younger, what's his name."

"Milton."

"You know what he does?"

"He never told me," he replied quietly. "Said he ain't police, though."

Bizness sucked his teeth. Police didn't typically burn down crack houses, so he was happy that the old man wasn't lying about that. "If he ain't police, you know why he's putting his nose in our business?"

"Dunno—honest."

"He's been staying with your mums, though. Right?"

Fear washed over the boy's face. "Not staying. One night."

"Like a boyfriend or something?"

"Dunno."

"Is it to do with her some way or another?"

"Dunno—"

"Come on, younger. There's no need to worry. Nothing's gonna happen to you or your mums, I just need to know what's going on so I can make sure he don't do no more damage than he's already done. Is he helping her?"

"I think maybe she asked him to keep an eye on me. I ain't told him nothing, though, I swear. I don't want nothing to do with him."

"A'ight, younger. That's all I needed to know. That'll do for now. Stop the car, Mouse—we'll let him out here."

They were near Bethnal Green now, nowhere near where they had picked him up. Another big group of hooded kids had gathered, heading along Mare Street towards Hackney's High Street. They passed the blacked-out windows of the Beamer, some of them staring, fire in their eyes. The busses weren't running; JaJa was going to have to walk home. Bizness didn't care about that. He picked up his phone and shuffled through his contacts for the number he wanted. He watched Elijah shuffling away with his head down as the call connected.

"You there?" he said.

"Yeah, man," Tookie said.

"Do it."

Chapter Forty-Five

MILTON STOPPED to fill up with petrol and then drove across to Blissett House. The traffic was heavy, and it had taken him longer than usual. A large crowd of teenagers, their faces covered by bandanas and hoods, suddenly swept across the street, bringing the traffic to a halt. Milton clenched his jaw as he sat waiting for them to clear out of the way. An Audi was three cars behind him; Milton watched in the rear-view mirror as bricks started to bounce off the roof and bonnet. The windscreen caved in, a missile landing square in the middle of it. A police Matrix van was behind the Audi, the officers inside it powerless to do anything. A kid, his face wrapped in the purple bandana of the LFB, ran up to it and swung the golf club he was carrying into the side of the van, swinging it again and again and again until the wing was crumpled and bent.

He banged his fist against the dash. The stakes had been raised, and he was suddenly very afraid. He had not expected Bizness to back down, but neither had he expected him to do what he had done. He operated without compunction, with no regard for restraint. Milton was concerned that he would do something else, something worse.

He took his mobile and called Aaron. The phone rang five times, then six before the call connected.

"Hello?"

Milton did not recognise the voice. "Can I speak to Aaron, please?"

"Who is this?"

He hesitated. "I'm a friend of Aaron's. Who are you?"

"Detective Constable Wilson, Stoke Newington CID. Who is this, please?"

"Where is Aaron?"

"I'm afraid Aaron has been shot, sir."

"Is he all right?"

"I'm sorry. No, he's not—he's dead, sir. Please—"

Milton cut off the call and bounced his mobile across the passenger seat. The lights were still red. He felt a tightening in his gut, a cold knot of fear and dread. He slammed his palms on the steering wheel.

Come on, come on, come on!

The lights changed, and he stamped on the accelerator, the rubber shrieking as he took a hard right turn. The traffic thinned out a little, and he was able to make better progress, pulling out and bullying his way along the opposite lane whenever it slowed.

He knew something was wrong as soon as he reached the Estate. A thick plume of smoke was rising into the darkening sky. As he got closer, he saw that it was wreathed around the side of the block, lit by the spotlights on the corners of the building as it crawled up and pitched into the sky as a dirty, clotting cloud. He swerved the car onto the forecourt. A crowd had gathered around the foot of the building, their eyes fixed on the sixth floor. Thick smoke was gushing from one of the flats. A window shattered and more spilled out. Milton stared into the source of the smoke and saw the orange-red of the fire.

Sharon's flat.

He sprinted across the forecourt to the stairwell, shouldered the door aside, and took the stairs three at a time. He reached the sixth floor, slammed through the door and onto the walkway. He recognised Sharon's neighbours among the group that had gathered at the end of the walkway. He grabbed one, the old lady who lived next door, and tugged her to one side. "Is she still in there?" he asked.

"I haven't seen her come out. Her boy, neither."

Milton released her arm and ran down the corridor. The heat climbed until it started to singe his eyebrows, a solid wall that washed over him and made it hard to breathe. He took off his coat and wrapped it around his hand, reaching out to the red-hot door handle and twisting it open. The room beyond was an inferno: the carpets, the furniture, even the walls and the ceiling seemed to be on fire. The flames lapped across the ceiling like waves. The smoke was dense and choking, and the sound of the hungry fire was threatening.

Milton heard a single scream for help, quickly choked back.

He draped his coat over his head and shoulders and stepped inside.

Chapter Forty-Six

RUTHERFORD LEFT THE HOUSE, locking the door behind him. It was another sultry, sticky night. The sound of sirens was audible in the distance, an up-and-down ululation that seemed almost constant and seemed to be coming from several directions at once. He paused at the door of his car, took off his jacket and tossed it onto the passenger seat. There was something else in the atmosphere tonight, an almost tangible edge. He could not define it, but it made him uneasy. This part of Hackney often had the hint of menace to it, especially at night, but this was different. Something was wrong.

Milton had called him five minutes earlier. He had sounded anxious. Rutherford hardly knew him, but he was not the sort of man that he would have associated with worry. He had explained that there had been an accident, and that Elijah's mother was in Homerton hospital. Rutherford asked what had happened, but Milton had ignored the question, asking him to find the boy and bring him to the hospital as quickly as he could. Rutherford had been eating a takeaway curry in front of a film, but he had put the plate aside at once and put on his shoes.

Rutherford opened the door and settled in the driver's seat. He had asked Milton where he could find Elijah. Milton said that he wasn't at home, but save that, he had no idea. That wasn't helpful, but Rutherford said that he would do his best.

He started the car, put it into gear, and drove west.

There were more kids on the streets than usual, gathered in small groups on the corners and outside shops. They wore their hoods up, and some had scarves and bandanas around their faces.

He reached for the radio and switched it on. Capital FM would normally have been playing chart music at this hour, but instead, there was a news bulletin. There were serious disturbances across London, and Hackney was said to be especially bad. Rutherford had read the reports in the newspaper about the gang banger who had been shot and killed, and it seemed that the protests in Tottenham and Enfield had spread, metastasizing into something much bigger and more dangerous.

As he turned off the main road, a bus hurried towards him from the opposite direction, driving quickly and erratically. As it rushed by, Rutherford saw that it had no passengers. All of its windows had been shattered. He drove on until he reached Mare Street; he had to slow to a crawl as the crowd on the pavement started to drift out into the road. Ahead of him, the crowd was a solid mass. He stared in stupefaction as a group of teenagers smashed the window of a parked police car. One of them reached in with a black bin bag and spread it across the passenger seat. He lit the bag, the flames taking at once, the upholstery going up and flames quickly curling back down again from the ceiling. The crowd cheered jubilantly. The windows that had been left intact blackened and then started to crack. Someone marshalled the crowd to stand back and then, on cue, the petrol tank exploded. A hundred mobile phones were held aloft, videoing the scene.

Rutherford had seen shit like this before in Baghdad, but this was London.

He found a side road and reversed the car into an open parking space. He set off, walking briskly. He didn't know where Elijah was, but he did know what youngers would be like with something like this happening on their doorstep. They would be drawn to it like cats to free crack. His best chance was just to follow the mayhem.

Shop owners were closing their businesses early, yanking down the metal shutters to cover the doors and windows. People looked up and down the street anxiously.

Rutherford stopped at the stall where he liked to get his coffee in the morning. "You know what's going on?" he asked the owner.

"Trouble," he said. "It's already crazy, and they say it's going to get worse. I'm closing up."

Rutherford and the man turned and watched as a young boy, no older than twelve, sprinted down the pavement towards them. He was struggling with a large box pressed against his chest. The youngster ran past, screaming, "I got an Xbox, bruv, believe it! There's bare free stuff down there."

Rutherford made his way further up the road. The shops were all shut now.

A large crowd had gathered in the high street. Forty or fifty of them, their faces covered with bandanas or hoods, were attacking the shuttered windows of the shops. Another two or three hundred were watching, laughing and pointing at what they were seeing, on the cusp of getting involved themselves. A large industrial bin had been wheeled into the centre of the street, next to the bus stop, and set alight. Thick black smoke gushed out of it as the rubbish inside caught fire. The crowd whooped and hollered as young men took it in turns to launch kicks into the window of a Dixons. The glass was tough and resistant, but kick after kick thudded into it, and it gradually started to weaken. A spider web of cracks appeared and spread, the glass slowly buckling inwards. "Out of the way!" yelled one of the crowd, a fire extinguisher held above his head. He ran at the window and threw the extinguisher into the middle of it. The glass crunched as it finally cracked open, the fire extinguisher tumbling into the space beyond. The crowd set on the wrecked display like jackals, kicking at it and clearing away the shards with hands wrapped in the sleeves of their coats. The televisions inside were ferried out, some of them put into the back of waiting cars, others wheeled away in shopping trolleys. The looters climbed into the window and disappeared into the shop beyond. Others moved on to the next one along.

Rutherford's attention was drawn to a scuffle at the mouth of an alley fifty yards ahead of him. Four larger boys were surrounding a fifth person; his face was obscured by the T-shirt that had been put over it like a hood, and he was identifiable as a police officer only by his uniform. The boys were dragging him into the alley, occasionally pausing to kick or punch him. Another one was tearing a fence down for the planks of wood it would yield; Rutherford knew what they would be used for. He changed course to head in their direction, shouldering people out of the way as he picked up speed.

"Oi!" he shouted to them. "That's enough. Let him go."

One of the boys turned, an insolent retort on his lips, but his expression changed as he saw what he was facing. Rutherford was big, and there was fire in his eyes. He called out to the others, and they all faded back into the crowd.

Rutherford pulled the T-shirt from the officer's head. He could only have been in his early twenties: a new recruit tossed into the middle of the worst disturbances London had seen for years. His nose was streaming with blood, and Rutherford used the shirt to mop away the worst of it. "You all right, son?"

The man wore an expression of terror. "There's nothing we can do," he said, his voice taut with hysteria. "They're like animals."

Rutherford took him by the shoulders and looked right into his face. "You don't want to be here," he said, loosening the straps that secured his stab vest. "Ditch your gear and get back. It's not going to take much more for it to get worse. Lynching, you know what I mean? Go on—breeze, man."

People buffeted Rutherford as he was swept further up the street. He had never seen anything like it. There were no police anywhere, and the crowd continued to grow and swell. The atmosphere was manic, and the riot seemed to be gathering momentum, a life all of its own. Glass smashed and shattered, shards tumbling into the street to be trodden underfoot. Alarms clamoured helplessly, the sirens swallowed by the deafening noise of the mob. At the far end of the High Street someone had set fire to another bin, and plumes of dark smoke billowed upwards into the dusk. A police helicopter swooped overhead, hovering impotently, its spotlight reaching down like a finger to stroke over the mob.

He was tall enough to look out over the top of the crowd, but there was no sign of him. A teenage girl slammed into him and turned him to the left, and there he was: with a group of boys, each of them taking turns to shoulder-barge the door to a newsagent's.

"Elijah!"

He turned. His face was full of exhilaration, but it softened with shame as he recognised him. "What you want, man?" he said, the false bravado for the benefit of his friends.

"I need to talk to you."

"Nah. Don't think so."

Rutherford reached out and snagged the edge of his jacket. "You need to come with me."

"Get off me!" He saw Rutherford's face, and the sudden anger paled. "What is it?"

"It's your mum."

"What about her?"

"Better come with me, younger."

Elijah's face blanched. Rutherford made his way back through the angry crowd, holding the edge of Elijah's jacket in a tight grip. The boy did not resist.

Chapter Forty-Seven

RUTHERFORD PARKED his car in the car park and led the way to the entrance of the hospital. Elijah had asked what the matter was as they made their way to the car. Rutherford had explained that he didn't know, that he had received a message from Milton and that was it. The boy had been quiet during the ride, and he remained silent now. Rutherford reached down and folded one large hand around the boy's arm, just above the bicep, his fingers gripping it loosely. Elijah did not resist.

Rutherford stopped at the reception and asked, quietly, for directions to the Burns Unit. The hospital was sprawling and badly organised, and it took them ten minutes to trace a route through the warren of corridors until they found the correct department. A long passageway gave access onto a dozen separate rooms. A nurse was sat behind a counter at the start of the corridor.

"Sharon Warriner?"

"Are you related to her?"

"This is her boy."

The nurse looked at Elijah, a small smile of sympathy breaking across her face. "Room eight."

They walked quickly and in silence, the soles of their shoes squeaking against the linoleum floor. The door was closed, with a sign indicating that visitors should use the intercom to announce themselves.

Rutherford paused. "Are you all right?" he asked Elijah.

The boy's throat bulged as he swallowed. "Yeah," he said, his voice wobbling.

"It might not look good now, but your mum is going to be all right. You hear me? She'll be fine."

"Yeah."

"And I'm here if you need me."

Rutherford buzzed the intercom and opened the door. He stepped inside, leaving his hand on Elijah's shoulder as they made their way into the ward. A series of private rooms were accessed from a central corridor. Milton was standing outside a room at the end. They walked up to him, and he stepped aside.

It was a small space, barely enough room for a bed and the cheap and flimsy furniture arranged around it. A window looked out onto a patch of garden, the ornamental tree in the centre of the space overgrown with weeds and bits of litter that had snared in its lifeless branches. A woman was lying in the bed, most of her body wrapped in bandages. The skin on her face was puckered across one side; angry blisters and weals started at her scalp and disfigured her all the way down to her throat. Her head had been shaved to a stubbled furze, and the eyebrow to the right had been singed away. An oxygen masked was fitted to her mouth, and her breathing in and out was shallow, a delicate and pathetic sound. Her eyes were closed.

Rutherford felt a catch in his throat. He squeezed Elijah's shoulder.

The boy's hard face seemed to break apart in slow motion. The hostility melted and the premature years fell away until he looked like what he really was: a fifteen-year-old child, confused, helpless and desperate for his mother. Rutherford's hand fell away as the boy ran across the room to the bed.

Rutherford stepped back from the bed to give the boy some space. He turned. Milton was standing at the back of the room, his arms folded across his chest. His face relayed a mixture of emotions: concern for the woman, sympathy for the boy, and beneath everything else, the unmistakeable fire of black anger. Rutherford knew all about that, it had landed him in trouble as a young man, and he had learnt to douse it down whenever it started to flicker and flame. He could see it smouldering behind Milton's eyes now. His fists clenched and unclenched, and his jaw was set into an iron-hard line. He was struggling to keep it under control. It didn't look as if he wanted to. As he looked at the darkness that flickered in those flinty, emotionless eyes, he was afraid.

"What happened?"

"Arson."

"Do you know—"

"I know."

Rutherford lowered his voice even lower and flicked his eyes towards Elijah. "You said he was in trouble—is it because of something he was mixed up in?"

Milton nodded.

"Have you told the police?"

His voice was flat. "It's gone beyond that."

"So?"

Milton put his hand on Rutherford's arm. "You need to do me a favour. Look after the boy. Keep an eye on him, keep on at him to train, he needs something like that in his life, and we both know he's got talent."

"What about you?"

Milton ignored the question. "He needs a strong figure in his life. Someone to look up to. It's not me—it was never going to be me. I'm the last sort of example that he needs."

"What you talking about, man?"

"It doesn't matter. Just say you'll look out for him."

"Of course I will."

"Thank you."

Rutherford pressed. "What about you?"

The feeling was suddenly bleached from Milton's expression again. It became cold and impassive and frightening. "There's something I have to do."

"Let me help."

"Not for this."

"Come on, man. I don't know what you're thinking about, but whatever it is, it'll go better if you've got someone to watch your back."

"Look after the boy."

"You're going after them, aren't you?"

"Look after the boy. That's more than enough."

Chapter Forty-Eight

JOHN MILTON set off for Dalston. The radio said that the rioting was getting worse, and the evidence bore that out: the streets were choked with people, groups of youngsters making their way into the centre of Hackney. A girl was standing on a corner wearing her shorts and bra, her T-shirt wrapped around her face, both middle fingers extended towards a police car as it sped by. Shop windows were smashed: broken TVs were left on the street, unwanted T-shirts were scattered about, empty trainer and mobile phone boxes and security tags lying where they had been thrown. Milton watched as a young boy cradling a PlayStation box was punched by two older boys and the box stolen, in turn, from him. The occasional police van went past, lights flashing, but not as many as Milton would have expected.

He passed a police station. It was surrounded by a large crowd, and as he watched, he saw the thick line of looters bulge and surge and then pour inside through a smashed door. Lights were turned on, and within moments, thick smoke started to pour through the windows. Rioters emerged again, some of them wearing police stab vests and helmets. They launched the helmets at the police and turned over the cars parked in the yard. Surely the authorities had not been caught out? he thought as he carefully skirted the crowd. Milton didn't mind. This would serve as a valuable distraction for what he was intending to do.

The main road was eventually blocked by the sheer number of people in the street, so he picked a way to Bizness's studio around the back streets, driving slowly and taking a wide path around clutches of rioters, their faces obscured by scarves and hoods, hauling away the goods they had looted from wrecked shops. He was stared down by huddled groups of people on the corner. They had boxes at their feet: consoles, stereos, flat-screen TVs.

He parked the car two hundred yards away and went around to the back. The light inside the boot cast a sickly light on the interior, a travel blanket lay across a collection of items that revealed themselves as bumps through the fabric. He looked around cautiously. There was no one close enough to see what he was doing.

He took a pair of latex gloves from a cardboard dispenser and fitted them carefully onto his hands. He checked the street again and, satisfied, pulled the blanket aside. A sawn-off shotgun was laid across the floor of the boot and, next to it, his Sig 9mm automatic. He took a rag and wiped both guns carefully. He checked the Sig was fully loaded and holstered it under his shirt, inside the waistband of his jeans, the metal pressed into the small of his back. There was a box of shells next to the shotgun, and he stuffed a handful into his pocket. He wiped the gun with the rag, carefully removing any prints, and wrapped it in the travel blanket. It was eighteen inches from tip to stock, and he slipped the bundle underneath his jacket, barrel pointing downwards. He had a dozen shells for the shotgun and seventeen rounds in the Sig. Twenty-nine in total. He hoped it would be enough. He dropped a pair of flashbangs into his pocket and closed the boot.

The sound of alarms filled the air, loud and declamatory, and beneath their sharp screech came the occasional noise of windows shattering and the hubbub of shouts and shrieks from the rioters on the street. Police riot vans raced down the street towards Hackney Central, and at the same time tens of kids with scarves over their faces came running in the other direction, laughing and screaming.

Milton made his way towards the main road.

Chapter Forty-Nine

"SHIT'S GOING *ON* OUT THERE," Mouse whooped. "You see that brother? He just put a dustbin through the window of the Poundland."

"Brother needs his head examined, looting a motherfucking Poundland."

Pinky was speaking on the phone. "It's going down at the shopping centre, too," he reported. "They've bust in through the front doors, and there ain't no security or police nowhere doing anything about it. There's a Foot Locker in there. What we doing here, anyway? It can wait. I want me some new Jordans, man. Come on, bruv. Let's get involved. We can be there in five minutes."

Bizness looked at Pinky. The boy was immature. He was enthusiastic and full of energy, but he was going to get on his nerves if he didn't take it easy.

"It's hot in here, man. Don't you ever open no windows?"

"Have a beer. Smoke something. Just stop fucking getting in my face, a'ight?"

They had been in the room for two hours, and it smelled of dope, sweat and cigarettes. Mouse had been out to find out the news and had returned to report that Pops's body had been found in the park and that Elijah's mother's flat had been razed to the ground. Bizness was not worried. He had been careful, and there was nothing to connect him to either crime. The best policy, in a situation like this, was to sit tight for a few hours until the initial fuss had blown over. If the police wanted to talk to him, they knew where he was. They would say that they had been in the studio all day.

He had told himself he wouldn't do any of the blow, but it had been a long wait. They had a lot of it, and there wasn't anything else to do. He felt twitchy, and a vein in his temple jumped now and again, a nervous tic that was beginning to irritate him.

Mouse took out his phone. "I'm gonna go call my woman."

"Do it in here," Bizness said.

"Place smells rank, man," Mouse countered. "If I don't get some fresh air, I swear I'm gonna faint. I'll speak to her for a bit, have a look on the street, see what's happening, then get back inside. Won't be long."

Chapter Fifty

MILTON WALKED briskly to the entrance to the studio. Bass was thumping through the walls of the building, rattling the door in its frame. He scouted it quickly. If there had been time, he would have prepared a careful plan for getting inside and taking Bizness out. He would have found a distraction, perhaps disabled the electricity to put them on the back foot. Or he could have broken into the building opposite and sniped them from the second floor. The road was only twenty metres wide, and he could have managed that in his sleep. He dismissed both ideas. There wasn't time for either of them, and anyway, he wasn't inclined to be subtle.

He tried the handle: it was locked. Milton took a step back and was preparing to kick it in when the lock clicked, the handle turned, and the door was pulled open. A man was standing there, shock on his face, an unlit cigarette dangling from his lip. Milton released his grip so that the blanket fell away from the sawn-off and shoved the stock into the man's face. His nose crumpled, and blood burst across his face. He lost his legs and began to fall. Milton followed him as he staggered back inside, swiping the stock like a club, the end catching the man on the chin as he went down. He was unconscious before he fell back and bounced off the stairs.

The light over the stairs was on. Milton flicked it off.

"Mouse?" came a voice from upstairs. "You alright?"

Milton turned the sawn-off in his hands, holding it loosely and aiming it diagonally upwards. He stepped over Mouse and started up the stairs, slowly, one at a time.

"Mouse?"

Milton climbed.

"You hear something?" came an angry voice from upstairs.

"Nah."

"Go and check."

"He's outside on the phone. It's nothing, Bizness."

"Then there's nothing to worry about going and making sure, is there?"

"Fuck it, man, all I want is a smoke and a relax."

"Get down there."

Milton kept climbing the stairs.

He thought of Aaron: shot dead in the park like an animal.

He thought of Sharon: breathing through a tube in a hospital bed, bandages wrapped around her face.

He thought of Elijah and his brutally short future if he let Bizness live.

No, he could not go back. Too much blood had been spilt. Milton had

232

offered Bizness a way out, but he had decided not to take it. That was his choice. Ignoring his offer came with consequences, and those had been explained to him, too. There was nothing else to do; he had to finish it, tonight.

A second man appeared at the top of the stairs. Milton recognised him from the crack house. He squeezed the trigger and shot him in the chest, the impact peppering him from his navel to his throat. He staggered, his hand pointlessly reaching for the knife in his pocket. Milton fired a second spread. Spit and blood foamed at the man's lips as he pirouetted back into the room above, dropping to the floor.

The music suddenly cut out.

Milton paused, crouching low.

"A'ight," Bizness called down to him. "That you, Milton?"

He gripped the barrel in his left hand, the index finger of his right hand tight against the trigger.

"I know it's you. I don't know what your beef is with me, but I ain't armed. Come up. Let's sort this out."

Milton took another step, then another.

"We can settle this thing. It's about JaJa, right? That's what you said. You want the younger, man, you can have him. Little shit ain't worth all this aggravation. Come up. We'll shake like men."

Milton was at the top of the stairs.

He took a quick step and flung himself into the room.

Two Mac-10s spat out.

Tck-tck-tck-tck-tck.

The bullets thudded into the sofa, spraying out fragments of leather and gouts of yellowed upholstery. Milton landed next to the table and scrambled into the studio beyond, more spray from the automatics studding into the floor and wall as he swung his legs inside and out of the line of fire.

Tck-tck-tck-tck-tck.

Chunks of wood sprayed out as bullets bit into the frame. The wide glass panel spider-webbed and then fell inwards in a hundred razored fragments as bullets cracked into it. Milton crabbed backwards so that the solidness of the mixing desk was between him and Bizness's dual autos.

He had dropped the shotgun. He fumbled for the Sig, pulled out the magazine and checked it, slapping the seventeen-shot load back into the butt. He cranked a bullet into the chamber and held the weapon in front of his face.

"What—you thought you could embarrass me in front of my friends and my fans with no consequences? You could burn down my place and that would be that, no hard feelings, let bygones be fucking bygones? You must be out of your mind, man, coming here. You're a dead man."

There was a moment of peace. It was not silence—bits of debris still spattered down and the crowd was loud outside the window—but the firing had ceased.

"You dropped your shotgun," he called. "Got anything else?"

Milton gritted his teeth.

"You ain't got nothing like what I got here."

"I gave you a choice," Milton called out. "You just needed to leave Elijah alone."

"See—there it is again, *arrogance*. What makes you think you can tell me what to do? You don't tell me nothing, bruv."

Tck-tck-tck-tck-tck.

The Mac-10s fired again, and the room flashed, bullets spraying into the recording booth opposite Milton. He glanced up and saw the twin muzzle-flash reflected in the jagged remains of the booth window before bullets stitched across it and sent the shards crashing down on top of him. Bizness was behind the sofa. The bullets thudded softly into the upholstered sound insulation, and the studio was filled with a fine shower of powder and dust.

"Come on. Come out, and let's get it over with. You know there's no way out for you. What you got—a nine? You just pissing in the wind, bruv. I got two Mac-10s and enough ammo for a month. Stop hiding like a bitch. I ain't gonna lie, you ain't getting out of here alive. Come on. But you come out now, I promise I'll do you quick."

Milton straightened his back against the mixing desk and reached inside his jacket. His fingers touched a smooth, rounded cylinder. The flashbang fitted snugly into his palm.

"Funny thing is, even this won't stick on me. You and my two boys had a gunfight, and you all got done. There won't be no sign of me. I've got a woman in Camden, she'll alibi me up for now and earlier. All this—you gonna get dooked for nothing, bruv."

Milton pulled the pin, reached up, and tossed the grenade through the broken window and into the room beyond.

There was a fizz and a burst of the brightest white light as the phosphorous ignited.

Milton rolled out of the door, bringing the Sig up, and fired. The first shot missed, but there was enough light from the flashbang for Milton to see Bizness just as he popped up from behind the sofa to return fire. He brought the Sig around and aimed quickly, squeezing the trigger twice. Bizness staggered backwards through a sudden pink mist, the Mac-10s firing wildly into the ceiling. The boy toppled into the sofa. It tipped over so that he lay across it on his back, his legs splayed out over the now vertical seats. He was pressing his hand against his chest. A bullet had hit him there, and blood was pulsing out between his fingers.

Milton had seen plenty of gutshots before. The boy was finished. No treatment could save him now.

He advanced on him, the Sig aimed at his head.

"You think you're better than me, don't you?" Bizness gasped out, the words forming between bloody gurgles. Milton kicked away the machine guns. He crouched down at Bizness's side. The boy took a ragged, wheezing breath. "You know what you are?" he said. "You people? You're a bunch of fuckin' hypocrites."

A ringing sound danced in Milton's ears, and his eyes stung with sweat. The smell of cordite was acrid, and he gagged a little. A trickle of blood, specked with bubbles of breath, dribbled from Bizness's mouth.

"You sit in your cosy homes… with your soft, comfy lives… nothing bad ever happens…" He coughed, a tearing cough that brought blood to his lips. "You look at us and… you shake your head. You *need* people like me so you can shake your fuckin' heads and say, 'See that guy, he's bad,' just so you can feel better about yourselves."

Milton reached down and collected one of the cushions that had scattered away from the sofa.

"And you know why you… people are scared of a proud black man? I'm a threat to the way you see the world to be. The black kid in school… his mums can't put food on the table. The black kid who's got no future… no prospects 'cept slaving for some fucked-up… system that sees him as a second-class citizen." He gasped. "You should be scared, bruv… Those kids running around outside tonight… I give them a purpose. I'm proof, man, living proof… that there ain't no need to bow down to fuckers like you and those fuckers you represent. You want something, it's a'ight, you go on and take it. JaJa, you can tell him what you want… but see how he feels this time next year when you've fucked off and he's doing twelve-hour shifts in Maccy D's because that's the only place that'll give him a job." He gasped again; the words were harder and harder to form. "He'll think about me… the taste I gave him of the life… and he'll ask himself, 'Why not me? Why can't I have me some of that good stuff?' You know I'm right. You've seen it in his eyes… same as I have."

"You don't know that. Maybe he will. Maybe he won't. But he'll see he's got choices. You can take the short cut or do things properly. You chose the short cut. The easy choice. It hasn't worked out so well for you."

"Fuck you, bruv. You don't know shit."

"I know he wouldn't think your life looked so appealing now."

Bizness tried to retort, but he coughed on a mouthful of blood.

Milton took the pillow and placed it over his head, one hand on each side, pressing down. The boy struggled, but Milton had his knees pressed down so that his arms were pinned to his side. His legs thrashed impotently, the kicks becoming less frequent until they subsided to spasms.

The spasms stopped.

Milton gently released the pressure, and the cushion, covered in blood, fell aside. Milton had it smeared across his trousers and on the latex gloves, too. He looked up and was suddenly aware that there was another person in the room. He stared into the eyes of a teenage boy, the same age as Elijah. He was tall and skinny, his chin pressed down hard into his chest, just his eyes showing. It took a moment, but then he recognised him: it was the boy from the park, the one who had threatened him on his first night in Hackney. He was in the corner of the room, pressed tight against the wall. He had a Makarov revolver in a trembling hand. The gun hung loosely from his fingers, pointed down at the floor. The boy looked young and frightened.

For a moment, Milton was back in France again, on the road in the mountains.

He stood and walked across the room, reaching down for the Makarov. The boy released it without speaking. He located the spent cartridges from the shotgun and pocketed them. He collected the sawn-off and put it, the Sig and the revolver into a Nike holdall he found in a cupboard. The boy's eyes followed him about the room, wide and timid, but he stayed where he was against the wall. He checked the room one final time to make sure that he had not left anything behind, and satisfied that he had not, he closed the door behind him and descended to the chaotic street below.

PART FIVE

Group Fifteen

Chapter Fifty-One

NUMBER TWELVE SAT IN HIS CAR. He was parked on the opposite side of the road to the church hall. The street was eerily quiet. A battered old minibus was parked directly in front of him, the stencilled sign on its dirty flanks advertising a Camden gym. He had watched the dozen youngsters pile out of the bus and file into the hall, different sizes and ages, all of them carrying sports bags. The local kids had arrived within the space of half an hour, all similarly equipped. Milton's car was parked fifty yards away; Callan had followed the tracking beacon from across London. He had not seen him and assumed that he was inside.

His mobile chirped.

"I have orders for you."

Callan recognised Control's voice. "Yes, sir."

"Do you know where Number One is?"

"He's in the East End. I have him under surveillance now. What do you want me to do?"

"The Committee has reviewed your report. It's been decided that he is a risk we cannot take. His behaviour, his likely mental condition—national security is at risk. We have decided that he needs to be retired."

Callan kept his voice calm and implacable. "Yes, sir. When?"

"Quickly."

"Tonight should be possible."

"Very good, Twelve. Let me know when it is done."

The line went dead.

Callan put the phone back into his pocket. He would have preferred a little longer to plan an operation like this, against a target of Number One's pedigree, but he didn't think it an impediment that need detain him. Number One had no idea that he had been marked for death. Callan had the benefit of the element of surprise, and that would be the only advantage that he would need.

He opened the door, went around to the boot of the car, and popped it open. He pulled up the false floor and ran his gaze across the row of neatly arranged weapons. He reached down and stroked his fingers across the cold metal stock of a combat shotgun. He pulled a bandolier over his shoulder and filled the pouches with shells. He didn't think he'd need more than the two that were already loaded, but it didn't hurt to be prepared. He shut the boot and locked it and got back into the car again. All he needed to do was wait for the right moment.

Chapter Fifty-Two

MILTON STOOD with Rutherford next to the ring, both of them watching the action. Elijah was fighting one of the boys from the Tottenham club. The two of them were well matched: the Tottenham boy was a year older and a little bigger, but Elijah was faster and his punches were crisper, with a natural technique that couldn't be taught.

"Boy's doing good," Rutherford said, his eyes fixed on the action. "Landing everything he throws. If he don't knock him out, he'll take him on points, easy."

Milton thought that was probably right, but it didn't mean that he wasn't nervous. His own fists jerked a little with each punch, and he caught himself holding his breath as the other boy moved in tight and clinched, snagging Elijah around the shoulders and hugging him. Elijah tried to struggle free, but the Tottenham boy was strong. The referee called for the break, but before he could step in, the boy released his right hand and punched, twice, into Elijah's groin.

The bell sounded.

Elijah spat out his mouthguard. "You hit me low!" he yelled at him.

"Yeah?" the boy called back across the ring at him. "What you gonna do about it, Hackney?"

Rutherford stepped between the ropes. "Elijah!"

"I'm gonna fuckin' dook you!"

Rutherford reached out a long arm, snagged the collar of Elijah's singlet, and dragged him back to the corner. "Deep breath, younger."

"He hit me in the nuts!"

Rutherford put one big hand on each shoulder and turned him away. "Yeah, he did, and you lose your temper like you're fixing to do, chances are this boy ain't got what it takes to hold you off, and you'll probably knock him out. But losing your temper like that gets to be a bad habit, and eventually, you'll come up against someone who's good enough to get you all fired and take advantage of it. You're good enough to go a long way, younger, maybe even make a nice career out of it. You don't want to get into bad habits that'll get you in trouble in a fight that really means something— like for your future. You hear what I'm saying?"

Elijah scowled down at the canvas. "Yeah."

"Now then—you know why he hit you low?"

"'Cos I'm better than him."

"That's right, younger. Better than him. Much better than he'll ever get to be, too. There's one more round coming, a'ight? I'm going to let you go, and you're going to get back out there, touch his gloves in the middle of the ring like you respect him even though we know you don't, and then you're going to box him. You keep your cool, follow the plan we talked about, and wait for the opening. When he gives it to you, *then* you punish him for hitting you low—you got it?"

"Yeah."

"All right then." Rutherford pushed the mouthguard back into Elijah's mouth and let go of his shoulder. "Touch his gloves and away you go."

The bell was rung to signal the start of the third round, and the two boys met in the centre of the ring again. They tapped gloves and then sprang apart. Elijah did exactly as Rutherford had instructed: he kept his opponent at arm's length, stinging him with his jab whenever he tried to get in too close. The older boy tried to rush him, but Elijah skipped out of the way, banging in straight rights and lefts into the side of the boy's face as he sailed harmlessly past. As the seconds wound down, he stepped back and lowered his guard, indicating his chin with a clumsy touch of his glove. He's showboating, Milton thought, a grin breaking out across his face. The other boy swore at the goading, his words muffled by his guard, and rushed in again. Elijah took a step to the side, pivoted on his right foot, and swung a strong right hook into the boy's guts. His momentum was stopped at once, and his guard dropping to shield his stinging ribs, Elijah powered a left hook that knocked him backwards, and after a comical stumble, he landed on his behind.

The bell sounded, and the fight came to an end.

That's my boy, Milton thought, before he caught himself. Elijah ducked his head to the referee and bumped his right fist against Rutherford's. He turned to look at Milton but looked away again quickly. Milton nodded at that. Fair enough, he thought. He didn't know anything about what had happened, and as far as he was concerned, he had caught Milton in bed with his mother. All things considered, he deserved his mistrust.

A week had passed since the riots. Milton had spent most of the time with Elijah in the hospital. Sharon's condition had stabilised to the extent that the doctors were happy to plan the skin grafts that would fix some of the damage that had been done to her face and the rest of her body. Elijah had refused to leave her side, so Milton had arranged for him to have a spare bed in a suite that was held back for relatives. He made sure that the boy ate and did whatever he could to reassure him that his mother would make a recovery, although he kept some of the information to himself. The doctors were confident that they would be able to help, but she had been very badly burnt, they said, and she was always going to be badly scarred. On the sixth day, Sharon was moved from the Burns Unit to a general ward, and Milton started to feel more confident that things would start to improve.

He had returned to the hospital after disposing of Bizness. He said nothing about it to Rutherford, but he didn't need to. The story was on the news that night, buried beneath the clamour of the riots, but once the streets had calmed down again, it rose to the top of the bulletins. Bizness, referred to by his given name of Israel Brown, had been murdered by a person or persons unknown. Two of his associates had also been shot and killed. It was quickly dismissed as a gangland argument that had escalated into something more. Bizness was revealed to be a man of many enemies and, when it all came down to it, not many friends. It was difficult to find anyone who was prepared to say that he would be missed.

Milton had been ready to find a hotel, but Rutherford told him there was no need for that: he could stay with him. Eventually, Milton had agreed. There was a long list of things that needed to be done to make the hall more suitable for the club's business and staying nearby enabled him to start earlier and finish later. Rutherford had a small house with two bedrooms, the second used as the office from where he ran the club. There was a sofa bed, and once the desk was pushed to the wall, there was enough space for Milton and the handful of things he had rescued from the rented house. They had spoken about Elijah, and once he was ready to leave the hospital, Rutherford had promised that he would be able to stay, too. Milton doubted that there would be space for all three of them, but he knew that that was moot: he didn't plan to stay for much longer.

Milton had quickly settled into a routine: he would rise early, at half-five, and go for his run. He would work until eight, and then, after showering at the club, he would drive across to the hospital to see Elijah and Sharon. After an hour with them, he would return to Hackney and work through until five, stopping only to buy his lunch from the arcade of takeaways at the end of the road. He stayed at the hospital for a second time until visiting closed for the night, worked until nine or ten and then, finally, returned to the house for something to eat. Rutherford would usually be watching the television, and he would join him for half an hour before calling it a day.

It was a hard schedule, but it had allowed him to get a lot done. He had fixed the roof properly, replacing the tiles that had been dislodged. He had given the equipment a thorough cleanse, scrubbing the canvasses in both rings until the stains that had been trodden in over years of use had been mostly scoured away. He had whitewashed the walls and mended the damaged fixtures in the toilets.

Rutherford approached him. "You coming?"

"In a couple of hours? I want to finish wiring the plugs." The biggest task left to do was to renew the wiring, but he had made a start and was keen to press on.

"You work too hard."

"It'll get done sooner this way."

"I'm still not sure why you're being so good about this."

"It's nice to be able to help," he said. "I'll see you later."

"A'ight," he said, clapping Milton on the back.

Rutherford went to collect his coat. Milton was about to fetch his tools from the office when Elijah stepped in front of him.

"Hey," he said, a little awkwardly.

"All right, Elijah?"

"Thanks for coming."

"Are you kidding? I loved it. I said you'd be cut out for this, didn't I?"

He paused awkwardly. "I never said thanks."

Milton smiled at him. "There's no need."

"It was—you know…"

"You don't have to say anything. I didn't handle things as well as I could have done, either. That's how things get to be, sometimes."

Elijah was struggling for the words. "It's just—I don't want you to think I'm ungrateful, that's all."

"You've done well. That fight, tonight, the way you handled him—I'm telling you, Elijah, that was something. I know a little bit about boxing, and when Rutherford says you've got potential, I reckon he's about right. You keep working hard and stay away from the street, I'd say there's a very good chance you're going to end up doing something pretty useful with these." He tapped the back of the boy's hands. "That left hook of yours"—he exhaled theatrically—"it's something, Elijah, it really is. I wouldn't want to get on the other side of it. Your mother will be proud of you when she sees what you've been doing."

The mention of Sharon quietened him for a moment.

"You know she'll be all right," Milton said.

He looked up at him. "Why did you help us? You never said." His eyes were wet.

Milton didn't know how to answer that.

"JaJa!" Rutherford called. The three of them were the last people in the hall. "I want a curry. You coming?"

Elijah hadn't taken his eyes off Milton's face.

It was his turn to feel discomfited. "Doesn't have to be a reason, does there?"

Elijah paused for a moment and then reached out his hand. Milton took it and held it for a moment. "See you later, Milton," the boy said. He self-consciously scrubbed the back of his hand across his damp eyes. "We're getting take-out curries. What do you want?"

"You choose. I'm not fussed."

"You like it hot?"

"Not really."

Elijah grinned. "Pussy."

Milton watched the boy make his way back to Rutherford. They made their way out, shutting the door behind them. Milton headed to the back and the small office. There was a desk, a filing cabinet and a battered leather sofa. He collected his bag of tools and went over to the plug that he was fitting. A curry with them sounded good. He was planning on leaving tomorrow, and it would be nice to have had an evening with them before he did.

Chapter Fifty-Three

RUTHERFORD AND ELIJAH walked along the perimeter of the park. All the boy wanted to do was recount the fight from earlier, constantly asking Rutherford for his opinion and his suggestions for how he could eliminate his faults. It made him smile to see the boy so animated. The evening had been an escape for him, Rutherford could see that, a distraction that meant that he did not have to think about his mother or the ordeal of the last few days. He was a lively, engaged boy, and in his enthusiasm Rutherford could see the premature aging endowed by the street quickly peeled back. He saw him for what he was: a sweet fifteen-year-old boy full of the usual insecurities, the usual need for encouragement and acceptance. He was a little full of himself at times, but what young boy wasn't? Rutherford remembered that he had been much worse.

"Damn it," Rutherford said.

"What's the matter?"

"I put the alarm on. Milton will set it off if he opens the door."

"Want me to run back and tell him?"

"I better do it." He handed over a set of keys and pointed. "No need for you to come too—we're nearly there. You know my house? Last one on the left. Let yourself in, make yourself at home. I'll get the takeaway on the way back—what do you want?"

"Curry," he said. "Milton, too. Chicken korma for him. Beef madras for me."

"Two chicken kormas and a beef madras, then. There are DVDs in the living room—put one on if you want. Go on, get inside. Don't hang around outside, you hear? It still ain't right around here."

Rutherford waited until Elijah had crossed the road and was at the door to the maisonette. The door opened and closed, the boy disappearing inside. Satisfied, Rutherford turned on his heel and retraced his steps back to the church hall.

Chapter Fifty-Four

MILTON PUT down his screwdriver and concentrated on the aches and pains that registered around his body. His joints throbbed with a dull ague, his muscles felt stiff, and there was a deep-seated fatigue all the way in the marrow of his bones. There was no point in pretending; he was getting old. Old and stiff.

He recognised, dimly, that he needed sleep more than anything else.

He was screwing the cover onto the new socket when he heard a knock on the door from outside. He waited, wondering whether he had misheard, but the knock was repeated. Three times, quite hard, urgent. He stood. His eye fell on his Sig Sauer hanging in the shoulder holster against the back of the nearby chair. There was no need. It was Rutherford or, in the worst case, kids who were mucking about. He tossed it behind the ring, out of sight.

He crossed the wide space to the front door, unlocked it, and pulled it back.

Milton did not recognise the man outside.

The man brought up a gun and pointed it directly at his chest.

"Back inside," he said.

The gun was a Sig Sauer 9mm, like his own. He knew what that meant.

"About time," he said.

"Inside."

"Control sent you?"

The man didn't answer.

"I don't think I've seen you before. Who are you? Eleven? Twelve?"

"Twelve," he said. The muzzle was aimed at his heart, unwavering in a steady hand, and the man's face was blank and inscrutable. There would be no sense in appealing to his better nature. He would have no better nature. Twelve followed him into the hall and pushed the door closed with his foot. Milton assessed him. He looked like an athlete with wide shoulders and a tapered trunk. The eyes stared out coldly from beneath pale lashes.

"What's this about?"

"Are you armed?" Twelve said. His voice was flat, the sentence trailing away on a dead note.

"No."

"Pull up your shirt."

Milton did as he was told.

"Turn around."

He did.

"Where is it?"

"In the car."

"Anyone else here?"

"No. Just me. Why don't you tell me what this is all about?"

Again, there was no response. Milton assessed. Was there any way of putting Twelve off his stride? Upsetting his balance? He knew with grim certainty that there was not. Twelve and all the other young agents in Group Fifteen were brutally professional. Milton knew how well he had been trained—he would have gone through the same programme as he had, after all—and he was able to anticipate all of the variables that he would be considering. First, he would assess the threat that Milton posed: significant, but limited as it stood. Second, he would confirm that the surroundings were suitable for an elimination: perfect. Once those quick assessments had been made to his satisfaction, he would carry out his orders. It would be quick and efficient. Milton guessed that he had a handful of seconds. A minute if he was lucky and could muddy the waters.

He would not go down without a fight. If there was a chance, a half-chance, he would take it. He assessed the situation himself. Six feet separated him from Twelve. Another indication that the agent was good; not enough to compromise his aim but enough to make sure that Milton could not attack before he could fire. Milton explored his own body, his posture, tensing his muscles and assessing how quickly he might be able to move. The position of his feet. The angle of his hips, of his shoulders. He would need to be decisive, but even then, he knew that his chances were slim. He would certainly be shot before he could reach him, and even if he was not, he did not fancy his chances in unarmed combat with Twelve. He was younger, his muscles more pliant and less damaged and scarred than Milton's.

"Control sent you?" he asked again, probing for a weakness, some conversational gambit he could spin out into hesitation, then work the hesitation into doubt.

Nothing. He took a step into the hall. The gun did not waver.

"He doesn't trust me?"

Nothing.

"Come on, Twelve. I'm owed a reason."

Finally, he answered the question. "Your mental health is in question."

"Don't be ridiculous."

Twelve's eyes darted left and right, taking in his surroundings, scanning for threats. "Look at this place! What are you now, a handyman?"

Milton ignored that. "It might have been in question before, but it isn't now. Ten years doing what we do, it's enough to make you hate the world. I'm not doing it anymore. I'm finished—I've never been more certain of anything in my life."

Twelve turned his gaze back onto Milton. "I used to look up to you," he said, a cruel smile briefly creasing his alabaster-white skin. "You were a legend. But that was then, wasn't it? Before whatever it is that's happened to you."

"Is that what Control thinks? That I've gone mad?"

"I've been following you. Moving into that dump of a place down the road. That woman you've been seeing. And going to those meetings. You're saying you're an alcoholic now, with all the intelligence you're privy to? Fuck, after what happened in France, what did you think he'd think? How could he possibly let that stand? You've been classified as a security risk. 'Most Urgent, Marked for Death.' What else did you expect? He can't have you running around like that, can he? You're a liability."

He tried to think of something that might deflect Twelve from his mission, but there was nothing. "There's no need for this," he said hopelessly.

"Comes to us all in the end. And I can't lie—this will be the making of me. I'm the one who gets to retire the famous Number One."

Behind them, the door handle pressed down. Milton saw it first, an advantage of a second or two that his body spent readying itself for sudden action. Twelve heard it too, and the gun continuing to cover Milton, he took a sideways step and then a quarter turn, allowing him to see both Milton and the doorway at the same time. The door opened inwards.

Rutherford stood there.

Oh no.

A warning caught in Milton's throat, stifled by the steady gun.

"Forgot to tell you about the alarm—" Rutherford said, the sentence trailing away as he noticed the tension in Milton's posture. His face creased with confusion as he looked to the right, at Twelve, and then that became anxiety as he saw the gun.

"Come inside, and shut the door," Twelve instructed him in the same cold, flat voice.

Milton knew Rutherford had seconds to live. He was a witness, and there could be no witnesses. He had to act, right now, but the gun remained where it was, as if held by a statue, pointed implacably at his heart. Rutherford did as he was told, stepping inside and pushing the door behind him. The mechanism closed with a solid click.

"You don't need to shoot him," Milton said, desperately trying to distract Twelve from the course he would already have determined the moment Rutherford set his hand on the door. "He doesn't know who you are. He doesn't know who I am. Let him go. We can settle this between us."

"We're going to settle it," Twelve said.

He swung the gun away from Milton and aimed it at Rutherford.

Chapter Fifty-Five

IN ONE VIOLENT corkscrew of motion, Milton threw himself across the room.

The gun spat out once and then swung back towards Milton again.

Twelve's reflexes were unbelievably quick, and a second—unaimed—shot rang out.

The bullet caught Milton in the shoulder, razor shards of pain lancing down his arm. Milton disregarded it, shut it down, and threw himself into the younger man. He tackled him around the waist, his momentum sending them both stumbling backwards until they clattered against the wall. Twelve tried to bludgeon him with the butt of the gun, but he blocked the clumsy swipe, their wrists clashing and the gun falling to the floor. They collapsed downwards, Milton ending up on top, and he drove the point of his elbow into Twelve's face. He felt the bones of his nose crumple and snap as they crunched together, blood immediately running over the pale white skin. Milton rolled away and scrambled for the gun. His fingers closed around it as Twelve sprang up to his feet, his face twisted with fury.

"Don't," Milton said. The pain from his shoulder washed over him in nauseous waves, but he managed to aim the pistol.

Twelve stopped. He was six feet away. Blood ran freely from his broken nose. His eyes shone with anger.

Milton slowly got to his feet. His left shoulder felt as though it had been mangled, the arm hanging uselessly down by his side. He was woozy from the pain. He knew, from experience, that it would get worse. It was the adrenaline that was holding him together, but the pain would overwhelm him eventually. He held the advantage, but he would not have it for long.

"Put the gun down," Twelve said.

Milton looked across the room. Rutherford's body was sprawled across the floor. Twelve's shot had struck him in the forehead. He had landed in an untidy sprawl, his arms outflung. His body was still. There was no hope for him.

Milton tightened his grip on the pistol. He felt the old, familiar flick of his anger. His finger tightened around the trigger.

"Put it down," Twelve said calmly.

He tried to tune out the pain. Twelve had sunk down a little, spreading his weight between both legs. He could see that Milton was injured. He would have noticed the way that his aim was slowly dropping, his gun arm gradually falling towards the floor. He would be making the same calculations that Milton had made moments earlier. The distance between them. How quickly he could close it. The odds of a shot stopping him before he could reach his target. Milton knew his weakness was obvious; Twelve would be able to smell it like a shark smells blood.

Milton fought the anger and the pain. "I'm not going to kill you," he said, his voice quiet. "I'm finished with that, not unless there's no other choice, and if you're sensible, you won't back me into a corner."

"All right," Twelve said, showing him his open palms, placating him. "I won't. Take it easy."

"I'm not going to kill you, but you know I can't have you following me."

Milton stiffened his arm, switched to a lower aim, and pulled the trigger.

The bullet struck Twelve in the right knee. His face distorted with agony, and he fell back.

Milton closed in and swept his good leg. Twelve dropped to the floor. Milton backed away, covering him with the gun until he reached the door. "Tell Control not to come after me."

"He'll come after you," he gasped through the pain.

"Tell him I'm out."

Twelve grunted; Milton realised that he was laughing. "We're never out."

"I am. Tell him if he sends anyone after me, I'll send them back in boxes. And then I'll bring him down."

He looked again at Rutherford's unmoving body, then at Twelve, staring up at him through a mask of pain. He reached around and pushed the gun into the waistband of his jeans and pulled out the tails of his shirt to cover it. The pain was reaching a crescendo.

He had to move now.

Right now.

He opened the door and hurried across the road towards the unlit stretch of park. He passed through the open gate and kept going until the darkness swallowed him.

Chapter Fifty-Six

THE HOUSE WAS EMPTY. Milton had forced his way in through a door to the garden; he'd put his fist through the glass and unlocked the door from the inside. It was on one of the most expensive streets in the neighbourhood, a long curved cul-de-sac that faced onto the peaceful expanse of a common adjacent to the main area of the park. Expensive SUVs and four-by-fours competed for space on the road. The houses were large, set behind railed front gardens with wide bay windows and broad front doors.

Milton had started to feel faint as he crossed the common. The pain had started to dull and fade; a sensation he knew was dangerous. He kept his hand clamped to his shoulder, but the blood kept coming. He knew enough about battlefield medicine to know that a lodged bullet could sometimes be a blessing, plugging up the entry wound until it could be carefully removed and the blood staunched. Milton had not been so fortunate. This bullet had nicked a vein, and the blood continued to seep out around it, squeezing through his fingers and soaking into the fabric of his shirt.

He found a packet of ibuprofen in a first aid box in the bathroom cabinet. He tapped out three and swallowed them dry and then laid out his tools on the kitchen table. He placed an adjustable mirror before the chair and stood an anglepoise lamp next to it, the shade turned so that the bright cone of light was cast back onto the chair. He opened the first aid box again and took out a tube of antiseptic gel, a gauze dressing and a roll of bandages. He crossed the room to the gas hob and removed the small kitchen knife from where he had rested it, the blade suspended in the blue flame. He raised the knife before his cheek; the metal glowed red and radiated heat. That was good. He lodged the blade of a larger, broader metal spatula in the flame instead.

He went back to the table and took off his shirt, using it to mop the blood from around the wound. He sat in the wooden chair, adjusting the lamp so that its light fell on the wound, and then turned the mirror so that he could stare right into it. A neat hole had been burrowed out, blackened around the edges and scabbed in parts with partly congealed blood. He grimaced with pain as he reached his left hand back up to his left shoulder and then gasped as he used his forefinger and thumb to spread the edges of the wound, opening it so that he could look a little way inside.

He took the knife and, biting down hard on a dish cloth, prodded the hot and sharp tip into the wound, digging deeper until he saw the silver sparkle of the bullet, lodged like a spiteful tumour an inch deep in his flesh.

He took a deep breath and pushed the knife further into his flesh, the sharp point sliding through the skin and into the muscle beneath. The pain yanked him back to wakefulness and then kept climbing; every millimetre of progress, every nudge and tap, was rewarded with a lance of agony that seared into his brain.

He thought about Elijah and Sharon.

He thought about Rutherford.

He felt the tip of the blade touch against the bullet, and with the pain and his weakness shimmering like heat haze before his face, he pressed down harder and then prised the blade back, levering the slug from its burrow and pressing it out until it dropped from out of the wound and onto the table.

The pain flared once, a crescendo that Milton met by slamming his fist against the table, and then slackened off.

Halfway there.

He swallowed another two ibuprofen and reached over to the hob for the spatula. Closing his eyes and pressing his teeth together, he took the blade and pressed it against the wound, the skin sizzling as the red-hot metal cauterised it. Milton gasped at another vicious wave of pain, clenching the edge of the table until it, too, passed. He inspected the seared, puckered flesh in the mirror. A huge, purple bruise had already bloomed around the wound, but the bleeding had stopped. He had done a decent job.

There was no time to pause.

Milton went upstairs and stripped off, taking Twelve's Sig Sauer into the bathroom with him, and showered in the en suite bathroom. He dried himself, daubing antiseptic gel onto the clean wound and then dressing it with the gauze pad, fixing it in place with the roll of bandage. He went into the bedroom and tore through the wardrobe, finding a T-shirt and jeans that fitted him and putting them on.

He had noticed a key fob on the radiator cover in the hall. The fob was attached to a leather swatch decorated with a BMW badge. He left the house through the front door, his pistol hidden beneath a leather jacket he had taken from where it had been slung over the end of the banister. He aimed the fob at the line of parked cars and pressed. There came the familiar double blip and the illumination of the courtesy lights of a large black BMW X5 that had been parked a little way down the road.

Milton opened the door and slid inside. He put Twelve's pistol on the passenger seat and pressed the engine start. The display reported a full tank of diesel. He let the handbrake out, put the car into gear, and pulled slowly into the quiet road.

EPILOGUE

Chapter Fifty-Seven

PINKY TOOK A SEAT on the see-saw and looked around. They were in the playground next to Blissett House. He looked up at the sixth floor. The fire had been contained there, but Elijah's old flat and the ones on each side had been gutted. Black ash and soot were everywhere, the windows and doors had been boarded up, the damage sticking out like an ugly bruise on the concrete face of the block. Pinky didn't have strong feelings about what had happened. Elijah and his mums had brought it on themselves. What else was Bizness supposed to have done, the two of them sending that man after him like that? Pinky had no sympathy for them.

He had sent messages to the other boys, and they had been waiting for him when he had arrived five minutes earlier. They were all there: Little Mark, Chips, Kidz and a couple of the primary school kids from the Estate who had been hanging around with him for the last week. Time they got promoted, Pinky thought, time they had something useful to do. The boys were spread out; Chips and Kidz sat on the swings, Little Mark leant against the chain-link fence, the youngsters kept together, eyeing the older boys with a mixture of bravado and nervousness. The older boys were smoking from the joint that Pinky had rolled and passed around.

It had been a crazy few days, and Pinky had not slept much. It didn't matter, though; he still felt good. There was no point in pretending that he hadn't been frightened, but nothing had happened to him, and now he was in the clear. He had searched the studio after Milton had left; he figured he had a little time before the feds came, and he knew that there was bound to be stuff worth taking. He had been right about that: he had found more than ten grand in a holdall and dozens of little bags filled with cocaine, ready to be distributed to Bizness's dealers, the network of shotters that he had on the street. Pinky had put the Mac-10s and the drugs into another bag he found and left the studio by the fire escape at the back.

It had been hairy getting back. London had been a war zone that night, police cars and vans speeding through the back streets under blue lights, but he had not been stopped. He had stored the guns and money under his bed at home, hiding it beneath his empty trainer boxes and dirty clothes. His mums had given up trying to get him to keep the room tidy long ago, and she had stopped going inside. He knew they would be safe there for a day or two until he could think of somewhere better.

Pinky cast his gaze around the group. They all knew Pops was gone, but no one had said anything about it. Pinky guessed that they had heard that he was responsible, and while he wasn't stupid enough to admit that it had been him, he was happy for them to speculate. He wouldn't own up to it, but he wouldn't deny it, either. A little bit of fear was a good thing, especially with what he had planned. It helped to build respect. That had been a long time coming, and he was going to make sure that he took advantage of it.

Pinky reckoned that he had been given an opportunity. After always being second best, now he had a chance to really do something with his life. Make a name for himself, make some money; he wasn't going to fuck it up, no way.

He got up from the see-saw. "A'ight," he said. "First things first. I'm in charge now. Anyone have a problem with that?"

No one spoke.

"Didn't think so." He grinned. He lifted the holdall onto the roundabout and pulled back the zip. Dozens of little bags full of white powder were snuggled together inside. "Pay attention," he said, making sure that they had all seen the stash. "Things are going to change around here. We're going to make some mad cash. I'm going into business, boys—if you got the balls to be a part of it, listen up. This is what we're gonna do."

Chapter Fifty-Eight

GROUP FIFTEEN had its own private medical facilities attached to a well-known London teaching hospital. State-of-the-art facilities, the best doctors in the country, absolute discretion. Control watched through the window as the surgeon bent low to examine the damage that had been done to Twelve's knee. The man—and his three colleagues—were wearing green smocks, their faces covered by surgical masks and latex gloves over their hands. Twelve had been anaesthetised and was laid out on the operating table, covered by a sheet with a long vertical slit that allowed easy access to his right leg. The surgeon had already sliced open his knee, a neat incision that began just below the quadriceps and curved around the line of his leg. The opening was held open by medical clips, and a miniature camera on an articulated arm had been positioned overhead, its feed visible on the large screen that was fixed to the wall in the observation suite.

Milton's bullet had ruined the knee, smashing through the anterior and posterior ligaments and shattering the patella. They had examined the damage with an arthroscope first and determined that repairs were not possible; a full arthroplasty was necessary. The surgeon had removed what was left of the patella and had shaved the ends of the femur and tibia so that he could fix the replacement joint. One of his colleagues was preparing the bone cement while the other was checking that the prosthesis was ready to be implanted.

Control watched the screen, his eyes a little glazed. He was not bothered by the blood and the gore; Heaven knows, he had seen enough of it over the years, and much worse than this. He was not really concentrating on Twelve at all. His mind was on Milton.

His liquidation should have been straightforward. Twelve had had the benefit of surprise, and Milton was not as young as he had once been. And, yet, here they were, with a badly injured agent and Milton a ghost.

He had been working on damage control ever since Twelve had limped out of the church hall and called for emergency pickup. He had taken the response team himself to ensure that there was no trace of Twelve ever having been there. The blood from his leg had been scrubbed away and footage from local CCTV cameras had been deleted. The dead man—Rutherford—was left where he was. Twelve had explained what had happened. The surprise of Rutherford's appearance had saved Milton's life, so now, in death, he would have to pay back the damage that he had caused. His body would prove to be useful. It was easy to fabricate the story. CCTV footage placed Milton at the scene and showed Rutherford arriving moments before he was shot.

A camera at the entrance to the park had footage of Milton heading north. He was wounded, too, a bullet to the shoulder. They had immediately checked local hospitals for admissions, but it was perfunctory; Milton was much too savvy to do something as foolish as that. An hour later they had intercepted a call to local police of a break-in. A couple had returned to their house on the edge of the nearby park to find that someone had forced the door to the garden. Their car and a few clothes had been stolen. That, in itself, would have been enough for Control to have investigated, but they had also reported that their first aid cabinet had been ransacked, that a lamp had been moved onto the kitchen table, and that kitchen utensils had been found covered in blood.

Control took command of the investigation himself and visited the house. He went through into the kitchen and sat at the table, glancing at his reflection. He knew that Milton had been sitting in the same chair a couple of hours earlier. He had operated on himself, cleaned the wound, and made it safe until he found someone that he could trust to do the job properly. He had showered, changed clothes, taken their car and fled. The police were looking for the vehicle, but they had not located it yet. It wouldn't matter. They would find it eventually, abandoned at the side of the road when Milton switched vehicles. It would be too late then. He would stay ahead of them unless he made a mistake or he chose to be found.

Control focussed on the screen again as the prosthesis was carefully placed into Twelve's wrecked joint.

John Milton was a chameleon. He had twenty years' experience of blending into the background, surfacing only to do the bloody work of his trade before sinking out of sight again. Control felt an icy knot in the pit of his stomach. Milton was the most dangerous man he had ever met, and now he knew that the State wanted him dead. He had no idea what he would do next, and that was the kind of thought that would keep a man up at night.

Chapter Fifty-Nine

THE MOTORWAY stretched away into the distance, the slow-moving row of tail lights painting a lazy swipe across the valley. There had been a crash outside Wolverhampton, and the traffic had backed up, filtering slowly through two lanes while the grim wreckage was craned away. Milton cursed the accident. He knew that it would only be a matter of time before the details of the stolen BMW were added to the national registry. The motorway was equipped with the CCTV masts that serviced the police's number-plate recognition system, and the longer he stayed on the road, the greater the chance that the car would be noticed. He felt vulnerable, and even though he knew it would make no difference, he tugged down the brim of the baseball cap he had found in the glove compartment so that his face was partially obscured.

He was tired, and his shoulder throbbed. He had been driving for three hours. His instinct was not to stop until he reached Manchester, but as he passed the sign advertising the services at Stafford South, he decided it was worth the risk for a strong cup of coffee.

Milton moved carefully into the crawler lane and pulled off the motorway.

The car park was quiet, a wide-open space lit by a series of tall overhead lights. Milton parked in a shadowed area and walked across to the complex of buildings. There were very few drivers around, a handful of red-eyed travellers drinking coffee in the small Starbucks concession. Milton bought a packet of Nurofen from WH Smith and then ordered a double espresso and a bottle of water from the bored-looking barista.

Milton looked up at the screen fixed to the wall. The BBC's rolling news channel was showing. He sipped from the Styrofoam cup as the anchor recapped the day's news. The riots were the main focus. The worst of the disturbances had abated, but the police were short-handed, and there was talk of calling in the army. Milton was stunned by their severity. Large parts of Croydon had been set alight, and a furniture store that he recognised had been razed to the ground by a ferocious blaze. There was footage from Hackney and Tottenham, crowds of rioters with scarves obscuring their faces, packs of looters that descended on retail parks and local businesses alike, taking whatever they could lay their hands upon. A police superintendent was interviewed, and promised that the culprits would be caught and punished. Milton thought of Elijah. Had they got to him in time?

"And in other news, police have launched a murder hunt after a man was found dead in the boxing club he ran in London's East End. Dennis Rutherford was found this evening by one of his students. He had been shot."

A picture of Rutherford was displayed. He was with a group of youngsters, holding a trophy and smiling into the camera. The picture switched to an outside broadcast. A reporter was standing in front of the boxing club, a policeman standing guard at the entrance.

The reporter spoke into the camera. "The Metropolitan police and London ambulance service were called here at 10.20pm, where the victim, from Hackney, was subsequently pronounced dead. A post-mortem is due to take place tomorrow, but it is understood that he died from a single gunshot wound. Police sources say that they want to speak to John Milton, last seen in the London area. He is described as a middle-aged white male, six foot tall, well built and with short dark hair. They recommend that he is not approached and that members of the public with information on his whereabouts should contact officers as soon as possible."

A head-and-shoulders picture of Milton flashed onto the screen. He recognised it: the picture had been taken from his Group file. Control was behaving exactly as he knew that he would. He would organise a manhunt, co-opting all the other agencies: the intelligence service, the police, everyone. His picture remained on the screen as the report continued. Milton looked around at the other customers anxiously. No one was paying the television much attention, but he replaced the cap on his head regardless.

He took his coffee with him and went back out into the hot night. The steady hum of the motorway was loud, the stand of trees that had been planted at the edge of the car park doing little to dampen the noise. Milton ignored the BMW. It had served him well, but he knew that it would have been reported by now. He found a spot that was poorly served by CCTV and approached a Ford Mondeo. He forced the door, slid inside, and hot-wired the engine.

The digital clock on the dashboard showed a little after three in the morning as he rejoined the motorway heading north. He passed through the gears, making sure to stay below the speed limit. In an hour and a half, the lights of Liverpool sparkled in the distance. Milton turned off the motorway and drove into town.

Saint Death

A John Milton Novel

Mark Dawson

"Put on the whole armour of the God, that ye may be able to stand against the wiles of the Devil / Because we wrestle not against flesh and blood, but against principalities, against powers, against the rulers of darkness of this world, against spiritual wickedness in high places."

Ephesians, Chapter 6, Verses 11 to 17

PROLOGUE

Samalayuca
South of Ciudad Juárez
Mexico

ADOLFO GONZÁLEZ lowered his AK, and the others did the same. They were stood in a semicircle, all around the three stalled trucks. There was no noise beyond the soporific buzz of the earth baking and cracking under the heat of the sun. Dust and heat shimmered everywhere. He looked out at their handiwork. The vehicles were smoking, bullet holes studded all the way across the sheetmetal. They were all shot up to high heaven. The windscreens had been staved in by the .416 calibre rounds that the snipers had fired. Some of the holes that ran across the cars were spaced and regular from the AKs, others were scattered with uneven clumps from number four buckshot. The Italians had come to the meet in their big, expensive four-wheel-drive Range Rovers. Tinted windows, leather interiors and xenon headlamps. Trying to make a big impression. Showing off. Hadn't done them much good. One of them had tried to drive away, but he hadn't got far. The tyres of the car were flat, still wheezing air. The glass was all shot out. Steam poured from the perforated bonnets.

Adolfo looked up at the hills. He knew Samalayuca like the back of his hand. His family had been using this spot for years. Perfect for dumping bodies. Perfect for ambushes. He'd put three of his best snipers up on the lava ridge. Half a mile away. They had prepared covered trenches and hid in them overnight. He could see them coming down the ridge now. The sun shone against the dark metal of their long-barrelled Barretts and reflected in glaring flickers from the glass in the sights.

He approached the nearest Range Rover, his automatic cradled at his waist. Things happened. Miracles. It paid to be careful. He opened the door. One of the Italians, slumped dead over the wheel, swung over to the side. Adolfo hauled his body out and dumped it in the dust. Bad luck, *pendejo*. There were two more bodies in the back.

Adolfo walked around the end of the truck. There was another body behind it, face up, mouth open. Vivid red blood soaked into the dirt. A cloud of hungry flies hovered over it.

He went to the second truck and looked through the window at the driver. This one had tried to get away. He was shot through the head. Blood everywhere: the dash, the seats, across what was left of the window.

He walked on to the third vehicle. Two men inside, both dead.

He walked back to the first truck to where the body lay.

He nudged the man's ribs with his toe.

The man moved his lips.

"What?"

The man wheezed something at him.

Adolfo knelt down. "I can't hear you."

"*Basta*," the man wheezed. "*Ferma*."

"Too late to stop, *cabrón*," Adolfo said. "You shoulda thought of that before."

He put the automatic down and gestured to Pablo. He had the video camera and was taking the footage that they would upload to YouTube later. Leave a message. Something to focus the mind. Pablo brought the camera over, still filming. Another man brought over a short-bladed machete. He gave it to him.

The dying man followed Adolfo with his eyes.

Adolfo signalled, and his men hauled the dying man to his knees. They dragged him across to a tree. There was blood on his face, and it slicked out from the bottom of his jacket. They looped a rope over a branch and tied one end around the man's ankles. They yanked on the other end so that he fell to his knees, and then they yanked again, and then again, until he was suspended upside down.

Adolfo took the machete with his right hand and, with his left, took a handful of the man's thick black hair and yanked back to expose his throat.

Adolfo stared into the camera.

He went to work.

DAY ONE

The City of Lost Girls

I have fought a good fight
I have finished my course
I have kept the faith

2 Timothy 4:7

From: <redacted>
To: <redacted>
Date: Monday, September 16, 5.21 P.M.
Subject: CARTWHEEL

Dear Foreign Secretary,

At our meeting last week you requested sight of a report detailing the circumstances in which the agent responsible for the botched assassination in the French Alps has disappeared.

I attach a copy of that report to this email.

While writing, please allow me to reiterate that all efforts are being made to locate and recover this agent. He will not be easy to find, for the reasons that we discussed, but please do be assured that he will not be able to stay undetected forever.

If there is any follow-up once you have considered this report, please do, as ever, let me know.

Sincerely,

M.

>>> BEGINS

* * * EYES ONLY * * *

CODE: G15
PUBLICATION: analysis/background
DESCRIPTION: n/a
ATTRIBUTION: internal
DISTRIBUTION: Alpha
SPECIAL HANDLING: Orange
CODENAME: "Cartwheel"

Summary

Following the unsatisfactory elimination of the Iranian nuclear scientists Yehya Moussa and Sameera Najeeb, John Milton (aka G15/No. 1/ aka "John Smith"/ aka "Cartwheel"), the agent responsible, has gone AWOL. Location presently undetermined. Milton is extremely dangerous and must be recovered without delay.

Analysis

>>>extracted

Control records that Milton evinced a desire to leave the service on returning to London following the completion of his assignment in France. The meeting is said to have been heated and ended with Milton being put on suspension prior to a full assessment and review.

<redacted>

His subsequent behaviour was observed to be erratic. He began to attend meetings of Alcoholics Anonymous (almost certainly in contravention of his obligations under the Official Secrets Act). He rented a house in a poor part of Hackney, East London, and is believed to have become emotionally involved with a single mother, Sharon Warriner. Our investigations are ongoing, but it is believed that he was attempting to assist Ms. Warriner's son, Elijah, who is believed to have been on the fringes of a local gang. We suspect that Milton was involved in the death of Israel Brown (the successful rapper who performed under the *nom de plume* of "Risky Bizness"), whom we understand to have been the prime mover in the relevant gang.

The order to decommission Milton was given on Monday, 15 August. A second G15 agent, Christopher Callan (aka G15/No. 12/"Tripwire"), had located Milton at a boxing club set up for local children by a Mr. Dennis Rutherford. As Callan was preparing to carry out his orders, he was disturbed by Mr. Rutherford. In the confusion that followed, Callan killed Mr. Rutherford and shot Milton in the shoulder. This was unfortunately not sufficient to subdue him, and he was able to overpower Callan—shooting him in the knee to prevent pursuit—and then make his escape. ANPR located him driving a stolen car northwards. The last sighting was on the M62 heading into Liverpool. The working hypothesis is that he boarded a ship to leave the country.

<redacted>

Analysis of Milton's psychological assessments (attached) suggests that his mental state has been deteriorating for some time. Feelings of guilt are not uncommon in Group 15 operatives, and Milton has worked there for a decade. It is regrettable that warning signs were missed, but perhaps understandable: Milton's performance has always been superb. He was perhaps the most effective of all our operatives. Subsequent analysis has led us to the conclusion that he is suffering from insomnia, depression and possible re-experiencing of past events. PTSD is a fashionable diagnosis to make, but it is one that we are now reasonably confident is accurate.

Regardless of his mental condition, Milton is far too dangerous to be ignored. He was a key part of several key British and NATO intelligence successes, not all of which have been reported in the press, and his value to the enemy is difficult to assess. The damage that he could do by going public is similarly incalculable.

>>> ENDS

From: <redacted>
To: <redacted>
Date: Wednesday, September 19, 5.21 P.M.
Subject: Re: CARTWHEEL

Dear M.,

Thank you for the report. I have shared it with the P.M., who is not, as you might well imagine, best pleased with its contents. You are to convey his displeasure to Control personally and to remind him that it is of the highest importance that Mr. Milton is located. We simply cannot have a man with his skills and knowledge running around outside of the reservation, as our American cousins would undoubtedly say. I am not sure which grubby little euphemism our mutual friend would prefer, but let's settle on "retirement."

<u>All due haste</u>, please.

Regards, etc.,

James

Chapter One

JOHN MILTON got off the bus and walked into the parking lot of the first restaurant that he found. It was a hot day, baking hot, brutally hot, the noon sun battering down on Ciudad Juárez as if it bore a grudge. The sudden heat hit him like a steel-yard furnace. The restaurant was set back from the road, behind a wide parking lot, the asphalt shimmering like the water in an aquarium. A large sign, suspended from a tall pole, announced the place as La Case del Mole. It was well located, on Col Chavena, and near to a highway off-ramp: just a few miles to the border from here, plenty close enough for the place to snag daring Americans coming south for a true taste of *la vida loca*. There were half a dozen similar places all around it. Brightly painted, practically falling to bits, garish neon signs left on day and night, a handful of cars parked haphazardly in the lot. Awful places, dreadful food, and not the sort of establishment that Milton would have chosen to visit. But they churned through the staff so fast that they were always looking for replacements, and they didn't tend to be too picky about who they hired. Ex-cons, vagabonds, vagrants, it didn't matter. And there would be no questions asked so long as you could cook.

Milton had worked in places like this all the way up through Mexico. He knew that they appealed to tourists and the uncritical highway trade and that this one, in particular, was still in business for three main reasons: It was better advertised than the tumbledown shacks and chain restaurants around it, the parking lot was big enough that it would be almost impossible to fill, and the daily seafood special was just $19.95, three dollars cheaper than the seafood special of any of the nearby competitors. Milton had worked in a place in Mazatlán until he had had to move on two weeks ago, and he was willing to bet that this would be just the same.

It would do him just fine.

He crossed the parking lot and went inside. The place really was a dive, worse when viewed in the middle of the day when the light that streamed through the grime-streaked windows revealed the peeling paint, the mice holes in the skirting, and the thick patina of dust that lay over everything. It was seven hundred miles west to the Pacific and eight hundred east to the Gulf, but the owner wasn't going to let small details like that dissuade him from the nautical theme he obviously hankered after: a ship's wheel, netting draped down from the walls, fronds of fake seaweed stapled to the net, lobster pots and shrimper's buoys dangling from the ceiling, a fetid and greening aquarium that separated the bar from the cavernous dining room beyond.

270

A woman was sitting at the bar, running a sweating bottle of Corona against the back of her neck.

"Hello."

She nodded in response: neither friendly nor hostile.

"Do you work here?"

"I ain't here for the good of my health, baby. What you want?"

"Came in to see if you were hiring."

"Depends what you do."

"I cook."

"Don't take this the wrong way, honey, but you don't look like no cook."

"I'm not bad. Give me a chance, and I'll show you."

"Ain't me you gonna have to show." She turned to the wide-open emptiness of the restaurant and hollered, "Gomez! New blood!"

Milton watched as a man came out of the back. He was big, fat and unhealthy, with a huge gut, short arms and legs, and an unshaved, pasty complexion. The T-shirt he was wearing was stretched tight around his barrel chest, and his apron was tied right to the limit of the strings. He smelt bad, unwashed and rancid from rotting food.

"What's your name?"

"Smith."

"You cook?"

"That's right."

"Where?"

"Wherever. I've been travelling up the coast. Ensenada, Mazatlán, Acapulco."

"And then Juárez? Not Tijuana?"

"Tijuana's too big. Too Californian."

"Last stop before America?"

"Maybe. Maybe not. Are you the owner?"

"Near enough for you, *cabrón*. That accent—what is it? Australian?"

"English. I'm from London."

Gomez took a beer from the fridge and cracked it open. "You want a beer, English?"

"No, thanks. I don't drink."

Gomez laughed at that, a sudden laugh up from the pit of his gut that wobbled his pendulous rolls of fat, his mouth so wide that Milton could see the black marks of his filled teeth. "You don't drink, and you say you want to work in my kitchen?" He laughed again, throwing his head all the way back. "Hombre, you either stupid or you ain't no cook like what I ever met."

"You won't have any problems with me."

"You work a fryer?"

"Of course, and whatever else you need doing."

"Lucky for you I just had a vacancy come up. My fry cook tripped and put his arm into the fryer all the way up to his elbow last night, stupid *bastardo*. Out of action for two months, they say. So maybe I give you a spin, see how you get on. Seven an hour, cash."

"Fifteen."

"In another life, *compadre*. Ten. And another ten says you won't still be here tomorrow."

Milton knew that ten was the going rate and that he wouldn't be able to advance it. "Deal."

"When can you start?"

"Tonight."

Chapter Two

MILTON ASKED Gomez to recommend a place to stay; the man's suggestion had come with a smirk. Milton quickly saw why: it was a hovel, a dozen men packed into a hostel that would have been barely big enough for half of them. He tossed his bag down on the filthy cot that he was assigned and showered in the foul and stained cubicle. He looked at his reflection in the cracked mirror: his beard was thick and full, the black silvered with flecks of white, and his skin had been tanned the kind of colour that six months on the road in South America would guarantee. The ink of the tattooed angel wings across his shoulders and down his back had faded a little, sunk down into the fresh nutty brown.

He went out again. He didn't care that he was leaving his things behind. He knew that the bag would be rifled for anything worth stealing, but that was fine; he had nothing of value, just a change of clothes and a couple of paperbacks. He travelled light. His passport was in his pocket. A couple of thousand dollars were pressed between its pages.

He took a scrap of paper from his pocket. He had been given it in Acapulco by an American lawyer who had washed up on the shores of the Pacific. The man used to live in New Mexico and had visited Juárez for work; he had been to meetings here and had written down the details. Milton asked a passer-by for directions and was told it was a twenty-minute walk.

He had time to kill. Time enough to orient himself properly. He set off.

Milton knew about Juárez. He knew it was the perfect place for him. It was battered and bloodied, somewhere where he could sink beneath the surface and disappear. Another traveller had left a Lonely Planet on the seat of the bus from Chihuahua, and Milton had read it cover to cover. The town had been busy and industrious once, home to a vibrant tourist industry as Texans were lured over the Rio Bravo by the promise of cheap souvenirs, Mexican exotica and margaritas by the jug (served younger than they would have been in El Paso's bars). There was still a tourist industry but the one-time flood of visitors had dwindled now to a trickle.

That was what the reputation of being the most murderous place on the planet would do to a town's attractiveness.

The town was full of the signs of a crippled and floundering economy. Milton passed the iron girder skeleton of a building, squares of tarpaulin flapping like loose skin, construction halted long ago. There were wrecked cars along the streets, many with bullet holes studding their bodywork and their windscreens shot out. Illicit outlets—*picaderos*—were marked out by shoes slung over nearby telegraph wires and their shifty proprietors sold cocaine, marijuana, synthetic drugs and heroin. Everything sweated under the broiling desert sun.

Milton walked on, passing into a residential district. The air sagged with dust and exhaust and the sweet stench of sewage. He looked down from the ridge of a precarious development above the sprawling *colonia* of Poniente. Grids of identical little houses, cheap and nasty, built to install factory workers who had previously lived in cardboard shacks. Rows upon rows of them were now vacant and ransacked, the workers unable to pay the meagre rent now that Asian labourers would accept even less than they would. Milton saw one street where an entire row had been burnt out, blackened ash rectangles marking where the walls had once stood. Others bore the painted tags of crack dens. These haphazard streets had been built on swampland, and the park that had been reserved for children was waterlogged; the remains of a set of swings rusted in the sun, piercing the muddy sod like the broken bones of a skeleton. Milton paused to survey the wide panorama: downtown El Paso just over the border; burgeoning breeze-block and cement housing slithering down into the valley to the south; and, in the *barrio*, dogs and children scattered among the streets, colourful washing drying on makeshift lines, radio masts whipping in the breeze, a lattice of outlaw electricity supply cables and satellite dishes fixed to the sides of metal shacks.

He reached the church in thirty minutes. It was surrounded by a high wire fence, and the gate was usually locked, necessary after thieves had broken in and made off with the collection one time too many. The sign hanging from the mesh was the same as the one Milton had seen around the world: two capitalised letter A's within a white triangle, itself within a blue circle. His first meeting, in London, seemed a lifetime ago now. He had been worried sick then: the threat of breaching the Official Secrets Act, the fear of the unknown, and, more, the fact that he would have to admit that he had a problem he couldn't solve on his own. He had dawdled for an hour before finding the guts to go inside, but that was more than two years ago now, and times had changed.

He went inside. A large room to the left had been turned into a crèche, where parents with jobs in the factories could abandon their children to listless games of tag, Rihanna videos on a broken-down TV and polystyrene plates divided into sections for beans, rice and a tortilla. The room where the meeting was being held was similarly basic. A table at the front, folding chairs arranged around it. Posters proclaimed the benefits of sobriety and how the twelve steps could get you there.

It had already started.

A dozen men sat quietly, drinking coffee from plastic mugs and listening to the speaker as he told his story. Milton took an empty seat near the back and listened. When the man had finished, the floor was opened for people to share their own stories.

Milton waited for a pause and then said, in his excellent Spanish, "My name is John, and I'm an alcoholic."

The others welcomed him and waited for him to speak.

"It's been 870 days since my last drink."

Applause.

"Why can't we drink like normal people? That's the question. It's guilt for me. That's not original, I know that, but that's why I drink. Some days, when I remember the things I used to drink to forget, it's all I can do to keep away from the bottle. I spent ten years doing a job where I did things that I'm not proud of. Bad things. Everyone I knew then used to drink. It was part of the culture. Eventually I realised why—we all felt guilty. I was ashamed, and I hated what I'd become. So I came to these rooms, and I worked through the steps, like we all have, and when I got to step four, "make a searching and fearless moral inventory," that was the hardest part. I didn't have enough paper to write down all the things that I've done. And then step eight, making amends to those people that you've harmed, and well, that's not always possible for me. Some of those people aren't around for me to apologise to. So what I decided to do instead was to help people. Try to make a difference. People who get dealt a bad hand, problems they can't take care of on their own, I thought maybe I could help them.

"There was this young single mother—this was back in London before I came out here. She was struggling with her boy. He was young and headstrong and on the cusp of doing something that would ruin the rest of his life. So I tried to help, and it all went wrong—I made mistakes, and they paid the price for them. That messed me up even more. When the first people I tried to help end up worse than when I found them, what am I supposed to do then?"

He paused, a catch in his throat. He hadn't spoken about Rutherford and Sharon before. Dead and burned. He blamed himself for both of them. Who else was there to blame? And Elijah. What chance did the boy have now after what had happened to him? He was the one who had found Rutherford's body.

"You can't blame yourself for everything," one of the others said.

Milton nodded, but he wasn't really listening. "I had to get out of the country. Get away from everything. Some people might say I'm running away from my problems. Maybe I am. I've been travelling. Six months, all the way through South America. I've helped a few people along the way. Small problems. Did my best, and by and large, I think I made a difference to them. But mostly it's been six months to think about things. Where my life's going. What I'm going to do with it. Do I know the answers yet? No, I don't. But maybe I'm closer to finding out."

Milton rested back in his chair: done. The others thanked him for his share. Another man started with his story. The meetings were meditative, a peaceful hour where he could shut out the clamour of the world outside.

Ignore his memories.

The blood on his hands.

He closed his eyes and let the words wash across him.

Chapter Three

THE MAN they called El Patrón was in his early seventies, but he looked younger. There had been a lot of plastic surgery in the last decade. That pig Calderon would have paid handsomely for his capture—the bounty was ten million dollars the last time he had checked—and it had been necessary for him to change the way he looked. The first few operations had been designed to do that: his nose had been reshaped, new hair had been transplanted onto his scalp, his teeth had been straightened and bleached. The recent operations were for the sake of vanity: wrinkles were pulled tight with a facelift, bimonthly Botox injections plumped his forehead, filler was injected into his cheeks. In a profession such as his, when Death was always so close at hand, it gave him a measure of satisfaction to be able—at least superficially—to thumb his nose at the passing of time.

His name was Felipe González, although no one outside of his family used it any more. He was El Patrón or, sometimes, El Padrino: the Godfather. He was of medium height, five foot eight, although he added an inch or two with Cuban-heeled boots. He had a stocky, powerful build, a bequest from his father, who had been a goatherd in the Sierra Madre Mountains, where he still maintained one of his many homes and where he had learned how to cook methamphetamine, cultivate the opium poppy crop, and move cargos without detection. He had large, labourer's hands, small dark eyes, and hair coloured the purest black, as black as ink or a raven's feathers.

He opened the door to the laboratory. The work was almost done. The equipment that he had been acquiring for the better part of six months—bought carefully, with discretion, from separate vendors across the world—had all been installed. The room was two thousand square feet, finished with freshly poured concrete floors and walls, everything kept as clean as could be. The largest piece of equipment was the 1200-litre reaction vessel, a huge stainless steel vat that had been positioned in the middle of the large space. There were separate vats for the other processes and a hydraulic press to finish the product. The top-of-the-line filtration system had been purchased from a medical research company in Switzerland and had cost a quarter of a million dollars alone. There were large tanks for the constituent parts: ephedrine, red phosphorous, caustic soda, hydrogen chloride, hydrochloric acid, ammonia hydroxide, and other chemicals that Felipe did not recognise nor was interested in understanding. The actual operation of the lab was not his concern. He had hired a chemist for that, a man from a blue-chip pharmaceutical company who felt that he was not receiving a salary commensurate with his talents. Felipe could assuage all doubts on that score. He would make him a millionaire.

Felipe considered himself an expert in the tastes and preferences of his clientele, and so far as he was concerned, meth was the drug of the future. He had been a little slow in getting into it, but that would all change now.

He had seen enough and went back outside. They were high in the mountains. The lab was stuffy, but the air was fresh and clean. It was a perfect spot for the operation: the only way to get to the lab was along a vertiginous road that wound its way around the face of the mountain, slowly ascending, an unguarded drop into a ravine on the right-hand side as the road climbed. There were shepherds and goatherds all along the route, each of them furnished with a walkie-talkie that Felipe had provided. In the unlikely event that an unknown vehicle attempted to reach the summit, they would call it in, and the *sicarios* who provided security for the laboratory would take to their posts and, if necessary, prevent further progress. The government made all the right noises about closing down operations like this one, but Felipe was not concerned. He knew the rhetoric was necessary for the public's consumption, but there would always be the cold, hard impracticality of putting those fine words into action. They would need helicopters and hundreds of men. It wasn't worth the effort.

His second-in-command, Pablo, was behind him. The man was as loyal as a dog, perhaps a little too enamoured of the white powder, but very dependable.

"It is done, El Patrón," he said.

"You have spoken to Adolfo?"

"I have."

"It was straightforward?"

"Apparently so. They killed them all. One of them was still alive. Adolfo cut off the man's head and posted the footage on YouTube."

Felipe tutted. His son had a weakness for the grand gesture. There was a time and a place for drama—it was practically de rigueur among the younger narcos these days—but Felipe preferred a little more discretion.

Pablo noticed his boss's disapproval. "It will be a message for the Italians."

"Yes," Felipe said shortly.

Pinche putas. Traitors. They had it coming.

La Frontera had been doing business with them for five years, and until recently, it had been a fruitful and mutually beneficial relationship. The Italians needed his drugs and his ability to get them over the border; he needed their distribution. In recent months, they had overestimated how much he needed them and underestimated how much they needed him. He had tried to make them understand, but they were stubborn and wrong-headed and kept asking for more. In the end, he had had to withdraw from the arrangement. It had to be final, and it needed to provide an idea of the consequences that would flow should they not accept his decision. For all his son's drama, at least that had been achieved.

"What about the gringos?"

"It is in hand," Pablo said. "The plane will collect them tomorrow morning. They will be in Juárez by the evening. I thought you could conclude the business with them there and then fly them here to see all this."

"They will be impressed, yes?"

"Of course, El Patrón. How could they not be?"

"Is there anything else?"

"There is one other thing, El Patrón. Your son says that they have located the journalists."

"Which? Remind me."

"The bloggers."

"Ah, yes." He remembered: those irritating articles, the ones that promised to cast light on their business. They had started to get noticed, at home and abroad, and that was not something that Felipe could allow to continue. "Who are they?"

"A man and a woman. Young. We have located the man."

"*Estúpido!* Take care of them, Pablo."

"It is in hand."

Chapter Four

CATERINA MORENO stared out into the endless desert, grit whipped into her face by the wind. It was just past dawn, and she was on the outskirts of Lomas de Poleo, a shanty that was itself in the hinterland of Ciudad Juárez. They had passed through a fence marked PRIVATE PROPERTY and out onto land that was known to have connections with La Frontera cartel. There were rumours that there was an airstrip here for the light planes that carried cocaine north into America and roads used by no one except the *traficantes*.

Caterina looked up into the crystal-clear blue sky and searched for the buzzards that would be circling over a possible cadaver.

She was standing with a group of thirty others, mostly women but a handful of men, too. They were from *Voces sin Echo*—Voices Without Echo—an action group that had been established to search for the bodies of the girls who were disappearing from the streets of Juárez. She was young and pretty, with her finely boned face and jet black hair just like her mother's, long and lustrous. Her eyes were large and green, capable of flashing with fire when her temper was roused. Her eyes were unfocussed now; she was thinking about the story she was halfway through writing, lost deep within angles and follow-ups and consequences.

She already had the title for the post.

The City of Lost Girls.

That was what some people were calling Juárez these days. It was Murder City, too, and people were dying in the drug wars every day, more than seven hundred this year already and not yet Easter. Caterina was obsessed with the drug wars; it was the bread and butter of Blog del Borderland: post after post about the dead, mutilated bodies left in plain sight on the city's waste ground, drive-by shootings with SUVs peppered with hundreds of bullets, babies boiled in drums of oil because their parents wouldn't do what they were told, bodies strung up from bridges and lamp posts. Grave pits were being dug up all around the city, dozens of bodies exhumed, the dead crawling out of their holes. And all the awful videos posted to YouTube and Facebook showing torture and dismemberment, warnings from one cartel to another, messages to the government and to the uncorrupted police and to the people of Mexico.

We are in control here.

We own this city.

Caterina reported on all of it, three thousand posts that had slowly gathered traction and gathered pace, so much so that Blog del Borderland was attracting a hundred thousand visitors every day. She had an audience now, and she was determined to educate it.

People had to know what was happening here.

The City of Lost Girls.

She kept coming back to it. The drug war was Juárez's dominant narrative, but there were other stories, too, drowned out in the static, stories within the story, and the one Caterina had found was the most compelling of them all. They were calling it *feminicidio*—femicide—the mass slaughter of women. In the last five years, three hundred women and girls—mostly girls, fifteen, sixteen years old—had been abducted as they made their way home from the *maquiladoras* that had sprung up like mushrooms along the southern banks of the Rio Bravo. The multinationals had hurried in under the auspices of one-sided trade agreements to exploit wages a fraction of what they would have to pay their workers north of the border. Sweatshops and factories staffed by young women who came from all over the country for the chance of a regular pay check and a better life. Women were favoured over men: their fingers were nimbler and more dextrous, and they could be paid even less.

These girls were nobodies, anonymous ghosts who moved through the city, barely disturbing its black waters. The kind of women who would not be missed. Some of them were abducted from the streets. Others were taken from bars, lured to hotels and clubs and other rendezvous, promised work or money or romance or just an evening when they could forget the mind-numbing drudgery of their workaday lives.

No one ever saw them alive again.

Their bodies were dumped without any attempt to hide them: on patches of waste ground, in culverts and ditches, tipped out of cars and left in the gutters. The killers did not care and made no attempt to hide their handiwork. They knew that they would not be caught. Not all of the missing were found, and desperate parents glued posters to bus shelters and against walls.

Caterina photographed the posters, published them all, noted down the names.

Alejandra.

Diana.

Maria.

Fernanda.

Paulina.

Adriana.

Mariana.

Valeria.

Marisol.

Marcella.

Esperanza.

Lupe.

Rafaela.

Aciano.

She had a notebook full of names, ages, dates.

This one was called Guillermina Marquez. She had worked for Capcom, one of the large multinationals who made transistors for Western appliances. She would normally have walked home from the bus stop with her friends, but the company had changed her shift, and she had walked alone. It was dusk; there should have been plenty of people to intervene, and police officers were around, including a special downtown patrol. But Guillermina disappeared. After she failed to return home, her mother went to the police. They shrugged and said that there was nothing they could do. Her mother made a thousand flysheets and posted them around the neighbourhood. Caterina had seen the posters and had interviewed the mother. She had posted an appeal for information on the blog, but nothing had come of any of it. And this was two weeks ago.

Caterina knew that they wouldn't find her this morning. Her body would appear, one day, in a place very much like this. She was here to write about the search. She took photographs of the participants scouring the dirty sand and the boiling rocks for anything that might bring some certainty to the idea that they must already have accepted: that the girl was dead.

Because only a handful of them ever came back alive.

They gave up the search for the morning and headed back to the place where they had parked their cars. Young women were emerging from their shacks and huts, huddling by the side of the road for the busses that would take them to the factories. As they passed through the fence again, Caterina watched a dirt-biker cutting through the dunes to intercept them, plumes of dust kicked up by his rear wheel. He rolled to a stop fifty feet away and removed his helmet. He was wearing a balaclava beneath it. He gunned the engine two times, drawing attention to himself, a reminder that they were trespassing and that they needed to get out.

Chapter Five

SIX HOURS LATER, Caterina sat in front of her laptop, willing a response to her last message. She bit her lip anxiously, but the cursor carried on blinking on and off, on and off, and the message did not come. She ran her fingers through her long dark hair, wincing as she stared at the screen. She had scared the girl off. She had pushed too hard, gone too fast, been too keen for her to tell her story, and now she had lost her.

Damn it. Damn it all. She kicked back, rolling her chair away from the desk a little, and stretched out her arms above her head. She was tired and stiff. She had spent eight hours at her desk, more or less, just a five-minute break to go and get lunchtime gorditas and quesadillas from the take-out around the corner, bringing them back and eating them right here. The papers were still on the floor, next to the overflowing bin where she had thrown them. Yesterday had been the same, and there had been little sleep during the night, either. When she was in the middle of a story like this, she allowed it to consume her. She knew it was a fault, but it was not one that she was prepared to correct. That was why she didn't have a boyfriend or a husband. It would take a very particular type of man—a very patient, very understanding man—to put up with a woman who could become so single-minded that she forgot to wash, to eat properly, to go out, to do anything that was not in the service of furthering the story.

But that was just how it had to be, she reminded herself.

The story was the most important thing.

People had to know.

The world had to know what was happening in Ciudad Juárez.

She did her work in the living room of her one-bedroom flat. The walls had been hung with large sheets of paper, each bearing scribbled ideas for stories, diagrams that established the hierarchy of the cartels. One sheet was a list of three hundred female names. There was a large map to the right of the desk, three hundred pins stuck into the wall to mark where the bodies had been found. Caterina's second-hand MacBook Pro sat amidst a whirlwind of papers, books and scrawled notes. An old and unreliable iMac, with an opened Wordpress document displayed, was perched on the corner of the desk. Minimised windows opened out onto search results pages and news stories, everything routed through the dark web to ensure that her presence was anonymous and untrackable. Caterina didn't know whether the cartels themselves were sophisticated enough to follow the footprints from the Blog del Borderland back to this flat in the *barrio*, but the government was, and since most of the government was in the pocket of the cartels, it did not pay her to be blasé. She was as sure as she could be: nothing she wrote could be traced, and her anonymity—shielded behind a series of online pseudonyms—was secure. It was liaisons like this one, with a frightened girl somewhere in the city, that were truly dangerous. She would have to break cover to write it up, and all she had to go on with regard to the girl's probity was her gut.

But the story was big. It was worth the risk.

She checked the screen.

Still nothing.

She heard the sound of children playing outside: "*Piedra, papel, tijeras, un, dos, tres!*" they called. Scissors, paper, stones. She got up and padded to the window. She was up high, third floor, and she looked down onto the neighbourhood. The kids were playing in front of the new church, the walls gleaming white and beautiful new red tiles on the domed roof. The money to build it came from the cartels. Today—and yesterday, and the day before that—a row of SUVs with tinted windows had been parked in front of the church, a line of men in DEA windcheaters going to and from the garden at the back of the house three doors down from her. She could see all the gardens from her window: the backs of the whitewashed houses, the unused barbeques, rusted satellite dishes, the kids' trampoline torn down the middle. The third garden along was dominated by pecan trees and an overgrown creosote bush. The men in the windcheaters were digging a deep pit next to the bush. Cadaver dogs sat guard next to the pit, their noses pointing straight down, tails wagging. Every hour they would pull another body out.

Caterina had already counted six body bags being ferried out.

Like they said.

Ciudad Juárez.

Murder City.

The City of Lost Girls.

She pulled her chair back to the desk and stared absently at the computer.

"I am here."

The cursor blinked at the end of the line.

Caterina sat bolt upright, beginning and deleting responses until she knew what to say.

"I know you're scared."

There was a pause, and then the letters tapped out, one by one, slow and uncertain: "How could you know?"

"I've spoken to other girls. Not many, but a few. You are not the first."

"Did they tell you they could describe them, too?"

"They couldn't."

"Then the stakes are much higher for me."

"I accept that."

"What would I have to do?"

284

"Just talk."

"And my name?"

"Everything is anonymous."

"I don't know."

"You're right to be scared. I'm scared, too. These men are dangerous. But you can trust me."

The cursor blinked on and off again. Caterina found she was holding her breath.

"If I come, it would just be to talk?"

"It would be whatever you want it to be. But talking is fine."

"Who would be there?"

"Me and my partner—he writes, too. You can trust him."

Another pause and Caterina wondered whether she should have said that it would just be her alone. Leon was a good man, but how was she to know that? A fear of men whom she did not know would be reasonable enough after what Delores had been through.

The characters flickered across the screen again. "I can choose where?"

"Wherever you want—but somewhere public would be best, yes?"

"La Case del Mole—do you know it?"

Caterina swept the papers from the iMac's keyboard and typed the name into Google. "The restaurant on Col Chavena?"

"Yes."

"I know it."

"I could meet you there."

"I'll book a table. My name is Caterina Moreno. I will be there from 8PM. Okay?"

There was no immediate reply.

And then, after a pause, three letters: "Yes."

Chapter Six

LIEUTENANT JESUS PLATO stopped at the door of his Dodge Charger police cruiser and turned back to his three-bedroom house on the outskirts of Juárez. His pregnant wife, Emelia, was at the door, with their youngest—Jesus Jr—in her arms. She was calling him.

"What is it?"

"Come here," she said.

He tossed his shoulder holster, the Glock safely clipped within it, onto the passenger seat, and went back to the house. "What did I forget?"

"Nothing," his wife said, "I did." She stood on tiptoes, and he bent a little so that she could plant a long kiss on his lips. "Be careful, Jesus. I don't want to hear about you taking any risks, not this week. Lord knows you've done enough of that."

"I know. I won't—no risks."

"You got a different life from next Monday. You got me and this one to think about, the girls, and the one on the way. If you get into trouble on your last week, it's going to be much worse as soon as you get back, all right? And look at that lawn—that's your first job, right there, first thing, you hear me?"

"Yes, *chica*," he said with an indulgent grin. The baby, just a year old, gurgled happily as Plato reached down and tickled him under the chin. He looked like his mother, lucky kid, those same big dark eyes that you could get lost in, the slender nose and the perfect buttery skin. He leant down again to kiss Emelia on the lips. "I'll be late back tonight, remember—Alameda and Sanchez are taking me out for dinner."

"They're just making sure you're definitely leaving. Don't go getting so drunk you wake the baby."

He grinned again. "No, *chica*."

He made his way back down the driveway, stopping where the boat he was restoring sat on its trailer. It was a standing joke between them: there he was, fixing up a boat, eight hundred miles from the coast. But it had been his father's, and he wanted to honour the old man's memory by doing a good job. One day, when he was retired, maybe he'd get to use it. Jesus had been brought up on the coast, and he had always hoped he might be able to return there one day. There would be a persuasion job to do with his wife, but when his job was finished, there would be little to hold them to Juárez. It was possible. He ran the tips of his fingers along the smooth wooden hull and thought of all the hours that he had spent replacing the panels, smoothing them, varnishing them. It had been his project for the last six months, and he was looking forward to being able to spend a little more time on it.

Another week or two of good, hard work—time he could dedicate to it without having to worry about his job—that ought to be enough to get it finished.

He returned to the cruiser and got inside. He pulled down the visor and looked at his reflection in the vanity mirror. He was on the wrong side of fifty now, and it showed. His skin was old and weathered, a collection of wrinkles gathered around the corners of his eyes. His hair was salt-and-pepper where it had once been jet black, and his moustache was almost entirely grey. Age, he thought, and doing the job he had been doing for thirty years. He could have made it easier on himself, taken the shortcuts that had been offered, made the struggle of paying the mortgage a little easier with the backhanders and bribes he could easily have taken. He could have avoided getting shot, avoided the dull throbbing ache that he felt in his shoulder whenever the temperature dipped. But Jesus Plato wasn't made that way, never had been and never would. Honour and dignity were watchwords that had been driven into him by his father, a good man who had also worked for the police, shot dead by a *sicario* around the time that it all started to go to hell, the time that dentist was shot to death. The rise of El Patrón and La Frontera. Plato had been a young cadet then, and while he had been green, he had not been blind. He could see that plenty of his colleagues had already been bought and sold by the narcos, but he vowed that he would never be the same as them, and thirty years later, he still wasn't.

He looked down and saw that Emelia was laughing at him, watching him stare at his own reflection. He waved her away with an amused flick of his hand and gunned the Dodge's big engine. One more week, he thought, flipping the visor back against the roof. He reversed off the drive and onto the street, his eye drawn to the overgrown lawn, and wondered if he could justify buying that new sit-down mower he had seen in The Home Depot the last time he had crossed over the bridge into El Paso. A retirement present for himself; he deserved it. Just five more days and then he could start to enjoy his life.

Chapter Seven

THE CALL had come through as Plato was cruising down the Avenida, Juárez's main drag. The street had two-storey buildings on each side, the once garish colours bleached out by the sun, the brickwork crumbling and broken windows sheltering behind boards that had themselves been daubed with graffiti. The shops that were still open catered to the baser instincts: gambling, liquor, whores. East of the main street was the red-light district, a confusing warren of unlit streets where if the unwary escaped after being relieved just of their wallets, then they were lucky. Plato had seen plenty of dead bodies in those dirty, narrow streets and the rooms with single bare light bulbs where the hookers turned their tricks. But then he had seen plenty of dead bodies, period.

The call had been a 415, just a disturbance, but Plato was only a couple of blocks away, and he had called back to say that he would handle it. He knew that if he took it, there would be less chance he would be assigned one of the day's 187s or 207s. Those were the calls you didn't want to get, the murders and the kidnappings that always turned into murders. Apart from the risk that the killers were still around—first responders had been shot many times—they were depressing, soul-sickening cases that were never really resolved, and the idea of having one or two of them on his docket when he finally hung it up wasn't the way he wanted to go out.

No, he reminded himself as he pulled the Dodge over to the kerb. Taking this call wasn't cowardice. It was common sense, and besides, hadn't he had more than his fair share of those over the years? He had lost count, especially recently.

The disturbance was on the street outside one of the strip clubs. Eduardo's: Plato knew it very well. Two college boys were being restrained by the bouncers from the club. One of the boys had a bloody nose.

Plato looked at the dash. Inside was sixty degrees. Outside was one hundred and ten. He sighed and stepped out of the air-conditioned cool and onto the street. The heat on his body hit him like a hammer.

"What's going on?" Plato asked, pointedly addressing the nearest bouncer first. It was a man he knew, "Tiny" Garcia, a colleague from years ago who had been chased out of the force for taking a cartel's money. Plato abhorred graft and despised the weakness in the man, but he knew that treating him respectfully was more likely to get him back to the station with the information that he wanted with the minimum of fuss.

"*Teniente*," the big man said. "How you doing?"

"Not bad, Tiny."

"You still in?"

"Only just. Coming to the end of the line. This time next week and I'll have my pension and I'm done."

"Good for you, brother. Best thing I ever did, getting out."

Plato looked at him, his shabby dress and the depressing bleakness of the Avenida, and knew that that was his pride talking.

"So—these two boys. What have we got?"

"A little drunk, a little free with their hands with one of the girls, you know what I mean, not like it's the first time. We ain't got many rules back in there, but that's one of them, no touching none of the girls at no time. She calls me over, and I say to them, nice and polite like you know I can be, I says to them that it's time to leave."

The boys snorted with derision. "That's not what happened," one of them said.

Plato nodded to the boy's bloodied face. "And his nose?"

"He didn't want to go, I guess. He threw a punch at me, I threw one back. I hit, he didn't."

"Bullshit!" the boy with the bloody nose spat out.

Plato looked at the two of them more carefully. They were well dressed, if a little the worse for wear. They had that preppy look about them: clothes from Gap, creases down the trousers, shirts that had been ironed, deck shoes that said they would be more at home crewing up a regatta schooner. Plato recognised it from the university at El Paso. A little too much money evident in their clothes and grooming, the supercilious way they looked at the locals. He'd seen it before, plenty of times. A couple of young boys, some money in their pocket and a plan to take a walk on the wild side of the border. They usually got into one sort of scrape or another. They'd end up in a rough, nasty dive like this, and then they didn't like it when they realised that they couldn't always get their own way. On this occasion, Plato knew that the boys had just been unlucky or tight. There was plenty of touching in Eduardo's, and a lot more besides that, if you were prepared to pay for it.

He shepherded them towards the Dodge. As they reached the kerb, one of them—blond, plenty of hair, good looks and a quarterback's physique—reached out and pressed his hand into Plato's. He felt something sharp pricking his palm. It was the edge of a banknote. He turned back to the boy and grasped it between thumb and forefinger.

"What is this?" Plato asked, holding up the note.

"It's whatever you want it to be, man."

"A bribe?"

"If you want."

"You've got to be kidding me. You're trying to buy me off?"

"It's a Benjamin, look! Come on, man! There's no need for all of this, right? A hundred bucks makes it all go away. I know how things work round here. I been here before, lots of times. I know the way the land lies."

"No," Plato said grimly. "You don't. You just made things worse. Turn around, both of you."

Garcia gave out a deep rumble of laughter. "They don't know who they're talking to, right, Jesus? You dumb fucks—I know this man, I worked with him. I doubt he's ever taken so much as a peso his whole life."

"Come on, man. I know we fucked up. What do we have to do to make it right? Two notes? Come on, two hundred bucks."

"Turn around," Plato said, laying his hand on the butt of the Glock.

"Come on, man—let's say three hundred and forget all about this."

"Turn around now."

The boy saw Plato wasn't going to budge, and his vapid stoner's grin curdled into something more malevolent. He craned his neck around as Plato firmly pressed him against the bonnet of the car. "What's the point of that? If you won't take my money, I know damn straight one of your buddies will. You *federales* are so bent you can't even piss straight; everyone knows it. You're turning down three hundred bucks bonus for what, your fucking *principles*? We all know it won't make a fucking bit of difference, not when it comes down to it. We'll be out of here and on our way back to civilisation before you've finished your shift and gone back to whatever shithole you crawled out of."

"Keep talking, son." Plato fastened the jaws of his cuffs around the boy's right wrist and then, yanking the arm harder than he had to, snapped the other cuff around the left wrist, too. The boy yelped in sudden pain; Plato didn't care about that. He opened the rear door, bounced the boy's head against the edge of the roof, and pushed him inside. He cuffed the second boy and did the same.

"Later, Garcia," he said to the big man as he shut the door.

"Keep your head down, Jesus."

"You too."

Chapter Eight

THE LEACH HOTEL in Douglas, Arizona, was a handsome relic from a different era. It had served an important purpose in the frontier years, the best place to stay in the last town before the lawlessness and violence of the borderlands. The hotel, built at the turn of the century, bore the name of the local dignitary for whom it was a labour of love. Mr. Robert E Leach was a southern nationalist, a supporter of slavery and, in later years, the US Ambassador to Mexico. It was Leach who, in 1853, had overseen the purchase of all land, including southern Arizona, south of the Gila River for the United States from the Mexicans. His hotel, a last beacon of respectability among the gun stores and bike repair shops of hard scrabble Cochise County, was the only monument to him now. It was still a fine building; it had seen better times, perhaps, but the Italian marble columns in the lobby and the marble staircase that curled up to the first floor were still impressing newcomers as they made their way to the reception desk to check in. The place was a relic of the Wild West, of Wyatt Earp and Geronimo, and the sounds of that time still echoed around the wood-panelled walls.

Beau Baxter knew everything there was to know about the Leach. He had a fondness for history, and the faded glamour of the hotel, the sense of a place caught out of time, appealed to him. This area of Cochise County had been frequented by desperados, including celebrities like Clay Hardin, who had killed forty men by the time he was forty years old, and Billy the Kid, who had laid twenty-one men in their graves by the time he was twenty-one. Local outlaws who had stayed in the hotel included Clay Allison, Luke Short, Johnny Ringo and Curly Bill Brocius. Beau had read up on all of them. And the great Pancho Villa was reputed to have ridden his horse right up the marble staircase.

He often met his clients here—those who didn't require him to travel to Houston or Dallas, anyway—and he had been pleased that the man who had asked to see him today had been conducting business on the border and had not been averse to coming to him.

Beau was in his early sixties, although he looked younger. His face was tanned and bore the traces of many dust storms and rancorous barroom brawls. He was wearing a light blue suit, nicely fitted, expensive looking. He wore a light blue shirt, a couple of buttons open at the throat, and snakeskin boots. He was sitting at a table in the lobby, his cream Stetson set on the table in front of him. The light was low, tinted green and blue by the stained-glass skylights that ran the length of the lobby.

A man was at the door, squinting into the hotel. He recognised his client:

he was a man of medium height, heavy build, olive brown skin and quick, suspicious eyes. His hair was arranged in a low quiff, a dye job with delicate splashes of silver on each side that made Beau think of a badger. He often dressed in bright shirts that Beau found a little distasteful. He did not know the man's full name—it wasn't particularly important—and he referred to himself just as Carlo. He was Italian, of a certain vintage, and belonged to a certain family of a certain criminal organisation. New Jersey. It was the kind of organisation about which one did not ask too many questions, and that suited Beau fine, too. They always paid their debts on time, and their money was just as good as anyone else's, as far as he was concerned.

He stood and held out his hand. "Carlo."

"Baxter. This is a nice place. Impressive. Is it authentic?"

"Been here nigh on a hundred years. I know they make a big play of it, but the history here's the real deal."

"Can't believe, all this time we been working together, you've never once brought me here."

Beau shrugged. "Well, you know—never had the opportunity, I guess."

They sat on a sofa in the corner of the lobby, and the man took out a brown envelope and set it on the table. "That's yours," he said. "Good job."

Beau took the envelope and opened it a little. He ran his finger against the thick bundle of notes inside. "Thank you." He folded the envelope and slipped it into the inside pocket of his jacket. "I hope you got what you wanted from our friend."

"We did. How did you find him?"

"What difference does it make?"

"I'm curious."

"You don't have to worry about that. That's why you pay me."

"A trade secret, Baxter?"

"Something like that." Beau smiled at him. "All right, then. You said you had something else?"

"Yes. But it's not easy."

"Ain't never easy, else anyone could do it. Who is it?"

Carlo took out his phone and scrolled through his pictures to the one that he wanted. He gave the phone to Beau. "You know him?"

He whistled through his teeth. "You ain't kidding this ain't going to be easy."

"You know him?"

"Unless I'm much mistaken, that's Adolfo González. Correct?"

"Correct. Know him by sight?"

"I believe so."

"Have you come across him before?"

"Now and again. Not directly."

"But you know his reputation?"

"I do."

"Is that a problem?"

"Not for me, maybe for you. A man like that's going to be mighty expensive."

"Go on."

Beau sucked air through his teeth as he thought. "Well, then, there's how difficult it'll be to get to him, and with the connections he has, I got to set a price that takes into account how dangerous it'll be for me both now and in the future if they ever find out it was me who went after him. That being said—I'd say we're looking at an even fifty, all-in. Half now, half later."

Beau found his eye drawn to the scruffy bush of chest hair that escaped from between the buttons of Carlo's patterned shirt. "Fifty?"

"Plus expenses."

"Fine."

"As easy as that?"

"You think you should have asked for more?"

"The price is the price."

"You can have the first twenty-five by two thirty."

"You got a hurry-up going on for this fellow, then?"

"How well do you know him?"

"I knew him when he was younger. Busted him coming over the border this one time."

"And what do you think?"

"If he was bad then, he's worse now."

"How bad?"

"I'd say he's a mean, psychopathic bastard. Want to tell me what he's done so that you want him so bad?"

"We had an arrangement with his old man—the buying and selling of certain merchandise. But then we had a problem: he changed the terms, made it uneconomic. We went to discuss it, and Señor González murdered six of my colleagues."

Beau remembered. "That thing down south of Juárez?"

Carlo spread his hands wide. "Let's say we would like to discuss that with him."

"Alive, then?"

"If you can. There'll be a bonus."

"Understood." Beau didn't need to enquire any more than that. He'd been working bounties long enough to reckon that revenge came in a lot of different flavours.

"Do you need anything else?"

"No, sir," Beau said. "That's plenty good enough."

"Then we're done." He rose. "Happy trails."

Beau followed him to his feet and collected his Stetson from the table. "You know what they call our boy over the border?"

Carlo shook his head.

Beau brushed the dust from his hat. "Oh yeah, this man, on account of his reputation, he's made quite the impression. Last time I heard anything about him they were calling him Santa Muerte."

"The wetbacks are superstitious fucks, Baxter."

"Maybe so. Fifty thousand? For a man like that, my friend, I'd say you've got yourself a bargain."

Chapter Nine

THE BORDER. They called it The Reaper's Line. Beau Baxter edged forward in the Cherokee. The checkpoint was busy today in both directions: trucks and cars and motorbikes heading south and a longer, denser line coming north. He looked at the trucks coming out of Juárez with a professional eye. How many of them were carrying drugs? Every tenth truck? Every twentieth? Vacuum-packed packets of cocaine dipped in chemicals to put the dogs off the scent. Packets stacked in secret cavities, stuffed in false bumpers, hidden amongst legitimate cargo. Billions of dollars.

Beau regarded the high fence, the watchtowers and the spotlights. It had changed a lot over the years. He had been working the border for all of his adult life. He had graduated from the Border Patrol Academy in 1975 and had been stationed in Douglas. His work had taken him across the continent and then to the Caribbean in the immigration service's anti-drugs task force, eventually returning him full circle. For two decades, he had been a customs special agent in this wild and untamed corner of the frontier, patrolling the border on horseback, a shotgun strapped onto his saddle.

He looked out at the guards circulating between the cars and trucks. Those boys doing the job today would have thought he was an anachronism, relying on a horse when he could have had one of the brand-new Jeeps they were driving around in. He could read the signs that told him exactly when movement occurred, whether his quarry was near or far.

But Beau was a realist, too, and he knew that time had moved on. A man like him was from a different era. He'd fought regular battles with the narco traffickers of Agua Prieta over the border. During his career, he had seen the territory between Nogales and Arizona's eastern border with New Mexico become known as "cocaine alley" and then quickly get worse. Juárez was the worst of all. The dirty little border *pueblo* was a place where greed, corruption and murder had flourished like tumbleweed seeds in souring horse manure. Now, with the cartels as vast and organised as multinationals, with their killing put onto an industrial scale and with the bloodshed soaking into the sand, Beau was glad to be out of it. In comparison to that line of work, hunting down bounties was a walk in the park.

But perhaps not this one.

His thoughts went to Adolfo González. On reflection, fifty grand was probably a generous quote for a job that was fixing to be particularly difficult.

He had heard about the six dead Italians on the news this morning. Ambushed in the desert, shot to shit, and left out for the vultures. He had seen the video on YouTube before it had been taken down. He recognised

Adolfo's voice. The cartels were all bad news, but La Frontera was the worst. Animals. And Adolfo was the worst of all. Getting him back across the border wasn't going to be easy.

He wondered whether he should have turned the job down.

There were easier ways to make a living.

He edged the Jeep forwards again and braked at the open window of the kiosk.

"Ten dollars," the attendant said.

Beau handed it over.

"Welcome to Mexico."

He drove south.

Chapter Ten

MILTON PAUSED in the restaurant's locker room to grab an apron and a chef's jacket. He sat down on the wooden bench and smoked a cigarette.

He changed and went through into the kitchen.

It was a big space, open to the restaurant on one side. The equipment was a mixture of old and new, but mostly old: four big steam tables; three partially rusted hobs; two old and battered steamers at the far end of the line; three side-by-side, gas-fired charcoal grills with salamander broilers fixed alongside; a flattop griddle. The double-wide fryer was where he would be working. The equipment was unreliable, and the surfaces were nicked and dented from the blows of a hundred frustrated chefs. Most of the heat came from two enormous radiant ovens and two convection units next to the fryer station. A row of long heat lamps swung to and fro from greasy cables over the aluminium pass. It was already hot.

Gomez came in and immediately banged a wooden spoon against the pass. "Pay attention, you sons of bitches. We got a busy night coming up. No one gets paid unless I think they're pulling their weight, and if anyone faints, that's an immediate twenty-percent deduction for every ten minutes they're not on their feet. And on top of all that, we got ourselves a newbie to play with. Hand up, English."

Milton did as he was told. The others looked at him with a mixture of ennui and hostility. A new cook, someone none of them had ever seen working before, no one to vouch for him. What would happen if he wasn't cut out for it, if he passed out in the heat? He would leave them a man down, the rest hopelessly trying to keep pace as the orders piled up on the rail. Milton had already assessed them: a big Mexican, heavily muscled and covered in prison tattoos; a sous chef with an obvious drinking problem who lived in his car; a cook with needle scars on his arm and a T-shirt that read BORN FREE – TAXED TO DEATH; and an American ex-soldier with a blond Vanilla Ice flattop.

"Our man English says he's been working up and down the coast, says he knows what he's doing. That right, English?"

"That's right."

"We'll see about that," Gomez said with a self-satisfied smirk, his crossed arms resting on the wide shelf of his belly.

Milton went back and forth between the storeroom, the cold cupboard and his station, hauling in the ingredients that he knew he would need. He looked around at the others methodically going through the same routine that they would have repeated night after night in a hundred different restaurants: getting their towels ready, stacking their pans right up close so that they could get to them in a hurry, sharpening their knives and slotting them into blocks, drinking as much water as they could manage.

The front-of-house girl who Milton had met earlier put her head through the kitchen's swing door. "Hey, Gomez," Milton heard her call out. "Coach of gringo tourists outside. Driver says can we fit them in? I said we're pretty full, but I'd ask anyway—what you wanna do?"

"Find the space."

The machine began rattling out orders. Milton gritted his teeth, ready to dive into the middle of it all. The first time he had felt the anticipation was in a tiny, understaffed restaurant in Campo Bravo, Brazil. He needed a way to forget himself, that had been the thing that he had returned to over and over as he worked the boat coming over, the desire to erase his memories, even if it was only temporary. After five minutes in that first restaurant he had known that it was as good a way as any. A busy kitchen was the best distraction he had ever found. Somewhere so busy, so hectic, so chaotic, somewhere where there was no time to think about anything other than the job at hand.

The first orders had barely been cleared before the next round had arrived, and they hadn't even started to prepare those before another set spewed out of the ticket machine, and then another, and another. The machine didn't stop. The paper strip grew long, drooping like a tongue, spooling out and down onto the floor. They could easily look out into the restaurant from the kitchen, and they could see that the big room was packed out. It got worse and worse and worse. Milton worked hard, concentrating on the tasks in front of him, trying to adapt to the unpleasant sensation that there suddenly wasn't enough air on the line for all of them to breathe. Within minutes he felt like he was baking, sweat pouring out into his whites, slicking the spaces beneath his arms, the small of his back, his crotch. His boots felt like they were filling with sweat. It ran into his eyes, and he cranked the ventilation hood all the way to its maximum, but with it pumping out the air at full blast, the pilots on his unused burners were quickly blown out. He had to keep relighting them, the gas taps left open as he smacked a pan down on the grate at an angle, hard enough to draw a spark.

The floor was quickly ankle-deep in mess: scraps of food that they swept off the counters, torn packaging, dropped utensils, filthy towels; it was all beneath the sill of the window and invisible from the restaurant, so Gomez didn't care. Still the heat rose higher and higher. Milton stripped out of his chef coat and T-shirt because the water in them had started to boil.

It was hard work, unbelievably hard, but Milton had been doing it for months now, and he quickly fell into the routine. The craziness of it, the random orders that spilled from the machine, the unexpected disasters that had to be negotiated, the blistering heat and the mind-bending adrenaline highs, the tunnel vision, the relentless focus, the crashing din, the screams and curses as cooks forgot saucepan handles were red-hot. The rest of his world fell away and everything that he was running away from became insignificant and, for that small parcel of a few hours at the end of a long day, for those few hours, at least, it was all out of mind and almost forgotten.

Chapter Eleven

CATERINA SAT on the bus and stared through the cracked window as they moved slowly through the city. It was getting late, seven in the evening, yet the sun still baked at ninety, and Juárez quivered under the withering blows of summer, a storm threatening to blow in from the north, tempers running high. A steady hum of traffic rose from the nearby interstate, and the hot air blowing in through the open windows tasted of chemicals, car exhaust, refinery fumes, the gasses from the smelter on the other side of the border, and the raw sewage seeping into what was left of the river. The bus was full as people made their way out for the evening.

Caterina had made an effort as she left the flat, showering and washing her hair and picking out a laundered shirt to go with the jeans and sneakers she always wore.

She was thinking about all the girls that she had been writing about. Delores was different. She had dodged the fate that had befallen the others. She had managed to escape, and she was willing to talk.

And she said she could identify one of them men who had taken her.

The brakes wheezed as the bus pulled over to the kerb and slowed to a halt. Caterina pulled herself upright, and with her laptop and her notes in the rucksack that she carried over her shoulder, she made her way down the gangway, stepping over the outstretched legs of the other passengers, and climbed down to the pavement. The heat washed over her like water, torpid and sluggish, heavy like Jell-O, and it took a moment to adjust. The restaurant was a hundred yards away, an island in the middle of a large parking lot, beneath the twenty-foot pole suspending the neon sign that announced it.

Leon was waiting for her. She stepped around a vendor with a stack of papers on his head and went across to him.

"This better be good," he said, a smile ameliorating the faux sternness of his greeting. "I had tickets for the Indios tonight."

"I would never let you pick football over this."

"It's good?"

"This is it. The story I want us to tell."

She was excited, garbling a little and giddy with enthusiasm. Leon was good for her when it came to that. She needed to be calm, and he was steady and reliable. Sensible. It seemed to come off him in gentle waves. Smiling with a warm-hearted indulgence she had seen many times before, he rested his hands on her shoulders. "Take a deep breath, *mi cielo*, okay? You don't want to frighten the poor girl away."

She allowed herself to relax and smiled into Leon's face. It was a kind face, his dark eyes full of humanity, and there was a wisdom there that made him older than his years. He was the only man she had ever met who could do that to her; he was able to cut through the noise and static of Juárez, her single-minded dedication to the blog and the need to tell the story of the city and its bloodied streets, and remind her that other things were important. They had dated for six months until they had both realised that their relationship would never be the most important thing in her life. They had cooled it before it could develop further, the emotional damage far less than it would have been if it had been allowed to follow its course. There were still nights when, after they had written stories into the small hours, he would stay with her rather than risk the dangerous journey home across the city, and on those nights, they would make love with an appetite that had not been allowed to be blunted by familiarity. Being with Leon was the best way to forget about all the dead bodies in the ground, the dozens of missing women, the forest of shrines that sprouted across the wastelands and parks, the culverts and trash heaps.

"Are you ready?" he asked her.

"Let's go."

DELORES KEPT them waiting for fifteen minutes, and when she eventually made her way across the busy restaurant to them, she did so with a crippling insecurity and a look of the sheerest fright on her face. She was a small, slight girl, surely much younger than the twenty years she had claimed when they were chatting earlier. Caterina would have guessed at fourteen or fifteen, a waif. She was slender and flat chested, florid acne marked her face, and she walked with a slight but discernible limp. She was dressed in a *maquiladora* uniform: cheap, faded jeans that had been patched several times, a plain shirt, a crucifix around her neck. Caterina smiled broadly as she neared, but the girl's face did not break free of its grim cast.

"I'm Caterina," she said, getting up and holding out her hand.

"Delores," she said quietly. Her grip was limp and damp.

"This is my colleague, Leon."

Leon shook her hand, too, then pulled a chair out and pushed it gently back as Delores rather reluctantly sat.

"Can I order you a drink? A glass of water?"

"No, thank you." She looked around the room, nervous, like a rabbit after it has sensed the approach of a hawk. "You weren't followed?"

"No," Caterina said, smiling broadly, trying to reassure the girl. "And we'll be fine here. It's busy. Three friends having a meal and a talk. All right?"

"I'm sorry, but if you think a busy restaurant would stop them if they had a mind to kill you, then you are more naïve than you think."

"I'm sorry," Caterina said. "I didn't mean to be dismissive. You're right."

"Caterina and I have been working to publicise the cartels for two years," Leon said. "We know what they're capable of, but you're safe with us tonight. They don't know our faces."

Delores flinched as the waiter came to take their orders. Caterina asked for two beers, a glass of orange juice and a selection of appetisers—tostadas, cheese-stuffed jalapenos, enchilada meatballs and nachos—and sent him away. She took out her notebook and scrabbled around in her handbag for a Biro. She found one and then her Dictaphone. She took it out and laid it on the table between them.

"Do you mind?" she asked. "It's good to have a record."

Delores shook her head. "But no photographs."

"Of course not. Let's get started."

Chapter Twelve

LIEUTENANT JESUS PLATO decided that the two gringo college boys needed to cool their heels for the night. They were becoming boisterous and disruptive when he brought them back to the station to book them, and so, to make a point, he chose to delay the fine he had decided to give them until tomorrow. They could spend the night in the drunk tank with the junkies, the tweakers and the boozers; he was confident that they would be suitably apologetic when he returned in the morning. And besides, he did not particularly want to go to the effort of writing them up tonight. He was tired, and he had promised Alameda and Sanchez that he would go out with them for something to eat. The meal was a self-justifying camouflage, of course; the real purpose was to go out and get drunk, and he had no doubt that they would end up on the banks of the Rio Bravo, drinking tins of Tecate and throwing the empties into what passed for the river around here. Plato had been on the dusty street all day, more or less; he certainly had a thirst.

His shift had been straightforward after booking the two boys. He had pulled over a rental car driven by a fat American sweating profusely through layers of fat and the synthetic fibres of his Spurs basketball shirt, a pimpled teen beauty in the seat next to him with her slender hand on his flabby knee. A warning from Plato was all it took for him to reach over and open the door, banishing the girl as he cursed the end of the evening that he had planned. The girl swore at Plato, her promised twenty bucks going up in smoke, but she had relented by the time he bought her a Happy Meal at the drive-thru on the way home. He had finished up by writing tickets for the youngsters racing their souped-up Toyota Camrys and VW Golfs tricked-out with bulbous hubcaps and tweaked engines, low-slung so that the chassis drew sparks from the asphalt. They, too, had cursed him, an obligatory response that he had ignored. They had spun their wheels as he drove off, melting the rubber into the road, and he had ignored that, too.

Captain Alameda waved him across to his office.

"Your last week, *compadre*," he said.

"Tell me about it."

"How was today?"

"Quiet, for a change. Couple of drunk gringo kids. Thought a couple of hundred bucks would persuade me to let them off."

"They picked the wrong man, then. Where are they?"

"In the cells. I'll see if they've found some manners tomorrow."

"You heard about what happened at Samalayuca?"

"Just over the radio. What was it?"

"Six men. They didn't even bother to bury them. Shot them and left them out in the desert for the vultures."

"Six? *Mierda.* We know who they are?"

"American passports. The *federales* will look into it."

Plato slumped into the seat opposite the desk.

"Jesus?"

"I'm fine." He sighed. "Just tired is all. How is it here?"

"Twenty-eight no-shows today. Worst so far."

Plato knew the reason; everyone did. Three weeks ago, a wreath had been left on the memorial outside police headquarters on Valle Del Cedro Avenue. A flap of cardboard, torn from a box, had been fastened around the memorial with chicken wire. It was a notice, and written on it were two lists. The first, headed by FOR THOSE WHO DID NOT BELIEVE, contained the names of the fifteen police officers who had been slain by the cartels since the turn of the year. The second, FOR THOSE WHO CONTINUE WITHOUT BELIEVING, listed another twenty men. That section ended with another message: THANK YOU FOR WAITING. The wreath and the notice had been removed as quickly as they had been found but not before someone had snapped them with their smartphone and posted it on Facebook.

The press got hold of it, and then everyone knew.

It had terrified the men.

"Twenty on long-term sick now. Stress. Another fifteen won't go out on patrol. It's not safe, apparently."

"Ten men for the whole district, then?"

"Nine."

"*Hijo de puta.*"

"Halfway to last year's murders and it's only just turned Easter. You're getting out at the right time, *compadre.*"

"Feels like I'm abandoning you."

Alameda chuckled. "You've done your time, Jesus. If I see you here next week, I'll arrest you myself."

"What about you?"

"If a transfer came up? I'd probably take it."

"If not?"

"What else can I do? Just keep my head down and hope for the best."

Plato nodded. It was depressing. There was a lot of guilt. He couldn't deny that. But, and not for the first time, he was grateful his time was up.

"You ready for that beer?" Alameda asked.

"Let me get changed. Ten minutes?"

"I'll get Sanchez and see you outside."

Plato went into the locker room and took off his uniform, tracing his finger across the stencilled POLICIA MUNICIPAL that denoted him as a member of the *municipio*, the local police force that was—laughably, he thought—charged with preventing crime. There was no time to be doing any of that, not when there was always another murder to attend to, another abduction, and then the flotsam and jetsam like the two drunken college boys from this afternoon. Prevention. That was a fine word, but not one that he recognised any more. He had once, perhaps, but not for many years.

The cartels had seen to that.

He clocked out, collected his leather jacket from the locker room, and followed Alameda and Sanchez to the restaurant.

Chapter Thirteen

THE GIRL talked in a quiet voice, her hands fluttering in her lap, her eyes staring down at the table except when they nervously flicked up to the entrance. Caterina took notes. Leon sat and listened.

"I moved to Juárez from Guadalajara for a job," she said. "It was in one of the *maquiladoras* on the banks of the river. Making electrical components for an American corporation. Fans for computers. Heat sinks and capacitors. I started work there when I was fourteen years old. A year ago. They paid me fifty-five dollars a week, and I sent all of it back to my mother and father. Occasionally, I would keep a dollar or two so that I could go out with my friends—soda, something to eat. It was hard work. Very hard. Long hours, no air-conditioning, so it got hot even by nine or ten in the morning. Complicated pieces to put together. Sometimes the parts would be sharp, and when you got tired—and you *always* got tired—then they would cut your fingers. I worked from seven in the morning until eight at night. Everything was monitored: how fast you were working, the time you spent on your lunch, the time you spent in the bathroom. They would dock your pay if they thought you were taking too long. None of us liked the job, but it was money, better money than I could get anywhere else, so I knew I had to work hard to make sure they didn't replace me.

"It wasn't just the work itself, though. There were problems with the bosses—there are more women than men in the factories, and they think it is all right for them to hit on us and that we should be flattered by it, give them what they want. The bosses have cars, and the women never do. Some girls go with the bosses so that they can get rides to work. It's safer than the busses. I never did that."

"They hit on you?"

"Of course."

"But you were fourteen."

"You think they care about that?" Delores smiled a bitter smile. "I was old enough." She sipped at the glass of orange juice that Caterina had bought for her. "They have those busses, the old American ones, the yellow and black ones they use to take their children to school. They were hot and smelly, and they broke down all the time, but it was better than walking and safer, too, once the girls started to disappear. I had a place in Lomas de Poleo—you know it?"

"I do." It was a shanty of dwellings spread in high desert a few miles west of Juárez. Caterina had been there plenty with the *Voces sin Echo*.

"It was just a bed, sharing with six other girls who worked in the same *maquiladora* as I did. The bus picked us up at six in the morning and took us up to the river; then, when we were finished at eight or nine, then they would take us back again."

Caterina's pen flashed across her pad. She looked at the recorder, checking that it was working properly. "What happened to you?"

"This was a Friday. The other girls were going out, but I was tired and I had no money, so I told them I would go home. The bus usually dropped us off in Anapra. The place I was staying was a mile from there, down an unlit dirt track, and it was dark that night, lots of clouds and no moon, darker than it usually was. I was always nervous, and there were usually six of us, but I was on my own, and it was worse. I got off the bus and watched it drive up the hill and then walked quickly. There was a car on the same side of the street as me. I remember the lights were on and the engine was still running. I crossed to the other side of the street to avoid it, but before I could get there, a man came up from behind me, put his hand over my mouth, and dragged me into the car. He was much stronger than I am. There was nothing I could do."

"Where did they take you?"

"There is a bar in Altavista with a very cheap hotel behind it where the men take the women that they have paid for. They took me there. They put me in a room, tied my hands and my feet, and left me on the bed. There was another girl there, too, on the other bed. She had been taken the night before, I think. She was tied down, like me. There was blood. Her eyes were open, but they did not focus on anything. She just stared at the ceiling. I tried to speak to her, but she did not respond. I tried again, but it was no use—she would not speak, let alone tell me her name or where she was from or what had happened to her. So I screamed and screamed until my throat was dry, but no one came. I could hear the music from the bar, and then, when that was quiet, I could hear noises from the other rooms that made me want to be quiet. There were other girls, I think. I never saw any of them, but I heard them. I must have been there for two or three hours before he came in."

"Just one?"

"Yes. I don't know if it was the same one who took me. I can remember him and yet *not* remember him, if you know what I mean. He was nothing special, by which I mean there was nothing about him that you would find particularly memorable. Neither tall nor short, neither fat nor thin. Normal looking. Normal clothes. He reminded me of the father of a girl I went to school with when I was younger. He was a nice man, the father of my friend. I hoped that maybe this man would be nice, too, or at least not as bad as I expected. But he was not like him at all. He was not nice."

"You don't have to tell me what happened."

But she did. She drew a breath and explained, looking down at the table all the time. She was a little vague, relying on euphemism, but Caterina was able to complete the details that she left out. Delores's bravery filled her with fury. She gripped her pen tighter and tighter until her knuckles were pale against the tanned skin on the back of her right hand. A fourteen-year-old girl. Fourteen. She vowed, for the hundredth time, the thousandth, that she would expose the men who were responsible for this. She did not care about her own safety. The only thing that mattered was that they were shamed and punished. Now that she had her blog and the thousands of readers who came to read about the disintegration of Juárez, now she was not just another protester. She had influence and power. People paid attention when she wrote things. This would be the biggest story yet.

Femicide.

The City of Lost Girls.

She would make them listen, and things would be done.

"How did you get away?"

"He untied my hands while he—you know—and then he did not tie them again when he went to use the bathroom. I suppose he was confident in himself, and he had made it plain that they would kill me if I tried to run. I knew that my prayers had been answered then and that I had been given a chance to escape, but at first, I did not think that my body would allow me to take advantage of it. It was as if all of the strength in my legs had been taken away. I think it was because I was frightened of what they would do to me if they caught me. I know that is not rational, and I know that they would have killed me if I had stayed—I knew about the missing girls, of course, like everyone does—but despite that, it was as much as I could do to take my clothes and get off the bed."

"But you did."

"Eventually, yes. I tried to get the other girl to get up too, but she told me to leave her alone. It was the first thing she had said to me all that time. She looked at me as if I had done something terribly wrong. She was still tied, too, and I am not sure I would have been able to free her, but it would not have mattered—she did not want to leave. I opened the door—he had not locked it—and I ran. I ran as fast as I could. I ran all the way to the Avenue Azucenas, and I found a policeman. I did not know if I could trust him, but I had no other choice. I was lucky. He was a good man. One of the few. He took me to the police station, away from there."

"Do you know his name?"

"The policeman? Yes—it was Plato. I think his first name was Jesus."

"And the man in the hotel?"

"I do not know his real name. But he liked to talk, all the time he would talk to me and the other girl, and this one time, just before I escaped, he told me about the things that he did for the cartels. He said his father was an important man in El Frontera and that he was a killer for them, a *sicario*, but not just any *sicario*—he said that he was the best, the most dangerous man in all of Juárez. He said that he had killed a thousand men and that, because he was so dangerous, the men who worked with him had given him a name. 'Santa Muerte.'"

Caterina wrote that down in her notebook, underlining it six times.

Santa Muerte.

Holy Death.

Saint Death.

Chapter Fourteen

"SO, OLD MAN—you going to stay in Juárez?"

Plato looked at Alameda and then at Sanchez. They had been goofing around all evening—mostly at Plato's expense, about how it felt to be so old—and this felt like the first proper, serious question. "I don't know," he said after a moment. "The girls are settled here, they got their friends, they're in a decent school. The little one's just been born; do I want to put him through the hassle of moving? There's another one on the way. The wife was born here, her old man's in a home half a mile from the house."

"Come on, man," Sanchez said. "Seriously?"

And Plato admitted to himself then that he had already decided. Ciudad Juárez was no place to bring up a family. Forty years ago, when he was coming up, even twenty years ago when he was starting to do well in the police, maybe he could've made a case that things would have been all right. But now? No, he couldn't say that. He'd seen too much. He had investigated eleven killings himself this month: the man in the Ford Galaxy who was gunned down at a stop sign; three beaten and tortured municipal cops found in the park; a man who was executed, shot in the head; and six narcos shot to pieces in the *barrio* by the army. In the early days, at the start, he had kept a list in a book, hidden it in the shed at the bottom of the garden. They called it Murder City for a reason. It took him two months to learn and give up.

"Maybe," he said.

"Maybe?" Alameda tweaked the end of his long moustache. "You ask me, Jesus, you'd be out of your mind if you stay here. Think what it'll be like when your girls are all grown. Or Jesus Jr, you want him hanging out on the corners when he gets a little hair on his chin? I'm telling you, man, as soon as I got my pension I'm getting the family together and we are out of here, as far away as we can."

"Me too," Sanchez said. "I've got family in New Mexico."

"Yeah, I guess we will move," Plato admitted. "I fancy the coast. Down south, maybe."

"Get to use that boat you're wasting all your time on."

"That did cross my mind."

Sanchez got up. "I'm gonna drain the lizard."

Alameda got up, too, indicating the three empty glasses. "Another?"

He watched Alameda and Sanchez as they made their way across the restaurant, Alameda heading to the bar and Sanchez for the restroom. They had chosen La Case del Mole tonight. It was a decent enough joint. The food was a little better than average, the beer was reasonably priced and plenty

310

strong enough, and the owner—a fat little gringo from El Paso—owed the police a favour, so there would always be a hefty markdown on the bill at the end of the night.

He relaxed in his chair, stretching out his legs so that the ache in his muscles might ease a little. He was getting old, no point hiding it. It had been a long day, too, and if those two had their way, it would be a long night. He thought of his wife trying to get the two girls to behave while she struggled to get the baby to settle, and then feeding them, the chaos of bedtime, and then tidying the house, and for a moment, he felt guilty. He should get home; there were chores to be done, there were always chores, and it wasn't fair to live it up here with the boys and leave her to do everything herself. But then he caught himself; there wouldn't be many more chances to do this, to knock off after a shift and have a beer to wind down, maybe stop at a taco stand and shoot the breeze. He would keep in touch with his old colleagues, that was for sure, but it would be different when he was a civilian. He should enjoy himself. Emelia didn't mind. And she'd given him a pass.

It was almost nine, and as he waited for the busboy to clear the plates away so they could get down to the serious drinking, he idly played with his empty glass and looked out into the parking lot outside. Darkness was falling, the sodium oranges and reds slowly darkening, and the big overhead lights were on. A nice new SUV rolled in, an Audi Q5, the same model that he had had his eye on for a while, the one he knew he probably couldn't afford. He took in the details: silver, El Paso plates, premium trim, nearly a hundred grand if you bought it new. The truck stopped, not in a bay but right out in front of the restaurant, and Plato sat up a little in his chair. The engine was still running—he could see the smoke trailing out of the exhaust—and the doors on both sides slid open, four men getting out, too dark and too far away for him to see their faces well enough to remember them. There was something about the way they moved that he had seen before: not running but not walking either, quick, purposeful. He didn't even notice that he had stopped trailing his finger around the rim of the beer glass, that his hand had cautiously gone to his hip, that his thumb and forefinger were fretting with the clip on the holstered Glock.

Plato heard a woman's voice protesting, saying, "No, no," and then the crisp thud of a punch and something falling to the floor. The men were into the restaurant now, all four of them, fanning out around the room, each of them with something metallic in their hands. Plato had seen enough firearms in his time to pick them all out: two of them had machine pistols, Uzis or Mac-10s, another had a semi-automatic Desert Eagle, and the last one, keeping watch at the door, had an AK-47. Plato had unfastened the clip now, his hand settling around the butt of the Glock, the handgun cold and final in the palm of his hot hand. He looked around, knowing that there were fractions of seconds before the shooting started, looking for Alameda or

Sanchez or anyone else who might be able to back him up, but Sanchez was still in the john, and Alameda had his back to him, facing the bar. The other diners, those that had seen the newcomers and recognised what was about to go down, were looking away, terrified, frozen to their chairs and praying that it wasn't them.

Twenty feet away to Plato's left, a fifth man rose from his seat. He recognised him: his name was Machichi. He was a mouthy braggart, early twenties, with oily brown shoulder-length hair and a high-cheekboned Apache face. Two yellow, snaggled buck teeth protruded from beneath a scraggly moustache and an equally scrubby goatee. Machichi had a small Saturday night special in his hand, and he pointed to the table a couple away to his left. Plato knew what was playing out: Machichi was the tail-man, his job was to ID the targets so the others could do the shooting. They were *sicarios*: cartel killers, murderers for El Patrón. But their targets didn't look like narcos. It was just a table of three: two young women and a man. One of the women—pretty, with long dark hair—saw Machichi and his revolver, shouted, "No," and dragged the other woman away from the table, away from the *sicarios*.

Plato felt a pang of regret as he pulled the Glock and pushed his chair away. One week to go, less than a week until he could hang it up, and now this? Didn't God just have the wickedest sense of humour? He thought of Emelia and the girls and little Jesus Jr as he stood and aimed the gun.

"Drop your weapons!"

The *sicario* with the AK fired into the restaurant, hardly even aiming, and Plato felt his guts start to go as slugs whistled past his head. A woman at the next table wasn't so lucky: her face blew up as the hollow point mashed into her forehead, blood spraying behind her as her neck cracked backwards and she slid from her chair. Plato hid behind the table, the cold finger of the Glock's barrel pressed up against his cheek. He hadn't even managed to get a shot off, and now he knew he never would. He couldn't move. Emelia's words this morning were in his head, he couldn't get them out, and they had taken the strength from his legs. He knew he was probably being flanked, the man with the rifle opening an angle to put him out of his misery. Plato knew it would be his wife's words that would be repeating in his head when the bullets found their marks.

Be careful, Jesus.

You got a different life from next Monday.

It was crazy: he thought of the lawn and how it would never get cut.

Gunfire.

The *tic-tic-tic* of the machine pistols.

A jagged, ripping volley from the Kalashnikov.

Screams.

The man who was with the two women had been hit. He staggered against his toppled chair, leaning over, his hand pressed to his gut, then wobbled across the room until he was at Plato's table. Blood on his shirt, pumping between his fingers. He reached for the table, his face white and full of fear, and then his hand slipped away from the edge and he was on his knees, and then on his face, his body twitching. Plato could have reached out to touch him.

He was facing at an angle away from the kitchen, but he glimpsed something move in the corner of his eye, cranked his head around in that direction and saw a cook, covered in sweat and shirtless save for a dirty apron, vaulting quickly over the sill of the wide window that opened onto the restaurant. The man moved with nimble agility, landing in a deep crouch and bringing up his right hand in a sudden, fluid motion. Plato saw a pair of angel wings tattooed across his back as his right arm blurred up and then down, something glinting in his hand and, then, leaving his hand. That glint spun through the air as if the man had unleashed a perfect fastball, like Pedro Martinez at the top of the ninth, two men down, the bases loaded. The kitchen knife—for that was what it was—landed in Machichi's throat.

He dropped his revolver and tottered backwards, clawing at the blade that had bisected his gullet.

It was the spur Plato needed: he spun up and around, firing the Glock. The *sicario* with the Kalashnikov took a round in the shoulder and wheeled away, wild return fire going high and wide, stitching a jagged trail into the fishing net that was hanging from the ceiling. Sanchez appeared and fired from the doorway to the restroom; Alameda was nowhere to be seen. All the diners were on the floor now; the cook fast-crawled on his belly between them, a beeline to the man with the Kalashnikov and, with a butterfly knife that had appeared in his hand, he reached down and slit the man's throat from ear to ear. He picked up the AK.

He popped out of cover, the muzzle flashing.

One of the *sicarios* was hit, his head jerking back.

The cook was beneath the line of the tables, firing a quick burst that left most of the top of the man smeared across the carpet and the wall behind him. The gun made a throaty chugging sound. Like someone with a hacking cough.

The remaining pair scrambled back to the door. Plato watched through the restaurant's large picture window as they hurried to the Q5. The cook stepped around to the window. The car was just fifteen feet away outside. The cook raised the Kalashnikov, calm and easy, braced the stock expertly against his shoulder, and fired a concentrated volley straight through the window. The pane shattered in an avalanche of shards, the bullets puncturing the driver-side window, none going astray, all of them within a neat ten-inch circle.

The car swerved out of control and hit another. The door swung open. The airbags had deployed. The driver fell out, his head a bloody mess. The passenger was hit, too.

Plato brought up his Glock and aimed at the cook.

"Police! Get down, Señor! Down! On the floor!"

The man got to his knees, put the Kalashnikov on the carpet, then lay down.

Chapter Fifteen

MILTON HAD lost track of time. Suddenly, there had been sirens, police, ambulances. Six men and two women were dead. It was obvious who the gunmen had been after: two of the dead were from the same table. The police fussed around the bodies, taking photographs and judging trajectories, and then, when they were done, the paramedics were called over to lift the dead onto gurneys, covering their faces as they hauled them away. Milton was detained by the older, silver-haired municipal cop who had shot the gunman with the Kalashnikov; he was a little plump around the middle, the wrong side of fifty, and he had the smell of alcohol on his breath. The man told him to get a shirt, told him he was going to have to come back to the station with him to give a statement. Milton said that wasn't necessary, he could just do it there and then, but the cop had been insistent. Then, when they had arrived, he had insisted that he be photographed and have his fingerprints taken. Milton said he wasn't a criminal. The cop said maybe, but he just had his word for that. Milton could have overpowered him easily and could have gotten away, sunk under the surface again, but there was something about the cop that said he could trust him and something about the night itself that said he better stick around.

He let them take their photographs, front and profile. He let them take his prints.

The man was sitting in front of him now.

"So—you're Mr."—he looked down at his notes—"Smith. Right?"

"That's right."

"First name John. Correct?"

"Correct."

"John Smith? Really?"

"Yes, really."

"All right then, Señor Smith. Sorry about bringing you down here."

"That's all right. Why don't you tell me what you want?"

"I just wanted to visit with you a little bit. Talk to you about what happened. That was some trick with the knife. What are you, ex-military?"

"I'm just a cook."

"Really? You don't look like a cook."

"So you say. But that's what I am."

"Don't know many cooks who can handle a Kalashnikov like that, either."

"Lucky shot, I guess." The man shrugged. "Who are you?"

"Lieutenant Jesus Plato. Where you from?"

"England."

"Of course you are. That's a fine accent you got there."

"Thank you very much."

"You want to tell me what happened back there, Señor Smith?"

"You saw it just about as well as I did."

"Why don't you tell me—give me your perspective."

"I was in the kitchen, and I heard shooting. No one seemed to be doing anything much about it."

"And so you did."

"That's right."

"Seriously, Señor, please—you must have been a soldier at some point?"

"A long time ago."

"Don't think I'm ungrateful—you saved my life and plenty of others in that room. It's just—"

"It's just that you have to make a report. It's fine, Lieutenant. Ask your questions. I understand."

"You want a drink of water?"

"I'm fine," Milton said.

"Smoke?"

He nodded.

Plato took out a packet of Luckies and tapped out two cigarettes. Milton took one and let the man light it for him.

Plato inhaled deeply. "You know who those men were?"

"Never seen them before."

"Those boys were from the cartel La Frontera. You'll have heard of them, no doubt."

"A little."

"A word of advice, John. Do you mind if I call you John?"

"If you like."

"Keep your eyes open, all right, John? What you did back there, that's like poking a stick in a termites' nest. People round here, they learned a long time ago that it's best not to fight back when the *sicarios* come around. It's better to let them get on with their business and pray to whatever God it is you pray to that it's not your name they got on their list."

"Let them kill?"

"Most people couldn't make the kind of difference you made."

"I couldn't just stand aside and do nothing, Lieutenant."

"I know. I'm just saying—be careful."

"Thanks. I'll bear that in mind." He drew down on the cigarette, the tobacco crackling. "Who were they after?"

"We're not sure yet."

"But you think it was the kids on the table?"

"Most likely. They missed one of them. Probably thanks to you."

"The girl."

"Yes."

"Was she hit?"

"In the shoulder. She'll live."

"But she's not safe, is she?"

"No."

"What's her name?"

"You know I can't tell you that."

"Where is she?"

"I can't tell you that, either. It's confidential. I've already said more than I should've."

He leant forwards. "You won't be able to keep her safe, will you?"

"Probably not."

"I can, Lieutenant."

"I doubt that."

"I can."

"How long have you been in Juárez?"

"Just got into town today."

"You know what it's like here? You know anything about La Frontera?"

"This isn't my first dance." He rested both forearms on the table and looked right into Plato's eyes. "I can help. I know what they've done to the police. I know about the messages they hang off the bridges when they leave their bodies, I know about the threats they make on police radio, and I know they've got a list with your names on it. I saw what that means tonight. There were three of you. Only you and one of your colleagues did anything at all. The other one was hiding behind the bar."

"This might not be your first dance, John, but if you haven't been to Juárez before, I can guarantee you that you haven't seen anything like the cartels." As he spoke, he took out a notebook from his breast pocket and turned to a page near the back. He wrote quickly, then turned it upside down and left it on the table between them. "You sure you don't want that drink of water? I know I do. Dying of thirst here."

"That's not such a bad idea. I would. Thanks."

"All right, then. I'll be right back."

Plato went out. Milton took the notebook and turned it over.

There were two lines of writing in Plato's untidy scrawl.

Caterina Moreno.

Hospital San José.

Chapter Sixteen

EL PATRÓN made it a habit to dress well, and this morning, his tailor had presented him with a fine new suit. It was cut from the most luxurious fabric—slate grey with the faintest pinstripe running through it—and it had been fitted expertly, measured to fit his barrel-like frame. His snakeskin boots disturbed small clouds of dust as he disembarked from the armour-plated Bentley, nodding to his chauffeur and setting off for the restaurant. Six of his bodyguards had already fanned out around the street, armed with a variety of automatic weapons. They would wait here while he ate. No one else would be allowed to go inside.

The place had been open for six months and was already the finest in Juárez. That was, perhaps, not the most impressive of accolades since local restaurants did not tend to last very long before they were shot up or firebombed or the management was murdered, but that was all beside the point; it had a fine reputation for its cuisine. Felipe considered himself something of a gourmet, and it was his habit to try all of the best new places. Now, with business to attend to in the city, he had the perfect excuse. He did not often venture down from the sixty thousand square miles of land he owned in the Sierra, not least because the vast space, the battery of gunmen and the fealty of the locals made it an almost impregnable redoubt. But this business was important, and it needed his attention.

The other members of his retinue had already been inside to inform the proprietor that El Patrón would be dining with them tonight. They had collected the cell phones of the other customers and staff and told them—politely but firmly—that no one would be allowed to leave until El Patrón had finished his meal. Of course, no one had protested. As compensation for their inconvenience, their meals would all be paid for. A couple celebrating their marriage had reserved the best table in the house, but they had needed little persuasion that it was in their best interests to move. The room was silent save for the muffled noise of the busy kitchen and the crisp retorts of Felipe's raised heels as they struck the polished wooden floorboards. He went from table to table, beaming his high-voltage smile at each of his fellow diners, clasping the hands of the men and kissing the women on both cheeks. He introduced himself to them and apologised for their inconvenience. They looked at him with fear or admiration or both; the power of his reputation gave him enormous pleasure. El Patrón was almost a mythical figure in Mexico, his exploits the subject of countless ballads and stories. He had outlived enemies and accomplices alike, defying the accepted bargain of a life in the drug trade: your career might be glittering, but it would be brief, and it would always end in prison or the grave.

Not for him.

He left the newlyweds until last. He stood beside their table and treated them to a wide, white-toothed smile.

"Do you know who I am?"

"Yes," the man said. His fear was evident, although he was trying to hide it. "You are El Patrón."

"That is right. I am. And I understand that you are celebrating your marriage?"

"Yes."

"Congratulations. May I ask, when was the happy day?"

"Yesterday."

"And you are not on honeymoon?"

"Money is difficult," the woman said.

Felipe took out the bankroll that he kept in the inside pocket. He had heard that one of his lieutenants had joked that the roll was thick enough to choke a pig, and it probably was. He removed the money clip and started to count notes from the roll—each was a $100 bill—got to twenty and then stopped. Smiling widely, knowing that everyone in the restaurant was watching his display of munificence, he put the roll on the table. He did not know precisely how much money there was—ten thousand, at least—but it didn't matter. Felipe González was responsible for over half of the illegal narcotics imported into the United States every year. He had appeared in Forbes' annual billionaires list. Ten thousand dollars was nothing to him. Chump change.

"Congratulations," he said. "You must take a holiday. You are only married one time, after all."

The woman looked ready to refuse his offer. "Thank you," her husband said quickly before she could speak. He did not want to displease him with ingratitude. He glared at her, and his message understood, her frown became an uneasy smile.

"You are very welcome."

His son, Adolfo González, was waiting for him at the table.

He rose. "*Padre*."

"Adolfo." Felipe hugged him. He was impetuous and prone to dangerous predilections, but he was still his son, and he loved him. There were other children—other brothers, even—but Adolfo was his oldest still alive and the only one who was born of his first wife. The boy reminded him of her often: she had been impetuous and wild, too, a seventeen-year-old beauty from a village near to his in the heart of the Sierra. She had been the most beautiful girl he had ever laid eyes upon, and his wedding day had been the happiest of his life. That it did not last did not sour the affection he felt for her whenever he recalled her memory. She had eventually become a little too wild, a little too free with her affections and too loose with her tongue, and he had been left with no other option than to do away with her. They had dissolved her body in a vat of hydrochloric acid and poured her into the river.

Adolfo and Raymondo had been twins. Raymondo was the oldest, and as such, he had been the real apple of his father's eye. He had arrived ten minutes before his twin, a protracted delivery that was contrasted by the ease with which Adolfo had followed. Felipe often joked to his wives that that had been the first indication of his character; if he could, Adolfo would always let someone else do all the hard work for him. Raymondo had been shot dead by the army two years ago. Felipe knew that the older boy had exercised a degree of control over his brother. Adolfo had reacted badly to his death, and that, combined with the sudden removal of his brother's restraint, had led to all this blessed nonsense with the girls.

"It is good to see you, *Padre*."

Felipe sat and made busy with the menu. "Have you eaten here before?"

"When it opened."

"What is good?"

"The steak. Excellent. And we should get some wine. They have a very well-stocked cellar."

He summoned the waiter and ordered an especially fine Burgundy. The man offered to pour, but Felipe dismissed him.

"Adolfo," he began, pouring for his son, "there are things we need to discuss."

"Yes, *Padre*."

"The Italians?"

"*Pendejos!* It was easy. No survivors."

"Good."

"Have they tried to contact you?"

"No," Felipe said. "And they won't."

He looked at the boy. He was wide-eyed and avid, desperate for his approval. He wondered, sometimes, if that need was the reason for the way he was. Amongst other things, the men called him *El Más Loco*.

The Craziest One.

"You did well, Adolfo. I couldn't have asked for more. But tonight?"

He frowned. "Yes. I know."

"What happened?"

"I'm as unhappy as you, *Padre*."

"That is doubtful."

"I'm still trying to find out."

"Were you there?"

"No."

"She was just a girl. It is a simple thing, is it not?"

"It should have been simple."

"And yet it wasn't."

"She has been difficult to find. Her *culo* boyfriend was less careful. We have been following him, and he led us to her. There was a third person, a girl; they were meeting her there—another of her stories, no doubt. I put five men on the job. Good men. They have always been reliable. As you say, it should have been easy. They went into the restaurant, but as they were carrying out their orders, they were attacked."

"By whom?"

Adolfo could not hide his awkwardness. "One of the cooks."

"A *cook*, Adolfo?"

"At first. And then two policemen."

"This cook—who is he?"

"I'm going to visit the proprietor. I'll know more after I have spoken with him. Whoever this *puto* is, he isn't just a cook. He threw a knife halfway across the room and hit Javier, and then he knew how to use an AK. I'm thinking he was a soldier."

"And the police?"

"They will be easier to find. Don't worry—they will all be punished."

"Make sure that they are. They work *for* us, Adolfo, not *against* us. Remind them. Make an example out of them."

"I will."

"It is important, Adolfo. I'm meeting the gringos tomorrow. They are cautious men. There must not be any doubt that we are in control. This kind of fuck-up makes us look bad. If they think we cannot get rid of a journalist who has been writing about us, how will they trust us to control this *plaza*? Do you understand?"

He looked crestfallen. "Yes."

He steepled his fingers and looked over them at his son, his brows lowering, his Botoxed forehead crinkling a little into what passed for a frown. "This whole mess would have been unnecessary if it wasn't for your"—he searched for the right word, each one more distasteful than the last—"*problem*. I will hear no more excuses about it; it has to stop. I've told you too many times already. Do you understand me?"

"Yes, *Padre*. It will—it has. No more."

"Very good. You have money, connections, power—you don't need to take your women. They will come to you." Felipe looked up; the waiter was at the edge of the room, shuffling nervously from foot to foot. Felipe smiled and beckoned him over. "Now then. Shall we order?"

Chapter Seventeen

LATER THAT NIGHT, smelling like grease and blood and cigarettes, Milton stepped out of the police station and stood with his back to the wall for a quiet smoke. There, away from the noise of the kitchen, the snarled abuse in the holding pens, the smell of gunpowder, away from the familiarity of boiling fat and plates that burned to the touch, away from the sudden shock of violence and death, all of reality came crashing back in on him.

Here was only the night, the dark, the fecund stink of uncollected trash and the distant highway roar, the ticking sound as the earth gave up the stored heat of the day, the wet pressure of breathing in the humid soup and the fat black cockroaches that crawled through the gutters. The night was warm and fuzzy from the refinery stacks on the other side of the border, from street dust and smoke. The low sky glowed orange. Milton knew that he had travelled far from London and what had happened there, far away from his job and the blood that still dripped from his hands. Suddenly, the thought of going back to the squalid dormitory room with the other men, of smoking cigarettes through the window, trying to read his paperbacks in the glow of his torch or watching Mexican football on Telemundo, too exhausted to sleep, was not what he wanted to do at all. Standing rigid, eyes aching, feet throbbing, blood humming in the hollows behind his ears to fill the sudden quiet, he stared up into the night and the stars, and decided. He pushed himself off the wall. He would get as much sleep as he could, and then, first thing tomorrow, he would head for Hospital San José.

That girl, whoever she was, was in trouble.

And he was going to help.

DAY TWO

"Just a Cook"

Chapter Eighteen

"TAKE A SEAT, Miss Thackeray," the man said.

Anna Thackeray did as she was told. The office was impressive, well appointed, spacious and furnished in the tastefully understated fashion that said that money had not constrained the choices that had been made. There was a wide picture window that offered a view of the Thames toiling sluggishly under a gunmetal grey sky. The room was light and airy. Military prints on the walls. Silver trophies and two photographs in luxurious leather frames: one was of the man on the other side of the desk in his younger days, in full battle dress; the other was of a woman and three children. A central table held a bowl of flowers, and there were two comfortable club chairs on either side of an empty fireplace.

The international HQ for Global Logistics was on the same side of the Thames as the more imposing building in Vauxhall where the important decisions were taken, but that was as far as the similarities went. It was built in the sixties, with that decade's preference for function over form, constructed from red brick and concrete, its anonymous five floors all rather squat and dowdy when compared to the Regency splendour of its neighbours or the statement buildings of government that had been constructed more recently. A grand terrace had been smashed down the middle by a three-hundred-pound Luftwaffe bomb, and this unpromising building had eventually sprouted from the weed-strewn bombsite that had been left. The windows were obscured with Venetian blinds that had been allowed to fade in the sunlight; the staircase that ascended the spine of the building was whitewashed concrete and bare light bulbs; the lift—when it worked—was a dusty box with four walls of faux wooden panels and dusty mirror. And yet the drab obscurity of the building was perfect to cloak its real purpose. The government organisation that did its work here lived in the shadows, a collection of operatives that was secret to all but those with the highest security clearances.

Anna had never even heard of it until yesterday, and she prided herself in knowing *everything*.

"You asked to see me, sir?"

His codename was Control. Only a handful of people knew his real name, and even fewer his background. He was a plump, toad-like man, dressed with the immaculate good taste of the best class of public schoolboy. A well-tailored suit, an inch of creamy white cuff, a regimental tie fastened with a brass pin. His hands were fleshy, his glistening nails bearing the unmistakeable signs of a recent manicure. Anna found that, above everything else, rather distasteful. He was oleaginous and slippery, undoubtedly brilliant but as far removed from trustworthiness as it was possible to be. That, of course, made him ideal for his position. Like the building from which he worked, he was perfect for his purpose. Control commanded Group Fifteen, otherwise known as the Section, Pegasus and the Department. He supervised two hundred civil servants, mostly seconded from MI5, MI6 and the Foreign Office, analysts and spooks that were simply the network that facilitated the work of the twelve men and women who carried out the jobs that Group Fifteen was allocated. When the government found itself with a particularly intractable problem and every other route had failed—commercial, diplomatic, political—Group Fifteen would occasionally be put out into the field. And, for them, all solutions were in play.

"Thank you for coming to see me, Miss Thackeray," Control said.

"Not a problem, sir."

She tried to project a feeling of ease, but she did not find that simple to do. The occasion was not suited to that, for one, and the formality of the place bothered her. She had already made more concessions than she was comfortable with making: she had removed her earrings, scrubbed the black nail varnish from her fingers and borrowed a trouser suit and a shirt. And of course, there was her hair. She had dyed it red over the weekend, and she was damned if she was going to spend the night before this meeting changing it to something more ... conservative.

There were limits.

"Everything I tell you this morning is beyond top secret—I'm sure that goes without saying?"

"It does."

"Very good. I'll be as brief as I can be. Six months ago, one of our most valuable agents went AWOL. Have you read the file?"

"Yes—John Milton."

"Indeed. It is our belief that Mr. Milton suffered a mental breakdown following an unsuccessful operation in France. The decision had been taken to bring him in for observation and treatment, but as one of our agents approached him for that purpose, he opened fire on him. A member of the public was killed, and the agent was badly wounded. We suppressed that from the report for obvious reasons."

"Yes."

"Following those events, Milton has dropped off the grid. We tracked him north to Liverpool, and our working assumption is that he either found work on a boat or stowed away on one. The trail went cold from there, and we have seen neither hide nor hair of him since. That is a state of affairs that we cannot allow to stand. Mr. Milton was our most experienced operative. He has intimate, first-hand knowledge of operations that would cause the government enormous embarrassment if their existence was ever to be disclosed, and that's not even considering the operational knowledge that would be of great interest to our enemies—and to our friends."

"You want me to find him."

"We do. We've been working with your department for some time but, so far, with disappointing results. Your predecessor made no headway, so he has been reassigned, and you are replacing him. I understand from your supervisor that you're the best analyst that GCHQ has to offer."

"No question."

"You don't suffer from false modesty, do you?"

"I don't see the point in it."

"You might come to wish you had been more circumspect because now I expect you to meet with more success." He sipped at his cup of tea; Anna found the sight of his pursed, fleshy lips nauseating.

"I have the file. Is there anything else I need to know?"

"You should be under no disillusions here: John Milton has been trained to be totally invisible. His profession for ten years was to be a ghost. He has operated in some of the most inhospitable, dangerous places you can imagine—if he was not as good at this as he is, he would have been captured and killed years ago. He is not married, he has no children, he has no real friends. No ties, not to anyone or anything. It will not be an easy task to find him, but I must re-emphasise: he *must* be found. This could be the making of your career or"—he paused and spread his hands—"not. Do I make myself clear?"

The implication was very clear.

Find him, or else.

"You do," she said.

Chapter Nineteen

IT WAS early the next day when Anna stooped to position her eye over the iris scanner, the laser combing up and down and left to right before her identity was confirmed and the gate opened to allow her inside. The guard, his SA80 machine gun slung loose across his shoulder, smiled a greeting as she passed him. An exhibit in the main entrance hall contained treasures from the history of British code-breaking: the Enigma machine was her favourite, but she passed it without looking and went through the further two checks before she was properly inside. GCHQ had the feel of a bustling modern airport, with open-plan offices leading off a circular thoroughfare that was known as the Street, offering cafés, a bar, a restaurant and a gym. Anna walked to the store and bought a copy of the *Times* and a large skinny latte with an extra shot of espresso.

Most of the staff were dressed conservatively; the squares on their morning commute might have mistaken them for workers on their way in to the office. Suits and blouses, all very proper. But they would not have mistaken Anna like that. She wasn't interested in conformity, and since she was not ambitious and didn't care whether she impressed anyone or not, she wore whatever made her comfortable. She was wearing a grey Ministry T-shirt, a black skirt, a battered black leather jacket, ripped Converse All-Stars and red tights. She cocked an eyebrow at the attendant working at the X-ray portal; the man, beyond the point of being exasperated with her after the last six months, readied his wand and waved her through. She smiled at him, and when he smiled back, she winked. She had a sensuous mouth, a delicate nose, and well-defined cheekbones that would have suited a catwalk model.

She followed the thoroughfare to the junction that, after another five minutes and a flight of stairs, led to the first-floor SigInt Ops Centre where she had her desk. It was a busy, open-plan area, staffed by mathematicians, linguists and analysts scouring the internet for intel on terrorism, nuclear proliferation, energy security, military support, serious organised crime and counter-espionage in different regions. Computer engineers and software developers helped make it possible; the Tempora program alone, responsible for fibre-optic interceptors attached to subsurface internet cabling, siphoned off ten gigabits of information every second. Twenty-one petabytes a day. The Prism and Boundless Informant programmes added petabytes more. That huge, amorphous mass of data needed to be sorted and arranged. GCHQ's gaping larders were stuffed full of data to be harvested by their algorithm profiles against a rainy day.

There were hackers here, too. A small team of them, including Anna.

Most of them had never considered a career in intelligence.

Anna had wanted the job specifically.

They had instructed her to get it.

And as it turned out, it had been easy.

Thackeray was an anglicised name that she had adopted when she had moved to London. She was born Anna Vasilyevna Dubrovsky in Volgograd in 1990. Her father was a middle-ranking diplomat in the Russian diplomatic service, and her mother worked for the party. She was their only child, and her prodigious intelligence—obvious from a very early age—was a source of tremendous pride to them. She had been precocious in school, a genius mathematician, quickly outpacing her peers and then her teachers. There was an annual children's chess competition in the district, and she had won it for two straight years; she had been banned from entering for a third time. She had been inculcated in data and analysis almost before she could read.

The day she had been given her first computer—a brand-new American-built Dell—was the day that the scales had truly fallen from her eyes. She was taught everything there was to know about it, and then, once again, she outpaced her teachers. Volgograd was a dreary backwater, and the internet spread out like a vast, open vista, a frontier of unlimited possibility where you could do anything and be anyone. She was taught how to live online. It became her second life. She became addicted to hacking forums, the bazaars where information was exchanged, complex techniques developed and audacious hacks lauded. It became difficult to distinguish between her real self and "Solo," as she soon preferred to be called.

Her instructors were pleased with her.

The family travelled with Vasily when he was assigned to the Russian embassy in London.

Her hacking continued. Questions of legality were easily ignored. Property was effectively communal; if she wanted something, she took it. She set up dummy accounts and pilfered Amazon for whatever she fancied. A PayPal hack allowed her to transfer money she did not have. She bought and sold credit card information. She joined collectives that vandalised the pages of corporations with whose politics—and often their very existence— she disagreed. After six months, they told her to draw attention to herself. She left bigger and bigger clues, not so big as to have been left obviously— or to have been the mark of an obvious amateur, which would have disqualified her from her designated future just as completely—but obvious enough to be visible to a vigilant watcher. She was just twenty-two when, from the bedroom of her boyfriend's house, she had hacked into ninety-seven military computers in the Pentagon and NASA. She was downloading a grainy black-and-white photograph of what she thought was an alien spacecraft from a NASA server at the John Space Centre in Houston when she was caught. They tracked her down and charged her. Espionage. The

Americans threatened extradition. Life imprisonment. The British pretended to co-operate, but then, at the last minute, they countered with a proposal of their own.

Come and work for us.

She appeared to be all out of options.

That was what she wanted them to think.

She had accepted.

Anna sat down at her desk. It was, as usual, a dreadful mess. The cubicle's flimsy walls were covered with geek bric-a-brac: a sign warning DO NOT FEED THE ZOMBIES; a clock designed to look like an oversized wristwatch; replicas of the Enterprise and the TARDIS; a Pacman stress ball, complete with felt ghosts; a Spiderman action figure. A rear-view mirror stuck to the edge of a monitor made sure it was impossible to approach without her knowledge.

She took a good slug of her coffee and fired up both of her computers, high-performance Macs with the large, cinema screens. On the screen to her right, she double-clicked on Milton's file. Her credentials were checked, and the classified file—marked EYES ONLY—was opened. A series of pictures were available, taken at various points throughout his life. There were pictures of him at Cambridge, dressed in cross-country gear and with mud slathered up and down his legs. Long, shaggy hair, lively eyes, a coltish look to him. A handsome boy, she caught herself thinking. Attractive. A picture of him in a tuxedo, some university ball perhaps, a pretty but ditzy-looking redhead hanging off his arm. A series of him taken at the time that he enlisted: a blank, vaguely hostile glare into the camera when he signed his papers; a press shot of him on patrol in Derry, camouflage gear, his rifle pointed down, the stock pressed to his chest; a shot of him in ceremonial dress accepting the Military Medal. Maybe a dozen pictures from that part of his life. There were just two from his time in the SAS: a group shot with his unit hanging out of the side of a UH-60 Blackhawk and another, the most recent, a head and shoulders shot: his face was smothered with camouflage cream, black war paint, his eyes were unsmiling, a comma of dark hair curled over his forehead. The relaxed, fresh-faced youngster was a distant memory; in those pictures he was coldly and efficiently handsome.

Anna turned to the data. There were eight gigabytes of material. She ran another of her homebrew algorithms to disqualify the extraneous material— she would return to review the chaff later, while she was running the first sweep—reducing it to a more manageable three gigs. Now she read carefully, cutting and pasting key information into a document she had opened on the screen to her left. When she had finished, three hours later, she had a comprehensive sketch of Milton's background.

She went through her notes more carefully, highlighting the most useful components. He was an orphan, his parents killed in an Autobahn smash when he was twelve, so there would be no communications to be had with them. There had been a nomadic childhood before that, trailing his father around the Middle East as he followed a career in petrochemicals. There were no siblings, and the aunt and uncle who had raised him had died ten years earlier. He had never been married nor was there any suggestion that he enjoyed meaningful relationships with women. There were no children. It appeared that he had no friends, either, at least none that were obviously apparent. *Milton*, she thought to herself as she dragged the cursor down two lines, highlighting them in yellow, *you must be a very lonely man.*

David McClellan, the analyst who worked next to her, kicked away from his desk and rolled his chair in her direction. "What you working on?"

"You know better than that."

McClellan had worked opposite Anna for the last three months. He'd been square—for a hacker, at least—but he had started to make changes in the last few weeks. He'd stopped wearing a tie. He occasionally came in wearing jeans and a T-shirt (although the T-shirts were so crisp and new that Anna knew he had just bought them, probably on the site that she used, after she had recommended it to him). It was obvious that he had a thing for her. He was a nice guy, brain as big as a planet, a little dull, and he tried too hard.

"Come on—throw me a bone."

"Above your clearance," she said, with an indulgent grin.

McClellan returned her smile, faltered a little when he realised that she wasn't joking, but then looked set to continue the conversation until she took up her noise-cancelling headphones, slipped them over her ears, and tapped them, with a shrug.

Sorry, she mouthed. *Can't hear you.*

She turned back to her screens. Milton's parents had left a considerable amount in trust for him, and his education had been the best that money could buy. He had gone up to Eton for three terms until he was expelled— she could not discover the reason—and then Fettes and Cambridge, where he read law. He passed through the university with barely a ripple left in his wake; Anna started to suspect that someone had been through his file, carefully airbrushing him from history.

She watched in the mirror as McClennan rolled back towards her again.

Coffee? he mouthed.

Anna nodded, if only to get him out of the way.

Milton's army career had been spectacular. Sandhurst for officer training and then the Royal Green Jackets, posted to the Rifle Depot in Winchester, and then Special Forces: Air Troop, B Squadron, 22 SAS. He had served in Gibraltar, Ireland, Kosovo and the Middle East. He was awarded the Distinguished Conduct Medal, and that, added to the Military Medal he had been given for his service in Belfast, briefly made him the army's most decorated serving soldier.

She filleted the names of the soldiers who had served with him. Emails, telephone numbers, everything she could find.

McClennan returned with her coffee. She mouthed thanks, but he did not leave. He said something, but she couldn't hear. With a tight smile, she pushed one of the headphones further up her head. "Thanks," she repeated.

"You having trouble?"

"Why—?"

"You're frowning."

She shrugged. "Seriously, David. Enough. I'm not going to tell you."

He gave up.

She pulled the headphones down again and turned back to her notes.

The next ten years, the time Milton had spent in the Group, were redacted.

Classified!

"Dammit!" she exclaimed under her breath.

She couldn't get into the contemporaneous stuff?

They were tying both hands behind her back.

It was impossible.

She watched McClellan scrubbing a pencil against his scalp, and corrected herself: impossible for most people. Hard for her, not impossible.

Anna picked up the fresh coffee and looked at her précis for clues. Where should she start looking? Nothing stood out. Control had been right about him: there was no one that she could monitor for signs of contact. She clicked over into the data management system and calibrated a new set of "selectors," filters that would be applied to internet traffic and telephony in order to trigger flags.

She started with his name, the nub of information around which everything else would be woven. She added his age—five years either way— and then the names of his parents, his aunt and uncle. She ran a search on the soldiers who shared record entries with him, applied a simple algorithm to disqualify those who only appeared once or twice, then pasted the names of the rest. She inputted credit card and bank account details, known telephone numbers and email addresses. He hadn't had a registered address since he had left the army, but she posted what she had and all the hotels that he had visited more than once.

His blood group, DNA profile and fingerprints had been taken when he joined the Group, and miraculously, she had those. She dragged each of them across the screen and dropped them in as new selectors.

Distinguishing marks: a tattoo on his back, a large pair of angel wings; a scar down his face, the memento of a knife fight in a Honolulu bar; and a scar from the surgery to put a steel plate in his right leg after it had been crushed in a motorcycle crash.

Each piece of data and metadata narrowed the focus, disambiguating whole exabytes held on the servers in the football-pitch-sized data room in the basement. She spun her web around that central fact of his name, adding and deleting strands until she had a sturdy and reliable net of information with which she could start filtering. Dozens of algorithms would analyse the data that her search pulled back, comparing it against historical patterns and returning probability matches. "John Milton" alone would generate an infinitesimally small likelihood rate, so small as to be eliminated without the need for human qualification. Adding his age might nudge the percentage up a fraction. Nationality another fraction. Adding his blood group might be worth a whole percentage point. The holy grail—a fingerprint, a DNA match—well, that happened with amateurs, but not with a man like this. That wasn't a break she was going to catch.

She filed the selectors for approval, took another slug of coffee, applied for capacity to run a historic search of last month's buffer—she guessed it would take a half day, even with the petaflops of processing power that could be applied to the search—and then leant back in her chair, lacing her fingers behind her head and staring at the screens.

Control was right. Milton was a ghost, and finding him through a digital footprint was going to be a very long shot. GCHQ was collecting a vast haystack of data, and she was looking for the tiniest, most insignificant needle. Control must have known that. If Milton was as good as he seemed to be, he would know how to stay off the grid. The only way that he would surface was if he chose to, or if he slipped up.

She stood, eyes closed, stretched out her arms, and rolled her shoulders.

Anna doubted John Milton was the kind of man who was prone to mistakes.

She started to wonder if this job was a poisoned chalice.

The sort of job that could only ever make her look bad.

Chapter Twenty

FIVE IN the morning. Plato looked at the icon of Jesus Christ that he had fixed to the dashboard of his Dodge. Feeling a little self-conscious, he touched it and closed his eyes. Four days, he prayed. Please God, keep me safe for four days. Plato was not usually a prayerful man, but today he felt that it was worth a try. He had been unable to sleep all night, the worry running around in his mind, lurid dreams of what the cartel would do to him and his family impossible to quash. In the end, with the red digits on the clock radio by his bed showing three, he had risen quietly from bed so as not to disturb Emelia and had gone to check on each of his children. They were all sleeping peacefully. He had paused in each room, just listening to the sound of their breathing. Satisfied that they were safe, he had gone downstairs and sat in the lounge for an hour with a cup of strong black coffee. His loaded service-issue revolver was laid on the table in front of him.

The kitchen light flicked on, and Emelia's worried face appeared at the window. Plato waved at his wife, forcing a broad smile onto his face. She knew something had happened last night, but she had not pressed him on it, and he had not said. He didn't want to cause her any more anxiety than he could avoid. What was the point? She had enough on her plate without worrying about him. He might have been able to unburden himself, but it would have been selfish. Far better to keep his own counsel and focus on the light at the end of the tunnel.

Four days.

He started the engine and flicked on the headlights. He backed the car down the drive, putting it into first and setting off in the direction of Avenue 16 de Septiembre and the Hospital San José. He turned off the road and rolled into the underground car park. As he reversed into a space, he found himself thinking of the Englishman. It was out of character for him to break the rules, and he was quite clear about one thing: giving a man he did not know the details of where the witness in a murder enquiry was being taken was most definitely against the rules. The man wasn't a relation, and he had no obvious connection to her. He was also, very patently, a dangerous man who knew how to kill and had done so before. Plato had wondered about him during his night's vigil. Who was he? What was he? What kind of ex-soldier. Special Forces? Or something else entirely? He had no reason to trust the man apart from a feeling in his gut that they were on the same side. Plato had long since learnt that it was wise to listen to his instincts. They often turned out to be right.

Plato rode the elevator to the sixth floor. The girl was being kept in her own room; they would be better able to guard her that way. Sanchez was outside the door. He had drawn the first watch, and his eyes were red rimmed from lack of sleep.

"About time," he grumbled.

"How is she?"

"Sleeping. The shoulder is nothing to worry about—just a flesh wound. They've cleaned it and tidied it up."

"But?"

"But nothing. They shot her up to help her sleep, and she's been out ever since."

"Has anyone told her about the others?"

"No. I didn't have the chance."

Plato sighed. It would fall to him to do it. He hated it, bringing the worst kind of news, but it was something that he had almost become inured to over the course of the years. How many times had he told relatives that their husband, son, wife or daughter had been murdered over the last decade? Hundreds of times. These two would just be the latest. He hoped, maybe, that they would be the last.

"All right," he said. "I'll take over. Have you spoken to Alameda?"

Sanchez nodded. "He called."

"All right?"

"Seemed to be."

"He's still relieving me? I've got to start looking into what happened, for what it's worth. I can't stay here all day."

"He said he was."

Sanchez clapped him on the shoulder and left him.

The room was at the end of the corridor. There was a chair outside it and, on the floor, a copy of *El Diario* that Sanchez had found from somewhere. The front page had a number as its headline, capitalized and emboldened—SEVEN HUNDRED—and below it was a colour picture of a body laid out in the street, blood pooling around the head. It would be seven hundred and eight once they had processed the victims from last night. Plato tossed the newspaper back down onto the ground, quietly turned the handle to the door, and stepped inside.

The girl was sleeping peacefully. She had been dressed in hospital-issue pyjamas, and her right shoulder was swaddled in bandages. He stepped a little closer. She was pretty, with a delicate face and thick, black hair. The silver crucifix she wore around her neck stood out against her golden-brown skin. He wondered if it had helped her last night. She had been very, very lucky. Lucky that the cook had been there, for a start. And lucky that the *sicarios* had, somehow, failed to complete their orders. That was unusual. The penalty for a *sicario*'s failure would be his own death, often much more protracted and unpleasant than the quick and easy ending that he planned for his victims. It was a useful incentive to get the job done, and it meant that they very rarely made mistakes.

It also meant that they often visited hospitals to finish off the victims that they had only been able to wound the first time around.

Plato was staring at her face when the girl's eyes slid open. It gave him a start. "Hello," he said.

She looked at him, a moment of muddied confusion before alarm washed across her face. Her feet scrambled against the mattress as she pushed herself away, her back up against the headboard.

"It's all right," Plato said, holding his hands up, palms facing her. "I'm a policeman."

"That's supposed to make me feel better?"

"I know I'd say this even if I wasn't, but I'm one of the good ones."

She regarded him warily, but as he took no further step towards her, smiling what he hoped was his most winning and reassuring smile, she gradually relaxed. Her legs slid down the bed a little, and she arranged herself so that she was more comfortable. The movement evidently caused her pain; she winced sharply.

"How's the shoulder?"

"Sore." The pain recalled what had happened last night, and her face fell. "Leon—where is he?"

Plato guessed that she meant the man she was with. "I'm sorry, ma'am," he said.

Her face dissolved, the steeliness subsumed by a sudden wave of grief. Tears rolled down her cheeks, and she closed her eyes, her breathing ragged until, after a moment, she mastered it again. She buried her head in her forearms with her hands clasped against the top of her head, her breathing sighing in and out. Plato stood there helplessly, his fingers looped into his belt to stop them fidgeting. He never knew what to do after he had delivered the news.

"Caterina," he said.

She moved her arms away. Her eyes were wet when she opened them again, and they shined with angry fire. "The girl?"

Plato shook his head.

"Oh God."

"I'm very sorry."

She clenched her teeth so hard that the line of her jaw was strong and firm.

"I'm sorry," he said again, not knowing what else he could say.

"When can I get out of here?"

"The doctors will want to see you. It's early, though. I don't think they'll be here until morning. A few hours."

"What time is it?"

"Half five. Why don't you try to get a little extra sleep?"

She gave him a withering look. "I don't think so."

"One of my colleagues watched over you through the night, and I'm going to stay with you now," he said. "The men who did this might come back when they find out that you're still alive."

"And you can stop them?"

There was the thing; Plato knew he would have no chance at all if they came back, and the girl looked like she was smart enough to know that too. "I'll do my best," he told her.

Chapter Twenty-One

PLATO SPOKE to the girl for an hour. He got more of the story and wrote it all down. Eventually, her eyelids started to fall, and as dawn broke outside, she was asleep again. Plato covered her with the coarse hospital blanket and picked up her chart from the end of the bed. They had given her a mild dose of secobarbital, and he guessed that there was still enough of it in her system to make her drowsy. It was for the best, he thought. She would need all her strength about her when she was discharged. He wasn't sure how best to go about that. There was no question that she was in a perilous situation. The cartels wanted her dead, and his experience suggested that they wouldn't stop until that had happened or until she was put out of reach. There was no easy way for him to help her with that. Once she was out of the hospital, she was on her own.

He looked down at his notebook. Her name was Caterina Moreno. She was twenty-five, and she was a journalist, writing for the Blog del Borderland. He wasn't as savvy with computers as some of the others, but even he had heard of it. It was generating a lot of interest, and the cartels had already murdered several of its contributors. The dead man was another of the blog's writers, and the dead girl was a source who was to be interviewed for a story she was writing.

He sat down on the chair outside the room, his pistol in his lap. He watched as the hospital switched gears from the night to day: nurses were relieved as they went off shift, the doctors began to do their rounds, porters pushed their trolleys with their changes of linen, medicines and breakfasts. Plato watched all of them, looking for signs of incongruity, his mind prickling with the anticipation of sudden violence, his fingers never more than a few inches from the stippled barrel of his Glock. They might come in disguise, or in force, they might come knowing that the power of their reputation was enough to grant them unhindered passage. The girl was helpless. Plato resolved to do his best to slow them down.

His vigil was uninterrupted until Alameda arrived at nine.

"*Capitán*," Plato said.

"How is she?"

"Not so good."

"How much does she know?"

"I told her enough."

Alameda scrubbed his eyes. "Stupid kids."

"That's harsh."

"Pretending to be journalists."

"They'd say they *were* journalists."

"Hardly, Jesus."

"We're out of touch."

"Maybe. But writing about the cartels? *Por dios*, man! How stupid can you get? They got what's coming to them."

Plato did not reply. He stood and stretched out his aching muscles.

"How did she take it?" Alameda asked, looking into Caterina's room.

"She's tough. If I were a betting man, I'd say it's made her more determined."

"To do what?"

"This—it won't shut her up."

"You ask me, she should get over the border as fast as she can. She won't last five minutes if she stays here." Alameda sighed. Plato thought he suddenly looked old, as if he had aged ten years overnight. "*Diablo*, Jesus. What are we going to do?"

Plato holstered his pistol. "We're gonna stand guard here until she's discharged, which I guess will be when the doctor comes to see her this morning. We'll make sure she's safe getting to where she wants to go. And then it's up to her." He put a hand on Alameda's shoulder. "Are you all right?"

"Not really. Couldn't sleep."

"Me neither."

"Go on," he said. "I'm fine. Take a break."

"Won't be long. I want to talk to her again when she wakes up."

He said he would take twenty minutes to get them both some breakfast from the canteen, and when Alameda lowered himself into the chair, his hand on the butt of his pistol, he quickly made for the elevator.

He did not mean to be very long.

Chapter Twenty-Two

MILTON CHANGED INTO his jeans and a reasonably clean shirt and walked to the hospital. He stopped in the coffee shop for an espresso and a copy of the morning paper. He scanned it quickly as he waited in line. There'd be nothing about the shooting at the restaurant yet. Instead, he saw a picture of some sort of memorial, a stone cross with a wreath propped up against it and a notice fixed up with wire. When he got to the checkout he asked the girl what time they got the afternoon edition.

"I don't know," she said. "I don't read it."

"Can't say I blame you."

"Haven't read it for years."

"Is that right?"

"Don't you think it's all too depressing? When was the last time you read anything good in the newspaper?"

Milton shook his head. "I don't know," he said. "Probably quite a long while."

"I'll say," she said. "A long while."

He handed her a ten-dollar bill. "I'm looking for a friend," he said. "Young girl. Brought in last night. Gunshot wound. You know where they would've taken her?"

"Try up on the sixth floor," she advised.

Milton told her to keep the change and followed her directions. There was a triage area and then a corridor with separate rooms running off it. He went down the corridor, looking into each room, looking for the girl. There was an empty chair at the door to the last room from the end. He walked quietly to the door and looked inside: the girl was there, asleep, her chest rising and falling gently beneath a single white bed sheet. A man in a white doctor's coat was leaning over her. A loose pillow was lying across the girl's legs. The man reached out his right hand, the fingers brushing against the pillow, then closing around it.

Milton opened the door all the way. "Excuse me."

The man looked up and around.

"Hello."

"Who are you?"

He had smooth brown skin, black hair, an easy smile. There was nothing remarkable about him. The kind of man you would never see coming. "My name is Martinez," he said. "I'm a doctor here. Who are you?"

Milton ignored the question. "What are you doing?"

"Checking that she is okay." He picked up the pillow and tossed it onto the armchair at the side of the bed. "Just making her comfortable."

Milton tapped a finger to his breast. "You don't have any credentials."

The man looked down at his white medical jacket, shrugging with a self-deprecating smile. "I've just come on shift. Must've left it in my locker. Thanks."

"You're welcome."

"Do you know her?"

"I'm a friend."

The doctor looked over Milton's shoulder, and for a tiny moment, a flicker of something—irritation, perhaps, or frustration—fell across his face. He replaced it with a warm, friendly smile. "Nice to meet you, Señor—?"

"Smith."

"Señor Smith. I'm sure I'll see you again."

The man smiled again, stepped around him, and left the room. Milton turned to watch him go just as the policeman from last night, Lieutenant Plato, came in the other direction. The two met in the corridor, Plato stepping to the side to let the other man pass.

Plato was carrying two wrapped burritos. He didn't look surprised to see him. "Who was that?"

"Said he was a doctor, but there was something about him. Seen him before?"

"No."

Milton started to move.

"Was there anyone else here?" Plato asked. "There should've been—"

"No one else."

Plato's face twisted with anxiety. "Is she all right?"

"You better check."

Milton walked quickly and then broke into a jog, passing through the busying triage area to the lobby beyond. The elevator was on the first floor, so he couldn't have taken that. He pushed the bar to open the door to the stairs and looked up and then down. There was no sign of Martinez anywhere. He quickly climbed to the seventh floor, but as he opened the door onto a paediatrics ward, he couldn't see him. He went back down, then descended further, to the fifth, but there was still no sign of him. The man had disappeared.

Chapter Twenty-Three

PLATO SAT on the chair, and Milton stood with his back to the wall. They ate the breakfast burritos that Plato had purchased in the canteen.

"How many people died last night?"

Plato looked at him evenly. "Two of the three on the table—the girl died at the scene, the guy was DOA by the time they got him here. Apart from them, one woman eating her dinner got shot in the head. Three dead, all told, and that's not even counting the five *sicarios* you took out. *Caramba*, what a world."

"The girl who died?"

"That's the coincidental part. Her name was Delores. Poor little thing. I knew I recognised her when they were wheeling her out. I found her a month ago on Avenue Azucenas. Half undressed and beside herself with panic. She was a worker in the *maquiladoras*. She'd been abducted and raped, but she managed to get away."

"You think that had something to do with it?"

He shrugged. "Looks to me like she was there to talk to Caterina. Tell her story, maybe. I don't know—maybe that's why they got shot."

"Why would Caterina want to talk to her?"

Milton knew that the information was confidential, but after just a moment of reluctance, Plato shrugged and said, "She's a journalist. This isn't a safe place to write about the news. The cartels don't like to read about themselves. The dead guy was another writer."

"Newspaper?"

"No," Plato said, shaking his head. "They're online. They call it Blog del Borderland. It's started to be a pretty big deal, not just here but over the border, too. There was a piece in the El Paso *Times* just last week, all about them, and someone told me they've got a book coming out, too. The cartels are all they write about. The shootings, the abductions. It's like an obsession. Most papers won't touch that stuff, or if they do, they don't write about it truthfully. It's all under control, there's nothing to worry about—you know the sort of thing. These kids are different. They've had writers go missing and get murdered before, but it hasn't stopped them yet. This time, though? I don't know, maybe they'll listen now."

"What would you do—if you were her?"

"I'd try to get over the border. But that won't be easy. As far as I can make out, she doesn't have any family here. No ties. She doesn't have a job. She's not the kind of person who gets a visa. As far as I know, no journalist has ever been given one. And I doubt she'd even get a border crossing card.

They'll say the chances of her staying over there illegally are too great."

"So?"

"Join the dots. If she's going to get across, she'll have to do it the other way."

Milton finished the burrito, screwed up the paper, and dropped it into the bin. "That doctor—?"

"Who knows. My guess? He was someone they sent to finish her off, and you got here just in time."

"You didn't recognise him?"

"No. No reason why I would."

"Why was she unguarded?"

He frowned. "You'd have to ask my captain that."

"But you're still here."

"How can I leave her on her own?" he said helplessly. "I've got daughters."

"I'll stay with her."

Plato finished his burrito and wiped his hands with a napkin. "Why would you want to do a thing like that?"

"Like you say—how can we leave her on her own. I'm guessing you boys will have to leave her as soon as they discharge her, right?"

"Right."

"And how long do you reckon she'll last without any protection at all? Christ, they almost got her when she was supposed to be guarded. She won't last five minutes, and you know it."

Plato exhaled wearily. "What's your story?—really?"

"You don't want to know."

"You need to give me a reason to let you stay."

"I can help. Come on—you know I can. You saw what I can do. You know I could be useful. That's why you told me where to find her."

"Maybe it was. And maybe I shouldn't've done that, putting you in harm's way as well as her."

"I can look after myself."

"They'll come back again. What makes you think you can stop them?"

"Because I'm not afraid of them, Lieutenant."

Chapter Twenty-Four

THE GIRL was awake. She had shuffled back in bed so that she was resting against the headboard, her knees bent beneath the sheet. Her black hair fanned out behind her, long strands running across her shoulders and across the pastel blue hospital pyjamas and the white of the bandage on her right shoulder. She was staring at Milton through the window. He got up from the chair, knocked on the door, and went inside.

"Hello," he said.

"Who are you?"

"My name's Smith."

"Have we met?"

"Not really."

She looked at him. "No. I recognise you. You were there last night. You work in the restaurant, don't you?"

"I did. Doubt there's a job for me there any more."

"You helped us."

"I did my best."

The conversation tailed off. She was nervous, and Milton felt awkward about it. He pointed to the armchair next to the bed. "Do you mind?"

She shrugged. Her right hand tensed and gripped the edge of the sheet. He could see the tendons moving in her wrist.

He moved the pillow out of the way and sat down. "How are you feeling?"

"Like I just got shot in the shoulder."

"You were lucky—it could've been much worse."

A bitter laugh. "Lucky? I wouldn't call that luck. And my friends—"

"Yes. They were very unlucky. I'm sorry about them."

Her chin quivered a little. She controlled it, a frown furrowing her brow. He turned his head and looked at her. She was slender and well put together. He saw that her nails were trimmed and painted. She had an intelligent face, sensitive, but her smoky eyes looked weary.

"Do you have any next of kin I could call?" he said.

"No. My parents are dead. I had a brother, but he's dead, too."

"Husband? Boyfriend?"

Her lip quivered again. "I'm not married. And my boyfriend—my boyfriend got shot last night."

"I'm sorry," he said.

She went quiet again. She stared out into the corridor and blinked, like she was about to cry. Like she was ready for it all to come out. Milton found that he was holding his breath. He didn't know what he would do if she started to cry. He wasn't particularly good with things like that.

"I spoke to Lieutenant Plato," he said.

"Does he think I killed her?"

"Who?"

"Delores—the girl—it's my fault she's dead."

"How could it be your fault?"

"She was safe as long as she kept out of the way."

"Of course it isn't your fault."

"I persuaded her to come and talk to me. I went on and on and on at her. Because of that, now she's dead."

Milton didn't know what to say to that. He started to mumble something that he hoped might be reassuring, but she cut him off.

"Why are you here?"

"Because you're not safe, Caterina."

"I can look after myself," she said, her eyes shining fiercely.

"They came back this morning. A man pretending to be a doctor. I saw him off, but it'll get worse as soon as they discharge you."

"Then I'll hide," she said angrily. "I've managed until now."

"I'm sure you have."

He watched her. She was pretty, and her fieriness made her even more attractive.

"Caterina—I want to help."

"You're wasting your time. I don't have any money, and even if I did, I wouldn't give it to you."

"I don't want money."

"Then what?"

"I help people who need it."

"Like some sort of charity?"

"I wouldn't put it like that."

"And I do? Need help?"

"The odds are against you. I can even the odds. That's what I do."

"You know what the cartel is capable of. You saw it. Last night was just them being playful. If they really want to come after me, there won't be anything that anyone can do about it. I'm sorry, Señor Smith, it's not that I don't appreciate the offer, and I don't want to be rude, but at the end of the day, you work in a kitchen."

He let that settle for a moment. And then he said, staring at her evenly, "I did other things before that."

Chapter Twenty-Five

BEAU'S SNAKESKIN cowboy boots clipped and clopped as he stepped out of the red Jeep Cherokee and walked across the pavement and into the hospital. There was a florist in the reception—a pathetic display of flowers, most of them half-dead and fading away in the broil of the early morning sun—but he found a halfway decent bunch of bougainvillea, then went to the shop and supplemented it with a bag of withered and juiceless grapes. He went to the desk and, putting on his friendliest smile, said he was looking for the girl who had survived the shooting at the restaurant last night, said he was her brother. The nurse looked down to the bouquet, bright colours against the blue of the suit, looked up at the warm smile, bought the story all the way, and told him that he could find her on the sixth floor, towards the back of the building, and that he hoped he had a nice day. Beau thanked her most kindly and made his way to the elevator.

He got in and pressed the button for the second floor. The doors closed and the elevator ascended. He stood with his back to the wall, looked down at the toe of his boot, lifted his leg and rubbed the toe against the back of his jeans to clean it off. The lights for each passing floor glowed on the display until the elevator reached the sixth. The doors opened. He reached inside his jacket, his fingers brushing against the inlaid handle of the revolver that was holstered to his belt, and stepped out.

The place smelt of hospitals: detergent and, beneath that, rot. The girl was in a room at the end of a corridor. Beau walked easily down towards it, his heels striking the floor noisily. As he approached, a man who had been leaning against the door jamb, just out of sight, peeled off the wall and stepped out into the corridor. He took a step forwards and blocked the way.

"Who are you?" the man said.

"Beau Baxter. Who are you?"

"Smith."

Beau grinned. "Mr. Smith—?"

The man smiled, or at least, his taut, thin lips rose a little at the edges. "John Smith. What do you do, Mr. Baxter?"

Beau looked him over. Not much to him, really, at least on the surface: a little taller than average, a little slimmer than average for someone his size, running two hundred, maybe two ten. Caucasian, a nasty scar on his face. Salt-and-pepper hair. Heavy, untidy beard. Around forty, maybe. The kind of man who'd be swallowed up by the crowd. He knew that sort. He was anonymous, at least until you looked a little harder. His eyes were different; they were cold and dark, enough to give a man a moment of reflection, a chance to think about things.

Beau shrugged. "I'm thinking you know what I do. Me and you, I'm guessing we're in the same line of work."

"I doubt that. Let me put it a different way: what are you doing here?"

He held up the wilting bouquet. "I brought the girl some flowers."

"She doesn't want them."

"I want to speak to her."

"I don't think so. Not while I'm here."

They both looked through the dirty window into the room. Caterina was sitting up in bed as a doctor examined the wound on her shoulder.

"You're the cook, right? I heard what you did."

"And how would you know about that?"

"My line of business, it pays me to know people who know things."

"Police?"

"Sure—among others."

"What do you want?"

"She had any visitors? Unexpected ones?"

Milton looked at him. He didn't answer.

"Let me describe him for you, tell me how close I am: he's in his forties, his hair is perfectly black, plain skin, smiles a lot but there's something going on beneath the smile that you don't feel too comfortable about. How am I doing?"

"Close enough."

"Thought so—can we talk about him?"

"Talk, then."

"When was it?"

"Half an hour ago."

"And what happened?"

"I scared him off."

"I doubt that. He's a bad man."

"There are a lot of bad men."

"Not like him. He's one of a kind."

"I wouldn't be so sure about that."

"I can get him out of the way."

"You think I can't do that myself?"

"I doubt it. You don't know what you're up against."

"And you don't know who I am."

"I know you ain't no cook." He smiled at him. "Okay. What do you know about him?"

The man didn't answer.

"You speak Spanish?"

"Enough."

"They call him Santa Muerte. Know what that means?"

"Saint Death."

"That's right: Saint Death. Bit grandiose, I'll give you that, but believe me, this dude, my word, he backs it up. This is not a man you want to know. Those people he takes a personal interest in, they tend not to be around for long after he's introduced himself, you know what I mean?"

"I've met people like that before. I'm still here."

He held Beau's gaze without flinching. It was rare to meet a man like this. It didn't look as if he had an ounce of fright in him. He was either brave or he had no idea what he was dealing with. "You're a long way from home, bro. That accent—English, right?"

"Yes."

"All right, then, old partner. Let me just lay it out for you. Imagine living in a place where you can kill anyone you want and nothing happens except they drop down dead. You won't get arrested. Your name won't get in the papers. You can just carry on with things like nothing has happened. You can kill again, too, just keep on going, and nothing will be different. Look at your friend in there—you can take a woman, anyone you want, and you can rape her for days and nothing will happen. And, once you're done with her, you can kill her, too. Nothing will happen. That kind of place? You're in it. That's Juárez, through and through."

"Sounds awful."

He stripped the good humour from his voice. "You need to pay attention, Mr. Smith. This man, Santa Muerte, even in a place as fucked up as this, he's the worst of the worst. Top of the food chain. What you'd call the apex predator. And you have his attention now. Undivided. All of it. I know what you did in the restaurant. I know what you did here, too, sending him away. And now he's not going to stop. Men like him, they survive because of their reputations. People start to think he's lost his edge, maybe they start getting brave, maybe someone who bears a grudge decides now's the time to get their revenge and stamp his ticket for him. *Reputation*, man. He has to kill you now. And there's nothing you can do to stop him short of putting a bullet in his head."

"What does this have to do with you?"

"I can help you. My line of work: I find people, I settle accounts, I solve problems. And my employers—this group of Italians, not men you'd want to cross—these men, well, see, they have good reason to speak to him. They had a business arrangement with the organisation he works for. Didn't go to plan. He sent them a video, one of theirs hung upside down from a tree while he sawed off his head with a machete. They're paying me to bring him back to the States. They'd prefer him alive, but that don't really matter, not really, they'll take him dead if that's the only way I can get him to them. And I will get him eventually. The only question is whether it's after he's killed you and your friend in there or before. I don't have any reason to protect you, but I will if you help me out."

"I'll take my chances."

Beau stood up and straightened out the fall of his trousers. "I don't know why, but he wants the girl. He'll drop out of sight now. You won't be able to find him. He'll bide his time, and then he'll come after her. And that's when you'll need me." He took a pen from his pocket, and tearing off a square of the brown paper sheaf that was wrapped around the flowers, he wrote down a number. He handed it to the man. "This is me. When you're ready to start thinking about how to get her out of the almighty motherfucking mess she's got herself into, you give me a call, all right?"

"What's his name?"

"His real name? I've heard lots of possibilities, but I don't know for sure."

"You're sure I can't find him?"

"Have you been listening to me? You don't find him, man. He finds you."

Chapter Twenty-Six

THEY DISCHARGED Caterina a little before midday. The doctor said that she would be fine; there were no vascular injuries, no bones had been clipped, it was all just flesh. They had performed a quick fasciotomy while she was out cold and had cleared away the fabric from her shirt that had been sucked into the wound, and removed the dead tissue. The doctor checked the sutures were holding, gave her a tetanus shot, told her to take it easy, and sent her on her way. Milton led her to the elevator, shielding her as they stepped out into the lobby downstairs.

Lieutenant Plato was waiting for them.

"How are you feeling?" he asked her.

"Better now. Thank you."

"Do you know where you're going?"

"A hotel."

"I was going to ask you," Milton said to him. "What would be a good hotel?"

Plato chuckled. "You know all the hotels get booked?"

"By who?"

"The narcos own them," Caterina answered. "They book the room, but no one ever stays. Perfect way to launder all their money."

"There is a place," Plato said. "La Playa Consulado, up by the border. You should be able to get in there."

"Thanks."

"And then?"

"New Mexico. Señor Smith says he's going to help me. Doesn't seem I have much choice in the matter."

"All right, then. You keep your head down. If I need to speak to you about what happened—the investigation and what have you—I'll be in touch." He reached out a hand, and she took it. "Good luck, Caterina."

Milton led Caterina out of the hotel. The midday heat was like a furnace. It was so fierce that it had just about cleared the streets, forcing everyone inside. A siesta sounded pretty good right around now, he thought. Those people who were out looked punch-drunk and listless. He led the way down to the cab stand, opened the door of the cab parked there, and ushered her inside.

The car was air-conditioned.

"You know the La Playa Consulado?" he said.

The driver looked at him in the mirror. "Near the US Consulate?"

"That's the one."

"*Si*—I know it."

They drove out, Milton checking that they were not being followed. If the narcos were good, there would be no way of knowing, but they would have to be very good, and Milton didn't see anything suspicious.

"What about you?" Caterina asked him suddenly.

"What about me?"

"I told you about me. What about you? You married?"

"I was, once. She left me."

"Oh—I'm sorry."

"Don't be."

"Family?"

"My parents died when I was little. No brothers or sisters."

"Girlfriend?"

"I'm never in the same place long enough to get attached."

"You must have someone?"

"Not really," he said with a wry smile. "This is it."

"I'm sorry about that," she said.

"For what?"

"That you're alone."

"Don't be. I choose to be that way."

"You're not lonely?"

"No. It's the way I like it. To be honest, I'm not the best company. I doubt anyone would put up with me for all that long, not unless they had to."

"And you move around a lot?"

"All the time."

"Why Mexico?"

"Why not? I've been heading north the best part of six months. Mexico was just the next place on the way."

"And Juárez? How long have you been here?"

"I got in on Monday."

She stared out of the window. "Good timing."

"I don't know," he said. "I'm glad I was there. It could've been a lot worse."

"But why here? Most people would go a hundred miles in either direction."

"Then I suppose I'm not most people."

"Why do you move around so much? Are you running from something?"

My history, he thought, but rather than that he said, "Not really. I just needed some time alone. To clear my head."

"From what?"

"That doesn't really matter, Caterina."

She thought about his answer. He saw her tension coming back, and she was quiet again.

La Playa Consulado was on Paseo De La Victoria. A two-storey motor court set around a large parking lot, an ugly sign outside advertising Restaurant Cebollero and its flautas, tacos and *hamburguesas*. Milton got out first, his hand resting on the burning roof of the cab as he checked again that they had not been followed. Satisfied, he stepped aside so that Caterina could get out, paid the driver, and went into the reception. Net curtains, wood panels, décor from deep into the eighties. A woman was sitting watching a chat show on TV. She got up and went around behind the desk.

"We need two rooms, one next to the other."

"I can do that. How many nights?"

"I don't know. Let's say a week."

"Weekly rate's forty-five dollars per night plus two dollars seventy-five tax. Cash or card?"

"Discount for cash?"

She took out a calculator and tapped it out. "No discount, sir. Forty-seven dollars, seventy-five cents per night, times two, times seven. That's six hundred and sixty-eight dollars and fifty cents."

Milton took out a roll of notes from his pocket and peeled off seven hundred-dollar bills. He gave them to the woman. "If anyone asks, we're not here. No visitors. No messages, at any time. No one cleans the rooms." He peeled off another note and laid it on the desk. "Is that going to be all right?"

"Absolutely fine, sir."

Milton took the two keys and led the way outside again, following a scrappy path around the parking lot to the row of rooms. He opened the door to the first room, number eleven, and went inside. He waited until Caterina had followed, shut the door again, and closed the curtains. He checked the room: a queen-sized bed with a heavy wooden headboard and a garish quilt cover; purple carpets, stained in places; an artexed asbestos ceiling; a print of a vase of flowers on the wall; and a bathroom with shower. Light from outside came in through the net curtains. Milton switched on the overhead light.

Caterina sat down heavily on the bed.

Milton stood at the window, parted the curtains a little, and looked out through them at the courtyard outside. A few cars, lots of empty spaces, plastic rubbish and newspaper snagged in the branches of sickly creosote bushes. He ran things over in his mind. He got two glasses of water from the bathroom and came back and went to the window again. He took a sip and set the water on the cheap bedside table. Halfway there, he thought.

Caterina slumped back on the bed. "This is crazy. I can't hide here forever."

"Just for a few days."

"So you can do what?"

"I know someone who'll be able to help you get across the border."

"In exchange for what? I told you I don't have any money."

"He has a problem I can help him with. And there's no harm in you staying here until I can do that, is there?"

She shook her head and stared straight up at the stippled ceiling. "I don't suppose so. I know I can't go home."

"Is there anything you need?"

"Nothing we can't get in New Mexico."

"Sure?"

"There is something—we've got another couple of writers. I have to get word to them."

"Call them?"

"Their details are on my laptop. I need that; then I can mail them."

"Where is it?"

"In my apartment."

"All right—I'll get it. Write down your address."

She did, writing it on a page that she tore from the Gideon's Bible in the drawer. Milton closed the curtains.

"You're not just a cook, are you?"

"No."

"You were a soldier."

"Yes."

"What kind of soldier?"

He thought about what to say. He had a sudden urge to be completely truthful, but he knew that might not be the best policy with her—good for him, bad for her—so he evaded the question a little. "I was in the special forces for a while. And then I was transferred to work for a special detail. I can't really tell you very much about that."

"You were good at it?"

"Very good," he said.

"Have you've killed people before?"

"I have."

She fell silent.

He found the TV remote and tossed it across to the bed. "Try to get some sleep," he said. "And I know you're not stupid, but lock and chain the door, and don't open it to anybody but me. All right?"

"You're going now?"

"There are some things I need to get, too. I might be back late. Maybe this evening. All right?"

She said that she was.

"Don't open the door."

Chapter Twenty-Seven

MILTON TOOK a taxi to the border and then got out and walked. The Paso del Norte Bridge spanned the Rio Bravo, and he took his place in the queue of people waiting to cross. He paid three pesos at the kiosk and pushed through the turnstile. A couple of hundred strides to reach the middle, where Mexico ended and the United States began. He paused there and looked down. The floodplain stretched beneath him, the Rio Bravo a pathetic trickle slithering between stands of Carrizo cane—a chain-link fence on either side, tall guard-posts with guards toting rifles, spotlights and CCTV.

The American gatepost was worse, bristling with security. He walked towards it and joined the queue. Well-to-do housewives chatted about the shopping they were going to do. Bored children bounced. Kids slung book bags over their shoulders, waiting to pass through to their Methodist schools. Vendors hawked hamburgers, cones of fried nuts and bottles of water. A woman in a white dress with a guitar sang folk songs, a handful of change scattered in the torn-off cardboard box at her feet.

It took an hour for Milton to get to the front.

"Hello, sir," the wary border guard said. "Your passport, please."

Milton took out the fake American passport that he had been using since he arrived in South America. He handed it to her.

"Mr. Smith," she said, comparing him with the photograph. "You've been away for a while, sir."

"Travelling."

She stamped the passport. "Welcome home, sir."

He walked through into America.

Milton had a fifteen-minute cab ride to get to where he was going. He fished out his phone from his pocket and took the scrap of paper that the man in the hospital had given to him from out of his wallet. He dialled the number and put the phone to his ear.

"Baxter?"

"Who's this?"

"John Smith."

"Mr. Smith. How are you, sir?"

"Our friend—how much is he worth to you?"

"He's worth plenty—why? You ready to help?"

"If you help me—then perhaps."

"How much do you want?"

"Nothing. No money. I need you to do me a favour."

"I'm listening."

"Those Italians you work for—I'm guessing it's a reasonably simple thing for them to bring someone across the border?"

"Sure. I've got to get our mutual friend across, and I'm damn sure I ain't taking him over the bridge. I don't reckon it'd be any great shakes to add another to the trip. Who do you got in mind?"

"The girl."

"Makes sense. Yeah—I reckon I could do that. Anything else?"

"A new life for her on the other side. Legitimate papers in a different name. Away from El Paso. Somewhere where they'll never find her."

"That's a bit more demanding. But maybe."

"What would you have to do?"

"Make a couple of calls. You on this number all day?"

Milton said that he was.

"I'll call you later."

The taxi had arrived. Milton put the telephone away, paid the driver, and got out.

The El Paso gun show was held every Saturday at the El Maida Shrine Centre at 6331 Alabama Street. A sign outside the venue advertised roller derbies, pet adoption fairs and home and garden shows, but it was obvious that guns were the big draw. He paid sixteen bucks at the entrance and went inside.

He had seen the show advertised in *El Diario*, a whole-page advert that promised that every gun that he could imagine would be available to buy. Milton could imagine a lot of guns, but after just five minutes, he saw the claim wasn't fanciful. The place was like a bazaar. Several long aisles had been formed by tables arranged swap-meet style, dozens of vendors on one side of them and several hundred people on the other. Milton recognised the hunters, but there were plenty of people buying for other reasons, too. He watched with a detached sense of professional interest as a rotund and cheerful white-bearded man, easily in his seventies, walked past with an ArmaLite and attached bayonet slung casually over his shoulder. A blue-rinsed lady of similar age negotiated hard for extra ammunition for the Smith & Wesson she was purchasing. Other shoppers were pushing handcarts of ammunition out to their trucks.

Milton sauntered along the aisle, looking for the right kind of seller. It didn't take long to find one: the man had a table covered in blue felt, with a selection of weapons sitting on their carry cases, a handwritten sign on the table reading PRIVATE SELLER/NO PAPER. The slogan on the man's black wifebeater read "When All Else Fails, Vote from the Rooftops!" and revealed sleeves of tattoos up both arms. He wore a baseball cap with a camouflage design.

"Afternoon, sir," he said.

"What do I need to buy from you?"

"Cash and carry. No background check, I don't need no address—don't really need nothing, no sir. This is a private party sale. What are you looking for?"

"What have you got?"

The man cast his hand across the heaving table. "I keep a nice selection. All the way from these little stainless steel Derringers, good for concealment, to the long guns. I got the Ruger .22—extremely popular gun. I got weapons with pink grips, for the ladies, engraved pieces with inlaid handles and decorative stocks. Walthers, Smith & Wessons. A lot of people are shooting .40 calibres. Those are pretty vicious. I got revolvers—"

"No, automatic."

"I have nice automatics. I got modern plastic guns. I got the Glock, I got the Springfield. And then, over here, I got the Mac semi-autos all the way up to the rifles: the .208s, the .223s. I got an AK-47 and an AR-15, a .50 calibre with fluted barrel and sniper green finish."

Milton looked down at the metalware lined up across the table. They were all expertly made, although he found it easier to feel affection and admiration for the collector's items with the wooden butts than for the coldly efficient and inorganic weapons that made sense only in combat. The cold grey foreboding of an AR-15. The leaden heaviness of the Czech MFP, modelled on the Kalashnikov.

He picked up a Springfield Tactical .45 auto.

"How much?"

"$480, cash money, and it's all yours, out the door you go."

"I'll take it."

"You want ammo with that, too?"

The Springfield boxed thirteen rounds per magazine; Milton bought four, mixed factory hardball and jacketed hollow points from Federal and Remington, for a straight hundred.

He paid the man, thanked him and went back outside. It was seven in the evening by now, and the winds had picked up. The faint orange dust that had hung in the windless morning had been whipped up into a storm, and now it was rolling in off the desert. He took a taxi back to the border and was halfway across the span of the bridge when the storm swept over Juárez. Sand and dust stung his face and visibility was immediately reduced: first the mountains disappeared, then the belching smokestacks on the edge of town, and then, as the storm hunkered down properly over the city, details of the immediate landscape began to fade and blur. The streetlights that ran along the centre of the bridge shone as fuzzy penumbras in the sudden darkness.

Milton's phone buzzed in his pocket. He took it out and pressed it to his ear.

"It's Beau Baxter."

"And?"

"Smith, are you outside in *this*?"

Milton ignored the question. "Get to it. Can you help?"

"Yeah, it can be done. You help me with our mutual friend, I'll help get the girl where she wants to get and set her up with a nice new identity. Job, place to live, everything she needs. Want to talk about it?"

"We should."

"All right, buddy—tomorrow evening. There's a joint here, does the best huaraches you've ever tasted, and I'm not kidding. I always visit whenever I'm in Juárez, compensation for having to come to this godforsaken fucking town in the first place. It's at the Plaza Insurgentes, on Avenida de los Insurgentes. Get a taxi, they'll know. Eight o'clock, all right?"

Milton said that he would be there and ended the call.

The lights of Juárez faded in and out through the eddies of dust and grit. The Hotel Coahuila's neon throbbed on and off, a huge sign with a girl wearing *bandolero* belts and brandishing Kalashnikov machine guns. He passed a police recruitment poster with a ninja-cop in a balaclava and the slogan *"Juárez te necesita!"*—Juárez Needs You. There was no one in the gate shack on the Mexican side of the river. No passport control, no customs checks, no one to notice the Springfield that was tucked into the back of his jeans or the clips of ammunition that he had stuffed into the pockets of his jacket. There was no queue, either, and he pushed his way through the creaking turnstile and crossed back into Juárez.

Chapter Twenty-Eight

THE STORM gathered strength. Milton took a taxi to the address that Caterina had given him. He told the driver to stop two blocks earlier and, paying him with a twenty-dollar bill, told him to stay and wait if he wanted another. He got out, the sand and grit swirling around him, lashing into his exposed skin, and walked the rest of the way. It was a cheap, dingy area, rows of houses that had been sliced up to make apartments. He passed one house, the road outside filled with SUVs with tinted windows. The cars were occupied, the open door of one revealing a thickset man in the uniform of the *federales*. The man turned as Milton passed, cupping his hand around a match as he lit a cigarette, the glow of the flame flickering in unfriendly eyes. Milton kept going.

Caterina's apartment was just a few doors down the street. Milton felt eyes on his back and turned; two of the SUVs were parked alongside one another, their headlights burrowing a golden trough through the snarling, swirling dust. He turned back to the house, walking slowly so that he could squint through the sand at the third floor. There was light in one of the windows; a shadow passed across it. A quick, fleeting silhouette, barely visible through the darkness and the grit in the air.

Her window?

He wasn't sure.

A narrow alleyway cut through the terrace between one address and its neighbour, and Milton turned into it, gambling that there was another way inside around the back. The roiling abated as he passed inside the passageway, but it wasn't lit, the darkness deepening until he could barely see the way ahead. He reached around for the Springfield and pulled it out, aiming it down low, his finger resting gently on the trigger.

The passageway opened into a narrow garden, fenced on both sides, most of the wooden panels missing, the ones that were left creaking on rotting staves as the wind piled against them. The ground was scrub, knee-high weeds and grasses, scorched clear in places from where a dog had pissed. There was a back extension attached to the ground-floor property, no lights visible anywhere. He looked up: there was a narrow Juliet balcony on the third floor. There was his way inside. Milton climbed onto a water butt and then boosted himself onto the flat roof, scraping his palms against the rough bitumen. He stuffed the Springfield back into his trousers and shinned up the drainpipe until he was high enough to reach out for the bottom of the balcony, shimmied along a little and then hauled himself up so that he could wedge his feet between the railings.

He leaned across and risked a look inside.

There was no light now.

He took the gun and pushed the barrel gently against the doors. They were unlocked, and they parted with a dry groan. He hauled his legs over the railing, and aware that even in the dim light of the storm he would still be offering an easy target to anyone inside, he crouched low and shuffled forwards.

He heard movement in the adjacent room: feet shuffling across linoleum.

Milton rose and made towards the sound. He edged carefully through the dark room, avoiding the faint outlines of the furniture.

He reached the door. It was open, showing into the kitchen. The digital clock set into the cooker gave out enough dim light to illuminate the room: it was small, with the cooker, a fridge, a narrow work surface on two sides and cupboards above. A man was working his way through the cupboards, opening them one by one and going through them. Looking for something.

Milton took a step towards him, clipping his foot on the waste bin.

The man swivelled, a kitchen knife in his hand. He slashed out with it.

Milton blocked the man's swipe with his right forearm, taking the impact just above his wrist and turning his hand over so that he could grip the edge of the man's jacket. The man grunted, trying to free himself, but Milton plunged in with his left hand, digging the fingers into the fleshy pressure point behind the thumb, pinching so hard that the knife dropped out of his hand. It had taken less than three seconds to disarm him. Maintaining his grip, Milton dragged the man's arm around behind his back and yanked it up towards his shoulders, pushing down at the same time. The man's head slammed against the work surface.

"Who do you work for?" he said.

"Fuck you, gringo."

Milton raised his head a little and slammed it back against the work surface.

"Who do you work for?"

"Fuck you."

Milton reached across and twisted the dial on the hob, the gas hissing out of the burner. He pushed the button to ignite it, the light from the blue flame guttering around the dark kitchen. He guided the man towards the hob, scraping his forehead across the work surface and then the unused burners, raising him a little over the lit one so that he could feel the heat.

His voice remained steady and even, implacable, as if holding a man's face above a lit flame was the most normal thing in the world. "Let's try again. Who do you work for?"

The man whimpered. There was a quiet yet insistent crackle as his whiskers started to singe. "I can't—"

"Who?"

"They'll—they'll kill me."

Milton pushed him a little closer to the flame. His eyebrows began to crisp. "You need to prioritise," he suggested. "They're not here. I am. And I will kill you if you don't tell me."

He pushed him nearer to the flame.

"El Patrón," the man said in a panicked garble. "It's El Patrón. Please. My face."

"What are you looking for?"

"The girl—the girl."

"But she's not here. What else?"

"Contacts."

"Why?"

"They've been writing about La Frontera. El Patrón—he wants to make an example of them."

Milton turned the man's head a little so he could see him better. "Where can I find him?"

The man laughed hysterically. "I don't know! Just look around. He's everywhere." He squinted at him. "Why would you even wanna know that?"

"I need to speak to him. He needs to leave the girl alone."

"And you think he'll listen?"

"I think he will."

"Who *are* you, man?"

"Just a cook."

The man laughed again, a desperate sound. "No, I tell you what you are—you're fucked. What you gonna do now? Call the *federales?* How you think that's going to go down, eh? You stupid gringo—El Patrón, he *owns* the cops."

"I won't need the cops."

Milton snaked his right arm around the man's throat and started to squeeze. The man struggled, got his legs up, and kicked off the wall. Milton stumbled backwards, and they went to the floor. The man was trying to get his hands inside Milton's arm, but he could not. Milton squeezed, the man's throat constricted in the nook of his arm. He braced his left arm vertically against his right, his right hand clasped around his left bicep, and he pulled back with that, too, tightening his grip all the time, his face turned away. The man was flailing wildly, his arms windmilling, and he scrabbled sideways over the floor, kicking over the waste bin, treading dusty prints up the kitchen cupboards. His sneakers squeaked against the linoleum floor. He was gurgling, a line of blood trickling from his mouth. He was choking on his own blood. Milton squeezed harder. The man's legs slowed and then stopped. Milton relaxed his grip. The man lay jerking. Then he stopped moving altogether.

Milton got up and flexed his aching arm. He poured himself a glass of water and drank it, studying the dead man gaping up from the floor. Early twenties, a cruel face, even in death. His eyes bulged, and his tongue lolled out of blue-tinged lips. He crouched down next to the body, frisking it quickly: a mobile phone, a wallet with three hundred dollars, a small transparent bag of cocaine. Milton took the money and the phone, discarding the wallet and the cocaine, and then took a dishcloth and a bottle of disinfectant he found under the sink and cleaned down anything that he might have touched. He wiped the glass and put it back in the cupboard. He wiped the tap. He wiped the hob.

Milton took the man's torch and went into the bedroom. The laptop, covered in stickers and decals—WikiLeaks, DuckDuckGo, Megaupload— was under the mattress, where Caterina said it would be. He slipped it into a black rucksack he found in the closet and dropped the Springfield and the ammunition in after it. He climbed down from the balcony and followed the passageway back to the front of the house. The storm had still not passed. Visibility was poor. Milton walked back in the same direction from which he had arrived. He passed the parked SUVs, ignoring the man smoking a cigarette in the open door, his eyes fixed straight ahead. He found the taxi again and got in.

"La Playa Consulado," he said.

He bought cheeseburgers, fries and Big Gulps from the take-out next to the hotel. He could hear the sound of the television as he approached the door to Caterina's room. The curtains were drawn, but light flickered against the edges. Milton stopped in his room first, taking out the revolver and ammunition and the things that he had taken from the dead man, hiding them under the sheet. He locked the door behind him and knocked for Caterina.

"Who is it?"

"It's John."

He heard the bedsprings as she got to her feet and then her footsteps as she crossed the room. The lock turned, and the door opened. Milton went inside.

"You were hours."

"I'm sorry. It took longer than I thought. Was everything all right?"

"The cleaner tried to come in, but I sent her away."

"Nothing else?"

"No. I've been watching TV all day."

She looked tired, and despite the permanent glare of defiance, her red-rimmed eyes said that she had been weeping.

"Here." Milton put the wrapped meals on the bed. Caterina was hungry and so was he; he realised that he hadn't had anything to eat since breakfast this morning. The meat in the cheeseburgers was poor, but they both finished quickly, moving onto the little cardboard sheaths of greasy fries.

Milton watched the TV as he put the food away; Caterina had tuned it to a channel from El Paso: news about local Little League sports, a fun run to raise money for cancer research, the pieces linked by glossy presenters with white teeth and bright eyes. It was a different world north of the river, he thought. They had no idea what it was like down here.

Milton put the rucksack on the bed and took out the laptop. "Is this what you wanted?"

"Perfect, thank you," she said. "Did you—did you have any trouble getting it?"

"No trouble at all."

Chapter Twenty-Nine

THREE MORE DAYS.

Jesus Plato reminded himself, again and again, as he stared up at the bridge.

It was Wednesday today.

Just three more days and then an end to all this.

It was a fresh morning, a cool wind blowing after the fury of the storm last night. Plato was at the concrete overpass known as Switchback Bridge. The bodies had been called in as dawn broke over the endless desert, ropes knotted beneath their armpits, tied to the guard rail, and the dead tossed over the side. They both dangled there, the rope creaking as they swung back and forth in the light breeze, twenty feet above the busy rush of traffic at the intersection. A small crowd of people had gathered to watch as a fire truck was manoeuvred around so that the ladder could get up to them. Former school busses from across the border, now ferrying workers to and from the sweatshops, jammed up against one another, and behind them, a queue of irate drivers leant on their horns. Just another day in Ciudad Juárez. Another morning, another murder. No one was surprised or shocked. It was an inconvenience. This was just how it was, and that, Plato thought, was the worst of it.

He could see that the bodies had both been decapitated. Hands had been tied behind their backs, and their feet flapped in the wind. He hadn't had a proper breakfast yet, just a Pop-Tart as he left the house, and he was glad. The bodies revolved clockwise and then counterclockwise, bumping up against each other, a grotesque and hideous display. They were suspended between advertising hoardings for Frutti Sauce and Comida Express fast food, and the *sicarios* had left their own message alongside their prey. A bed sheet was tied to the guard rail, and painted on it was a warning: "FREEDOM OF THE PRESS" and then "ATENCION—LA FRONTERA." A fireman scaled the ladder, and with help from colleagues on the bridge, the carcasses were untied, lowered to the ground, and wrapped in canvas sacks to be taken to the morgue.

Plato was about to head back to the station when he saw John Milton and Caterina Moreno. The girl was crouched down, leaning her back against the side of his Dodge, hugging her knees tight against her chest. Her face was pale, and on the ground next to her, there was a puddle of drying vomit. Milton was leaning against the bonnet, his face impassive and his arms folded across his chest.

"What are you doing here?" Plato asked him.

"She knows who they are."

"Who?"

"Up there." He pointed. "She knows them."

"Even without their—you know—without their heads?"

"They used to write for her blog."

"Shit."

"I know." Milton pushed himself away from the car and led Plato out of the girl's earshot. "She wanted to see them before I get her over the border. Warn them that they should get out, too. We went to their address, but—well, we were too late, obviously. The place had been turned over. We saw the bodies from the taxi as we were driving back to the hotel. Went right underneath them. They were husband and wife. Daniel and Susanna Ortega."

"This is what happens if you get on the wrong side of the cartels. There's nothing anyone can do about it."

He pointed to the bridge. "That wasn't a five-minute job. There must have been witnesses—passing traffic?"

"They don't care. No one's going to say anything." Plato nodded to Caterina. "And it'll happen to her, too—they won't stop. When are you taking her across?"

"I'm working on that."

The white morgue van backed up and drove away. The fire truck was lowering its ladder.

"Work faster."

Chapter Thirty

FELIPE WATCHED from the car as the Cessna 210 touched down on the rough gravel runway that had been constructed right down the middle of the arid field. It had big tyres and metal strips under the nose to protect the engine from stones. It was one of several that Felipe owned. He had sent it north this morning, touching down in a similar field in New Mexico to collect its passengers and refuel, and then returned to deliver them to him here. He stepped out of the Jeep. Adolfo had already disembarked and was leaning against the bonnet, watching as the plane taxied across the field, dust kicking up from the oversized tyres. Felipe shielded his eyes against the sun and waited for the plane to come to a halt.

"Wait here," he said to his son.

"*Padre?*"

"Stay here."

He stared at him sourly. "Yes, *Padre.*"

"Pablo."

Felipe and Pablo crossed the desert to the plane. He was not particularly concerned about his guests. They would have been frisked before they got onto the plane, and he knew very well that the fear of his reputation was the most effective guarantee of his own security. That said, you couldn't be too careful, and with that in mind, Adolfo and the men in the second Jeep were all equipped with automatic rifles.

The ramp was lowered, and the three passengers inside descended. Felipe was wearing a Stetson; he removed it, wiped inside the rim with his handkerchief, wiped his forehead, and put the hat back on. He paused and allowed the gringos to come to him.

"El Patrón?" said the man who had stepped to the front.

"That's right." He smiled at them. "Welcome to Mexico. How was your flight?"

"Was good—thanks for arranging it." He was a thick-limbed Texan, tall, a little colour in his face.

"You are Isaac?"

"I sure am."

"And your friends?"

"Kevin and Alejandro."

"Your business partners?"

"That's right."

Felipe smiled at the other two. His first impression: they were not particularly impressive. Isaac was the owner of the business that they were going to use and was, not surprisingly, the most interesting.

Felipe turned and indicated in the direction of the two Jeeps. Adolfo and the other two men were lounging against the vehicles, the brims of their hats pulled down to shield their eyes from the glare of the sun. "We'll drive back to Juárez and discuss our business."

"Forgive me, El Patrón," Isaac said. "Before we do, there's something I'd like to clear up."

Isaac was standing with the sun behind him, and Felipe couldn't see his face through the glare. Why hadn't he made sure that he had approached the plane from the opposite direction? He clenched his teeth in frustration at his error and Isaac's presumption. "Of course," he said, squinting a little and yet managing to smile.

"Listen, I hope you can forgive me—I don't mean to be blunt, but there's no point in pussyfooting around it, so I'm gonna come right out and get to the point. I'm sure you know all about this, but there's a whole lot of coverage about the girls that are going missing over here. Someone's been writing about it, and now the TV channels and newspapers and suchlike over the border have got hold of it."

"How is this relevant?"

"It's extra heat, right? More attention? Makes things more—what would you say—more *precarious.*"

"I would say you shouldn't worry. And that you should trust me."

"I'd like to be able to say that I can, El Patrón, truly I would. I'm sure, in time, we'll come to trust each other like brothers. But now, well, we don't even know each other."

His tone suddenly lost the avuncular tone he had been working hard to maintain. "What does that have to do with us?"

"The word over the border is that your men are behind it. They say they're doing it for sport. Now, I'm sure that ain't true, El Patrón, because if it was, well, yessir, if someone was allowing them to get away with hijinks like that, then we'd have to question whether that someone was the sort of someone we'd want to get into business with. Not morally—I don't care about none of that. It's business—a person who'd allow someone to bring so much attention to his operation, well then, that wouldn't make no sense."

Besa mi culo, puto! Felipe breathed in and out: the sun in his eyes, the *huevos* on this man, coming over to Mexico as his guest and insulting his hospitality like this! It would have taken a moment for him to signal to Adolfo and his goons to bring up their rifles and perforate them, blow them away. All he would have to do would be to click his fingers. It was tempting, but he could not. Since he had ended his business relationship with the Luciano family— and ended it in such a way that a reconciliation was impossible—he needed Isaac and his *pajero* friends to distribute his product in the south-west. He had tonnes to move. Without them he would have to split the product between small-time operators, and that would mean less leverage for him, less profit and much greater risk. It was impossible.

So he forced himself to swallow his anger and cast out a bright smile. "I know the stories, Isaac, and I can assure you, they are nothing to do with La Frontera. If I found out that my men were responsible, they would be dealt with. But they are not. The police here suspect a group of serial killers. In fact, they have already charged one man—perhaps you have read about that, too?"

Isaac shrugged. "That's what I thought."

"As I say, you needn't worry. Now—shall we go? There is much to discuss."

Chapter Thirty-One

ANNA THACKERAY had almost forgotten about John Milton. The results of the first sweep had come back negative and then the second and then the third. She had tried everything she could think of trying, feeding every combination of selectors through every megabit of data that they had. She ran it again and again and again, working well into the night, but every variation, every clever rephrasing, none of them returned anything that she could use. Since he had disappeared, it appeared that Milton had neither used the internet in any way that could be traced back to him, nor been referred to by anybody else.

No emails.

No social media.

No banking activity.

No credit cards.

No immigration data.

Anna had been warned that he would be good at this, and she had not doubted it. But she had not expected him to be *this* good. Control had been right. It was as if he had sunk beneath the surface of the world, leaving not even a ripple behind him.

"What are you missing?" she said aloud.

"I don't know—what?" David McClellan said.

"Excuse me?"

"Talking to yourself again."

"Sorry," she said, managing a laugh. "Just frustrated."

"Going to tell me what about?"

"Not really, it's—"

"—classified," he finished for her.

"I don't know—all this computing power, all this information, but if you really want to drop out of sight, if you can drop everything and get off the grid, all of this is useless. You can still do it. I keep thinking I'll think of something different—anything—something that'll change the results, but I know that's not going to happen. This guy is either a hermit, living in some jungle somewhere, or he's dead. If I was going to find anything at all, I'd have found it long before now."

But she couldn't give up, so she thought it through again.

Eventually, she knew, they would have to go out into the field. The realistic plan was to confirm her assumption that nothing concerning John Milton existed in any data that GCHQ or the NSA held. After that, she would appeal to Control to broaden the scope of the exercise. Interviews with victims, witnesses, reporting parties, informants. Anything that might buy her more information, more selectors to add to the sweep. She knew from unredacted excerpts from his file that he had been in contact with people in East London before he had disappeared. Elijah and Sharon Warriner. They would be a good place to start.

"Coffee," McClellan said. "Look at you. You need caffeine. Fancy it?"

She stood and stretched, working the kinks out of her stiff muscles. "Sorry, David, I would, but I'm meeting someone tonight."

He looked almost comically crestfallen. "A boyfriend?"

"A friend," she said. She logged off and collected her leather jacket from the back of the chair. "I'll see you tomorrow."

THE RENDEZVOUS had been arranged the day before and was to take place in the Beehive, a pub two miles away in the centre of town. Anna made her way into the car park where she had left her motorbike. It was her one concession to luxury in an otherwise ascetic life: it was a Triumph Thruxton, built in the style of the '60s, an authentic café racer in Brooklands green, with low-rise bars, eighteen-inch spoked wheels and megaphone-style silencers. It was a beautiful machine, and she loved it. She lowered her helmet over her head, straddled the bike, and gunned the 850cc engine. David was coming down the steps into the car park as she pulled away; he looked flustered, the wind billowing his open coat around him. He started as she twisted the throttle and revved the big engine.

The cloud was low and leaden, and the wind was cold. She was thankful for her leathers as she hurried along the A40. She arrived at the pub ten minutes later, parked the bike, and went inside to her usual table before the fireplace. A man was waiting for her. She didn't recognise him, and that made her nervous.

"Haven't I seen you before," she said as she paused beside him. "Waterloo station?"

He was plain, early middle age, a receding hairline, nondescript, just like they all were.

"I think it was Liverpool Street," he corrected, completing the introduction.

Satisfied, she sat down. "Where is Alexei?" she said curtly.

The man spoke in quiet Russian. "He has gone home. Don't worry about him. You deal with me from now on."

"Fine. But in English, please. You are less likely to draw attention."

"Sorry." The man switched languages. "Yes, of course."

"Have you done this before?"

"No. You are my first."

She sighed. "Wonderful. Why couldn't this wait until Saturday as normal?"

"Your last report has been passed to the highest levels. There are some questions."

"A little more information about you before we can talk, please."

"Very well. I work in the same department as you, but I work in the consulate. My name is Roman. I know you are going back to Moscow in two weeks, and I know they want to sit down with you and talk officially about your work, your performance, and so on, but before that, we need further details after your last report."

"Okay. What do you want to know?"

"The English spy—are you any nearer to finding his location?"

"Not yet. And I'm not sure that I'll be able to. He's good."

"Too good for you?"

"Probably not. But they are withholding information from me. It makes it very much harder."

"Have you seen Control again?"

"Daily progress reports. It's all one-way, though. I get nothing back."

"Do you know why they're looking for him?"

"He tried to resign. They wouldn't tell me why. But they're not happy."

"The fuss with the other agent—in London?"

"Classified. Like almost everything else. But obviously connected."

"What about him?"

"Milton? He knows how to drop out of sight."

"But they value him?"

"Yes—very much. I get the impression he was one of their best. I'd say this has caused them serious problems. They are very keen to have him back."

"Colonel Shcherbakov is to be kept up to date. You must contact me if you make a breakthrough."

"Why is he so interested?"

"You know better than to ask that."

"Yes. But—?"

"I believe they have something planned for Mr. Milton."

Anna's iPhone bleeped.

Roman cocked an eyebrow.

She took it out of her pocket and checked it. She had set up the system to ping her if any of her selectors were tripped. The message said that that was precisely what had happened.

"What is it?"

"The spy. I might have found him."

SHE GUNNED the Triumph on the way back to headquarters, touching seventy as she weaved through the slow-moving evening traffic. She didn't wait to strip out of her leathers as she hurried through security for the second time.

The report that the system had emailed to her indicated that the selector that had been triggered was for fingerprints.

A fingerprint?

Seriously?

She jogged to her desk and sat down, and there it was: a scanned PDF of a row of fingerprints inked onto a strip of paper with instructions in Spanish printed along the side in green ink. The strip had, at some point, been scanned and dumped into a database. The NSA's XKEYSCORE program had picked it up in transit.

"No fucking way."

She sat down and fumbled for her mouse, scrolling through the metadata.

```
NAME: JOHN SMITH
ALIAS: None
DOB: Unspecified
SEX: M
RACE: White, Caucasian
HEIGHT: 182
WEIGHT: 80
EYE COLOUR: Blue
HAIR COLOUR: Black
SCARS/TATTOOS: Scar on face // Tattoo (angel
wings) on back.
RESIDENCE: None
OCCUPATION: Cook
SOC. SEC. NO.: Unspecified
STATE ID NO.: Foreign
LOCATION: Ciudad Juárez, Chihuahua, MEX
ORGINATING AGENCY: Juá. Muncipal Police,
District 12
OFFICIAL TAKING PRINTS: Lt. Jesus R Plato
```

"Fuck," she said. The probability matrix was off the charts: the name, personal statistics, identifying features, the metadata all ringing back super-strong hits. But the prints themselves were the thing: the system had matched them with the positive set that she had taken from Milton's SAS file, and they were unquestionably the same.

The loops and ridges, whorls and arches, delta points and type lines.

One set fitted snugly over the other when they were overlaid.

That kind of thing couldn't be a mistake or a coincidence.

It was him. There was no doubt about it.

She moused over to the second data packet that had been marked for her and opened it.

She nearly fell off her chair.

Pictures, too?

There were two: front and profile. In the first, Milton stared out into the camera. His eyes were the iciest blue and his expression implacable. He had a full beard, and his hair was unkempt. The second offered a clear angle of the scar that curled down from his scalp. He was holding a chalkboard with his name and a reference number. Again, the board was written in Spanish. It was marked Ciudad Juárez.

"Hello, Milton," she said. "I found you, you sneaky *ublyudok*. I *found* you."

DAY THREE

Desperado

"If Juárez is a city of God, it is because the Devil is scared to come here."

Street *dicho*, or *saying*.

Chapter Thirty-Two

ADOLFO GONZÁLEZ slammed the door of the hotel behind him and stalked to his car. He had been furious, and the girls had borne the brunt of his temper. There were two of them this time, just the right age, plucked from outside the car park of the *maquiladora* that made the zips for the clothes that bargain retailers sold over the border and in Europe. His men had called him and told him that the two were waiting for him in the usual place. He had bought the hotel a year ago, just for this purpose, and it had earned back the hundred thousand dollars he had paid for it. Earned it back and then some.

Esmeralda and Ava.

They had struggled a little. More than usual, anyway. He preferred it like that.

He'd leave the cleanup to the others.

He took off his bloodied latex gloves and dropped them into the trash. He opened the door of his car and slipped into the front seat. His ride was a 1968 Impala Caprice, *"Viva La Raza"* written across the bonnet in flaming cursive, the interior featuring puffy cream-coloured cushions and a child's doll on the dash, dressed in a skirt bearing the colours of the Mexican flag. The car seats were upholstered in patriotic green, white and red.

He took off his dirty shirt, took a replacement from the pile on the rear seat, tore off its plastic wrapping, and put it on. He opened the glove compartment, took a packet of baby wipes, and cleaned his face. His movements were neat and precise: the shallow crevices on either side of his nose, the depressions at the edge of his lips, the hollows in the corners of his eyes. He pulled a fresh wipe to mop the moisture from his brow, tossed the shirt and the wipes into the trash, took a bottle of cologne and sprayed it on each side of his throat, then quickly worked a toothpick around his teeth. Better. Once he was finished, he enjoyed his "breakfast"—a generous blast up each nostril from the cocaine-filled bullet that he carried in the right-hand hip pocket of his jeans. The cocaine was unadulterated, fresh from the plane that had brought it up from Colombia. It was excellent, and he had another couple of blasts. He hadn't slept for two straight nights. He needed something to keep him alert. That should do the trick.

Adolfo was always angry, but last night had been unusually intense. His father had been the cause of it. The old man had castigated him as they drove back to Juárez yesterday evening. The gringo *bastardos* had angered him, so he had taken out that anger on his son. He had told him—ordered him—to find the journalist and the cook. They were to be found and killed without delay.

Fine.

With pleasure.

He started the car and crossed town, the traffic slowing him up, cars jamming behind the big busses that took the women to and from the factories. The busses stirred up layers of grey dust that drifted into the sky and rendered the sun hazy, settling back down again on the lanes and the labyrinth of illicit electricity cabling that supplied the *colonia* shacks. When he pulled into the vast car park that surrounded La Case del Mole, he was hot and irritated. He shut off the engine and did another couple of blasts of coke. He got out. He took a pistol from the trunk, slotted home a fresh magazine, pushed it into his waistband, pulled his shirt over it, and walked across the asphalt. There was blood there: a pool of blood so thick that it was still sticky underfoot two days later, the still-congealing red glistening in the sunlight.

He climbed the steps and knocked on the glass door. Nothing. He turned to look out at the city: the belching smokestacks, the traffic spilling by on the freeway on the other side of the border, the heat haze. He turned again and tried the handle. It was locked. He took a step back and kicked the glass; it took another kick to crack it and a third to stave it all the way through. He reached through the broken glass, unlocked the door from the inside, and stepped into the lobby.

He paused, listening. He sniffed the air. He heard someone in the other room, hurrying in his direction.

"What the fuck you doing?"

He was a fat man, his belly straining against a dirty T-shirt.

"You in charge here?"

"What the fuck you doing, man, breaking the fucking door like that?"

"Are you in charge?"

"Who's asking?"

"Better just answer the question, friend."

"All right, yeah, sure—as far as you're concerned, I am in charge. And unless you tell me what the fuck you think you're doing, busting the door like that, I'm going to call the cops."

Adolfo pulled back his jacket to show a holstered Glock. "Wouldn't do that."

"Oh, Jesus, I'm sorry—I didn't mean to cause offence."

"You didn't?"

"No, sir. I'm sorry if I did. I've had a hell of a couple of days."

Adolfo fingered one of the lobster pots that had been fixed to the wall. "What's the point of this? We're nowhere near the sea."

"Just a bit of decoration."

"It's plastic. It's not even real."

"It's just for atmosphere."

Adolfo let the lobster pot fall back again. "What's your name?"

"Gomez."

"Well, then, Gomez. I'm looking for one of your cooks."

Gomez looked at him anxiously. "I don't ever get to know them that good. We get a high turnover here—in and out, all the time. There's always someone new practically every day."

"But you know the one I want to find."

"The Englishman."

"English?"

"Sounded like it. The accent—"

"What else?"

"That's all I got."

"What does he look like?"

Gomez thought. "Six foot tall. Muscular, but not too much. Black hair. Scruffy. Had a beard. And cold eyes—no light in them."

"What else?"

"He just started Monday. He was pretty good on a fryer, but you know, I—"

Adolfo let his jacket swing open again. "Come on, Gomez," he said. "This is poor. Really—very, very poor."

The man turned away and scrubbed his fist against his head. "Oh, shit, wait—there is something. He asked if I could recommend a place to stay, so I told him about that place on Calle Venezuela. Shitty place, bums and drunks—just a flophouse, really—I could give you the address if you want."

"I know where it is."

Gomez spread his flabby arms. "That's it—I ain't got no more."

"That's it?"

"I don't know what else I can tell you."

A toilet flushed somewhere.

"Who's that?"

"Maria. Front of house."

"Tell her to come through."

The man called out.

"Jesus, Gomez, it's dark in here." A woman stood in the doorway. Her hand drifted slowly away from the switch as she saw him. "I knew this wasn't done with."

"He wants to know about the cook. The Englishman. Did you speak to him?"

"Only when he came in. Not really."

Adolfo pulled the pistol from the holster and shot both of them once each through the head, one after the other, and put the gun back in the holster. The woman had just enough time to open her mouth in surprise as she fell. Adolfo walked back out to his car. He got in, started it, and backed around and drove out onto the busy road and back towards the middle of town.

Chapter Thirty-Three

HE WOUND THE window down as he drove through the city, an old Guns and Roses CD playing loud, his arm out of the window, drumming the beat with his fingers. "Welcome to the Jungle." That was just about right. Welcome to the fucking jungle. He turned off the road and onto the forecourt of the hostel and reverse parked. He took out the bullet and did another couple of blasts of cocaine. He went through to the office.

The office was hot. No AC. A television tuned to Telemundo was on in the back, a football match on. The heat made it all woozy. A dazed fly was on its back on the desk, legs twitching. The man behind the desk was dripping with sweat.

"*Hola*, Señor," he said. "Can I help you?"

"You have an Englishman staying here?"

"Who's asking?"

"Yes or no, friend?"

"I can't tell you anything about our guests, Señor."

Adolfo smiled, pulled his shirt aside, and took out the pistol. "Yes or no?"

The man's eyes bulged. "Yes. He ain't here."

"How long has he been staying?"

"Got in the day before yesterday."

"Say much?"

"Just that he wanted a bed."

"That it?"

"Quiet type. Hardly ever here."

"What time do you expect him back?"

"I don't know, Señor. He left pretty early yesterday; don't think he's been back."

"He leave any things?"

"Couple of bags."

"Show me."

The dormitory was empty. Ten beds pushed up close together. Curtains drawn. Sweltering hot. A strong smell of sweat, dirty clothes, and unwashed bodies. The man pointed to a bed in the middle of the room. It had been neatly made, the sheets tucked in snugly. All the others were unmade and messy. Adolfo told the man to leave, and he did. He stood before the bed and sniffed the air. He took the pistol and slid the end inside the tightly folded sheets, prising them up an inch or two. He yanked the sheets all the way off and looked inside them. He prodded the pillows. He looked beneath the bed. There was a bag. He took it and opened it, tipping the contents out onto the bed.

A pair of jeans.

Two T-shirts.

A pair of running shorts.

A pair of running shoes.

Underwear.

Books. English.

The Unbearable Lightness of Being.

Great Expectations.

No money. No passport. No visas.

Adolfo's cellphone vibrated in his pocket. He fished it out and pressed it to his ear.

"Yes?"

"It's Pablo."

"What do you want?"

"You know Beau Baxter?"

"Works for our friends?"

"He's in town. Spotted him an hour ago."

"Where?"

"Plaza Insurgentes. Avenida de los Insurgentes. Driving a red Jeep Cherokee."

Adolfo ended the call and went back to the office. The television was still on, but the man wasn't there. He went outside, got into his car, and left.

Chapter Thirty-Four

ANNA STRAIGHTENED the hem of her skirt and knocked on the door.

"Come in."

There were two men with Control.

"Anna," he said. "Thank you for coming."

"That's all right."

"Do you know the Foreign Secretary?"

"Only from the newspapers," she said. She took the man's outstretched hand.

"Hello, Anna. I'm Gideon Coad."

"Pleased to meet you."

Anna noticed Control was fidgeting with his pen, and as she glanced at him, she heard him sigh. He was uncomfortable introducing her to the politician; that much was obvious. She turned to the older man and gave him a polite smile. She was not nervous at all. She felt comfortable, not least because she had done a little illicit research before leaving the office last night. There had been rumours of Coad's extramarital affair with a male researcher, and true enough, it had been easy enough to find the evidence to demonstrate that those rumours were true. Emails, bank statements, text messages, hotel receipts. Anna would have been fired on the spot for an unauthorised and frivolous deployment of GCHQ's resources for the purposes of muckraking, but if you were good enough—and she most certainly was good enough—there were simple enough ways to hide your footsteps.

There was another reason for her amusement: she was right at the heart of government now.

That was good. It was confirmation that they knew nothing about her at all.

Control turned to the second man. "And this is Captain Pope."

He was tall and grizzled. Slab-like forehead. A nose that had been broken too many times. Cauliflower ears. Anna recognised the type: unmistakeably a soldier.

"Captain Pope is one of our agents," Control explained. "Like Captain Milton was." He cleared his throat. "As you know, the Foreign Secretary has asked for a briefing from you about your findings."

"Fine. Here."

She handed them each a folder labelled JOHN MILTON, CAPTAIN. The name was followed by his government record number neatly typed on the cover. It was a much slimmer volume than the reports she typically provided, but since her predecessor had found nothing at all, she felt that her smirk of pride was justified.

"You wanted everything I could find about him. I've written up his early history, plus sections on his time in the army and the SAS, his friendships—that's a short section—relationships with the opposite sex—even shorter—where he lives, his bank accounts, medical records, the cars he's driven, and so on and so forth. Everything I could get my hands on. I've found a decent amount. There are three hundred pages."

Coad looked at the report with a dismissiveness that Anna found maddening. "The potted version will be fine for now, please."

She mastered the annoyance that threatened to flash in her eyes, nodded with polite servility and, when she began to speak, her voice was clipped and businesslike.

"Milton is a very private man, but even so, I was able to build up a picture of his life in the years before he disappeared. He's forty years old, as you know. Single. He married a Danish national in 1999. Martha Olsen. A librarian. There were no children, and the marriage didn't last. They were divorced two years later. Olsen has remarried and has two children, and save a couple of emails and texts between them, they don't appear to have kept in touch. There have been affairs with other women: a businesswoman in Chelsea, a Swiss lawyer in Basel, a tourist in Mauritius. Nothing serious, though."

"Milton's not marriage material," Pope said.

"My main task was to find Mr. Milton's current location. That was not a simple assignment. He is evidently an expert in going off the grid, and it would appear that he has an unusual dedication to doing that—this is not the sort of man who makes silly mistakes. The task was made considerably more complicated by the fact that all the information after he started to work for you"—she nodded at Control—"remained classified. That was like having one hand tied behind my back."

She didn't try to hide the note of reproach. Control glared at her and then turned to the Foreign Secretary. "Some things about Milton must remain private."

"Quite. Get on with it, Miss Thackeray."

"I ran all of the usual searches, but none of them paid off. I wasn't able to find anything on him at all. No obvious sources of income—"

"Then how is he affording to live?"

"Frugally. There was a withdrawal of £300 in Liverpool before you lost him but nothing since. He has £34,534 left in the account. It's been untouched for six months. He's not stupid—he knows that's the first place a decent analyst would look. There is another savings account with another £20,000, also untouched. No pension."

Pope laughed. "He wouldn't have anticipated retirement. Not that sort of job."

"My guess would be that he has been picking up work on the way. Bar work? Bouncing? Something that attracts migrants. Cash-in-hand, no questions asked. I don't think we'll be able to find anything substantial. How detailed shall I be?"

"Whatever you think is relevant."

"There's been no correspondence with any of the few contacts I was able to find," she continued, casting a reproachful look at Control. "He has no family, and there have been no emails, calls or texts to the friends he does have. He dropped off the face of the earth."

"And yet you found him."

"Mostly down to a stroke of luck. He was fingerprinted in Mexico. Ciudad Juárez. The Mexican police upload all their data to a central database in Mexico City, and we picked it up en route. Pictures, too."

She flicked to the page with the picture of Milton in the police station.

"And there he is," Pope said.

"This was taken on Monday night. Standard procedure. The passport he gave to the local police is a fake."

"He'll have several," Pope observed.

"I'm sure he does."

"What else?"

"Knowing which passport he has been using made it much easier to get more on him—like where he's been for the last six months, for example." She flipped forwards to a double-page map of South America. "The red line marks the route that he's taken. Passport data is collected at most borders these days, and that data is very easy to find. Once I knew the number of the passport he was using, it was quick to find out where he's been. He landed in Santos in Brazil in August. He came ashore from the MSC *Donata*, a cargo ship registered in Panama. It sailed from Liverpool two weeks earlier. From there, he started west. He crossed into Paraguay at Pedro Juan Caballero, then into Bolivia and Peru. Since then, he's always headed north—Ecuador, Colombia, Nicaragua, Guatemala, then Mexico. Most of the time he was photographed at the border, and I have those pictures, too."

She flicked through to a series of photographs. The tall cranes of Santos appeared in one picture and the barren deserts of the Brazilian interior in another. Milton was looking into the camera for some of them, bored and impatient. Others had been taken without him noticing.

She scratched her head. The Foreign Secretary examined her with searching eyes. "So he's been in South America since you lost track of him," she said. "No idea what he's been doing in between his border crossings. But we do know where he is now. He came across the Mexican border at Tapachula four weeks ago, travelling by bus. He's been heading north, and it looks like he got to Juárez earlier this week. We've got the police pictures and the prints, so I tried to find something else. I ran face recognition on everything I could think of and picked up this. They're from CCTV from a restaurant in the city."

She turned to the series of stills she had grabbed. Milton was approaching the camera across a broad parking lot. He had a rucksack slung over his shoulder. Black glasses obscured his eyes. He was tanned and heavily bearded.

"How did you find that?" Coad asked.

"The software's pretty good if you can narrow the search for it a little. There was a disturbance at this restaurant the same day this was taken. A shooting. Seven people were killed. Footage from all of the cameras in the area was uploaded by the police. I was already deep into their data. Made it a lot easier to find."

Control scowled at the pictures. "Was he involved?"

"Don't know."

"Was he arrested?"

"Don't think so."

Coad held up his hand. He paused for a moment, drumming the fingers of his right hand on the armrest of his chair before turning to her again. "Do you know where he is?"

"No," she admitted.

"You've checked hotels?"

"First thing I checked. Nothing obvious. He'll be paying in cash."

"So where do we look first?"

"Lieutenant Jesus Plato—the policeman who fingerprinted him. He's the best place to start."

"And if we should decide to send agents to Mexico to find him ... what is your estimate of the odds that we would find him?"

"I can't answer that. I'd be speculating."

"Then speculate," Control said.

"If he's as good as I think he is, he won't stay in one place for more than a week or two, and he's been in Juárez since Monday. Plus there's the danger that what happened at the restaurant might have spooked him. But if you're quick? Like in the next couple of days? Decent odds, I'd say. He won't know you're coming. If he's moved on, he won't be far away. A decent analyst might be able to pick up a trail."

Control looked across at Coad, and at the latter's curt nod, he turned back to Anna. "We've been in contact with the Mexican government. They've given us approval to send a team into Mexico to bring him out. Captain Pope will be in charge. Six agents and you, Ms. Thackeray."

"Oh."

"Are you willing to go?"

"I'll do what I'm told."

Pope nodded at her. "Juárez is not a small place," he said, "and if you've done your research, you'll know it's not the easiest city in the world to find something. It's overrun with the drug cartels. Normal society has broken down completely. We might need help tracking him down. And you know him as well as anybody."

"Well?" Coad said.

"Of course," she said.

Control nodded brusquely. "You'll be flying from Northolt and landing at Fort Bliss in Texas. You'll go over the border from there. Do you have any questions?"

"When?" she said.

"First thing tomorrow."

ANNA RODE home, changed out of her leathers, and went out for a walk. Pittville Park was nearby, and she made her way straight for the Pump Room and the ornamental lakes. The building was a fine example of Regency architecture, and the lakes were beautiful, but Anna was not distracted by them. She slowed as she approached the usual bench. She sat and pretended to watch the dogs bounding across the grass. When she was satisfied that she was not observed, she reached down beneath the bench, probing for the metal bars that held the wooden slats in place. Her fingers brushed against the narrow plastic box with the magnetic strip that held it against the rusted metal. She retrieved the box, opened the end, and slid the memory stick inside. It contained her full report on Milton, plus the regular updates that she provided on the operation and scope of GCHQ's data-gathering activities. She didn't know how long she would be out of the country, and she did not want to be late in filing. She paused again, checked left and right, waited, and then reached back and pressed the case back into its place. As she left for home, she swiped the piece of chalk that she held in her hand against the side of the metal bin next to the chair.

Chapter Thirty-Five

CAPTAIN MICHAEL POPE took off his boots and his jacket and went through into his kitchen. It was late, and his wife was asleep upstairs. He looked in the fridge, but there was nothing that took his fancy. He took a microwave meal from its paper sleeve, pierced the film, and put it in the oven to heat. While he was waiting, he reached the bottle of whisky down from the cupboard, poured himself a double measure, added ice, and sipped it carefully to prolong it. He rested his hands on the work surface and allowed his head to hang down between his shoulders.

Did he know Milton?

He did. He knew him very well indeed.

THEY MET twenty years ago. They had both been in the sandpit for the First Iraq War, young recruits who were too stupid to be scared. They were in the same regiment, the Royal Green Jackets, but in different battalions. Milton had been in the Second and Pope in the First. They hadn't met in the desert, but once that was all over, Pope had transferred into the First Battalion. He was assigned to B Company.

That was the same company, and then the same rifle platoon, as Milton.

They were almost immediately sent to South Armagh.

B Company had been assigned to South Armagh. That was bandit country, and Crossmaglen, the town where they would be based, was as bad as it got. It was right on the border, which meant that the Provos could prepare in the south and then make the quick trip north to shoot at them or leave their bombs or do whatever it was that they had planned to do.

The men had been billeted in the security forces base, and their rifle company lived in "submarines," long corridors with beds built three high on one side. Milton had the top bunk, and Pope was directly beneath him. It was the kind of random introduction that the army was good at, but they quickly discovered that it was propitious; they had plenty in common. Both liked The Smiths and The Stone Roses and the films of Tarantino and de Palma. Both liked a drink. Both had girlfriends back home, but neither was particularly attached to them. Milton's sense of humour was dry, and Pope's was smutty. They were both obsessed with getting fitter and stronger, and both intended to attempt SAS selection when they had a little more experience. The chemistry just worked, and they quickly became close.

POPE WASN'T ONE for mementoes, but he had kept a couple of photographs from that part of his career. He took down an album and flicked through it, finding the photograph that he wanted: seven men arranged around a Saracen. In those days, the vehicles were fitted with two gallon containers at the rear. They called them Norwegians. The drivers filled them with tea before they left the sangar each morning, and although the tea grew lukewarm and soupy before too long, it was a life-saver during cold winter patrols. The photograph was taken in a field somewhere in Armagh. Three of them were kneeling, the other four leaning against the body of the truck, each of them saluting the camera with a plastic cup. Milton was at the back, his cup held beneath the Norwegian's tap, smiling broadly. Pope was kneeling in front of him. Milton was confident and relaxed. Pope remembered how he had felt back then: it had been difficult not to look up to him a little. That respect was something that remained constant, ever since, throughout their time together in the regiment and then the Group.

The microwave beeped. He knocked back the rest of the whisky, collected the meal, and took it into the lounge.

He sat down with the album on his lap.

Memories.

He didn't question his orders, but they were troubling. Control had said that Milton had suffered from some sort of breakdown. That didn't seem very likely to Pope. Milton had always been a quiet man, solid and dependable. Extremely good at his job. Impossible to fluster, even under the most extreme pressure. The idea that he might snap like this was very difficult to square. But there again, there was all the evidence to suggest that something *had* happened to him: the trouble he had caused in East London, shooting Callan, and then, after six months when no one knew where he was, turning up again in Mexico like this.

Something had happened.

He had his orders, and he would obey them as far as he could.

He would go and bring him back. But he wouldn't retire him unless there was nothing else for it. He would do everything he could to bring him back alive.

Chapter Thirty-Six

BEAU BAXTER DIDN'T even see him come in. He was hungry, busy with his plate of quesadillas, slicing them into neat triangles and then mopping the plate with them before slotting them into his mouth. It was a public place, popular and full of customers. He had let his guard down just for a moment, and that was all it took. Adolfo González just slid onto the bench seat opposite him, a little smile on his face. It might have been mistaken for a friendly smile, one that an old friend gives to another, except for the fact that his right hand stayed beneath the table and held, Beau knew, a revolver that was pointed right at his balls.

"Good morning, Señor Baxter."

"Señor González. I suppose you think I'm pretty stupid."

"Negligent, perhaps. I'm surprised. Your reputation is excellent."

"And yours," Beau said, with a bitter laugh.

"You know not to make any sudden moves, yes?" Adolfo's English was heavily accented, slightly lispy.

"No need to remind me."

"Nevertheless—"

"There's no need for this to end badly."

"It won't, Señor Baxter, at least not for me."

Beau tried to maintain his composure. He laid the knife and fork on the plate, nudging them so that they rested neatly alongside each other. "Let me go back to New Jersey. I'll tell them to lay off."

"I could let you do that."

"They'll listen to me. I'll explain."

"But they won't, Beau—do you mind if I call you Beau? You know they won't. I killed your employer's brother. I removed his head with a machete. I killed five more of their men. They want that debt repaid. I'd be the same if the roles were reversed, although I would do the business myself rather than hide behind a *panocha's* skirts."

"I've got money in the car. Twenty-five grand. I'll give it to you."

"That's the price they put on me?"

"Half. You're worth fifty."

"Fifty." He laughed gently. "Really? Beau, I'm disappointed in you. You think I need money?"

He realised how stupid that sounded. "I suppose not."

He indicated the half-finished quesadilla. "How is the food here?"

"It's all right."

"Do you mind?" González picked up Beau's knife, used it to slice off a triangle, then stabbed it and put it in his mouth. He chewed reflectively. "Mmmm," he said after a long moment. "That *is* good. You like Oaxaca?"

"I like it all right."

"It is a little too Mexican for most *Americanos*."

"I'm a little too Mexican for most Americans."

González took a napkin from the dispenser, folded it, and carefully applied it to the corners of his mouth. Beau watched Adolfo all the time. He looked straight back at him. Beau assessed, but there was nothing that he could do. The table was pressed up against his legs, preventing him from moving easily, and besides, he did not doubt that Adolfo had him covered. A revolver under the table, it didn't matter what calibre it was, he couldn't possibly miss. No, he thought. Nothing he could do except bide his time and hope he made a mistake.

"We're alike, you and I," he said.

González did not immediately answer. "Let me tell you something, Beau. I want to impart the gravity of your"—he fished for the correct word—"your predicament. Do you know what I did last night? I went out. Our business has a house in a nice neighbourhood. Lots of houses, actually, but this one has a big garden in back. Not far from here. We had two men staying there. *Hijos de mil cojeros*. They used to be colleagues, but then they got greedy. They thought they could take my father's money from him. Do you know what I did to them?"

"I can guess."

"Indeed, and discussing the precise details would be barbaric, yes? I'm sure a man such as yourself must have an excellent imagination. We had some enjoyment, but then, eventually, after several hours, I shot them both. And then, this morning, I visited the restaurant where a journalist and her friends were eating on Monday night. The owner and the *cuero* he was with, they didn't give me the information that I wanted. So I shot them, too. Just like that."

"I don't doubt it."

"Another question: do you know what a *pozole* is?"

"I'm pretty sure you're fixing to tell me."

He smiled, his small teeth showing white through his thin, red lips. "A *pozole* is a Mexican stew. Traditional. Hominy, pork, chillies. It's important to keep stirring the soup while it is on the stove so that the flavours blend properly. One of my men has acquired a nickname: he is known as *El Pozolera*. The Stewmaker. It is because he is an expert in dissolving bodies. He fills a plastic drum with two hundred litres of water, puts in two sacks of caustic soda, boils it over a fire, and then adds the body. You boil them for eight hours until the only things left are teeth and nails, and then you take the remains—the soup—to an empty lot and burn it up with gasoline. It is disgusting for those without the constitution necessary to watch. A very particular smell."

"Why are you telling me this?"

"Because, Beau, I need you to understand that, even though we might be in the same business, you are mistaken: we are *not* alike. You deliver your quarry alive. You even allow them to bargain with you. To negotiate, to offer you a better deal. Mine cannot. I do not make bargains, and I do not negotiate. I'm not open to persuasion, and I can't be dissuaded with whatever you have in your car, by the money in your bank account or by any other favour you might offer me. Once I have decided a man must die, that is it—they will die. A final question before we leave. You have killed people. Not many people, I know, but some. Tell me: what does it feel like for you?"

"Feels like business."

"Again, a point of difference. For me, it is *everything*. It is the sensation of having someone's life in the palm of your hand and then making your hand into a fist, tightening it, squeezing tighter and tighter until the life is crushed. That is power, Beau. The power of life and death."

"You're crazy."

"By your standards, perhaps, but it hardly matters, does it?" The man leaned back. He studied Beau. "I'll be honest. You will die today. It will not be quick or painless, and I will enjoy it. We will record it and send it to your employer as a warning: anyone else you send to Mexico will end up the same way. The only question is where, when and how. I will give you a measure of control over the first two of those. The how?—that you must leave to me."

Beau looked out of the restaurant's window. "I know where the girl is."

"Good for you."

"The Englishman—I know where he's taken her."

"Ah, yes, the Englishman. *Caro de culo.* An interesting character. I can find out nothing about him. What can you tell me?"

"I could give you him, too."

"You're not listening, Beau. I don't barter. You'll tell me everything I want in the end, anyway."

"I could deliver him to you in five minutes."

He smiled again, humouring him. "You said you know where the girl is?"

"Yeah."

"You know, Beau. It still doesn't matter."

"And why is that?"

"Because there is nowhere in Juárez where the Englishman could hide her from me. This city is mine, Beau. Every hovel in every *barrio*. Every street corner, every alleyway. Every hotel, every mansion, every last square inch. How do you think I found you? All I have to do is wait. She will be delivered to me eventually. They always are."

Chapter Thirty-Seven

MILTON WATCHED the conversation through the windows of the diner. The place was on Avenida de los Insurgentes in a strip mall with a large plastic sign in the shape of a lozenge that said Plaza Insurgentes. Milton's taxi had pulled over on the other side of the road, behind a 1968 Impala Caprice with *"Viva La Raza"* written across the bonnet. The passenger-side window was down, classic rock playing loudly.

He recognised the driver as the doctor from the hospital.

Milton stood quietly and watched.

The diner was busy. Beau Baxter was alone in a booth, and González made his way straight to him, slipping down opposite and beginning to talk. Beau's body language was stiff and stilted, and his face was pale; this was not a meeting that he had requested. Curious, Milton crossed the street to get a little closer, watching through an angled window so that neither man could see him. He looked closer and saw that González had not moved his right hand above the table. He was armed, or he wanted Baxter to think that he was.

Milton moved away from the window and leant against a telephone kiosk. He looked up and down the street and across the strip mall, but if González had other men here, they were good. Milton could see nothing that made him think that there was any sort of backup. González was on his own. He could feel the reassuring coldness of the Springfield's barrel pressed against his spine. Thirteen shots in the clip, one in the chamber. He hoped they would be enough.

Beau and González got up.

Milton moved to the entrance. There was a bench next to the door, an advertisement for a law firm on the backrest. He sat down behind a newspaper he found on the ground, the Springfield hidden in his lap. Beau came out first, González behind him. Milton let them pass, folded the newspaper over the arm of the bench, and picked up the gun. He followed. When they reached González's car, Milton pressed the barrel against González's coccyx.

"Nice and easy," he said.

González turned his head a little, looking back from the corner of his eyes.

"You again."

"That's right."

"I still don't know your name."

"I know."

"English, then. Why are you always involved in my business, English?"

Milton glanced at Baxter. "You all right?"

"Feel a bit stupid."

"Get his gun."

Baxter frisked him quickly, finding a gold-plated Colt .45 in a holster clipped to his belt. He unfastened the holster and removed it.

"Look at this. Gold? You might have money, but you can't buy class."

González said nothing. He just smiled.

"Beau," Milton said. "What are you driving?"

"The Jeep," he said, nodding to the red Cherokee with tinted windows.

"Get it started."

"You have already taken too long, English," González said. "My family has eyes everywhere. They are our falcons—waiters, barmen, newspaper vendors, taxi drivers, even the *cholos* on the street corners. A hundred dollars a week so that we may know everything about the comings and goings of our city. My *padre* will know what you are doing before he sits down to dinner. And then he will find you."

"You'll be halfway back to New Mexico by then, partner," Beau said.

Milton prodded González in the back and propelled him towards the Jeep. When they reached the car, the Mexican finally turned around to face him. "Every moment in your life is a choice, English. Every moment is a chance to go this way or that. You are making a choice now. You have picked an unwise course, and you will have to face the consequences of your decision."

Milton watched him carefully, a practiced assessment that was so automatic that he rarely realised he was making it. He watched the dilation in his eyes and the pulse in the artery in his neck. He saw the rate of his breathing. The man was as relaxed as if they were old friends, meeting up by coincidence and engaging in banal small talk about their families. Milton had seen plenty of disconcerting people before, but this man—Santa Muerta—this man was something else. A real piece of work.

"The way I'm coming at it," Beau said, "you ain't in a position to lecture anyone."

González kept his eyes on Milton. "Not everyone is suited to this line of work, English. Having a gun pointed at someone can sometimes lead people to exaggerate their own abilities. They tell themselves that they are in control of events where perhaps they are not."

"Don't worry yourself on my account," Milton said. "I'm as used to this as you are. Get in the car."

Baxter opened the door, and smiling serenely and without another word, González got in.

Chapter Thirty-Eight

EL PATRÓN had a small mansion on the outskirts of Juárez. He had dozens, all around Mexico. This was in the best part of the city, St. Mark's Close, a gated community approached through a series of arches and set around a pleasant green. It was a quiet retreat of mansions, each more garish than the next. Outside some were vehicles marked with the corporate logos of the owners of the *maquiladoras*. In other forecourts were SUVs with blacked-out windows and bulletproof panels; those belonged to the drug barons. The community had a private security detail that Felipe bolstered whenever he was in residence. His men were posted at the gates now, in the grounds of the mansion and in the watchtower that he had constructed at the end of the drive. Twenty of his very best men, most related to him by blood or marriage, vigilant and disposed towards violence. His doctor had advised him that sleep was important for a man of his age, and he made sure that he always slept well.

He had bought the place a year ago, persuading the prominent lawyer who had owned it that it was in his best interests to sell. He hadn't stiffed him on the price—he felt no need to drive a hard bargain—and he had sent three bags with a million dollars in each as a mark of his gratitude. He had visited the house before the lawyer had owned it, and he had always been fond of it. It was surrounded on all sides by tall brick walls. It had been built with a small cupola, an architectural shorthand for extravagance in Juárez. Inside, there were baroque tables mixed with minimalist leather couches, red velvet curtains and a disco ball, Oriental rugs and, on the wall above the fireplace, a knockoff of Picasso's "Guernica." The décor was not systematic thanks to the fact that it had been purchased, at various times, by several of Felipe's wives. There was a glass-enclosed pool. A room in the basement held a large pile of stacked banknotes—four feet cubed—a little over twenty million, all told. Another held his armoury, some of the guns plated in gold. There were just a few street-facing windows and, at his insistence, the best security system that money could buy.

Marilyn Monroe had owned the house at one time; the rumour was that the purchase was a drunken extravagance after a night in the Kentucky Bar following her divorce from that American writer. It reminded him of another time in Juárez, so different from how things were today that it was almost another place. Salaciousness and audacity, everything for sale, most of it carnal.

Not an innocent time, because Juárez could never be innocent, but innocent compared to what had followed in the wake of the narco wars. He was old enough to remember all of it, the town's history as evident to him as the rings on a split tree trunk.

The house was busy tonight. He was hosting a party for the gringos. Plenty of his lieutenants were present, together with a significant delegation from the city. The deputy mayor, representatives from the *federales*, senior officers from the army. They had erected a wrestling ring in the garden, and a tag team of *luchadores* were putting on an athletic display: wiry, masked wrestlers who grappled and fought, climbing the turnbuckles to perform ever more impressive dives and twists. The best *cueros* from the brothels that Felipe owned had been brought to the house to provide their own kind of entertainment. Drink and drugs were unlimited.

He and Isaac were enjoying a bottle of very expensive wine. Isaac's colleagues were partying with the women. They were gross *Americanos*. Both were drunk. No style or class. *Que te den por el culo,* he thought. He had no respect for them, none at all, but he put on a wide smile and played the generous host. Business was business, after all, and they stood to make him a lot of money.

"Are you happy, Isaac?" Felipe asked.

"Yes, El Patrón."

"Our arrangement is satisfactory to you?"

"Are you kidding? It's perfect."

They had discussed the arrangement for a couple of hours. Felipe would deliver his product across the border in a number of different ways: by truck and car through Juárez, by ultralight into the fields of New Mexico and Texas, and through the tunnel that he was in the process of building. Isaac owned several commercial ranches across the south-west and had a fleet of trucks to deliver the slaughtered cows and sheep to market. The product would be hidden inside the carcasses of the animals and distributed to a network of dealers that the two would arrange together.

Yes, he thought. It was satisfactory. Business came first, but there would come a time when another means of distribution was available to him, and when that happened, he would not forget the way that Isaac had spoken to him in the desert. The impudence. The unspoken threat: we will return north without speaking to you if you do not give us the reassurances that we want. Felipe had a long memory, and he bore a grudge. There would be an accounting.

"I'm looking forward to seeing your new facility," Isaac said.

"Ah, yes. The lab. It is nearly finished."

"When will it be ready?"

"By the end of the week. Twenty pounds of meth every day. Excellent quality, too. I will show you."

"Who is your cook?"

"An American. He used to work for a pharmaceutical company. Blue chip."

"How'd you find him?"

"I keep my eyes open, Isaac."

The man grinned at him. "When can we go see it?"

"Tomorrow. We will fly."

He was interrupted by Pablo. The man was scared. "El Patrón," he said, his face bleached of colour. "Please—may I have a word with you?"

"What is it?" he said mildly.

The man looked agonised. "In private, El Patrón, *por favor*."

"Excuse me," he said with an easy smile even as his temper was bubbling. He moved to the side, out of earshot, and glared at Pablo. "What *is* it?"

"Your son. It is Adolfo. He has been abducted."

"What on earth do you mean?"

"There is a gringo bounty hunter in town."

"Working for who?"

"The Lucianos. There is a price on your son's head—the killings in the desert."

"And this man—he has him?"

"Yes—him and another. Adolfo had surprised the bounty hunter. We were going to take him out into the desert and kill him, but as they left the place where they had met, he was stopped by a second man. We think he was the man at the restaurant on Monday night."

"And who is he?"

"We don't know, El Patrón."

His temper flared. "Do we know *anything*?"

"He's been protecting the journalist from the restaurant. Adolfo visited her this morning to finish her off, and this man was there. He is English. There is some connection between them."

"Then if we cannot find him, we must find her, and then he will come to us." He put down his glass of wine. Isaac was looking at him quizzically; he replaced the angry mask that had fallen across his face with a warm and reassuring smile. "Call the police," he said quietly to Pablo. "They are to put roadblocks on every road out of Juárez. No one leaves without the car being checked. And put the word out: a million dollars to whoever can bring me her. A million dollars if anyone can bring me him. Tell all our falcons. I want them found."

Chapter Thirty-Nine

ANNA HAD been picked up from her two-bedroom flat in Cheltenham High Street at four in the morning. The car was a black BMW with tinted windows and a uniformed driver. She wasn't used to being chauffeured, and she felt a little out of place, her grubby Doc Martens against the spotless cream carpet inside the car. The man said very little as they headed west, following the A40 until it became the M40. That suited her well. She slept for the first half hour, and then, roused as the sun rose into a sky of wispy low clouds, she took out her laptop and reviewed—for the hundredth time—the report she had made on John Milton.

She was excited. It wasn't unheard of for an analyst to be sent out into the field, but it was the first time that it had happened to her. The rationale was obvious and made sense: if Milton slipped beneath the surface again, it was best to have an expert in situ to help track him down again.

And they were right: she knew him as well as anyone.

The trip also promised to furnish her with a much better idea of how Group 15 worked. They had always been unable to find out much about them, save the rumour and gossip that occasionally reached the ears of the Federal Security Service; they had certainly never been on actual operations with them. That, she knew, would stand her in excellent stead with Colonel Shcherbakov.

The driver turned into Ickenham and then, after a further few minutes, turned and slowed to a stop outside the armed guards stationed at the entrance of RAF Northolt. He showed his credentials and drove onto the base, following a route that brought him straight onto the main runway. A Gulfstream G280 was being readied for flight. It was painted gleaming white, the sunlight sparking off the fuselage. The driver took her luggage from the boot and added it to the pile of gear that two technicians were loading into the hold. Anna got out and stared at them. A large black fabric bag was open, the contents being checked. Anna saw automatic rifles, the metal glinting black and icy in the early light.

She paused at the steps to the cabin.

The pilot, performing a final external check, smiled at her. "Miss Thackeray?"

"Yes."

"Good morning, ma'am. Up you go. They're waiting inside."

Anna climbed the steps and entered the jet. The cabin was plush. Decadent. Eight handcrafted leather seats, a workstation and a three-person sofa. Large porthole windows. Proper cutlery on the tables. Pewter crockery.

Crystal glasses. One of the portholes faced the door, and she glimpsed her reflection: the boots, the ripped jeans and the faded and frayed T-shirt looked completely out of place. She swallowed, daunted, her usual confidence knocked just a little. She almost wished that she had worn something more— well, something more *appropriate*.

Five men and a woman were arranging themselves around the cabin.

She felt self-conscious. "Hello," she said.

Captain Pope turned to her. "Good morning, Miss Thackeray."

"Morning."

He looked at her and frowned. It was quizzical—perhaps even amused— and not disapproving. "Get yourself settled. We'll be taking off soon."

"Introductions first?"

He smiled patiently. "You know who I am. Lance Corporal Hammond's over there with the headphones. That's Lance Corporal Callan. Corporal Spenser and Corporal Blake are playing cards. And Sergeant Underwood is sleeping."

Anna looked the others over.

The woman, Hammond, looked to be in her early thirties. Five eight, black hair cut severely. Compact and powerful. Callan was tall and slender. Strikingly handsome. Hair in tight curls, so blond as to almost be white. Skin was white, too, like alabaster. A cruelty to his thin lips and unfeeling eyes that Anna found unsettling. Alien. Spenser was shorter, bald and heavily muscled. Blake was darker skinned. Something about him was a little exotic. Foreign, perhaps. Underwood had a sleeping mask over his face, obscuring his features.

They looked up at her, but no one spoke.

Pope smiled at her. "Take your seat," he said. "Wheels up in five minutes."

Chapter Forty

THERE WAS a sign on the wall of the room that said that the motel had Wi-Fi. Caterina booted up her laptop, located the network, and joined it. She had installed police scanner software, and it was then, listening to those disinterested voices bracketed by static, that she heard about the body of the missing girl who had been found.

The police said that the girl had been identified as Guillermina Marquez.

The body had turned up on scrubland near to the Estadio Olímpico Benito Juárez. The Indios played there; Leon had taken her to see them once. It was close to the motel. A twenty-minute walk, maximum. Fifteen if she ran. She thrust her camera and her notepad into her rucksack, scribbled a quick note to Milton explaining where she was going, locked the door behind her, and set off towards the river.

It was growing late, and the light was leaving the city. Caterina crested a shallow hill and looked out across the border to El Paso, the lights twinkling against the spectrum of greys across the desert and the mountains beyond. She wondered what it was like over the border. She had never been. She had an idea, of course, on a superficial level—she was in contact with journalists on the other side of the line, there was television and the movies—but it was more than the superficial things that she wondered about. She wondered what it would be like to live in a city that was safe. Where you were not woken with yet another report of dead bodies dropped on your doorstep. Where the army and the police were not as bad as the criminals. Where children were not abducted, were not tortured, mutilated, bruised, fractured or strangled or violated.

The stadium was across a bleak expanse of scrub. Other girls had been found here: she thought of the map in her room, with the pins that studded this part of town, a bristling little forest of murders. She remembered two of them left in the dust with their arms arranged so that they formed crucifixes; she remembered those two particularly well.

She walked faster.

Dusk was turning into night. Two police cruisers were parked on the scrub next to a thicket of trees and creosote bushes. Blue and white crime scene tape had been strung around the trunks of three of the trees, fluttering and snapping in the breeze, forming a broad triangular enclosure. Uniformed officers were inside, gathered around a shapeless thing on the floor. Caterina ducked down, pulled the tape over her head, and went forwards. She could see the body covered with a blanket, the naked feet visible where the blanket was too short. She took out her camera, shoved in the flash, and started taking pictures.

One of the policemen turned. "Excuse me."

She moved away from him, circling the body, continuing to take pictures.

"Excuse me, Señorita. No pictures, please."

"What was her name?" she asked, the camera still pressed to her face.

"I recognise you," the policeman said.

She lowered the camera. "Do I know you?"

"I'm *Capitán* Alameda. You don't remember?"

"No, I—"

"It's Caterina, isn't it?"

"Yes—how do you know my name?"

"I was at the restaurant on Monday night. I was with you in the hospital."

"Oh."

He put a hand on Caterina's shoulder. "You shouldn't be here."

"Who was she?"

"We don't know yet."

"When was she found?"

"A couple of hours ago." He guided her back and away from the covered body. "Come on. It's not safe. I thought you were going over the border."

"Soon. Tomorrow, I think."

"You need to keep off the street until then. If they find out where you are— look, where are you staying?"

She paused.

"Don't worry—I know the cook is looking after you. My colleague— *Teniente* Plato—he's been speaking with him. I'll take you back there. We can talk about what happened here in the car. I'll answer all your questions."

She paused.

"Caterina—I'm the captain of the police. Come on. You can trust me."

She relented.

Chapter Forty-One

FELIPE EXCUSED HIMSELF from the party. It would continue in the grounds of the mansion, but out of sight, the garages were busy with activity. He had called in his best men. His best *sicarios*. Their cars were parked in the wide bay before the triple garage, and they were milling there, waiting for his instructions. Pablo had opened the arms cache and was in the process of distributing the heavy artillery. The way Felipe was thinking, if Adolfo wasn't returned to him soon, he would have to do something to focus the attention of the authorities. Firing a few AR-15s in the marketplace, tossing in a few grenades, that ought to do the trick. They knew, but perhaps they needed to be reminded: there were some things that could not be allowed to stand.

An unmarked police car rolled up the slope that curved around the mansion and parked next to the garages. Two of the men broke away from the rest, their hands reaching for their pistols. Felipe watched as the door opened and a man he recognised stepped out.

The municipal cop. *Capitán* Alameda.

The two men recognised him, too, and stepped aside.

"El Patrón."

"Not now, *Capitán*. I'm busy."

"I know about Adolfo."

"Then you'll understand why this is not a good time."

"No—I know who has him. And how you can get him back."

Felipe turned to Pablo. "You go in five minutes," he called.

"Yes, El Patrón."

"Be quick, Alameda. And don't waste my time."

"The girl from the restaurant. The one you didn't get. The Englishman is trying to keep her safe."

"And?"

"I have her. There was a body in the park next to the stadium. She was there. Taking pictures."

"Where is she?"

He nodded in the direction of his car. "In back."

"Get her."

Alameda went back to the car and brought the girl out. She was cuffed, her wrists fastened behind her back.

"Do you know who I am?" Felipe asked.

She spat at his feet.

"She's feisty," Alameda suggested. "Took a good swing at me before I got the bracelets on."

"Where is the Englishman?"

"*Come mierda y muerte.*"

"If you help me get my son back, I'll let you go. You have my word."

"Your word's no good."

Felipe shifted his weight. "Look around—you're on your own. The Englishman can't help you now. You don't have any other choice."

Chapter Forty-Two

BEAU PULLED the Jeep into the motel parking lot. Milton opened the rear door, stepped outside, and pulled Adolfo out with him. Beau followed close behind, the barrel of his pistol pushed tight into the small of the Mexican's back. Milton unlocked the door and opened it.

The room was empty.

"Caterina?"

The bathroom door was open. Milton checked. It was empty, too.

"Where is she?" Beau said anxiously.

"I don't know."

Her laptop was on. Milton checked it: a police scanner application was open, the crackle of static interrupted by occasional comments from the dispatcher. A scrap of paper was on the desk next to the computer. A note had been written down.

"There's been another murder. She's gone to cover it."

"We don't wanna be hanging around, partner. The sooner we get them both over the border, the better."

"Not without her."

"I know, but we're not on home turf here."

"It's not open to debate. You can go whenever you want, but he stays until I have her back."

Milton's phone started to ring.

He looked at the display: an unknown number.

"*Hola.*"

He didn't recognise the voice. "I think you have the wrong number," he replied in Spanish.

The caller spoke in accented English. "No, I have the right number."

"Who is this?"

"I am Felipe."

A pause.

"You know me now?"

"I've heard of you. Where's the girl?"

"In a minute. I don't know your name. What shall I call you?"

"John."

"Hello, John. You are the Englishman from the restaurant?"

"That's right."

"You have caused me some—awkwardness."

"I'm just getting started. Where's the girl?"

"She's here. Safe and sound. Where is my son?"

"With me."

"He is—?"

"He's fine."

"We seem to be at an impasse."

"Seems so. What do you want to do about that?"

Felipe paused. Milton knew he was trying to sweat him. Pointless. "I'm waiting," he said. There was not even the faintest trace of emotion in his voice.

Felipe was brusque. "We each have something the other wants. I don't know why you have involved yourself in my business, but I am going to propose a short truce. An exchange: the girl for my son."

"Where?"

"There is a village south of Juárez. Samalayuca. Turn right off the 45 and drive into the desert. We can meet there. Tomorrow morning. Nine."

"You wouldn't be thinking about trying to ambush me, would you, Felipe?"

"A truce is a truce."

"I know you don't know who I am."

"So why not tell me, John?"

"All you need to know is that you don't want to know me. Don't do anything stupid. You might think you're a frightening man, and people around here would say that you are, but you don't frighten me. There's nothing here I haven't seen before. If you try anything, if the girl is hurt—if anything happens at all that I don't like—I give you my word that I will find you and I will kill you. Do you understand me?"

When he replied, the man's voice was tight, with fury behind it. Milton knew why: he was not used to being threatened. "I believe I do," he said. "Let's make this exchange. After that—well then, *John*—after that, well, you know how this is going to turn out, don't you?"

"No. Do you?"

"Yes, I do. And so do you."

The line went dead.

"They have her?" Beau said.

Milton nodded.

"Ignorant dogs!" Adolfo gloated. "You—"

Milton did not even look at him; he just backhanded him with a sudden, brutal clip that snapped his head around and sent him toppling backwards onto the bed. When Adolfo sat back up, his lip was dripping with blood.

Milton wiped the blood from his knuckles. "Put him in the bath. If he tries to come out, shoot him."

Beau did as he was told. Milton took his phone and found the number he had been given at the police station three days earlier. He entered the number and pressed CALL.

It connected. "Plato."

"It's John Smith."

"John—what can I do for you?"

"I need to talk to you. It's the girl."

"What about her?"

"She's been taken."

An audible sigh. "When?"

"A couple of hours ago."

"You said you were going to the hotel."

"I'm here now. I went out, and she's gone.

"You left her?"

"Temporarily. She left on her own."

"You know that for sure?"

"She left a note."

"How do you know she—"

"I just had a call from Adolfo's father."

"*Cojer!*" Plato cursed.

"I'm guessing he's in charge around here?"

"Felipe González. El Patrón. He *is* La Frontera. What did he say?"

"I'd rather not talk on the phone. Can we meet?"

Milton heard the long sigh. "You better come over here. Do you have a pen and paper?"

"Yes."

Milton took down the address that Plato dictated.

Chapter Forty-Three

JESUS PLATO SLID underneath the hull of the boat, hooked the pot with his hand, and dragged it toward him. He dipped his brush into the paint and started to apply it. He had been looking forward to this part of the project for weeks. There were few things that made an old boat look better than repainting it. The *Emelia* had a tatty, ancient gel-coat finish, and Plato was going to replace it with two new coats of urethane paint. The paint wasn't cheap, but he figured it'd be worth it for the difference it would make. It was calming work, too—meditative—and something where the gratification from the job would be quick.

A taxi turned into the road. He looked up as it slowed to a halt. Milton got out, paid the driver, and walked up the driveway. Plato slid out from beneath the boat and then stood, pouring a handful of white spirit into his palms and wiping away the stained paint. "In here," he said, leading the way through the open garage door. He hadn't told Emelia that Milton would be coming over, and he didn't want her to worry.

The boat's gas engine was in pieces on his work desk. He had a small beer fridge in the corner, and he opened it, taking out a couple of cans.

"Thanks—but I don't drink."

"Suit yourself." Plato put one back, tugged the ring pull on the other, and drank off the first quarter. It was a hot day, and he had been working hard; the beer tasted especially good. "You better tell me what's happened."

"I met a man at the hospital. He's a bounty hunter. He's here for Adolfo González."

"Good luck with that."

"He says he can help get the girl over the border and set up on the other side."

"He's doing that out of the goodness of his heart?"

"Of course not. I said I'd help him find González."

Plato sighed.

"I was going to meet him to talk about it. A restaurant. González was there. We've got him."

Plato watched him carefully over the rim of his can. "You've got him?"

"Baxter does. The bounty hunter."

"Beau Baxter?"

"You know him?"

"I've heard of him. He used to work on the line before he got into what he does now. Border Patrol."

"And?"

"Back then he was old school. A hard man. But I don't know about now. You don't normally get much integrity out of men in his line of business. You saying he's got Adolfo now?"

Milton nodded.

"And you don't think he'll just up and leave? Get him over the border and get paid?"

His icy blue eyes burned with cold. "I saved his life. And he's not that stupid."

"All right."

Milton clenched and unclenched his fists. "When I got back to the hotel, the girl was gone. It didn't happen there. No sign of a struggle. Nothing disturbed. I looked through her stuff. She'd written this down."

Milton handed him a piece of paper. Plato recognised the address. The note said that she had gone to investigate a murder.

"There was a body found here earlier," Milton said. "Another of the dead girls."

"That's right. It was on the radio. She must have gone to cover it."

"I'll ask around. Maybe whoever was there might've seen her."

"Thank you."

"This phone call you had with Felipe—what did he say?"

"He knows we've got his son. He wants to exchange. Her for him."

"You do know you can't trust anything he says?"

"Of course. I've dealt with men like him before, Plato."

"I doubt it," he said, shaking his head. "Not like him. Where does he want to meet?"

"A village south of Juárez. Samalayuca."

"I know it. It's off the 45. Not a good place for you."

"Why?"

"Open ground. No one else around for miles. And he'll know it well. I've been out there more than a few times over the years. One of their favourite places for dumping bodies."

"That's one of the reasons I'm here. I'm going to need some help."

Plato shook his head.

"There's me and Baxter, but I don't think that's going to be enough."

"I'm sorry."

"I need someone who's good with a rifle."

"No, Smith, I'm sorry—I just can't."

"Don't think about me, Lieutenant. Don't think about Baxter. It's the girl. You know if we don't do something they'll kill her."

"I know that, and it's awful, but she knew the risks, and it doesn't make any difference. I still can't. Look—let me tell you a story. I've been dealing with the cartel about as long as they've been around, least in the form they're in at the moment. Before El Patrón, there was another boss. They called him

El Señor de Los Cielos. Lord of the Skies, on account of the jumbo jets they said he had, packed full of cocaine up from Colombia. He was Mr. Juárez for years. And then La Frontera came over from Sinaloa, trying to muscle in on his turf. There was a war, a proper one, a shooting war."

He took another long pull on his beer.

"Bad things happened. Over the years, I got to see some pretty awful shit. The line of work I think you're in, I'm guessing you've seen those things, too. And I've met bad men. But recently, things have gotten worse. The men have gotten worse—younger—and the old rules don't apply. The one I remember more than all the others, he was just a kid. Fourteen years old from out of the *barrio*. This kid had been given a gun and told to shoot two dealers for the Juárez cartel. They were trying to sell on a corner that La Frontera was claiming for itself. And he did it. Point blank, one shot each in the back of the head and then another while they were on the ground. We picked him up. He didn't try to run. I interviewed him. Looked like he wanted to talk about it. Like he was proud. He told me that he'd been wanting to kill someone since he was a little boy. Said that if he got out, he'd do it again, and I believed him. There are others like him. Dozens of them. What does that say for the future, John? What chance have we got?"

Milton looked at him. Had his face softened a little?

"Look around, man—I've got a family. Wife and kids. And look at me. I'm fifty-five years old. I retire on Friday. I'm going to fix up this boat, drink beer, and go fishing. There's no place for a man like me in a world like that. You always had to go to work knowing that there's a good chance you might get shot today. I could live with that. But now it's worse—now, they'll go after your family, too, and I won't do that. I've done my time. I'm out. You understand?"

Milton did not answer.

There was no disapproval, just a quick recalibration of circumstances.

"I understand. This place—Samalayuca. Can you give me directions?"

DAY FOUR

"One More Day"

Chapter Forty-Four

BEAU BAXTER had his face in the dust. The toes of his boots were against the gravel of the ridge, his pelvis pressed tight against it, his elbows prised up against rough stones. His Jeep was back up the ridge; his jacket was hanging from a Joshua tree. He pushed his Stetson back a little, loosening the hand-braided horsehair stampede string that was tight up against his neck. The rifle on the ground next to him was a Weatherby Mark V Deluxe with the claro walnut stock and highly polished blued barrelled action, chambered for the .257 Wetherby Magnum cartridge. He had been here since dawn, and it had been so quiet, he thought, that you could damn near hear your own hair grow. He had a pair of twenty-power Japanese binoculars he had bought in Tijuana. He swept the scrubland below with them. The valley floor was made up of a reddish-brown lava rock that, depending on the angle of the sun, could turn a blackish lavender. There were tracks of wiry javelina pigs and mule deer but nothing human. Beau stuffed his mouth with chewing tobacco and waited like a grizzled old buzzard guarding his roadkill.

He saw the dust cloud. It blurred in the shimmer and drifted north, the faint desert breeze catching it and pushing it back towards the city. It grew into a long yellow slash of dust, gradually rising, eventually growing to a mile long before he could make out the hire car Smith was driving at its head. It bumped off the asphalt and onto the rough track, greasewood bushes and pear cactus on either side, slowing to negotiate the deeper potholes. He put the glasses to his eyes and focussed. Eventually it was close enough for Beau to see Smith at the wheel and, in the back, Adolfo González. The cloud of dust kept drifting north.

Beau still wasn't sure that he was doing the right thing. He had Adolfo. All he had to do was cuff him, wrists and ankles, put him in the back of the Jeep, cross the border, pick up his money. Smith would have let him do it, too, if it hadn't been for the girl. Beau had watched as Smith spoke to El Patrón, and although he had kept his voice calm, he had seen the flashes of anger in his eyes. He would never agree to let him have Adolfo now, not until they had gotten Caterina back again. Beau wondered for a moment about drawing down on him, just taking the greaser and bugging out for the border, but there was something about the Englishman that told him that that would be a very bad idea. He didn't want a mean dude like that on his tail. That, and the fact that he had just saved his life.

They had agreed to meet El Patrón out here in the desert and get the girl but try and get away with Adolfo, too. Beau was taking the risk with the bounty, so Smith had agreed that he should be the one with the rifle. Much less dangerous away from the action. Smith would make the exchange, and Beau would provide cover, should Smith need it.

Beau knew that he would.

As a kid in the woods of southeast Texas, Beau had never really been good at much in particular with the exception of hunting. This talent was honed in Vietnam, where he was trained as a sniper by the 101st Airborne in Phu Bai. He did his stint on a hunt-and-kill team with the Fifth Infantry Division out of Quang Tri Province.

He learned plenty, like how to shoot.

The sun behind him was a good thing: there would be no reflection off his glasses or the scope. It was climbing into a perfect blue sky, already blazing hot. There was no wind. No cloud cover. No shelter. The air shimmered in the heat. The deep shadow of the ridge and the Joshua tree were cast out across the floodplain below him. A little vegetation: candelilla and catclaw and mesquite thickets. He put the binoculars down and mopped at his forehead with a handkerchief. He gazed out over the land. To the west and east were the mountains. To the south, the arid scrub of the *barrial* that ran out into the deeper desert. He saw another cloud of dust on the 45. He picked up the glasses again and found the road. It was another car, an SUV, with tinted windows. A narco car. It turned off the road and followed Smith down the same long track. He replaced the glasses, took a slug of water from the canteen shaded by his hat, and picked up the rifle. His vantage point was nicely elevated, not too much, well within the range of the Weatherby. He nudged the forestock around until he had the car in his sights. He slipped his finger through the trigger guard.

The narco who had climbed the mesa behind him had followed him all the way from Juárez. The man was a tracker, a coyote with experience of smuggling people over the border. He knew how to move quietly, how to avoid detection.

Beau never even saw him.

The first thing he knew about it was the click as the man cocked his revolver.

Chapter Forty-Five

MILTON GOT out of the hire car. The air was arid and clear all the way to both horizons, where it broke up into morning haze. The heat was already unbelievable. The sun was ferocious. He could feel the skin on his face beginning to burn. It seemed to coat him from the top of his head to the tips of his toes, and he broke out into a sweat almost immediately. He felt the moisture seeping into his shirt, sticking the fabric against his stomach.

The Mercedes Viano rumbled down the bare track towards him, a cone of dust pluming in its wake. The sun reflected off the windscreen with a dazzling glare. Milton took off his jacket, folding it neatly and laying it on the driver's seat. He opened the rear door, took Adolfo by the crook of the elbow, and dragged him out of the car. He shoved him forwards so that he fell forwards onto his knees, took the Springfield, and aimed at his back.

"Nice and easy," he said.

The Viano slowed and swung around, coming to rest opposite the hire car. Milton leant against the bonnet. The metal was already searing hot.

The passenger-side door of the SUV slid open. Milton looked inside. Too dark to make much out.

"Where's the girl?" he called.

Two men stepped down. One had a short-barrelled H&K machine pistol with a black leather shoulder strap. The other had a twelve-gauge Remington automatic shotgun with a walnut stock and a twenty-round drum magazine.

"She ain't here, *ese.*"

Milton racked the slide of the Springfield. "Where is she?"

"Don't worry. You'll see her."

He took a step forward and jabbed the muzzle into the nape of Adolfo's neck.

"Are you calling my bluff?"

Milton tightened his grip on the pistol.

"Shoot him!" Adolfo screamed at the men.

Milton glanced around. The sun dazzled him. What was Beau waiting for?

A plume of dust kicked up a foot to his left; the cracking report of the rifle echoed across the desert.

"Your friend can't help you. Drop the gun."

A second shot rang out, this one a foot to his right. The bullet caromed off the rocks and ricocheted away into the scrub.

Milton tightened his grip and half-squeezed the trigger. Another ounce or two of pressure and González's brains would be splashed across the sand. But what then? The two *sicarios* looked like they knew how to use their

411

weapons, and the man with Beau's Weatherby was a decent shot, too. He could shoot González, but then Caterina would be killed. He didn't know what the right play was, apart from the certainty that it wasn't shooting the man. Not yet.

He stepped back, released his grip, and let the pistol drop to the scrub.

Adolfo's cuffs were unlocked. He sneered at Milton. He took the shotgun and flipped it around. "Fuck you, English," he said. He swung the shotgun. The stock caught him on the chin and staggered him. The blazing bright day dimmed, just for a moment, but he did not go down. Adolfo flexed his shoulders, as if he was straightening out a kink, then swung again.

This time, the light dimmed for longer, and he went down. He dropped to the hard-packed dirt and sat there, the taste of his blood like copper pennies in his mouth. His instinct was to get up, so he did. He rose and stood, swaying. A wave of blackness came over him. He took an uncertain step forwards. Blood ran out of his mouth freely now. Adolfo stepped back for extra space and jabbed the stock into his unguarded chin as hard as he could. The black curtain fell and did not rise again. Milton fell face first into the dust.

Chapter Forty-Six

PLATO LEFT his cruiser at home and took the Accord. He was dressed in jeans and a white shirt and a trucker's cap. He had his shotgun in the footwell next to him, and there was a box of shells on the seat. He reversed out of his driveway and set off to the south. He didn't look back; he didn't want to see Emelia's face in the window. He wondered sometimes that the woman was practically psychic. She always knew when he had something on his mind. He had managed to avoid her this morning, creeping out of bed and leaving the house as quietly as he could. Even then, he had heard the floorboard in the bedroom creaking as she got out of bed. He'd nearly stayed, then, the reality of just how stupid this was slapping him right in the face. But then he thought of his old man, and his badge, and what that all meant, and he opened the door and set off.

The lights out of the city were all on green for him. One after the next, the whole sequence, all of them green. He wouldn't have minded if they were all red this morning. He couldn't help the feeling that they were hastening him towards something terrible.

Plato escaped the ring of *maquiladoras* arranged in parks on the outskirts and accelerated away. He knew Samalayuca. It was hardly a village, just a collection of abandoned huts. The road, the 45, cut right through the desert. The *barrial* was a prime cartel dumping spot. He had lost count of the number of early morning calls that had summoned him to Samalayuca, Ranchería or Villa Ahumada.

A trucker had seen a body on the side of the road.

A pack of coyotes observed tugging on fresh meat.

Vultures wheeling over carrion.

And those were just the bodies that La Frontera wanted them to find.

How many more hundreds—thousands—were buried out here?

The right-hand turn approached. The junction had no stop sign, just thick white lines that had melted into the blacktop. To the right, the road became a dirt track, cutting across the desert like a scar across sun-cooked skin. He slowed the car and pulled to the side of the road. He wound down the window, and hot air rushed inside. He glanced left and right, south and north, and saw nothing at all except heat shimmer and distant silver mirages. He left the engine running, reached across to the passenger seat, took his binoculars, and scanned the country, looking across the caldera towards a low ridge of rock. A mile away on the floodplain were two vehicles parked forty or fifty feet apart. A late-model Ford sedan and an SUV. He lowered the binoculars and looked over the country at large. It was already hot.

Stifling. He pushed back his cap and wiped his forehead with his bandana and put the bandana back in the hip pocket of his jeans.

He raised the glasses again. There were men in between the cars. Two of them were armed. One was motionless on the ground. A fourth man was above him, kicking and stamping at him.

Was he too late?

He watched. The man on the ground was hauled to his feet. It was Smith. He was unconscious. They dragged him through the dirt to the SUV. They tossed him inside, and then the other men got inside, too.

The SUV reversed.

Plato dropped the glasses on the seat, pulled out on to the highway, and continued south. After half a mile he swung around on the margin, rattled over the bars of a cattle guard, and stopped. He fetched the glasses. The SUV was on the road and heading back towards the city. There was little he could do: confronting them would be suicide, and he did not have a death wish. He was frightened, for himself and his family. His instinct told him to switch off the engine and let them drive away. But he couldn't do that. Finding out where were going would have to be enough. He put the car into gear, pulled onto the blacktop again, and keeping a safe distance behind them, he followed.

Chapter Forty-Seven

CATERINA MORENO had tried everything. The door was locked and the window, too. She had wondered whether she might be able to take a chair and smash it, but it was toughened glass, and anyway, it looked down onto a sheer thirty-foot drop. Then her thoughts had turned to weapons. Could she arm herself? The only cup in the room was plastic and too strong for her to break. There was the chair, again, but it was too well put together to be broken apart and too unwieldy as it was. There was a mirror in the bathroom, and eventually, her hopes focussed on that. She unplugged a table lamp and used the base to smash the glass. A jagged piece fell free, and she picked it up, wrapping the thicker end in a towel. It wouldn't be easy to use, but it was sharp, and perhaps, if she was careful, she might be able to maintain an element of surprise. She took it to the bed and hid it beneath the pillow.

She returned to the window. It was in the side of the house, looking out onto a stand of pecan trees. She heard the thump of bass from a powerful sound system. If she pressed her face against the glass, she could see a sliver of the rear garden, and occasionally, guests from the party would pass into and out of view. Servants ferried crates of beer and trays of food from a catering tent. They passed directly below her; she banged her fists against the window, but they either could not hear her or paid her no heed.

She went back to the bed but was unable to settle. She got up and started to pace. She returned to the window. The drive to the house snaked through the trees beneath her, and as she watched, a Mercedes SUV approached and stopped. The branches obscured her view a little, but she saw a door opening and then two men hauled John Smith out. It didn't look as if he was conscious: he was a deadweight, the two men dragging him across the driveway, his toes scraping against the asphalt. A second man followed. Caterina recognised him from the cowboy hat he was wearing: the man from the hospital who had wanted to speak to her, the man Smith had sent away.

She went back to the bed and sat.

Five minutes later, the door was unlocked and opened.

A man came into the room and locked the door behind him.

He was bland. Average. Nothing out of the ordinary about him at all.

"Hello, Caterina."

She backed away.

"You've caused us quite a lot of trouble."

She sat on the edge of the bed.

"This business of ours—we don't welcome publicity."

She shuffled backwards, her hand reaching beneath the pillow.

He tutted and waggled a finger at her. "Don't," he said, nodding towards the bed. He took out a pistol and pointed the barrel up to a tiny camera on the wall that Caterina had not seen.

"Who are you?"

"You can call me Adolfo." He stepped further into the room. "Let's have a talk."

"What do you want to talk about?"

"Why have you been writing about me?"

"What?"

"The girls."

She thought of what Delores had told them.

He was nothing special, by which I mean there was nothing about him that you would find particularly memorable. Neither tall nor short, neither fat nor thin. Normal looking. Normal clothes.

"It's you?"

"I can't take the whole credit. Me and a few friends."

She tore the pillow off the bed, grasped the shank, and rushed him. He pulled the gun quickly, expertly, and held it steady, right at her face. She stopped. She thought about it, calling his bluff, but her legs wouldn't move.

He nodded to the shank.

She dropped it.

"Your hand."

She had taken the glass too hastily and had cut her index finger.

"I'll send someone in to wrap that for you," he said.

"Don't bother. I don't need your favours."

"We'll see. I am going to speak with your friend, the Englishman, and then we have some business that needs to be seen to. Once I am finished, I will be back. We have lots to talk about."

Chapter Forty-Eight

ANNA STRAPPED herself into her seat as the captain of the Gulfstream announced that they were on their final descent into Fort Bliss. She had been working for most of the flight, ostensibly refining her report on John Milton but, in reality, observing everything she could about the six agents. There was very little conversation between them: some slept, others listened to music.

She pulled up the blind and looked out onto the New Mexico landscape five thousand feet below. It was desert for the most part, with nearly two thousand square miles of terrain within its boundaries and adjacent to the White Sands missile range. The populated area was set on a mesa, was six miles by six miles and housed several thousand soldiers and civilian personnel. It was practically a small city, and the biggest US Army base in the world. She watched as the plane arced away to port and then dropped into its glide path. Details in the desert became clearer, the mountains and the blue sliver of the Rio Bravo, and then the asphalt strip of the runway at Biggs Army Airfield. The pilot cut the speed, raised the nose, and executed a perfect landing, taxiing across to the parking area.

Anna disembarked, following Pope down onto the runway. It was unbearably hot. The heat wrapped around her like a blanket, and she quickly felt stunned by it. There was pressure in the air. A hundred miles away to the south-west she could see lightning flickering. Faint sheets and bolts of dry electricity discharging in a random display.

A soldier with colonel's pips was waiting for them. "Welcome to the United States," he said.

"Thank you."

"I'm Stark."

"Captain Pope."

"Good flight?"

"Straightforward, Colonel."

"Glad to hear it. I'll be your liaison here. Anything you need, you just holler. Can I do anything for you now?"

"Not really. We'd just like to get started."

"No sense in delaying."

"That's right."

"Thought you'd say that. We've got you a couple vehicles ready to go. We'll get your gear unloaded and repacked, and then you can be on your way."

"The border?"

"That's all arranged. The Mexicans know you're coming. We'll get you straight across."

"That's very helpful. Thank you, Colonel."

"My pleasure." He took off his cap and squinted against the sun. "Don't suppose you can tell me what you folks have come all this way to do?"

"Afraid not," he said.

He laughed. "Didn't think so. Completely understand."

Two identical SUVs were standing at the edge of the taxiway. Pope led Anna to the nearest.

"You'll be with me," he said. "We'll speak to the police. I'll send the others to the restaurant; see if they can find anything out there."

"Fine."

Anna turned to watch as the army technicians started to unload the cargo from the Gulfstream. The weapons were ferried to a cart and then wheeled across to the SUVs.

They had a lot of firepower.

She wondered whether they would need to use it.

Chapter Forty-Nine

MILTON CAME around. He was groggy, and as awareness returned, so did the pain. He assessed the damage. Red hot spears lanced up from his face. His head throbbed. His arm was difficult to move. A couple of ribs broken? He tried to open his eyes. His left was crusted with dried blood, and his right was badly swollen; he could only just open the first, and he could see nothing through the second. There were bones broken there: the orbital, perhaps, and something in the bridge of his nose. He felt a stubborn ache from his shoulders and realised that his hands were cuffed behind his back.

"You all right?"

He looked to his left. It was Beau.

"I'll live."

"You don't look so good. They worked you over some. I saw when they marched me down the mountain. They pretty much had to pull Adolfo off you."

"I've had worse."

"Really? Doubt that, partner."

Milton winced; his lips were cracked and bloodied.

He looked over at Beau. His shirt was ripped to the navel, revealing a tiger's tooth that he wore on a chain around his neck. He was sitting down, leaning back against the wall. His arms were shackled with FlexiCuffs behind his back.

"You got any bright ideas?" Beau asked.

"Not right at this moment. Has anyone been in to see us?"

"Not yet."

"Where are we?"

"Back in the city. South side. Looked like a pretty swanky neighbourhood, at least by standards around here. My guess is we're in one of El Patrón's houses."

"And this room?"

"First floor. End of a corridor. I didn't get the chance to see all that much."

"Anything else?"

"Only that I'm not sure why they didn't just cap us out in the desert."

"He strikes me as the kind who'd want to make a point."

"I reckon that's right. The way I'm thinking, that roughing up they gave you out there ain't going to be a pimple on a fat man's ass compared to what they're going to do to us next. It ain't going to be pretty for us."

"Or them."

Beau laughed bitterly. "Jesus, man. Has anyone ever told you you're full of it? Look around, will you? We're cuffed, in a locked room, waiting for a psychopathic motherfucker to come and do whatever the fuck he wants to us. This ain't the time for bravado."

"It's not bravado, Beau. They should have killed me when they had the chance. They won't get another."

Beau was quiet for a minute. Milton assessed himself again: save his face and some bruising down his arms and trunk, there were no major breaks or internal injuries. He flexed his muscles against the cuffs. The sharp edges bit into the skin on his wrists.

"You think the girl's still alive?" Beau asked him.

"I don't know."

"If she is, she probably don't want to be."

THEY DIDN'T have to wait long. The door was unlocked, and Adolfo and another man stepped inside. He was older and bore a passing resemblance to Adolfo. His skin was unnaturally smooth; Milton guessed there had been a lot of plastic surgery involved.

"Hey, Adolfo," Beau said.

"*Hola*, Beau."

"I'm guessing this is your old man?"

"I am Felipe," the man said calmly. "You are Señor Baxter, and you are Señor Smith?"

"That's right. I don't suppose you want to get these cuffs off me?"

The man smiled broadly. "I don't think so."

"I was saying to Adolfo earlier, things don't have to be unfriendly between us."

"It's a little late for that, isn't it? You came here to murder my son."

"Come on, man. Who said I was gonna murder him? I was paid to deliver him."

Another indulgent smile. "We both know that would have been the same thing."

Milton tensed against the FlexiCuffs again. The two men were close enough to him—if he could free his hands, he knew he could take them both—but the plastic was too strong. He tried again. There was no give at all. Dammit.

Felipe noticed him. "Señor Smith. Unlike Señor Baxter, I know very little about you."

"Not much to know."

"I doubt that. You are mysterious—hiding something, I think. You will tell me what it is."

"You think?"

"They always do."

"They're not like me."

"You talk a good game."

"Where's the girl?"

"She's here."

Milton sat forwards and then got onto his knees. "I'm going to give you one chance. Give her to me, give us a car, and let us leave."

"And if I don't?" Felipe asked.

"Then it won't go well for you."

Adolfo stepped over and backhanded him across the face. Fragments of broken bone in his nose ground against each other and his nerve endings.

Milton looked up at Adolfo and smiled. "Or you."

Adolfo drew back his foot and kicked him in the ribs. Pain flared, and Milton gasped.

Felipe put a restraining hand on his son's shoulder. "Enough. You will both stay here for now. We have business to attend to. We'll send for you when we are ready."

They stepped outside. The door was locked behind them.

"Come on, man," Beau said. "What was that about? You got a death wish?"

"Something like that."

Chapter Fifty

"LET ME do the talking," Pope told her. "All right?"

"All right."

"If there's anything I need to know, I'll ask you."

"Fine."

Anna, Captain Pope, Lance Corporal Hammond and Lance Corporal Callan had been the first across the border. The SUV was plenty big enough for the four of them and the extensive amount of weapons and other equipment that had been unloaded from the hold of the Gulfstream. The second SUV had followed behind. They had dispensation to cross the border, passing swiftly through a filter lane reserved for the army, border patrol and government agents. Anna had never been to Mexico before, and the sudden, abrupt change from the affluence of El Paso to the poverty of its twin was shocking. The buildings south of the border were dilapidated and scarred, and the people bore the fatigued look of the perpetually defeated. It was all a stark contrast to the optimistic, banal chatter of the hosts on Sunny 99.9FM, still within range as they drove south.

They had been busy. The second van had peeled off for the restaurant, but their first stop was to the headquarters of the municipal police for details on Lieutenant Jesus Plato. After being made to wait for an hour, they had finally been directed to a block station in the west of the city. It was a small, boxy building, cut off from the rest of the neighbourhood by a tall wire-mesh fence. There was a second line of concertina wire, the windows had bars, and they had to wait for the door to be unlocked.

"Pleasant neighbourhood," Pope said.

He led the way inside.

The receptionist regarded them with wary eyes.

"*Teniente* Plato, please."

"Take a seat."

Anna sat down. Pope did not. She watched him from behind a magazine as they waited. He stood, arms folded, impassive. There was no expression on his face. He made no effort to engage with her. The woman behind the desk tried to get on with her work, but she didn't find it easy; there was a restive presence about Pope that was impossible to ignore.

The officer who came out to see them was old. Anna would have guessed mid-fifties. His hair and moustache were greying, and he was a little overweight.

"I'm *Teniente* Plato. Who are you?"

"Pope. Is there somewhere we can talk?"

"I'm just going to smoke a cigarette. We can talk outside."

They went back out into the humid morning.

"We're here on behalf of the British government," Pope began.

"That right?"

Pope took out a passport.

Plato glanced at it. "Captain?"

"That's right."

"Army?"

He nodded.

"That's a coincidence."

"How's that?"

"Had an Englishman in here three days ago."

"The man you arrested?"

"Didn't arrest him."

"But you fingerprinted him?"

"Standard procedure."

"Name of John Smith?"

"That's right. How'd you know all that?"

"We need to see him."

"I need some reciprocation here, okay, Señor?"

"What did Mr. Smith tell you—about himself?"

"Next to nothing."

"That's not surprising.

"But there's more to him than he's letting on—right?"

"We're here to help him. We work together."

"Doing what?"

Pope made a show of reluctance. "Let's call it intelligence and leave it at that."

"You know he said he was a cook? What's he done?"

"*Lieutenant*, please—we need to speak to him. Please."

"You're going to have to move fast. He's in a whole heap of trouble." Plato dragged down on his cigarette. "Someone he's been helping out has got herself mixed up with the cartels. A journalist, writes about them, not a good idea. They abducted her yesterday night. This morning, your friend went out to the desert to try to negotiate with them to get her back. Didn't go so well—the cartels, they're not big on negotiating. Him and another man who went with him were taken away."

"How do you know that?"

"I was watching," he said. The answer seemed to embarrass him.

"Where?"

"Place out of town."

"Got any idea where they'd take him?"

"Better than that—I know. I followed. Place not too far from here."

"You'll take us?"

Plato shook his head. "That's not a place for a policeman like me." Again, Anna saw shame wash across his face. "I'm done with getting myself into scrapes like that. But no one's stopping you. You want, I'll give you directions."

Chapter Fifty-One

DUSK FELL as they travelled across the city. Anna sat at the back of the SUV and said nothing. No one spoke. There was a sense of anticipation among the three agents. Determination. Callan had disassembled his handgun and was cleaning the mechanism with a bottle of oil and a small wire brush, as ritualistic as a junkie with his works. Hammond was listening to music again, her eyes closed and her head occasionally dipping in time with the beat. Pope was driving, his eyes cold and resolute, fixed on the road ahead. Their equipment was laid out on the floor in the back of the van: MP-5 SD3 suppressed machine guns equipped with holographic sights and infrared lasers, a large M249 Squad Automatic Weapon, H&K machine pistols, a Mossberg 500 shotgun, three 9mm M9 Beretta pistols, M67 grenades and a Milkor Mk14 Launcher, M84 flashbangs, and night-vision goggles. The agents were each wearing jeans, T-shirts and desert boots with khaki load-carrying systems strapped on over the top. Each gilet was equipped with pouches for ammunition, hooks and eyelets for grenades and flashbangs, and each was reinforced with Kevlar plates.

The second SUV was directly behind them. They had visited the restaurant and found it closed down, boarding fixed across the front door. They had asked around at the other businesses nearby and discovered that there had been a second shooting, two days after the first. The owner and the woman who ran the front of house had both been shot dead. No clues as to who did it. It was them who they needed to talk to. Since they couldn't, that trail had run cold.

But it looked like they didn't need that trail after all.

Anna was nervous. She would have preferred to stay behind, but Pope had insisted that she come. If the operation proceeded as he hoped, they would not delay in getting out of the city and back across the border again. There would be no opportunity to detour and pick her up. Pope had explained what she would have to do calmly and without inflection: stay in the van, don't get out of the van, leave it all to us.

And Pope needed her help, too.

He parked a hundred yards away from the gated entrance to the compound. Anna saw a guard shack and two men, both of whom were armed with rifles.

"All right, Anna," Pope said. "There's the house. See it?"

"I'm not blind."

"Do your thing."

She opened her laptop and connected with the internet. Her slender fingers fluttered across the keyboard as she navigated to the website for the *Comisión Federal de Electricidad* and, after correctly guessing the URL for the firm's intranet, forced her way inside.

"I can't be surgical about this," she said. "It'll be the whole block."

"Doesn't matter. Can you do it?"

"Just say when."

"Ready?" Pope asked the others.

Hammond said, "Check."

"Check," said Callan.

"All right then. Here we go."

They quickly smeared camouflage paint across their faces. Pope put the van into gear again and slowly pulled forwards. When they were twenty feet away from the gatepost, the guards came to attention, one holding up his hand for them to stop. The van had tinted windows, and the two of them were unable to see inside. The men made no effort to hide the automatic rifles they were carrying. Pope pulled a little to the left, opening up an angle between the driver's side of the van and the gatepost. One of the man spat out a mouthful of tobacco juice and stepped into the road. Hammond brought her MP-5 up above the line of the window, aimed quickly, and put three rounds into each guard. Anna was shocked: the gun was quiet, the suppressor so efficient that all you could really hear was the bolt racking back. The men fell, both of them dead before they hit the ground.

Anna's heart caught. She had never seen a man shot before.

Suddenly, it all seemed brutally, dangerously real.

Pope calmly put the van into gear again and edged forwards through the gate.

Anna compared what she could see in the gloom with the map she had examined earlier. It was a crescent-shaped street that curved around a central garden. Mansions were set back behind tall fences. It was nothing like the rest of the city; it was as if all the money had fled here, running from the squalor and danger outside and cowering behind the gates. One of the gardens was lit up more brightly than the others: strings of colourful lights had been hung from the branches of pecan and oak trees, and strobes flashed. The sound of loud *norteño* music was audible. Pope pulled over outside the driveway of the mansion. They pulled down full-face respirators and added night-vision goggles.

They collected their weapons.

The time on the dashboard display said 21:59.

"Now, Anna."

She hit return.

Her logic bomb deployed.

The time clicked to 22.00, and all the lights went out.

The streetlights.

The lights in the mansion, the colourful lights in the grounds.
The music stopped.

"Go, go, go," Pope said.

Chapter Fifty-Two

PLATO AND SANCHEZ ended up on their usual jetty, looking out onto the sluggish Rio Bravo. The brown-green waters reached the city as a pathetic reminder of what it must have been, once, before the factories and industrial farmers choked it upstream for their own needs. They were beneath the span of the bridge, sitting on the bonnet of Plato's Dodge. The headlights were on, casting out enough light so that they could read the graffiti on the pillars. Several of the concrete stilts had been decorated with paintings of the pyramids at Teotihuacán. He could see the fence and the border control on the other side. The low black hills beyond El Paso. America looked pleasant, like it always did. The day was ending with the usual thickening soup of smog muffling the quickly dying light.

Sanchez pulled another two cans of Negra Modelo from the wire mesh.

Plato took a long draught of his beer. He sighed. His heart wasn't in the banter like he hoped it would be.

"What's on your mind, man?" Sanchez asked. "You've been quiet all night."

"Been coming here for years, haven't we?"

"At least ten."

"But not for much longer. All done and finished soon."

"What? You saying you won't still come down?"

"Think Emelia will let me?"

"You wait. She'll want you out of the house. You'll drive her crazy."

"Maybe." Plato tossed his empty can into the flow. It moved beneath him, slow and dark. Sanchez handed him another.

"What am I doing?"

"What?"

Plato looked at the can, felt it cold in his palm. He popped the top and took a long sip. "I can't stop thinking about that girl."

"From the restaurant?"

"And the Englishman. Going after her like that. Going after the cartels, Sanchez, on his own, going right at them. Makes me ashamed to think about it. That's what we're supposed to do—the police—but we don't, do we? We just stand by and let them get on with their murdering and raping and their drugs. We swore the same oath. Doesn't it make you ashamed?"

He looked away. "I try not to think about it."

"Not me. All the time. I can't help it. All that bravery or stupidity, whatever you want to call it, how do I reward him?—by sending him on his way to a death sentence and not doing anything to help him. And then three of his colleagues turn up, and I won't even take them to where he is. Didn't even try to help them. I just tell them where to find him. They go there, that'll be another three deaths that keep me up at night. All I can think about, all day, is what am I doing? I've just been trying to keep my head down. Get my pension and get out."

"You've done your years."

"Not yet. I've still got one more day."

"So keep that in mind. One more day, then all you need to worry about is your family and that stupid boat."

"No, Sanchez. I don't agree. I've been doing that for months, and it's selfish. I'm police for one more day. My oath should still mean something."

They heard a dog somewhere. An anguished, hungry howl.

The receiver crackled inside the car. "We got a 246 at St. Mark's Close. Repeat, a 246 at St. Mark's Close. Possible 187."

"That's the narco mansions, right?"

"Yep," Plato said.

"González's mansion?"

Plato nodded. He pushed himself off the bonnet. His bones ached.

"No one's answering *that* call."

"I will," Plato said.

"You're joking—right?"

"No. You coming?"

He gaped at him. "Someone's shooting up González's mansion, and you want to respond? It can only be another cartel. You want to get in the middle of *that?* Are you crazy?"

"That's what we're supposed to do."

"You promised Emelia—don't get shot. One more day, amigo. You stay away from shit like that. How stupid would it be to get yourself shot now?"

"I've been making the wrong decisions all week. And now I'm thinking what am I going to do to set them right?"

Chapter Fifty-Three

THE LIGHTS went first. The live music, which had been playing loud all evening, petered out and then stopped. Milton winced as he pushed himself upright against the wall. Small-arms fire rattled from the grounds outside the house. Beau got up, went to the window, and put his eye to the crack between the shutters.

"Can you see anything?"

"Not really."

"Yes or no?"

"It's too dark."

The door opened, and a guard came into the room. "*Bajar*," he told Beau, waving his ArmaLite at him. *Get down.* He unlatched the shutters, threw them aside, switched the rifle, and used the stock to smash out the glass. He swept away the shards still stuck to the frame and then put the stock to his shoulder, glancing down the sight and opening fire.

All right, then. Milton winced as he moved forwards onto his knees, sliding his hands all the way down his back, his shoulders throbbing with pain as he passed them over his backside and then down into the hollow behind his knees. He rolled his weight forwards until the momentum brought him to his feet, stepping over the loop of his closed hands, raising himself up. Milton dropped his cuffed hands around the man's throat, and with his left shoulder pressed as near to perpendicular to the man's head as he could manage, he yanked quickly to the right and snapped his neck.

"You've done that before."

Milton frisked the dead guard, found a butterfly knife in his pocket, shook it open, and sliced through the plastic shackles. He did the same for Beau. He stooped to collect the ArmaLite, checked the magazine, added a second from the guard's pocket, and went out into the corridor.

"We're getting out, right?"

"Not without the girl."

"Come on, man, we're fucked as it is. You want to waste time looking for her? Forget what they said—they were pulling your chain. That psychopath probably did her yesterday. She's already dead, man. Dead."

"We get her first."

"She's dead, and you know it. And we got to get out. I don't know who that is outside, but I'm willing to bet they ain't gonna be too friendly with us. Another cartel. Military. Anyone in here's gonna be fair game."

"We get her; then we get González. How much if you bring him back?"

"Twenty-five large."

"So why do you want to leave?"

"Can't spend it when you're dead."

"If you want to go, there's the door. Go. I'm not stopping you."

Beau sighed helplessly. "I'm gonna regret this."

"Stay behind me."

"You're as crazy as they are." He settled in behind him. "I need a gun."

Milton brought the ArmaLite up and tracked down the corridor. As he passed a window, all the glass fell out of it. He hadn't even heard the shot. He looked out of the next window: a pandemonium of gunfire had broken out. Muzzle flashes spat out, three of them, shots aimed by the guards, and as Milton watched, all three were taken out by a single frag grenade. That portion of the garden was subdued; Milton saw a flash of khaki as a figure in night-vision goggles crab-walked to a forward position, an MP-5 cradled easily between practiced hands.

"It's not a cartel," he muttered.

The next room to the one in which they had been held was occupied by two men. They were pressed against the wall on either side of an open window. One had a shotgun; the other had an M-15. Shots from outside passed through the window and jagged across the ceiling. Milton turned into the doorway and raked both men with a quick burst of fire.

"Smith! Look out!"

A third Mexican was coming up the stairs, reaching for a small machine gun he carried on a strap. Milton turned and fired, the ArmaLite cracking three times, blowing the top of his head against the wall and sending his body spinning back down the stairs.

"There's your gun," he said. "Help yourself."

Beau took the shotgun.

There was a window at the end of the corridor. It smashed loudly, a six-inch canister crashing through it and then bouncing once, twice, before it came to rest against the wall.

Gas started to gush from both ends.

Milton's mouth was filled with the impossibly acrid taste of tear gas before he covered his face with his sleeve. Whoever was attacking the mansion was professional. They'd cut the power, and now they were going to disable everyone inside. Too organised and too well equipped for a cartel. There was precision here. A plan.

If he didn't know better, he would have said it was Special Forces.

Chapter Fifty-Four

FELIPE GONZÁLEZ watched as the grenade looped in a graceful arc over the swimming pool, bounced against the tiled floor, and collected against the cushion of one of the loungers. It immediately started to unspool a cloud of brown-tinged smoke, and within moments, the guests on that side of the garden started to choke. Women screamed. One of the guests—it was the mayor, for fuck's sake—stumbled and fell into the water. Felipe turned back to the mansion—the lights had all been extinguished there, too—and then he heard the first rattle of automatic weaponry.

What?

Que Madres?

More screams.

What the fuck was going on?

"El Patrón?" Isaac said.

"Come with me—all of you."

He hurried around the pool, away from the spreading cloud of gas. The gringos stumbled after him, drunk.

"Sir," Pablo said. "Come."

"Who is it? Army?"

"I do not know. But whoever they are, they are very good."

"Los Zetas?"

"We need to get you away from here."

"Where is Adolfo?"

"Inside—with the girl."

Felipe cursed. "Get him."

"Javier has gone for him. Come, please, El Patrón."

"Bring the gringos," he said, pointing back to the three Americans.

"We will. But we must leave—now."

There was a garage at the end of the garden. Pablo hurried him down the path towards it. A BMW was waiting, the engine running. An Audi waited behind that. The automatic gates did not function without power, so they were being dragged open by hand. Two other men were waiting with AKs, aiming back towards the house. Felipe allowed himself to be jostled into the back of the car. The gringos were loaded into the Audi. He turned and looked back towards the mansion, his fists clenched in impotent rage. There was an explosion from the first floor. Debris plumed upwards and out, falling down onto the patio below: bricks, bits of window frame, shards of glass.

He thought of his son.

The driver stamped on the gas, the wheels spinning until the rubber bit, the car lurching for the gate and the road beyond.

Chapter Fifty-Five

MILTON STOOD listening at the door. He took a step back and kicked it open. A bedroom, plush, thick carpets, art on the walls. Caterina was on the bed. A Mexican stood at an open door across the room. Milton dropped him where he stood. He stepped out of the doorway and stood with his back to the wall. He ducked his head around to look in again. Now the second door was shut. He locked eyes with Caterina. She looked at the door and nodded. Milton pressed in the second magazine and fired a steady burst through the door. A jagged hole was torn from the middle of the panel. He looked through it and saw a spray of pink blood across a white-tiled wall.

"Beau," he said, indicating the bathroom. "Check it."

"Right you are."

He went forwards and fired three more rounds through the door, then kicked it open and went in, the shotgun held out.

Milton went to the girl. "Are you all right?"

She nodded.

"They didn't—?"

She shook her head.

"What happened?"

"The police captain—Alameda—he is working for them."

"Well, lookit here," Beau called out. He stepped back, the shotgun still aimed into the bathroom. "Out you come."

Adolfo González came into the bedroom. His hands were above his head. "Don't," he said, staring at the business end of the Remington.

"Hiding in the bath," Beau said. "On your knees, boy. Hands behind your back."

There was a nest of FlexiCuffs on the dresser. Beau looped one around Adolfo's right wrist, then his left, and yanked them tight. He kicked the man behind the knees, forcing him to the floor, and went to the wide window that looked down onto the gardens outside. Beau edged carefully alongside it and looked down below.

"Hey, Smith," he called. "You want to see this."

"What is it?"

"The firefight outside? Them fellas ain't Mexican."

Milton counted six attackers, each of them wearing load-carrying systems and night-vision goggles. Five moved with easy confidence, passing from cover to cover, popping out to fire tight and controlled rounds that were unerringly accurate. The sixth looked to be limping. Even from this distance, and despite the goggles and the darkness, he recognised them. Five because he had fought alongside them before. The other because he had looked into the barrel of the man's pistol six months ago, in an East End London gymnasium with Dennis Rutherford's body laid out in a bloody mess behind him.

Pope, Hammond, Spenser, Blake, Underwood and Callan.

Oh, shit.

"It's not the cartels," he said. "I know them. It's much worse."

"Wanna tell me what's going on, partner?"

"We don't have enough time."

He was in the window for too long, and Callan saw him. For a moment, their eyes locked, but then the man brought up his M-15. The red laser dazzled his eyes. Milton swung around just in time: the fusillade of bullets shredded the blind and chewed gouts of dusty plaster from the ceiling.

"When you say you know them—?"

"Not in a good way. Look, Beau—you have to listen to me. Get her out of here. Stay away from them. They're coming from the south. I doubt they'll be any more of them—they won't think it's necessary. Get her back to where they had us—there's a fire escape there, end of the corridor, go down and then out the back. I'll hold them off as long as I can."

"There's only the six of them. They'll never take the house."

"They count double. At least. Please, Beau, go—get her over the border."

"All right, all right."

"And fast. They know I'm here. They'll be coming up now."

"All right."

"Caterina—you have to go with him."

"What about you?"

"I'm going to buy you a little time and then make a run for it. I'll see you in America."

Beau hauled Adolfo to his feet and shoved him towards the door. He looped an arm around his throat and held the shotgun, one-handed, to the side. Using him as a shield, Beau edged out into the corridor.

Another barrage peppered the ceiling.

"Get going," Milton implored her, and after a moment, she did.

Chapter Fifty-Six

MILTON KNEW there was no sense in running. The only chance Beau and Caterina had was if he gave the agents what they wanted; if he didn't, they would chew through the house, room by room, taking out anyone and everyone they found until they had who they were there for.

Him.

He thought about it: six months.

It had been a good run, but it was always going to end, eventually.

He wondered, vaguely, how they had found him.

He started downstairs to meet them.

The first-floor half-landing gave him a good view into the darkened gardens. The cartel members were either dead or gone. A few people from the party that he had heard from earlier were scattering. One man—older, portly—was pulling himself out of the swimming pool. A lost hairpiece floated towards the filter. Pope and Callan were working through the gardens and poolside area, the flash of their laser sights raking ahead of them. Emptying canisters leaked gas into the night. A dead narco was draped over a piece of topiary pruned into the shape of a machine gun. Another was laid out in an elaborate swing set as if he was gently reclining, everything normal apart from the smoking hole in his guts.

The patio doors had been blown in.

Hammond was crouched in the empty doorway.

Milton propped the ArmaLite against the balustrade, raised his hands, and came down the rest of the stairs. "Here I am."

She brought her MP-5 to bear. The red laser sight blinded him as she brought it to rest on his forehead, right between the eyes.

"Knees," she said, nodding her head downwards.

Milton did as he was told.

She tapped a throat mic to open the channel. "Got him."

THEY TOOK him outside, to the front of the house. There was an SUV parked in the road with a young woman inside. Milton did not recognise her. They took off their goggles and scrubbed their faces, puckered red outlines around their eyes. Pope, who had swapped his MP-5 for a pistol, took him by the arm, and led him towards the van.

"John."

"Mike."

"You've led us on a merry dance."

"Sorry about that."

"You didn't think it could last forever, did you?" he said quietly.

"I don't know. It was going pretty well."

"What the fuck's been going on?"

"What did he tell you?"

"That you're a couple of sandwiches short of a picnic."

He shrugged. "Well, you know—"

"Fine," Pope qualified. "Even more than usual. Control's been crucified about this. He's made you his personal project."

"Trying to make me feel special?"

"And Callan—"

"Probably best not to get me started on him."

"Callan was all for putting a bullet in your brain right now. You really fucked up his knee."

"He's lucky that's all I did."

"Well, that's as may be, but you're not on his Christmas card list. I don't have the same predisposition, and luckily for you, I'm the ranking officer. So that's not going to happen."

"And what is?"

"I have to take you back, John. Back over the border to Fort Bliss. We've got a jet there. Back to the UK. I'll help as best as I can, but whatever comes next is between you and Control."

"Do whatever you have to do."

Pope paused and looked at him with sudden concern. "What's this all about, John? Really? What's going on?"

"It got to the stage where I'd just had enough. I'm not interested in doing it anymore."

"So what have you been doing instead?"

Milton paused.

"Something useful."

He could hear sirens.

"Come on," Pope said.

The sirens grew louder. Milton turned to the development's ostentatious gate as a police car rushed through, past the two dead bodies on the pavement and towards them.

Chapter Fifty-Seven

JESUS PLATO got out of his car. There were six soldiers. The oldest of the three, the one who had spoken to him at the station, was with Smith. Plato could see dead bodies in the gardens behind him. He saw three, at least, maybe four. A massacre. His stomach turned over. Whoever these six were, they were armed to the teeth and ruthless as hell, and they had just subdued El Patrón's mansion and all of the *sicarios* that he had at his disposal.

And now Captain Pope had a gun pointed at Smith's chest.

"Someone going to tell me what's happening here?"

"This is the man we're here for. We're taking him back over the border."

"You told me he was a colleague."

"He is a colleague."

"And you were going to help him."

"That's true."

"This is helping him?"

"He's also a wanted man."

"For what?"

"That's classified."

"Not good enough."

"I'm afraid it's going to have to do."

Plato shook his head. He drew his Glock and aimed at Pope.

"What are you doing, Lieutenant?"

"Let's just keep it nice and easy."

"Put that down, please."

"I'm going to need you to explain to me why you think you can take him. You got a warrant?"

"We don't need one."

"Afraid you do. Can't let you do anything without one."

"Don't be an idiot," the woman said. "Step aside."

"Wish I could, Señorita, but I'm afraid I just can't. This man is wanted for further questioning—that ruckus at the restaurant on Monday, seems there's a bit more to that than we thought there was. And unless I'm mistaken, this is Mexico, and I'm an officer of the law. The way I see it, that gives me jurisdiction."

Pope spoke calmly. "Think about this for a moment, *Teniente*. We are here with the approval of your government and with the co-operation of the American military. This man is a fugitive. There'll be serious consequences if you interfere."

"Maybe so."

"Your job, for one."

He laughed. "What are they going to do? Fire me? I retire tomorrow. That's what you call an empty threat. Drop your weapons."

They did no such thing.

Plato tightened his grip on his pistol.

A stand-off.

There were six of them and one of him.

He had no second move.

He heard a siren; another cruiser hurried through the gates and pulled over next to his car.

Sanchez got out. He was toting his shotgun. "All right, Jesus?"

"You sure about this, buddy?"

Sanchez nodded. "You were right."

Pope turned to Sanchez. "You too?"

"Let him go."

The shotgun was quivering a little, but he didn't lower it.

"Now, then," Plato said, stepping forward. "I'm going to have to insist that you drop those weapons, turn around, and put your hands on the car."

The younger man fixed him with a chilling gaze. "Don't be a fool. We're on the same side."

"I think in all this noise and commotion it's all gotten to be a little confusing. I think the best thing to do is, we all go back to the station and work out who's who in this whole sorry mess."

"If we don't want to do that?"

"I suppose you'd have to shoot us. But do you want to do that? British soldiers in a foreign country, murdering the local police? Imagine the reaction to that. International outrage, I'd guess. Not what you want, is it?"

"All right," Pope said. "Do as he says."

He took a step backwards.

Sanchez raised the shotgun and indicated the car with it. "Now, then, please—the guns on the floor, please."

They finally did as they were told.

"Señor Smith," Plato said. "You're riding with me. Señor Pope—you and your friends stay with *Teniente* Sanchez, please."

Sanchez said that he had called for backup and that it was on its way. Plato turned to Smith and took him by the arm. As he moved him towards the waiting cruiser, he squeezed him two times on the bicep.

Chapter Fifty-Eight

MILTON SAT AND watched the streets of Ciudad Juárez as they rushed past the windows of the Dodge.

Plato looked across the car at him for a moment. "You all right?"

"Fine."

"You don't look fine."

Milton saw his reflection in the darkened window of the car: his right eye was swollen shut, lurid purples and blues in the ugly bruise; there was dried blood around his nose and from the cuts on his face. He probed his ribs gently; they were tender. "Looks worse that it is."

"Want to tell me who they are?"

"Ex-colleagues."

"They seem pretty keen to meet with you."

"They've been looking for me for six months."

"You think it was my fault they found you?"

"Those fingerprints you took get emailed anywhere?"

"Mexico City."

"Probably was you, then. Doesn't matter."

"What do they want?"

He sighed. "I used to do the same kind of job that they do. Then I didn't want to do it anymore."

"I know the feeling."

"But the problem is, mine's not the kind of job you can just walk away from."

"And they want you to go back to it again?"

He chuckled quietly. "We're well beyond that."

Plato mused on that. "Where's the girl?"

"With Baxter."

"He got her out?"

"As far as I know."

"Did you speak to her?"

"Briefly."

"And?"

"I don't think they touched her. But you've got a problem."

"I know," he said grimly.

Milton nodded. "Alameda."

"I think I've known for a while. He ducked out when they attacked the restaurant, and if you asked me to bet, I'd say it was him who called González from the hospital, then disappeared so he could do what he came there to do. I checked who responded to that murder, too, when she was taken. It was him."

"She said he took her."

Plato sighed.

"What are you going to do?"

"Haven't worked that out yet."

"What's the plan now?" Milton said.

"You don't wanna see them again, right?"

"Not if I can help it."

"Thought so. Sanchez will keep them busy for an hour or so. Papers to fill out and suchlike. Give you a bit of a head start. The only thing to decide is where do you want to go?"

"North, eventually."

"My opinion? El Paso's too obvious. I'm guessing your passport is shot now, and even if you could bluff your way across, it'd be easy to find you again from here."

"I think so."

"So, if it was me, I'd go east and then go over. You can walk across, somewhere like Big Bend. It's not easy—it's a long walk—but the coyotes take people over there all the time. I've been hunting there, too. I can show you the best place. You'll need some gear. A tent, for one. A sleeping bag. A rifle."

"I'm not going yet."

Plato glanced across at him. "Why not?"

"There's something I need to do first. But I'm going to need your help."

"Am I going to regret that?"

"Probably. Can we go to your house?"

"That's where we're headed. I was going to kit you out."

He slowed, turned left across the flow of traffic, and headed into a pleasant residential estate. Milton recognised it from before. Oaks and pecan trees lined the broad avenue. After five minutes they pulled into the driveway of the house and parked behind the boat. A light flicked on in a downstairs window, and a woman's face appeared there. Plato waved up at the window and made his way to the garage at the side of the house.

Plato led the way inside, switched on the overhead strip light, and started to arrange things: he took out a one-man tent, a rucksack, and a canteen that he filled with water.

"What are you going to do?" Milton asked him.

"About what?"

"Juárez."

"Stick it out like I've always done."

"And El Patrón?"

"Nothing's changed there."

"But if he finds out you were involved with me? And the girl?"

"Look, man, if he wanted to take me out, he could've done it a long time ago. There's nothing I could do about it if he has it in his mind to make an example out of me. You get used to the thought of it. That's just Juárez."

"And your family?"

Plato looked away. "I'm thinking about that."

"Where do you think he's gone?"

"Don't know for sure—he has a lot of places—but I could hazard a pretty good guess. I reckon, given that you and your friends back there just gave him a bloody nose, he'll go back to where he feels most secure. The Sierra Madre. That's where he's from originally. The whole place out there, it's all La Frontera: hundreds of cartel men, even the locals are on his side. The mountains, too. Inhospitable. You'd need an army to get him out again if that's where he's gone. And I'm not exaggerating."

There was a gun cabinet on the wall. Milton pointed at it. "What have you got in there?"

Plato took a key from his belt and opened the cabinet. There was a rifle, a revolver and several boxes of ammunition.

"The rifle," Milton said.

"I'm guessing you know plenty about guns?"

A small smile. "A little."

"You'll like this, then." Plato took it down and handed it across. "That's the Winchester Model 54. They started making those babies in 1925. Chambered for the .30-06 Springfield. They've developed it some over the years, and some people will tell you the Model 70 is the better of the two, but I don't have any truck with that."

Milton ran his fingers across the walnut stock and the hand chequering. The gun had good rifling and a strong muzzle. The bolt throw still had a good, crisp action. It had been oiled regularly and kept in pristine condition.

"You ever shot with it?" Plato asked.

"Now and again."

"Most accurate gun I ever used. Belonged to my father originally—he took it to war with him. I killed my first deer with it. Must've been no more than ten years old. Had it ever since."

"Do you think I could borrow it?"

"Don't suppose there's any point me asking you what for?"

"You don't need to ask, do you?"

"No. I don't suppose I do."

Milton put the rifle next to the tent and the rest of the equipment that Plato had assembled. He added a box of bullets.

"Your car, too, if that's all right?"

Plato chuckled. "Why not? Lending my rifle and my car to someone I don't know wouldn't be the stupidest thing I've done this week."

"Don't worry, Plato. I won't be long. And I'll bring it all back."

Chapter Fifty-Nine

BEAU HAD STOLEN a Pontiac Firebird from the street near the mansion. Caterina was in the front with him, and González was in back. He was cuffed, his arms behind his back. They had cuffed his ankles together, too. Beau had a pistol laid out on the dash in front of him, and he had threatened González that he would gag him with the duct tape he had found in the glovebox if he made a nuisance of himself. So far, Caterina thought, he had not. She guessed that he was facing something very unpleasant on the other side of the border, and his compliance—up until now, at least—made her nervous. He did not strike her as the kind of man who would just go quietly.

Beau had not explained their route to them, but it was easy enough to guess. They were going to head south and then west, probably to Ojinaga, and then cross into Presidio and Texas. They were close enough to the border for the car radio to pick up the channels on the other side of the Rio Bravo, and as the miles passed beneath their wheels, the channels blurred from stoner rock to throbbing *norteño* and then to the apocalyptic soothsaying of fire and brimstone preachers.

They cut through the savannah and scrub on the 45, the distant buttes of the mountains visible as darker shadows on the horizon. The road was quiet, shared only with trucks, each cab decorated with the coloured lights that the teamster used to distinguish his from the next. A freight train rattled along the tracks to their right, the huge half-mile-long monster matching their pace for a minute or two before splitting off to disappear deeper into the desert. Caterina watched it and then stared out into the night until the swipes of its lights faded from her retinas and she could see the darkness properly again, the quick flashes that were the eyes of the rabbits and prairie dogs watching them from the side of the road as they passed.

They reached the edge of Chihuahua, found the 16, and headed back to the north-east.

"Do you really think this is going to work?"

Beau stiffened a little next to her. She glanced into the rear-view mirror and straight into González's face. He was calm and placid; there was even the beginning of a playful smile on his thin lips.

"Don't reckon you need worry yourself on account of that," Beau said.

"You won't even get across the border. My father owns the border. What is it? Where will you try? Ojinaga? Ciudad Acuña? Piedras Negras?"

"Thought I'd just take a little drive, see which one caught my fancy."

"Fifty thousand is very little to be forever watching your back, Beau."

"It'll do for now."

"I could give you five hundred thousand."

"Haven't we been here before? Shoe was on the other foot, then, as I recall. Answer's still the same."

"The offer stands until the border."

"You know something, Adolfo? You're a piece of work. You might be a scary fucker when it's on your own terms, but when it gets to the nut-cutting, like now, the moment of true balls, all you've got is talk."

The dawn's first light fell upon them as they turned off the highway and headed directly north. The landscape changed suddenly, the flat scrubland replaced by ridges and plateaus, the mountains filling the distance all the way to the horizon. The rock turned from black to blue and then to green as the sun climbed in the sky. Dust devils skittered across the road. The next twin towns on the line east from Juárez and El Paso, Ojinaga and Presidio clung together against the awesomeness of the mountains. It was the most isolated of the crossings. Here, the Rio Bravo was supplemented by the waters from the Conchos, and rather than the insipid trickle that apologetically ran between Juárez and El Paso, it was a surging, throbbing current that was full of life.

Beau stepped on the gas.

"Caterina," González said.

Beau turned to her. "Don't."

"I'm not frightened of him."

"Long as he's trussed up like that, there ain't no need to be. But a feller like him, the only thing he wants to do is put things in your head, thoughts you'll worry about, cause problems down the line."

Caterina set her face and turned a little. "What do you want?" she said into the back of the car.

"Those girls—you want to know what it was like?"

"Shut your trap," Beau ordered.

"Come on, Caterina. You're a writer. You're curious, I know you are. This is your big story. What about that girl you were with in the restaurant? You want to know how it was for her?"

"No, she don't."

"Delores. That was her name. I remember—she told me. I don't normally remember the names—there've been so many—but she stood out. She kept asking for her mother."

"I won't tell you again. Any more out of you and you're getting gagged."

"She's the proof, though, isn't she? Look at what happened to her. You can't escape from us. It doesn't matter where you are. It doesn't matter who is protecting you. Eventually, one way or another, you'll be found and brought back to me."

Beau slammed on the brakes. "All right, you son of a bitch," he said, reaching for the roll of duct tape. "Have it your way."

THEY FOUND a motel on the outskirts of Presidio. The place was a mongrel town, full of trailer parks and strip malls. They had crossed the border an hour ago. Beau had pulled the Firebird to the side of the road as the steep fence and the squat immigration and customs buildings appeared ahead of them. He had taken out his cellphone and made a quick call. A few shops had collected next to the crossing: Del Puente Boots, a Pemex gas station, an Oxxo convenience store, a dental clinic. An all-night shack with flashing lights advertised "Sodas, Aguas, Gatorades." It was practically empty, and only one of the northbound gates was open. Beau slotted the car into it, wound down the window, and reached out to hand over his passport. The customs agent, a nervous-looking forty-something man who reminded Caterina of a rabbit, made a show of inspecting the documents as he removed the five hundred-dollar bills from within their pages. He handed the passport back. "Welcome to America," he had said, opening the gate. Beau had thanked him, put the car into gear, and driven them across the bridge and into the United States.

It was as simple as that: they were on the 67 and across. A neat line of palm trees on either side of the road. A smooth ribbon of asphalt. A large sign that welcomed them to America and invited them to "Drive Friendly – The Texas Way."

The Riata Inn Motel was a low, long line of rooms on the edge of the desert, set alongside a parking lot. They had taken a single room, and now the dawn's light was glowing through the net curtains. They had cuffed González to the towel rack in the bathroom.

"Is this it?" Caterina asked him.

"It is for him. My employer will be here in a couple of hours."

"And then?"

"Not our problem any more. He'll take him off our hands, and then he'll sort you out with what you need: papers, money, someplace to live."

Beau sat and tugged off his boots. He unbuckled his holster and tossed it onto the bed.

"What do you think happened to Smith?"

"I don't know. That boy's as tough as old leather, though. I wouldn't count him out."

Beau looked at her. She was tired, but there was a granite strength behind it. After all she had been through, well, Beau thought, if it had've been him? He might've been ready to pack it all in.

"Long night," she said.

"Tell me about it."

"I'd kill for a cold drink."

"There's an ice machine outside. I'll get some. Thirty seconds?" He pointed at the door to the bathroom. "Don't—well, you know, don't talk to him."

Her smile said that she understood.

The machine was close, but even though the door to the motel room was going to be visible the whole time, he didn't want to tarry. González was resourceful and smart—thirty or forty or however the hell old he was, practically ancient in narco-years—and although Caterina was smart, too, he didn't want to leave him alone with her for any longer than he had to. He went outside in his stockinged feet and walked across to the machine. He filled the bucket with crushed ice, took a handful and scrubbed it on the back of his neck and then across his forehead and his face.

He was getting too old for this shit.

When he got back to the room, Caterina had taken his Magnum .357 out of the holster. The bathroom door was open. González was on his knees, his hands in front of his face. She was pointing the gun at his head.

"How do you get paid?" she asked him.

"Cash on delivery."

"So, what?—he's got to be alive?"

"He don't got to be. More for me if he is, though."

"Ah," she said. "Sorry about that."

The gunshot was audible all the way across the scrubby desert.

Chapter Sixty

CAPITÁN VICENTE ALAMEDA lived with his wife and three children in the upscale neighbourhood of Campestre. The district rubbed against Highway 45, just before the crossroads with Highway 2, and massive *maquiladoras* were gathered on one edge of the neighbourhood. Plato continued along an avenue that could have been in any city north of the border: a Starbucks, Chili's, Applebee's and strip malls. He turned into Alameda's street and parked. Razor wire lined the top of brick and stucco walls. Uniformed guards stood watch at gated entryways. Gold doors on one home reflected the lamplight. Parked in the driveways were BMWs and Lexuses, many with Texas license plates. Alameda's house had an Audi in the driveway. There was a large garden. A pool. Four or five bedrooms judging from the windows on the second floor. A set of gates, although they hadn't been closed.

It wasn't a policeman's house.

Plato got out of the car and looked up. The sky was full of stars, a rind of moon hanging over the silhouette of the factories on the edge of the neighbourhood. He made his way up the street to a small *zócalo* where the grackles in the eucalyptus trees called out in drowsy alarm.

He pressed the intercom.

"Yes?"

"*Capitán*—it's Jesus Plato."

"Plato? It's late. Do you know what time it is?"

"I know. But I need to talk to you."

"Tomorrow, Jesus, all right?"

"No, sir. It has to be now."

The intercom cut out. Plato stood at the gate, staring through the bars at the home beyond. The curtains in one of the large windows on the first floor twitched aside, and Plato saw Alameda's face.

He held his finger on the intercom for ten seconds.

He would wait as long as it took.

After a minute, the front door opened, and Alameda came outside. He was wearing slippers and a dressing gown.

Plato slipped between the gates and met him in the garden.

"What the fuck are you doing?" Alameda hissed. "You've woken the children!"

"I must be some kind of idiot. How long have we known each other?"

"Ten years."

"Exactly. Ten years and you've never invited me here. We've had barbeques at my place and at Sanchez's, but you never did the same. Don't know why that never struck me as odd. Now I can see why."

"What are you talking about?"

"The first thing I would've asked is where you could possibly be getting the money to afford a place like this. It's not on a captain's salary, I know that much. Not wondering about that could all have been stupidity on my part, I'm capable of that, but I don't think so, not this time. I think it was wilful blindness. I didn't want to look at what was staring me in the face."

"I had an inheritance. My father-in-law."

"No, you didn't. Drug money bought all this."

"Come on, Jesus. That's crazy."

"I don't think so. I'm sorry it's come to this, sir, but you're under arrest."

"You want to do this now? *Now?* You're retiring."

"I've been thinking about that. I'd have to talk to Emelia, of course, but I'm thinking maybe I can stay on another six months. There's a lot of cancer that needs to be cut out. Now's a good a time as any. Maybe I can do something about that."

"You know what that'll mean for you and your family?"

"I know I swore an oath. When I retire, I aim to have done what I promised to do."

"You've lost your mind, Jesus."

"That's as may be, *Capitán*. But you're still under arrest."

Plato took out his cuffs, and with Alameda's wife and children watching open-mouthed from the windows, he fastened them and led him back out and onto the street.

Chapter Sixty-One

"AND THERE YOU HAVE IT," Felipe said with a grand gesture. "The best equipped methamphetamine lab in Mexico."

Isaac and his two colleagues looked suitably impressed. That was good. Felipe had been struggling to maintain their confidence after what had gone down at the mansion. He had struggled a little during the flight south to maintain his mood. The day since the attack had been an ordeal. There was nothing from Adolfo. One of the men thought that he had seen the foolish boy led out of the house at gunpoint, but he couldn't be sure. There had been no word from him. No ransom. No gloating message. Nothing.

Felipe had very little idea of who had been responsible. He only knew who it was not. It wasn't the cartels. Only Los Zetas had the kind of military training to do what had been done, and even then, it would have taken more of them than the six that had been counted. But if not them, then who? The army? Special Forces? The Americans? His sources said not. The Luciano family seeking revenge? Hired mercenaries? Again, there was no suggestion that it was them.

Who, then?

The Englishman?

He was at a loss.

Isaac was admiring the thorium oxide furnace. The gleaming new laboratory had restored his faith.

Felipe knew why: greed.

The promise of great wealth had a way of doing that.

The American Drug Enforcement Agency classified a lab as a "superlab" if it could produce more than ten pounds of meth every week.

The one that Felipe had built could produce twenty pounds *a day*.

Wholesale, a pound of methamphetamine was worth $17,000.

The lab could produce one hundred forty pounds a week.

One hundred forty pounds had a value of over two million dollars.

The lab stood to make him over one hundred million dollars a year.

Isaac wandered further down the line: the hydrofluoric acid solution vat, the aluminium strip and sodium hydroxide mixing tank, the huge reaction vessel, the filtration system, the finishing tanks. The first cook had been completed overnight, and the meth had been broken down and packed in plastic bags, ready to be moved. "May I?" he asked, looking down at the bags.

"Please," Felipe replied.

The gringo opened the bag and took out a larger-than-usual crystal. He held it up to the light and gazed into it.

Felipe knew it was pure.

$C_{10}H_{15}N$.

Eight-tenths carbon.

One-tenth nitrogen.

One-tenth hydrogen.

The formula didn't mean much to him apart from this: it would make him a whole lot of money.

"I knew it was good," Isaac said, "but this is remarkable. How pure is this?"

"Ninety-eight per cent," the chemist said. He looked up and down the line like a proud father.

"Very good," Isaac said. "Very good indeed."

"Have you seen enough, my friend?"

"I think so."

"We should get you back to the plane. You have a long flight ahead of you."

Felipe stepped out of the laboratory and into the baking heat. The land dropped down on all sides, covered with scrubby brush. The horizon shimmered as if there was another mountain range opposite this one, a thousand miles away. A trick of the heat. His cellphone rang. He fished it out of his pocket and looked at the display. He hoped it might be Adolfo. It was not a number he recognised.

"Hello, Felipe."

"Who is this?"

"You know who I am."

He frowned. "The Englishman?"

"That's right."

"Then I am talking to a dead man."

"Eventually. But not today."

"What do you want?"

"I told you."

"You told me what?"

"That I'd find you."

There was a loud *crack*, and one of Felipe's guards fell to the ground. He looked over at the man; the initial response was one of puzzlement, but as he noticed the man's brains scattered all across the dusty track, the feeling became one of panic. Isaac screamed out. Felipe spun around, staring into the mountains for something that would tell him where the Englishman was—a puff of smoke from his rifle, a glint against a telescopic sight, anything—but there was nothing, just the harsh glare of the sun, a hateful kaleidoscope of refulgent brilliance that lanced into his eyes and obscured everything.

"Felipe."

He still had the phone pressed to his ear.

"Listen to me, Felipe."

"What?"

"I wanted you to know—your son is in America now. He's been delivered. The Mafia, isn't it? How will that go for him?"

Felipe pulled his gold-plated revolver from its holster and shot wildly into the near distance. "Where are you, you bastard?"

He started in the opposite direction, towards his second guard. The man was on one knee, his AK-47 raised, scanning the landscape. A second *crack* echoed in the valley, and a plume of blood fountained out of the guard's neck, bursting between his fingers as he tried to close the six-inch rent that had suddenly been opened there.

"Felipe."

"Show yourself!"

Isaac and his men ducked down behind the car.

"I should thank you, really," the Englishman said.

He crept backwards towards the entrance to the lab. "For what?"

"I thought I was bad. Irredeemable. And maybe I am."

He backed up more quickly.

A bullet whined through the air, slamming into the metal door and caroming away.

"Stay there, please."

He wailed at the rocks, "What do you want from me?"

"You reminded me—there are plenty worse than me. I'd forgotten that."

The rifle shot was just a muffled pop, flat and small in the lonely quiet of the mountain. He turned in time to see the muzzle flash, fifty feet to his left and twenty feet above him. A stinging pain in his leg and then the delayed starburst that crashed through his head. His knee collapsed. Blood started to run down his leg, soaking his pants. He dropped forwards, flat onto his face, eating the dust. He managed to get his arm beneath him and raised his head. Through the sweat that was pouring into his eyes and the heat haze that quivered up off the rocks, he could see a man approaching him. The details were fuzzy and unclear. He had black camouflage paint smeared across his face, the sort that gringo football players wore. He had a thick, ragged beard. He was filthy with dust and muck. He had a long rifle at his side, barrel down.

Felipe tried to scrabble away, his good leg slipping against the scree.

"Isaac!" Felipe yelled. "Help me!"

There was no sign of him.

The hazy figure came closer.

"Please," Felipe begged.

The man lowered himself to a crouch and blocked the way forwards.

"I'll give you anything."

Felipe raised his head again. The sun smothered him. The pain from his leg made him retch. The barrel of the rifle swung away, up and out of his field of vision. The Englishman straightened up. Felipe saw a pair of desert boots and the dusty cuffs of a pair of jeans. He scrabbled towards them.

The muzzle of the rifle was rested against the top of his skull.

He heard the thunk of a bolt-action rifle, a bullet pressed into the chamber.

The click-click of a double-pulled trigger, and then nothing.

Chapter Sixty-Two

LIEUTENANT SANCHEZ had delayed them for an hour. Captain Pope had made an angry phone call, and eventually, Sanchez had been contacted by someone from the Ministry of Justice in Mexico City and had been ordered to stand down. The six agents had dispersed into the streets to take up the search. Anna had taken a room in a hotel with a decent internet connection, hooked into GCHQ's servers, and spent hours running search after search. She was tired, but she did not sleep. She stayed awake with pots of strong coffee and nervous tension.

She hacked into the municipal police database and withdrew everything she could find about Jesus Plato. She started with his address, plotting alternative routes to his house from the mansion and then looking for CCTV cameras that might have recorded his Dodge as it passed along its route. There were half a dozen hits—the best was a blurred shot from the security camera at a Pemex gas station showing Milton sitting in the front seat of the car while Plato filled the tank—but nothing that was particularly useful.

She extracted the details of Plato's private car and ran that through the number plate recognition system that had recently been installed on the Mexican highway system. That was more successful. The Honda Accord was recorded heading south: first on the 45, then past Chihuahua and onto the 16. It was picked up again on the outskirts of Parral, leaving the city on the 24 and heading south-west.

Towards the Sierra Madre.

Fourteen hours of driving.

She told Pope. He left with two of the others.

It was a long shot. They were hours behind him.

Then she skimmed intelligence from the army that said that Felipe González, the boss of La Frontera cartel, had been shot to death in the mountains.

It was all across the mainstream news hours later.

It started to make more sense.

The Accord was recorded heading north again, on highway 15 this time, heading up the coast. The camera had taken a usable picture, too. Milton was driving. He turned west at Magdalena, back towards Juárez.

She warned Pope that Milton might be meeting with Plato.

They put his house under surveillance.

They watched the police station.

No sign of Milton.

Plato went out in a taxi the next day. They followed him. He picked up the empty Accord in the car park of a *maquiladora* on the edge of town. He drove it back home. They saw him take a rifle from the back of the car and lock it in a gun cabinet in his garage.

The gun that killed González?

It didn't matter.

They had struck out.

Milton was a ghost.

Gone.

ANNA EXCUSED HERSELF for half an hour and found a payphone in a grocery store. The phone was in the back, inside a half booth that was fitted to the wall. It looked private enough. She dialled the number she had been given several years before. She had never had the need to dial it before, and she was anxious as she waited for it to connect.

It did.

"My garden is full of weeds this year, the herbicide isn't working."

"Perhaps you should use a shear to clip the weeds."

"Shears are too indiscriminate; besides, weeds must be pulled out by the roots."

"Thank you," the operator said. "Please wait."

After a moment, the call was transferred.

"Anna Vasilyevna Dubrovsky."

She held the mouthpiece close to her mouth. "Hello, Roman."

"How is Mexico?"

"Hot."

"Did you find the man?"

"We did, but then we lost him again."

"And now?"

"He is still lost. They are looking for him."

"Are you still working on the case?"

"I believe so."

"And do you think you can find him again?"

"It depends on him doing anything foolish like allowing himself to be fingerprinted."

"And if he doesn't?"

"Maybe. I have a better idea where he is headed now. And I know where he has been in the last couple of weeks. There might be something there that I can use. So maybe."

"Shcherbakov wants to talk to you about him."

"The colonel?"

"Your trip to Moscow is postponed. He is coming to speak to you instead."

"In London?"

"Next Monday. Be at the usual place at eight. You will be collected."

Now she really was nervous. The colonel was coming to London? "Fine."

"The man—you saw him?"

"Very briefly."

"What did you make of him?"

"He had been beaten. But there is something about him. He is not the sort of man you would want to have as your enemy. Why is he suddenly so important?"

"The colonel will explain. But an opportunity has arisen that requires a special kind of operative. Someone just like him."

"You know he won't work for us?"

"We think he will. We have something—someone—that he wants."

EPILOGUE

The Coyote

Chapter Sixty-Three

MILTON LOOKED up into the sky. It was midnight, and the stars, spread out across the obsidian canvas like discarded fistfuls of diamonds, burned with a fierceness that was more vivid than usual. He thought of those stars, dead for millions of years, their light only just now reaching the Earth. He paused for a moment to straighten out a kink in his boot and, realising that he was tiring, dropped his pack and allowed himself to sink back down into the sand. He sat and gazed up, lost in the glorious celestial display. The black blended away into infinity and unbeing, and he felt utterly and completely alone, as if he was the only man in the universe. It was a sensation that he recognised, one that had been with him for most of his adult life, and certainly for the last ten years.

He was comfortable with that.

Part of his solitary journey through South America had been to give himself time to come to terms with what, he knew, was the only possible way that he could live out the rest of his life. He had done too many bad things to deserve happiness, and even if he could have accepted that he did deserve it, he was too dangerous to allow anyone else to drift into his orbit. That had been demonstrated to him in spades in London, with what had happened to Sharon and Rutherford. Burned half to death and shot in the head, all because they had allowed him to cross their paths. Death followed him, always close at heel, always avid, always hungry. And now Control had found him again and flung his agents at him from half a world away. What if he had allowed himself to draw closer to someone, perhaps one of the women whose bed he had shared over the last six months? What if he had allowed himself a wife? Children? The thought was preposterous. The Group would offer him no quarter, and anyone who was found with him would be executed. It would have to be that way. What might he have told them? What secrets divulged? The shoe had been on the other foot before, and he knew what the orders would be. No loose ends.

No.

There had already been too much innocent blood spilt.

He could only ever be alone.

He took off his boot and massaged his heel. He had been travelling for thirty-eight hours straight. He had taken a couple of naps in the car, parked on the side of the road, but that was it. He was as tired as a dog. It was absolutely still, the quiet so deep that it was all-consuming, enough to make you wonder if you had gone deaf. As he listened to his own heartbeat keeping him company, he wondered whether death could possibly be more serene.

He had returned Plato's car, left it in the car park of a *maquiladora* at one in the morning. The rifle was in the back, hidden beneath a travelling blanket. He exchanged it for a stolen Volkswagen and crossed the city. He drove carefully for fear of attracting attention, only accelerating properly once he was among the scrubland and the start of the desert. He had followed the highway for two hundred miles, and then he had pulled over to the side of the road, soaking siphoned diesel into the upholstery and tossing in a match. With the heat of the burning car braising his cheeks, he turned to the north and set his face to America.

He walked.

Big Bend National Park was ahead, the Chisos Mountain range welcoming him to the border. Milton picked the distinctive shape of Emory Peak at the end of a deep valley as his waypoint. He walked. It hardly seemed to draw closer at all, but distance was almost impossible to judge, that was the way of it in the desert, and especially so at night. Milton was not concerned. He had navigated through bleaker landscapes than this.

He was close.

He walked.

He came across an abandoned railway track, an idle row of orphaned boxcars daubed with graffiti across the rust. The dawn was coming up now. The darkness was weakening, lilac blooming at the edges of the horizon, the light fading the constellations, the herald of the glorious golden desert sunrise that would be on him all too quickly. Somewhere on the mesa, a coyote howled. The long, mournful wail was followed by a yipping chuckle until it almost sounded as if the dog was laughing.

He kept walking.

John Milton trudged across the border as the light turned from black to mauve, the sun coming around again.

The Driver

A John Milton Novel

Mark Dawson

We stood at the turning point. Half-measures availed us nothing.
— *The Big Book of Alcoholics Anonymous*

"Each man's death diminishes me,
For I am involved in mankind,
Therefore, send not to know,
For whom the bell tolls,
It tolls for thee."
— *'For Whom the Bell Tolls,' John Donne*

#1 TABITHA BETTY WILSON

TABBY WILSON updated her Craigslist profile on the night she was murdered. She tweaked her personal information a little and added a new selfie that she had taken that same afternoon. It was a good likeness of her: she was wearing wispy red lingerie, her skin was smooth and blemish-free, and she was wearing a crazy blonde wig that made her look a little like Lana Del Rey. She looked fine, she thought. Her expression was sultry and provocative, almost daring men to contact her. She was slender and had big eyes, androgynous with that alien look that was so popular on the blogs that she bookmarked and the magazines she thumbed through in Walmart or when she was waiting at the laundromat.

It was important that she looked her best. The Craigslist ad was her shop window, and as she touched up the blemishes in Photoshop, she was pleased with the results. She had porcelain skin, a short bob of dark hair, and those big eyes were green and expressive. She was twenty-one and had left school when she was seventeen to have a baby. She never went back. She had two children now, each with a different father, although she never saw either man. Her mom helped to bring up the kids. Until recently, she had worked in telemarketing. She lived in a one-bedroom apartment in Vallejo funded by the alimony that her son's father had been ordered to pay. Apart from the fact that cold-calling saps to sell them new windows wasn't what she had in mind for her career, the alimony and her wages didn't cover all of her expenses. Things got worse when she was fired for missing her sales targets. Delivering pizza or running the register at Walmart were not what she had in mind as her career, either, and those jobs ended just as soon as they had started.

Tabby liked to think that she was a positive person, so she concentrated on her ambitions. She had always wanted to be a model. There was money in that, lots of money, and she was sure that she was pretty enough and had a good enough figure to make a go of it. She created Pinterest and Instagram pages that she filled with photographs: selfies with the camera held as far away from her face as possible, others showing her in the full-length bedroom mirror, and a selection that she had culled from the shoot that a photographer friend had conducted in exchange for a night with her.

She knew that she needed to do something to get her career moving in the right direction. She spent a lot of time working on her page, and it wasn't long before she noticed the ads for modelling. She clicked on a site called ModelBehavior.com, which offered free hosting for the portfolios that girls sent in. She set up an account and uploaded the best photos from the shoot.

She started to see enquiries right away. She was hoping for offers from catalogues and magazines, but they were all from agencies that said that they could book her for those kinds of jobs, but when she clicked on their sites, it was obvious that what they were really looking for were hookers and escorts.

She started to take the offers more seriously when she saw how much money she could earn. Escorting was like webcam stripping, only in person, with no sex involved. And it wasn't hard to be tempted by the money she could make if she did have sex. But she couldn't see the point of signing up for a service and giving them half of the money she made.

She could do it all herself.

That was when she had started advertising on Craigslist.

THAT NIGHT'S JOB had been booked on the phone. The john had emailed her to say that he was interested, and she had done what she always did: gave him the number of her work phone so that she could talk with him and lay out the prices and what he could expect to get in return. Insisting on a call also gave her the chance to screen the guys who had never booked her before. There were always weirdos, and she'd been knocked around by a couple. Talking to someone was better than reading an email to get an idea of what they were like. She had refused bookings with several men who had just sounded wrong on the phone. Tabby liked to say that she was a good judge of character. She was careful, too.

This guy, though? He sounded all right. A Southern accent, a bit of a hillbilly twang going on, but he'd been polite and well spoken. He'd explained to her that he was a police officer, in town for a law enforcement conference, and said that he wanted a little bit of fun. He had no problem with her charges, so she had arranged to meet him.

She was on the corner of Franklin and Turk at eight, just as they had arranged, smoking a cigarette and watching the traffic go by. She was thinking about her kids and about how she had made enough money already this week to pay the rent, pay for the groceries, and maybe even take them to Six Flags for a treat. There was one at Vallejo. She was thinking about that as the Cadillac slowed to a stop beside her. Her old man had been a mechanic, and she had been big into cars when she was younger so that she could impress him; she recognised it as an Eldorado, probably twenty years old. It wasn't in the best condition. The front-right wing was dinged, the registration plate was barely attached to the chassis, and the engine backfired as the driver reached over and opened the passenger-side door for her.

He called out her name in the same redneck accent that she remembered from the phone call.

She picked up her bag and stepped into the car.

She was never seen again.

PART ONE

Regular John

Chapter One

THE GREY SEPTEMBER MIST had rolled in off the bay two days earlier, and it hadn't lifted yet. It softened the edges of objects within easy sight, but out beyond ten or fifteen feet, it fell across everything like a damp, cold veil. June was often the time when it was at its worst—they called it June Gloom for a reason—but the fog was always there, seeping down over the city at any time, without warning, and often staying for hours. The twin foghorns—one at either end of the Golden Gate Bridge—sounded out their long, mournful, muffled ululations. John Milton had been in town for six months, and he still found it haunting.

It was nine in the evening, the streetlamps glowing with fuzzy coronas in the damp mist. Milton was in the Mission District, a once-blighted area that was being given new life by the artists and students who swarmed in now that crime had been halted and rents were still low. It was self-consciously hip now, the harlequinade of youth much in evidence: long-haired young men in vintage suits and fur-trimmed Afghans, and girls in short dresses. The streets looked run-down and shabby. The girl Milton had come to pick up was sitting on a bench on the corner. He saw her through the fog, difficult to distinguish until he was a little closer. He indicated right, filtered out of the late evening traffic, and pulled up against the kerb.

He rolled the passenger-side window down. The damp air drifted into the car.

"Madison?" he called, using the name that he had been given.

The girl, who was young and pretty, took a piece of gum out of her mouth and stuck it to the back of the bench upon which she was sitting. She reached down for a rucksack, slung it over her shoulder, picked up a garment bag, and crossed the pavement to the Explorer. Milton unlocked the door for her, and she got in.

"Hi," she said in a lazy drawl.

"Hi."

"Thanks for being so quick. You're a lifesaver."

"Where do you want to go?"

"You know the McDonald's in Balboa Park?"

He thought for a moment. Six months driving around San Francisco had given him a decent grasp of local geography. "I know it."

"That's where we're headed."

"Okay then."

Milton changed into first and pulled back out into the sparse traffic. The rush hour had dissipated. He settled back into his seat and nudged the car up to a steady forty-five. He looked in the mirror at his passenger; Madison had opened her rucksack and taken out a book. It looked thick and substantial; a textbook, he thought. The dispatcher had told him to look for a blonde when she had relayed the booking although her skin was a very dark brown, almost black. Her hair was light and straightened, and Milton wondered whether it might be a wig. She was curvaceous and small, and dressed in jeans and a chunky sweater. Definitely very pretty. She read her book in silence. Milton flicked his eyes away again and concentrated on the road.

They passed through Mission Bay, Potrero Hill and into Balboa Park. The McDonald's, a large drive-thru, was in the grid of streets south of Ocean Avenue. There were advertisements for three-for-two on steak burritos and cups of premium roast coffee for a dollar.

"Here you go," he said.

"Thanks. Is it okay to wait?"

"What for?"

"A call. We're just stopping here."

"Fine—but I'll have to keep the clock running."

"That's okay. I got to wait until the call comes, and then we'll be going someplace else. Is that okay with you?"

"As long as you can pay, we can stay here all night."

"I can pay," she said with a broad smile. "How much do I owe you?"

Milton looked down at the meter. "Twenty so far."

"Twenty's no problem." She took a purse out of her bag, opened it, and took out a note. She reached forward and handed it to him. It was a hundred.

He started to feel a little uncomfortable.

"That should cover it for a couple of hours, right?"

Milton folded it and wedged it beneath the meter. "I'll leave it here," he said. "I'll give you change."

"Whatever." She nodded at the restaurant, bright light spilling out of the window onto the line of cars parked tight up against it. "I'd kill for a Big Mac," she said. "You want anything?"

"I'm fine, thanks."

"You sure?"

"I ate earlier."

"All right."

She got out. He clenched and unclenched his fists. He rolled the window down.

"Actually," he said, "could you get me a coffee? Here." He reached in his pocket for a dollar bill.

She waved him off. "Forget it. My treat."

Milton watched as she crossed the car park and went into the restaurant. There was a queue, and as she slotted into it to await her turn, Milton undid his seat belt and turned around so that he could reach into the back. She had left her bag on the seat. He checked that she was facing away and quickly unzipped it, going through the contents: there was a clutch bag, two books, a mobile phone, a bottle of vodka, a box of Trojans and a change of clothes. He zipped the bag and put it back. He leant back against the headrest and scrubbed his forehead with the palm of his hand.

He had been very, very stupid.

The girl returned with a bagged-up Happy Meal, a tall soda and a large coffee. She passed the Styrofoam cup through the open window, slid into the back seat, took the bottle of Stolichnaya from her bag, flipped the plastic lid from the soda, and poured in a large measure.

"Want a drop in your coffee?"

"No, thanks," he said. "I don't drink."

"Not at all?"

"Never."

"Wow. What is that, like, a lifestyle choice?"

He wasn't about to get into that with her. "Something like that," he said vaguely.

"Suit yourself."

She put the straw to her mouth and drew down a long draught.

"Madison," Milton said, "I need you to be honest with me."

She looked up at him warily. "Yeah?"

"There's no delicate way to put this."

She stiffened, anticipating what was coming next. "Spit it out."

"Are you a prostitute?"

"You're a real charmer," she said.

"Please, Madison—no attitude. Just answer the question."

"I prefer 'escort.'"

"Are you an escort?"

"Yes. You got a problem with it?"

"Of course I do. If we get pulled over, I could get charged with promoting prostitution. That's a felony."

"If that happens, which it won't, then you just tell them that I'm your friend. How they gonna say otherwise?"

"You make it sound like it's happened to you before."

"Hardly ever, and whenever it has, it's never been a big deal."

"No," Milton said. "I'm sorry. It's a big deal for me."

"Seriously?"

"I don't need a criminal record. You're going to have to get out. You can call another cab from here."

"Please, John," she said. He wondered for a moment how she knew his name, and then he remembered that his picture and details were displayed on the laminated card that he had fixed to the back of his seat. "I can't afford this right now."

"And I can't take the risk."

"Please," she said again. He looked up into the mirror. She was staring straight at him. "Come on, man. If you leave me here, I'll never get a ride before they call me. I'll miss the party, and these guys, man, this agency I work for, they've got a zero-tolerance policy when the girls no-show. They'll fire me for sure, and I can't afford that right now."

"I'm sorry. That's not my problem."

"Look, man, I'm begging you. I've got a little kid. Eliza. She's just two years old—you've got no idea how cute she is. If I get fired tonight, then there's no way I'm going to be able to pay the rent. Social services will try to take her away from me again, and that just can't happen."

Milton stared out at the queued traffic on Ocean Avenue, the glow of a hundred brake lights blooming on and off in the soupy fog as they waited for the junction to go to green. He drummed his fingers on the wheel as he turned the prospect over in his mind, aware that the girl was looking at him in the mirror with big, soulful, hopeful eyes.

He knew he was going to regret this.

"On one condition: no drugs."

"Sure thing. No drugs."

"You're not carrying anything?"

"No, man. Nothing, I swear."

"No cocaine. No pills. No weed."

"I swear it, on my daughter's life, I haven't got a thing. I'm already on probation. I got to pee in a cup twice a week, man. If I get caught with anything in my system, they take her away from me just like that. People say a lot of things about me, John, but one thing they don't say is that I'm stupid. It's not worth the risk."

He watched her answer very carefully. She was emphatic and convincing, and he was as satisfied as he could be that she was telling the truth.

"This is against my better judgment," he said, "but, all right."

"Thanks, John. You don't know how much I appreciate this."

He was about to answer when her cellphone buzzed. She fumbled for it in her bag and put it to her ear. Her tone became deferential and compliant. He didn't catch any names, but it was obviously about where they were headed next. The conversation was short. She put the phone back into her bag.

"You know Belvedere?"

"Don't get up there very often."

"Full of rich folks."

"I know that. That's where we're headed?"

"Please."

"You got an address?"

She gave it to him, and he entered it into the satnav slotted into a holder that was suction-cupped to the windshield. The little unit calculated and displayed the best route.

"The 101 up to the bridge," he said, reading off the screen. "It's going to take forty minutes. That all right?"

"Perfect."

"You going to tell me what's out there?"

"Like I say, rich folks throwing a mad party. That's where it's at."

Chapter Two

MADISON WAS TALKATIVE as they drove north through Sunset, Richmond and Presidio, hanging a left at Crissy Field and joining the 101 as it became the Golden Gate Bridge. She explained how the business worked as they drove north. She met her driver at a prearranged spot every night. She said he was called Aaron and that he was twitchy but, generally, a stand-up kind of guy. He had let her down badly tonight. They were supposed to have met at eight at Nob Hill, but he hadn't showed, and when she finally got through to him on his cell, he said that he was unwell and that he wouldn't be able to come out. There was a number for a taxi firm on the back of the bench she had been sitting on. She called it. It was one of the firms that sent jobs Milton's way. The dispatcher had called him with her details, and he had taken the job.

She wasn't shy about her work. She explained how she got jobs through an agency, with the rest coming from online ads she posted on Craigslist. The agency gigs were the easiest; they made the booking, and all she had to do was just show up, do whatever it was that needed to be done, collect the cash, and then go. The money was split three ways: the driver got twenty percent, and the rest was split equally between the agency and the girl. Milton asked how much she made, and she was a little evasive, saying that she did okay but skimping on the detail. There was a moment's silence as he thought of the flippant way that she had given him the hundred. He concluded that she was probably earning rather a lot, and then he chastised himself for his credulity. The story about the struggle to find the rent suddenly seemed a little less likely. He wondered whether there even was a little girl. Probably not. He chuckled a little as he realised that he had been well and truly suckered.

The bridge was lit up rusty gold as they passed across it, the tops of the tall struts lost in the darkness and the sterling-grey fog.

He heard the sound of a zipper being unfastened. He looked into the mirror and saw her taking a black dress from the garment bag.

"I need to get changed," she said. "No peeking, John, all right?"

"Of course."

"Don't be a pervert."

He concentrated on the gentle curve as the bridge stretched out across the bay, but he couldn't resist a quick glance up at the mirror. She had removed her jumper, and now she was struggling to slip out of her jeans. She looked up into the mirror, and Milton immediately cast his eyes back down onto the road ahead; she said nothing, but when he flicked his eyes back up again, there was a playful smile on her lips.

They crossed over into Sausalito and then Marin City.

"Done," she said. "You can look now."

He did. Milton knew very little about women's clothes, but the simple black cocktail dress she was wearing had obviously been purchased in an expensive boutique. It was sleeveless, with a plain design and a deep collar that exposed her décolletage.

"You look very pretty," he said, a little uncomfortably.

"Thank you, John."

It was coming up to ten when Milton took the ramp off the interstate at Strawberry and negotiated the traffic circle around the tall brick spire that marked the turning onto Tiburon Boulevard. It was a long, narrow stretch of road that cut north to south right along the coast. White picket fences marked the boundaries of vast paddocks where million-dollar horses grazed. The lights from big houses that commanded impressive estates glowed from the crowns of the darkened headland to the left. They reached Belvedere proper and turned up into the hills.

The fog was dense here, and as they drove on, the vegetation closed in on both sides, the beams of the headlights playing off the trunks and briefly lighting the deep darkness within. Milton could only see fifty feet ahead of them. The flora grew a little wilder and less tended. To the left and right were thickets of bayberry and heather, a thick jumble of branches that tumbled right up to the margins of the road. There was poison ivy, as tall as two men and thick as the branches of a tree. There was shining sumac and Virginia creeper and salt hay and bramble. Light reflected sharp and quick in the eyes of deer and rabbits. The road was separate from the houses that sat at the end of their driveways, and that night, the darkness and the fog enveloping the car like a bubble, Milton knew that they were alone.

"You know where we're going?" he asked.

"Turn onto West Shore Road. There's a private road at the end."

He looked into the mirror. Madison had switched on the courtesy light and was applying fresh lipstick with the aid of a small mirror. She certainly was pretty, with nice skin and delicate bones and eyes that glittered when she smiled, which was often. She was young; Milton would have guessed that she was in her early twenties. She was small, too, couldn't have been more than five-three and a hundred pounds soaking wet. She looked vulnerable.

The whole thing didn't sit right with him.

"So," he said, "you've been here before?"

"A few times."

"What's it like?"

"All right."

"What kind of people?"

"I told you—rich ones."

"Anyone else you know going to be there?"

"Couple of the guys," she said. Was she a little wistful when she said it?

"Who are they?"

She looked into the mirror, into his eyes. "No one you'd know," she said, and then he knew that she was lying.

He thought she looked a little anxious. They drove on in silence for another half a mile. He had been in the area a couple of times before. It was a beautiful location, remote and untroubled by too many visitors, full of wildlife and invigorating air. He had hiked all the way down from Paradise Beach to Tiburon Uplands and then turned and walked back again. Five miles, all told, a fresh autumnal afternoon spent tracking fresh prints into the long grass and then following them back again in the opposite direction. He hadn't seen another soul.

He looked in the mirror again. "You mind me asking—how long have you been doing this?"

"A year," she said, suddenly a little defensive. "Why?"

"No reason. Just making conversation."

Her temper flickered up. "As long as you don't try to tell me I should find something else to do, okay? If you're gonna start up with that, then I'd rather you just kept quiet and drove."

"What you do is up to you. I'm not in any place to tell you anything."

"Fucking A."

"I'm just thinking practically."

"Like?"

"Like how are you getting back?"

"I'll call another cab."

"Back to the city?"

"Sure."

"That's if you can find someone who'll come out this late at night. The fog as bad as this and supposed to get worse? I know I wouldn't."

"Lucky I'm not calling you, then."

He spoke carefully. He didn't want to come over like some concerned father figure. He guessed that would put her on the defensive right away. "You got no one to look out for you while you're here?"

She hesitated, looking out into the gloom. "My guy usually waits and then drives me back again. Keeps an eye on things, too, makes sure I'm all right."

"I can't do that for you."

"I wasn't asking."

"I've got a day job. I need to get back to sleep."

"I told you—I wasn't asking. Jesus, man! This isn't the first time I've done this. I'll be all right. The men are okay. Respectable types. Bankers and shit. A frat party, maybe I'm a little concerned to be out on my own. But here? With guys like that? Nothing to worry about. I'll be fine."

The GPS said the turn was up ahead. Milton dabbed the brakes and slowed to twenty, searching for the turn-off in the mist. He found it; it was unlit, narrow and lonely, and the sign on the turn-off read PINE SHORE. He indicated even though there was no one on the road ahead or behind him, and then slowed a little more.

He looked at the clock in the dash; the glowing digits said that it was half-ten.

The road ran parallel to West Shore Road for half a mile or so, and then Milton saw lights glowing through the trees. It turned sharply to the left and then was interrupted by an eight-foot brick wall and, in the midst of that, a majestic wrought-iron gate that looked like it belonged on a Southern plantation. A white gatehouse was immediately ahead. Beyond the gate, on the right-hand side of the road, a blue wooden sign had been driven into the verge. The sign said PINE SHORE ASSOCIATION in golden letters that sloped right to left. There was a model lighthouse atop the gate. Milton considered it: a private community, prime real estate, close enough to the city, and Silicon Valley not too far away. It all smelt of money.

Lots and lots of money.

"Through there," she said.

"How many houses in here?"

"Don't know for sure. I've only ever been to this one. Twenty? Thirty?"

"How do we get in?"

"They texted me the code." The glow of her cellphone lit up her face as she searched for the information she needed. "2-0-1-1."

He nudged the car forwards and lowered his window. The low rumble of the tyres on the rough road surface blended with the muffled chirping of the cicadas outside. He reached out to the keypad and punched in the code. The gate opened, and they passed along a long driveway enclosed on both sides by mature oaks. Large and perfectly tended gardens reached down to the road. There were tree allées, expansive lawns, follies, knot gardens, and boxwood parterres.

They reached the first house. It was a large modern building set out mostly on one level with a two-storey addition at one end. It spread out across a wide parcel of land. There were two separate wings, each with floor-to-ceiling windows that cast oblongs of golden light that blended away into the grey shroud that had fallen all around. A series of antique lamps cast abbreviated, fuzzy triangles of illumination out across the immaculate front lawn. There was a motor court verged by espalier fruit trees. Milton reversed parked in a space; there was a Ferrari on one side and a new Tesla convertible on the other. Two hundred thousand dollars of peerless design and engineering. His Explorer was old and battered and inadequate in comparison.

Milton switched off the engine. "You weren't kidding."

"About what?"

"There's money here."

"Told you." She unclipped her safety belt, put her hand on the handle, but then paused for a moment, as if unwilling to open the door.

"Are you all right?"

"Sure. It's just—"

"You're nervous? I could take you back if you want."

She shook her head. "I'm not nervous."

"Then what?"

"I'm here to meet someone except I haven't seen him for a while, and he doesn't know I'm coming. The last time I saw him it—well, let's say it didn't go so well, didn't end well for either of us. There's probably a very good chance he tells me to get the fuck out as soon as he sees me."

"I'm going back into the city. It's not a problem."

"No. I don't have any choice. I want to see him."

"It'd be no trouble. No charge."

"I'm fine. Really. It's completely cool. I'm just being stupid."

She opened the door and got out, reaching back inside for her coat and bag.

She shut the door.

She paused.

She turned back to him. "Thanks for driving me," she said into the open window. She smiled shyly and suddenly looked very young indeed. The chic dress and stratospheric heels looked out of place, like a schoolgirl playing dress-up. She turned towards the house. The door opened, and Milton noticed a male face watching them through the gloom.

Milton wondered, again, how old she was. Nineteen? Twenty?

Too young for this.

Her footsteps crunched through the gravel.

Dammit, Milton thought.

"Madison," he called through the window. "Hang on."

She paused and turned back to him. "What?"

"I'll wait."

She took a step closer to the car. "You don't have to do that."

"No, I do. You shouldn't be out here on your own."

She liked to keep her face impassive, he could see that, but she couldn't stop the sudden flicker of relief that broke over it. "Are you sure you're okay with that? I could be a couple hours—maybe longer if it goes well."

"I've got some music and a book. If you need me, I'll be right here."

"I'll pay extra."

"We'll sort that out later. You can leave your bag if you want."

She came back to the car and took a smaller clutch bag from the rucksack. She put the condoms inside and took a final swig from the bottle of vodka. "Thanks. It's kind of you."

"Just—well, you know, just be careful, all right?"

"I'm always careful."

Chapter Three

MILTON GOT OUT of the car and stretched his legs. It was quiet with just the occasional calls of seals and pelicans, the low whoosh of a jet high above and, rolling softly over everything, the quiet susurration of the sea. A foghorn boomed out from across the water, and seconds later, its twin returned the call. Lights hidden in the vegetation cast an electric blue glow over the timber frame of the building, the lights behind the huge expanses of glass blazing out into the darkness. Milton knew that the house was high enough on the cliffs to offer a spectacular view across the bay to Alcatraz, the bridge and the city, but all he could see tonight was the shifting grey curtain. There was a certain beauty in the feeling of solitude.

Milton enjoyed it for ten minutes, and then, the temperature chilled and dropping further, he returned to the Explorer, switched on the heater, took out his phone, and plugged it into the dash. He scrolled through his music until he found the folder that he was looking for. He had been listening to a lot of old guitar music, and he picked *Dog Man Star*, the album by Suede that he had been listening to before he picked Madison up. There had been a lot of Brit-pop on the barrack's stereo while he had slogged through Selection for the SAS, and it brought back memories of happier times. Times when his memories didn't burden him like they did now. He liked the swirling layers of shoegazing and dance-pop fusions from the Madchester era and the sharp, clean three-minute singles that had evolved out of it. Suede and Sleeper and Blur.

He turned the volume down a little and closed his eyes as the wistful introduction of "Stay Together" started. His memories triggered: the Brecon Beacons, the Fan Dance, hours and hours of hauling a sixty-pound pack up and down the mountains, the lads he had gone through the process with, most of whom had been binned, the pints of stout that followed each exercise in inviting pubs with roaring log fires and horse brasses on the walls.

The credentials fixed to the back of the driver's seat said JOHN SMITH. That was also the name on his driver's licence and passport, and it was the name he had given when he had rented his nine-hundred-dollar-a-month single-room occupancy apartment with no kitchen and shared bathroom in the Mission District. No one in San Francisco knew him as John Milton or had any idea that he was not the anonymous, quiet man that he appeared to be.

He worked freelance, accepting his jobs from the agencies who had his details. He drove the night shift, starting at eight and driving until three or four. Then he would go home and sleep for seven hours before working his second job from twelve until six, delivering boxes of ice to restaurants in the city for Mr. Freeze, the pseudonym of a cantankerous Ukrainian immigrant Milton had met after answering the "positions vacant" ad on an internet bulletin board. Between the two jobs, Milton could usually make a hundred bucks a day. It wasn't much in an expensive city like San Francisco, but it was enough to pay his rent and his bills and his food, and that was all he needed, really. He didn't drink. He didn't have any expensive habits. He didn't have the time or the inclination to go out. He might catch a movie now and again, but most of his free time was spent sleeping or reading. It had suited him very well for the six months he had been in town.

It was the longest he had been in one place since he had been on the run, and he was starting to feel comfortable. If he continued to be careful, there was no reason why he couldn't stay here for even longer. Maybe put down some roots? He'd always assumed that that would be impossible, and had discouraged himself from thinking about it, but now?

Maybe it would be possible after all.

He gazed out of the window. He could see the glow from other houses further down the road. The nearest was another big building with lights blurring through the murk. As he watched, a sleek black town car turned into the driveway and parked three cars over from him. The doors opened, and two men stepped out. It was too dark and foggy to make out anything other than their silhouettes, but he watched as they made their way to the door and went into the house.

The dull thump and drone of bass was suddenly audible from the house. The party was getting started. Milton turned up the stereo a little to muffle it. He changed to The Smiths. Morrissey's melancholia seemed appropriate in the cloying fog. Time passed. He had listened to the whole of "Meat is Murder" and was halfway through "The Queen is Dead" when he heard a scream through the crack in the window.

His eyes flashed open.

He turned down the stereo.

Had he imagined it?

The bass throbbed.

Somewhere, footsteps crunched through the gravel.

A snatch of angry conversation.

He heard it again, clearer this time, a scream of pure terror.

Milton got out of the car and crossed the forecourt to the front door. He concentrated a little more carefully on his surroundings. The exterior was taken up by those walls of glass, the full-length windows shining with the light from inside. Some of the windows were open, and noise was spilling out: the steady bass over the sound of drunken voices, conversation, laughter.

The scream came again.

A man was standing with his legs apart on the front porch.

"You hear that?" Milton said.

"Didn't hear nothing."

"There was a scream."

"I didn't hear anything, buddy. Who are you?"

"A driver."

"So back to your car, please."

The scream sounded for a fourth time.

It was hard to be sure, but Milton thought it was Madison.

"Let me in."

"You ain't going in, buddy. Back to the car now."

Milton sized him up quickly. He was big, and he regarded Milton with a look that combined distaste and surliness. "Who are you?"

"I'm the man who tells you to go and fuck off. Like already, okay?" The man pulled back his jacket to reveal a shoulder holster. He had a big handgun.

Milton punched hard into the man's gut, aiming all his power for a point several inches behind him. The man's eyes bulged as the pain fired up into his brain, and he folded down, his arms dropping to protect his groin. Milton looped an arm around his neck and yanked him off the porch, dragging him backwards so that his toes scraped tracks through the gravel, and then drove his knee into the man's face. He heard the bones crack. He turned him over, pinning him down with a knee into his gut, reached inside his jacket and took out the gun. It was a Smith & Wesson, the SW1911 Pro Series. 9mm, ten rounds plus one in the chamber. A very good, very expensive handgun. Fifteen hundred bucks new. Whoever this guy was, if he bought his own ironwork, he must have been getting some decent pay.

Milton flipped the S&W so that he was holding it barrel first and brought the butt down across the crown of the man's head. He spasmed and then was still.

The scream again.

Milton shoved the gun into the waistband of his jeans and pushed the door all the way open. A central corridor ran the length of the building with doors and windows set all along it. Skylights were overhead. The walls were painted white, and the floor was Italian marble. The corridor ended at a set of French doors. Vases of orchids were spaced at regular intervals across the marble.

He hurried through into the bright space beyond. It was a living room. He took it all in: oak parquetry floor inlaid with ebony, a gilded fireplace that belonged in a palazzo as the focal point of the wall, rich mahogany bookshelves and fine fabric lining one wall, and the rest set with windows that would have provided awesome views on a clear day. The ceiling was oak, and downlighters in the beams lit the room. The furnishings were equally opulent, with three circular sofas that would each have been big enough to accommodate ten or eleven people. The big windows were ajar and gleaming white against the darkness outside. A night breeze blew through the room, sucking the long curtains in and out of the windows, blowing them up toward the ceiling and then rippling them out over a rust-coloured rug.

Milton took in everything, remembering as much as he could.

Details:

The DJ in a baseball cap mixing from two laptops set up next to the bar.

The lapdancing pole with two girls writhing around it, both of them dressed as nuns.

The girl dancing on the well-stocked bar, wearing a mask of President Obama.

The music was loud, and the atmosphere was frantic. Many of the guests were drunk, and no attempt had been made to hide the large silver salvers of cocaine that had been placed around the room. Milton watched a man leading a half-naked woman up the wide wooden staircase to the first floor. Another man stuffed a banknote into the garter belt of the girl who was dancing for him.

The scream.

Milton tracked it.

He made his way farther inside. The windows at the rear of the room looked out onto wide outdoor porches and manicured grounds. He could just see through the fog to the large illuminated pool, the spa, the fire flickering in an outdoor fireplace. He passed into a library. Silk fabric walls blended with painted wainscoting. There was a private powder room and a large wood-burning fireplace. A handful of guests were there, all male.

Madison was cowering against the wall, slowly rocking backwards and forwards.

There was a man next to her. He put his hand on her shoulder and spoke to her, but she pulled away. She looked vulnerable and frightened.

Milton quickly crossed the room. "Are you all right?"

She looked right through him.

"Madison—are you all right?"

She couldn't focus on him.

"It's John Smith."

Her eyes were glassy.

"I drove you here, remember? I said I'd wait for you."

The man who had been speaking to her faded back and walked quickly away. Milton watched him, caught between his concern for her and the desire to question him.

"They want to kill me," she said.

"What?"

"They want me dead."

Another man appeared in the door and came across to them both. Another guard.

Milton turned his head to look at him. "What's going on?"

"Nothing."

"Look at her. What's happened?"

He snorted out a derisive laugh. "She's tripping out, man. Look at her! They said she went into the bathroom, and when she came out, she was like that. But you don't need to worry. We'll look after her. We're going to drive her back to the city."

"She says someone wants to kill her."

"You want me to repeat it? Look at the state of her. She's off her head."

Milton didn't buy that for a moment. Something was wrong, he was sure of it, and there was no way he was going to leave her here.

"Who are you?" the man asked him.

"I drove her out here. You don't need to worry about another car. I'll take her back."

"No, you won't. We're taking care of it, and you're getting out of here. Right now."

"Not without her."

Milton stood slowly and turned so that they were face to face. The man was about the same height as him but perhaps a little heavier. He had low, clenched brows and a thick, flattened nose. He had nothing in common with the well-dressed, affluent guests next door. Hired muscle in case any of the guests got out of hand. Probably armed, too, like his pal with the broken nose and the headache outside. Milton took another deep breath. He stared forward with his face burning and his hands clenching and unclenching.

"What?" the man said, squaring up to him.

"I'd be careful," Milton advised, "before I lose my temper."

"That supposed to be a threat, pal? What you gonna do?"

Milton's attention was distracted for just a moment, and he didn't notice Madison sprint for the door. He shouldered the man out of the way and gave chase, but she was quick and agile and already halfway across the library and then into the living room beyond. Milton bumped into a drunken guest, knocking him so that he toppled over the back of the sofa and onto the floor, barely managing to keep his own balance. "Madison!" He stumbled after her, scrambling through the room and into the foyer and then the cool of the night beyond.

He could barely make her out as she headed up the driveway.

He called out to her. "Madison! Wait!"

She crossed the driveway and kept going, disappearing into the bushes at the side of the gardens.

She vanished into the fog.

The man outside was on his knees, still dazed, struggling to get to his feet.

Milton started in pursuit but came to a helpless stop. He clenched his teeth in frustration. He couldn't start crashing across the neighbours' properties. They would call the police, and then he would be arrested, and they would take his details. He had probably stayed too long as it was. Perhaps they had already been called. Bringing attention to himself was something that a man in his position really couldn't afford.

He rolled the car up the road. He turned right, further into Pine Shore, and as the headlights raked through the murky gloom, he saw Madison again, at the front door of the next house, knocking furiously. He watched as the door opened and an old man with scraps of white hair and an expression that flicked from annoyance to concern came out and spoke with her. She shrieked at him, repeating one word—"help"—before she pushed her way into the house. Milton stepped out of the car and then paused, impotent, as the sounds of an argument were audible from inside. Madison stumbled outside again, tripping down the porch steps, scrambling to her feet as Milton took a step towards her, the old man coming outside after her, a phone in his hand, calling out in a weak and uncertain voice that he had called 911 and she needed to get off his property. He saw Milton, glared at him, and repeated that he had called the cops. Milton paused again. Madison sprinted to the old man's fence and clambered over it, ploughing through a flower bed and a stand of shrubs, knocking on the front door of the next big house, not waiting to have her knock answered and continuing on down the road.

Milton heard the growl of several motorcycle engines. Four sets of lights blasted around the corner, powerful headlamps that sliced through the fog. He turned and looked into the glare of the high beams. The shape of the bikes suggested big Harleys. The riders slotted the hogs in along the side of the road. The engines were killed, one by one, but the headlights were left burning.

A car rolled up alongside them. It was difficult to make it out for sure, but it looked like an old Cadillac.

He got back into the Explorer and drove slowly up the road after Madison. It was poorly lit, with dense bushes on the left. He couldn't see where she had gone. He dialled the number she had used to book him earlier. There was no answer.

Another set of headlights flicked on behind him, flashing across the rear-view mirror. The town car from before had pulled out of the driveway to the party house. Milton redialled the number as he watched its red tail lights disappear into the fog, swerving away behind the shoulder of dark trees at the side of the road.

He turned around and went through the gate in case she had doubled back and tried to make her way back up towards West Shore Road. The vegetation was dark and thick to either side, no light, no sign of anyone or anything. No sign of her anywhere. He parked. After five minutes, he heard the engines of the four motorbikes and watched as they looped around in a tight turn and roared away, heading back out towards the road, passing him one after the other and then accelerating sharply. The Cadillac followed. Five minutes after that he heard the siren of a cop car. He slid down in the seat, his head beneath the line of the window. The cruiser turned through the gate and rolled towards the house. He waited for the cruiser to come to a stop, and then, with his lights off, he drove away. He had already taken more risks than was prudent. The cops would be able to help her more than he could, and he didn't want to be noticed out here.

That didn't mean that he didn't feel bad.

He flicked the lights on and accelerated gently away.

Chapter Four

MILTON STIRRED AT twelve the next day. His first waking thought was of the girl. He had called her cell several times on the way back to the city, but he had been dumped straight to voicemail. After that he had driven home in silence. He didn't know her at all, yet he was terribly worried. He made his bed, pulling the sheets tight and folding them so that it was as neat as he could make it, a hang-up from a decade spent in the army. When he was done, he stared out of the window of his room into the seemingly never-ending shroud of fog in the street beyond. He feared that something dreadful had happened.

His apartment had a shared bathroom, and he waited until it was unoccupied and then showered in the lukewarm water. He ran his right hand down the left-hand side of his body, feeling for the broken ribs that he had suffered after Santa Muerte had stomped him in the dust and dirt outside Juárez. There had been no time to visit a doctor to fix them, but they had healed well enough. It was just another fracture that hadn't been dealt with properly, and he had lost count of the number of times that that had happened. He took his razor and shaved, looking at his reflection in the steamy mirror. He had short dark hair with a little grey. There was a scar on his face, running horizontally from his ear lobe, across his cheek, and terminating just below his right nostril. He was even-featured although there was something "hard" about his looks. He looked almost swarthy in certain lights, and now that he had shaved away the untidy beard that he had sported while he travelled north through South America, his clean, square, sharply defined jaw line was exposed.

His day work was physically demanding, and hefting the weighty boxes from the depot into the back of the truck had been good for his physique. His old muscle tone was back, and he felt better than he had for months. The tan he had acquired while he was in South America had faded in the grey autumnal gloom, and the tattoo of angel's wings on his back and neck stood out more clearly now that his skin was paler. He dried himself and dressed in jeans and a work shirt, locked the door, and left the building.

TOP NOTCH BURGER was a one-room restaurant at the corner of Hyde and O'Farrell. Milton had found it during his exploration of the city after he had taken his room at the El Capitan. It was a small place squeezed between a hair salon and a shoe shop, with frosted windows identified only by the single word BURGER. Inside, the furniture was mismatched and often broken, the misspelt menu was chalked up on a blackboard, and hygiene looked as if it was an afterthought. The chef was a large African-

American called Julius and, as Milton had discovered, he was a bona fide genius when it came to burgers. He came in every day for his lunch, sometimes taking the paper bag with his burger and fries and eating it in his car on the way to Mr. Freeze, and on other occasions, if he had the time, he would eat it in the restaurant. There was rarely anyone else in the place at the same time, and Milton liked that; he listened to the gospel music that Julius played through the cheap Sony stereo on a shelf above his griddle, sometimes read his book, sometimes just watched the way the man expertly prepared the food.

"Afternoon, John," Julius said as he shut the door behind him.

"How's it going?"

"Going good," he said. "What can I get for you? The usual?"

"Please."

Milton almost always had the same thing: bacon and cheddar on an aged beef pattie in a sourdough bun, bone marrow, cucumber pickles, caramelized onions, horseradish aioli, a bag of double-cooked fries and a bottle of ginger beer.

He was getting ready to leave when his phone rang.

He stopped, staring as the phone vibrated on the table.

No one ever called him at this time of day.

"Hello?"

"My name's Trip Macklemore."

"Do I know you?"

"Who are you?"

Milton paused, his natural caution imposing itself. "My name's John," he said carefully. "John Smith. What can I do for you?"

"You're a taxi driver?"

"That's right."

"Did you drive Madison Clarke last night?"

"I drove a Madison. She didn't tell me her second name. How do you know that?"

"She texted me your number. Her usual driver wasn't there, right?"

"So she said. How do you know her?"

"I'm her boyfriend."

Milton swapped the phone to his other ear. "She hasn't come home?"

"No. That's why I'm calling."

"And that's unusual for her?"

"Very. Did anything happen last night?"

Milton paused uncomfortably. "How much do you know—"

"About what she does?" he interrupted impatiently. "I know everything, so you don't need to worry about hurting my feelings. Look—I've been worried sick about her. Could we meet?"

Milton drummed his fingers against the table.

483

"Mr. Smith?"

"Yes, I'm here."

"Can we meet? Please. I'd like to talk to you."

"Of course."

"This afternoon?"

"I'm working."

"After that? When you're through?"

"Sure."

"Do you know Mulligan's? Green and Webster."

"I can find it."

"What time?"

Milton said he would see him at six. He ended the call, gave Julius ten bucks, and stepped into the foggy street outside.

THE BUSINESS had its depot in Bayview. It was located in an area of warehouses, a series of concrete boxes with electricity and telephone wires strung overhead and cars and trucks parked haphazardly outside. Milton parked the Explorer in the first space he could find and walked the short distance to Wallace Avenue. Mr. Freeze's building was on a corner, a two-storey box with two lines of windows and a double-height roller door through which the trucks rolled to be loaded with the ice they would deliver all around the Bay area. Milton went in through the side door, went to the locker room, and changed into the blue overalls with the corporate logo—a block of motion-blurred ice—embroidered on the left lapel. He changed his Timberlands for a pair of steel-capped work boots and went to collect his truck from the line that was arranged in front of the warehouse.

He swung out into the road and then backed into the loading bay. He saw Vassily, the boss, as he went around to the big industrial freezer. His docket was fixed to the door: bags of ice to deliver to half a dozen restaurants in Fisherman's Wharf and an ice sculpture to a hotel in Presidio. He yanked down the big handle and muscled the heavy freezer door open. The cold hit him at once, just like always, a numbing throb that would sink into the bones and remain there all day if you stayed inside too long. Milton picked up the first big bag of ice and carried it to the truck. It, too, was refrigerated, and he slung it into the back to be arranged for transport when he had loaded them all. There were another twenty bags, and by the time he had finished carrying them into the truck, his biceps, the inside of his forearms and his chest were cold from where he had hugged the ice. He stacked the bags in three neat rows and went back into the freezer. He just had the ice sculpture left to move. It was of a dolphin curled as if it was leaping through the air. It was five feet high and set on a heavy plinth. Vassily paid a guy fifty bucks for each sculpture and sold them for three hundred. It was, as he said, "A big-ticket item."

Milton couldn't keep his mind off what had happened last night. He kept replaying it all: the house, the party, the girl's blind panic, the town car that only just arrived before it had pulled away, the motorcycles, the Cadillac. Was there anything else he could have done? He was embarrassed that he had let her get away from him so easily when it was so obvious that she needed help. She wasn't his responsibility. He knew that she was an adult, but he also knew he would blame himself if anything had happened to her.

He pressed his fingers beneath the plinth, and bending his knees and straining his arms and thighs, he hefted the sculpture into the air, balancing it against his shoulder. It was heavy, surely two hundred pounds, and it was all he could manage to get it off the floor. He turned around and started forwards, his fingers straining and the muscles in his arms and shoulders burning from the effort.

He thought about the call from her boyfriend and the meeting that they had scheduled. He would tell him exactly what had happened. Maybe he would know something. Maybe Milton could help him find her.

He made his way to the door of the freezer. The unit had a raised lip, and Milton was distracted; he forgot that it was there and stubbed the toe of his right foot against it. The sudden surprise unbalanced him, and he caught his left boot on the lip too as he stumbled over it. The sculpture tipped away from his body, and even as Milton tried to follow after it, trying to bring his right arm up to corral it, he knew there was nothing he could do. The sculpture tipped forwards faster and faster, and then he dropped it completely. It fell to the concrete floor of the depot, shattering into a million tiny pieces.

Even in the noisy depot, the noise was loud and shocking. There was a moment of silence before some of the others started to clap, others whooping sardonically. Milton stood with the glistening fragments spread around him, helpless. He felt the colour rising in his cheeks.

Vassily came out of the office. "What the fuck, John?"

"Sorry."

"What happened?"

"I tripped. Dropped it."

"I can see that."

"I'm sorry."

"You already said that. It's not going to put it back together again, is it?"

"I was distracted."

"I don't pay you to be distracted."

"No, you don't. I'm sorry, Vassily. It won't happen again."

"It's coming out of your wages. Three hundred bucks."

"Come on, Vassily. It doesn't cost you that."

"No, but that's money I'm going to have to pay back. Three hundred. If you don't like it, you know where to find the door."

Milton felt the old, familiar flare of anger. Five years ago, he would not have been able to hold it all in. His fists clenched and unclenched, but he remembered what he had learnt in the rooms—that there were some things that you just couldn't control, and that there was no point in worrying about them—and with that in mind, the flames flickered and died. It was better that way. Better for Vassily. Better for him.

"Fine," he said. "That's fine. You're right."

"Clean it up," Vassily snapped, stabbing an angry finger at the mess on the floor, "and then get that ice delivered. You're going to be late."

Chapter Five

MILTON DROVE the Explorer back across town and arrived ten minutes early for his appointment at six with Trip Macklemore. Mulligan's was at 330 Townsend Street. There was a small park opposite the entrance, and he found a bench that offered an uninterrupted view. He put the girl's rucksack on the ground next to his feet, picked up a discarded copy of the *Chronicle*, and watched the comings and goings. The fog had lifted a little during the afternoon, but it looked as if it was going to thicken again for the evening. He didn't know what Trip looked like, but he guessed the anxious-looking young man who arrived three minutes before they were due to meet was as good a candidate as any. Milton waited for another five minutes, watching the street. There was no sign that Trip had been followed and none that any surveillance had been set up. The people looking for him were good, but that had been Milton's job for ten years, too, and he was confident that they would not be able to hide from him. He had taught most of them, after all. Satisfied, he got up, dropped the newspaper into the trash can next to the seat, collected the rucksack, crossed the road, and went inside.

The man he had seen coming inside was waiting at a table. Milton scanned the bar; it was a reflex action drilled into him by long experience and reinforced by several occasions where advance planning had saved his life. He noted the exits and the other customers. It was early, and the place was quiet. Milton liked that. Nothing was out of the ordinary.

He allowed himself to relax a little and approached. "Mr. Macklemore?"

"Mr. Smith?"

"That's right. But you can call me John."

"Can I get you a beer?"

"That's all right. I don't drink."

"Something else?"

"That's all right—I'm fine."

"You don't mind if I do?"

"No. Of course not."

The boy went to the bar, and Milton checked him out. He guessed he was in his early twenties. He had a fresh complexion that made him look even younger and a leonine aspect, with a high clear brow and plenty of soft black curls eddying over his ears and along his collar. He had a compact, powerful build. A good-looking boy with a healthy colour to his skin. Milton guessed he worked outside, a trade that involved plenty of physical work. He was nervous, fingering the edge of his wallet as he tried to get the bartender's attention.

"Thanks for coming," he said when he came back with his beer.

"No problem."

"You mind me asking—that accent?"

"I'm English."

"That's what I thought. What are you doing in San Francisco?"

Milton had no wish to get into a discussion about that. "Working," he said, closing it off.

Trip put his thumb and forefinger around the neck of the bottle and drank.

"So," Milton said, "shall we talk about Madison?"

"Yes."

"She hasn't come back?"

"No. And I'm starting to get worried about it. Like—seriously worried. I was going to give it until ten and then call the police."

"She's never done this before?"

"Been out of touch as long as this?" The boy shook his head. "No. Never."

"When did you see her last?"

"Last night. We went to see an early movie. It finished at eightish, she said she was going out to work, so I kissed her goodnight and went home."

"She seemed all right to you?"

"Same as ever. Normal."

"And you've tried to call her?"

"Course I have, man. Dozens of times. I got voicemail first of all, but now I don't even get that. The phone's been shut off. That's when I really started to worry. She's never done that before. She gave me your number last night—"

"Why did she do that?"

"She's careful when she's working. She didn't know you."

Milton was as sure as he could be that Trip was telling the truth.

The boy drank off half of his beer and placed the bottle on the table. "Where did you take her?"

"Up to Belvedere. Do you know it?"

"Not really."

"There's a gated community up there. She said she'd been up there before."

"She's never mentioned it."

"There's a couple of dozen houses. Big places. Plenty of money. There was a party there. A big house just inside the gate. She didn't tell you about it?"

He shook his head. "She never told me anything. Can't say it's something I really want to know about, really, so I never ask. I don't like her doing it, but she's making money, thousand bucks a night, sometimes—what am I gonna do about that? She makes more in a night than I make in two weeks."

"Doing what?"

"I work for the electric company—fix power lines, maintenance, that kind of thing."

"What does she do with the money?"

"She saves it."

"She have a kid?"

"No," he said.

Milton nodded to himself: suckered.

"She's saving as much as she can so she can write. That's her dream. I suppose I could ask her to stop, but I don't think she'd pay much attention. She's strong willed, Mr. Smith. You probably saw that."

"I did."

"And anyway, it's only going to be a temporary thing—just until she's got the money she needs." He took another swig from the bottle. Milton noticed his hands were shaking. "What happened?"

"I dropped her off, and then I waited for her to finish."

"And?"

"And then I heard a scream."

"Her?"

"Yes. I went inside to get her." He paused, wondering how much he should tell the boy. He didn't want to frighten him more than he already was, but he figured he needed to know everything. "She was in a state," he continued. "She looked terrified. She was out of it, too. Wouldn't speak to me. I don't even know if she saw me."

"Out of it? What does that mean?"

"She ever do drugs?"

"No way," Trip said. "Never."

"That's what she told me, too." Milton frowned. "I went in to see her, and look, if I had to say one way or another, then I'd say she was definitely on something. She said everyone was trying to kill her. Very paranoid. Her eyes wouldn't focus, and she wasn't making any sense. I'm not an expert, Trip, I'm not a doctor, but if you asked me to testify to it, I'd say she was definitely on something."

"Maybe her drink was spiked?"

"Maybe," Milton said. But maybe not. He thought it was more likely that she was doing drugs. A job like that? Milton had helped a girl in the Balkans once during the troubles over there, and she had worked up a ferocious heroin habit. The way she had explained it, she'd needed something to deaden herself to the things she had to do to stay alive, and that had been as good as anything else. And Madison had kept the details of her hooking away from Trip, so wasn't it likely that she'd keep this from him, too? Didn't it stand to reason? No sense in pushing that now, though.

"What happened after that?"

"She ran. I went after her, but she was too quick for me, and to be honest, I'm not sure what I would've done if I'd caught her anyway. I got in the car and drove up and down, but there wasn't any sign of her. I called her cell but didn't get anywhere. In the end, I waited as long as I could, and then I came back. I was hoping she might have found her way home."

Trip blanched with worry. "Fuck."

"Don't panic," he said calmly. "It's only been a day. There might be a reason for it."

"I don't think so. Something's wrong."

Milton said nothing. He pushed Madison's rucksack along the floor with his foot. "Here," he said. "She left this in the car. You better take it."

He picked up the bag, put it on his lap, opened it, and idly picked out the things inside: her books, the bottle of vodka, her purse. "What do I do now?"

"That's up to you. If it was me, I wouldn't wait to call the police. I'd do it now—"

"But you said."

"I know, and the chances are that there's a perfectly good explanation for what's happened. She'll come home, and you'll just have to explain to them that it was a false alarm. They won't mind—happens all the time. But if something is wrong, if she is in trouble, the sooner you get the police onto it, the better it's likely to be."

"How do I do that? Just call them?"

"Better to go in."

"Yes," he said, nodding vigorously. "I'll go in."

"You want some backup?"

"What—you'll come too?"

"If you like."

"You don't have to do that," he said, although his relief was palpable.

It was the right thing to do. The way he saw it, they would want to speak to him, and it would save time if he was there at the same time. It would show willing, too; Milton was a little anxious that there might be questions about him driving a prostitute to a job, and he thought it would be better to front it up right from the start. He would deny that he knew what was going on—which was true, at least up to a point—and hope for the best. And, he thought, the boy was becoming increasingly anxious. He thought he might appreciate a little moral support.

"Come on," he said. "You drive here?"

"I don't have a car. I got the bus."

"I'll give you a ride."

Chapter Six

THEY WERE met in the reception area by a uniformed cop who introduced himself as Officer Francis. He was an older man with the look of a long-standing veteran. His hair was shot through with streaks of grey, his face was creased with lines, and he sat down with a sigh of contentment that said that he was glad to be off his feet. He wasn't the most vigorous officer that Milton had ever seen, but he wasn't surprised by that: with something like this, why waste the time of a more effective man? No, they would send out one of the older guys, a time-server close to his pension, someone who would listen politely and give them the impression that they had been given the attention that they thought their problem deserved, and then he would send them on their way.

"You're Mr. Macklemore?"

"That's right."

"You're the boyfriend."

"Yes."

"And you, sir?"

"John Smith."

"How are you involved in this?"

"I'm a taxi driver. I dropped Madison off last night."

"You know Mr. Macklemore?"

"We just met."

"So you're here why?"

"I'd like to help. I was one of the last people to see Madison."

"I see." He nodded. "All right, then, Mr. Macklemore, why don't you tell me what's happened, and then we can work out what to do next."

Trip told the story again, and Officer Francis listened quietly, occasionally noting down a detail in a notebook that he took from his breast pocket. When Trip was finished, Francis asked Milton a few questions: how had Madison seemed to him? Did he have any idea why she had run off the way she did? Milton answered them all honestly.

"You know she was hooking?"

"I didn't," Milton said.

"Really?"

"No. I didn't. Not until we got there. It was just another job for me. I know the law, Officer."

"And you've come here without being asked," he said, pursing his lips.

"Of course. I'd like to be helpful."

"Fair enough. I'm happy with that. What do you think happened?"

"I don't know. Whatever it was, she was frightened."

"Whose party was it?"

"I'm afraid I don't know that."

"A lot of rich folks up there," Francis mused. "I can remember when you could buy a place with a nice view of the bay for a hundred grand. You wouldn't get an outhouse up there for that these days. Plenty of the tech guys have moved in. Driven up the prices like you wouldn't believe."

Francis closed the notebook and slipped it back into his breast pocket.

"Well?" Trip said.

"I gotta tell you, Mr. Macklemore, this isn't what we'd call a classic missing persons case. Not yet, anyway. She's only been gone a day."

"But it's totally out of character. She's never done anything like this before."

"That may be, sir, but that don't necessarily mean she's missing. She's young. From what you've said, it sounds like she's a little flighty, too. She's got no history of mental illness, no psychiatric prescriptions, and you say she wasn't on drugs. Just because you can't find her, that don't necessarily mean that she's missing, you know what I mean?"

"No," Trip said. "I don't agree."

"Not much I can do about that, sir," Francis said, spreading his hands.

Milton shook his head. "I agree with Mr. Macklemore, detective. I'm not sure I'm as relaxed about it as you are."

The policeman looked up at Milton with a look of mild annoyance. "What do you mean?"

"You didn't see the state she was in last night."

"That may be—I'm sorry, what was your name again?"

"Smith."

"That may be, Mr. Smith, but she wouldn't be the first working girl I've seen freak out, then check out for a bit."

"Not good enough," Trip complained angrily. "It's because she's a hooker you're not going to assign someone to this, right? That's the reason?"

"No. That's not what I said."

"But it's what you meant."

He stood and held out his hands, palm first. "Take it easy, son. If she's still not back tomorrow, you give us another call, and we'll see where we are then. For now, I'd go back home, make sure your phone's switched on, and try to relax. I've seen plenty of cases like this. Plenty. Seriously. I'm telling you, ninety-nine times out of a hundred, they come back, a little embarrassed about the whole thing, and everything gets explained."

"And the other time?"

"Not going to happen here, Mr. Macklemore. Really—go home. She'll turn up. You'll see."

THEY MADE THEIR way outside and onto the street.

"What the fuck was that?"

"Take it easy," Milton said.

"You think he was listening to a word we said?"

"Probably not. But I'm guessing that's standard operating procedure. And he's right about one thing, it's been less than a day."

"You agree with him?"

"I didn't say that. And no, I don't. Not with everything."

Milton had expected a reluctance to get involved, and part of him could accept the logic in what the officer had said; it *was* still early, after all. But the more he thought about what had happened last night, the more he had a bad feeling about it.

The way she had looked.

The way she had run.

The car speeding away.

The bikers. What were they doing at a high-end party like that?

Milton had made a living out of relying on his hunches. Experience told him that it was unwise to ignore them. And they were telling him that this didn't look good.

Trip took out a packet of Luckies. He put one into his mouth and lit it. Milton noticed that his fingers were trembling again. "That was a total waste of time. Total waste. We could have been out looking for her." He offered the packet to Milton.

"It wasn't," he said, taking a cigarette and accepting Trip's light. "At the very least, he'll file a report that says that you came in tonight and said she was missing. Now, when you call them back tomorrow, they'll have something to work with. And the clock will have started. I wouldn't be surprised if they treat it more seriously then."

"So what do I do now? How long do we have to wait before they'll do something? Two days? Three days? What's the right time before they accept that something is wrong?"

"If she's not back in the morning, I'd call again. I'd make a real nuisance of myself. You know what they say about the squeaky hinge?"

"No."

"It gets the oil. You keep calling. Do that until ten or eleven. If it doesn't work, and if she's still not back by then, go back to the precinct and demand to see a detective. Don't leave until you've seen one. Authority's the same the world over: you give them enough of a headache, eventually they'll listen to you even if it's just to shut you up."

"And until then? It's not like I'm gonna be able to sleep."

"There are some things you can do. Do you know anything about the agency she was working for?"

"No. She never said."

"Never mind. Google all the emergency rooms in a twenty-mile radius. There's one in Marin City, another in Sausalito, go as far north as San Rafael. That's the first place to look. If something's happened to her, if last night was some sort of episode or if she's hurt herself somehow, then that's probably where she'll be. And when you've tried those, try all the nearby police stations. Belvedere, Tiburon, the Sheriff's Department at Marin. You never know. Someone might've said something."

"Okay."

"Does she have a laptop?"

"Sure."

"There might be emails. Can you get into it?"

"I don't know. There'll be a password. I might be able to guess it."

"Try. Whoever booked her is someone we'll want to talk to. The police will get to it eventually, assuming they need to, but there's nothing to stop us having a look first."

He looked at him, confused. "Us?"

"Of course."

"What—you're going to help me?" He was almost pitifully grateful.

"Of course I'm going to help."

"But you don't even know us. Why would you do that?"

"Let's just say I like helping people and leave it at that, all right?"

His time in A.A. had taught him plenty of things. One of them was that it was important to make amends; recovering alcoholics considered that almost as important as staying away from the first drink. It wasn't as easy for him to do that as it was for others. Most of the people that he would have had to make amends to were already dead, often because he had killed them. He had to make do with this. It wasn't perfect, but it was still the best salve he had yet discovered for soothing his uneasy conscience.

Chapter Seven

GOVERNOR JOSEPH JACK ROBINSON II was a born talker. It was just what he did. Everyone had a talent: some men had a facility for numbers, some for making things, some for language; hell, others could swing a bat and send a ball screaming away to the fences. Governor Robinson was a speaker, and Arlen Crawford had known it within five seconds of hearing him for the first time. That was why he had given up what could have been a very profitable career in law and turned down the offer of a partnership and the millions of dollars he would have been able to make. He had postponed the chance to take an early retirement and the house on the coast he and his wife had always hankered after. The governor's gift was why he had given all that up and thrown in his lot with him. That was back then, two years ago, back when Robinson was governor, just starting out on this phase of his political career, but he had never regretted his decision, not even for a second. It could have gone wrong, a spectacular flameout that took everyone and everything around him down too. But it hadn't, and now J.J.'s star was in the ascendant, climbing into the heavens, streaking across the sky.

Arlen Crawford had seen nothing to make him think that he had misjudged him.

He took his usual place at the back of the room and waited for the governor to do his thing. There had been plenty of similar rooms over the course of the last few months all the way across the country from the Midwest to the coast of the Pacific: school gymnasia, town halls, factory dining rooms, warehouses, anywhere where you could put a few hundred seats and fill them with enthusiastic voters who were prepared to come and listen to what the candidate had to say.

It was like that today; they were in the gymnasium where the Woodside Cougars shot hoops, a polished floor that squeaked when he turned his shoe on it, a banked row of seats where moms and pops and alumni and backers of the school would gather to cheer on the kids, a scoreboard at one end that said COUGARS and AWAY, the neon numerals set to zero. A lectern had been placed against the wall that faced the bleachers with enough space for six rows of folded chairs to be arranged between the two. A poster that they had fixed to the lectern said AMERICA FIRST. A larger banner that they had fixed to the wall behind it read ROBINSON FOR PRESIDENT.

The room was full. Crawford guessed there were five hundred people inside. There were a few curious students, not Robinson's normal constituency, but Crawford had insisted. It made him look more hip and helped in his campaign to broaden his appeal to a younger audience. He knew, too, that the governor was occasionally prone to phoning it in if the room was too friendly; it did him no harm at all to think that there was the possibility of awkward questions in the Q&A that would follow his speech. The rest of the audience were naturally right-leaning voters from the area, all of them given a little vim and vigour by the dozen or so backers that the campaign brought with them on the bus. They were doing their thing now, hooting and hollering as they watched a video of the governor's achievements as it played on the large video screen that had been fixed to the wall.

The video ended, and Robinson walked through a storm of applause to the lectern.

"Thank you, Woodside. Thank you so much. The sign over there that says, 'Thank you, Joe,' no, I thank *you*. You are what keeps me going, keeps so many of us going. Your love of country keeps us going. Thank you so much. Woodside, you are good people. You are all good people. Thank you."

Crawford looked around the room: five hundred avid faces hanging on every word.

"So what brought us here today? Why aren't we catching a game, the 49ers or the Raiders, grilling up some venison and corn on the cob, maybe some steak with some friends on this Labor Day weekend? What brought us together is a love of our country, isn't it? Because we can see that America is hurting. We're not willing to just sit back and watch her demise through some 'fundamental transformation' of the greatest country on earth. We're here to stop that transformation and to begin the restoration of the country that we love. We're here because America is at a tipping point. America faces a crisis. And it's not a crisis like perhaps a summer storm that comes in from the Pacific—the kind that moves in and hits hard, but then it moves on. No, this kind will relentlessly rage until we restore all that is free and good and right about America. It's not just fear of a double-dip recession. And it's not even the shame of a credit downgrade for the first time in U.S. history. It's deeper than that. This is a systemic crisis due to failed policies and incompetent leadership. And we're going to speak truth today. It may be hard-hitting, but we're going to speak truth because we need to start talking about what hasn't worked, and we're going to start talking about what will work for America. We will talk truth."

Robinson stopped. He waited. One of the women in the audience called out, "We're listening!"

He grinned. "Now, some of us saw this day coming. It was three years ago on this very day that I gave my acceptance speech after I was re-elected as governor. And in my speech I asked: 'When the cloud of rhetoric has passed, when the roar of the crowd fades away... what exactly is the president's plan? What does he actually seek to accomplish after he's done turning back the waters and healing the planet?' The answer is to make government bigger, and take more of your money, and give you more orders from Washington, and to reduce the strength of America in a dangerous world. I spoke of this, but back then it was only my words that you had to go by. Now you have seen the proof yourself. The president didn't have a record back then, but he sure does now, and that's why we're here today. He pledged to fundamentally transform America. And for all the failures and the broken promises, that's the one thing he has delivered on. We've transformed from a country of hope to one of anxiety.

"Today, one in five working-age men are out of work. One in seven Americans are on food stamps. Thirty percent of our mortgages are underwater. In parts of Michigan and California, they're suffering from unemployment numbers that are greater than during the depths of the Great Depression. The president promised to cut the deficit in half, and instead he turned around and he tripled it. And now our national debt is growing at $3 million a minute. That's $4.25 billion a day. Mr. President, is this what you call 'winning the future'? I call it losing—losing our country and with it the American dream. Mr. President, these people—these good, hard-working Americans—feel that 'fierce urgency of now.' But do you feel it, sir?"

He went on in the same vein for another ten minutes. It was a bravura display, yet again. In his two years as Robinson's chief of staff, Crawford had probably heard him speak a thousand times, and that, right there, was another in a long line of brilliant speeches. It wasn't so much the content. That didn't matter, not at this stage of the game. It was the way he effortlessly connected to his audience, made them feel like he was one of them, the kind of fellow you could imagine having a beer with, shooting the breeze and setting the world to rights. That was what summed up the man and made him so exciting. He measured his audience so well and connected so precisely, and more incredible even than that was the fact that he did it all so effortlessly. It wasn't a conscious thing, a talent he calibrated and deployed with care and consideration; it was totally natural, so much so that he didn't even seem to realise what he was doing. It was an impressive bit of politics.

He stepped away from the lectern and made his way along the front row of the folding chairs, pumping offered hands, sometimes taking them in both of his and beaming that brilliant megawatt smile. They were all over him, clapping his back, hugging him. He didn't back off or fend them away, the way that some politicians would; instead, he hugged them back, seeming to get as much satisfaction from touching them, draping his big arm over their shoulders, as they got from him.

Crawford watched and smiled and shook his head in admiration.

No doubt about it: Joseph Jack Robinson was a natural.

He stayed with them for half an hour, listening to their stories, answering their questions and signing autographs. The principal pitched him about the need for more money to fix a leaking roof, and the governor said that increasing funding for education was one of his campaign priorities; that was news to Crawford, who tapped out a note in his phone to remind himself to look into that later. Then they all followed him back downstairs and out to the campaign bus. Crawford and Catherine Williamson, the press manager, trailed the crowd. Catherine looked at Crawford and raised her manicured eyebrow, an inverted tick of amusement that the governor had done it again. Crawford looked back at her and winked. J.J. did that, now and again, surprised even the staffers who had been with him the longest. It seemed to be happening more often these days. As the speeches got more important, as the television crews that tailed them everywhere grew in number, as his polling numbers solidified and accrued, Robinson pulled the rabbit out of the hat again and again and again.

It was why they were all so excited.

This felt real.

It felt like they were with a winner.

Crawford followed the governor up the steps and onto the bus.

"Great speech," he told him as he opened his briefcase and took out the papers he needed for the trip.

"You think?"

"Are you kidding? You had them eating out of your hand."

Robinson shrugged and smiled. Crawford found that habit of his a little annoying, the aw-shucks modesty that was as false as the gleaming white veneers on his teeth. The governor knew he was good. Everything was done for a reason: every grin, every knowing wink, every handshake and backslap and beam of that radiant smile. Some of the rivals he had crushed on the way had been good, too, but not as good as him. They had a nagging sense of the ersatz that stuck with their audiences and curdled over time, seeds of doubt that grew into reasons why the voters chose Robinson instead of them when they finally got to the polling booths. The governor didn't suffer from that. He was a good man, completely trustworthy, honest to a fault, or, more relevantly, that was what they thought. The greatest expression of his genius was to make the whole performance look so effortlessly natural.

"Those questions on immigration," Robinson began.

"Go vague on the numbers. We don't want to get caught out."

"Not the numbers. The message. It's still holding up?"

"People seem to agree with you."

"Damn straight they do. If I can't say it like it is, what's the point?"

"I know—and I agree."

"These fucking wetbacks," he said with a dismissive flick of his wrist, "taking jobs that belong to Americans; damn straight we should be sending them back."

Crawford looked around, making sure they weren't overhead. "Easy," he advised.

"I know, I know. Moderation. I'm not an idiot, Arlen." He dropped down into the chair opposite and unbuttoned the top button of his shirt. "Where next?"

"Radio interview," Catherine said. "And we're an hour late already."

Robinson was suddenly on the verge of anger. "They know that?" he demanded.

"Know what?"

"That we're gonna be late."

"Don't worry. I told them. They're cool."

They were all used to his temper. He switched unpredictably, with even the smallest provocation, and then switched back again with equal speed. It was unnerving and disorientating for the newest members of the entourage, who had not had the opportunity to acclimate themselves to the vagaries of his character, but once you realised it was usually a case of bark over bite, it was just another vector to be weighed in the calculus of working for the man.

She disappeared further up the bus.

"No need to snap at her," Crawford said.

"You know I hate being late. My old man used to drill it into me—"

"You'd rather be thirty minutes early than a minute late. I know. You've told me about a million times. How's the head?"

"Still pretty sore. You should've told me it was time to go."

"I did."

"Not early enough. We should have left about an hour before we did. You didn't insist."

"Next time, I will."

"We probably shouldn't even have been there."

"No," he said, "we should."

The party had been a little more raucous than Crawford would have preferred, but it was full of donors and potential donors, and it would've been unseemly to have given it the bum's rush or to have left too early. The hour that they had been there had given the governor plenty of time to drink more than he should have, and Crawford had spent the evening at his side, a little anxious, trying to keep him on message and making sure he didn't do anything that would look bad if it was taken out of context. It had been a long night for him, too, and he knew he would have to find the energy from somewhere to make it through to the end of the day.

"You get the Secret Service if you have to. Tell them to drag me out." He paused theatrically. "Do I have a detail yet?"

"Not yet," Crawford said, playing along.

"You know what I'm looking forward to most? The codename. You know what they called Kennedy?"

"No, sir."

"LANCER. And Reagan?"

"No, sir."

"RAWHIDE. What do you reckon they'll call me?"

"You want me to answer that? Really?"

"No." He grinned. "Better not."

Chapter Eight

CRAWFORD SETTLED BACK in his seat as the bus pulled out of the school car park, closed his eyes, and allowed himself to reminisce. They had come a long way. He remembered the first time he had met J.J. God, he thought, it must have been at Georgetown almost twenty years ago. He had been involved in politics ever since he'd arrived on campus, standing for various posts and even getting elected to a couple of them. J.J. had been the same. They had both been in the same fraternities—Phi Beta Kappa and Kappa Kappa Psi—and they had served on the same committees.

Eventually, they stood against each other for president of the Students' Association. After a convivial two-week campaign, Robinson had defeated him. But defeated was too polite a word; it had been an annihilation. A good old-fashioned straight-up-and-down slobberknocker. Crawford knew the reason. Joe had always been a handsome boy, something of a surfer dude back in those days, and the aura of charisma that clung to him seemed so dense as to be able to deflect all of Crawford's clever thrusts. It was like a suit of armour. The campaign was civil enough so as to require them to temper their attacks, but the list of deficiencies in his opponent that he had hoped to exploit—his vanity, his privileged background, the suspicion that he was doing this for his résumé rather than from a spirit of public service—were all neutralised the moment he switched on his smile and dazzled his audience with a serving of his West Coast charm. They had debated each other twice, and both times, even the most biased of observers would have had to admit that Arlen had destroyed J.J. on the issues at hand. It didn't seem to make the slightest scrap of difference; J.J.'s election victory was the largest landslide in college history.

It was a good lesson learned: style trumped substance every single time. It was ever thus.

Crawford retired from student politics with good grace. He was better as the man in the background, the overseer with the long view to better plot strategy and tactics, and he was happy to cede the spotlight to characters like J.J. They had both become friendly during their jousting, despite the occasional low blow, and Crawford had agreed to work with him to make his term of office productive and useful. By and large, it was. They stayed in loose touch as they went their separate ways on graduation.

Crawford was always going to go into the law. His father was an attorney, and he had known that he would follow in his footsteps since he was young. He made a career for himself in property and taxation, esoteric subjects that were complicated enough to be remunerative for the few who could master them. His firm served the nascent technology industry in Silicon Valley, and his roster of clients included Microsoft and Apple. He did well. There was the big house in Palo Alto, the BMW in the driveway, and a boat. The trophy wife who wouldn't have looked twice at him if they had met at college. Two healthy and happy kids. And it still wasn't enough. Law was never what he would have described as fun or even satisfying, even though he was good at it. Eventually, each month became a long and depressing slog that was made bearable only by the massive pay check at the end of it.

He stayed at the firm more than long enough for it to lose its lustre. Stuck in a rut. Law had been the easy decision out of school, cashing in his degree for the easy money despite the nagging suspicion that he would have been better satisfied doing something else: academia, perhaps, or something where he could write. And then he turned forty, and he realised, with a blinding flash of self-awareness that was frightening in its certainty, that he was wasting his life. He quit the next day, called an old friend at Georgetown, and asked him for a job.

The man had obliged. He had been teaching the legislative process to keen young up-and-comers for three years when two very different offers came at the exact same time: the first was the offer of millions as a partner at a lobbying firm in Washington; the second was J.J. Robinson inviting him out to dinner.

He had watched his old opponent's career with a strange mixture of jealousy and relief that it wasn't him. Robinson had run for the House of Representatives as a twenty-eight-year-old Republican but had been handily defeated by the incumbent. Instead, he had switched his target to the Attorney Generalship, and after defeating a host of minor opponents, he had been elected at the age of thirty. Two years later, he defeated the Democratic governor of California and finally took the high office that he had always craved. He had managed to hold onto his youthful appearance, a fact that gave his opponents something to latch onto when they laid into him; he was routinely derided as the 'Boy Governor' and not to be taken seriously. He lost popularity over misjudged taxation and immigration policies and was ousted by his Democratic challenger after just one term of office. He licked his wounds in a lobbying practice for a short while before winning the governorship again, this time serving for ten years.

Crawford had taken up his offer of dinner. He remembered the conversation. There had been some small talk, nothing consequential, until Robinson explained the reason for getting back in touch. He was forty-six now, a political veteran, and he was looking for a new challenge.

He was running for president.

And he wanted Crawford to be his chief of staff.

THE BUS PULLED UP outside the campaign office, and the entourage duly decamped. The office was the same as the other ones, all the way across the country. It was entirely generic. It didn't seem to matter where they were, everything looked the same. There was some comfort to be had in that, Crawford thought. There was the usual clutch of pollsters working the phones, entering data into laptops, pecking at the platter of sandwiches from the deli around the corner, the cellophane wrapper still halfway across. Empty soda cans were stacked on desks. Some wore headphones, nodding their heads to the music that seeped out. Crawford knew some of them from the convention last year, but most were new recruits, drawn into the candidate's orbit by the tractor beam of his charisma, offering their time for free.

He saw Sidney Packard standing to one side, a half-eaten sandwich in one hand and his phone in the other. It was pressed to his ear, and he had an expression of deep concentration on his face. Packard was older, bald-headed and wrinkled, and when he moved, his limbs flowed with a lazy confidence. He had been in the police before, and before that, there was talk of the army. He was head of the security detail, and he had been working with the governor for the last ten years. It was an interesting job. Crawford watched him speaking, and eventually, the other man noticed that he was looking at him and gave him a single, curt nod. Crawford interpreted that as good news, went to the nearest platter of sandwiches, and loaded up a plate.

The radio crew had already set up their gear in the conference room, so Crawford went looking for the governor. He opened the door to the bathroom, and there he was; he was buttoning his shirt and fastening his belt. He recognised the young staffer, too. She was adjusting her clothes in the stall behind the governor.

"I'm sorry," Crawford said.

The woman seemed confused. Robinson drew her out and put his arm around her. "This is Karly Hammil," he said. "She's working for us now."

"Yes," Crawford replied. "I know. I hired her. Hello, Karly."

She seemed to brace herself against the washbasin and just about managed a shy smile, an attempt to maintain the appearance of propriety that was redundant in the circumstances. Robinson, on the other hand, did not appear to have the capability of being embarrassed. It was as if he had just come out of the stall after using the toilet. Nothing unusual. Nothing out of order. It was an act he had, no doubt, perfected over many years. My God, Crawford thought, there had been plenty of practice. He had seen that shit-eating grin many times since he had started working for him.

"Well, then," Robinson said. "We ready?"

"We are," Crawford said.

Robinson winked at Crawford as he stepped outside and moved over towards the food.

Crawford followed behind him.

"You can't keep doing this," he said, and the note of resignation he heard in his voice made him feel even more pathetic.

"Relax."

"How many times do I have to tell you?"

"No lectures today, Arlen."

"If just one of them tells their story, you do know what'll happen, right? You do understand?"

"Arlen—"

"I'm just checking, because I don't think you've thought about it."

"No one's saying anything, are they?"

He bit his lip. "If they did, that'll be the end of it for you. End of the road. That kind of thing—Jack, I'm telling you, you need to listen to me. This isn't the '60s. You're not JFK."

"Not yet."

Arlen clenched his teeth; the man was infuriating. "It's toxic," he protested.

Robinson took Crawford's right hand in his and squeezed it tight. Depending on his mood and what was required, the governor had several ways of shaking hands. He might place his left hand by the elbow or up around the biceps or take your hand in both of his. That meant that he was especially interested, underscoring a greeting and making the recipient feel as if they were the most important person in the room. Other times, he would squeeze the shoulder, or for those he really wanted to bring within the dazzling aura of his personality, he might loop the arm across the shoulders and bring them in for a hug. He did this now, releasing Crawford's hand, draping his arm around his shoulders and squeezing him tight.

"I'm keeping a lid on it," he said. "You need to stop worrying. You'll get an ulcer."

Crawford felt like sighing at the sheer boring predictability of it and the frustration that despite it all—despite increasingly doom-laden warnings of what would happen to the campaign if any of his indiscretions were to be aired in public—that the governor would just not listen to him.

Chapter Nine

MILTON DROVE BACK to Belvedere. It was a little after eight as he drove the Explorer out of the city, heading north out of the Mission District until he picked up the 101 and then passed through Presidio. He paid more attention this time, orientating himself properly and memorising as much of the landscape as he could. Newly formed whitish fog filtered through the harp strings of the bridge and then puffed out its chest as though pleased with its dramatic entrance; its only applause was the regular blare of the two foghorns, the lapping of the waves as they disappeared under the silent mass, and the constant hum of the traffic. He passed turn-offs for Kirby Cove Campground and the Presidio Yacht Club, continued on after Southview Park and Martin Luther King Jr Park, the big cemetery at Fernwood and then, as he turned east and then back south, Richardson Bay Wildlife Sanctuary and McKegney Field with the placid waters of Richardson Bay off to the west. The darkness and the fog—deep and thick—reduced visibility to a handful of yards. Milton drove carefully.

The price of living down here on the coast was high, but the benefits were valuable, too: clean air, untamed beauty and, weather allowing, incredible views. If that was the kind of thing you wanted, you would be hard-pressed to find a better example of it anywhere on this side of the continent.

Milton had done a little internet research before setting out. Pine Shore was governed by a residents' association, with an executive board that was elected from residents who became eligible after living in the area for ten years. The presidency of the board had transferred over the years from Vera Schulman, a lawyer; to Pauline Bridges, an artist; to, most recently, Harvey Dell, another lawyer. It was a precarious kind of place. The thirty houses had been built on land that did not belong to the residents. Towards the end of the nineteenth century a Presbyterian pastor named Peter Rogers Casey had negotiated a seventy-year lease from the nearby town of Tiburon, which owned the land of Pine Shore. The original purpose was to build a retreat for sailors who had fallen upon hard times. Those plans grew, and the months passed, and soon afterwards, the pastor's flock constructed a community building that was sufficient to seat five-hundred people.

Five years later Tiburon was persuaded to grant a ten-year lease to the Pine Shore Residents' Association. In return for two hundred dollars a year, they would be permitted to build houses on the land. The lease had been renewed throughout the years, each extension for another ten years and each, as it neared its expiry, carrying the threat that the townsfolk would exorcise their perpetual jealousy of the people who made their homes there and the city dwellers who made the place their summer retreat, and either inflate the rent to uneconomic amounts or refuse to renew it. That kind of tenuous year-to-year existence could only be tolerated by a small slice of the population, and as a result, you would only find a particular kind of person in Pine Shore: very rich, upper middle class, usually white. It also generated something of a siege mentality.

Milton turned off the coast road and continued to the gate. The radio was on and tuned in to a talk radio channel; the presenter was speaking to one of the candidates for the Republican nomination for the presidential election. He sat for a moment, half listening to the conversation: immigration, how big government was wrong, taxation. The man had a deep, mellifluous voice accented with a lazy West Coast drawl. Milton had heard of him before: the governor of California, seen as a front-runner in the race. Milton had little time for politicians, but this one was convincing enough.

He counterclockwised the dial to switch the radio off, lowered the window, and entered the code that Madison had given him last night.

2-0-1-1.

The final number elicited a buzz, and the gate remained closed.

The code had been changed.

Milton looked at the gate and the community beyond and thought. Why had it been changed? He tried the combination a second time, and as the keypad buzzed at him again, he noticed the dark black eye of a CCTV camera pointed at him from the gatehouse. He hadn't noticed that being there last night.

He put the car into reverse, and the camera jerked up and swivelled as it tracked him. He turned around and drove slowly back down the drive until he was around the corner and out of sight. He killed the lights and then the engine and reached into the back for the black denim jacket he had stuffed into the footwell. He had a pair of leather gloves in the glove compartment, and he put them into the pockets of the jacket. He took the S&W 9mm that he had confiscated from the guard outside the house and slipped it into the waistband of his jeans. He put the jacket on, opened the door and, keeping within the margin of the vegetation at the side of the road, made his way back towards the gate again.

About fifteen yards from the gate, a wooden pole carried the high-tension power cabling from the substation into the estate. Three large cylindrical transformers were rigged to the pole, twenty feet in the air, and the wire crossed over to a corresponding pole on the other side of the wall. From there, individual wires delivered the current to the houses. Milton took out the S&W and racked a bullet into the chamber. There were better ways to disable a power supply—Mylar balloons filled with helium would have shorted it out very nicely—but he was working on short notice, and this would have to do. He took aim at the ceramic insulators that held the wire onto the pole. It was a difficult shot; the insulators were small targets at a reasonable distance, it was dark, and the fog was dense. He fired once, but the shot missed. He re-sighted the target, braced his right wrist with his left hand, and fired again. The insulator shattered, and the wire, sparks scattering into the gloom, swept down to earth in a graceful arc.

The light above the gate went out.

Milton cut into a dense copse of young fir that crowded close to the left of the road and, using it as cover, moved carefully to the wall. It was made of brick and topped with iron spikes. He reached up and dabbed a finger against the top, feeling for broken glass or anti-climb paint. All he could feel was the rough surface of the brick. Satisfied, he wrapped each gloved hand around a spike and, using them for leverage, hauled himself up, his feet scrabbling for purchase. He got his right foot onto the lip of the wall and boosted himself up until he was balancing atop it. The vantage offered an excellent view of the community beyond. He could see half a dozen big houses in the immediate vicinity and, as the road turned away to the east, the glow of others. There was no one in sight. He stepped carefully over the spikes and lowered himself down.

The big house where the party had been held was quiet. All the windows were dark. Milton moved stealthily into the cover of a tree and, pressing himself against it, scoped out the road. It was empty in both directions. There was no one visible anywhere. He ran quickly across, vaulting the low fence and making his way through the large garden to the back of the house. He remembered the layout from the quick glimpse through the window last night: the T-shaped swimming pool with the underwater lamps; the series of terraces on different levels; trees and bushes planted with architectural precision; the fire pit; the dark, fogged waters of the bay. A redwood platform abutted the house here, a sheer drop down the cliff to the rocks below on the right-hand side. The surf boomed below, crashing against the cliff, and the air was damp with salty moisture.

Milton followed the platform.

He pressed himself against the back wall and risked a glance through the windows. The living room beyond was very different now from how it had been the previous night. It was empty. The furniture had been returned to more usual positions around the room. The DJ equipment was gone. The bar, which had been strewn with bottles and glasses, was pristine. The salvers of cocaine that had been so ostentatiously left on the tables had been removed. The room was cool and dark and quiet. The windows were still open a little at the tops, and the curtains shivered in and out on each breath of wind, the only movement that Milton could see.

It was as if the party had never even happened.

Milton flitted quickly across the window to a door that was set into a long extension that had been built across one side of the house. He tried the door.

It was locked. Taking off his gloves, he took a pair of paperclips from his pocket and bent them into shape. He slid one into the lower portion of the keyhole, used it to determine which way the cylinder turned, applied light tension and then slid the other clip into the upper part of the keyhole and felt for the pins. He pressed up and felt the individual pins with the tip of the clip, finding the stiffest one and pushing it up and out of the cylinder. He repeated the trick for the remaining four pins, adjusting the torque for each. He turned the cylinder all the way around, and the door unlocked.

Milton scrubbed the lock with the sleeve of his shirt, put the gloves back onto his hands, and went inside. It was a utility room. He closed the door behind him, leaving it unlocked, and then paused for a moment, listening carefully. He could hear nothing. He was confident that the house was empty. He walked quickly into a huge kitchen with wide windows, then a hallway, then into the living room. It was gloomy, but there was just enough suffused moonlight from outside for him to see his way.

He checked the downstairs quickly and efficiently. There was another formal living room with a large, carved stone mantel. A secret doorway in the bookshelves led to a speakeasy-style wet bar. The dining room looked like it was being used as a conference room, with a speakerphone in the middle of the table and videoconferencing equipment at the other end. A spiral staircase led down to a wine cellar that had been built around crouching monk corbels that had been turned into light fittings; there were hundreds of bottles, thousands of dollars' worth of wine, but nothing of any obvious interest.

He found the stairs and climbed to the first floor. There were four bedrooms, all with en-suite bathrooms. He climbed again to the second floor: three more bedrooms, all enormous. He searched them all quickly and expertly. There were no clothes in the closets and no products in the bathrooms. No signs of habitation at all.

It looked as if the house was vacant.

Distantly, down the stairwell, two storeys below, Milton heard the sound of the front door opening.

He froze.

Footsteps clicked across the wooden floor.

"Power's out," the voice said.

"The fuck?"

"Whole road from the look of things."

"Place like this, millions of dollars, and they lose the power?"

"Shit happens."

"You say so."

"I do."

"You got a flashlight?"

"Here."

There was a quiet click.

"You know this is a waste of time."

"It's gotta get done."

"What we looking for?"

"Just make sure everything looks the way it should."

"What would look like the way it shouldn't?"

"Anything that looks like there was a crazy-ass party here."

"Looks clean to me."

"Had professionals in—everything you can do, they did."

"So what are we doing here?"

"We're making sure, okay? Double-checking."

Milton stepped further back, to another door. He moved stealthily. He could hear footsteps down below. He opened the door; it led to another bedroom. The footsteps downstairs were hard to make out. Was that somebody walking up the stairs to the floor below, the first floor? Or somebody walking through the foyer on the ground floor? He couldn't tell, but either way, he was stuck. If he crossed the landing there, he would have to go past the stairwell, and then he might be visible from below for a certain amount of time.

"You ever seen a place like this? Look at all this shit. This is where the real money's at."

"Concentrate on what you're doing."

They were definitely up on the first floor now.

"Go up there. Check it out."

"Just gonna be more bedrooms."

"And crazy-ass parties end up in the bedroom, so go up and check them all out."

"What about you?"

"I'm calling the boss."

Milton could hear scuffed footsteps coming up the stairs; it was the unenthusiastic, resentful one of the pair. That was probably fortunate.

He dropped to the floor and slid beneath the bed.

"It's me," the other man was saying, his voice muffled now by the closed door. "We're at the house. Yeah—looks good. Clean as a whistle. Power's out, though. Alarm was off. Whole neighbourhood. I don't think that's anything to bother us. One of those things."

Milton held his breath as the door to the bedroom opened and heavy footsteps sounded against the boards. A flashlight swept the room. The bed was low down, the boards and the mattress snug against his back, and he couldn't see his feet; he thought they were beneath the valance, but he couldn't be completely sure. He felt horribly vulnerable and suddenly cursed himself for picking the bed over the walk-in cupboard he could have sheltered in. He could have pulled the gun in there, too. If the man saw him under here, there would be nothing he could do. It was a rookie mistake. He was trapped.

He turned his head to the right and looked through a gap between the fabric and the floor. He saw the soles of a pair of boots: heavy treads, worn and scuffed leather uppers, lots of buckles.

The boots made their way from one end of the room to the other.

A door opened, creaking on rusty hinges, and then closed again.

The man downstairs was still on the phone. "Up to you, obviously, but I say we check the garden, then get out of here. All right? All right. Sweet. We'll see you there."

The flashlight swept across the floor, the light glowing through the thin cotton valance.

The boots came closer, shoes on polished wood. He saw them again, closer this time. He could have reached out and touched them.

The boots moved out of sight, away to the door; steps sounded, going away again.

"Nothing up here," the man said.

"You sure? They want us to be absolutely sure."

"Check yourself if you don't believe me."

"If you say it's okay, it's okay. Take it easy."

Milton slid carefully out from under the bed and stayed low, crouching, listening. He heard steps, a pause, more steps, a door opening downstairs, then closing, then another door, a heavier door, then closing, and then silence.

He moved quickly but quietly out onto the landing, gently pulled the door closed and then descended, treading on the sides of the steps as he made his way down to minimise the risk of putting weight on a creaking board. He did the same on the next set of stairs. He was halfway down the final flight, facing the big front door and about to make the turn to head back along the long hall to the kitchen and the rear door, when he heard the sound of a key in the front door's lock.

He froze: too late to go back up, too late to keep going down.

The door didn't open.

He realised what it was: they had forgotten to lock it.

The fresh, cool evening air hit his face as he opened the rear door and stepped out into the garden. He breathed it in deeply. He heard the sound of two powerful motorcycle engines grumbling and growling into life, the sound fading as they accelerated away. He shut the door behind him and walked carefully and quickly to the road.

Chapter Ten

MILTON MADE HIS WAY towards the house that Madison had run to last night, the one with the old man who had threatened to call the police. It was another big place, a sprawling building set within well-tended gardens and fronted by a stone wall topped with ornamental iron fencing. Milton buzzed the intercom set into the stone pillar to the right of the gates and waited. There was no answer. He tried again with the same result. He was about to leave when he saw the old man. He came out of a side door, moving slowly and with the exaggerated caution of advanced age. Behind him was a wide lawn sloping down to the shore. A collie trotted around the garden with aimless, happy abandon, shoving its muzzle into the flower beds in search of an interesting scent.

"Can I help you?"

"I hope so," Milton said. "Could I have a word?"

Milton assessed him as he approached. He was old; late eighties, he guessed. He was tall, but his frame had withered away with age so that his long arms and legs were spindly, sharply bony shoulders pointing through the fabric of the polo shirt that he was wearing.

"What can I do for you?"

"I was here last night."

The man thought for a moment, the papery skin of his forehead crinkling. He remembered, and a scowl descended. "This morning, you mean?"

"That's right."

"She woke me up, all that racket, my wife, too. You with her?"

"No, sir. But I drove her out here."

"So what are you? A taxi driver?"

"That's right."

"What's your name, son?"

"John Smith. And you?"

"Victor Leonard."

"Sorry about all the noise, Mr. Leonard. The disturbance."

"What the hell was she so exercised about?"

"I was hoping you might be able to tell me—did she say anything?"

Milton watched through the bars of the gate as he pursed his withered lips. "Didn't make a whole heap of sense. She was in a terrible panic. Just asking for help. I've no idea what she wanted help for. She had her cellphone out and kept trying to make a call, but it didn't look like she was getting through. I could see she needed help, so I told her she could come in. My wife, Laura, she sleeps downstairs because she's just had her knee replaced,

511

she was up too, all that noise. I got her inside, but then she got a whole lot worse. Couldn't make any sense out of her. Laura picked up the phone and started talking to the dispatcher, 'This girl here is asking for help, can you send someone to help her,' and as she finished the call and turned to her and told her to sit down and relax, the police were on their way, as soon as she said that, out the door she went."

"And?"

"And nothing much. Police came around half an hour later. It was a single officer; he had a look around the place. Said he looked around the whole neighbourhood, but he couldn't find her anywhere. They asked me the questions I guess they ask everyone: what did she look like, what was she wearing, what did she say, all that. I told them what I could remember." He paused. "I've got six kids, Mr. Smith, and I'm sure one or two of them could probably tell you more about drugs than I could. But you ask me, that girl was pretty well drugged up. She had her hand on the sideboard to help her stay upright. Big eyes—pupils practically as big as saucers. She almost fell over twice while I was talking to her. And she wasn't making any sense. If that's not someone under the influence of something or another, I don't know what is. You ask me, whatever she thought her problems were, they were in her mind—hallucinations or whatever you want to call them."

"Did you see where she went?"

"Over the fence. Straight into Pete Waterfield's garden, I guess because he had his security light on, looked like maybe he was in. She pounded on his door, but he's off on vacation with his grandkids, and when she didn't get an answer, she kept on going—into his back garden and then away."

"That leads down to the cliffs?"

"Sure does. You see the boat he's got parked down there? Behind the car?" Milton said that he did. "She crouched down there, between the two, as if she was hiding from something. I saw her try to make a call on her phone again, but I guess it didn't get anywhere, like the others, because she upped and made a run for it. And that's the last time I saw her."

"Yes," Milton said. "Me too. The cliffs are fenced off there?"

"Around the house, sure they are. But not further down."

"You think she might have gone over the edge?"

"I hope not. That's a fifty-foot drop right onto the rocks." He paused. "What's it got to do with you, anyway? She's just a customer, right?"

"I'm worried."

"Ain't like no taxi drivers I know, get worried about the people they drive."

"I think something bad has happened to her."

"Nothing bad happens around here, Mr. Smith."

"I don't know about that." Milton took a business card for his taxi business from his pocket. "I appreciate you talking to me. Maybe I am worrying too much, but maybe I'm not. The police won't even treat this as a missing person enquiry until she's been gone a couple more days, and even then, it's not going to be very high up their list of priorities. I wonder, if you think of anything else, or if you hear anything, or if anyone says anything to you, could you give me a call?"

"Sure I can."

Milton passed the card through the bars of the gate.

"One more thing," he said. "The house over there"—he pointed to the house he had just been inside—"do you know who owns it?"

"The company place?"

"What do you mean?"

"It's owned by a company, one of the tech firms down in Palo Alto. Was on the market last year. Ten million dollars. What do you think of that?"

Milton made a show of being impressed.

"Good for the rest of us, too. They send executives there to stay—guys they've just hired before they can find a place of their own. None of them ever make much of an effort round here with the rest of us. Not unreasonable, I suppose. Why would they? They're only stopping on the way to something else."

"Know who's in there now?"

"Afraid not. It's empty, I think."

"Apart from last night."

"You can say that again."

Milton thanked him, and the old man went back to his front door. Milton turned back to the big house again. The place was quiet, peaceful, but there was something in that stillness that he found disturbing. It was as if the place was haunted, harbouring a dark secret that could only mean bad things for Madison.

Chapter Eleven

MILTON PRESSED THE buzzer on the intercom and then stepped back, waiting for it to be answered. It was early, just before nine, and the sun was struggling through thinning fog. The brownstone was in Nob Hill, a handsome building that had been divided into apartments over the course of its life. Rows of beech had been planted along both sides of the street twenty or thirty years ago, and the naked trees went some way to lending a little bucolic charm to what would otherwise have been a busy suburban street. The cars parked beneath the overhanging branches were middle-of-the-road saloons and SUVs. The houses looked well kept. Both were good indications that the area was populated by owner-occupiers with decent family incomes. Milton thought of Madison and her reticence to talk about the money she was making. It must have been pretty good to be able to live here.

"Hello?"

"It's John Smith."

The lock buzzed. Milton opened the door and climbed the stairs to the second floor.

Trip was waiting for him inside the opened door.

"Morning, Mr. Smith."

"Anything?"

He shook his head.

Milton winced. "Two days."

"I know. I'm worried now."

He led the way into the sitting room.

"You've spoken to the police?"

"About ten times."

"What did they say?"

"Same—they won't declare her missing until this time tomorrow. Three days, apparently, that's how long it has to be. It's because of what she does, isn't it?"

"Probably."

"If this was a secretary from Sacramento, they would've been out looking for her as soon as someone says she's not where she's supposed to be."

Milton gestured to indicate the apartment. "Do you mind if I have a look around? There might be something you've missed. The benefit of fresh eyes?"

"Yeah, that's fine. I get it."

"Could you do me a favour?"

"Sure."

"Get me a coffee? I'm dying for a drink."

"Sure."

That was better. Milton wanted him out of the way while he looked around the apartment. He would have preferred him to have left the place altogether, but if he worked quickly, he thought he would be able to do what needed to be done.

The place was comfortably sized: two bedrooms, one much smaller than the other, a bathroom, a kitchen-diner. It was nicely furnished. The furniture was from IKEA, but it was at the top end of their range; Milton knew that because he had visited the store to buy the things he needed for his own place. There was a sofa upholstered in electric blue, a large bookcase that was crammed with books, a coffee table with copies of *Vogue* and *Harper's Bazaar* and a crimson rug with a luxurious deep pile. A plasma screen stood on a small unit with a PlayStation plugged in beneath it and a selection of games and DVDs alongside. There was a healthy-looking spider plant standing in a pewter vase.

Milton went straight to the bedroom. It was a nice room, decorated in a feminine style, with lots of pastel colours and a pretty floral quilt cover. He opened the wardrobe and ran his fingers along the top shelf. He opened the chest of drawers and removed her underwear, placing it on the bed. The drawer was empty. He replaced the clothes and closed the drawer again. Finally, he took the books and magazines from the bedside table. He opened the magazines and riffled their pages. Nothing. Once again, beyond the detritus of a busy life, there was nothing that provided him with any explanation of what might have happened to her in Pine Shore.

He went back into the sitting room. A MacBook sat open on the coffee table.

"Is this hers?"

"Yes."

"Did you have any luck?"

"No. Couldn't get into it."

He tapped a key to kill the screensaver, and the log-in screen appeared. He thought of the specialists back in London. Breaking the security would have been child's play for them, but his computer skills were rudimentary; he wouldn't even know where to start.

"The police will be able to do it if they have to."

"You think that'll be necessary?"

"Maybe."

Trip had left a cup of coffee next to the laptop. Milton thanked him and took a sip.

"So," he said, "I went back to Pine Shore last night."

"And?"

"It was quiet. Peaceful. I had a look in the house—"

"You went in?"

"Just looked through the window," he lied. "It was clean and tidy, as if nothing had ever happened."

"Who lives there?"

"One of the neighbours told me it belongs to a company."

"Which one?"

"I don't know. It was sold last year. I looked it up online. It was bought by a trust. The ownership is hidden, but the deal was for ten million, so whichever company it was has plenty of cash."

"A tech firm. Palo Alto."

"I think so."

"Apple? Google?"

"Someone like that."

"You get anything else?"

"I spoke to one of the neighbours. She ran into his house. He said she was out of it, didn't make much sense. He called the police, and that was when she ran off again. He's not going to be able to help much beyond that."

The boy slumped back. "Where is she?"

He took a mouthful of coffee and placed the cup back on the table again. "I don't know," he said. "But we'll find her."

"Yeah," he said, but it was unconvincing.

"You know what—you should tell me about you both. Could be something that would be helpful."

"What do you want to know?"

"Everything you can think of. Maybe there's something you've overlooked."

He sparked up a cigarette and started with himself. He was born and raised in Queens, New York. His father worked as a janitor in one of the new skyscrapers downtown. His mother was a secretary. His father was Irish and proud of it, and it had been a big family with three brothers and six sisters. The children had all gone to Dickinson, the high school on the hill that drivers passed along the elevated highway connecting the New Jersey Turnpike to the Holland Tunnel. Trip explained that he was a bad pupil—lazy, he said—and he left without graduating. The area was rough, and he found himself without a job and with too much time on his hands. He drifted onto the fringes of one of the gangs. A string of petty robberies that passed off without incident emboldened him and the others to go for a bigger score. Guns were easy enough to find, and he had bought a .22 and helped hold up a fast-food joint on Kennedy Boulevard. They had gotten away with a couple of hundred dollars, but they hadn't worn gloves, and they left their prints all over the place.

The police had taken about three hours to trace them.

Trip was sentenced to three years in a juvenile facility. He served most of the time at the New Jersey Training School for Boys in Jamesburg. He did thirty months, all told, most of it spent in boot camp, living in barracks with fifty other young convicts. He was twenty when he finally came out. He had relatives in San Francisco, moved west to get out of the way of temptation, and enrolled at community college to try to round out a few qualifications so that he could fix himself up with a job. He found out that he had an aptitude for electronics, and he took a course in electrical engineering. He parlayed that into an apprenticeship, and now he was employed fixing up the power lines.

He met Madison while he was out celebrating his first pay packet. She had been at the bar on her own, reading a book in the corner and nursing a vodka and Coke. He introduced himself and asked if he could buy her a drink. She said he could, and they had started to get to know each other. She was a big talker, always jawing, and he said how it was sometimes impossible to get a word in edgeways. (Milton said he had noticed that, too.) She was living out of town at the time, taking a bus to get into work. She said she was a secretary. Trip figured out the truth by the time they had been on their third date, and he had been surprised to find that it didn't bother him. If he didn't think about it, it was bearable. And of course, the money was great, and it was only ever going to be temporary. He always tried to remember that. She had big plans, and she was just escorting until she had saved enough to do what she wanted to do.

"She wants to write," Trip said. "A journalist, most likely, but something to do with words. She's always been into reading. You wouldn't believe how much. All these"—he pointed at the books on the bookcase—"all of them, they're all hers. I've never been into reading so much myself, but you won't find her without a book. She always took one when she went out nights."

Milton looked at the bookcase, vaguely surprised to see so many books, always a clue to a personality. They were an odd mixture: books on astrology and make-up, novels by Suzanne Collins and Stephanie Meyer. Some books on fashion. The collected poems of Ralph Waldo Emerson. Milton pulled it out to look at the cover. Several pages had their corners turned down. Not what he would have expected to find. He slipped it back into its slot on the shelf.

"That's one of the things I love about her, Mr. Smith. She gets so passionate about books. She writes, too. Short stories. I've seen a couple of them, the ones she doesn't mind showing me. And I know I'm no expert and all that and I don't know what I'm talking about, but the way I see it, I reckon some of her stuff's pretty good."

"What's she like as a person?"

"What do you mean?"

He searched for the right word. "Is she stable?"

"She gets bad mood swings. She can be happy one minute and then the whole world is against her the next."

"You know why?"

He screwed the cigarette in the ashtray and lit another. "Family."

He explained. Madison had been born and raised in Ellenville. The place was up in the foothills of the Catskills, right up around Shawangunk Ridge, and it was on its uppers: the local industry had moved out, and Main Street had been taken over by dollar stores and pawn shops. Madison had two sisters and a brother; she was the oldest of the four. Her father had left the family when she was five or six. Her mother, Clare—a brassy woman full of attitude—told the children it was because he was a drunk, but Madison had always suspected that there was something else involved. She had no memories of her father at all, and whenever she thought of him, she would plunge into one of her darker moods. Clare moved a series of increasingly inappropriate men into the house, and it was after one of them started to smack her around that the police were called. He had been sent to jail, and the children had been moved into foster care. Clare got Madison's sisters and brother back after a year once she was able to demonstrate that she could provide a stable environment for them, but she had left Madison with the family who had taken her in. She would run away to try to get back home and then be taken back into the foster system. There was a series of different places, several well-meaning families, but she never settled with any of them.

"Have you spoken to her mother?"

"Last night. She hasn't seen her. Same goes for her sisters and brother."

"Does she get on with them?"

"They used to go at it all the time, but I think it's better now than it was."

"Why?"

"The others got to grow up at home, and she didn't. She hates that. She said it felt like no one wanted her. Always on the move and never where she wanted to be."

"Why didn't her mother take her back?"

"She never said. I think Madison was a little wild when she was younger, though. Maybe they didn't know what to do with her. She has triggers like we all do, I guess—she'll go off if she thinks somebody has lied to her, or if we're running low on money, or if she's having one of her arguments with her mom or her sisters. If she feels like she's being ignored or rejected, it all comes back again, and then, you know"—he made a popping noise—"look out."

"Could that be a reason for what's happened? Something's upset her?"

"No," he said. "She's been really good with her mom for the last couple of months. They've been speaking a lot. Now she's got money, she's been buying things for them—for her mom, her sisters, for her nieces and nephews, too. I've tried to tell her she shouldn't need to do that, but she likes it. They never had much money growing up, and now she has some, she likes to spread it around, I guess."

"All right," Milton said. "Go on."

He did. Around the time of seventh grade, Madison moved across country to live with her aunt in San Diego. The woman was young, and Madison felt that they had something in common. It was a better town, too, with better schools, and she was encouraged to work hard. That was where her love of reading and writing found expression, and she started to do well. For the first time in her life, he said, she felt wanted and useful, and she started to thrive.

"Have you spoken to her? The aunt?"

"No. I don't have her number."

Milton's cellphone vibrated in his pocket. He scooped it up and looked at the display. He didn't recognise the number.

"John Smith," he said.

"Mr. Smith, it's Victor Leonard from Pine Shore. We spoke last night."

"Mr. Leonard—how are you?"

"I'm good, sir," the old man said. "There's something I think you should know —about the girl."

"Yes, of course—what is it?"

"Look, I don't want to be a gossip, telling tales on people and nonsense like that, but there's a fellow who's been saying some weird things about what happened up here the other night. You want to know about it?"

Trip raised his eyebrows: who is it?

"Please," Milton said.

Chapter Twelve

MILTON WAS GETTING USED to the forty-minute drive to Pine Shore. Trip was in the passenger seat next to him, fidgeting anxiously. Milton would have preferred to go alone, but the boy had insisted that he come, too. He had been quiet during the drive, but the mood had been oppressive and foreboding; Milton had tried to lighten it with some music. He had thumbed through his phone for some Smiths but then, after a couple of melancholic minutes, realised that that hadn't been the best choice. He replaced it with the lo-fi, baggy funk of the Happy Mondays. Trip seemed bemused by his choice.

Milton drove to the address that Victor Leonard had given him and parked. It was eleven in the morning. They walked toward the house, a Cape-style cottage raised high, with a carport at ground level. Milton climbed up a set of steps that rose up beyond the level of the sidewalk and rapped the ornate iron knocker three times. There was a vertical panel set into the side of the door, and Milton gazed inside. He made out the shape of a telephone table, a flight of stairs leading up to the first floor, a jumble of shoes against the wall, coats draped off the banister. It looked messy. A man turned out a doorway to the left of the lobby and came towards the door; Milton stepped away from the window.

The door opened.

"Dr. Brady?"

"Yes? Who are you?" Andrew Brady was very tall, with a plump face, greasy skin and a pendulous chin. His hair was chestnut streaked with grey, and his small eyes had retreated deep into their sockets. He was unshaven, and despite his height, he was overweight and bore his extra pounds in a well-rounded pot belly. He was wearing a fuchsia-coloured windbreaker, a mesh cap and a pair of wading boots that were slicked with dried mud up to just below his knees.

"My name is John Smith. This is Trip Macklemore."

"I'm sorry, fellas," he said. "I was just going out. Fishing." He indicated the waders and a fishing rod that was propped against the wall behind him.

"Could we speak to you? It would just take a moment."

He glared out from the doorway at them with what Milton thought looked like an arrogant sneer. "Depends on what about."

"The commotion around here the other night."

"What commotion?"

"There was a girl. You didn't hear?"

"The girl—oh, yes."

"I understand you spoke to her?"

Brady's eyes narrowed suspiciously. "Who told you that?"

Milton turned and angled his face towards the house diagonally opposite. "Mr. Leonard. I spoke to him earlier. Is it true?"

"No," Brady said. "It isn't."

"Do you think we could have ten minutes of your time? It's important."

"What do you both have to do with her?"

"I'm her boyfriend," Trip explained.

"And you, Mr. Smith?"

"I'm a taxi driver. I drove her up here the night she went missing. I'd like to see that she gets home safely again."

"How honourable," he said with a half-smile that could have been derisory or amused, it was difficult to tell. "A knight of the road." The bluster was dismissed abruptly, and Brady's face broke out into a welcoming smile. "Of course, of course—come inside."

Milton got the impression that this was a man who, if not exactly keen to help, liked people to think that he was. Perhaps it was a doctor's self-regard. He bent down to tug off his boots and left them against the wall amidst the pile of shoes. As he led the way further into the house, Milton noticed a small, almost imperceptible limp. He guessed he was in his early fifties, but he might have been older; the greasy skin made it difficult to make an accurate guess.

He led them both into the main room of the house, a double-height living room that captured the light from large slanted windows. There was a galley kitchen in the far corner, and a breakfast bar with bar stools arranged around it. There was a large television tuned to CNN, a shelf of medical textbooks and, on the wall, a picture of a younger Brady—perhaps ten years younger—posing in army uniform with a group of soldiers. The photograph was taken in a desert; it looked like Iraq. He cleared the sofa of discarded remnants of the newspaper so that they could sit down.

"Could I get you something to drink?"

"No, thanks," Trip said, struggling with his impatience.

Milton smiled encouragingly at the boy. "No," he repeated. "That's all right. We're fine."

Brady lowered himself to the sofa. "So what did Victor have to say about me?"

"Just what he said that you've been saying."

"Which was—"

"That she—the girl, Madison—was here. That she knocked on the door and you took her in. He says you used to specialise in getting kids off drugs and that you run a retreat here. Kids with problems come up here, and you help them get clean. That true?"

"Yes, that's true."

"And Madison?"

"No, that isn't true. And I don't know why he'd say that."

"It didn't happen?"

"I heard the clamour—my God, the noise she was making, it'd be impossible not to hear her. She must've clambered over the wall at the bottom of the garden and went straight across, screaming for help at the top of her lungs. I was up working."

"At that hour?"

"I was an army doctor, Mr. Smith. Served my country in the Gulf, both times." He indicated the photograph on the wall. "Second time, one of our men ended up with both legs blown off after he stepped on an IED. I went to try to help stabilise him before we got him out. Didn't notice the second IED." He closed his hand into a fist and rapped it against his leg; it sounded a hollow, plastic knock. "Gets painful sometimes so that I can't sleep. It was like it that night. Kept me awake, so I thought I might as well make myself useful."

"I'm sorry," Milton said.

"No one notices. That's the beauty with prosthetics these days. You wouldn't know unless you're told. They're not quite so inconspicuous if you have to wear one, though. But you know, we're getting better at it all the time. Another five years..." He spread his arms wide. "It'll be good as new. You won't even know it's there."

"Nevertheless."

"I manage."

He tried to make a connection with him. "I served, too," he said.

"Iraq?"

"Yes. Both times."

"Doing what?"

"Just a squaddie the first time. Then Special Forces."

"SAS?"

"That's right."

"You boys are tough as hell. Came across a few of your colleagues."

"That right?"

"Helped one of them out. Crashed his jeep. Ended up with a broken leg."

"You know what," Milton said, smiling at him. "I will have that coffee."

Brady smiled. "Not a problem. Young man?"

"No," Trip said. "I'm fine."

Brady got up and went to the kitchen. There was a coffee machine on the countertop, and Brady made two cups of black coffee. "You been to Afghanistan, too?" he asked.

"Several times," Milton replied.

"What's it like?"

"It wouldn't be on my bucket list, put it like that."

"Never been out there myself, but that's what I heard from the guys I know who have. Ragheads—you ask me, we leave them to get on with whatever it is they want to do to each other. One thing you can say about them, they know how to fight—right?"

Milton ignored his distaste for the man. "They do."

"Gave the Russians a bloody nose when they tried to bring them in line, didn't they? They'll end up doing the exact same thing to us. If it was my decision, I'd get us out of there as soon as I could. We should never have gone in the first place."

Brady rambled on for a moment, his remarks scattered with casual racism. Milton nodded and made encouraging responses, but he was hardly listening; he took the opportunity to scan the room more carefully: the stack of unpaid bills on the countertop; the newspaper, yellow highlighter all over a story about the Republican primary for the presidential elections; a precarious stack of vinyl albums on the floor; the textbooks shoved haphazardly onto the shelves; framed photographs of two children and a woman Milton guessed must have been Brady's wife. Nothing stood out. Nothing out of the ordinary. Certainly nothing that was a reason for suspicion.

"Milk and sugar?"

"No, thanks. Black's fine."

He passed him a mug of coffee and went back around to sit. "So—the girl."

Trip leaned forwards. "Madison."

"That's right."

"Did you speak to her?"

"Not really. I went to the door and called out, but she didn't even pause. Kept going straight on."

"She didn't come in?"

"No, she didn't. Like I said, she ran off."

"Why would Mr. Leonard tell me that you said she did come in?" Milton asked.

"You'll have to ask him that. Between us, Victor's an old man. His faculties... well, let's be charitable about it and say that they're not what they once were."

"He's lying?"

"I'm not saying that. Perhaps he's just mistaken. It wouldn't be the first time."

"Right."

Brady spoke easily and credibly. If he was lying, he was good at it.

The doctor sipped his coffee and rested the mug on the arm of the chair. "You've reported her missing?"

"Of course," Trip said tersely.

"And?"

"They were useless."

"Well, of course, in their defence, this isn't a lost child, is it? She's a grown-up. I suppose they might be inclined to think she's gone off somewhere on her own and she'll come back when she feels like it."

"She's missing," Trip said, his temper up a little. Milton felt the atmosphere in the room change; the boy was angry, and the doctor's air of self-importance would only inflame things. They had got all they were going to get from this visit. It was time to go.

He stood. "Thanks for the coffee. I'm sorry we had to bother you."

Brady stood, too. "I'll tell you what," he said, reaching into his pocket and fishing out a business card. "This is my number. I'll be happy to help out if you need anything. I'm on the board of the community association here. If you want to speak to anyone else or if you want to put flyers out, that sort of thing, please do just give me a call. Anything I can do, just ask."

Milton took the card. "Thank you," he said as they made their way back down the corridor. They shook at the door. Brady's hands were bigger than his, but they were soft, and his grip was flaccid and damp, unimpressive. Milton thanked him again, and impelling Trip onwards with a hand on his shoulder, they made their way down the steps to the pavement. Milton turned back to the house and saw Brady watching them from a side window; the man waved at him as soon as he realised that he had been seen. Milton turned back to the car, went around, and got inside.

"Bullshit," Trip said. "One of them is lying, right?"

"Yes," Milton said. "But I don't know who."

Chapter Thirteen

MILTON MET TRIP in Top Notch Burger at noon the next day. Julius bagged up Milton's cheeseburger and the "original" with jalapeños that the boy had ordered, and they ate them on the way back to Pine Shore. Trip had printed a missing person poster overnight, and they had stopped at a Kinko's to run off two hundred copies. The poster was a simple affair, with a picture of Madison smiling into the camera with a paper birthday hat perched on her head. MISSING was printed above the photograph in bold capitals, her name was below the photograph, and then at the foot of the flyer were Trip's cellphone number and his email address.

Milton parked outside Andrew Brady's house, and they split up and set to work. He had purchased a stapler and staples from the copy-shop, and he used them to fix flyers to telegraph poles and fences. He went door to door, knocking politely and then, if the residents were home, explaining what had happened and what he was doing. Reactions varied: indifference, concern, a couple of the residents showing mild hostility. He pressed a copy of the flyer into the hands of each and left one in the mailboxes of those who were not home. It took Milton an hour to cover the ground that he had volunteered to take.

He waited for Trip at the car and stared up at the plain wooden door to Andrew Brady's house. The doctor had been the subject of several conversations with the other residents. He had visited the library that morning, and his research, together with the information he was able to glean, enabled him to build up a more comprehensive picture. He was an interesting character, that much was obvious, and the more he learnt about him, the more questions he had.

Brady had moved into Pine Shore in the middle 1990s. There was the doctor himself; his French wife, Collette; and their two young children, Claude and Annabel. Brady was the son of an army general who had served with distinction in Korea. He had followed his father into the military and had apparently enjoyed a decent, if not spectacular, career. Unable to work on the frontline after he lost his leg, he was moved into an administrative role. It had evidently been a disappointment after his previous experience. He gave an interview to the local press upon his appointment as chief of surgery at St Francis Memorial Hospital explaining that while he would always love the army and that his military career had made him the man he was, he was a man of action and not suited to "riding a desk." He wanted to do something tangible and "make a difference in the community."

The family appeared to be affluent. Their house was one of the more expensive in the neighbourhood, and there was a Lexus and an Audi in the driveway. A couple of the neighbours made awkward reference to his leg; it wasn't usually obvious that he was lame, a fact that Milton could attest to. He wore shorts in the summer, though, and then it was evident. The prosthesis was a cream colour, mismatched with the tan that he always developed from working in his garden. One of the women that Milton spoke with, a blue-rinsed matriarch who was full of spite, said that she found it distasteful that he would put his leg "on show" like that. Milton humoured her and was about to take his leave when she looked at him with a mixture of lasciviousness and conspiracy.

"You know how he lost it? He told you what happened?"

"Yes—a bomb in Iraq."

She chuckled. "He usually tells people that."

"There's another story?"

"It was a car crash," she said, delivering the news with an air of self-satisfied smugness. "I don't know all the details, but the story is that he'd been drinking. It was on the army base out there. He got drunk and drove his car into a tree. They had to amputate the leg to get him out."

There were some who spoke with a guarded warmness about the Bradys. Andrew and Collette were gregarious to a fault, becoming friends with their immediate neighbours. Andrew had been elected to the board of the residents' association, and it appeared that most of the other members were on good terms with him. There was Kevin Heyman, the owner of a large printing business. There was Charles Murdoch, who ran a real estate brokerage with another neighbour Curtis McMahon. Those families were close, and there was talk of barbeques on the Fourth of July and shared festivities in the winter. The closeness wasn't shared with all, and for all those who described Brady as friendly and approachable, there were others who described him as the head of a closed and overbearing clique. While some spoke of his kindness, often visiting the sick to offer the benefit of his experience, others saw him as a loud-mouthed braggart, looking down on his neighbours and claiming status in a way that invited resentment.

Apart from the suggestion that he might not have lost his leg in Iraq, Milton heard other stories that called his honesty into question. The most troubling concerned his professional reputation. During his time at the hospital, there had been a serious road crash on the interstate outside of San Mateo. A truck loaded with diesel had jacknifed across the 101, slicking the asphalt with fuel so that a series of cars had ploughed into it. The resulting fireball had been hot enough to melt the metal guardrails that ran down the median. Brady had been forced to resign in the aftermath of the crash after local reporters suggested that he had embellished his role in the recovery effort. He had claimed that he had driven himself to the scene of the disaster, and badging his way past the first responders, he had made his way into the heart of the inferno and administered first aid to survivors as they were pulled from the wreckage of their vehicles. The fire service later denied that he had been present at all and stated that he would never have been allowed to get as close to the flames as he had claimed. In another incident, Brady recounted the story of being on his boat in Richardson Bay when a yacht had capsized and started to sink. He boasted that he had swum to the stricken boat and pulled a man and his son to safety. It was subsequently found that there was no record of a boat getting into difficulty that day and no father and son to corroborate the story. An anonymous source even suggested that Brady had not even been on the water.

He had not taken another job since his resignation, and the suggestion had been made that there had been a large pay-off to get rid of him. He had retreated to Pine Shore and made himself busy. He took it upon himself to act as the resident physician, attending neighbours and offering help that was sometimes not welcome. He rather ostentatiously attached a police beacon to the top of his car and monitored a police scanner for the barest sniff of an emergency so that he could hurry to the scene and offer his help. He had assisted locals with minor ailments and had attended the owner of a chain of delicatessens in the city when he complained of a soreness in his arm and a shortness of breath. He worked hard, seemingly intent on gaining the trust and respect of the community, but continually told tales that were simple enough to debunk, and when they were, they damaged the good that he had done. He suggested that he had worked with the police. He boasted that he was a qualified pilot. He spoke of having obtained a degree in law through distance learning while he was in the army. He seemed almost too eager to resolve any given crisis, no matter how small.

It seemed to Milton that Brady was intent upon making himself the centre of the community. His role as the chair of the residents' association seemed particularly important to him, and there was grudging acceptance from many that he did good and important work to make Pine Shore a better place to live. But not everyone felt the same way. More than one person confided to Milton that there was bad blood when it came to the committee. The chairmanship was an elected post, and it had been contested when the previous incumbent had stood aside.

The other candidate in an election that was described as "pointlessly vicious" was Victor Leonard.

Trip opened the passenger door and slid inside.

"How did it go?" Milton asked him.

"Got rid of all of them."

"Learn anything?"

"That this place is full of crap. You?"

"The same."

Milton told him what he had learned about Brady.

"He told others that he worked in Washington after coming out of the army. Homeland Security. He's full of shit, Mr. Smith. How can we trust anything he's told us?"

"I'm not sure we can," Milton admitted.

"So where does that leave us? You ask me, Madison was in there." He stabbed his finger angrily against the window three times, indicating Brady's house.

"I don't know. But we need to find out."

Chapter Fourteen

ONE OF THE CAMPAIGN BOOSTERS was a big wine grower, exporting his bottles all over the world for millions of dollars a year, and one of the benefits of that largesse was an executive box at Candlestick Park. Arlen Crawford could take it or leave it when it came to sports, but his boss was an avid fan. The 49ers were his team, too, so the prospect of taking in the game against Dallas was something that had kept him fired up as they approached the end of the week. It wasn't all pleasure, Crawford reminded him as they walked through the busy stadium to the level that held the luxury suites. Plenty of potential donors had been invited, too, not all of them on board with the campaign yet. They needed to be impressed. Robinson needed to deploy that beguiling grin, and his charisma needed to be at its most magnetic.

They reached the door, and Robinson opened it and stepped through into the box beyond. There was a long table laden with cold cuts, beers and snacks and, beyond that, an outside seating area. The governor's smile was immediate and infectious; he set to work on the other guests, working his way through the room, reaching out to take hands, sometimes pressing them between both of his, rewarding those who were already on the team with jovial backslaps or, for the lucky few, a powerful hug. It took him fifteen minutes to reach the front of the box and the open French doors that allowed access to the outside seats. Crawford stepped down to the front of the enclosure and allowed himself a moment to breathe.

The field was brilliant green, perfectly lush, the gridiron markings standing out in vivid white paint. The stadium PA picked up the intensity as the teams made their way out through an inflatable tunnel in the corner of the stadium. Fireworks shot into the air, flamethrowers breathed tendrils of fire that reached up to the upper decks, music thumped, cheerleaders shimmied in formation. The 49ers' offense was introduced by the hyperbolic announcer, each armoured player sprinting through a gauntlet fashioned by the defense, chest-bumping those that had made the procession before him.

Crawford turned away from the noise and the pageantry to watch the governor deep in conversation with the multimillionaire who owned cattle ranches all the way across the south. Two good old boys, Crawford thought to himself. Winning him over would be a slam dunk for Robinson. They would be drinking buddies by the end of the afternoon, and a cheque with a lot of zeroes would be on its way to them first thing in the morning.

Suddenly tired, he slid down into a seat and closed his eyes. He thought about the sacrifices he had made to get them as far as this. Robinson was the

529

main draw, the focus, but without Crawford and the work that he did for him, he would just be another talker, high on star-power but low on substance, and destined for the level he was at right now. If Robinson was the circus, Crawford was the ringmaster. You couldn't have one without the other. It just wouldn't work.

He opened his eyes as the home team kicked off, the kicker putting his foot through the ball and sending it high into the air, spinning it on its axis all the way to the back of the end zone. The return man fielded it and dropped to one knee. Touchback.

The others settled into their seats. Robinson saw Crawford, grinned, and gave him a wink.

He hoped that all this effort was going to be worth it.

Chapter Fifteen

TUESDAY NIGHT'S A.A. meeting was Milton's favourite. He stopped at a 7-Eleven and bought two jars of instant coffee and three different types of cookies. Yet more mist had risen from the ocean and was beginning its slow drift across the town. It was a soft, heavy night, too cloudy for a moon. The streetlights were dim, opalescent in the mist; there was a slight neon buzzing from the signage of a bar on the opposite side of the street from the church. Milton parked and left the engine idling for a moment, the golden beams of the headlights glowing and fading against the banked fog. He killed the engine, got out and locked the door, and crossed the street. He took the key from his pocket, unlocked the door, and descended into the basement of the church.

It was a tired room, with peeling beige paint and cracked half-windows that were set far up towards the ceiling, revealing the shoes and ankles of the pedestrians passing by. Milton filled the urn with water and set it to boil. He took the coffee from the cupboard and then arranged the biscuits that he had brought on a plate, a series of neat concentric circles. The mugs hadn't been washed from the last meeting that had used the room, so he filled the basin and attended to them, drying them with a dishcloth and stacking them on the table next to the urn.

Milton had been coming to meetings for more than three years. London, all the way through South America, then here. He still found the thought of it counter-intuitive, but then the complete honesty that the program demanded would always be a difficult concept for a man who had worked in the shadows for most of his adult life. He did his best.

It had been more difficult at the start, in that church hall in West London. There was the Official Secrets Act, for a start, and what would happen to him if it came out that he had a problem. He had hidden at the back, near the door, and it had taken him a month to sit all the way through a meeting without turning tail and fleeing. He had gradually asked a regular with plenty of years of sobriety and a quiet attitude if he would be his first sponsor. He was called Dave Goulding, a musician in his late forties, a man who had been successful when he was younger and then drank his money and his talent away. Despite a life of bitter disappointment, he had managed to get his head screwed on straight, and with his guidance, Milton had started to make progress.

The first thing he insisted upon was that he attend ninety meetings in ninety days. He had given him a spiral-bound notebook and a pen and told him that if he wanted him to remain as his sponsor, he had to record every meeting he attended in that notebook. Milton did that. After that, a little trust between them developed, and they worked on his participation in the meetings. He wasn't ready to speak at that point—that wouldn't come for more than a year—but he had been persuaded to at least give the impression that he was engaged in what was going on. Dave called the back row at meetings the Denial Aisle, and had drummed into him that sick people who wanted to get well sat in the front. Milton wasn't quite ready for that, either, but he had gradually moved forwards. Each month he moved forward again until he was in the middle of the action, stoic and thoughtful amidst the thicket of raised arms as the other alcoholics jostled to speak.

He had found this meeting on his first night in 'Frisco. It was a lucky find; there was something about it that made it special. The room, the regulars, the atmosphere; there was a little magic about it. Milton had volunteered to serve the drinks on the second night when the grizzled ex-army vet who had held the post before him had fallen off the wagon and been spotted unconscious in the parking lot of the 7-Eleven near Fisherman's Wharf. Milton always remembered Dave explaining that service was the keystone of A.A., and since taking care of the refreshments was something he could do without opening himself up to the others, it was an excellent way to make himself known while avoiding the conversations that he still found awkward.

He opened the storage cupboard, dragged out the stacked chairs, and arranged them in four rows of five. The format of the meeting was the same as all of the others that Milton had attended. A table was arranged at the front of the room, and Milton covered it with a cloth with the A.A. logo embroidered on it in coloured thread. There were posters on the wall and books and pamphlets that could be purchased. Milton went back to the cupboard, took out a long cardboard tube, and shook out the poster stored inside. It was made to look like a scroll; he hung it from its hook. The poster listed the Twelve Steps.

Milton was finishing up when the first man came down the stairs. His name was Smulders, he worked on the docks, he had been sober for a year, and he was the chairman of this meeting. Milton said hello, poured him a coffee, and offered him a biscuit.

"Thanks," Smulders said. "How've you been?"

"I've had better days."

"Want to talk about it?"

"Maybe later," he said, the same thing he always said.

"You know what I'm going to say, right?"

"That I shouldn't brood."

"Exactly. Get it off your chest."

"In my own time."

"Sure. Mmm-hmm. Good cookies—gimme another."

Milton had already begun to feel a little better.

IT WAS a normal meeting. The chair arranged for a speaker to share his or her story for the first half an hour, and then they all shared back with their own experiences. Smulders had asked one of the regulars, a thirty-something docker that Milton knew called Richie Grimes, to tell his story. They sat down, worked through the preliminaries, and then Smulders asked Richie to begin.

"My name is Richie," he said, "and I'm an alcoholic."

Milton was dozing a little, but that woke him up. Richie was a nice guy.

"Hi, Richie," the group responded.

"I'm pleased I've been asked to share tonight. I don't always talk as much as I know I ought to, but I really do need to share something. I've been holding onto it for the last six months, and unless I deal with it, I know I'll never be able to stay away from coke and the bottle."

The group waited.

"I'm grandiose, like we all are, right, but not so much that I'd argue that mine is an original problem. You know what I'm talking about—money." They all laughed. "Yeah, right. Most alkies I know couldn't organise their finances if their lives depended on it, but if I'm not the worst in the room, then I'd be very fuckin' surprised, excuse my French. I lost my job a year ago for the usual reasons—attendance was shitty, and when I did turn up, I was either drunk or thinking about getting drunk—and instead of taking the hint, I decided it'd be a much better idea to get drunk, every day, for the next month. By the end of that little binge, the savings I had managed to keep were all gone, and the landlord started making threats about throwing me onto the street. I couldn't work; no one would even look at me not least give me a job. If I got evicted, it was gonna get a hundred times worse, so I thought the only thing I could do was borrow some money from this dude that I heard would give me credit. But he's not like the bank, you know? He's not on the level, not the kind of dude you'd want to be in hock to, but it wasn't like anyone legit was about to give me credit, and my folks are dead, so the way I saw it, I didn't have much of a choice. I went and saw him and took his money, and after I dropped a couple of Gs on a massive bender, the one that took me to rock bottom, then I found the rooms, and I haven't drunk or drugged since."

A round of warm applause was punctuated by whoops from the eager alkies in the front row.

"I know, it's good, best thing I've ever done, but despite it being his cash that allowed me to stay in my place, give me somewhere to anchor myself, the stability I need to try to do all this stuff, he don't necessarily share the sentiment. He's not into community outreach, know what I mean? So he sent a couple of guys around yesterday. They made it clear that I'm running out of rope. He wants his money back. With the interest and 'administration charges' and all that shit, I'm looking at the thick end of six grand."

He laughed at this as if it was a particularly funny joke, then put his head in his hands and started to sob. His shoulders quivered, and Milton watched him awkwardly until one of the other guys shuffled across the seats and put his arm around him.

There was silence for a moment until he recovered himself. "I got a job now, like you all know about, but even though it's the best thing that's happened to me for months, it still barely covers my rent and groceries, and if I can save twenty bucks a month, then I reckon I'm doing well. That don't even cover the interest on the loan, not even close. I don't expect any of you to have any clever ways for me to fix this. I just wanted to share it because, I gotta be honest, I've felt the urge to go and buy a bottle of vodka and just drink myself stupid so I can forget all about it. But I know that'd be a crazy idea, worst thing I could do, and now, especially after I've shared, I think maybe I can keep it behind me, at least for now. But I've got to get this sorted. The more it seems like a dead end, the more I want to get blasted so I can forget all about it."

Chapter Sixteen

MILTON WAS STACKING the chairs at the end of the meeting, hauling them across the room to the walk-in cupboard, when he noticed that the woman he knew as Eva was waiting in the entrance hall. She was sitting against the edge of the table, her legs straight with one ankle resting against the other, with a copy of the Big Book held open before her. Milton watched her for a moment, thinking, as he usually did, that she was a good-looking woman, before gripping the bottom of the stack of chairs, heaving it into the air and carrying it into the cupboard. He took the cloth cover from the table, tracing his fingers over the embroidered A.A. symbol, and put that in the cupboard, too. He shut the cupboard, locked it, then went through. Eva had stacked all the dirty cups in the kitchen sink.

"Hello," she said, with a wide smile.

"Hello. You all right?"

"Oh, sure. I'm great. Just thought you could do with a hand."

"Thanks."

She stood and nodded down at the table. "Where does that go?"

"Just over there," Milton said. "I've got it." He lifted the table, pressed the legs back into place, picked it up, and stacked it against the wall with the others. He was conscious that she was watching him, and allowed her a smile as he came back to pick up the large vat, the water inside cooling now that the element had been switched off. She returned his smile, and he found himself thinking, again, that she was very attractive. She was slim and petite, with glossy dark hair and a Latino complexion. Her eyes were her best feature: the colour of rich chocolate, smouldering with intelligence and a sense of humour that was never far from the surface. Milton didn't know her surname, but she was a voluble sharer during the meetings, and he knew plenty about her from the things that she had said. She was a lawyer, used to work up in Century City in Los Angeles doing clearance work for the networks. Now she did medical liability work at St Francis Memorial. She was divorced with a young daughter, her husband had been an alcoholic too, and it had broken their relationship apart. She had found the rooms; he hadn't. She shared about him sometimes. He was still out there.

"Enjoy it tonight?" she asked him.

"Enjoy might not be the right word."

"Okay—get anything from it?"

"I think so."

"Which other meetings do you go to?"

"Just this one. You?"

"There's the place on Sacramento Street. Near Lafayette Park?"

Milton shook his head.

"I do a couple of meetings there. Mondays and Fridays. They're pretty good. You should—well, you know."

He turned the urn upside down and rested it in the sink.

"How long is it for you?" she asked.

"Since I had a drink?" He smiled ruefully. "One thousand and ninety days."

"Not that you're counting."

"Not that I'm counting."

"Let's see." She furrowed her brow with concentration. "If you can manage to keep the plug in the jug for another week, you'll be three years sober."

"There's something to celebrate," he said with an ironic smile.

"Are you serious?" she said, suddenly intense. "Of course it is. You want to go back to how it was before?"

He got quick flashbacks. "Of course not."

"Fucking right. Jesus, John! You have to come to a meeting and get your chip."

Anniversaries were called birthdays in the rooms. They handed out little embossed poker chips with the number of months or years written on them, all in different colours. Milton had checked out the chip for three years: it would be red. Birthdays were usually celebrated with cake, and then there would be a gathering afterwards, a meal or a cup of coffee.

He hadn't planned on making a fuss about it.

He felt a little uncomfortable with her focus on him. "You've got more, don't you?"

"Five years. I had my last drink the day my daughter was born. That was what really drove it home for me—I'd just given birth, and my first thought was, 'God, I really need a gin.' That kind of underlined that maybe, you know, maybe I had a bit of a problem with it. What about you? You've never said?"

He hesitated and felt his shoulders stiffen. He had to work hard to keep the frown from his brow. He remembered it very well, but it wasn't something that he would ever be able to share in a meeting.

"Difficult memory?"

"A bit raw."

The flashback came back. It was clear and vivid, and thinking about it again, he could almost feel the hot sun on the top of his head. Morocco. Marrakesh. There had been a cell there, laid up and well advanced with their plan to blow up a car loaded with a fertiliser bomb in the middle of the Jemma el-Fnaa square. The spooks had intercepted their communications, and Milton had gone in to put an end to the problem. It had been a clean job—three shots, three quick eliminations—but something about one of them had stayed in his head. He was just a boy, they said sixteen but Milton guessed younger, fourteen or fifteen at the outside, and he had gazed up at him and into his eyes as he levelled the gun and aimed it at his head and pulled the trigger. Milton was due to extract immediately after the job, but he had diverted to the nearest bar and had drunk himself stupidly, horribly, awfully, dangerously drunk. They had just about cashiered him for that. Thinking about it triggered the old memories, and for a moment, it felt as if he was teetering on the edge of a trapdoor that had suddenly dropped open beneath his feet.

He forced his thoughts away from it, that dark and blank pit that fell away beneath him, a conscious effort, and then realised that Eva was talking to him. He focussed on her instead.

"Sorry," she was saying, "you don't have to say if you'd rather not, obviously."

"It's not so bad."

"No, forget I asked."

A little brightness returned, and he felt the trapdoor close.

"It's fear, right?" she said.

"What do you mean? Fear of what?"

"No, F.E.A.R." She spelt it out.

He shrugged his incomprehension.

"You haven't heard that one? It's the old A.A. saying: Fuck Everything and Run."

"Ah," Milton said, relaxing a little. "Yes. That's exactly it."

"I've been running for five years."

"You still get bad days?"

"Sure I do. Everyone does."

"Really? Out of everyone I've met since I've been coming to meetings, you seem like one of the most settled."

"Don't believe it. It's a struggle just like everyone else. It's like a swan, you know: it looks graceful, but there's paddling like shit going on below the surface. It's a day-to-day thing. You take your eye off the ball and, bang, back in the gutter you go. I'm just the same as everyone."

Milton was not surprised to hear that—it was a comment that he had heard many times, almost a refrain to ward off complacency—but it seemed especially inapposite from Eva. He had always found her to have a calming, peaceful manner. There were all sorts in the rooms: some twitchy and avid, white-knuckling it, always one bad day from falling back into the arms of booze; others, like her, had an almost Zen-like aspect, an aura of meditative serenity that he found intoxicating. He looked at them jealously.

"What are you doing now?" she asked him impulsively.

"Nothing much."

"Want to get dinner?"

"Sure," he said.

"Anywhere you fancy?"

"Sure," he said. "I know a place."

THEY WERE THE ONLY people in Top Notch. Julius took their order and set about it with a cheerful smile, and soon, the aroma of cooked meat filled the room. He brought the burgers over on paper plates and left them to get on with it, disappearing into the back. Milton smiled at his discretion; there would be wry comments when he came in tomorrow. The food was as good as ever, and the conversation was good, too, moving away from A.A. to range across work and family and life in general. Milton quickly found himself relaxing.

"How are you finding the Steps?"

"Oh, you know…" he began awkwardly.

"Which one are you on?"

"Eight and nine."

"Can you recite them?"

He smiled a little ruefully. "'We made a list of all persons we had harmed, and became willing to make amends to them all.'"

"And?"

"'We made direct amends to such people wherever possible, except where to do so would injure them or others.'"

"Perfect," she said. "My favourites."

"I don't know. They're hard."

"You want my advice? Do it in your own time. They're not easy, but you do feel better afterwards. And you want to be careful. Plenty of people will be prepared to take your amends for you—"

"—and they can, too, if they're prepared to *make* my amends."

"You heard that one before?"

He smiled. "A few times. Where are you? Finished them?"

"First time around. I'm going back to the start again now."

"Step Ten: 'We continued to take a personal inventory.'"

"Exactly. It never stops. You keep doing it, it stays fresh."

Eva was an easy talker, something she affably dismissed as one of her faults, but Milton didn't mind at all; he was happy to listen to her, her soft West Coast drawl smoothing the edges from her words and her self-deprecating sense of humour and easy laughter drawing him in until it was just the two of them in an empty restaurant with Julius turning the chairs upside down on the tables, a hint that he was ready to call it a night and close.

"That was really nice," she said as they stood on the sidewalk outside.

"It was."

"You wanna, you know—you wanna do it again next time?"

"I'd love to."

"All right, then, John." She took a step toward him, her hand on his shoulder as she raised herself onto tiptoes and placed a kiss on his cheek. She lingered there for a moment, her lips warm against his skin, and as she stepped back, she traced her fingertips across his shoulder and down his arm to the elbow. "Take it easy, all right? I'll see you next week."

Milton smiled, more easily and naturally than was normal for him, and watched her turn and walk back towards where she had parked her Porsche.

Chapter Seventeen

PETER GLEASON was the park ranger for the Golden Gate National Recreation Area. He had held the job for twenty years, watching all the communal spaces, making sure the fishermen and water sports enthusiasts observed the local regulations, keeping an eye on the wildlife. Peter loved his job; he was an outdoorsman at heart, and there couldn't be many places that were as beautiful as this. He liked to say that he had the best office in the world; his wife, Glenda, had heard that quip about a million times, but he still said it because it was true and it reminded him how lucky he was.

Peter had been a dog-lover all his adult life, and this was a great job to have a hound. It was practically a requirement. He had had four since he had been out here. They had all been Labradors. Good dogs, obedient and loyal; it was just like he always said, you couldn't go far wrong with a Lab. Jethro was his current dog. He was two years old and mongrel, part Labrador and part pointer. Peter had picked him out as a puppy and was training him up himself. He had the most even temperament out of all the dogs, and the best nose.

It was an early Tuesday morning in December when Peter stopped his truck in the wide, exposed and bleak square of ground that served visitors to Headlands Lookout. It was a remote area, served by a one-track road with the waters of Bonita Cove at the foot of a sheer drop on the left. He stepped carefully; yet another dense bank of fog had rolled in overnight and visibility was down to twenty yards. It was cold and damp, the curtain of solid grey muffling the sound. The western portion of San Francisco was just on the other side of the bay, usually providing a splendid vista, but it was invisible today. The only sign that it was there was the steady, eerie boom of the foghorns, one calling and the other answering.

There were only two other cars in the lot. Fishermen still visited with reels to try to catch the fluke, bluefish, winter flounder, mackerel, porgy and weakfish that abounded just offshore, and as he checked, he noticed that a couple of them had followed the precarious path down the cliff face to get to the small beach. Oystermen came, too, even though the oyster beds, which had once been plentiful, had grown more scarce. There was still enough on the sea bed to make the trip worthwhile: hard-shelled clams, steamers, quahogs, bay scallops, blue-claw crabs and lobsters. Others came with binoculars to watch the birds and the seals. Kayakers, clad in neoprene wetsuits, cut across the waves.

The margins between the road and the cliff had grown too wild in places for a man to get through, but the dog was keen to explore today, and Peter watched as he forced himself into thickets of bramble. He walked on, following the headland around to the west. He watched the dog bound ahead, cutting a line through the sumac and salt hay that was as straight as an arrow. Peter lived on the other side of the bay, in Richmond, and he had always had a keen interest in the local flora and fauna. He found the rough natural world interesting, which was reason enough, but it was also professionally useful to have some knowledge of the area that you were working in. As he followed Jethro through the salt hay that morning, he found himself thinking that this part of the world would not have changed much in hundreds of years. Once you were down the slope a ways and the city was out of sight, the view would have been unchanged for millennia.

He stepped carefully through the bracken, navigating the thick clumps of poison ivy before breaking into the open and tramping down the suddenly steep slope to the water's edge. All along the beach were stacks of tombstones brought over from Tiburon. They had been piled into makeshift jetties to help combat the constant erosion, and the salty bite of the tide had caused them to crumble and crack.

The dog paused for a moment, frozen still, his nose twitching, and then as Peter watched with a mixture of curiosity and anticipation, he sprinted towards the deep fringe of the undergrowth. He got six feet in and stopped, digging furiously with his forepaws. Peter struggled across the soft, wet sand as the dog started to bark. When he got there, the dog had excavated the sand so that a flap of canvas sacking had been exposed. He called for Jethro to stay, but he was young and excited and knew he was onto something, so he kept digging, wet sand spraying out from between his hind legs.

By the time the ranger had fastened the lead to the dog's collar, he had unearthed a skull, a collarbone and the start of a ribcage.

PART TWO

The Man Who Would Be King

#2 MEGAN MELISSA GABERT

MEG GABERT had always wanted to act. She was a born performer, that was what she would tell anyone who cared to ask her about her ambitions, and as far as she was concerned, she was going to make it. She hadn't decided exactly what her talents best suited—acting or singing, she could do both—but there was no question about it in her mind: she was going to be famous. It wasn't in doubt.

When she was in seventh grade, she had taken to the stage in her school's production of *Bugsy Malone*. She had hoped to play Tallulah, Fat Sam's moll and Bugsy's old flame, but that role had been assigned to a rival. She ended up playing Blousey Brown, a sassy dame who had designs on Hollywood, and once she had gotten over her disappointment, she decided that this was the better role, one that was more suited to her. She had a great voice, and everyone said that she was brilliant on opening night. The local paper exclaimed that she stole the show. It was something she would never forget: the excitement she felt while she was standing there in the single spotlight, belting out the numbers to a roomful of parents and friends. If she had needed any confirmation about the course she had chosen for herself, this was it. From that point forwards, performing would be the only thing she was interested in doing.

Getting to the stage where she could make enough money to support herself through her acting was going to take some time, and until that happened, she had paid her way with a little hooking. It had started with webcams, but then she had realised there was more to be made by going a little further. She had posted an ad on the Fresno/Adult Services page of Craigslist a year after she graduated from high school. She had a killer photo from a session she did for her acting portfolio, and the replies had been instantaneous.

She was hanging out with a guy in those days, this dude called Clay, nothing serious, just messing around, and she had persuaded him to come along and keep an eye on her. He drove her from job to job. They worked out a routine to keep her safe: he called her cell ten minutes after she went inside, and if there was no answer, then he would know that she was in trouble. If she answered, everything was fine. She charged a hundred bucks an hour and gave him twenty.

It was going okay, but she was always a little nervous that she'd bump into a john again when she was off the clock. She knew, too, that there was better money to be made in a bigger city. She thought of Los Angeles, but the idea of being closer to Hollywood and her dream frightened her; she wasn't ready for that yet. San Francisco seemed like a good compromise.

The difference in the city was stark. It was full of johns, and they were of a much higher class than the bums and stiffs she was used to in Fresno. There were plenty of out-of-towners away from home and bored and looking for a little fun. She would take her laptop to a hotel room, post an ad, and wait for the calls. She could get through four or five appointments and clear a thousand bucks every night, easy. The men were a real mixture: some were old and wanted to daddy her; others were young and trim and good-looking. The money was amazing. She took rooms in the nicest hotels with views of the Golden Gate and ate in the best restaurants. She never had any problems with what she was doing. It was another performance, in a way. The johns were prepared to pay to spend time with her. She could play any number of parts for them: schoolgirl, vamp, prim secretary. Their adulation was instant and obvious. For as long as she was with them she was desired: full of potential, the centre of attention, loved, rich. And what was wrong with that?

SHE HEARD THE CADILLAC before she saw it. It backfired loudly from a couple of blocks away, the noise carrying down the street and around the corner to where she was waiting at 6th and Irving. The engine sounded throaty and unhealthy, as if it was about to expire, and she had been nonplussed as it pulled over to stop at the edge of the sidewalk opposite her. The man she had spoken to on the phone had said that he was an executive from a company that dealt in cattle all the way across the south-west. He certainly had the accent for it, a mild Southern burr that lent his voice a musical quality. She hadn't expected him to be driving a beat-up car like this, but as she crossed the sidewalk to the open window, she chided herself for jumping to conclusions.

A bum begging for change next to the entrance to J.C. Penney watched as the door was opened for her. He watched as she carefully slid into the car, her hands pressing down her skirt as she lowered herself into the seat. The man didn't think twice about it, and she hardly registered; he was hungry and more interested in adding to the couple of bucks in change that had been tossed into the cap on the sidewalk before his folded legs. If he had paid attention, perhaps he would have noticed the look of confusion on the girl's face as she looked, for the first time, at the man who had picked her up. He might have remembered more if he had known that he would be the last person to see the girl alive.

Chapter Eighteen

MILTON LEANT BACK and traced his fingers against the rough vinyl surface of the table. It had been marked by years of graffiti: gang tags, racial epithets and unflattering remarks about the police, some of them quite imaginative. There was a dirty glass of water, an ashtray that hadn't been emptied for days and, set against the wall, a tape recorder. He crossed his arms and looked up at the police officers who were sitting opposite him. The first was a middle-aged man with several days of growth on his chin, an aquiline face and a lazy left eye. The second was a little older, a little more senior, and from the way the two of them had behaved so far, Milton could see that he was going to keep quiet while his partner conducted the interview.

The young one pressed a button on the tape recorder, and it began to spool.

"Just to go through things like we mentioned to you, we're gonna do a taped interview with you."

"That's fine," Milton said.

"There's my ID. And there's my partner's."

"Okay."

"So I'm Inspector Richard Cotton. My colleague is Chief of Detectives Stewart Webster."

"I can see that."

"Now, first of all, can you please state your name for me?"

"John Smith."

"And that's S-M-I-T-H."

"Correct."

"Your date of birth, sir?"

"Thirty-first of October, 1973."

"That makes you forty, right?"

"It does."

"And your address at home?"

"259 Sixth Street."

"What's that?"

"A hotel."

"An SRO?"

"That's right."

"Which one?"

"The El Capitan."

"How are you finding that? Bit of a dive, right?"

"It's all right."

"You say so. Phone number?"

He gave them the number of his cellphone.

"Are you all right for water?"

"Yes."

He tossed a packet of cigarettes on the table. "Feel free to light up. We know this can be stressful."

Milton had to stifle a long sigh of impatience. "It would be stressful if I had something to hide. But I don't, so I'll pass, but thanks anyway. Now, please—can we get started? There's already been too much waiting around. Ask me whatever you like. I want to help."

Cotton squinted one eye, a little spooky. "All right, then. John Smith—that's your real name, right?"

"It is."

"And you're English, right?"

"That's right."

"I've been to England. Holiday. Houses of Parliament, Buckingham Palace, all that history—one hell of a place."

Milton rolled his eyes. Was he serious? "Just ask me about Madison."

"In a minute, John," the man said with exaggerated patience. "We just want to know a little bit about you first. So how come you ended up here?"

"I've been travelling. I was in South America for six months, and then I came north."

"Through Mexico?"

"That's right."

"How long you been here?"

"Nine months. I was here once before, years ago. I liked it. I thought I'd come back and stay a while."

"How have you been getting by?"

"I've been working."

Cotton's good eye twitched. "You got a visa for that?"

"Dual citizenship."

"How's that?"

"My mother was American." It was a lie, but it was what his passport said. Dual citizenship saved unnecessary nonsense that would have made it more difficult for him to work. Being able to claim some connection to the United States had also proven to be useful as he worked his way north up the continent.

"All right, John. Let's change the subject—you want to talk about Madison, let's talk about Madison. You know we've dug up two bodies now, right?"

"I've seen the news."

"And you know none of them are her?"

That was news to him. "No. I didn't know that."

"That's right—none of them. See, Madison had a metal pin in her hip. Fell off her bike when she was a girl, messed it up pretty good. They had to put one in to fix it all together. The remains in the morgue are all whole, more or less, and none of them have anything like that."

Milton felt a moment of relief but immediately tempered it; it was still surely just a matter of time.

"That doesn't mean we won't find her," Cotton went on. "If you've been watching the news, you'll know that we're still searching the beach, and we're very concerned that we're gonna find more. So, with all that being said, let's get down to meat and potatoes, shall we?"

"Please."

"Why'd you do it, John?"

Milton wasn't surprised. "Seriously?"

"What did you do with her body?"

"You've got to be kidding."

"I'm not kidding, John."

"No, you've got to be. It's nothing to do with me."

"Answer the question, please."

He looked dead straight at the cop. "I just answered it. I didn't do it. I have absolutely no idea where she is."

"So you say. But on your own account you were the last person to see her alive."

He clenched his fists in sudden frustration. "No—that's not what I said."

"You got a temper, John?"

"I don't know that she's dead. I hope she isn't. I said that I was one of the last people to see her before she disappeared. That's different."

"We know the two girls we've got in the morgue were all hookers. Madison was hooking when she disappeared. It's not hard to join the dots, is it?"

"No, it isn't. But it has nothing to do with me."

"All right, then. Let's change tack." He took a cigarette from the packet and lit it, taking his time about it. He looked down at his notes. "Okay. The night after she disappeared—this is the Friday—we've got a statement from Victor Leonard that says you went back to Pine Shore. He said he saw you coming out of the garden of the house where the party was the night before. Is that right?"

"Yes."

"We checked the security camera, Mr. Smith. There's one on the gate. We looked, and there you are, climbing over the wall. Why'd you do something like that?"

Milton gritted his teeth. The camera must have run off rechargeable batteries that would cut in when the power went out. "The gate was locked," he said.

"Why didn't you buzz to get in?"

"Because someone had changed the code to the gate after Madison disappeared. Rather than wasting your time with me, I'd be asking why that was. A girl goes missing, and the next day the code to the gate is changed? Why would they want to keep people out? Don't you think that's a little suspicious?"

"We'll be sure to bear that in mind. What were you looking around for?"

"Anything that might give me an idea what caused Madison to be so upset that she'd run away."

"You spoke to Mr. Leonard?"

"Yes."

"Why?"

"Madison went to his house. I wanted to know what she said to him."

"He say anything useful?"

He thought of Brady. "Not really."

"And you don't think all this is something that the police ought to do?"

"Yes, I do, but Madison's boyfriend had already reported her missing, and he got the cold shoulder. Most crimes are solved in the first few hours after they happen. I didn't think this could wait."

Cotton chain-smoked the cigarette down to the tip. "Know a lot about police work, do you, John?"

"Do you have a sensible question for me?"

"Got a smart mouth, too."

"Sorry about that. Low tolerance level for idiots."

"That's it, John. Keep giving me attitude. We're the only people here keeping you from a pair of cuffs and a nice warm cell."

Milton ignored the threat.

Cotton looked down at his notes. "You said she was frightened?"

"Out of her mind."

"That's not what security at the party said."

"What did they say?"

"Said you barged in and went after her."

"I heard her screaming."

"How'd you explain how one of them ended up with a concussion and a broken nose?"

"He got in my way."

"So you broke his nose and knocked him out?"

"I hit him."

"It raises the question of that temper of yours again."

Milton repeated himself patiently. "I heard Madison screaming."

"So?"

"So I went in to see if she was all right."

"And?"

"I told her I'd take her home."

"And?"

"She got around me and ran."

Cotton got up and started to circle the table. "You mentioned Trip Macklemore. We've spoken to him. He said you had Madison's bag in the back of your taxi."

"I did. I gave it to him afterwards."

"What was it doing in your car?"

"She left it there."

"But you'd already taken her where she needed to go. Why would she have left it?"

"I said I'd wait for her."

"You didn't have another job to go to?"

"She was nervous. I didn't think it was right to leave her there, on her own, with no way to get back to the city."

"You were going to charge her for that?"

"I hadn't decided. Probably not."

"A favour, then? Out of the goodness of your heart?"

"It was the right thing to do."

"He's English," the other man, Webster, offered. "What is it you call it?"

"Chivalry?"

"That's right, chivalry."

"Don't know about that, boss. Doesn't strike me as all that likely. Taxi drivers aren't known for their charity."

"I try to do the right thing," Milton said.

He looked down at his notes. "You work for Vassily Romanov, too, right? Mr. Freeze—the ice guy?"

"Yes."

"We spoke to him. He had to have words with you the afternoon she went missing. That right?"

"I dropped some ice."

"He says you were agitated."

"Distracted. I knew something was wrong."

"Tell me what happened."

"I already have."

Cotton slapped both hands on the table. "Where is she?"

Milton stared at him and spoke calmly and carefully. "I don't know."

He drummed the table. "What did you do with her body?"

"It's got nothing to do with me."

"Is she on the headland?"

"I don't know."

"Let me share a secret with you, John. The D.A. thinks you did it. He thinks you've got a big guilty sign around your neck. He wants to throw the book at you."

"Knock yourself out." Milton calmly looked from one man to the other. "We can go around the houses on this all day if you want, but I'm telling you now, if anything has happened to Madison, it has absolutely nothing to do with me, and it doesn't matter how you phrase your questions, it doesn't matter if you shout and scream, and it doesn't matter if you threaten me—the answers will always be the same. I didn't do it. It has nothing to do with me. And I'm not a fool. You can say what you want, but I know you don't think that I did it."

"Really? How would you know that, John?"

"Because you would have arrested me already and this interview would be under caution. Look, I'm not a fool. I understand. I know you need to eliminate me. I know that I'm going to be a suspect. It stands to reason. I'll do whatever you need me to do so that you can be happy that I'm not the man you want. The car I was driving that night is parked outside. Get forensics to have a look at it. You can do it without a warrant—you don't need one, you have my authorisation. If you want to search my room, you've just got to ask." He reached into his pocket and deposited his keys on the table. "There. Help yourself."

"You're awfully confident, John."

"Because I have nothing to hide." Webster was fingering the cigarette packet. Milton turned to him. "You're the ranking officer here, right? I'm not going to tell you your job, but you've got to put a lead on your friend here and get off this dead end—right now. You're wasting time you don't have. If Madison is still alive, every minute we're doing this makes it less likely she'll be alive when you find her."

Webster cocked an eyebrow. "You like telling us what we should be doing so much, Mr. Smith—what would you be doing?"

"I'd be looking at the footage from that CCTV camera. Maybe you'll see what happened. And everyone who went to the party that night will have gone through the gate. You should start looking into them."

"The footage has been wiped," he said.

"What?"

"There's nothing from the Friday night."

"Who wiped it?"

"We don't know."

"You need to talk to whoever did that, then. Right?"

"It was three months ago. It's not unreasonable."

Cotton took over. "You got anything to tell us, John?"

Milton thought about the two men in the house after the party. He would have told the cops what had happened, what he had overheard, but how could he do that without telling them that he had broken in? Why would he have done something like that? It wasn't going to be possible. That was a lead that he would have to follow for himself.

"All right, officers. Is there anything else?"

They said nothing.

"I'm going to be on my way. You know where I am, and you've got my number. If you want me to stay, you're going to have to arrest me."

He pushed the chair away and stood up from the table.

Chapter Nineteen

MILTON NEEDED A MEETING. As he drove across town, he felt as if he needed one even more than usual. He wasn't overly worried—he knew he would be able to run rings around the police—but the interview had still left him angry and frustrated. He had known that the police would treat him as a suspect—he would have done the same, if the roles had been reversed—but they seemed fixated. The longer they wasted on him, the worse it would be for Madison. And also, for a man in his particularly precarious position, there was the overriding need to be careful. More than careful. An arrest, his fingerprints and mugshot taken, metadata passing between anonymous servers, he knew that was all the spooks at GCHQ or the NSA would need to pin him down, and then it would all kick off again. The firestorm that had blazed around him in Juárez would spark back to life. Worse this time. He knew the prudent thing to do would have been to jump town the moment that there had been even a sniff of trouble. The day after Madison had disappeared. Now, though, he couldn't. The city had closed around him like a fist. If he ran, the police would see it as a sign of guilt. They would have all the evidence they needed to push their suspicions about him up a notch. There would be a manhunt. His name would be in the papers. His picture on the internet.

He might as well telephone Control.

I'm in San Francisco.

Come and get me.

No, he thought, as he drove across town.

He had to stay and see this through until the end.

He gripped the wheel tightly and concentrated on the pattern of his breathing. The rooms had taught him that anger and frustration were two of his most delicate triggers. A good meeting was like meditation, and he knew that it would help him to put the lid back on his temper.

Eva was waiting for him, leaning against the wall by the door. She was wearing a woollen jumper, expensive, long enough to reach well down beyond her waist, a pair of jeans and chunky leather boots. She had a black felt beret on her head. She looked supremely cute.

"Hello, John."

"You're early."

She leaned forward, pressing herself away from the wall. "Thought maybe I'd give you a hand. That all right?"

"Course," he said.

They worked quickly and quietly: preparing the room, setting up the table with the tea and coffee, washing the crockery. Milton's thoughts went back to the meeting with the police. He thought about everything he knew. Two escorts found dead on the same stretch of headland. Madison going missing just five miles from the same spot. It looked bad for her. Maybe there was another explanation for what had happened, but then again, maybe there wasn't. The most obvious explanation was often the right one.

"You all right?" Eva asked him.

"I'm fine," he said.

"Looks like you're a thousand miles away."

"Sorry," he said. "I've got some stuff on my mind."

"A problem shared is a problem halved."

"I know."

The regulars started to arrive twenty minutes before the meeting was scheduled to start. Milton went behind the table and made their coffees. The room was quickly busy. Eva was waylaid by a young actor who obviously had a thing for her. She rolled her eyes, and as he nudged her towards the room for the start of the meeting, she paused by the table.

"You want to get dinner again?"

"I'm not sure I'll be the best company tonight."

"I'll take the risk." She looked straight at him and winked.

"Okay." He smiled. "That'd be great."

The room emptied out as it got closer to the top of the hour, and Milton quickly poured himself a coffee.

Smulders hijacked him as he was about to go inside. "About time you opened that mouth of yours in a meeting, John."

"Do I get to say no?"

Smulders looked at him with an intense sincerity. "Man, you need me to remind you? You need me to explain? You're sick. And the cure for your sickness, the best cure I ever found, is to get involved and participate." He enunciated that last word carefully, each syllable pronounced slowly, and then pressed a pamphlet into his hands. The title on the pamphlet was THE TWELVE PROMISES. "Here they are, Smith. Read them out when I tell you and think on them when you do. All right?"

"Fine."

Milton sat down as Smulders brought the gavel down and opened proceedings. He had recruited a speaker from another meeting that he attended, a middle-aged woman with worry-lines carved in deep grooves around her eyes and prematurely grey hair. She started to speak, her share focussed on the relationship with her ex-husband and how he had knocked her around. It was worthy, and she was a powerful speaker, but Milton found his thoughts turning back to the interview and the police. They had already wasted too much time, and now they threatened to waste even more. It was three months already. Milton didn't know if Madison was still alive, but if she was and if she was in danger, the longer they wasted with him made it less likely that they would be able to help her.

The speaker came to the end of her share, wiping away the tears that had fallen down her cheeks. Smulders thanked her, there was warm applause, and then the arms went up as men and women who had found similarities between the speaker's story and their own—that was what they were enjoined to look for, not differences—lined up to share their own feelings. Milton listened for ten minutes but couldn't help zoning out again.

Richie Grimes put his hand up. He had come into the room late, and Milton hadn't noticed him. He looked now and saw, with shock, that the man's face was badly bruised. His right eye was swollen and almost completely shut, a bruise that ran from black to deep purple all the way around it. There was a cut on his forehead that had been sutured shut and another beneath his chin. Milton watched as he lowered his arm again; he moved gingerly, pain flickering on his face. Broken ribs.

"My name is Richie, and I'm an alcoholic."

"Hi, Richie," they all said.

"Yeah," he said. "Look at the fucking state of me, right? It's like what I was sharing about last time, you know, the trouble I'm in? I guess maybe I was hoping it was all bluster, that it'd go away, but I always knew that was just wishful thinking. So I was coming home from work last night, and— boom—that was it, I got jumped from behind by these two goons with baseball bats. Broken nose, two broken ribs. I got a week to pay back all the money that I owe or they're coming back. I'd tell the police, but there's nothing they can do—what are they gonna do, put a man on me twenty-four hours? Nah"—he shook his head—"that ain't gonna happen. If I can't find the money, I'm gonna get more of the same, and now, with the ribs and everything, I'm not sure I can even work properly. I gotta tell you, I'm closer to a drink today than I have been for months. I've been to two other meetings today already. Kinda feel like I'm hanging on by my fingertips."

The others nodded their understanding and agreement. The woman next to him rested her hand on his shoulder, and others used his story to bounce off similar experiences of their own. If Richie was looking for advice, he didn't get any—that was "grandiose," and not what you came to A.A. to find—but he got sympathy and empathy and examples that he could use as a bulwark against the temptation of getting drunk. Milton listened to the simple tales that were told, his head down and his hands clasped tightly on his lap.

The meeting drew towards a close, and Smulders looked over to him and nodded. It was time. Milton took the pamphlet that his fingers had been fretting with all meeting and cleared his throat.

"'If we are painstaking about this phase of our development, we will be amazed before we are halfway through. We are going to know a new freedom and a new happiness. We will not regret the past nor wish to shut the door on it.'" He cleared his throat awkwardly. "'We will comprehend the word serenity and we will know peace. No matter how far the scale we have gone, we will see how our experience can benefit others. The feeling of uselessness and self-pity will disappear. We will lose interest in selfish things and gain interest in our fellows. Self-seeking will slip away. Our whole attitude and outlook upon life will change. Fear of people and of economic insecurity will leave us. We will intuitively know how to handle situations which used to baffle us. We will suddenly realize that God is doing for us what we could not do for ourselves. Are these extravagant promises?'"

The group chimed back at him, "We think not."

"'They are being fulfilled among us—sometimes quickly, sometimes slowly. They will always materialise if we work for them.'"

Peace.

Serenity.

We will not regret the past nor wish to shut the door on it.

We will not regret?

Milton doubted that could ever possibly come to pass. Not for him. His transgressions were different to those of the others. He hadn't soiled himself in the office, slapped his wife, crashed his car. He had killed nearly one hundred and fifty men and women. He knew that he would always regret the past, every day for as long as he lived, and what was the point in even trying to shut the door on it? The room behind his door was stuffed full of bodies, stacked all the way up to the ceiling, one hundred and fifty corpses and gallons of blood, and the door wouldn't begin to close.

They said the Lord's Prayer and filed out. Milton put away the coffee and biscuits and started to clean up. The usual group of people were gathering in the lobby to go for their meal together, and Eva was with them, smoking a cigarette and waiting for him to finish up. Milton was turning the tea urn upside down in the sink when the door to the bathroom opened and Richie Grimes hobbled out.

Milton turned to Eva and mouthed that he would be five minutes. She nodded and went outside.

"You all right?" Milton asked Grimes.

"Yeah, man."

Milton held up the plate that had held the biscuits; it was covered with crumbs and one solitary cookie. "Want it? Last one."

"Sure." He reached across and took it. "Thanks. It's John, right?"

"Right."

"Don't think I've ever heard you share."

"I'm more of a listener," he said. "How are you feeling?"

"Like I've been ten rounds with Tyson."

"But it was good to get it off your chest?"

"Sure. Getting rid of the problem's another matter. I ain't barely got a cent to my name. How am I gonna manage to find six large?"

"There'll be a way."

"I wish I shared your confidence. The only way I can think is to get another loan, but that's just putting it off." He gave him an underwhelming smile. "Time to run. See you next week?"

The man looked like a prisoner being led out to the gallows. Milton couldn't let him go like that.

"This guy you owe the money to—who is he?"

"What good's it gonna do, telling you that?"

"Try me. What's his name?"

"Martinez."

"Works down in the Mission District?"

"That's right. You know him?"

Milton shrugged. "Heard the name."

"I should never have gotten involved with him."

"If it were me, Richie, I'd make sure I stayed in my place apart from when I was at work or at meetings. I wouldn't put myself somewhere where I could get jumped again."

"How am I gonna get the cash if I hide out at home?"

"Like I say," Milton said, "there'll be a way. That's what they tell us, right—we put our faith in a power greater than ourselves."

"I've been praying for six months, John. If there's a power, it ain't been listening."

"Keep praying."

Chapter Twenty

ARLEN CRAWFORD WAS NERVOUS. The first debate was two weeks to the day before the primary. It was held in a converted hat factory that had been turned into a new media hub with start-ups suckling the teats of the angel investor who owned the building, offering space in exchange for a little equity. There was a large auditorium that had only recently been done out, still smelling of fresh plaster and polyethylene. There was a live audience, card-carrying local party members packed into the cramped seating like sardines in a tin. There was a row at the front—fitted with much more comfortable seating—that was reserved for the heavy-hitters from Washington, who had made the trip west to see the candidates in action for the first time.

Crawford looked down from the back of the room and onto the temporary stage, bathed in the glare of the harsh television lights. Each candidate had a lectern with a name card placed along the top. Governor Robinson's was in the centre; that had been the prize following an hour's horse-trading with the other candidates. The prime position would be fought over for the remaining two debates. Other bargaining chips included the speaking order, whether or not there would be opening and closing remarks, and a host of other ephemera that might have appeared trivial to the unenlightened observer. Crawford did not see them that way at all; to the politicos who were guiding the campaigns of the candidates, they were almost worth dying for. You lose the little battles and you better get ready to lose the war.

The negotiations before the debate had been exhausting. Crawford had had little sleep, and the evening had already taken on a surreal tinge that was accentuated by his fatigue. It was already a strange scene. The building wasn't big enough to offer the candidates individual rooms before the debate, so a communal greenroom had been arranged, with each combatant ensconced in a corner with his or her spouse and seconds close at hand. Food had been laid on—platters of sandwiches—together with cans of soda and an urn of coffee. Robinson was the only candidate who looked totally at ease in the room, his monumental confidence sweeping out of him in great waves. He overwhelmed the room, or so it seemed. His backup team was as frantic as the others, making last minute calibrations to his opening statement and preparing a series of stock lines to fall back on should he need them. It was a little late for that, Crawford thought, but he understood the need to be busy with something if only as a distraction from the nerves.

Robinson moved among his rivals like a Mafia don, giving them his double-clasped handshake, clapping them on the shoulders, squeezing their biceps, all the while shining out his gleaming smile. He laughed at their jokes and made his own, the consummate professional. Crawford didn't have that ease with people, and never had. It was an unctuousness that you had to possess if you were going to make it as a player on the national stage. That was fine. He was happy with his strengths, and he recognised his weaknesses. That kind of self-awareness, in itself, was something that was rare to find and valuable to possess. Robinson had amazing talents, but his instincts were off. Crawford's instincts were feral, animal. He was a strategist, a street fighter, and you needed a whole different set of skills for that. Robinson was surface, but Crawford was detail. He devoured every tiny bit of public life. He hovered above things like a hawk, aware of the smallest nuances yet always conscious of the whole. He could see how one small change might affect things now or eleven moves down the line. It wasn't a calculation he was aware of making; it was something that he processed, understood on a fundamental level.

One of the local party big shots came into the room and announced that it was time. Robinson, who was talking to the senator for New Mexico, wished everyone good luck and led the way to the door. Crawford waited at the back, absorbing the energy of the room and the confidence—or lack thereof—that he could see in other candidates. The retinues filtered into the auditorium. He hooked a doughnut from the refreshment table and followed them.

THE DEBATE COULDN'T have started any better. Robinson was totally in control, delivering his opening position with statesmanlike charm, so much so that Crawford found himself substituting the drab surroundings of the auditorium for what he imagined the General Assembly of the United Nations might look like with his boss before the lectern, or with the heavy blue drapes of the Oval Office closed behind him during an address to the nation. He was, Crawford thought with satisfaction, presidential. The first question was posed—something on healthcare reform—and Robinson stayed away from it, letting the rest tear strips out of one another. Crawford watched and could hardly believe their luck. It wasn't hard. They were murdering themselves. Scott Martin tried to explain his very elaborate health-care scheme and got so bollixed up that he threw up his hands and said, "Well, this thing makes a lot more sense on paper."

"Next question," the moderator said.

"Delores Orpenshaw." A shrew in a green dress and white pearls. "The way folk around here see it, this country is broken. My question for the candidates is simple: how would they fix it?"

"Governor Robinson?"

Crawford felt the momentary chill of electricity: nerves. Robinson looked the questioner right in the eye. "How would I fix it? Well, Delores, there are some pretty fundamental things that we need to do right away. We need to reverse the flood of Third World immigration. The Mexicans, the Puerto Ricans—we need to stop the flow, and we need to send back the ones who are here illegally. It's only logical that the more a country gets a Third World population, the more it will suffer from Third World problems. We need to reverse globalisation to bring back real jobs to this great country. That will help bring back personal pride, and that helps restore pride in the community. We need to expose the climate change lies. That's the constant claim of the technocrats, but not everyone agrees. As an army of global-warming zealots marches on Washington, the truth is that their Orwellian consensus is based not on scientific agreement, but on bullying, censorship and fraudulent statistics. We need to restore discipline in our schools and respect for others. We need to rebuild a sense of national unity and pride. Only if we do those things can we start to take back this great nation from the political elite in our nation's capital."

There was a smattering of applause that grew in intensity, triggering more applause and then more, and then, suddenly, it had become a wave as the audience—almost all of them—rose to their feet and anointed the governor with an ovation. The moderator struggled to make her voice heard as she asked the others for their views.

It went on for another hour in the same vein. Robinson picked his spots and was rewarded volubly every time he finished speaking. Eventually, the moderator brought the debate to an end. They all dashed to the spin room, another wide space that had been equipped with folding tables with trailing multi-plugs for laptops and cellphones. Crawford and the rest of his team split up and worked the room, button-holing the hacks from the nationals and talking up the points that Robinson had made that had gone down well, quietly de-emphasising the points that hadn't found their marks. There was no need to spin things.

Crawford remembered the old political adage: losers spin, winners grin.
And they were winners.

Chapter Twenty-One

MILTON TURNED THE KEY. The ignition fired, but the engine didn't start. He paused, cranked it again, but still there was nothing. He had serviced the car himself a month ago, and it had all looked all right, but this didn't sound good. He drummed his fingers against the wheel.

Eva paused at the door of her Porsche and looked over quizzically.

He put his fingers to the key and twisted it a final time. The ignition coughed, then spluttered, then choked off to a pitiful whine. The courtesy light dimmed as the battery drained from turning over the engine. He popped the hood, opened the door, and went around to take a look.

"Not good?" Eva said, coming over as he bent over the engine.

"Plugs, I think. They need changing."

Eva had insisted they come back to Top Notch. Julius had never let him down, and the meal had been predictably good. The unease that Milton had felt after reading the Promises had quickly been forgotten in her company. He almost forgot the interview with the police. They had talked about the others at the meeting, slandering Smulders in particular; they agreed that he was well meaning, if a little supercilious, and she had suggested that he had form for coming onto the new, vulnerable, male members of the fellowship. She had cocked an eyebrow at him as she had said it. Milton couldn't help but laugh at the suggestion. His troubles were quickly subsumed beneath the barrage of her wit as she took apart the other members of the group. The gossip wasn't cruel, but nevertheless, he had wondered what she might say about him in private. He said that to her, feigning concern, and she had put a finger to her lips and winked with unmistakeable salaciousness. By the end of the main course Milton knew that he was attracted to her, and he knew that the feeling was mutual.

She watched now as he let the hood drop back into place.

"What are you going to do?"

"Walk, I guess."

"Where's your place?"

"Mission District."

"That's miles."

That much was true. He wouldn't be home much before midnight, and then he would have to come back out in the morning—via a garage—to change the plugs. He was a little concerned about his finances, too. He had been planning to go out and drive tonight. He needed the cash. That obviously wasn't going to happen.

"Come on—I'll give you a ride."

"You don't have to do that."

"You're not walking," she said with a determined conviction.

Milton was going to demur, but he thought of the time and the chance to get some sleep to prime him for the day tomorrow, and he realised that would have been foolish. "Thanks," he conceded as he locked the Explorer and walked over to her Cayenne with her.

The car was new and smelt it. It wasn't much of a guess to say that her job paid well—her wardrobe was as good a giveaway as anything—but as he settled back in the leather bucket seat, he thought that perhaps he had underestimated how well off she really was.

She must have noticed his appraising look as he took in the cabin. "I've got a thing for nice cars," she said, a little apologetically.

"It's better than nice."

"Nice cars and nice clothes. It used to be Cristal and coke. The way I see it, if you're going to have an addiction, it better be one that leaves you with something to show for it."

She put on the new Jay-Z as she drove him across town. Milton guided her into the Mission District, picking the quickest way to his apartment. The area was in poor condition; plenty of the buildings were boarded up, others blackened from fire or degraded by squatters with no interest in maintaining them. The cheap rents attracted artists and students, and there was a bohemian atmosphere that was, in its own way, quite attractive. It felt even cheaper than usual tonight, and as he looked out of the window of the gleaming black Porsche, he felt inadequate. They shared a weakness for booze, but that was it; he started to worry that there was a distance between the way they lived their lives that would be difficult to bridge.

The El Capitan Hotel and Hostel was a three-storey building with eighty rooms. The frontage was decorated with an ornate pediment and a cinema-style awning that advertised OPEN 24 HOURS A DAY and PUBLIC PARKING—OPEN 24 HOURS. It was a dowdy street, full of tatty shops and restaurants. To the left of the hotel was the Arabian Nights restaurant and, to the right, Modern Hair Cuts. Queen's Shoes and Siegel's Fashion for Men and Boys were opposite. There were tall palm trees, and the overhead electricity lines buzzed and fizzed in the fog.

"This is me," Milton said.

She pulled up outside the building.

She killed the engine. "Thanks for dinner."

"Yeah," he said. "That was fun."

There was a moment's silence.

"So—um...?" she said.

He looked at her with an uncertainty that he knew was ridiculous.

"You gonna invite me up?"

"You sure that's a good idea?"

She smiled. "What do you mean? Two recovering addicts? What could possibly go wrong?"

"That's not what I meant."

"Really?"

"Maybe it was."

"So?"

He paused, couldn't find the words, couldn't even think what he could have been thinking when he said it, and laughed at the futility of it. "Come on, then. It's at the top of the building, so you're going to have to walk. And I'll warn you now, save the view, it's nothing to write home about. It's not five star."

"Not what I'm used to, you mean?" She grinned. "Fuck you too."

She locked the Cayenne and followed him to the door of the building. The narrow heels of her shoes clacked against the pavement as she took his arm and held it tightly. He was aware of the powerful scent of her perfume and the occasional pressure of her breast against his arm. He opened up and accepted her hand as she pressed it into his.

The reception was incredibly bright; the fluorescent tubes did not flicker, shining down with unflattering constancy onto the occupants roaming the stairs and hallways, occasionally stopping by the front desk with its glass partition and signs apologizing for the inability to lend money and forbidding the use of hot plates in the rooms. The night manager, Ahmed, nodded at them from behind the glass enclosure. There were all manner of people here. For some, it was a permanent residence, and for others, a room for the night. Many of the residents had mental problems, and Milton had seen plenty of disturbances in the time he had been there. No one had ever bothered him— the cold lifelessness behind his eyes was warning enough—and the place had served him well.

They climbed the stairs together, and he gently disengaged as he reached into his pocket for the key to his door. A short, unkempt man with stringy grey hair and an oversized brown jacket peered around a potted plant at them. He stared at them, vigorously rubbing his eyes, and after Milton returned the stare with interest, he darted back around the corner again.

"A friendly neighbour," he explained. He didn't mention the man who was found hanging in his room across the other side of the building, or the woman who stood in her underwear in the corridor complaining about "the radiation."

Milton opened the door. Inside was simple and ascetic, but it was all he could afford. The owner was happy enough to take cash, which saved him from the necessity of opening a bank account, something he was very reluctant to do.

Milton's apartment was tiny, an eight-by-twelve room that was just big enough for a double bed with a chair next to it and a small table next to that.

There wasn't much else. The bathroom and kitchen were shared with the other rooms on the floor. Milton had always travelled light, so storing clothes wasn't an issue; he had two of everything, and when one set was dirty, he took it down to the laundromat around the corner and washed it. He had no interest in a television, and his only entertainment was the radio and his books: several volumes of Dickens, Greene, Orwell, Joyce and Conan Doyle.

"What do you think?" he said, a slightly bashful expression on his usually composed face.

"It's... minimalist."

"That's one way of describing it."

"You don't have much—stuff—do you?"

"I've never been much of a one for things," he explained.

She cast a glance around again. "No pictures."

"I'm not married. No family."

"Parents?"

"They died when I was a boy."

"Sorry."

"Don't be. It was years ago."

"Siblings?"

"No. Just me."

He had a small pair of charged speakers on the windowsill; he walked across and plugged these into his phone, opening the radio application and selecting the local talk radio channel. The presenter was discussing the Republican primary; the challengers had just debated each other for the first time. The candidates were trying to differentiate themselves from their rivals. J.J. Robinson, the governor of California, was in the lead, by all accounts. They were saying that the primary was his to lose. He killed the radio app and scrolled through to his music player. He selected *Rated R* by the Queens of the Stone Age and picked out the slow, drawled funk of "Leg of Lamb."

"Good choice," she said.

"I thought so."

The room was on the third floor, and the window offered a good view of the city. She stood and looked out as he went through the affectation of boiling the kettle for a pot of tea. It was a distraction; they both knew that neither would drink a drop. He took the pot to the table and sat down on the edge of the bed; she sat on the chair next to him. She turned, maybe to say something, maybe not, and he leant across to press his lips gently to hers. He paused, almost wincing with the potential embarrassment that he had misjudged the situation even though he knew that he had not, and then she moved towards him and kissed harder. He closed his eyes and lost himself for a moment. He was only dimly aware of the physical sensations: her breath on his cheek, her arms snaked around his shoulders as her mouth held his, her fingers playing against the back of his neck. She pulled away and looked into his face. Her fingers reached up and traced their way along the scar that began with his cheek and ended below his nose. She kissed it tenderly.

"How'd you do that?"

"Bar fight."

"Someone had a knife?"

He had no wish to discuss the events of that night—he had been drunk, and it had ended badly for the other guy—so he reached for her again, his hand cupping around her head and drawing her closer. Her perfume was pungent, redolent of fresh fruit, and he breathed it in deeply. He pulled off her sweater and eased her back onto the bed with him. They kissed hungrily. He cupped her neck again and pulled her face to his while her hands found their way inside his shirt and around, massaging his muscular shoulders. They explored their bodies hungrily, and Milton soon felt dizzy with desire. Her lips were soft and full; her legs wrapped around his waist and squeezed him tight; her underwear was expensively insubstantial, her breasts rising up and down as she gulped for air. He kissed her sweet-smelling neck and throat as she whispered out a moan of pleasure. He brushed aside the hair that framed her face. They kissed again.

His cellphone buzzed.

She broke away and locked onto his eyes with her own. Her eyes smiled.

"Don't worry. I'm not answering."

The phone went silent.

He kissed her.

Ten seconds later it rang again.

"Someone wants to speak to you."

"Sorry."

"Who is it? Another woman?"

He laughed. "Hardly."

"Go on—the sooner you answer, the sooner they'll shut up. You're all mine tonight."

Milton took the call.

"Mr. Smith?"

The boy's voice was wired with anxiety. "Trip—is everything all right?"

"Did you see the police today?"

"Yes," he said.

"They say you're a suspect?"

"Not in as many words, but that's the gist of it. I'm one of the last people to see her before she disappeared. It stands to reason."

"They had me in, too. Three hours straight."

"And?"

"I don't know. I think maybe they think I'm a suspect, too."

"Don't worry about it. They're doing what they think they have to do. Standard procedure. Most murders are committed by—well, you know."

"People who knew the victim? Yeah, I know."

Milton disentangled himself from Eva and stood. "You haven't done anything. They'll figure that out. This is all routine. Ticking boxes. The good thing is that they're taking it seriously."

"Yeah, man—like, finally."

Milton took out his cigarettes and shook one out of the box. He looked over at Eva. She was looking at him with a quizzical expression on her face. He held up the box, and she nodded. He tossed it across the room to her, pressed the cigarette between his lips, and lit it. He threw her the lighter.

"There was another reason for calling."

"Go on."

"I had a call ten minutes ago. There's this guy, Aaron, he says he was the driver who usually drove Madison to her jobs. He was the guy who didn't show the night she went missing, so she called you. He heard about what's happened on the TV."

"How did he get your number?"

"Called the landline. Madison must've given it to him."

"You need to tell him to go to the police. They'll definitely want to talk to him."

"He won't, Mr. Smith. He's frightened."

"Of what?"

"He knows the agency she was working for. He says they're not exactly on the level. If he rats them out, they'll come after him."

"You need to tell the police, Trip."

"I would, Mr. Smith, but this guy, he says he'll only speak to me. He says he'll tell me everything."

"When?"

"Tomorrow morning. I said I'd meet him at Dottie's. Nine."

Milton knew it. Dottie's was a San Francisco institution, and conveniently enough, it was right at the top of Sixth Street, just a couple of minutes from the El Capitan. Milton yanked up the sash window and tossed the cigarette outside. "I'll be there."

The relief in Trip's thanks was unmistakeable.

"Don't worry. Try to sleep. We'll deal with this tomorrow."

Milton ended the call.

"What was that?"

Milton hadn't told her anything about Madison, but he explained it all now: the night she disappeared, Trip and the days that he had helped him to look for her, the dead bodies that had turned up on the headland, the interview with the police.

"Did you have a lawyer there?" she said. There was indignation in her voice.

"I didn't think I needed one."

"They spoke to you without one?"

"I haven't done anything."

"Are you an idiot?" she said angrily. "You don't speak to the police investigating a murder without a lawyer, John."

"Really," he said, smiling at her. "It was fine. I know what I'm doing."

"No," she said, sitting up. "You don't. Promise me, if they bring you in again, you tell them you're not speaking until I get there. All right?"

"Sure," he said. "All right."

"What did he want?"

Milton related what Trip had told him.

"All right, then. This is what we're going to do. I'm taking tomorrow morning off. I'll drive you so you can get your car fixed, and then you can go and see him."

"You don't have to do that."

"You don't listen much, do you, John? This isn't a democracy. That's what we're doing. It's not open to debate."

Chapter Twenty-Two

EVA DROVE MILTON to the garage to pick up a new set of spark plugs and then to the meeting hall. She waited while he changed the plugs and until the engine was running again.

He went over to the Porsche. They hadn't said much during the ride across town to his car, and he felt a little uncomfortable. He had never been the best when it came to talking about his feelings. He had never been able to afford the luxury before, and it didn't come naturally to him.

"Thanks for the ride," he said.

"Charming!"

He laughed, blushing. "I didn't mean—"

"I know what you meant," she said, the light dancing in her eyes. "I'm joking."

The words clattered into each other. "Oh—never mind."

"You're a funny guy, John," she said. "Relax, all right? I had a nice night."

"Nice?"

"All right—better than nice. It was so nice that I'd like to do it again. You up for that?"

"Sure."

"Be at the next meeting. My place for dinner afterwards. Now—come here."

He leant down and rather awkwardly kissed her through the window.

"What's up?"

"I was wondering," he said. "Could you do me a favour?"

"Sure."

He told her about Doctor Andrew Brady and his potential involvement on the night that Madison went missing. He explained that he had worked at St Francis, like she did, and asked if she could find out anything about him.

"You want me to pull someone's personnel file?" she asked with mock outrage. "Someone's *confidential* personnel file?"

"Could you?"

"Sure," she said. "Can you make it worth my while?"

"I can try."

"Give me a couple of days," she said.

"See you," he said.

"You will."

TRIP WAS WAITING outside Dottie's, pacing nervously, catching frequent glances at his watch. He was wearing a woollen beanie, and he reached his fingers beneath it, scratching his scalp anxiously. His face cleared a little when he saw Milton.

"Sorry I'm late. Traffic. Is he here?"

"Think so. The guy at the back—at the counter."

"All right. That's good."

"How we gonna play this?"

"I want you to introduce yourself and then tell him who I am, but it might turn out best if I do the talking after that, okay? We'll play it by ear and see how we get on."

"What are we going to do?"

"Just talk. Get his story."

"And then the police?"

"Let's see what he's got to say first—then we decide what we do next."

The café was reasonably large, with exposed beams running the length of the ceiling with a flat glass roof above. The brickwork was exposed along one side, there was a busy service area with a countertop around it, and the guests were seated at freestanding tables. Blackboards advertised breakfast and a selection of flavoured coffees. A counter held home-made cakes under clear plastic covers, and quartered wooden shelving bore crockery and condiments. A single candelabra-style light fitting hung down from the ceiling, and there were black-and-white pictures of old Hollywood starlets on the walls. The room was full.

Milton assessed the man at the counter automatically: the clothes were expensive, the empty mug suggested that he was nervous, the Ray-Bans he still hadn't removed confirming it. He was sitting so that he could see the entrance, his head tilting left and right as he made constant wary assessments of the people around him. Milton paused so that Trip could advance a step ahead of him and then followed the boy across the room.

"Aaron?" Trip asked.

"Yeah, man. Trip, right?"

"Yes."

He looked up, frowned, stabbed a finger at Milton. "He with you?"

"Yes."

"So who is he?"

"It's all right. He's a friend."

"Ain't my friend, bro. I said just you. Just you and me."

"He was driving Madison the night she went missing."

That softened him a little. "That right?"

"That's right," Milton said.

"I don't like surprises, all right? You should've said. But okay, I guess."

"Shall we get a table?"

A booth had emptied out. Aaron and Trip went first; Milton bought coffees and followed them.

"Thanks," Aaron said as Milton put the drinks on the table. "What's your name, man?"

"I'm Smith."

"You a driver, then?"

"That's right."

"Freelance or agency?"

"Mostly freelance, bit of agency."

"Police been speaking to you?"

"All afternoon yesterday."

The hardness in his face broke apart. "I'm sorry about you being involved in all this shit. It's my fault. It should've been me that night, right?—I mean, I'd been driving her for ages. The one night I didn't turn up, that one night, and... I can't help thinking if it had've been me, she'd still be here, you know?"

There was an unsaid accusation in that, too: if it were me, and not you, she would still be here. Milton let it pass. "You were good friends?"

"Yeah," he said with an awkward cough. "She's a good person. Out of all the girls I've driven, she's the only one I could say I ever really had any kind of fun with." He looked at Trip and, realising the implication of what he had just said, added, unpersuasively, "As a friend, you know—a good friend."

Milton found himself wondering if that disclaimer was insincere, the way his eyes flicked away from Trip as he delivered it, and he wondered whether Aaron and Madison had been sleeping together. The boy was certainly all broken up about what had happened. Milton wondered whether Trip had started to arrive at the same conclusion. If he had, he was doing a good job of hiding it.

"What do the police think has happened to her?"

"They've got no idea," Trip said. "It took them finding the bodies on the headland for them to start taking it seriously. Up until then she was just a missing person, some girl who decided she didn't want to come home, nothing worth getting excited about."

"Jesus."

"Why didn't you call before?" Milton asked him. "She's been gone three months."

"I don't know," he said. "I felt awkward about it, I guess, you being her boyfriend and all."

"Why would that matter?" Trip said tersely.

"No, of course, it wouldn't—"

Milton nudged Trip beneath the table with his knee. "You said you could tell us who Madison was working for."

"Yeah," he said vaguely. "Same agency I work for, right?"

"Has it got a name?"

"Fallen Angelz. It's this Italian guy, Salvatore something, don't know his second name. I was out of work, got fired from the bar I was working at; I had a friend of a friend who was driving for them. I had no idea what it was all about until he explained it to me. I had no job, no money, not even a car, but I had a clean licence, and I thought it sounded like an easy way to make a bit of cash, maybe meet some people, a bit of fun, you know? Turns out I was right about that."

"How did it work?"

"Straightforward. The girls get a booking, some john all on his own or a frat party or something bigger, some rich dude from out of town wants company all night, willing to pay for the convenience of having a girl come to his hotel room. Celebrities, lawyers, doctors—you would *not* believe some of the guys I drove girls to see. Each girl gets assigned a driver. If it's me, the dispatcher in the office calls me up on my cell and tells me where I have to go to pick her up. They gave me a sweet whip, a tricked-out Lexus, all the extras. So I head over there, drive her out to wherever the party's at, then hang around until the gig's finished, and drive her back home again or to the next job, whatever's happening. It's a piece of cake; the more girls I drive, the more money I make. I get a slice of their takings. The agency gives all the drivers and girls a chart—kinda like a tip calculator—with the different hourly pay rates, everything broken down into separate shares for the agency, the driver, the girl. The drivers always get the least, about a quarter, max, but when you've got a girl charging a grand for an hour and she's out there for two, maybe three hours, well, man, you can imagine, you can see how it can be a pretty lucrative gig, right? I was getting more money in a night than I could earn in two weeks serving stiffs in a bar."

"What about drugs?" Milton asked.

Trip shot a glance at him.

"What about them?" Aaron said.

"They ever involved?"

He shifted uncomfortably. "Sure, man, what do you think? These girls ain't saints. Some bring coke to help stretch the calls out beyond an hour or two. The dispatcher asks the john whether he wants any brought over— 'party material', they call it—they give it to me, and I deliver it. Sometimes I'll get some to sell myself—I've lived here my whole life; it's not like I don't know the right guys to ask, you know what I'm saying?" He delivered that line with a blasé shrug of his shoulders, like it was no big thing, but Milton wasn't impressed and fixed him in a cold stare. "I ain't endorsing it," Aaron backtracked. "Can't say I was ever totally comfortable with having shit in the car, but the money's too good to ignore. You can make the same on top as you do with the girls. This one time, I was out of the city, and we got pulled over. It was me and Madison, actually, way I recall it. Apart from the fact that they were looking for guys driving girls, going after us for procuring prostitution, we had three grams on us. I said she was my girlfriend, and we got away with it." He looked apologetically over at Trip.

"What about Madison?" Milton asked. "Does she use at all?"

"Yeah, man, sure she does."

"Bullshit," Trip said.

Aaron looked at Trip with a pained expression. "You don't know?"

"She doesn't."

"It's the truth, dude, I swear. They use, all of them do."

Trip flinched but held his tongue.

"What does she use?"

"Coke. Weed."

"Anything hallucinogenic?"

He shook his head. "Never seen that."

"All right. Tell us about her."

He shifted uncomfortably. "What do you want to know?"

"Everything."

He shrugged again. "I don't know, man. I'd driven her before, this one time, maybe a year ago. We hit it off right away. She's a great girl, a lot of fun—the only girl I ever drove who I looked forward to seeing. Most of them—well, most of them, let's just say they're not the best when it comes to conversation, all right, a little dead behind the eyes, some of them, not the smartest cookies. But she's different."

"Go on."

He looked over at Trip and then back to Milton. He looked pained. "Is this really necessary?"

"Come on," Trip insisted. "Don't pussy out now." He must have known where this was going, but he was tough, and he wasn't going to flinch.

He sighed helplessly. "All right, man. I guess this was seven, eight months ago, before she went missing. The dispatcher said it was her, and I was happy about it. I'd had the same girl for a week, and she was driving me crazy. I went over to Nob Hill and picked her up in the Lexus, the same place we always met, and she got up in front with me, not in the back like they usually do. Sometimes there'd be more than one girl, but it was just me and her this time, and she talked and talked, told me everything that was going on in her life, said she was into books. I mean, that shit was never my bag, I ain't the best in the world at reading, but she was into it big time, loved it, writing too, and I thought that was kind of cool. Turns out that they put us together for two shifts after that. That's like almost two whole days and nights. The third time out, we were together the whole time. It was a day shift, and it was quiet, just two or three gigs, and we kind of kept getting closer. The next night was the same. The shift ended, and we kept talking. I found a place to park the car, and she pulled out a fifth of vodka, and we drank it. Then I had an eight ball of coke in the glove box, and we ended up doing bumps of that, too. She said things about the work that I hadn't heard from the other girls."

"Like what?" Trip said, suddenly with a little aggression.

He cleared his throat and looked down at the table.

"Keep going," Milton said, knowing what was coming next and hating himself for pressing, hating what it was going to do to Trip.

"Then—I guess it just sort of happened. We had the cash to get a hotel, but I guess we didn't want to wait. We had sex in the car."

"And?"

"She said she liked it. I didn't really believe it, but then, the next time I was driving her, like a couple of days after that, it happened again."

Trip stood abruptly. Without saying a word, he turned on his heel and stalked out of the café.

"I'm sorry, man," Aaron said helplessly. "I didn't want to say—"

Milton stared at him. "Keep going."

He frowned, his eyes on the table again. "I had a girlfriend then, but I ended it. I couldn't stop thinking about Madison. I knew it wasn't right. My girl was cut up, and I knew Madison had a guy, but I couldn't help it, neither of us could help it. I was getting pretty deep into working for the agency then, and my girl had always been jealous about that, the girls I was driving, but Madison didn't have any of that. No jealousy, just totally cool about it all. She got me, totally, understood where I was coming from. Sometimes I drove her, and sometimes I didn't, but it didn't matter. We were both cool with how it was. When I drove her, we slept together between calls. Sometimes she'd pretend to be on call during the day, but she'd meet me, we'd check into a hotel and stay there all day. We'd get room service, watch movies on the pay-per-view, I'd usually have a couple of grams on me, and we'd work our way through that."

"What was she like?"

"How do you mean?"

"Ever think she was depressed?"

"She had her moments, like all the girls, but no—I don't think so. If you mean do I think she's run away or done something worse, then, no, I'd say there was no chance. That'd be completely out of character. You want my opinion, I'd say that something bad has happened. No way she stays out of touch this long. She says nothing to me, nothing to your friend—no, no way, I ain't buying that."

"You know you have to tell the police, don't you?"

"About us?"

"Yes, and about the agency."

His eyes flickered with fear. "No way, man. Talk to the cops? You mad? Salvatore, he's connected, you know what I mean? *Connected.* It's not like I know everything about how it works, but my best guess, the things I heard from the girls and the other drivers, he's fronting it for the Lucianos. You know them, man? The fucking Lucianos? It's fucking Mafia, right?—the

Mafia! Ain't no way I'm getting myself in a position where they might think I was ratting them out to the cops. No way. You know what happens to guys they reckon are rats, right?"

"Your name doesn't have to come out."

"Fuck that shit, man! What you been smoking? That kind of stuff don't ever stay under wraps. They got cops on the payroll; everyone knows it. My name would be on the street in minutes, and then they'll be coming over to talk to me about it, and that ain't something that I want to think about. Next thing, I'd be floating in the bay with my throat cut. Fish food, man."

"All right," Milton said, smiling in the hope that he might relax a little. "It's okay. I understand."

Aaron looked at him suspiciously. "You're just a driver, right?"

"That's right."

"So why you asking all the questions, then?"

He spoke with careful, exaggerated patience. "Because I'm one of the last people to have seen Madison before she disappeared. That means I'm a suspect, and I'd rather that I wasn't. Trip is a suspect now, too, and it'll probably get worse for him when the police find out that you were sleeping with his woman. Jealousy, right? That's a good motive. The more information you can give us, maybe that makes it easier for us to find out what happened to her, and then maybe the police realise me and him had nothing to do with it. Understand?"

"You wait for her that night?"

"Yes."

"Why didn't you help her, then? If it was me out there, I guarantee nothing would've happened."

Milton looked at him dead straight, staring right into his eyes; the boy immediately looked down into the dregs of his coffee. "She didn't give me a chance," Milton said sternly. "Something happened to her at that party, and there wasn't anything I could do about it. By the time I got to her, she was already in a mess."

"So where is she?"

"She ran. That's all I know."

He gestured towards the door. "That dude—you tell him I'm sorry, will you? I didn't want to say anything, and you know, muscling in on another guy's girl, that ain't the way I do things, that ain't my style at all, you know what I'm saying?"

"I'm sure it isn't," Milton said.

"All right," he said. "I'm done."

"The agency. How can I get in touch with them?"

"What are you gonna do?"

"I'm going to visit them."

"And?"

"And get as much information as I can."

"No way, man. I can't. That shit's gonna come back to me, right? They'll figure out I've been talking. I don't know. I don't know at all."

He got up quickly, the chair scraping loudly against the floor. He made to leave, but Milton reached out a hand, grabbed the boy around the bicep, and squeezed.

"Shit, dude!" he exclaimed. "That hurts."

Milton relaxed his grip a little, but he didn't let go. "Have a think about it," he said, his voice quiet and even. "Think about Madison. If you care about her at all, you give me a call and tell me how I can get in touch with the agency. Don't make me come and find you. Do we understand each other?"

"Shit, man, yeah—all right."

Milton took a pen from his pocket, pulled a napkin from the chrome dispenser, and wrote his number on it. "This is me," he said, putting it in the boy's hand. "Take the rest of the day to think about it, and call me. Okay?"

The boy gulped down his fear and nodded.

Milton released his grip.

Chapter Twenty-Three

MILTON DROVE THEM as near to Headlands Lookout as he could get. Trip was nervous, fidgeting next to him, almost as if he expected them to find something. The police had blocked the road a hundred yards from the parking lot, a broad cordon cutting from the rocky outcrop on the right all the way down to the edge of the cliff on the left. Half a dozen outside broadcast trucks had been allowed down to the lot, and they were crammed in together, satellite dishes angled in the same direction and their various antennae bristling. Milton slowed and pulled off the narrow road, cramming the Explorer up against the rock so that there was just enough space for cars to pass it to the left. The skies were a slate grey vault overhead, and rain was lashing against the windscreen, pummelling it on the back of a strong wind coming right off the Pacific. Visibility was decent despite the brutal weather, and as Milton disembarked, he gazed out to the south, all the way to the city on the other side of the bay.

They made their way through the cordon and down to the parking lot. There were several dozen people there already, arranged in an untidy scrum before a man who was standing on a raised slope where the phalanx of cameras could all get a decent view of him. Milton recognised him. It was Commissioner William Reagan, the head of the local police. He was an old man, close to retirement, his careworn face chiselled by years of stress and disappointment. The wind tousled his short shock of white hair. He pulled his long cloak around him, the icy rain driven across the bleak scene. An officer was holding an umbrella for him, but it wasn't giving him much shelter; he wiped moisture from his face with the back of his hand.

"Ladies and gentlemen," he said into the upheld microphones, "before I get into my remarks, let me identify those who are here with me. I got Chief of Detectives Stewart Webster, everyone knows the chief, and I got Inspector Richard Cotton." He cleared his throat and pulled out a sheet of paper. "As you know, we've found two bodies along this stretch of the headland. I wish we hadn't, but that's the sad fact of it. I don't think it's a coincidence that two bodies ended up in this area. It appears that they were taken down from the road into the foliage and hidden there so that they wouldn't be seen. We're assuming they were dumped here by the same person or persons."

A brusque man from cable news shouted loudest as he paused for breath. "You identified them yet?"

"No," Reagan said. "Not yet."

"So you're saying you've got a serial killer dumping victims along this stretch of land?"

"I don't think it's a coincidence that two ended up in this area."

"You expect to find anyone else?"

"That's impossible to say. But we're looking."

"There's snow forecast for the weekend. Does that add pressure?"

"It doesn't help. We want to make sure we don't miss anything."

"So are you or are you not looking at it being the same guy?"

"Well, you know, I'm not gonna say that, but certainly, we're looking at that."

THE PRESS ROADSHOW decamped and moved to Belvedere. A slow crawl of traffic worked slowly along the narrow road, Milton and Trip caught in the middle of it. Their purpose in driving out of the city had been to go and speak to Brady, but Milton had not anticipated all this extra company. It made him nervous. The vehicles turned left and headed north, taking the right and doubling back to the south. Milton gripped the wheel tightly and ran the morning's developments through his mind. It wasn't surprising that they had reached the conclusion that Madison's disappearance must have been connected. Why not? Two working girls turning up murdered just a few miles away, another working girl goes missing: it was hardly a stretch to think that she was dead, too, and dead at the hands of the same killer.

As they reached Pine Shore, it was obvious that the prospect of a community of potential suspects was just too tempting to ignore. The gates stood open—it looked as if they had been forced—and the cavalcade had spilled inside. Reporters and their cameramen had set up outside the two key properties: the house where the party had taken place and Dr. Brady's cottage. Police cruisers were parked nearby, but the cops inside seemed content to let them get on with things. Milton parked the Explorer and joined Trip at the front of the car. They watched as two reporters for national news channels delivered their assessments of the case so far—the discovery of the two bodies, the fact that a third girl had gone missing here—and suggested that the police were linking the investigations.

Milton looked at the cameras.

"We shouldn't be here," he said, more to himself than to the boy.

"What are they doing outside his place?" Trip said, his eyes blazing angrily as he started up the street towards Brady's cottage.

"Trip—stop."

"They think he did it, right? That must be it."

Milton followed after him and took him by the shoulder. "We need to get back in the car. They'll be all over us if they see us and figure out who we are."

Trip shook his hand away. "I don't care about that. I want to speak to him."

He set off again. Milton paused. He knew he should leave him, get back into the car, and drive back to the city. He had been stupid to come up here. He should have guessed that it would be swarming with press. It stood to reason. He didn't know if they would be able to identify him, but if they did, if he was filmed and if the footage was broadcast?—that would be very dangerous indeed.

Milton's phone vibrated in his pocket.

"Hello?"

"Mr. Smith?"

"Speaking."

"It's Aaron Pogue—from this morning."

Milton put his hand over the microphone. "Trip!"

He paused and turned. "What?"

"It's Aaron."

The boy came back towards him.

"You there?" said Pogue.

"Yes, I'm here. Hello, Aaron."

"I've been thinking about what you said."

"And?"

"And I'll tell you what you need. The agency, all that."

"That's good, Aaron. Go on."

"I don't have a number for the agency—the number they use when they call, it's always blocked, so there's nothing I can do to help you there. But Salvatore, the guy who runs it, I know he owns the pizza house in Fisherman's Wharf. That's just a cover—the agency is his main deal, that's his money gig; he runs it from the office out back. That's it."

"Thank you."

"You'll keep my name out of it?"

"I'll try."

"I hope you find her."

Milton ended the call.

"What did he say?"

"He told me where to find the agency."

The thought of confronting Brady seemed to have left his mind. "Where?"

"Come on," he said. "It's in the city. Want to come?"

Chapter Twenty-Four

MILTON PARKED THE CAR on the junction of Jefferson and Taylor. He had explained his plan to Trip during the drive back into the city and persuaded him that it was better that he go in alone. He had objected at first, but Milton had insisted and, eventually, the boy had backed down. Milton didn't know what he was going to find, but if the agency was backed by the Mafia, what he had in mind was likely to be dangerous. He had no intention of exposing Trip to that.

"I won't be long," he said as he opened the door. "Wait here?"

"All right," Trip said.

Milton stepped out and walked beneath the huge ship's wheel that marked the start of Fisherman's Wharf. He passed restaurants with their names marked on guano-stained awnings: Guardino's, The Crab Station, Sabella & LaTorre's Original Fisherman's Wharf Restaurant. Tourists gathered at windows, staring at the menus, debating the merits of one over another. A ship's bell clanged in the brisk wind that was coming off the ocean, the tang of salt was everywhere, the clouds pressed down overhead. It was a festival of tacky nonsense, as inauthentic as it was possible to be. Milton continued down the road. The Classic Italian Pizza and Pasta Co. was between Alioto's and The Fisherman's Grotto.

He climbed the stairs to the first floor and nodded to the maître d' as he passed him as if he were just rejoining friends at a table. It was a decent place: a salad and pasta station, tended to by a man in a chef's tunic and a toque, was positioned beneath a large Italian tricolour; string bags full of garlic and sun-dried tomatoes hung from a rack in the area where food was prepared; a series of tables was arranged on either side of an aisle that led to the bar; the tables were covered with crisp white tablecloths, folded napkins and gleaming cutlery and glassware. Two sides of the restaurant were windowed, the view giving out onto the marina beyond on one side and the wharf on the other. It was busy. The smell of fresh pizza blew out of the big wood kiln that was the main feature of the room.

He went into the kitchen. A man in grimy whites was working on a bowl of crab meat.

"I'm looking for Salvatore."

The man shifted uncomfortably. "Say what?"

"Salvatore. The boss. Where is he?"

"Ain't no one called Salvatore here."

Milton was in no mood to waste time. He stalked by the man and headed for the door at the end of the kitchen. He opened the door. It was a large office. He surveyed it carefully, all eyes. First, he looked for an exit. There was one on the far wall, propped open with a fire extinguisher. There was a window, too, with a view of the wharf outside, but it was too small to be useful. There was a pool table in the middle of the room and a jukebox against the wall. There was a desk with a computer and a pile of papers. A man was sitting at the computer. He was middle-aged, burly, heavy shoulders, biceps that strained against the sleeves of his T-shirt, meaty forearms covered in hair. Both arms were decorated with lurid tattooed sleeves, the markings running all the way down to the backs of his hands and onto his fingers.

The man spun around on his chair. "The fuck you want?"

"Salvatore?"

He got up. "Who are you?"

"My name is Smith."

"And?"

"I want to talk to you."

"You think you can just bust into my office?"

"We need to talk."

"Then make an appointment."

"It's about your other business."

The man concealed the wary, nervous turn to his face behind a quick sneer. "Yeah? What other business?"

Milton looked at him with dead eyes. He had always found that projecting a sense of perfect calm worked wonders in a situation like this. It wasn't even a question of confidence. He knew he could take Salvatore, provided there were no firearms involved to even the odds. Milton couldn't remember the last time he'd lost a fight against a single man. He couldn't remember the last time he'd lost a fight against two men, either, come to that.

"Your escort business, Salvatore."

"Nah."

"Fallen Angelz."

"Never heard of it."

"It would be better to be honest."

"I don't know nothing about it, friend."

Milton scanned for threats and opportunities. There were drawers in the desk that might easily contain a small revolver. No way of knowing that for sure, though, so he would just have to keep an eye on the man's hands. There was a stack of cardboard trays with beer bottles inside, still covered by cellophane wrap, but Milton wasn't worried about them. Bottles made for poor weapons unless you had the chance to smash them, and it would take too long to tear through the plastic to get at these ones for them to be useful. No, he thought, the pool table was the best bet. There were the balls, hard balls made up of six ounces of phenolic resin that were good for throwing or for using as blunt weapons in an open fist. There were half a dozen cues held in a vertical rack on the nearest wall. A pool cue was a good weapon. Nice and light and easy to wield, balanced with lead shot in the fat end, long enough to offer plenty of range.

Milton watched the Italian carefully. He could see from the way that the veins were standing out in his neck and the clenching and unclenching of his fists that it would take very little for things to turn nasty.

"So—let's talk about it."

"Don't you listen? I don't know what you're talking about."

"So I wouldn't find anything in those papers if I were to have a look?"

"Reckon that'd be a pretty dumb thing to go and try to do."

Salvatore reached down slowly and carefully pulled up the bottom of his T-shirt, exposing six-inches of tattooed skin and the stippled grip of a Smith & Wesson Sigma 40F. He rested the tips of his fingers against it, lightly curling them around the grip.

"This isn't the first time I've seen a gun."

"Could be your last."

Milton ignored that. "Let me tell you some things I know, Salvatore. I know you run girls out of this office. I know you distribute drugs on the side. And I know you sent Madison Clarke to a party at the house in Pine Shore."

"Yeah? What party was that?"

"Three months ago. The one where she went missing."

He stared at him. A flicker of doubt. "Madison Clarke? No. I don't know no one by that name."

"I don't believe you."

"You think I care what you believe?" He stood up now, his right hand curled more tightly around the grip of the handgun. He pointed to the telephone on the desk with his left hand. "You know who I'm gonna call if you don't start making tracks?"

"I've no idea."

"I'm gonna call an ambulance. I'm telling you, man, straight up, you don't get out of here right now, you won't be leaving in one piece. I'm gonna fucking shoot your ass."

"I tell you what—you tell me all about the escorting business and maybe I won't break your arm. How's that sound?"

He slapped his hand against the gun. "You miss this, man? Who the hell are you to tell me what to do?"

"Let's say I'm someone you don't want to annoy."

"What's that supposed to mean?"

"I'm a concerned member of the public. And I don't like the business you're running."

He assessed the distance between them—eight feet—and couldn't say for sure that he would be able to get all the way across the room before the man could draw and shoot. And if he could get the gun up in time and shoot, it would be point-blank and hard to miss.

That wasn't going to work.

Plan B.

Milton stepped quickly to the table, snatched up the eight-ball and flung it. His aim was good, and as Salvatore turned his head away to avoid it, the ball struck him on the cheekbone, shattering it.

Milton already had the pool cue, his fingers finding the thin end.

Salvatore fumbled hopelessly for the gun.

Milton swung the cue in a wide arc that terminated in the side of his head. There was a loud crunch that was clearly audible over the ambient noise from the restaurant, and a spray of blood splashed over the computer monitor. Salvatore slid off the chair and onto the floor. Milton stood over him and chopped down again three more times, fast and hard into his ribs and trunk and legs until he stayed down.

He discarded the cue and started to look through the papers on the desk.

TRIP WAS LISTENING to the radio when Milton reached the Explorer again. He opened the door and slid inside, moving quickly. He started the engine and pulled away from the kerb.

"You get anything?"

"Nothing useful."

"So it wasn't worth coming down here? We should've stayed in Belvedere?"

"I wouldn't say that. I made an impression. There'll be a follow-up."

Chapter Twenty-Five

MILTON HEARD THE buzzer as he was cleaning his teeth. He wasn't expecting a delivery, and since very few people knew where he lived, he was about as sure as he could be that whoever it was who had come calling on him at eight in the morning wasn't there for the good of his health. He put the brush back in its holder and quietly opened the window just enough that he could look downwards. The window was directly above the entrance to the building, and he could see the three men who were arrayed around the door. There was a car on the corner with another man in the front. It was a big Lexus, blacked-out windows, very expensive.

Four men. An expensive car. He had a pretty good idea what this was.

Milton toggled the intercom. "Yes?"

"Police."

"Police?"

"That's right. Is that Mr. Smith?"

"Yes."

"Could we have a word?"

"What about?"

"Open the door, please, sir."

"What do you want to talk to me about?"

"There was an incident yesterday. Fisherman's Wharf. Please, sir—we just need to have a word."

"Fine. Just give me five minutes. I work nights. I was asleep. I just need to get changed."

"Five minutes."

He went back to the window and looked down at them again. There was no way on earth that these men were cops. They were dressed too well in expensive overcoats, and he saw the grey sunlight flickering across the caps of well-polished shoes. And then there was the car; the San Francisco Police Department drove Crown Vics, not eighty-thousand-dollar saloons. He waited for the men to shift around a little and got a better look at them. Three of the men he had never seen before. The fourth, the guy waiting in the car, was familiar. Milton recognised him as he wound down the window and called out to the others. It was Salvatore. His face was partially obscured by a bandage that had been fixed over his shattered cheek. Milton waited a moment longer, watching as the men exchanged words, their postures tense and impatient. One of them stepped back, and the wind caught his open overcoat, flipping his suit coat back, too, revealing a metallic glint in a shoulder holster.

584

That settled it.

The three guys at his door were made guys; that much was for sure. So what to do? If he let them in, then the chances were they'd come up, subdue him, and Salvatore would be called in to put the final bullet in his head. Or if he went down to meet them, maybe they would take him somewhere quiet, somewhere down by the dock, perhaps, and do it there. He had known exactly what he was doing when he beat Salvatore, and the way he saw it, he hadn't been given any other choice. There were always going to be consequences for what he'd done, and here they were, right on cue. An angry Mafioso bent on revenge could cause trouble. Lots of trouble.

So maybe discretion was the better part of valour this morning. He dropped his cellphone in his jacket pocket and went through into the corridor. There was a window at the end; he yanked it up. The building's fire escape ran outside it. He wriggled out onto the sill, reached out with his right hand, grabbed the metal handrail, and dropped down onto the platform.

He climbed down the stairs and walked around the block until he had a clear view onto the frontage of the El Capitan. The Lexus was still there, and the three hoodlums were still waiting by the door. One of them had his finger on the buzzer; it looked like he was pressing it non-stop.

He collected the Explorer. It was cold. He started the engine and then put the heater on max. He took out his cellphone and swiped his finger down, flipping through his contacts. He found the one he wanted, pressed call, and waited for it to connect.

Chapter Twenty-Six

THE SIGN in the window said BAXTER BAIL BONDS. The three words were stacked on top of one other so that the three Bs, drawn so they were all interlocked, were the focus that caught the eye. The shop was in Escondido, north of San Diego, and Beau Baxter hardly ever visited it these days. He had started out here pretty much as soon as he had gotten out of the Border Patrol down south. He had put in a long stint, latterly patrolling the Reaper's Line between Tijuana, Mexicali, Nogales and, worst of them all, Juárez. Beau had run his business from the shop for eighteen months until he came to the realisation that it was going to take years to make any serious coin, and, seeing as he wasn't getting any younger, he figured he needed to do something to accelerate things. He had developed contacts with a certain Italian family with interests all the way across the continental United States, and he started to do work for them. It paid well, although their money was dirty and it needed to be laundered. That was where having a ready-made business, a business that often ran on cash and dealt in the provision of intangible services, sometimes anonymously, came in very handy indeed.

So Beau had kept the place on and had appointed an old friend from the B.P. to run it for him. Arthur "Hank" Culpepper was a hoary old goat, a real wiseacre they used to call "PR" back in the day because he was the least appropriate member of the crew to send to do anything that needed a diplomatic touch. He had always been vain, which was funny because he'd never been the prettiest to look at. That didn't stop him developing a high opinion of himself; Beau joked that he shaved in a cracked mirror every morning because he thought of himself as a real ladies' man. His airs and graces might have been lacking, but he had made up for that by being a shit-hot agent with an almost supernatural ability to nose out the bad guys.

He wasn't interested in the big game that Beau went after nowadays; there was a lot of travel involved in that, and there was the ever-present risk of catching a bullet in some bumble-fuck town where the quarry had gone to ground. Hank was quite content to stick around San Diego, posting bond for the local scumbags and then going after them whenever they were foolish enough to abscond. He had his favourite bar, his hound and his dear old wife (in that order), and anyways, he had a reputation that he liked to work on. Some people called him a local legend. He was known for bringing the runners back in with maximum prejudice, and stories of him roping redneck tweakers from out of the back of his battered old Jeep were well known among the Escondido bondsmen. It was, he said, just something that he enjoyed to do.

Beau pulled up and took a heavy black vinyl sports bag from the rear of his Cherokee. He slung it over his shoulder, blipped the lock on the car, crossed the pavement, and stopped at the door. He unlocked it, pushed down the handle with his elbow, and backed his way inside. The interior was simple. The front door opened into the office, with the desk, some potted plants, a standard lamp and a sofa that had been pushed back against the wall. There was a second door, opposite the street door, that led to a corridor that went all the way to the back of the building. There was a kitchenette, a bathroom and, at the end, a small cell that could be locked.

The safe was in the kitchen, the kettle and a couple of dirty mugs resting atop it. Beau spun the dial three times—four-nine-eight—and opened the heavy cast-iron door. He unzipped the bag and spread it open. It was full of paper money.

Fifteen big ones.

The smell of it wafted into the stuffy room. Beau loved that smell.

He took out the cash, stacked the fifties in neat piles, and locked the safe.

He locked the front door, got back into his Cherokee, and headed for the hospital.

HANK WAS SITTING up in bed, his cellphone pressed between his head and shoulder while his right hand was occupied with tamping tobacco into the bowl of the pipe in his left hand. He was in his early sixties, same as Beau was, and lying there in bed like that, he looked it. Man, did he ever look *old*. The whole of his right side was swathed in bandages, and there was a drip running into a canula in the back of his hand. He hadn't shaved for a couple of days, and that added on a few extra years. The colour had leeched from his face, and now his skin was as white as the sheets the Klan folks used to bleach up special for a Saturday night cross-burning session. He wasn't wearing anything above the waist, and his arms—Beau remembered them when they were thick with muscle—looked withered and old. The tattoo of the snake that he had had done in Saigon was wrinkled and creased where once it had been tightly curled around his bicep.

Old age, Beau thought. That was the real reaper. Coming for all of us. Still, he thought, I'd rather eat five pounds of cactus thorns and shit-sharp needles than look like that.

He raised a hand in greeting, and Hank reciprocated with a nod, mouthing that he would be two minutes before speaking into the receiver again: "I'm telling you, Maxine, the judge don't give a sweet fuck about that. What he's gonna get now ain't a pimple on a fat man's ass compared to what he's gonna get. If he don't make it for the hearing tomorrow, he'll make an example out of him. I'm telling you, no shit, he's looking at five years before he even gets a sniff of parole. Five. Is that what you want for him? No? Then you better tell me where he's at."

Beau could hear the buzz of a female voice from the receiver.

There was a coffee machine in the hall, and Beau went outside for two brews in white Styrofoam cups. He searched the small wicker basket next to the machine for a packet of Coffee-mate, came up empty, went back through into the room, and found a bowl of sugar instead. He spooned a couple into both cups, stirring the sludgy brown liquid until it looked a little more appealing.

"Fine. Where—Pounders? All right, then. I'm gonna send someone to go and get him."

Beau sat down and stared at his old friend. He thought about the first time they had met. 1976. They'd graduated from the Border Patrol Academy and been posted up in Douglas at about the same time. Hank had been a uniformed cop near the border in El Centro, California, before coming on duty with the B.P.

"I'm serious, Maxine," Hank was saying. "If he comes back, you call me right away. He really doesn't want to rile me up right now. I'm not in the mood to go chasing him down all over the state, and if he makes me do that, I ain't promising he don't get brought back in cuffs and with a bloody nose. You hearing me straight, darling? I ain't messing. Don't you dare make me look like a fool, now."

He ended the call.

"You ain't chasing anyone tonight, partner," Beau said, dropping down onto the room's small sofa.

"She don't know that."

"Who is it?"

"Fellow named George Bailey. Been stealing cars. This time, though, the dumb fuck had a pistol on him while he was doing it. 'Possession of a concealed weapon,' he's looking at five, minimum, probably seven or eight depending on which judge he gets. He decided he'd take his chances on the road; I'm trying to persuade his lovely girlfriend"—that word was loaded with sarcasm—"otherwise. He's out getting drunk, so I'm going to send George McCoy to go pick him up. Unless you wanna do it?"

"Uh-huh," Beau said with a big smile, shaking his head. "I'm not into that no more."

"Only the big game for you now, partner?"

"That's right."

"What was the last one?"

"Mexican."

"And?"

"Not so bad."

Beau had finished the job the night before. It had been an easy one by his usual standards. The Lucianos had interests in a couple of big casinos in Vegas, and one of their croupiers, this wiry beaner by the name of Eduardo del Rio, had entertained the thought that he could run south with fifty grand of their money. The family had sent Beau after him. He must have been the most dumbshit robber in the Mexican state of Sonora that night, and it had been a simple bust. He had run straight home to his wife, and Beau just had to wait there for him. He'd been a little punchy when Beau confronted him, but his attitude had adjusted just as soon as he started looking down the barrel of Beau's 12-gauge pump.

"Boy was as dumb as you like," Beau said. "He wouldn't have found his way to the kitchen for a taco in his own one-room hut." He sipped his coffee; it was foul. "All right." Beau crossed his legs, the hem of his right trouser riding up a little to show more of his snakeskin cowboy boot. "Now then. You wanna tell me what in God's name has been going down round here?"

"Meaning what?"

"Meaning what? Which sumbitch shot you up, Hank?"

"Ever heard of Ordell Leonard?"

Beau shook his head. "Can't say I have."

"Big, black brother from 'Bama. Quiet fella until he gets on the drink, then you never know what you're gonna get. They had him for driving under the influence and resisting arrest. All he was looking at was a couple of months, but he reckons they're prejudiced against black men from the South round here, so he decides he's gonna take his chances and takes off. I ended up in Arkansas before I could catch him. Fucking Little Rock, can you believe that shit? Two thousand miles, man. It took me three days there and three days back, although, course, he was in the back coming home, so I had to listen to his goddamn problems the whole way. The whole experience made me think I ain't getting a good enough shake out of this here thing we got going on."

He was grinning as he said it; Beau knew he was fooling around.

"And then?"

"And then I got lazy, I guess. We was right back up at the store when I let him out. I was going to put him in the cell until I could transfer him to the courthouse. He'd been on best behaviour for the whole trip, and I'd taken off his cuffs. Clean forgot. Dude cold-cocks me, knocks me down, then gets my shotgun from the front, and fires off a load. I'm not sure how he missed, to be honest with you. Ended up catching me in the shoulder, but it could've been a helluva lot worse."

"Know where he's headed?"

"Got a brother in Vallejo. I'd bet you a dime to a doughnut that's where he's gone."

"All right, then. You can leave that one to me."

"You sure? Not much money in it, Beau."

Beau looked at Hank again. He was getting on. Couldn't have that many years left in him doing what they were doing. A shotgun at close range? He'd got lucky. Maybe it was time Beau suggested Hank took it easy. Maybe it was a message. "Ain't about money all the time, partner. Dude shot you all up. I can't stand for that. Bad for our reputation."

"Ah, shit—I'll be fine. I was gonna enjoy seeing him again."

"How long they going to keep you in?"

"Couple more days."

"By which time he'll be long gone. Nah, Hank, don't worry about it. Leave him to me."

Hank sucked his teeth and, eventually, nodded his assent. "Shit," he said. "I remembered something; you had a call back at the office. Jeanette took the details down and told me about it."

Jeanette was the secretary who kept things ticking over. "Who from?"

"She said he called himself Smith. Sounded like he was English, she said; he had that whole accent going on. She says you weren't around and could she take a message for you, and he says yes, she could, and he tells her that he wants you to call him pronto. He gave her a number—I've got it written down in my pants pocket."

"He say what he wanted to speak to me about?"

"Nope," Hank said, shaking his head, "except it was urgent."

Chapter Twenty-Seven

BEAU DROVE NORTH. It took him eight hours on the I-5, a touch under five hundred miles. He could have flown or caught a northbound Amtrak from San Diego, but he liked the drive, and it gave him some time to listen to some music and think.

He spent a lot of time thinking about duties and obligations. He had always lived his life by a code. It wasn't a moral code because he couldn't claim to be a particularly moral man; that would be fatuous, given the profession he had latterly chosen for himself. It was more a set of rules that he tried to live his life by, and one of those rules insisted that he would always pay his debts. It was a matter of integrity. Beau's father had always said that was something you either had or you didn't have, and he prided himself that he did; he was made of integrity from the guts out. Getting the Mexican journalist away to safety had been the right thing to do, but he couldn't in all honesty say that he thought it had completely squared the ledger between them. He figured the Englishman had done him two solids down in Mexico: he had saved him from Santa Muerta and then drew the fire of whoever it was who hit El Patrón's mansion so that he and the girl could get away. Helping the girl had paid back only half of the debt. At the very least, he could drive up to San Francisco and hear what the Englishman had to say. If it wasn't something he could help him with, then he would book into a nice hotel for a couple of nights and enjoy the city. He really had nothing to lose.

And if nothing else, he could find out how on earth Smith had gotten out of Mexico. It hadn't looked so good for him when Beau and the girl had made tracks. That guy, though, he was something else. He could fall into a tub of shit and come out smelling like a rose every time.

Beau could mix in a spot of business, too. Ordell Leonard was up there, and there was no way on God's green earth Beau was going to let him have even an extra second of liberty. He would never have admitted it to another person, but seeing Hank in the hospital like that, old and shot up, it had reminded him of his own advancing years. He had been thinking about his own mortality a lot recently. He was sixty-two years old. Every morning he seemed to wake up with another ache. Everyone came to the end of the road eventually, that was the one shared inevitability, but Beau was determined that he wasn't there yet. The more he thought about it, the more he understood his own reaction: Ordell Leonard was a bad man, a dangerous man, and he would have been a challenge to collar ten years ago, when he and Hank were fitter and meaner than they were now. Bringing him in now would be his way of thumbing his nose at the notion that he was ready to retire.

Ordell would be the proof that Beau wasn't ready to hang it up just yet.

HE BOOKED a suite at the Drisco, and five minutes before the time that they had agreed to meet, he was waiting in the bar downstairs.

John Smith was right on time.

"Beau," he said, sitting down opposite him.

"All right, English," Beau said. "Didn't think I'd ever be seeing you again."

"I guess you never know what's around the corner."

"I guess you don't."

"What happened to the girl?" Smith asked.

"As far as I know, she's safe and sound."

"As far as you know?"

"That's all I can say. The man who makes people disappear, this guy my employers use when they need to send someone out of harm's way, the arrangement is strictly between him and the client. No one else gets to know anything about it. She could be in Alaska for all I know. She could be back in Mexico, although I hope for her sake she ain't. But what I can say for sure is that I got her into the country like I said I would, and she was just fine and dandy when I dropped her off."

Smith nodded at that. "You get paid for the job?"

"Sure did," Beau said.

He had delivered the body of Adolpho González to the Lucianos nine months ago. The job had been to bring him in dead or alive, yet there had been consternation that it was in the latter condition that Santa Muerta was delivered. Beau had explained what happened—that the girl journalist from Juárez had put a bullet in the Mexican's head while he was outside their motel room getting ice—but his honesty had led to recriminations. The awkwardness had been underscored by the requirement, stipulated by Beau, that the girl was to be given a new identity and kept hidden from the cartels. There had been a moment when Beau had been unsure that they were going to let her leave in one piece, but he had stuck to his guns and, eventually, they had conceded. Beau didn't necessarily care about her either way—she wasn't his problem, after all—but he had promised Smith that he would get her out of Mexico and set up in the States, and Beau wasn't the sort of man who went back on his word. Doing the right thing had eventually lightened his payment by fifteen grand; the Italians docked ten from his bounty for spoiling the fun they had planned for González and the other five went to pay the fee of the professional who made people disappear.

Fifteen thousand!

Beau hadn't been happy with that, not at all.

"I appreciate it," Smith said.

"No sweat, English. Least I could do, circumstances like they were." He paused and lit up a smoke. "So—how'd you get out alive?"

"There was a lot of confusion. I took advantage of it."

"Who were those dudes?"

"Best not to ask."

"What about El Patrón?"

"What about him?"

"He got himself shot dead a couple of days later. That wouldn't have been anything to do with you, would it?"

"Me? No," Milton said. "Course not."

Beau laughed and shook his head. The Englishman was something else. Quiet and unassuming for the most part, but when he got all riled up, there weren't many people who would have concerned Beau more. He remembered the way he had strode through El Patrón's burning mansion, offing gangsters just like he was shooting fish in a barrel. He had been ruthlessly efficient. Not a single wasted shot and not a moment of hesitation. The man was private, too, and Beau knew that there was no point in pushing him to speak if he didn't want to. "You said you needed a favour," he said instead. "What can I do for you?"

"The syndicate you've been working for—it's the Lucianos?"

Beau paused and frowned a little. He hadn't expected that. "Could be. Why?"

"I have a problem—you might be able to help."

"With them? What kind of problem?"

"I put one of their men in the hospital."

"Why would you want to do a crazy-assed thing like that?"

"He pulled a gun on me. I didn't have much choice."

"By 'hospital'—what do you mean?"

"He's not dead, Beau. Broken nose, broken ribs. I worked him over with a pool cue."

"Jesus, English."

Smith shrugged.

"You wanna tell me why he was going to pull a gun on you?"

"They're running an escort business. This man fronted it for them. I had some questions about it, and he didn't like them."

"What were they?"

"They sent a girl to a party. She hasn't been seen since, and I was one of the last people to see her. Apart from anything else, the police have got me down as a suspect."

"For what?"

"You hear about those dead girls up north?"

"Sure."

"The party was right around there. I'd say there's a good chance her body'll be the next body they find."

"Murder, then."

"I'm not concerned about me, I know I didn't do it, and I know they're just going through the motions."

"Kicking the tyres."

He nodded. "Exactly. But I got talking to her before."

"An escort?"

"I was driving her. I have a taxi."

"Chef. Taxi driver. You're full of surprises."

Smith brushed over that. "She's a nice girl. And her boyfriend's a good kid. When they realise I don't have anything to do with it, they're going to go after him, and maybe he isn't quite as single-minded as me, maybe they need a conviction, and he looks like he could be their guy. Maybe they *make* him their guy. I'd like to get to the bottom of what happened, one way or another."

Beau shook his head. "You've got yourself in a mess over another woman? You got a habit for that. What is it with you, English?"

"I need to talk to them, Beau, but at the moment, I think they'd rather put a bullet between my eyes. I was hoping you might be able to straighten things out."

"Put a good word in for you, you mean?"

"If you like."

Beau couldn't help but chuckle. "You're unbelievable. Really—you're something else."

"Can you do it?"

"Can I ask them not to shoot you? Sure I can. Will they listen? I have absolutely no idea."

"Just get me in a room with whoever it is I need to speak to. It might not look like it, but we both have a stake in this. If she's dead, I'm going to find out who killed her. It's in their best interests that I do. Because if I don't, there's going to be a whole lot of heat coming their way. You'd be doing them a favour."

"Well," Beau said, "you put it like that, how can I possibly refuse?"

Chapter Twenty-Eight

"I KNOW YOU'VE GOT A TEMPER," Beau said to him as he reversed parked his Jeep into a space next to the bowling alley, "but you'll want to keep it under wraps today, all right? Apart from the fact that I vouched for you, which means it'll be me who gets his ass kicked if you start getting rambunctious, these aren't the kind of dudes you want to be annoying, if you catch my drift." He paused. "You *do* catch my drift, John, don't you?"

"Don't worry, Beau," Milton said. "I'm not an idiot."

"One other thing, let me do the talking to start with. Introduce you and suchlike. Then you can take the conversation whichever way you want. If you get off on the wrong foot with them, you'll get nowhere—you might as well just pound sand up your ass. This has to be done right."

The car park was half full, mostly with cheap cars with a few dings and dents in the bodywork, nothing too showy, the kind of first cars that kids new to the business of driving would buy with the money they had managed to scrape together. Beau had parked next to the most expensive car in the lot. It was a Mercedes sedan with darkened windows and gleaming paintwork. There was a driver behind the wheel. Milton could only just make him out through the smoked glass, but there he was; it looked like he was wearing a uniform, the cap of which he had taken off and rested against the dash. He had reclined the seat, and he was leaning back, taking a nap.

Milton followed Beau inside.

He looked around. It was a scruffy dive, dirty around the edges and showing its age, staffed by kids in mismatched uniforms trying to make beer money. There were two exits. One was the door they had just come through; the other was at the end of a long dark restroom corridor all the way in back. An air conditioner over the door was on its last legs, running so hard that it was trembling and rattling, but it wasn't making much difference to the humidity in the air. Seven bowling lanes had been fitted into what might once have been a large warehouse. It was a generous space, the roof sloping down towards the end of the lanes with dusty skylights at the other end. There was a bar at the back with ESPN playing on muted TVs, then some upholstered benches, then a cluster of freestanding tables, and then the lanes. There were computerised scoring machines suspended from the roof. All sorts of bottled beers behind the bar. The place was loud. Music from a glowing jukebox was pumped through large speakers, but that was drowned out by the sound of balls dropped onto wood, falling into the gully, smashing into the pins. The machinery rattled as it replaced the pins, and the balls rumbled as they rolled back to the players.

"What is this place?"

"What's it look like?"

"Looks like a bowling alley."

"There you go."

"The family owns it?"

"Sure they do. They own lots of things: pizza parlours, nail bars, couple of hotels."

"All useful if you've got money you need to wash."

"Your words, John," he said with a big smile that said it was all the way true.

Milton checked the clientele, counting people, scanning faces, watching body language. Kids, mostly, but there were a few others that caught his eye. At a table in a darkened corner away from the bar were two guys talking earnestly, their hands disappearing beneath the table, touching, then coming back up again. A dealer and his buyer. There were two guys further back in the room, sat around a table with a couple of bottles of beer. Big guys, gorillas in sharp suits. The first was a tall, wide man with collar-length hair and a black T-shirt under a black suit. The second was a little smaller, with a face that twitched as he watched the action on the nearest lane. They were a pair. Milton pegged them as bodyguards. Operators. Made men, most likely. He'd seen plenty of guys like that all around the world. They'd be decent, dangerous up to a point, but easy enough to take care of if you knew how to do it. There would be a point beyond which they were not willing to go. Milton had their advantage when it came to that; he didn't have a cut-off. The men were sitting apart from each other, but their twin gazes were now trained on the table in a private VIP area that was raised up on a small platform accessed by a flight of three steps and fenced off from the rest of the room.

A further pair of men were sitting there.

"Is that them?"

Beau nodded. "Remember—I'll do the introductions, and for God's sake, show them a little respect. You're not on home territory here, and I don't care how tough you think you are, they won't give two shits about that. Wait here. I'll go and speak to them."

Milton sat down at the bar. One of the televisions was tuned to CNN. They had a reporter out at Headlands Lookout, ghostly in the thick shroud of fog that alternated between absorbing and reflecting the lights for the camera. The man was explaining how the police had charted out a search area, breaking it down into eight four-foot sections of maps they kept in a mobile command centre. The item cut to footage of the search. The narrow road he had driven down four days ago was marked with bright orange arrows, pointing south to the two spots where remains had been found. Fluorescent orange flags were planted in the scrub and sand on each of the sites. Officers were weeding through the bramble, fanning outward from the flags.

Beau came back across. "All right," he said. "They'll see you. Remember, play nice."

"I always do."

Milton approached. One was older, wrinkled around the eyes and nose. He had a full head of hair, pure black, the colour obviously out of a packet. There was a beauty spot on his right cheek, and his right eyelid seemed to be a little lazy, hooding the eye more than the other. He was wearing a shirt with a couple of buttons undone, no tie, a jacket slung over the back of the chair. The second man was younger. He had a pronounced nose with flared nostrils, heavy eyebrows and beady eyes that never stayed still.

Beau sat down on one of the two empty seats.

Milton sat down, too.

"This is Mr. Smith," Beau said.

"How are you doing?" the older man said, nodding solemnly at him. "My name is Tommy Luciano."

He extended his hand across the table. Milton took it. His skin was soft, almost feminine, and his grip was loose. He could have crushed it.

"And my friend here is Carlo Lucchese."

Lucchese did not show the same hospitality. He glowered at him across the table, and Milton recognised him; he was the one who had been on the intercom to him, one of the four who had come to kill him.

He didn't let that faze him. "Thank you for seeing me."

"Beau said it was important. That wouldn't normally have been enough to interrupt my afternoon, but he told us that you were very helpful with a small problem we had in Juárez."

"That's good of him to say."

"And so that's why we're sitting here. Normally, with what you've done, you'd be dead."

Lucchese looked on venomously.

"Perhaps," Milton said.

"You had an argument with one of my men."

"I'm afraid I did."

"Want to tell me why?"

"I have some questions that I need to have answered. I asked him, and they seemed to make him uncomfortable. He threatened me with a gun. Not very civil. I wasn't prepared to stand for that."

"Self-defense on your part, then?"

"If you like."

Beau put a hand down on the table and intervened: "John's sorry, though—right, John?"

Milton didn't respond. He just kept his eye on the older man.

"He don't look sorry," Lucchese said.

"Carlo…"

"This douche broke Salvatore's face. Three ribs. Messed up his knee real good. And we're talking to him? I don't know, Tommy, I don't, but what the goddamn fuck?"

"Take it easy," the old man said, and Milton knew from the way that he said it that he was about to be judged. The next five minutes would determine what came after: he was either going to get the information he wanted, or he was going to get shot. "These questions—you wanna tell me what are they?"

He didn't take his eyes away from the older man. "There was a party in Pine Shore three months ago. September. I drove a girl up there."

"You drove her?"

"I'm a taxi driver."

Luciano laughed. "This gets better and better."

Milton held his eye. "Something happened at the party, and she freaked out. She ran, and she's never been seen since."

"Pine Shore?"

"That's right. Near where the two dead girls turned up."

"I know it. And you think this girl is dead?"

"I think it's possible."

"And what's any of it got to do with us?"

"Fallen Angelz. She was on the books."

He looked at him with an amused turn to his mouth. "Fallen Angelz? That supposed to mean anything to me?"

Milton didn't take his eyes away. "You really want to waste my time like that?"

Beau stiffened to Milton's right, but he said nothing. The younger man flexed a little. Milton stared hard at Luciano, unblinkingly hard. The old man held his glare steadily, unfazed, and then smiled. "You have a set of balls on you, my friend."

"Aw, come on, Tommy—you can't be serious. You said—"

"Go and do something else, Carlo. I don't need you around for this."

"Tommy—"

"It wasn't a suggestion. Go on—fuck off."

Lucchese left the table, but he didn't go far. He stopped at the bar and ordered a beer.

Milton didn't relax, not even a little. He was very aware of the two bodyguards at the table across the room.

"All right," Luciano said. "So suppose I said I do know about this business. What do you want?"

"A name—who booked the girls that night."

"Come on, Mr. Smith, you know I can't give you that. That business only works if it's anonymous. We got some serious players on the books. Well-known people who would shit bricks if they knew I was letting people know they took advantage of the services we offer. They need to trust our discretion. I start spilling their names, there are plenty of other places who'll take their money."

"You need to think bigger than that, Mr. Luciano. Telling me who booked her that night is the best chance you've got of keeping the business."

"That so? How you figure that?"

"One of your drivers told me that the girl was sent by the agency. You could say he's had a crisis of conscience about it. He knows he ought to be telling the police. So far, that hasn't been strong enough to trump the fact that he's terrified that talking is going to bring him into the frame. That's his worst-case scenario."

"No, Mr. Smith. His worst-case scenario is that I find out who he is."

"But you won't find out, not from me."

"So what's his worry?"

"If he goes to the cops? That he gets charged with procuring prostitution."

"So he's not saying anything."

"Not yet. But you know the way that guilt is. It has a way of eating at you. I'm betting that he's feeling worse and worse about what happened every single day, and the longer the police dig away without getting anywhere, the harder it's going to be for him to fight off going to them and telling them everything he knows. And if she turns up dead? I reckon he calls them right away. The first thing that's going to happen after that is that Salvatore gets a visit about the murders. The second thing is that he gets arrested and charged. The police need to be seen to be doing something. They'll go after the low-hanging fruit, and three dead prostitutes linked—rightly or wrongly—to an illegal agency like Fallen Angelz would be a perfect place to start. And, without wanting to cast aspersions, Salvatore didn't strike me as the kind of fellow with the character to stand up to the prospect of doing time when there's a plea bargain on the table. I don't need to go on, do I?"

"You sure Salvatore flips? Just like that?"

"Are you sure he won't?"

"You saying you can help me?"

"I've got a few days head start on the police. Maybe that's enough time for me to find out what happened. Maybe my girl isn't linked to the other two. Maybe something else has happened to her. And maybe, if I can find some answers, the driver decides he doesn't have to say anything."

"And if this girl is dead?"

"Provided it had nothing to do with you, maybe I can find a way that leaves you out. That agency's got to be valuable to you, right? It's got to be worth giving me the chance to sort things out. What have you got to lose?"

Luciano looked at him shrewdly. "I could speak to the driver myself. Find out what he knows."

"You don't know who he is."

"You do. You could tell me." He smiled thinly, suggestively.

"Forget it," Milton said, smiling back. "I'm not frightened of you."

"What did you do before you drove taxis, Mr. Smith?"

"I was a cook," he said.

"A cook?"

"He was working in a restaurant when I met him," Beau said.

"You think he's a cook, Beau?"

"No."

Luciano sucked his teeth.

Milton clenched his fists beneath the table.

"All right—let's say, just for the sake of discussion, that I give you what you want. Why are you so interested? What does it have to do with you?"

"The police have me down as a suspect, and it's not in my interest for my name to come out. The sooner I can clear this up, the better."

"Publicity is bad for you?"

"Very bad."

Luciano shook his head, a small smile playing on his lips. "You're a very interesting man, Mr. Smith. That's all I need for now. I'll speak to Beau. You can wait outside."

Milton made his way down from the raised area and across the wide room. As he passed the bar, he saw Carlo with another man. The newcomer held himself at an odd angle, his left arm clutched to his side as if he was in pain, and he had a huge, florid bruise on his cheek. There were purples and blues and greys in the bruise, and the centre was pure black and perfectly rounded, as if it had been caused by a forceful impact with something spherical. The nose was obscured by a splint. Salvatore glared at Milton as he crossed in front of him, his eyes dripping with hate. Milton nodded once, a gesture he knew he probably shouldn't have made but one that he just couldn't resist. The injured man lost it, aggrieved at the beating that he had taken, aggrieved at seeing Milton walk out of the bowling alley with impunity, not a scratch on him, and he came in at an awkward charge, moving painfully and with difficulty, his right fist raised. Milton feinted one way and moved another. The Italian stumbled past, Milton tapped his ankles, and Salvatore tripped and fell. He grimaced as he pushed himself to his feet again, but by then Milton had backed off and turned around and was ready for the second go-around. Salvatore came at him again, his fist raised, lumbering like a wounded elephant. Milton ducked to one side and threw a crisp punch that landed square on his nose, crunching the bones again. Salvatore's legs went, and he ate carpet. He stayed down this time, huffing hard.

Milton raised his hands helplessly and looked over at the VIP area, wondering whether things were going to get heated. Beau looked anxious, but neither Tommy Luciano or Carlo Lucchese did anything. Milton turned to look at Luciano, then to Lucchese, then to Salvatore; then he pushed out of the door and went outside to wait for Beau in the cold, bright afternoon sun.

Chapter Twenty-Nine

MILTON HAD GONE to a meeting that evening. It wasn't his usual, and Eva wasn't there. He had gone out for dinner afterwards with a couple of the guys, and by the time he returned to his flat, it was midnight. He was reasonably confident that there would be no more issues with the Lucianos—at least for the moment—but he couldn't completely rule out that Lucchese might ignore his boss and come at him again, so he had driven around the block twice before going inside. He saw nothing to make him anxious, and there was nothing in the blindingly bright lobby to suggest that his visitors had returned or that they intended to. He climbed to the third floor. He knew exactly where the light switch was, and it was with a single blur of motion that he opened the door, flicked it on, and stood in the threshold with the door open wide, scanning the room with practised eyes. Everything looked as if it was in order.

He stepped forward and locked himself inside, bending down to examine one of his own black hairs, which still lay undisturbed where he had left it before going out, placed carefully across the drawer of the coffee table. He had left a faint trace of talcum powder on the handle of the bedroom door and that, too, had not been disturbed. These were, he knew, extravagant measures to confirm his safety, but ten years in a business as dangerous as his had hardwired him with caution. Paying heed to that creed, and to his instincts, was the reason he was still alive. The precise application of a routine like this had saved his life on several occasions. The Mafia was a blunt instrument compared to the secret services of the countries that he had infiltrated—a cudgel as to a scalpel—but that was no reason to treat them with any less respect. A cudgel was still deadly.

He propped a chair beneath the door handle, locked the window that faced the fire escape, and slept with his fingers wrapped around the butt of the Smith & Wesson 9mm that he kept under the pillow.

HE ROSE EARLY the next morning. There was a lot to do. First, though, he dressed in his running gear, pulled his battered running shoes onto his feet, and went downstairs. It was a crisp, bright December day, the sun's cold rays piercing the mist that rose off the bay. Milton ran south on Mason Street, turned onto Montgomery Street, and ran until he reached the Embarcadero, the piers, the bridge to Oakland and, beyond it, the greenish-blue of the ocean. He ran north, following the road as it curved to the west, listening to the rhythmic cadence of his feet and clearing his mind. This had always been his preferred way to think. It was his meditation before he found the sanctuary of the rooms, a peaceful retreat where he had the time and the luxury to let his thoughts develop at their own speed, without even being conscious of them.

He ran onto Jefferson, turned left inside Aquatic Park, and then followed Hyde to Broadway and then, finally, Mason Street and home.

He passed through the lobby and took the stairs at a jog.

There were two men waiting outside the door to his room.

He recognised them both.

"Inspector Cotton. Detective Webster."

"Mr. Smith."

"How can I help you?"

"We're going to need to talk to you."

"Again? Really?"

"A few more questions."

"I answered them before. Is there anything else?"

"I'm afraid there is. We found another body this morning."

PART THREE

The Suspect

#3 MILEY VAN DYKEN

MILEY VAN DYKEN had been having second thoughts about how she had chosen to live her life. She'd told friends about them, how she was thinking about getting out. She knew that turning tricks could be a dangerous business, but it seemed to her that there had been more stories of psychos preying on working girls recently. There had been all those poor girls down on the beach in New Jersey, for one, and the police still had no idea who was responsible for their deaths. There were plenty of benefits that came from doing what she did—the money, obviously, but the freedom of working to your own schedule was another that other girls often overlooked—but it had been getting to the stage that her doubts and fears were starting to get so bad that she couldn't ignore them. She had nightmares and premonitions about running into a murderous john, and she had suffered with a really bad one the night before. She had recorded it on her Facebook page, telling her friends in vague terms (since not many of them knew what she did) that she was having serial-killer dreams that were more and more vivid each time they came around.

The john had hired a room in The Tuscan on North Point Street in North Beach, five minutes from Pier 39. Miley usually preferred to sort the room herself, charging a little extra as expenses so that she still cleared her two hundred per hour, but the guy had apologised that he couldn't very easily leave the hotel and, when he had sensed her reluctance, had offered to pay a further fifty bucks on top to "make up for her inconvenience." He sounded nice enough, kind, speaking with a lilting Southern accent that put her in mind of that guy Kevin Spacey played in the Netflix thing, and even though she had initially turned him down and hung up, she stewed on it for fifteen minutes and changed her mind. She didn't have another job booked, he had been polite on the phone, and most importantly, she needed the money.

Craigslist had started charging $5 per advert, and that had made it difficult to stay at the top of the list. Miley had used a JavaScript program that kept posting and reposting her ad so it was always on the first page, but the new charges meant that that wasn't an option any more. The cost of advertising was higher, and the competition was tougher. She worried about all of that as she rode the bus. The driver smiled at her as she disembarked outside the hotel.

He was the last person to see her alive.

It was a small hotel that catered to travelling business people. It was a two-storey building surrounded by a parking lot. It didn't appear to be very busy; the lot was almost empty, save for a couple of rentals and a beaten-up

Cadillac Eldorado. She went around the car on the way to the lobby when the driver's side door opened and a man got out. He was tall and skinny, dressed in a white T-shirt, jeans and a pair of cowboy boots. He said her name. She recognised his voice.

Chapter Thirty

COTTON AND WEBSTER didn't sit, so neither did Milton. Webster wandered absently to the window and looked down onto the street below. Cotton took a book from the shelf—it was *The Unbearable Lightness of Being*—made a desultory show of flicking through the pages and then put it back again. He looked around, his face marked by a lazy sneer.

"Nice place you got here," he said.

"It suits me very well."

"I don't know, Mr. Smith. We get called out to places like this all the time. Don't you find it a bit tawdry?"

"You didn't come here to critique my accommodation."

"No."

"And I have things to do. What do you want? If you've got questions, ask them."

The cop took out his phone and selected a picture. He slid it across the table. Milton looked at it; it was a picture of a woman, white, slender with a short-cropped elfin hairstyle. Very pretty. "Recognise her?"

Milton looked at the picture. "No."

"You sure about that? Scroll right for the next one."

Milton did as he was told. It was the same girl, this time in some sort of prom dress. She looked young. "No," he said. "I've never seen her before. Who is she?"

"Her name is Miley Van Dyken."

"I don't know her, detective."

"Where were you three weeks ago last Wednesday?"

"I'd have to check."

"Like I say, it's a Wednesday. Think."

Milton sighed exasperatedly. "I would've gone to work in the afternoon and driven my car at night."

"We can check the afternoon. What about the night—can anyone prove you were driving?"

"If my calls were from the agency, then maybe. If they came straight through to me, then no, probably not." He slid the phone back across the table to him. "Who is she? Number three?"

"That's right, Mr. Smith. We found her this morning. Same place as the other two."

"There's only so many times I can say it—I've got nothing to do with this."

"Can I ask you something else?"

"Please do."

"You own any firearms?'"

Milton felt his skin prickle. "No."

"So if we looked around, we wouldn't find anything?"

"Help yourself. I don't have anything to hide."

"Reason I'm asking, that guard at the party you put on the ground, he said you took his gun from him. Smith & Wesson. The Pro Series, 9mm— very nice gun. Then, yesterday, we found a couple of shell casings outside the gate for Pine Shore. Looks like the electricity was shot out. You wouldn't know anything about that, would you?"

Milton concentrated on projecting a calm exterior. He had left the gun under the bed. It wasn't even well hidden, all they would need to do would be to duck down and look. "No," he said. "I don't know anything about it. I don't own a gun. To be honest, I doubt I'd even know what to do with one."

"All right, then."

"Is that it?"

"No," Webster said from the window. "There is one more thing you can help us with."

"Please."

"When we spoke to you before, you said you came across the border from Mexico. Six months ago. July. That's right, isn't it?"

"Yes."

"Where did you cross?"

Milton started to feel uncomfortable. "Juárez into El Paso."

"That's weird," Webster said. "You know, there are forty-six places where you can legally cross over from Mexico. We spoke with Immigration. We checked El Paso, Otay Mesa, Tecate, Nogales. Hell, we even tried Lukeville and Antelope Wells. We found a handful of John Smiths who came across the border around about then. That's no surprise, really, a common name like that—but the thing is, the thing I just can't get my head around, is that when we looked at their pictures, none of them looked anything like you."

That, Milton thought, was hardly surprising. He had crossed the border illegally, trekking across country east of Juárez into the Chisos Mountains and then Big Bear National Park. The last thing he had wanted to do was leave a record that would show where he had entered the country. He had not been minded to give the agents pursuing him any clue at all as to his location.

"Mr. Smith?" Webster and Cotton were eyeing him critically.

Milton shrugged. "What do you want me to say to that?"

"Can you explain it?"

"I was working in Juárez. I crossed into El Paso. I can't explain why there's no record of it."

"Do you mind if we take your passport for a couple of days?"

"Why?"

"We'd just like to have a look at it."

Milton went over to the bedside table and took his passport from the drawer. He could see the dull glint of the brushed steel on the handgun, an inch from his toe. He handed the passport to Webster. "There you are," he said. "I've got nothing to hide."

"Thank you."

"Anything else?"

"Nah," Cotton said. "We got nothing more for you now."

"But don't leave town without telling us," Webster advised. "I'm pretty sure we'll want to talk to you again."

Chapter Thirty-One

MILTON HAD a lock-up at Extra Space Storage at 1400 Folsom Street. He had hired it within a couple of days of arriving in San Francisco and deciding that it was the kind of town he could stay in for a few months. The lock-up was an anonymous place, a collection of industrial cargo crates that had been arranged in several rows. Each crate had been divided into two or four separate compartments, and each was secured with a thick metal door padlocked top and bottom.

It cost Milton twenty bucks a week, and it was easily worth that for the peace of mind that it bought. He knew, eventually, that Control would locate him again and send his agents to hunt him down. He didn't know how he would react to that when it happened—he had been ready to surrender in Mexico—but he wanted the ability to resist them if that was what he chose to do. More to the point, he knew that his assassination of El Patrón and the capture of his son would not be forgotten by La Frontera. There would be a successor to the old man's crown, a brother or another son, and then there would be vengeance. They would have put an enormous price on his head. If they managed to find him, he certainly did not want to be unprepared.

Milton took out his key and unfastened the locks. He checked again that he was alone in the facility and, satisfied that he was, opened the door. He had stocked the storage crate with everything he would need in an emergency. There was a change of clothes, a cap, a packet of hair dye and a pair of clear-lensed spectacles. There was a go-bag with three false passports and the money he had found at El Patrón's superlab before he had torched it. Five thousand dollars, various denominations, all used notes.

At the back of the crate, hidden beneath a blanket, was a Desert Eagle .50 Action Express with a picatinny rail. It had been El Patrón's weapon, and like everything else in his comic-book life, it had been tricked out to clichéd excess. The gun was gold-plated with diamonds set into the butt. Milton had no idea how much it was worth—thousands, obviously—but he didn't really care about that. The semi-automatic was one of Milton's favourite weapons. It was gas-operated with a firing mechanism usually found in rifles as opposed to the more common short recoil or blowback designs. The mechanism allowed for far more powerful cartridges, and he had purchased a box of Speer 325-grain .50 AE ammunition for it the day after he arrived in town. He tore back the cardboard and tipped the bullets onto the floor of the unit; they glittered in the light of the single naked bulb that had been fitted to the roof of the crate. Lethal little golden slugs.

Milton detached the magazine and thumbed seven into the slot.

He slid the Desert Eagle into his jeans, his belt pressing it against his skin. The golden barrel was icy cold, the frame flat against his coccyx. He filled his pockets with the rest of the bullets. He dropped the Smith & Wesson 9mm into the go-bag and slung it over his shoulder.

He shut and locked the crate.

He wouldn't be coming back again.

Things were already too hot for him in San Francisco. He hadn't been named in any of the newspaper reports that he had read about the missing girls, but that was probably just a matter of time. It was a little irrelevant, too; his name would have been recorded by the police, and Control would sniff that out soon enough. They could be here tomorrow or next week; there was no way of knowing when, except that they were coming. Under normal circumstances, he would have moved on already, but he didn't feel able to leave until he had tried a little harder to find Madison. Trip would have no chance without him, and besides, he had a lead now. He would find out what he could and then disappear beneath the surface again.

The Explorer was parked close to the entrance of the facility.

He nodded to the attendant and made his way out to his car.

A SHORT DETOUR FIRST. Manny Martinez ran his operation out of a grocery shop in the Mission District, not far from Milton's place. Milton had called ahead to make an appointment, and when he arrived, he was ushered all the way to the back of the store. There was a small office with a desk and a computer. A clock on the wall. Martinez was a big man, wearing an old pair of cargo pants and a muscle top that showed off impressively muscled biceps and sleeves of tattoos on both arms. His head was shaved to a furze of rough hair, and he had a tattoo of a tear beneath his right eye. Prison ink. Milton checked the office; his eye fell on the cudgel with a leather strap that was hanging from a hook on the wall.

"You Smith?"

"That's right. Thank you for seeing me."

"How much you want?"

"I don't want anything."

"You said—"

"Yes, I know—and I'm sorry about that. It's something else."

He sat up, flexing his big shoulders. "That right?"

"One of your customers—Richie Grimes?"

"Yeah," he said. "I know Richie. Fucking reprobate. Drunk."

"How much does he owe you?"

"What's it got to do with you?"

"I'd like to buy his debt."

"Just like that?"

"Just like that."

"What if I don't wanna sell?"

"Let me make you an offer—if you don't want to sell after that, that's fair enough."

Martinez swivelled the chair so that he was facing the computer and clicked through a series of files until he found the one he wanted. "He's in the hole for fifty-eight hundred. He wanted four, and the vig was ten per cent."

"How'd you get to fifty-eight from there?"

"Compound interest, buddy. Interest on top of interest."

"Hardly ethical."

"Ethical? These are the streets, buddy. Ethics don't get much play here."

"I'll give you five."

Ramirez shook his head. "No."

"Debt's only worth what someone'll pay for it."

"What are you? An economist?"

"Five. That's a grand clear profit."

"I can get seven."

"Not from him."

"Don't have to be from him, does it?"

The second hand on the clock swept around the dial. Milton opened his bag and reached for the stolen drug money inside. He would put it to good use. He took out the five bundles, each secured by an elastic band around twenty fifties, and put them on the desk.

"Five thousand. Come on, Mr. Martinez—it's right there."

Martinez looked up at him with an amused cast to his face. "I said no."

"What's the point in dragging this out? He's got nothing."

"He told you that? Guy's an addict, like I said. You can't believe a thing they say."

"I believe him," Milton said. "He can't pay."

"Then he's got a problem."

"Is that your final word?"

"That's right."

Milton nodded. He picked up the money and put it back into his bag.

"Come back with seven, maybe we can talk."

Milton looked at him, then the cudgel. He was a big man, but he was lounging back in his chair. He was relaxed. He didn't see Milton as a threat, but Milton could have killed him, right there and then. He could have done it before the second hand on the clock had skirted another semicircle between the nine and twelve. Fifteen seconds. He thought about it for a moment, but that wouldn't solve Richie's problem. The debts would be taken over by someone else, and that person might be worse. There would have to be another way.

"See you around," Martinez said. A gold tooth in his mouth glittered as he grinned at him.

"You will," Milton said.

MILTON CALLED Beau Baxter as he drove to the airport.

"Morning, English. What can I do for you?"

"Did you get a name for me?"

"I did. You got a pen and paper?"

"Go on."

"You want to speak to Jarad Efron. You know who that is?"

"I've heard it before."

"Not surprising. He's a big noise on the tech scene."

"Thanks. I'll find him."

"Goes without saying that you need to leave the Italians out of this."

"Of course. Thanks, Beau. I appreciate it."

"Anything else?"

"There is, actually. One other thing."

"Shoot."

"Do our friends have an interest in the lending business?"

"They have interests in lots of things."

"So I'll assume that they do. There's a loan shark in the Mission District. A friend of mine owes him money. I just made him a very generous offer to buy the debt."

"And he turned you down?"

"Thinks he can get more."

"And how could our friends help?"

"I get the impression that this guy's out there all on his own. A lone operator. I wondered, if that's something they're involved in, whether the competition is something they'd be happy about. You think you could look into it for me?"

"What's this dude's name?"

"Manny Martinez."

"Never heard of him. I can ask around, see what gives. I'll let you know."

Milton thanked him and said goodbye, ended the call, and parked the Explorer. He took his go-bag and went into the terminal building. He found the Hertz desk and hired a Dodge Charger, using one of the false passports and paying the three hundred bucks in cash. He drove it into the long-stay car park, put the go-bag in the trunk, locked it, and then found his way back to the Explorer.

He felt better for the preparation. If he needed to get out of town on short notice, he could.

He put the car into gear and drove away.

There was someone he wanted to see.

Chapter Thirty-Two

THE MAN WAS in his early forties, in decent shape, just a little under six foot tall and with the kind of naturally lean frame that has gone a little soft with the onset of middle age. He had dark hair with flecks of grey throughout it, and the expensive glasses he wore were borne a little uncomfortably. His clothes were neat and tidy—a crisp polo shirt, chinos and deck shoes—the whole ensemble marking him out as a little vain. Milton had parked in the lot for thirty minutes, the angle good enough for him to see the place side on, and to see all the comings and goings. It was more like a campus than an office. It looked like a busy place. The lot was full, and there had been a steady stream of people going in to start their working day. He had been waiting for one man in particular, and now, here he was. Milton eyed him as he opened the passenger door of his red Ferrari Enzo and took out a rucksack.

Milton looked at the scrap of paper that he had stuck to the windshield of the Explorer.

It was a picture.

The man in the Ferrari and the man in the picture were the same.

Jarad Efron.

Milton got out of his car, locked the door, and followed the man as he exited the parking lot and started towards the office. The campus was out in the hills outside Palo Alto, surrounded by a lush forest bisected by streams, hiking paths and mountain bike trails. The wildness of the landscape had been transplanted here, too, with grasses and wildflowers allowed to grow naturally. Purple heather clustered around the paths, and coneflowers, evening primroses and asters sprouted from natural rock gardens. Milton quickened his pace so that he caught up with Efron and then overtook him. He gave him a quick sidelong glance: he had white iPhone earbuds pressed into his ears, something upbeat playing; his skin was tanned; his forehead was suspiciously plump and firm; and there was good muscle tone on his arms. He was gym fit.

Milton slowed a little and followed into the lobby just behind him.

After he had spoken with Beau yesterday morning, he had spent the afternoon doing research. Three hours at the local library. They had free internet and cheap coffee there, and he had had plenty of things that he wanted to check.

Jarad Efron was familiar to him from the news, and a quick Google search filled in the details: the man was CEO of StrongBox, one of the survivors of the first dotcom bubble that had since staked a claim in the cloud storage market. He was a pioneer. The company owned a couple of massive data farms in South Carolina, acres of deserted farmland rammed full of servers that they rented out to consumers and, increasingly, to big tech companies who didn't want to build facilities of their own. They offered space to Netflix and Amazon, among others. The company was listed on the NASDAQ with a price of $54 per share. Another search revealed that Efron had recently divested himself of five per cent of the company, pocketing thirty million bucks. He still owned another 2,000,000 shares.

A paper fortune of $108,000,000.

Efron was born and raised in Serbia, buying his first computer at the age of ten. He taught himself how to program, and when he was twelve, he sold his first piece of software, a game he created called Battlestation Alpha. At the age of seventeen, he moved to Canada to attend Queen's College, but he left to study business and physics at the University of Pennsylvania. He graduated with an undergraduate degree in economics and stayed for a second bachelor's degree in physics. After leaving Penn, he moved to Stanford to pursue a PhD in energy physics. The move was perfectly timed with the first Internet boom, and he dropped out after just two days to become a part of it, launching his first company. He sold that for $100 million and set up StrongBox with the proceeds.

Milton looked around quickly, taking everything in. The lobby was furnished sparsely, minimally, but every piece of furniture—the leather sofas, the coffee table—looked exceedingly expensive. Two security guards wore light blue uniforms and well-shined shoes, big boys with a stiff posture. They both had holstered .45s hanging from their belts. The staff behind the reception desk looked like models from a high-end catalogue, with glossy, airbrushed skin and preternaturally bright eyes. Milton knew he only had one opportunity at this, and straightening his back and squaring off his shoulders, he followed right alongside Efron as the man beamed a bright smile of greeting to the girls and headed for the elevators. One of the girls looked past him at Milton, a moment of confusion breaking across her immaculate face, but Milton anticipated it and shone out a smile that matched Efron's for brightness and confidence. Her concern faded, and even if it was with a little uncertainty, she smiled right back at him.

Milton dropped back again and let Efron summon an elevator. There were six doors; one of the middle ones opened with a pleasant chime, and he went inside.

Milton stepped forwards sharply and entered the car as the doors were starting to close.

"Which floor?" Efron asked him absently.

Milton looked: ten floors, and Efron had hit the button for the tenth.

"Five, please."

Efron pressed the button and stood back against the wall, leaving plenty of space between them.

The doors closed quietly, and the elevator began to ascend.

Milton waited until they were between the second and third floors and hit the emergency stop.

The elevator shuddered and came to a halt.

"What are you doing?" Efron protested.

"I've got a few questions. Answer them honestly."

"Who are you?"

Efron's arm came up and made a sudden stab towards the button for the intercom. Milton anticipated it, blocked his hand away with his right, and then, in the same circular motion, jackhammered his elbow backwards into Efron's gut. It was a direct hit, just at the right spot to punch out all the air in his lungs, and he staggered back against the wall of the car with his hands clasped impotently to his sternum, gasping for breath. Milton grabbed the lapels of his jacket, knotted his fists into the fabric, and heaved him backwards and up, slamming him into the wall so that his feet were momentarily off the ground. Then he dropped him.

"Hello?" said a voice through the intercom speakers.

Efron landed on his behind, gasping. Milton lowered himself to the same height, barred his forearm across the man's throat and pressed, gently.

"It's in your best interests to talk to me."

"They'll call… the police."

"Probably better for you if they didn't. The police are going to want to talk to you soon anyway, but you'll do better with a little time to prepare. If they show up now, they'll ask me what I was doing here. And I'm going to tell them all about the party you had in Pine Shore."

"What party?"

"I was there, Mr. Efron. I drove Madison Clarke. You remember—the missing girl? I went inside. I saw it all. The people. I recognised some of them. The drugs. I have an eye for detail, Mr. Efron, and I have a very good memory. You want the police to know that? The press? I know a man like you, in your position, you definitely don't want this in the papers. Bad publicity. It'd be a scandal, wouldn't it? So we can speak to them if you want—go right ahead. I'll wait."

Milton could see him working out the angles, a frown settling over his handsome face.

"Fuck," he cursed angrily, but it was from frustration backed by resignation; there was no fight there.

"Better sort that out." Milton indicated the intercom. "You hit the button by mistake. Tell them it's all right."

He stood aside.

Efron's breath was still a little ragged. He pushed the button to speak. "It's Jarad," he said. "I pressed the wrong button. Sorry. Can you reset it, please?"

"Yes, sir," the girl said.

The elevator started to rise again.

It reached the fifth floor. The doors opened, no one got on, the doors closed, and the car continued upwards.

"Is your office on the tenth?"

"Yes."

"We'll go inside and shut the door. Don't do anything stupid, and I'll be gone in five minutes."

They reached the tenth floor, and the doors opened again. Efron stepped out first, and Milton followed. The floor must have been reserved for StrongBox's executive team. Milton looked around. The big lobby was bright, daylight streaming in through huge floor-to-ceiling windows. One of the windows was open, leading out to a terrace area. The room was airy and fresh, very clean, the furniture and décor obviously chosen with great care and a generous budget. Efron led the way to an office with a wide picture window that framed the gorgeous landscape beyond: the deep green of the vegetation, the brown flanks of the distant mountains, infinite blue sky, crisp white clouds. There was a leather sofa, and Milton indicated that Efron should sit. He did as he was told. Milton shut the office door and sat on the edge of the desk.

"Don't get too comfortable," Efron said. "You're not staying."

"You better hope so. Tell me what I want to know, and I'll be on my way."

"What's your name?"

"You can call me Smith."

"So what do you want, Mr. Smith?"

"Just to find the girl."

"What girl?"

"The girl who went missing after the party."

"I really have no idea what you're talking about."

"Playing dumb is just going to mean this takes longer, Mr. Efron. And I'm not the most patient man in the world."

"What's her name?"

"Madison Clarke."

His shrug didn't quite mask a flicker of disquiet. "I don't know anyone by that name."

"But you own a house in Pine Shore."

"No, I don't. The company owns it. We're expanding. Hiring a lot of new talent. Time to time, we have new executives stay there while they're looking for places of their own. It's not mine."

"There was a party there."

"Okay. So there was a party there. Your point?"

"Madison is a prostitute. She was hired to be there."

"You're fucking crazy. We're gearing up for an IPO. Do you know how stupid it'd be to invite a hooker onto company property?"

"You weren't there?"

"I was in Boston."

"That's strange."

"Come on, man. Enough with this shit!"

"No, it's strange, Mr. Efron, because you hired her."

"What?"

Milton saw him swallow.

"I didn't!"

"You've never used Fallen Angelz?"

"No."

"Yes, you have. You paid, in advance, with a credit card registered to your company."

He was starting to panic. "Someone used a StrongBox credit card?" he gasped. "So? Maybe they did. Lots of people have a company card."

"Including you?"

"Of course. I'm the CEO. But it wasn't me."

"I thought you might say that, Mr. Efron, so I did a little extra checking. The things you find out when you speak to the right people, know what I mean? Here's what I know: I know it's not the first time you've used that agency. I know you're a valued customer. One of the regulars. I know the girls speak highly of you. A good payer, they said. A nice guy."

He swallowed again, harder.

It was a bluff. Milton looked at Efron, setting aside the bland mask and letting him see him as he really was: a seasoned, iron-willed operative. "Now," he said. "Bearing that all in mind, you want to reconsider?"

"Okay."

"Okay what?"

"Okay, yes. I hired her. All right?"

"Better. Keep going. And you were there."

"Yes."

"You saw her."

"Only briefly. I was hosting."

"What happened to make her so upset?"

"I didn't know she was—not until afterwards."

"You know she hasn't been seen since the party?"

"Yes—but only because the police said."

"Have they spoken to you?"

"Not to me, but to a couple of guys who work for me. We said it was their party, and that's how it needs to stay. The IPO is everything, man. I got three hundred people working here. Their jobs depend on getting it right. I get involved in a scandal now, we'll have to pull it."

"I don't care about that, Mr. Efron. I just want to find out what happened to Madison."

"And I told you I don't know."

"Someone who was there does know."

"Maybe it was nothing to do with the party at all."

"Give me a list of the people who were there."

"You're kidding?" He shook his head. "No way."

"Last chance. Don't make me ask you again."

"I can't do that."

Milton got up and walked straight at Efron. The man scrabbled backwards, into the chair, and held up his hands to ward him away. Milton swatted them aside, hauled him out of the chair, and dragged him across the room to the terrace. He struggled, guessing what Milton had in mind, but his right arm was jacked up behind his back with the fingers splayed, almost pointing all the way up. The more he tried to free himself, the harder Milton pushed his palm, flattening it, each added ounce of pressure closer to breaking Efron's wrist and fingers.

"Last chance."

"I can't tell you."

"Your choice."

Milton shoved him up against the wooden balustrades, the rail at waist height, then forced him over it until his feet were raised off the floor. He fixed his right hand in the waistband of his trousers, locking his bicep to bear the weight, and used his left to press him down. Efron's head went almost vertical, looking straight into the ten-story drop.

Milton kept his voice calm. "Who was there?"

"Jesus!"

"Who was there, Jarad?"

"Shit, man, please! I'll tell you, I'll fucking tell you!"

MILTON TOOK THE ELEVATOR back down to the ground floor. He had a sheet of A4 paper that Efron had printed for him; he halved it, then quartered it, and slipped it into his inside pocket. He waited patiently as the car descended, the floors ticking off with the same pleasant chime as before. He reached the ground floor, and the doors parted. He wasn't particularly surprised to see the two security guards waiting for him.

"It's all right, boys," he said. "No need for any trouble. Your boss is fine, and I'm leaving."

They each had their hands resting on the butts of their identical Colt .45s.

"Don't move," the nearest one ordered. He was a big boy—bigger than Milton—and stood with the kind of lazy confidence that a guy gets from being young, a little stupid, six-three and two-ten. The other one had a similar stance: quarterback type, jock, used to getting whatever he wanted. That age, Milton thought, they'd probably tried out for the police but been shitcanned because they weren't bright enough. They didn't fancy shipping out to the desert in the army, so private security was their best chance to wear a uniform—they probably thought they looked cute doing it—and wield a little authority.

"You sure you want to do this?"

"Turn around."

Milton shrugged, made it look like he was resigned to doing as they asked, but as he turned he flung out his right hand in a streaked blur of motion, his fingers held straight with his thumb supporting them beneath. The jab caught the first guard above the larynx, hard and sharp enough to dent his windpipe; he fell backwards, his mouth open in a wide O of surprise, his hands flapping impotently, gasping for breath that wasn't getting into his lungs as easily as it had done before. The second man went for his holstered .45. Milton hit him high on the cheekbone with his right fist, rocking him back, fired in a left jab, then shoved the guy in the chest to bounce him off the wall, and as he came back toward him, he delivered a head butt straight to his nose. He caught the man's wrist in his hand, yanked his arm around, and pivoted so that all of his weight propelled him back into the elevator. He bounced face-first off the wall of the elevator car and landed on his knees. Milton caught the second man by the belt and collar and boosted him into the elevator after him, reaching around the corner and slapping the button for the tenth floor.

"Tell your boss if he does anything stupid like that again, I'll be back."

He stepped back as the doors closed and the car began to ascend.

Then he turned. The two receptionists and the handful of staff in the lobby were all gawping helplessly at him. He pulled at his jacket to straighten it out, squared his shoulders again, wished them all a good morning, and then walked calmly and purposefully into the parking lot to his car.

Chapter Thirty-Three

ARLEN CRAWFORD SAT AT THE DESK in the hotel room with policy papers scattered around him. There was a stack on the desk, three distinct piles on the carpet by his feet, and a pile—ready to be read, digested and sorted—spread out across the bed. The speech at the Moscone Center that afternoon was starting to look a whole lot like a coronation, and he wanted to make sure that everything about it was perfect. He had CNN on the flat-screen TV that had been fixed to the wall inside a frame to make it look like a painting—it didn't work—and he was drinking from a glass of orange juice, staining a paper on fiscal prudence with wet, concentric circles.

He looked up at the TV. The newscaster was introducing a panel discussion on the San Francisco killings. A third girl had been found, and they were describing the perpetrator as a serial killer. The producers had a stable of pundits for the big crime stories—medical examiners, criminologists, forensic scientists, former prosecutors—and the serial-killer category had its own roster of subspecialists. Three had been deputed to discuss the case. They opined upon what could be discerned from bones that had been left outside and exposed to weather. They considered what the location of the bodies might say about the killer's signature. They made comparisons with the Green River Killer, explaining how Gary Ridgway had acquired his nickname after burying his victims near the river of the same name in Washington. They discussed methodology and how Denis Rader had been dubbed B.T.K. after his *modus operandi* of binding, torturing and killing had been made public. Then they focused on how the most pertinent recent historical analogue, the Zodiac Killer, had never been caught. One enterprising expert even swung for the fences by suggesting that this new killer might even *be* Zodiac. That hypothesis was quickly rubbished—if he was still alive, Zodiac would have been at least seventy by now—but the discussion was feverish and excited, and that, Crawford knew, could only be good for ratings. The discussion moved onto what the newcomer should be called.

The consensus seemed to settle on the Headlands Lookout Killer.

He was roused from his distraction by a soft knocking at the door.

Crawford got up, took a sip of the OJ, and padded across the room in his stockinged feet. It was just after breakfast, and he wasn't expecting anyone.

He opened the door. Karly Hammil, the young female staffer who had been with Robinson after the speech in Woodside, was on the other side.

"What is it, Karly?"

She was anxiously chewing her bottom lip. "Could I have a word?"

"Yes, of course. Come in."

He stood back, and she came into the room, closing the door behind her. "What is it?"

"This is difficult, Mr. Crawford."

"Call me Arlen." He felt a moment of apprehension. He pointed to the opened minibar. "You want anything? Water?"

"No, I'm fine."

"Want to sit?"

"I'd rather stand if that's all right."

"Well, I'm going to sit."

She stammered. "I-I—"

She was nervous, and that made him nervous, too.

"You better tell me what it is."

She drew a breath. "There's no point sugar-coating this, I guess. All right, then. Okay." Another breath. "Okay. I guess you know some of this already. Five weeks ago, the governor made a sexual advance to me. I know he has a reputation, everyone knows that, but I couldn't believe it. And I resisted it at first, I told him to forget about it, it was a crazy idea, but then he tried again the day after that. I told him no again, but he was more persistent. You know what he can be like, so persuasive, that feeling you get when he fixes his attention on you, like you're the most important person in the world. Well, that's what he made me feel like, and he persuaded me that he really meant all those things he was telling me."

Crawford felt himself deflate, the air running from his lungs.

"We've been sleeping together once or twice a week ever since."

"You have been—this is past tense?"

"He's stopped it. I saw him last night after the speech. He said he couldn't do it anymore. Something about his wife. It's bullshit, obviously. I guess he's just had what he wanted. He doesn't need me anymore. He's probably already onto the next one."

Crawford tried to marshal himself. He needed to deal with this. He needed to be diplomatic. He needed her to think that he was sympathetic and understanding. He had experience with this kind of motherfucking nonsense—plenty of experience—and he knew what he needed to do. "I'm sure it isn't like that, Karly. You know what he's like."

"He's unsafe for a woman to work around is what he is," she said angrily.

"Why are you telling me? What do you want me to do?"

She looked at him as if he was stupid. "Seriously?"

"Tell me."

"You need to look after me."

"Of course you'll be looked after. I'll make sure you get an apology. And it'll never happen again."

"Not like *that*."

"Then like what?"

"Come on, Mr. Crawford. You want me to spell it out?"

"Money?"

"Maybe I should sit tight, wait until he's better known. A story like this, what kind of book deal you reckon I'd get if I waited until later? His inauguration, maybe? The day before the election?"

Crawford felt the familiar, cold knot of anger tightening in his gut. "All right, I get it. I get it. How much do you want?"

"I don't know."

"You have to give me a number."

"Okay. Fifty thousand—that's what I would've earned this year."

"Fifty." He felt his temperature rising.

She hesitated uncertainly. "What do we do now?"

"First time you've shaken somebody down?" he spat sarcastically.

Her eyes flashed. "You're angry with me? Maybe you ought to think a little about him, Mr. Crawford."

He tried to defuse the tension. "Arlen—call me Arlen, please."

She ignored the attempt at conciliation. "You don't know how close I was to putting this out there. A man like him, a weak man, how is that good for our country to have him in high office?"

He forced himself to take a breath, to regain a little composure. "No, you're right. Quite right. I'm sorry, Karly. It'll take me a little while to sort this out. It's not quite as straightforward as you think, that much money. It needs to be done quietly. Is that all right?"

"Of course."

She exhaled.

He had a moment of empathy; it had probably been one of the most difficult conversations she had ever had. She didn't deserve his anger. It wasn't her fault. Robinson, on the other hand, did deserve it. His behaviour kept putting him in intolerable situations. He was irresponsible and childish, ignoring his clear instructions that he had to put this behind him and keep it zipped. Cleaning up the mess that he left in his wake was becoming a full-time job. An expensive full-time job.

Crawford told the girl that she just had to be patient, that he would sort it all out for her, and then he showed her to the door of his room. He switched channels on the television, lay back on his bed, and stared at the ball game that was playing on repeat for five minutes, not paying any attention to it, running the situation around in his head and wondering if there was any other way it could be resolved.

He decided that there was not.

He picked up his cellphone from the bedside table and called the usual number.

Chapter Thirty-Four

MILTON WAS HEADED to the Moscone Center when his cellphone buzzed in its cradle. He glanced at the display; Trip Macklemore was calling. He pulled out of the traffic, parked, and called him back.

"Have you heard?" Trip said as soon as he accepted the call.

"Heard what?"

"They've found another body—it's on the news."

"It isn't Madison."

"How do you know that?"

"The police brought me in again."

"You're kidding?"

"It's just routine. It's nothing."

"It might not be her now, but it's just a matter of time, isn't it? You know that—she'll be next."

"We don't know that."

"I do."

Milton thought he could hear traffic on the call. "Where are you?"

"In a taxi. I'm going up there."

"What for?"

"To see Brady."

"No, Trip—"

"Yes, Mr. Smith. He did it. It's fucking obvious. It's him. We know he's been lying to us right from the start. What else has he been lying about? I'm gonna make him admit it."

"How are you going to do that?"

"It's all right. I'll take it from here."

Milton gripped the wheel. "Don't," he said. "Turn around and come back. We just need to wait. Getting into an argument up there will make things worse."

"I'm sick of waiting. Nothing's happening. They're not doing shit."

Milton was about to tell him about Efron and what he had learned, but the call went dead.

He redialled, but there was no answer.

Dammit.

The boy had sounded terrible, wired, his voice straining with stress, as if at his breaking point. Milton had to stop him before he did something stupid, something that would wreck his life. He put the Explorer into gear, pulled out into traffic, and swung around. He drove as fast as he dared. Trip was already on the way. Where was he? The traffic was mercifully light as he accelerated across the Golden Gate Bridge, and it stayed clear all the way to the turning onto Tiburon Boulevard. He swung to the south, still clear, and reached Pine Shore without seeing the boy.

He drove inside the gates. There was an outside broadcast truck parked across the sidewalk and a reporter delivering a piece to a camera. Great, Milton thought. He was hoping the media would all have moved on by now, but the new body had juiced the story again, and with the police still floundering, they were going to focus on the place where the next presumed victim went missing. There was nothing else for them to go on.

An empty San Francisco cab was coming the other way.

Too late? .

Milton parked outside Brady's cottage and hurried up the steps. The door was ajar, and he could hear raised voices from inside.

He made out two bellowed words: "Tell me!"

He pushed the door and quickly followed the corridor through into the living room. Brady was on one side of the room, next to the wide window with the view down to the bay. Trip was opposite him.

"I know she was in here!" Trip said, angrily stabbing a finger at the doctor.

"No, she wasn't."

"Don't fucking lie to me!"

"Get out of my house!"

"I'm not going anywhere. What did you do to her?"

Milton was behind Trip, and it was Brady who noticed him first. "Get this meathead out of here," he ordered. "You got ten seconds, or I'm calling the cops."

"Go ahead and call them," Trip thundered back at him. "Maybe they'll finally ask you some questions."

"I've told you—I had nothing to do with whatever it was that happened to your girlfriend. You know what? Maybe you want to stop harassing me and start thinking that maybe if you'd done something to stop her from going out hooking, then none of this would have happened."

That really pushed Trip's buttons; he surged forward, knocking a chair out of the way. Brady's face registered stark fear as Trip raised his fist and drilled him in the mouth. The doctor stumbled backwards and, forced to compensate on his prosthetic leg, overbalanced and slammed against the low wooden coffee table, the impact snapping one table leg and tipping a fruit bowl onto the floor.

"Where is she?" Trip yelled.

Brady shuffled away from him on the seat of his pants. "I don't know," he stammered, blood dribbling out of the corner of his mouth.

"Trip!" Milton said. "Calm down."

"Fuck that. What's that got us so far? Nothing. We need to *do* something."

"We are doing something."

"Yeah? What are you doing? I don't see anything happening. Doing things your way hasn't got us anywhere, has it? It's my turn now. I'm telling you, man, this piece of shit is going to tell me what happened to my girl."

The boy reached down with his right hand, and Milton saw, just in time, the glint of silver that emerged from the darkness of his half-open jacket. He thrust his own arm out, his hand fastening around Trip's wrist.

"No," the boy said, struggling, and he was young and strong, but Milton knew all kinds of things that the boy could only dream about, and he slid his index and forefinger around to the inside of his arm, down until it was two fingers up from the crease of his wrist, and squeezed. The pressure point was above the median nerve, and Milton applied just enough torque to buckle the boy's knees with the unexpected shock.

"Don't," Milton said, looking at him with sudden, narrow-eyed aggression.

Trip gritted his teeth through the blare of pain. "He did it."

Milton kept the pressure on, impelling Trip back towards the hallway. "No, he didn't."

He looked at Milton in fuming, helpless entreaty. "Then who did?"

"I have a better idea," he said.

Confusion broke through the pain on the boy's face. "Who?"

"You're going to go outside now," Milton said in a firm voice that did not brook disobedience. "There's a reporter out there, down the road, so you need to be calm, like nothing's going on—we don't want there to be a scene. Understand?"

"Who is it?"

"I'll tell you on the way back. But you have to tell me you understand. Do you understand?"

Trip's eyes were red-raw, scoured and agitated. He looked as if he had gone without sleep. "Fine."

Milton gave him the keys to the car. "I'll be right after you."

"What are you going to do?"

"Just go."

Milton waited until he heard the squeak of the front door as Trip opened it.

He went across the room and offered a hand to Brady. The man took it, and Milton helped him back to his feet.

Brady went to the galley kitchen, picked up a tea cloth, and mopped the blood from his face. "If you think that's the end of this, you're out of your mind."

"It is the end of it," Milton said.

"You saw—he sucker-punched me!"

"I know, and he's sorry he did that. So am I. I know you've got nothing to do with what happened to Madison."

"Damn straight I don't."

"But I also know that it's better for you to forget that just happened and move on."

"You reckon? I don't think so."

"I do. A friend of mine works for St Francis. Legal department. You said you used to work down there, so once I found out that you were lying about what happened to your leg, I thought maybe it was worth getting her to have a look into your record, see if it stacked up like you said it did. And it turns out you have a pretty thick personnel file there."

"How dare you—"

"Here's what I know: you didn't choose to leave, you were asked to go. Two sexual harassment cases. The first one was a nurse, right?"

Brady scowled at him, but said nothing.

"And the second one was a technician. She had to be persuaded from going to the police. You had to pay her a lot of money, didn't you?" Milton was next to the picture of Brady in the desert; he picked it up and made a show of examining it. "It was an interesting read, Dr. Brady. You want me to go on?"

"Get out," Brady said.

TRIP WAS WAITING IN THE CAR. Milton leant across towards him and used his right hand to reach inside his coat. His fingers touched the butt of a small gun. He pulled it out. It was a small .25 calibre semi-auto, a Saturday Night Special. Milton slipped the gun into his own pocket.

"You're an idiot," Milton said. "What were you thinking?"

He stared out of the window. "I had to do something," he said with a surly inflection that made Milton think how young he really was. "Someone had to do something."

"And so you were going to threaten him with a gun?"

"You got a better plan?"

"You would've gone to prison."

"I don't care."

"Yes, you do. And so do I. And anyway, it would all have been for nothing; he didn't do it."

The boy frowned, confused. "How do you know that?"

"Brady is a talker. He likes to be the centre of attention. He has enemies in the neighbourhood, too, and maybe those enemies like other people to believe that he's up to no good. Victor Leonard and Brady hate each other. If you ask me, Leonard put us onto Brady because he wants to see him in trouble. But he's got nothing to do with this. If he's guilty of anything, it's being a fantasist and a braggart."

"I don't buy that," he said, although Milton could see that he was getting through to him.

"So are you going to let me drive you back into town?"

"You said you had something."

"I do. I have a very good lead."

"What do you mean?"

"I think I know what happened to Madison."

Chapter Thirty-Five

ARLEN CRAWFORD drove around the block three times until he was sure that he was not being followed. It was an abundance of caution, perhaps, but Crawford was an operator, experienced enough to know all the tricks. He knew staffers who had been tailed before, heading to meet a friendly journalist to leak something explosive, only to find that their meeting was photographed and reported, and before they knew it, they were the story and not the leak. There was no way that he was going to let that happen to him. He was too good. And the consequences didn't bear thinking about.

Not for this.

The guys operated out of a warehouse in Potrero Hill. It was a low-slung building in the centre of a wide compound surrounded by a perimeter of ten-foot-high wire. Floodlights stood on pylons, and there were security cameras all over. The warehouse was owned by a company that distributed beer, and the compound housed three trucks. Empty kegs had been stacked against the wall of the warehouse, and next to that, four big motorcycles had been parked. An old Cadillac Eldorado had been slotted alongside the bikes.

Crawford drew up against the compound gate and sounded his horn. The single black eye of the security camera gleamed down at him, regarding him, and then there was the buzz of a motor and a rusty scrape as the gate slid aside. Crawford put the car into gear and edged inside. He parked next to the Caddy and went into the warehouse. The main room had been fitted with comfortable chairs, a large television and a sound system that was playing stoner rock. The place smelt powerfully of stale beer; it was strong enough that Crawford felt like gagging.

The four men were arranged around the room. Their leader was a tall, skinny man with prison tattoos visible on every inch of exposed skin. There was a swastika etched onto the nape of his neck, just below the line of his scalp. His name was Jack Kerrigan, but they all referred to him as Smokey. Crawford had been introduced to him by Scott Klein, their head of security. He had recommended him and his boys as a solution for problems that could only be solved with the radical measures that they could implement. Strong-arm jobs, pressure that needed exerting to shut people up or to get them to do things they didn't naturally want to do. The others were cut from the same cloth as Kerrigan: tattoos, lank hair worn long, a lot of greasy denim.

Kerrigan got up and stretched, leonine, before sauntering across to him.

"Mr. Crawford," he said, a low Southern drawl.

"Jack."

The air was heady with dope smoke; Crawford noticed a large glass bong on the table.

"How's our boy doing?"

"He's doing good."

"Good enough to get it done?"

"He'll win," Crawford said. "Provided we keep him on the right track."

"That's all that matters."

Crawford nodded at that, then scowled a little; he had forgotten the headache he had developed the last time they had dragged him out here. It was the dope, the droning music, the dull grind of the necessity of making sure the dumbfuck rednecks stayed on the right path.

"Wanna beer?"

"No, thanks."

He nodded at the bong. "Smoke?"

"What do you think?"

"Nah, not your scene. All business today, then. I can work with that. What's up?"

"We've got a problem."

"If you mean the girls—I told you, you need to stop worrying."

"That's easy for you to say."

"I have a little update on that, something that'll make you feel better." He stooped to a fridge and took out a bottle of beer. He offered it to Crawford. "You sure?"

"No," he said impatiently. "What update?"

Jack popped the top with an opener fixed to his keychain and took a long swig.

"What is it, Jack?"

"Got someone who knows someone in the police. Friend of our persuasion, you know what I mean. Fellow soldier. This guy says that they have no clue. Those girls have been out there a long time—all that salty air, the animals, all that shit—there's nothing left of them except bones."

"Clothes?"

"Sure, but there's nothing that would give them any idea who they were."

"I wish I shared your confidence, Jack. What about the others?"

"You know, I can't rightly recall how many there were, and I ain't kidding about that."

"*Four.*"

"It'll be the same. You might not believe it, but we were careful."

"They're all in the same place."

"Give or take."

"You think that's careful?"

"The way I see it, the way we left them girls, all in that spot and all done up the same way, police are gonna put two and two together and say that there's one of them serial killers around and about, doing his business."

"I heard that on the TV already," one of the other men, Jesse, chimed in.

"They had experts on, pontificating types. They said they was sure. Serial killer. They was saying Zodiac's come back."

"Son of Zodiac," Jack corrected.

Crawford sighed.

"They're gonna say it's some john from the city, someone the girls all knew."

"The Headlands Lookout Killer. That's what they're saying."

"Exactly," Jack said with evident satisfaction. "And that's what we want them to think." He took a cigarette from a pack on the table and lit it. "It's unfortunate about our boy's habits, but if there's one thing we got lucky on, it's who they all were. What they did. In my experience, most hookers don't have anyone waiting for them at home to report them missing. They're in the shadows. Chances are, whoever those girls were, no one's even noticed that they're gone. How are the police going to identify people that they don't know is missing? They ain't. No way on earth. And if they can't identify them, how the hell they gonna tie 'em all back to our boy?"

"I don't know," he said impatiently.

"I do—I do know. They ain't." Jack said it with a sly leer. "Make you feel any better?"

"Oh, yes," he said, making no effort to hide his sarcasm. "I can't tell you how relieved I am. I would've felt even better if you'd done what I asked you to and made them all *disappear*."

"What happened to them, Mr. Crawford, it's the same thing. They are disappeared. You've got to relax, man. You're gonna give yourself a coronary you keep worrying about stuff that don't warrant no worrying about."

"Someone has to."

"Fine." He took another long pull of his beer. "You worry about it as much as you want, but I'm telling you, there ain't no need for it." He finished the beer and tossed it into an open bin. "Now then—you didn't come here to bitch and moan at us. What can we do for you?"

"There's another problem."

"Same kind of problem as before?"

"The exact same kind."

He shook his head. "Seriously? Number five? You want to get our boy to keep his little man in his trousers."

"You think I haven't tried? It's not as easy as you think."

"Who is it? Another hooker?"

"No, not this time. Worse. She's on staff. He's been schtupping her for a month, and now she's trying to shake us down. We either pay up, or she goes public. One or the other. It couldn't be any more damaging."

"And paying her wouldn't work?"

"What do you think?"

His greasy hair flicked as he shook his head. "Nah—that ain't the best outcome. She might get a taste for it. You want her gone?"

There it was, the power of life and death in the palm of his hand. It still gave him chills. And what choice did he have? Joseph Jack Robinson II, for all his faults, was still the medicine that America needed. He was the best chance of correcting the god-almighty mess that the country had become, and if that meant that they had to clean up his messes to keep him aimed in the right direction, then that was what they would have to do. It was distasteful, but it was for the greater good. The needs of the many against the needs of the few.

"Sort it," he said.

"Same as before. No problem."

"No, Jack. *Not* the same as before. Make it so she disappears. Properly disappears. This stuff on the news—"

"I'm telling you, that was just bad luck is what that was."

"No, Jack, it's fucking amateur hour, *that's* what it was. I never want to hear about her again. Not next week. Not next month. Not when some mutt puts its snout into a bush on the beach next fucking year. You get me? Never."

"Sure I do." Jack fixed him with gimlet eyes, and Crawford remembered what the man was capable of; the man was a snake—venomous, lethal—and like a snake, he needed careful handling. "You got her details? We'll get looking into it right away."

Chapter Thirty-Six

"THANK YOU SO MUCH. Thank you all very, very much. Thank you all. I can't tell you how wonderful that makes me feel. It happens everywhere I go, but it's still special here." The crowd laughed. "If you all will indulge me, I just learned that Fox, God love them, is televising this speech on the Fox News Channel, which means, ladies and gentlemen, that this is the first time that I've ever addressed the nation."

Robinson took the applause, raising his arm above his head and waving broadly, shining his high-beam smile out over the adoring crowd. He walked across to the right-hand side of the stage, paused to bask in the acclaim—occasionally pointing out people in the crowd who he recognised, or those who he wanted to give the impression that he recognised—and then came back to the left, repeating the trick.

Milton was almost entirely apolitical, a personal choice he had made so that he was able to carry out his orders dispassionately and without regard to the colour of the government that he was serving, but even he could feel the electricity in the air. The woman next to him was glassy-eyed and a little unsteady on her feet. The man at her side was booming out the three syllables of Robinson's name with no regard to what the others around him might think (not that it mattered; they were just as fervent as he was). The air thrummed with excitement. It was close to mania.

Robinson came down the steps. A path had been arranged right down the centre of the hall, maintained on either side by metal railings that slotted together to form a barrier. There were photographers there, their cameras ready to take a thousand snaps of the governor in the midst of his people.

Milton knew he would only have one chance to get at him, and he had to move fast. He pushed his way to the front of the crowd, muscling through the throng until he was pressed up against the barrier. Robinson was ten feet away, the crowd swelling until Milton was squeezed even tighter against the metal. He thrust his elbow back to free his right arm and extended it out, over the guardrail, bending his usually inexpressive face into a smile. "Great speech, Governor."

"Thank you, sir."

Robinson bathed him in that brilliant smile and took his hand, emphasising the gesture by placing his left on top of Milton's right. A nearby camera flashed, white streaks blasting across his eyes.

Milton maintained his own smile.

He tightened his grip.

He leant in even closer.

"I need to speak to you, Governor."

A flicker of concern. "I'm afraid I'm a little busy."

Milton didn't release his hand.

"And you need to talk to me. It's very important."

Robinson tried to pull his hand away, but Milton just tightened his grip, taking the strain easily.

Robinson took his left hand away and tugged again with his right. "Let go."

Milton did not. The governor's expression mutated; the fixed grin and the sparkle in his eyes were both washed away by a sudden flush of fear. The security man in the suit, less than five paces away, had noticed what was happening. He started to close in. Milton guessed he had a couple of seconds.

"I know about you and Madison Clarke."

The fear in Robinson's eyes was subtly altered. It graduated from an immediate fear, a response to the physical threat of the smiling man with the cold eyes who wouldn't let go of his hand, to a deeper fear, more primal, more fundamental, one that required calculation to properly assess.

Milton could see him begin to make that calculation.

"Let go of the governor's hand," the man in the suit said.

Milton held on.

His mouth was inches from Robinson's ear.

"I know about you both, Governor. You need to talk to me. Your campaign is going to end tomorrow if you don't."

Chapter Thirty-Seven

ARLEN CRAWFORD followed the governor into the back of the building. He was worried. He had seen the man to whom Robinson had been speaking. It could only have been a short conversation, a handful of words, but whatever had been said had spooked Robinson badly. Normally, after a speech that had been as well received as that one had been, the governor would have been exhilarated, anxiously seeking the redundant confirmation from Crawford that it had gone as well as it had appeared. He would have soaked up the acclaim. This was different; his eyes were haunted, there was a sheen of light sweat across his brow, and the tic in his cheek that was only noticeable when he was nervous had started to twitch uncontrollably.

Crawford hurried to catch up. "What did he say?"

"Something about me and Madison."

"What about her?"

"That he knows, Arlen. He knows about me and her. He said I needed to talk to him, and if I don't, he'll end the campaign."

Crawford's stomach immediately felt empty. "Let me handle it."

"No. Not this time."

Robinson walked quickly through a service corridor. Crawford had trouble keeping up with him.

"He's a crank. We've had them before, and there'll be more and more of them the better we're doing. Please, sir—let me speak to him first. If it's anything we need to worry about, I'll let you know. You speaking to him now is just asking for trouble."

"No, Arlen."

"We don't even know who he is!"

"We'll do it in private, out back. I want to hear what he has to say. I don't want you reporting it back to me, pulling your punches—you do that all the time."

Crawford trailed after him. "I don't understand. Why are you so worried about him?"

"I told you before—I still don't know what happened with me and Madison."

"It was nothing."

"No, Arlen, it was. She just stopped taking my calls. One day, it was great; the next, nothing. It was out of character. I never got an explanation."

"We spoke about that. It was for the best. If it came out... you and her... a prostitute... Jesus, J.J., that would sink us for good. There's no coming back from a story like that."

He stopped abruptly and turned to him. "Do you know what happened to her?"

Crawford took a quick breath and covered his discomfort with a vigorous shake of his head. "No, sir, I don't. But we've been lucky so far. No one has said anything about the two of you. I just don't see the point in pushing it."

"Noted."

"So you'll let me handle this?"

"No. I want to speak to him."

He pushed through wide double doors and into the kitchen that served the conference centre. The doors banged back against Crawford's shoulders as he followed in his wake. It was a large space, full of scratched and dented metallic work surfaces, large industrial ovens and burners, walk-in fridges and freezers, dinged pots and pans hanging down on racks suspended from the ceiling. Chefs in grubby white jackets were preparing the lunch that would be enjoyed by the governor's guests. The space was filled with noise, warm aromas and clouds of steam. Robinson walked right into the middle of the busy chaos; the man to whom he had been speaking was waiting for them at the edge of the room, standing next to the two security guards who had brought him back here. Crawford hurried in his wake, straining for a better glimpse of his interlocutor.

He didn't recognise the man. He was a little over six feet tall and slender, at least when compared to the muscular security on either side of him. He had dark hair and a scar across his face. A cruel mouth. His eyes were blue, crystal blue, and they were cold and calm. There was something unsettling about him. He looked perfectly composed, a centre of calm in the frantic activity that clattered and whirled around him. He wasn't fazed by the guards. He wasn't fazed by the governor, either.

"What's your name, sir?" Robinson asked him.

"John Smith."

"Let's get this over with as quickly as we can."

"I think that would be best."

"So—what is it you want to say?"

"Wouldn't you prefer this to be in private?"

Robinson told the security guards to stand aside.

"Who's this?" Smith asked, indicating Crawford.

"This is my chief of staff. I have no secrets from him. Now—please—what do you want to tell me?"

"I know that you were having an affair with her."

"How do you know that?"

"There was a party in Pine Shore. A fund-raiser for your campaign. Jarad Efron hosted it."

He frowned. "And? How is that relevant?"

"Madison Clarke was there. Obviously, you know she was an escort."

"The governor doesn't know that," Crawford interposed hurriedly. "And he doesn't know who the girl is, either."

"It would be better if we didn't waste time," he said, looking straight at Robinson rather than Crawford. "I spoke to Mr. Efron. He said you were at the party. And he said that you and Madison were seeing each other. I understand that he introduced the two of you—he said that he was a client of hers and then you took a shine to her. I believe you had been seeing her for several weeks. He arranged for her to be there."

Crawford felt a red-hot scorch of anger. Why had Efron said that? What was he thinking? And then, a flash of divination: there was something about Smith. It was self-evident what had happened. There was a deadness in the man's eyes. It was unnerving, a little menacing. Crawford guessed that he could be very persuasive.

"You were seeing her, weren't you?"

"I was," Robinson confirmed quietly. "She's special. I'm very fond of her."

"Did you see her at the party?"

"The governor wasn't at the party."

"Arlen—"

"You know she went missing afterwards?"

Robinson looked at Crawford, then back at Smith. "I had no idea."

Crawford felt a shiver of anxiety.

"She hasn't been seen since."

Crawford stepped forwards. "What does this have to do with you, Mr. Smith?"

"I drove her to the party."

"So, what—you're her friend? Her agent?"

"I'm a driver."

"And so what's this about? What's it *really* about? You want money or you're going to the papers? They won't believe you, Mr. Smith—"

"I don't want money," he interrupted. "I want to know what happened to her."

"Arlen—"

Crawford ignored the governor. "Let's say he did know her, just for the sake of argument. She was a prostitute, Mr. Smith. You said so yourself. Maybe she had money problems? Maybe she's hiding from someone? Maybe she had an issue with drugs? There could be any number of reasons."

"Arlen—"

Smith pressed ahead. "Those things are all possible, but unlikely, considering the circumstances. I waited for her that night. I was going to drive her back into the city again. But then I heard her screaming."

"It was *that* party?" Robinson said to Crawford. "I remember. You dragged me away? She was there?"

Crawford clenched his teeth.

"I went into the house to get her out," Smith said. "She was in a terrible state—panicking, she said someone had threatened to kill her."

"Arlen?"

"This is news to me."

"She ran away and disappeared."

"So she's hiding somewhere," Crawford said sharply. "Report it to the police."

"I did that. But now I think she might not be missing. I think she's been murdered. The bodies that have been turning up along the coast road—"

"How on earth is that relevant—"

"—up on the headland?" Robinson interrupted.

"Yes. You know about that?"

"Only vaguely."

"But your speech tonight?"

"I didn't write it," he said, as if the man was stupid. "I just say what they tell me to say."

"I think her disappearance might be connected."

"You think the governor has something to do with that?" Crawford managed to splutter.

"I didn't say that. But he might know something that could help find her, one way or another."

Crawford felt like he was losing control of the conversation and, beyond that, his tenuous grip on the whole situation. "That is all speculation," he protested. "Dangerous speculation with no basis in fact. And it has nothing to do with the governor."

"Of course it does, Arlen! I was seeing her, and then she disappears. Maybe something has happened to her. Of course it's relevant. At the very least, I need to speak to the police. Maybe I can help."

Smith pressed. "You've no idea what happened?"

"Of course he doesn't know!"

Smith ignored him; he moved around slightly so that he was facing away from him, placing his shoulder between himself and Robinson so that Crawford was temporarily boxed out of the conversation. "If there's anything you can tell me, sir, I would appreciate it."

"I can't think of anything. Really—I can't."

Crawford pressed himself back into the conversation. "What are you going to do?" he asked him.

"That depends. You need to speak to the police. I think you should do it right away. I'm not an expert at these things—crisis management, I suppose you'd call it—but it would probably be best for you and your campaign if you're seen to be volunteering information. Maybe they can keep it confidential, I don't know. But you have to speak to them. I'll wait until tomorrow, and then I'll tell them what I know."

"We'll tell them," Robinson said. "Right away. Thank you for speaking to me, Mr. Smith. I really do appreciate it."

The governor had a dazed look on his face. He shook the man's hand, an automatic reaction after these long months of campaigning, and made his way out of the kitchen. Crawford turned to follow, then paused, turning halfway back again, wanting to say something to the man, something that might make the problem go away, but he didn't look like the kind of person who could be intimidated or bought off or deflected from his course in any way whatsoever. His posture was loose and easy, and he returned Crawford's angry stare with implacable cool. It was unnerving.

Crawford turned back to the door again and hurried after the governor.

He was waiting for him in the service corridor.

"We need to think about this, sir."

"What's there to think about? It's obvious what we have to do."

"We mustn't act hastily. Everything is at stake."

"I have to speak to the police."

"That's a bad idea. A terrible idea."

"No, Arlen. It's the right thing to do."

"Jack, please—this doesn't have to be a threat. All he has is what Efron told him."

"But it's true."

"All he can say is that you were at the same party as she was."

"And I was seeing her."

"No one can prove that."

"It doesn't matter if they can or they can't. She's missing. Those girls have turned up not five miles from there. Maybe this is connected. And maybe there is something that I can help the police with. Don't you think it's possible?"

"No, I don't. But if you're determined, then, all right, fine—but let me speak to them."

"No," he said. "It has to be me."

Chapter Thirty-Eight

MILTON GOT INTO his car and drove. He wasn't sure how to assess the meeting. Had he scared Robinson enough? He was confident that he had. The governor had gotten the message, but it was obvious that Crawford held significant influence over him. There was a base cunning there, Milton had seen it clearly, and he could see that he would try to limit the governor's exposure. How would he do that? Milton wasn't sure. Would he be able to stop him from going to the police? Perhaps. All he had were guesses about what would happen next. Milton had meant what he said, though; he would give them until tomorrow to do the right thing. If they did not, he would take matters into his own hands and go to the police himself.

He checked his watch: six. He was late for his next appointment. He drove quickly across town to Pacific Heights and parked in a lot near to the Hotel Drisco. It was a boutique place, obviously expensive, everything understated and minimal. Milton climbed the steps to the smart lobby, all oak panelling and thick carpet, a little out of place in his scruffy jeans, dirty shirt and scuffed boots. The doorman gave him a disapproving look, but Milton stared him down, daring him to say anything, then walked past him and into the bar.

Beau was sitting at a table beneath an ornate light fixture, a copy of the San Francisco *Chronicle* spread out on the table before him. His glass was empty, so Milton diverted to the bar, paid for a beer and an orange juice, and ferried them across.

"Evening," Milton said, sitting down.

"Evening, English."

Milton pushed the beer across the table.

Beau thanked him and drank down the first quarter of the glass. "That name you got from the Lucianos—you do what you needed to do?"

"Yes."

"And?"

"And thanks for your help."

"I should know better than to ask what it was all for?"

"Probably best."

"You're a secretive fella, ain't you?"

Beau folded the paper but not before Milton saw the news on the front page: an article on the bodies that had been dug up on the headland. He said nothing and watched as Beau drank off another measure of the beer. "How long are you here for?" he asked him.

"Couple days. I've got some work to attend to."

"Anything interesting?"

"Not particularly. I ever tell you about my other business?"

"I don't think we ever had the chance."

Beau put the glass on the table. "I'm a bail bondsman—well, least I used to be. You have them in England?"

"It doesn't work like that."

"Guess the whole thing is a little Wild West. I got into it when I got out of the Border Patrol. Probably why I used to like it so much. I don't do so much of that no more, though, but it's still my good name above the door, still my reputation on the line. An old friend of mine who runs the show while I'm away got shot trying to bring a fellow back to San Diego to answer his obligations. This fellow's got family up here, and the word is that he's hiding out with them. Sure as the sun rises in the east and sets in the west, he's coming back down south with me. You calling was good timing—I was going to have to come up here anyways. Two birds with one stone. Now I'm going to have a look and see if I can find him."

Milton sipped his orange juice. Time to change the subject. "So—did you speak to the Italians?"

"About the other thing? The loan shark? I did."

"And?"

"They did a little looking into it. Like you thought—your Mr. Martinez has been running his operation without cutting them in. Strictly small-time, just a local neighbourhood kind of deal, but that ain't clever on his part. You want to play in that particular game, you got to pay your taxes, and he ain't been paying. They were unhappy about it."

"Unhappy enough to do something about it?"

"Oh, sure."

"What are they going to do?"

"Let's call it a hostile takeover. You just need to tell me where he's at, and I'll see that it gets sorted."

"I can do that. What about my friend?"

"They'll wipe out the debt."

"How much do they want for it?"

Beau held up his hands. "No charge. They'll be taking over his book— that's worth plenty to them. His debt can be your finder's fee. They'll give it to you."

Milton took his orange juice and touched it against the side of Beau's beer. "Thanks, Beau," he said. "I owe you."

"Yeah, well, about that. There's maybe something we can do to square that away. This fellow I've come to take back down to San Diego, there's no way he's going to play nice. Some of the runners we go after, they're real bad-ass until it comes down to the nut-cutting, and then, when the moment of true balls comes around, most of them capitulate. This guy, though? There's always one asshole in the crowd who has to be different, and I'm not getting any younger. I was thinking maybe I could use a hand."

"When?"

Beau finished his beer. "You doing anything now?"

Chapter Thirty-Nine

THE PLACE WAS in the hills outside Vallejo. It was a clear evening, and for once, there was a perfect view all the way down to the Golden Gate Bridge and the lights of the city beyond. Beau could see returning saltwater fishermen out in their boats on the San Pablo Bay and the wide, leafy streets of the town. Beyond it and across the straits, you could see the big iron derricks, the rotting piers, the grey hulks of battleships, and the brick smokestacks and derelict warehouses of Mare Island. It had been a pleasant place, once—Beau remembered coming here with his father when he was travelling on business—but the cheap housing units of plasterboard and plywood that had been thrown up to accommodate the boom years after the end of the Second World War had fallen quickly into disrepair. The seventies had seen the place struggle with race hatred that begat violence and unrest; the stain was only now being washed away.

Beau drove along Daniels Avenue until he found number 225. Hank had given him the address, and Beau had had it checked with an investigator they sometimes used when they had runners in Northern California. It was a small, two-storey house painted eggshell blue. There was a line of red brick steps that led up from a carport to the first-floor entrance. The brick wall was topped with imitation lanterns on the corners, the garden was overgrown and scruffy, and the car in the driveway was up on bricks. It was down-at-heel, the worst house on the street, and tonight, it looked like it was hosting a party. A couple of men in thick warm-up coats were smoking in the garden, and loud music was coming from inside.

"That the place?"

"It is." Beau drove on and parked out of sight.

"A busy place, drink, maybe drugs? That'll make things more difficult."

"I know."

"Still want to do it?"

"I'm picking him up come hell or high water. You don't ride your horse into a canyon you ain't willing to walk out of."

"How do you want to play it?"

Beau looked at the house, assessing it. "You got a preference?"

Milton looked at him with a smile. "Old man like you?" he said. "You go around the back, and get ready if he runs. I'll go in and flush him out."

"All right," he said. "You know what he looks like?"

Smith had studied Beau's photograph on the drive north from San Francisco. "Big. Nasty looking. I'll recognise him."

"Goes by the name of Ordell," Beau reminded him.

"Don't worry. I got it."

Beau held up the cosh. "Want this?"

"Keep it. I'll give you ten minutes to get yourself around the back, and then I'll go in."

Beau rolled the car around the block until he found an access road that ran between the back gardens of Daniels Avenue. It was a narrow street that climbed a hill with broken fencing on both sides, wooden garages that were barely standing, and unkempt trees that spread their boughs overhead. A row of cars, covered over with tarps, was parked along one side of the road. He recognised number 225 from the peeling blue paint and settled into place to wait behind the wing of a battered old Ford Taurus.

He had barely been there a minute when he heard the sound of raised voices and then crashing furniture.

He rose up quickly.

The back door exploded outwards, the limp body of a man tumbling through the splintered shards.

He took a step forward just in time to intercept the big, angry-looking man who was barrelling out of the shattered doorway. He looked madder than a wet hen. He held one hand to his nose, trying unsuccessfully to stem the flow of blood that was running down his lip, into his mouth and across his chin.

Beau stepped into his path.

"Oh shit," Ordell Leonard said.

Beau swung the cosh and caught him flush on the side of the head. He went jelly-legged and tripped, Beau snagging the lapels of his shirt as he went stumbling past him, heaving his unsupported weight and lowering him down to the road.

He was out cold before his chin hit the asphalt.

Smith came out of the house, shaking the sting out of his right fist.

"That was easy," he said.

Chapter Forty

ARLEN CRAWFORD was working on the preparation for the next debate. They were in Oakland, another anonymous hotel that was the same as all the others. They were all high-end, all luxury. All the same, one after another after another, a never-ending line of them. The sheets on the bed were always fine Egyptian cotton, the bathrooms were always Italian marble, the carpets were always luxuriously deep. They were all interchangeable. It was easy to forget where you were.

He put down his pen and leaned back in his chair. He thought of John Smith and his threats. That certainly was a problem, and if it had been left to metastasise, it would have grown into something much, much worse. But Crawford had it under control. He had been with Robinson when he reported his connection to the girl to the police. They had done it yesterday evening. He had called in a whole series of favours to arrange for a friendly detective to take the statement. The detective had come to them to avoid any whiff of it getting to the press. There would be no shots of the governor on the steps of a police precinct house. The process of the interview looked official, just as it should, but the statement would never see the light of day. It would never be transcribed, and the tapes onto which it had been recorded had already been shredded.

The detective had reassured Robinson that there was little chance that his liaison with Madison had anything to do with her disappearance. He went further, just as Crawford had suggested, saying that there was no evidence to suggest she had anything to do with the dead girls. The governor's conscience was salved, and now they would be able to get back to the business of winning an election.

Some things were just too important to be derailed.

There was Smith himself, of course. He would need to be dealt with, but that was already in hand. The background checks had turned up very little. He wasn't registered to vote. He didn't appear to pay any taxes. A shitty place in an SRO in the Mission District. He worked nights as a taxi driver and worked days hauling blocks of ice. He was a nobody. Practically a vagrant. They had two good men on his case now. Good men, solid tails, both with surveillance experience, the sort who could drift in and out of a crowd without being spotted. They had already got some good stuff. The man went to a meeting of Alcoholics Anonymous. That was useful to know. There was no family, but it looked like there was a girl.

That, too, might be helpful.

Leverage.

He turned his attention back to his work. Crawford had just been emailed the latest polling numbers, and the news was good. They were tracking nicely ahead of the pack, and the last debate ought to be enough to nail the lead down. They had blocked out the weekend for preparation. Crawford was going to be playing the role of Robinson's most likely rival, and he was putting together a list of questions that he knew would be difficult if they came up. Forewarned was forearmed, and all that. Fail to prepare, prepare to fail. Crawford knew all the questions, drilled them into the rest of the team, drilled them into the governor. That was a difficult proposition given his propensity to shy away from preparation and rely upon his instinct. Crawford preferred a balance, but...

There was a fierce knocking on the door of his hotel room.

He put his pen down. "What is it?" he called.

"Arlen!"

The banging resumed, louder.

He padded across the carpet and opened the door.

It was Robinson.

"Have you seen the news?"

He looked terrible; his face was deathly pale.

"No," Crawford said. "I've been working on the debate."

"Put it on. CNN."

Crawford rescued the remote from the debris on the desk and flipped channels to CNN. It was an outside broadcast. The presenter was standing on the margin of a road with scrub and trees. It was heavy with fog, a heavy grey curtain that closed everything in. The ticker at the bottom of the screen announced that the police had finally identified all three sets of remains that had been found at Headlands Lookout.

"Turn it up," Robinson demanded.

Crawford did as he was told.

"... the bodies of three women found near Headlands Lookout, just behind me here. The victims are twenty-one-year old Tabitha Wilson of Palo Alto, twenty-five-year old Megan Gabert of San Francisco and twenty-one-year old Miley Van Dyken of Vallejo. A police official has revealed to me that there were substantial similarities in how the women died but declined to reveal their causes of death. The same source suggested that the police believe that the three women were killed at a different location, but then their bodies were dumped here. Lorraine Young, Tabitha's mother, has said that police forensic tests, including DNA, have confirmed that one of the bodies belonged to her daughter. The bodies were found within fifty feet of each other in this stretch of rocky grasslands, hidden by overgrown shrubbery and sea grass."

Crawford felt his knees buckle, just a little.

"What the fuck, Arlen? What the fuck?"

Crawford muted the TV.

The muscles in his jaw bunched as he considered all the possible next moves.

None of them were any good.

"Arlen! Don't play dumb with me." He stabbed a finger at the screen. "What the fuck!"

"Calm down, sir."

"Calm down? Are you kidding? Seriously? Those girls—you know who they are. Jesus Christ, Arlen, you remember, I know you do."

Yes, he thought bitterly, *I do remember.* There were no next moves now. Check and mate. End of the line. The situation was all the way out of control, and it could only get worse before it got better. He had been managing it, carefully and diligently, nudging events in the best direction and very discreetly burying all of this so deep that it would never be disturbed. That, at least, had been his intention. The girls were never supposed to be seen again.

"I do remember," he said.

And then came the recrimination. He should have seen to this himself rather than trusting others; that was his fault, and now he would have to live with it. He had been naïve to think that those dumbass rednecks could be expected to handle something so sensitive the way it needed to be handled. The brakes were off now, and momentum was gathering. There was little to be done, and knowing that, Crawford almost felt able to relax. The sense of fatalism was strangely comforting. He had, he realised, been so intent on keeping a lid on events that he had neglected to notice the pressure that was building inside him. The stress and the constant worry. The campaign, twice-daily polling numbers, the places they were strong and the places they were weak, the governor's appeal across different demographics, how was he playing with the party, how would the Democrats go after him?

His erratic behaviour.

The suicidal appetite that he couldn't sate.

Time bombs.

He had done his best for as long as he could, but it was too much for one man to handle.

And he didn't have to handle it anymore.

Maybe this had always been inevitable.

Robinson gaped as if the enormity of what he was discovering had struck him dumb. "And—I—"

"Yes, Governor. That's right."

"I—"

"You were seeing them all."

"But—"

"That'll have to come out now, of course. There will be something that

649

ties them to you, something we couldn't clean up: a text message, a diary entry, anything, really. Nothing we can do about that, not now. That boat has sailed."

The governor put a hand down against the mattress to steady himself. He looked as if he was just about ready to swoon. "What happened?"

"You don't recall?"

"What's going on, Arlen?"

"You had your way with them for as long as it suited you, and then you put them aside, moved on to whoever you wanted next. The same way you always do. They all came to me. They were hurt and angry, and they wanted revenge. They threatened to go to the press. They asked for money. The problem with that, though, is that you can't ever be sure that they won't come back for more. They get their snouts in the trough, they're going to think that it's always going to be there. It's not hard to see why they might think that, is it? I would. They still have the story to sell. We can't run a campaign with that hanging over us, let alone a presidency."

"*You* did this?"

"I arranged for things to be sorted."

"'Sorted?'"

"That's right."

"You *murdered* them?" Robinson slumped.

"No, sir. You did."

"Don't be—"

"I arranged for things to be sorted. What else could I have done?"

"And Madison?"

He shrugged. "I shouldn't think it'll be long until she turns up."

"Oh, Jesus…"

"It's a bit late for that."

"Who did it?"

"Friends who share our cause. It doesn't matter who they are. There are some things that are more important than others, Governor. Country, for one. I love this country, sir. But I look at it, and I can see everything that's wrong with it. Immigration out of control, drugs, a government with its hand in everything, the way standards have been allowed to fall, weak foreign policy, the Chinese and the Russians making us look like fools at every turn. That's not what this country was founded to be. We haven't lived up to our potential for years. Decades. You were the best chance of making this country great again. You are… no"—he corrected himself, a bitter laugh—"you were… very electable. We would have won, Governor. The nomination, the presidency and then whatever we wanted after that. We could've started the work that needs to be done."

He was hardly even listening to him. "You killed them."

There was no anger there, not yet, although that would come. He had been stunned into a stupor. The life had been sucked from him. It was a depressing thing to see; the sight of him on a stage, in full flow, railing against the state of the world and promising that he would make things right—that, Crawford thought, *that* was something special. Something to experience. But it was also a mirage. The man was a fraud. No sense pretending otherwise. A snake-oil salesman. Joseph Jack Robinson II, the most inspirational politician that Arlen Crawford had ever seen, was just another man selling moonshine.

He went over to his suitcase and opened it.

"Why did you do it, Arlen?"

"What happened was necessary for the greater good, sir. It's regrettable, of course, but what were they? Four prostitutes and an intern. They were expendable."

"An intern? Karly?"

"That's in hand."

Robinson jacknifed over the edge of the bed and, suddenly and explosively, voided his guts. He straightened up, wiping the back of his hand across his mouth.

"It's all over now, sir. You had everything. The charisma, the way you command a room, the good sense to know when to listen and adopt the right ideas. You would have been perfect. Perfect, Governor, if it wasn't for the fact that you're weak. No discipline. I should have realised that months ago. There was always only ever going to be so much that I could do for you, and now, after this"—he pointed to the TV—"we've gone past the limit. The only thing we can do now is try to limit the damage."

The smell of his vomit was strong, acrid and cloying.

Crawford took out a gun with a silencer and pointed it at Robinson.

"Arlen—"

"I'm sorry it's come to this, sir, but I don't see any other way."

PART FOUR

No Half Measures

#4 KARLY HAMMIL

MR. CRAWFORD HAD SAID to meet her at a lookout point in Crissy Field. He had arranged for her to take a temporary leave of absence from the campaign, saying that she had contracted glandular fever and would be out of action for at least a month. That, he said, would be enough time for them to come up with something better, but she knew that she would never be going back. In the meantime, he had promised that he would see to the money, and the rendezvous was so that he could deliver her the first instalment. She had driven up to the park and sat in her car and watched as the sun went down over the bay. It had been a bright day, and as the sun slipped slowly beneath the horizon, the rusty red metal of the bridge glowed brightly in its dying rays. The lights of Treasure Island and, beyond that, Oakland began to flicker, twinkling in the gloaming, growing brighter.

Karly wound down the window and let the air into the car. She took a pack of cigarettes from the dashboard, held them to her mouth, and pulled one out with her lips. She lit it, sucking the smoke into her lungs, closing her eyes and enjoying the hit of the nicotine. The park was empty save for a couple of joggers who were descending the hill back towards the city. The night grew darker. The last ferry headed back to the mainland from Alcatraz. A jet laid down grey vapour trails as it cut through the star-sprinkled sky overhead. Gulls wheeled on lazy thermals. It was a spectacular view.

She saw the high beams of a car as it turned up the steep road that ended in the vantage point. Karly finished the cigarette and flicked the butt out the window. The car was an old Cadillac, and it was struggling with the incline. As it drew closer, she could see that it was dented on the front-right wing and the number plate was attached to the chassis with duct tape. It slowed and swung into the bay next to her. She squinted through the glare of the headlights, but they were bright, and she couldn't make out anything about the driver or the passenger. The door opened, and the driver came over to her side of the car.

Chapter Forty-One

JULIUS HAD A SMALL TV SET on a shelf above the door, and he was flicking between channels; they were all running with the same story. Joseph Jack Robinson II, the presumptive candidate as Republican nomination for president, had been found dead in his hotel room. Details were still sketchy, but the early indications were that he had taken his own life. Suicide. There was unconfirmed speculation that he had been found on his bed next to a bottle of scotch and empty bottles of prescription sleeping tablets. The anchors on all of the channels were reporting the news with the same breathless, stunned sense of disbelief. A major piece in the political life of the country had been swiped from the board. Friends and colleagues were interviewed, some of them fighting back tears. No one could believe that Robinson had killed himself. It didn't make sense, they said. He had been full of life. He had been determined to win the nomination, and now that he had almost achieved that, he was gearing up for election year. To do this, now, to end it all when he had so much to look forward to? It didn't make any sense at all.

There were four other customers in the place today. They were all watching the television.

"Unbelievable," Julius said as he slid a spatula beneath a burger and deftly flipped it. "Someone like that just topping himself? Don't make no sense."

"Goes to show," said one of the others. "You never know what's in a man's head."

The coverage switched to an outside broadcast. It was a hotel. Flashbulbs flashed as a figure emerged from the lobby of the hotel and descended until he was halfway down the steps, a thicket of microphones quickly thrust into his face.

"Turn it up, would you?" Milton said.

Julius punched the volume up.

Milton recognised the man. It was Robinson's chief of staff, Arlen Crawford.

"Mr. Crawford," a reporter shouted above the hubbub, "can you tell us what you know?"

"The governor was found in his room this afternoon by a member of the election team. Paramedics were called, but it was too late—they say he had been dead for several hours. We have no idea why he would have done something like this. I saw him last night to talk about the excellent progress we were making with the campaign. I saw nothing to make me think that this could be possible. The governor was a loud, enthusiastic, colourful man. This is completely out of character." He looked away for a moment, swallowing, and then passed a hand over his face. "More than just being my boss, Jack Robinson was my friend. He's the reason I'm in politics. He's the godfather to my son. He was a good man. The best." His voice quavered, almost broke. "What happened this morning is a disaster for this country and a tragedy for everyone who knew him. Thank you. Good day."

He turned back and made his way into the hotel.

"It might be a personal tragedy," Julius opined, "but a national one? Nah. Not for me. Boy had some pretty strident views on things, you know what I'm saying? He wouldn't have got my vote."

Milton's phone rang.

It was Eva.

"Afternoon," Milton said. "Are you watching this?"

There was no reply.

Milton checked the phone's display; it was definitely her. "Eva?"

"Mr. Smith," a male voice said. "You've caused us a whole heap of trouble, you know that? And now you're gonna have to pay."

"Who is this?"

"My name's not important."

It was a Southern accent. A low and lazy drawl. A smokey rasp.

"Where's Eva?"

"She's with us."

"If you hurt her—"

"You ain't in no position to make threats, Mr. Smith."

"What do you want?"

"To talk."

"About?"

"You know what about. We need to be sure you won't mention"—there was a pause—"recent events."

"The governor."

"That's right."

"And if I persuade you that I won't say anything, you'll let her go?"

"Perhaps."

"Right. I wasn't born yesterday."

There was a rasping laugh. "Perhaps and perhaps not, but if you don't play ball with us now, well then, it's a definite no for her, ain't it? How much does she know?"

"She doesn't know anything."

"Gonna have to speak to her to make sure about that."

Milton's voice was cold and hard. "Listen to me—she doesn't know anything."

"Then maybe we just need you."

"Where are you?"

"Nah, partner, it ain't gonna happen like that. We know where you are. We'll come to you. You stay right there, all right? Finish your meal. We'll be along presently."

Chapter Forty-Two

THEY ARRIVED IN AN OLD Cadillac Eldorado. Milton was sat in the back, in the middle, a large man on either side of him. He had checked the joint out after he had finished speaking to the man on the phone and could guess which of the other four patrons had followed him inside: a scrawny, weasely man with three days' worth of stubble and a face that had been badly scarred by acne. Milton stared at him, and the man had eventually found the guts to make a sly nod, emboldened, no doubt, by the prospect of imminent reinforcements and his opinion that they had the advantage. That knowledge wasn't enough to stiffen his resolve completely, and as Milton stared at him, his confidence folded and he looked away. Milton had wondered if there was some way he could use the man to even the odds, but he knew that there would not be. What could he have done? They had Eva, and that, he knew, eliminated almost all of his options.

The others had arrived outside the restaurant ten minutes after the call. Milton finished his burger, wiped his mouth, laid a ten-dollar bill on the counter, and went to the car. He got into the back without complaint. There was no point in making things difficult for them.

That would come later.

There were four of them in the car, each of them wearing a biker's leather jacket and each, helpfully, following the biker habit of having a nickname badge sewn onto the left shoulder lapel. The man in the passenger seat was Smokey. It looked like he was in charge. He was tall and slender, all knees and elbows, and Milton saw a tattoo of a swastika on the back of his neck. The driver was bigger, wearing a denim jacket with cut-off sleeves that revealed heavy muscle. His badge identified him as Dog. The men flanking him both had long hair, like the others, and they smelled of stale sweat, pot and booze. There wasn't much space in the back, and they were pressed up against him. The one on his right was flabby, Milton's elbow pressing into the side of his doughy gut, with a full red beard and shoulder-length red hair. His badge identified him as Orangutan. The one on his left was different, solid slabs of muscle, hard and unyielding. If it came down to it, he would be the one to put down first. His nickname was Tiny.

They had a radio on; it was a news channel, and the show was dominated by talk of the governor's death. They discussed it with animation, and Milton quickly got the impression that they considered it a tragedy.

The four of them seemed pretty secure in themselves and their ability to keep Milton in line. He noticed that they didn't blindfold him or do anything to prevent him from seeing where he was being taken. Not a good sign. They didn't plan on him making a return trip, and so, they reckoned, it made no difference what he found out. They were right about one thing: Milton wasn't planning on going back to wherever it was they were going. There would be no need after he was through. He would be leaving, though, and he would be taking Eva with him. And if they thought he would be as pliant as this once they had him wherever they were taking him?

Well, if they thought that, then more fool them.

They drove out to Potrero Hill, the gritty industrial belt on the eastern boundary facing the bay and, on the other side of the water, Oakland. There were warehouses, some old, others cheaply and quickly assembled prefabs. They navigated the streets to the water's edge, prickling with jetties and piers, and then drew up to a gate in a tall mesh wire fence. The compound contained a warehouse, and Milton saw stacks of beer barrels and trucks with the logo of a local brewhouse that he thought he recognised.

There were four big motorcycles parked under cover next to the warehouse.

Dog hooted the horn, and the gates parted for them.

They took him into the warehouse through a side door. He paid everything careful attention: ways in and out of the building, the number of windows, the internal layout. The place smelt powerfully of hops and old beer and sweat and marijuana. He watched the four men, assessing and reassessing them, confirming again which were the most dangerous and which he could leave until last when it came time to take them out.

They followed a corridor to a door, opened it, and pushed him inside.

It was empty, just a few bits and pieces. It looked like it was used as a basic kitchen and dining area. A trestle table with one broken leg. Rubbish strewn across the table. Three wooden chairs. Several trays with beer bottles stacked up against the wall. A dirty microwave oven on the floor next to a handful of ready meals. A metal bin overflowing with empty food packaging. Breeze block walls painted white. A single naked light bulb overhead. A pin-up calendar from three years ago. No windows. No natural light. No other way in or out.

Eva was standing at the end of the room, as far away from the door as she could get. There was another woman with her.

The skinny guy stepped forwards and shoved Milton in the back so that he stumbled further into the room.

Eva stepped forwards.

"Are you all right?" Milton asked her.

"Yes," she said.

He kept looking at her. "They haven't hurt you?"

"No," she said. She gestured to the other girl. "This is Karly."

"Hello, Karly," Milton said. "Are you okay?"

She nodded. There was no colour in her face. She was terrified.

"Don't worry," Milton told her. "We'll be leaving soon."

"That right?" Smokey said from behind him, his words edged by a braying laugh.

Milton turned back to him.

"All right then, partner. We got a few questions for you."

"You should let us leave."

"You'll go when I say you can go."

"It'll end badly for you otherwise."

Smokey snorted. "You're something, boy. You got some balls—but it's time for you to pay attention."

"Don't worry. I am."

"My questions, you gonna answer 'em, one way or another. No doubt you're gonna get slapped around some, don't really matter if you co-operate or not. Only issue is whether we do it the hard way or the fucking hard way. Your choice."

Milton glanced over. The three men were all inside the room. Smokey was just out of reach, but the big guy, Tiny, was close. The stack of beer bottles was waist high. The cellophane wrapper on the top tray had been torn away, some of the bottles had been removed, and the necks of those that remained were exposed.

"Who are you working for?" Milton asked.

"See, you say you're paying attention, but you ain't. I'm asking, you're answering."

"Is it Crawford?"

Smokey spat at his feet. "You gonna have to learn. Tiny—give him a little something to think about."

Tiny—the big man—balled his right hand into a fist and balanced his weight to fire out a punch. Milton saw and moved faster, reaching out and wrapping his fingers around a bottle, feeling it nestle in his palm, pulling it out of the tray and swinging it, striking the guy on the side of the head, just above his ear. He staggered a little, more from shock than from anything else, and Milton struck the bottle against the wall and smashed it apart, beer splashing up his arm, and then closed in and jabbed the jagged end of the bottle into the man's shoulder, then stabbed it into his cheek, twisting it, chewing up the flesh. He dropped the bloodied shards, grabbed Tiny by the shoulders and pulled him in close, driving his knee into his groin, then dropped him down onto the floor.

Three seconds, start to finish.

"The fucking hard way, I guess," he said. He wasn't even breathing hard.

Smokey pulled a revolver from his waistband and brought it up. "Get back. Over there. Against the wall."

Milton knew he wouldn't be able to take them all out, but that wasn't what he had in mind. He just wanted a moment alone with Eva. He knew they wouldn't kill him, not yet. They needed some answers before they could think about that, and he wasn't minded to give them any. He did as he was told and stepped back. The man waved the revolver, and he kept going until he was at the rear of the room, next to Eva and Karly.

"Get him out of here," Smokey said to the Orangutan and Dog, pointing at the stricken Tiny. They helped him up, blood running freely from the grisly rent in his cheek, and half-dragged him out into the corridor beyond.

"Last chance," Milton said.

"For what?" Smokey yelled at him.

"To let us out."

"Or?"

"I'll make what just happened to him look like a love bite."

His bravado seemed to confuse, and then amuse, the man. "Are you out of your fucking mind? Look at you—look where you are. You're fucked, brother. You can have a couple of hours to think about that until a friend of ours gets here."

"Mr. Crawford?"

"That's right. Mr Crawford. He wants to speak to you. But then that'll be the end of it after that. You're done. Finished."

Chapter Forty-Three

MILTON TRIED THE DOOR. It was locked. He paused for a moment, thinking. He could hear the deep, muffled boom of the foghorns from outside. Eva came to him. "Jesus, John," she said. "Look at you." She pointed to a spot on his shirt. "Is that yours?"

He looked down. A patch of blood. "No. I'm fine. It's his."

She turned to the front of the room and the splatter of blood across the bare concrete floor. Her face whitened as she took it in and what it meant. He could read her mind: the horror at what he was capable of doing, the ease and efficiency with which he had maimed the man. How did someone like him, so quiet and closed-in, explode with such a terrifying eruption of violence? How did he even have it in him? Milton recognised the look that she was giving him. He had seen it before. He knew that it would presage a change in the way that she felt about him. She was going to have to see more of it, too, before the day was over. Worse things. It couldn't possibly be the same afterwards. Tenderness and intimacy would be the first casualties of what he was going to have to do to get them out.

"Don't worry," he said. "It's fine. I'm going to get us out."

"Don't worry? John—?"

"Are you sure you're all right? They didn't hurt you?"

"No. They just threw me in here. They asked me a few questions about you, but that was it."

"What kind of questions?"

"Who you are, what you do, how long I've known you."

He took her by the shoulders. "I'm very sorry," he said, looking into her eyes. She flinched a little. "You should never have been involved. I don't know how they found out about you. They must've been following me."

"I don't understand why, though? Why would they follow you? What have you done?"

"Nothing."

"What you did to that man—Jesus, John, you fucked him up—are you some sort of criminal?"

"No."

"Then what?"

"It's to do with the girls they've found."

"Which girls? The ones on the beach?"

"I know who did it."

"Who?"

"Governor Robinson," the other girl, Karly, answered. "Right?"

"Do you know him?" Milton asked.

"I worked for him."

"And you had a relationship with him?"

She nodded.

Milton asked her to explain what had happened and she did: how Robinson had discarded her, how she had gone to Crawford for help, and how the bikers had abducted her and brought her here.

"You know he's dead?"

"No," Karly said, her mouth falling open.

"What do you mean?" Eva said.

"This morning. They found him in his hotel room. They're saying suicide, but I don't think it was that. Robinson was seeing the three girls they've found up on Headlands Lookout. I'm guessing the same thing happened with them as happened to you, Karly."

"He killed them?"

"I doubt he knew anything about it. Crawford found out about them, maybe they threatened to expose Robinson, and he covered everything up. I spoke to Robinson yesterday afternoon and told him I knew about him and Madison. I said if he didn't go to the police and tell them that he was seeing her, then I'd do it for him. The names of the girls came out this morning. If I had to guess, I'd say he found out. It wouldn't have been difficult to work out what had happened to them after that. He went to Crawford and confronted him, and Crawford killed him."

Eva listened, and as he explained more, her disbelief was replaced with incredulity. "So who are these men?"

"They're working with Crawford."

Eva's brow clenched angrily. "None of this has anything to do with me."

"I know it doesn't. They took you to get my attention. They've got it now, but they're going to wish they hadn't."

"John—look around. We're stuck."

"No, we're not. These boys aren't the smartest. There are plenty of things we can use in here."

She picked up a utensil from the table. "A plastic knife isn't going to do us much use against a gun, and I doubt they'll let you come at them with a bottle again."

He picked up a roll of duct tape from the table. "I can do better than a plastic knife."

HE DIDN'T KNOW how long they had. Two hours, Smokey had said, but it might have been more or it might have been less, and he wasn't sure how much time had already passed. He had to make his move now. Milton went to the stack of beer, tore away the rest of the cellophane wrapper on the top tray and took out three bottles. He took the duct tape and wrapped each bottle, running the tape around it tightly until they were completely sealed. He needed to make sure the caps didn't pop off. A little resin would have been perfect, but that was asking for too much. This should work well enough. It was the best he could do.

He opened the microwave and stood the bottles neatly inside.

"What are you doing?" Eva asked him.

"Creating a diversion." He closed the microwave door. "I've seen four men. One of them won't be a problem, so that makes three. Have you seen any more?"

"No."

"Karly?"

"Four, I think."

"Did you see any guns?"

"He had a gun."

"I mean big guns—a shotgun, anything like that?"

"I didn't see anything."

"I think I saw one," Karly said.

"Are you sure?"

"Pretty sure. Yes. I'm sure."

They would be wary of him now. It wasn't going to be easy.

"Both of you—get to the back of the room. In the corner. And when the time comes, look away."

"What are you doing?"

"Trust me, okay? I'm getting us out."

"'When the time comes'? What does that mean?"

"You'll know."

Milton set the microwave's timer to fifteen minutes and hit the start button.

He hammered on the door.

Footsteps approached.

"What?"

"All right," he called out.

"What you want?" It was the red-haired biker, Orangutan.

"I'll talk. Whatever you want."

Footsteps going away.

There was a pause. Milton thought he could hear voices. They were muffled by the door.

Minutes passed.

The foghorns boomed out.

He watched the seconds tick down on the counter.

14.12.

13.33.

12.45.

Footsteps coming back again.

"Stand back," Smokey called. "Right up against the far wall. I'm coming in with a shotgun. Don't try to do anything stupid, or I'll empty both barrels into your face."

Milton looked down at the microwave timer.

9.18.

9.16.

9.14.

It would be close. If they noticed it too quickly, it wouldn't work, and he didn't have a plan B. If the man did have a shotgun, he would be hopelessly outmatched. Too late to worry about that. He stepped all the way back, putting himself between the microwave and the two women.

The door unlocked.

It opened.

Smokey did have a shotgun, a Remington. The room was narrow and not all that long. A spread couldn't really miss him from that range, and the man was careful now, wary, edging into the room, his eyes fixed on Milton.

Once bitten, twice shy. He knew Milton was dangerous. He would be careful now. No more mistakes.

That was what Milton wanted.

It was the reason for the demonstration earlier.

He wanted all of his attention on him.

"Change of heart?"

"What choice do I have?"

"That's right, buddy. You ain't got none."

"What do you want to know?"

"The governor—you tell anyone what you know about him and the girls?"

"The dead ones?"

"Them, that one behind you, any others."

"No," he said.

"No police?"

"No police."

"What about her?" he said, chin-nodding towards Eva. "You tell her?"

"No," he said. "She doesn't know anything."

"You tell anyone else?"

"I told you—no one knows but me."

"All right, then. That's good. How'd you find out?"

"I had a chat with Jarad Efron."

"A chat? What does that mean?"

"I dangled him off a balcony. He realised it'd be better to talk to me."

"Think you're a tough guy?"

"I'm nothing special."

"I ain't scared of you."

"You shouldn't be. You've got a shotgun."

"Damn straight I do."

"So why would you be scared?"

Milton glanced down at the microwave.

7.17.

7.16.

7.15.

"You want to tell me what happened to the girls?" he asked.

"Obvious, ain't it?"

"They wanted money."

"That's right." He flicked the barrel of the shotgun in Karly's direction. "She wanted money."

"And then you killed them?"

"They brought it on themselves."

"Who told you to do it? Robinson?"

"Hell no. Robinson didn't know nothing about none of this shit. We took care of it on his behalf."

"Crawford, then?"

"That's right. Crawford and us, we just been cleaning up the governor's mess is what we been doing. He had his problems, y'all can see that plain as day, but that there was one great man. Would've been damn good for this fucked-up country. What's happened to him is a tragedy. Your fault, the way I see it. What you've done—digging your nose into business that don't concern you, making trouble—well, old partner, that's something you're gonna have to account for, and the accounting's gonna be scrupulous."

"What about Madison Clarke?"

"Who?"

"Another hooker. The governor was seeing her."

"This the girl you took up to the party in Pine Shore?"

"That's right. You all came out that night, didn't you?"

"That's right."

"You find her?"

"You know what? We didn't. We don't know where she is."

Milton glanced down at the microwave.

6.24.

6.23.

6.22.

Come on, come on, come on.

"We don't need to do this, right?" he said, trying to buy them just a little more time. "I'm not going to say anything. You know where I live."

Smokey laughed. "Nah, that ain't gonna cut it. We don't never leave loose ends, and that's what y'all are."

5.33.

5.32.

5.31.

Smokey noticed Milton looking down at the microwave.

"Fuck you doing with that?" he said.

"I was hungry. I thought—"

"Fuck *that*."

He stepped towards it.

"Please," Milton said.

The man reached out for the stop button.

He saw the beer bottles inside, turning around on the platter: incongruous.

Too late.

The liquid inside the bottles was evaporating into steam; several atmospheres of pressure were being generated; the duct tape was holding the caps in place; the pressure was running up against the capacity of the bottles. Just at that precise moment there was no more space for it to go. It was fortunate; it couldn't have been better timing. The bottles exploded with the same force as a quarter-stick of dynamite. The microwave was obliterated from the inside out. The glass in the door was flung across the room in a shower of razored slivers, the frame of the door cartwheeled away, the metal body was broken apart, rivets and screws popping out. Smokey was looking right at it, close, as it exploded; a parabola of debris enveloped his head, the barrage of tiny fragments slicing into his eyes and the skin of his face, his scalp, piercing his clothes and flesh.

Milton was further away, yet the blast from the explosion staggered him backwards, and instants later, the red-hot shower peppered his skin. His bare arms were crossed with a thin bloody lattice as he dropped his arm from his face and moved forwards.

He looked back quickly. "You all right?"

Neither Eva nor Karly answered, but he didn't see any obvious damage.

He turned back. Smokey was on the floor, covered in blood. A large triangular shard from the microwave's metal case was halfway visible in his trachea. He was gurgling, and air whistled in and out of the tear in his throat. One leg twitched spastically. Milton didn't need to examine him to know that he only had a minute or two to live.

The Remington was abandoned at his side.

Milton took it and brought it up. He heard hurried footsteps and ragged breathing and saw a momentary reflection in the long blank window that started in the corridor opposite the door. He aimed blind around the door and pulled one trigger, blowing buckshot into one of the other men from less than three feet away. Milton turned quickly into the corridor, the shotgun up and ready, and stepped over the second man's body. He was dead. Half his face was gone.

Three down.

One left.

He moved low and fast, the shotgun held out straight. The corridor led into a main room with sofas, a jukebox, empty bottles and dope paraphernalia.

The fourth man popped out of cover behind the sofa and fired.

Milton dropped flat, rolled three times to the right, opening the angle and negating the cover, and pulled the trigger. Half of the buckshot shredded the sofa, the other half perforated the man from head to toe. He dropped his revolver and hit the floor with a weighty thud.

He got up. Save the cuts and grazes from the explosion, he was unmarked.

He went back to the kitchen.

Smokey was dead on the floor.

Eva and Karly hadn't moved.

"It's over," he told them.

Eva bit her lip. "Are you all right?"

"I'm good. You?"

"Yes."

"Both of you?"

"I'm fine," Karly said.

He turned to Eva. "You both need to get out of here. We're in Potrero Hill. I'll open the gates for you, and you need to get out. Find somewhere safe, somewhere with lots of people, and call the police. Do you understand?"

"What about you?"

"There's someone I have to see."

Chapter Forty-Four

ARLEN CRAWFORD waited impatiently for the hotel lift to bear him down to the parking garage. He had his suitcase in his right hand and his overcoat folded in the crook of his left arm. The car had stopped at every floor on the way down from the tenth, but it was empty now, just Crawford and the numb terror that events had clattered hopelessly out of control. He took his cellphone from his pocket and tried to call Jack Kerrigan again. There had been no reply the first and second time that he had tried, but this time, the call was answered.

"Jack! Smokey!" he said. "What the fuck's going on?"

"Smokey's dead, Mr. Crawford. His friends are dead, too."

"Who is this?"

"You know who this is."

The elevator reached the basement, and the doors opened.

"Mr. Smith?"

"That's right."

"What do you want, Mr. Smith? Money?"

"No."

"What do you want?"

"Justice would be a good place to start."

"Jack killed the girls."

"We both know that's only half of the job done."

He aimed the fob across the parking lot and thumbed the button. The car doors unlocked and the lights flashed.

"I didn't have anything to do with it. There's no proof."

"Maybe not. But that would only be a problem if I was going to go to the police. I'm not going to go to the police, Mr. Crawford."

"What are you going to do?"

No answer.

"What are you going to do?"

Silence.

Crawford reached the car and opened the driver's door. He tossed the phone across the car onto the passenger seat. He went around and put the suitcase in the trunk. He got inside the car, took a moment to gather his breath, stepped on the clutch, and pressed the ignition.

He felt a small, cold point of metal pressing against the back of his head.

He looked up into the rear-view mirror.

It was dark in the basement, just the glow of the sconced lights on the wall. The modest brightness fell across one half of the face of the man who was holding the gun. The other half was obscured by shadow. He recognised him: the impassive and serious face, the cruel mouth, the scar running horizontally across his face.

"Drive."

PART FIVE

Collateral

Chapter Forty-Five

THE MEETING on the third anniversary of Milton's sobriety was a Big Book meeting. They were peaceful weekly gatherings, the format more relaxed than usual, and Milton usually enjoyed them. They placed tea lights around the room, and someone had lit a joss stick (that had been the subject of a heated argument; a couple of the regulars had opined that it was a little too intoxicating for a roomful of recovering alkies and druggies). Every week, they each opened a copy of the book of advice that Bill Wilson, the founder of the program, had written, read five or six pages out loud and then discussed what it meant to them all. After a year they would have worked their way through it and then they would turn back to the start and begin again. Milton had initially thought the book was an embarrassingly twee self-help screed, and it was certainly true that it was packed full of platitudes, but the more he grew familiar with it, the easier it was to ignore the homilies and clichés and concentrate on the advice on how to live a worthwhile, sober life. Now he often read a paragraph or two before he went to sleep at night. It was good meditation.

The reading took fifteen minutes and then the discussion another thirty. The final fifteen minutes were dedicated to those who felt that they needed to share.

Richie Grimes raised his hand.

"Hey," he said. "My name's Richie, and I'm an alcoholic."

"Hi, Richie," they said together.

"You know about my problem—I've gone on about it enough. But I'm here today to give thanks." He paused and looked behind him; he was looking for Milton. "I don't rightly know what happened, but the man I owed money to has sold his book, and the guys who bought it off him don't look like they're going to come after me for what I owe. I might be setting myself up for a fall, but it's starting to look to me like someone paid that debt off for me." He shook his head. "You know, I was talking to a friend here after I did my share last week. I won't say who he was—anonymity, all that—but he told me to trust my Higher Power. If I didn't know any better, I'd say he was right. My Higher Power has intervened, like we say it will if we ask for help, because if it wasn't that, then I don't know what the hell it was."

There was a moment of silence and then loud applause.

"Thank you for sharing," Smulders said when it had died down. "Anyone else?"

Milton raised his own hand.

Smulders cocked an eyebrow in surprise. "John?"

"My name is John, and I'm an alcoholic," Milton said.

"Hello, John."

"There's something I need to share, too. If I don't get it off my chest, I know I'll be back on the booze eventually. I thought I could keep it in, but… I know that I can't."

He paused.

Richie turned and looked at him expectantly.

The group waited for him to go on.

Eva reached across, took his hand, and gave it a squeeze.

Milton thought of the other people in the room and how they were living the program, bravely accepting "honesty in all our affairs," and he knew, then, with absolute conviction, that he would never be able to go as far down the road as they had. If it was a choice between telling a roomful of strangers about the blood that he had on his hands and taking a drink, then he was going to take a drink. Every time. He thought of what he had almost been prepared to say, and he felt the heat gathering in his face at the foolish audacity of it.

"John?" Smulders prompted.

Eva squeezed his hand again.

No, he thought.

Some things had to stay unsaid.

"I just wanted to say how valuable I've found this meeting. Most of you know me by now, even if it's just as the guy with the coffee and the biscuits. You probably wondered why I don't say much. You probably think I'm pretty bad at all this, and maybe I am, but I'm doing my best. One day at a time, like we always say. I can do better, I know I can, but I just wanted to say that it's my third year without a drink today, and that's as good a reason for celebrating as I've ever really had before. So"—he cleared his throat, constricted by sudden emotion—"you know, I just wanted to say thanks. I wouldn't be able to do it on my own."

There was warm applause, and the case of birthday chips was extracted from the cupboard marked PROPERTY OF A.A. They usually started with the newest members, those celebrating a day or a week or a month, and those were always the ones that were marked with the loudest cheers, the most high-fives and the strongest hugs. There were no others celebrating tonight, and when Smulders called out for those celebrating three years to come forward, Milton stood up and, smiling shyly, went up to the front. Smulders shook his hand warmly and handed him his chip. It was red, made from cheap plastic, and looked like a chocolate coin, the edge raised and stippled, the A.A. symbol embossed on one side and a single 3 on the other. Milton self-consciously raised it up in his fist, and the applause started again. He felt a little dazed as he went back to his seat. Eva took his hand again and tugged him down.

"Well done," she whispered into his ear.

Chapter Forty-Six

IT WAS TIME. He had already stayed longer than was safe. He had thought about skipping the meeting altogether, and he had gone so far as getting to the airport and the long-stay parking lot, but he had been unable to go through with it. He needed the meeting, and more than that, he needed to see his friends there: Smulders, Grimes, the other alkies who drank his coffee and ate his biscuits and asked him how he was and how he was doing.

And Eva.

He had needed to see her.

She stayed to help him clear away.

"You hear what happened to the governor's aide?"

"Yeah," Milton said vaguely. "They found him in his car up in the Headlands."

"He'd killed himself, too."

"Yes."

"Put a hose on the exhaust and put it in through the window."

"Guilt?" Milton suggested.

She bit her lip.

"You're sure he had something to do with those men? Those girls?"

"He did."

Milton looked at her, and for a moment, he allowed himself the thought: could he stay here? Could he stay with her? He entertained the thought for a moment, longer than was healthy or sensible, until he caught himself and dismissed it. Of course he couldn't. How could he? It was ridiculous, dangerous thinking. He had made so much noise over the last few days. The spooks back home would be able to find him without too much bother now. Photographs, references in police reports, all manner of digital crumbs that, if followed, would lead them straight to him. The arrival of the Group would be the first that he knew of it. They would be more careful this time. A sedative injected into his neck from behind; a hood over his head before being muscled into a waiting car; a shot in the head from a sniper a city block away. He'd be dead or out of the country before he could do anything about it.

Thinking about staying was selfish, too. He knew what Control would order. Anyone who had spent time with him would be a threat.

A loose end.

The guys at the meeting?

Maybe.

Trip?

677

Probably.

Eva?

Definitely.

"What are you doing now?"

It startled him. "What?"

She smiled at him. "Now—you wanna get dinner?"

He wanted it badly, but he shook his head. "I can't. I've got—I promised a friend I'd catch up with him."

If she was disappointed, she hid it well. "All right, then. How about tomorrow?"

"Can I give you a call?"

"Sure," she said.

She came over to him, rested her hand on his shoulder, and tiptoed so that she was tall enough to kiss him on the cheek. Her lips were warm, and she smelled of cinnamon. He felt a lump in his throat as she lowered herself down to her height. "It was good to hear you speak. I know you're carrying a burden, John, and I think it's very painful. You should share it. No one will judge you, and it'll be easier to carry."

He smiled at her. His throat felt thick, and he didn't trust himself to speak.

"See you around," she said, rubbing her hand up and down his right arm. "Don't be a stranger, all right?"

HE DROVE BACK to the El Capitan for the last time. He recognised Trip Macklemore as he slotted the Explorer into the kerb outside the entrance to the building. He scanned his surroundings quickly, a little fretfully, but there was no sign of anything out of the ordinary. The Group were good, though. If an agent was using the boy and didn't want to be seen, he would be invisible. Milton felt an itching sensation in the dead centre of his chest. He looked down, almost expecting to see the red crosshatch of a laser sight, but there was nothing there. He turned the key to switch off the engine and stepped outside.

"Hello Trip."

"Mr. Smith."

"Are you all right?"

"I'm fine."

"What can I do for you?"

"There's someone you need to talk to."

Milton noticed that there was someone else waiting at the entrance to the building.

She smiled nervously at him.

Milton couldn't hide his surprise. "Madison?"

"Hello, John."

"Where have you been?"

"Is this your place?" she said, rubbing her arms to ward off the chill. "Can we maybe go in? Get a coffee? I'll tell you."

SHE EXPLAINED. To begin with, she edged around some of the details for fear of upsetting Trip, but when he realised what she was doing, he told her—a little unconvincingly—that he was fine with it and that she should lay it all out, so that's what she did.

It had started in May when Jarad Efron booked her through Fallen Angelz for the first time. She had no idea who he was other than that he was rich and generous and fun to be around. They had had a good time together, and he booked her again a week or two afterwards, then several times after that. The eighth or ninth booking was different. Rather than the plush hotel room to which they usually retreated, this was a private dinner party. Some sort of fundraiser. He had bought her a thousand-dollar dress and paraded her as his girlfriend. It was a charade, and it must have been easy to see through it, but there were other escorts at the party, a harem of young girls with rich older men. Madison recognised some of them, but it didn't seem like any of it was a big deal.

One of the other guests came over to speak to Efron. She guessed within minutes that the conversation was an excuse; he was more interested in finding out about her. She hadn't recognised him at first; he was just another middle-aged john with plenty of cash, charming and charismatic with it. He didn't explain who he was, and when she asked what he did for a living, all he said was that he worked for the state government. They had exchanged numbers, and he had called the next morning to set up a meeting the same night. She reserved a room at the Marriott; they had room service and went to bed together.

He booked her two more times until, one day, she was idly watching the TV in a bar where she was waiting for Trip, and she had seen him on the news. The bartender made some quip about how they were watching the next president of the United States. She Googled him on her phone and nearly fell off her stool. He booked her again the day after her discovery, and she had told him, when they were lying on the bed together afterwards, that she knew who he was. He asked if that bothered her, and she said that it didn't. He asked if she could keep a secret, and she had said that she could. He had said that he was pleased because he thought that she could be special—"different from all the others"—and he wanted to see her more often. Mentioning that there were "others" didn't make her feel all that special, but she told herself that he was with her, and that she *was* special; she would make him see that, and then, maybe, eventually, it would just be the two of them.

Robinson had been good to his word, and they saw each other at least once a week all the way through the summer. She had persuaded herself that he really did see her as more than just another working girl and that, maybe, something might come of it. She dreamt that he would take her away from hooking and give her a better life: money, a car, a nice place to live. He had made promises like that, and she bought all of them. She read about him online and watched him on the news. The fact that a man like him, with so much to lose, had started a relationship with her and trusted her to keep it secret? Man, that was totally crazy. The proximity to power was intoxicating, too, and she admitted that she had let it get to her head. He told her that his wife was a bitch, and he would be leaving her as soon as the election was over. She started to believe his spin that, if she was patient, they could be together. At no point did she question how any of that could ever be possible for a working girl. She loved him.

"And then he dropped me," she said. "No warning. Just like that. He called me and said he couldn't see me again. I asked why, and he said it was one of those things—we'd had a good run, he said, we'd both had fun, but all good things have to come to an end. No hard feelings, goodbye, and that was it. Just like that."

She moped for a week, wondering whether there was any way she could put things back the way they were before. She blamed herself: she had pushed him too fast, talking about the future and the things they could do together once they were a couple. That, she saw then, had been childishly naïve. She had scared him off. She called the number he had given her, but the line had been disconnected. She saw that he was speaking at a rally in Palo Alto and had hitched down there in the vain hope that she might be able to speak to him, but that, too, had been a failure. She had found a space near the front, but he had been absorbed in his speech, and even as he beamed his brilliant smile into the crowd, his eyes passing right across her, she knew that he hadn't even noticed that she was there.

Two days later, Jarad Efron called.

"He was having a party," she explained. "A fundraising thing for the campaign. He was inviting people that he knew, CEOs and shit, these guys from the Valley, and Robinson was going to be there, too. He asked if I could come. I couldn't understand it at first, I mean, why would he want me to be there after what had happened between me and J.J., but then I realised, there was no way he could've known how involved we'd been and what had happened since. All he knew was that Robinson had taken a shine to me, so he thought he'd get me to be there too because he thought that'd make him happy." She laughed bitterly. "That's a laugh, right? I mean, he couldn't possibly have been much more wrong about that."

"What happened?"

"You drove me to the house. It was fine at first. Robinson wasn't there.

Jarad was sweet, looking after me—the place was jammed with rich guys, totally flush, and there was as much booze as you could drink."

"And drugs?"

"Yeah," she said, "but I didn't take any. I'm not into that."

Milton frowned, but he said nothing.

Madison said that Jack Robinson and Arlen Crawford arrived at a little after midnight. Milton remembered the town car that had pulled into the driveway and the two guys who had stepped out; he hadn't recognised them, it had been dark and foggy, but it must have been them.

Crawford had been aghast to see her. He sent Robinson into another room and came over to deal with her. He had been kind, she explained, taking her to one side and having a quiet drink with her. He explained that the governor couldn't see her that night, that there were people at the party who couldn't be trusted and that it would be damaging to the campaign if anything leaked out, but as she protested, he told her that the governor was missing her and that he would call her the next day. She had been overwhelmed with relief, and as Crawford refilled her glass, and keen to ingratiate herself more fully with him, she had accepted his offer to do a pill with him. He said it was ecstasy, and although she rarely did it these days, she had swallowed it, washing it down with a slug of Cristal. She realised afterwards that he had not taken his pill and then, after that, that it wasn't ecstasy but something that was making her feel woozy and out of it.

"I asked him what it was that I'd taken, and he said not to worry, it was just MDMA, and then when I told him I was feeling worse, he said it was just a bad trip and that he'd get me a car and take me home. He was on his cell, making a call, and he had this weird expression of concern and irritation on his face. Mostly irritation, like I was this big inconvenience for him, this big problem he was going to have to deal with. I knew then that Jack never wanted to see me again and that Crawford was getting rid of me. I told him that. He snapped at me, said I was a fucking embarrassment and a mistake and a liability and why couldn't I have stayed away? I shouted back at him. I went totally nuts, so he lost his cool too, and when I tried to get away, he grabbed me and told me I had to stay until they could drive me back, and that's when I screamed."

"Do you remember me being there?" Milton asked.

She shrugged. "Sort of."

"Why didn't you let me help you?"

"Because I was out of my head and terrified. I didn't believe Crawford, not then, not for an instant, and I knew I was in trouble. Whatever it was he'd given me was seriously messing me up. I didn't even know where I was. I just felt like I was underwater, and I kept trying to swim up, I was really trying, but it felt like I was going to fall asleep. I remember an argument, men shouting at each other, and then I knew I had to get out of there, right that instant, before it got worse and I couldn't move, and so I took off." She paused, frowning as she tried to remember what had happened next. "I know I went to a house over the road. There are bits after that that are a complete blank. The pill, whatever it was, it totally wiped me out. I woke up in the woods behind the houses. Five, six in the morning. Freezing cold. There was no way I was going back there, so I just kept going through the trees until I hit a road, and then I followed that until I got onto the 131. I hitched a ride back to San Francisco."

"After that?"

"I've got a girlfriend in L.A., so I got on the first Greyhound the next morning, this is like at seven, and went straight there. I didn't want to stick around. I didn't think it was safe. The first week down there I just kept my head down. Stayed in the apartment most of the time."

"Why didn't you call?"

"I heard about what had happened to them... those other girls."

"No one knew that they were connected to Robinson."

"Yeah," she said. "But it freaked me out. It just felt a little close to home. And then when they said who they were, like last week? I was about ready to get out of the state."

"Did you know them?"

"Megan—I met her once. This one time, at the start, before I was seeing Jack properly, there were two of us. Me and her. She was a sweet girl. Pretty. She was kind of on the outs then, but I liked her. I remember her face, and then, when they put pictures up on the news and said she was one of the girls they'd found, and then I thought what had nearly happened to me, I realised what was going on. I mean, it was obvious, right? Robinson likes to have his fun, and then, when it's all said and done and over, if they think the girl is gonna cause trouble, they get rid of her."

"You could've called the police," Trip said.

"Seriously? He is—was—the governor of California. How you think that's going to sound, I call and say I've been with him, and they ask how, and I say it was because I was a hooker, and then I say I think he wants to kill me? Come on, Trip. Get real, baby. They'd just laugh."

"You could've called me," he said sadly.

"Yeah," she said, looking away for a moment. "I know."

"You have to go to the police now, Madison," Milton said. "It's pretty much wrapped up, but you have to tell them."

"I know I do. Trip's going to take me this afternoon."

They finished their drinks quietly. Milton had packed his few possessions into a large bag. The apartment looked bare and lonely, and for a moment, the atmosphere was heavy and depressing.

"I'm gonna go and wait outside," Madison said eventually. They all rose, and she came across the room, slid her arms around his neck, and pulled him down a little so that she could kiss him on the cheek. "Probably wasn't what you were expecting when you picked me up, right?"

"Not exactly."

"Thank you, John."

She disengaged from him and made her way across the room. Milton watched as she opened the door and passed into the hallway, out of sight.

He looked over at Trip. He was staring vaguely at the open doorway.

"You all right?"

He sighed. "I guess," he said quietly. "Things aren't what they always seem to be, are they, Mr. Smith?"

"No," Milton said. "Not always."

Trip gestured at his bulging travel bag. "You going away?"

"I'm leaving town."

"For real?"

Milton shrugged. "I like to keep moving around."

"Where?"

"Don't know yet. Wherever seems most interesting. East, I think."

"Like a tourist?"

"Something like that."

"What about your jobs?"

"They're just jobs. I can get another."

"Isn't that a bit weird?"

"Isn't what?"

"Just moving on."

"Maybe it is, but it suits me."

"I mean—I thought you were settled?"

"I've been here too long. I've got itchy feet. It's time to go."

He walked across to the bag and heaved it over his shoulder. Trip followed the unsaid cue and led the way to the door. Milton took a final look around—thinking of the evenings he had spent reading on the sofa, smoking cigarettes out of the open window in the swelter of summer, staring out into the swirling pools of fog, and above all, the single night he had spent with Eva—and then he pulled the door closed, shutting off that brief interlude in his life. It was time. He had taken too many chances already, and if he had avoided detection, it had been the most outrageous luck. There was no sense in tempting fate. Quit when you're ahead.

He locked the door.

They walked down the stairs together.

"What are you going to do now?" he asked the boy as they crossed into the harsh artificial brightness of the lobby. "With Madison, I mean?"

"I don't know. We're right back to the start, I guess—that's the best we can hope for. And I'm not stupid, Mr. Smith. Maybe we're through. I can kinda get Robinson, how it might be flattering to have someone like that chasing after you. Efron, too, all that money and influence. But there's the other guy, the driver, I thought he was kinda dumb if I'm honest. I don't get that so much. All of it—I don't know what I mean to her anymore. So, yeah—I don't know. I've got a lot of thinking to do."

"You do."

"What would you do? If you were me?"

Milton laughed at that. "You're asking me for relationship advice? Look at me, Trip. I've got pretty much everything I own in a bag. Do I look like I'm the kind of man with anything useful to say?"

They stopped on the street. The fog had settled down again, cold and damp. Milton took out the keys to the Explorer. "Here," he said, tossing them across the sidewalk at the boy. He caught them deftly but then looked up in confusion. "It's not much to look at, but it runs okay, most of the time."

"What?"

"Go on."

"You're giving it to me?"

"I don't have any need for it."

He paused self-consciously. "I don't have any money."

"That's all right. I don't want anything for it."

"Are you sure?" he said awkwardly.

"It's fine."

"God, I mean, thanks. Do you want—I mean—can I drop you anyplace?"

"No," he said. "I'll get the bus."

"Thanks, man. Not just for this—for everything. For helping me. I don't know what I would've done if you hadn't been here."

"Don't worry about it," Milton said. "I'm glad I could help."

The corners of the books in his bag were digging into his shoulder; he heaved it around a little until it was comfortable and then stuck out his hand. Trip shook it firmly, and Milton thought he could see a new resolution in the boy's face.

"Look after yourself," Milton told him.

"I will."

"You'll do just fine."

He gave his hand one final squeeze, turned his back on him, and walked away. As the boy watched, he merged into the fog like a haggard ghost, melting into the long bleak street with its shopfronts and trolley wires and palm trees shrouded in fog and whiteness. He didn't look back. The foghorn boomed as a single shaft of wintry sunlight pierced the mist for a moment. Milton had disappeared.

EPILOGUE

Chapter Forty-Seven

THE TWO NEWCOMERS came into the bar with trouble on their minds. They were both big men, with broad shoulders and thick arms. The bar was full of riggers from the oil fields, and these two fitted right in. Milton had ordered a plate of BBQ chicken wings and fries and a Coke and was watching the Cowboys' game on the large flat-screen TV that was hanging from the wall. The food was average, but the game was close, and Milton had been enjoying it. The bar was busy. There were a dozen men drinking and watching the game. Three young girls were drinking next to the pool table. He watched the two men as they made their way across the room. They ordered beers with whiskey chasers, knocked back the whiskeys, and set about the beers. They were already drunk, and it looked like they were fixing to work on that a little more.

Milton had been in Victoria, Texas, for twelve hours. He had dropped the Dodge back at the Hertz office and was just wondering what to do next. He still had four thousand dollars in his go-bag, enough for him to just drift idly along the coast with no need to get a job just yet. He thought that maybe he'd get a Greyhound ticket and head east from Texas into Louisiana and then across to Florida, and then, maybe, he would turn north up towards New York and find a job. That was his rough plan, but he was taking it as it came. No sense in setting anything in stone. He had taken a room in a cheap hotel across the street from the bar, and rather than spend another night alone with just his paperbacks for company, he had decided to get out, get something to eat, and watch the game.

Milton took a bite out of one of the chicken wings.

"Good?" said the man sitting on the stool to his right. Milton looked at him: mid-twenties, slender, acne scars scattered across his nose and cheeks.

"Very good."

"All in the sauce. Hot, right?"

"I'll say."

"That's old Bill's original recipe. Used to call it Suicide 'til folks thought he ought to tone it down a bit. Calls it Supercharger now."

"So I see," Milton said, pointing to the menu on the blackboard above his head. "It packs a punch."

"Say—where you from?"

"Here and there."

"Nah, man—that accent, what is it? English, right?"

"That's right," Milton said. He had no real interest in talking, and eventually, after he made a series of noncommittal responses to the man's comments on the Cowboys' chances this year, he got the message and quietened down.

The two newcomers were loud. Milton examined them a little more carefully. One of them must have been six-five and eighteen stone, built like one of the offensive linemen on the TV. He had a fat, pendulous face, a severe crew cut and small nuggety eyes deeply set within flabby sockets; he had the cruel look of a school bully, a small boy transported into the body of a fully grown man. His friend was smaller but still heavyset and thick with muscle. His head was shaved bald, and he had dead, expressionless eyes. The other men in the bar ignored them. It was a rough place, the kind of place where the threat of a brawl was never far from the surface, but the way the others kept their distance from these two suggested that they were known and, probably, that they had reputations.

The bald man saw Milton looking and stared at him.

Milton turned back to the screen.

"Alright!" the man at the bar exclaimed as the fullback plunged over the goal line for a Cowboys' touchdown.

The two men sauntered over to the table where the girls were sitting. They started to talk to them; it was obvious that they were not welcome. The big man sat down, preventing one of the girls from leaving. Milton sipped on his Coke and watched as the girl pressed herself against the wall, trying to put distance between him and her. He reached across and slipped an arm around her shoulders, she tried to shrug it away, but he was persistent. The bald man went around to the other side of the table and grabbed the arm of the nearest girl. He hauled her up, encircled her waist with his arm and pulled her up against his body. She cursed him loudly and struggled, but he was much too strong.

Milton folded his napkin, carefully wiped his mouth with it, and then stood.

He walked to the table.

"Leave them alone," he said.

"Say what?"

"They're not interested."

"Says who?"

"I do. There's no need for trouble, is there?"

"I don't know—you tell me."

"I don't think so."

"Maybe I *do* think so."

Milton watched as he sank the rest of his beer. He knew what would come next, so he altered his balance a little, spreading his weight evenly between his feet so that he could move quickly in either direction.

The bald man got up. "You ought to mind your own business."

"Last chance, friend," Milton said.

"I ain't your friend."

The bald man cracked the glass against the edge of the table and rushed him, jabbing the sharp edges towards his face. Milton took a half-pace to the left and let the man hurry past, missing him completely with his drunken swipe. He reached out with his right hand and snagged the man's right wrist, pivoting on his right foot and using his momentum to swing him around and down, crashing his head into the bar. He bounced backwards and ended up, unmoving and face down, on the floor. The big man reached out for a pool cue from the table. He swung it, but Milton stepped inside the arc of the swing, took the abbreviated impact against his shoulder, and then jabbed his fingers into the man's larynx. He dropped the cue; Milton took a double handful of the man's shirt, yanked him down a little, butted him in the nose, and then dumped him back on his behind.

The bald man was out cold, and the big man had blood all over his face from his broken nose.

"You had enough?" Milton said.

"All right, mister! Get your hands up!"

Milton turned.

"Come on," he groaned. "Seriously?"

The man he had been talking to earlier had pulled a revolver and was aiming it at him.

"Put your hands up now!"

"What—you're police?"

"That's right. Get them up!"

"All right. Take it easy."

"On your head."

"You want me to put them up or on my head?" He sighed. "Fine—here." He turned away and put his arms behind his back. "Go on. Here we go. Cuff me. Just relax. I'm not going to resist."

The young cop approached him warily, moved his hands behind his back, and fixed handcuffs around his wrists.

"What's your name?"

"John Smith."

"All right then, buddy. You have the right to remain silent. Anything you say can and will be used against you in a court of law. You have the right to an attorney."

"Come on."

The fat man wiped the blood from his face and started to laugh.

"If you cannot afford an attorney, one will be provided for you. Do you understand the rights I have just read to you?"

"Of course."

"With these rights in mind, do you wish to speak to me?"

"Not particularly."

"John Smith—you're under arrest."

An extract from the next John Milton novel

GHOSTS

Chapter One

THE VAN WAS PARKED at the side of the road. It was a white Renault and it had been prepared to look just like one of the maintenance vehicles that Virgin Media used. It was parked at the junction of Upper Ground and Rennie Street. The spot had been chosen carefully; it allowed an excellent view of the entrance to the Oxo Tower brasserie on London's South Bank. The interior of the van had been prepared carefully, too. A console had been installed along the right-hand side of the vehicle, with monitors displaying the feed from the low light colour camera that was fitted to the roof. There was a 360-degree periscope that could be raised and lowered as appropriate, various recording devices, a dual band radio antenna and a microwave receiver. It was a little cramped in the back for the two men inside. The intelligence officer using the equipment had quickly become oblivious to any discomfort. He reached across to the console and selected a different video feed; they had installed a piggyback into the embassy's security system two weeks ago and now he had access to all those separate feeds as well as to an array of exterior cameras they had also hijacked. The monitor flickered, and then displayed the footage from the security camera that monitored the building. He could see the big Mercedes S280 that the chauffeur had parked there, but, apart from that, there was nothing.

The second man was sitting just to the side of the technician, watching the action over his shoulder. This man was anxious, and he knew that it was radiating from him. "Change views," he said tensely. "Back inside."

The technician did as he was told and discarded the view for another one from inside the restaurant. The targets were still in the main room, finishing their desserts. The first target was facing away from the camera but she was still recognisable. The second target was toying with an unlit cigarette, turning it between his fingers. The second man looked at the footage. It looked as if the meal was finally coming to an end. The two targets would be leaving soon.

"Group," the second man said into the headset microphone. "This is Control. Comms check."

"Copy that Control, this is One. Strength ten."

"Eight, also strength ten."

"Twelve, copy that."

"Ten, strength ten."

"Eleven, same here. Strength ten."

"Five. Ditto for me."

"Eleven, what can you see?"

The agent code-named Eleven was standing at the bar, enjoying a drink as he waited for a table. His name was Duffy and he had latterly been in the Special Boat Service. Control could see him in the footage from the camera and watched as he angled himself away from the couple and put his hand up to his mouth. "They're finishing," he said, his voice clipped and quiet as he spoke into the discreet microphone slipped beneath the strap of his watch. "The waiter just asked if they wanted coffees and they didn't. Won't be long."

Satisfied, Control sat back and watched. Very few people knew his given name. He was dressed well, as was his habit, in a pale blue shirt and tastefully spotted braces. He held his glasses in his right hand, absently tapping one of the arms against his lips. He had been in day-to-day command of Group Fifteen for several months but this was the first operation that he had overseen from the field. He was a desk man by nature. He preferred to pull the strings, the dark hand in the shadows. The puppet master. But this operation was personal and he wanted to be closer to the action. He would have preferred to smell the gun smoke, if that had been possible. He would have preferred to pull the trigger.

Watching would be an acceptable substitute.

It was an expensive and exclusive restaurant. The wall facing the river was one huge expanse of glass, with doors leading out onto a terrace. The views were outstanding and Control knew, from several meals there himself, that the food was just as good. The bright sunlight refracted against the watch that the first target wore on her wrist and the diamond earrings that must have cost her a small fortune. Control watched and felt his temper slowly curdle. He had been introduced to her by a mutual Iranian friend. The name she had given him was Alexandra Kyznetsov. He knew now that that was not her name. Her real name was Anastasia Ivanovna Semenko and, instead of being a businesswoman with interests in the chemical industry, she was an agent in the pay of the Russian Federal Security Service. She was in her early forties but she had invested heavily in cosmetic surgery and, as a result, she could have passed for a woman fifteen years younger. Control had found her attractive and he had enjoyed her flirtatious manner on the occasions that they had met.

Now, though, that just made her betrayal worse.

Control stared at the screen and contemplated the frantic action of the last three days. That was how long he had had to plan the operation. It was hopelessly insufficient, especially for something as delicate as this, but the role that Semenko played cast her as something of a globetrotter and it was difficult to find a reliable itinerary for her; she tended to change it on a whim. She had only just returned from business in Saudi Arabia. Control had only green-lit the operation when it was confirmed that she was stopping in London before returning to Moscow. The team had then been assembled and briefed. Control had considered the precise detail of the plan and, by and large, he was satisfied with it. It was as good as he would be able to manage in the limited time that he had available.

The second target laughed at something that Semenko said. Control switched his attention to him. He had introduced himself as Andrei Dragunov but, again, that was a lie. His real name was Pascha Shcherbatov. He, too, was Russian. He was in his early middle-age and he was a long-time KGB agent, an intelligence man to the quick; since the fall of the Wall he had amassed considerable influence in the SVR, the successor to his notorious previous employer, and was now considered to be something of an operator. A worthy opponent, certainly.

Semenko clasped the hand of the *maitre d'*, her face beaming. They both got up, leaving money on the table, and made for the archway that opened into the lobby.

"DOLLAR and SNOW are on the move," Control reported. "Stand ready."

Shcherbatov's phone rang and he stopped, putting it to his ear. Semenko paused, waiting for him. Control stared at the pirated feed, willing himself to read Shcherbatov's lips, but it was hopeless: the angle was wrong and the quality of the image was too poor. He watched, frowning hard. Shcherbatov smiled broadly, replaced the phone and spoke with Semenko. Control hoped that their plans had not changed. That would throw things into confusion.

"Control to One and Twelve," Control said into the mike. "They are on the move."

"One, Control. Copy that."

Control watched as Semenko and Shcherbatov headed towards the exit. The pair stepped beneath the camera and out of shot. "Keep on them," Control said, and the technician tapped out a command and switched views to a new camera. This one was in the elevator and, as he watched, the doors opened and the two of them stepped inside. Shcherbatov pressed the button for the ground floor. The camera juddered as the lift began to descend.

"Targets are in the lift," Control reported. "One and Twelve, stand ready."

"One, Control. Copy that."

The technician swung around on his chair and brought up another feed on the second monitor. It offered a wide angle view of the street outside the restaurant. Control could see Semenko's chauffeur. He was a large man, powerfully built, with a balding head. They knew he had a background in the Spetsnaz and would certainly be armed. He wore a pair of frameless glasses and was dressed in a dark suit and open-necked shirt. Control watched as he stepped out of the shadows, tossing a cigarette to the floor and stomping it out.

The lift came to a stop and the door opened.

Semenko emerged into the wide shot first, walking with a confident bounce across the space to the Mercedes. Shcherbatov followed, his phone pressed to his ear again. The chauffeur opened the rear door for his passengers and, as they slipped inside, he opened the front door and got in himself.

He started the engine. Control could see the fumes rising from the exhaust.

The Mercedes reversed and turned and then pulled away, moving quickly.

"Targets are in play," Control reported.

GHOSTS is available now!

GET EXCLUSIVE
JOHN MILTON MATERIAL

Building a relationship with my readers is the very best thing about writing. I occasionally send newsletters with details on new releases, special offers and other bits of news relating to the John Milton, Beatrix Rose and Soho Noir series.

And if you sign up to the mailing list I'll send you this free Milton content:

1. A copy of the John Milton introductory novella, 1000 Yards.

2. A copy of the highly classified background check on John Milton before he was admitted to Group 15. Exclusive to my mailing list – you can't get this anywhere else.

You can get the novella and the background check **for free**, by signing up at http://eepurl.com/M2105

IF YOU ENJOYED THIS BOOK...

Reviews are the most powerful tools in my arsenal when it comes getting attention for my books. Much as I'd like to, I don't have the financial muscle of a New York publisher. I can't take out full page ads in the newspaper or put posters on the subway.

(Not yet, anyway).

But I do have something much more powerful and effective than that, and it's something that those publishers would kill to get their hands on.

A committed and loyal bunch of readers.

Honest reviews of my books help bring them to the attention of other readers.

If you've enjoyed this book I would be very grateful if you could spend just five minutes leaving a review (it can be as short as you like) where you bought the book.

Thank you very much.

ABOUT THE AUTHOR

Mark Dawson is the author of the breakout John Milton, Beatrix Rose and Soho Noir series. He makes his online home at www.markjdawson.com. You can connect with Mark on Twitter at @pbackwriter, on Facebook at www.facebook.com/markdawsonauthor and you should send him an email at markjdawson@me.com if the mood strikes you.

ALSO BY MARK DAWSON

Have you read them all?

In the Soho Noir Series

Gaslight

When Harry and his brother Frank are blackmailed into paying off a local hood they decide to take care of the problem themselves. But when all of London's underworld is in thrall to the man's boss, was their plan audacious or the most foolish thing that they could possibly have done?

The Black Mile

London, 1940: the Luftwaffe blitzes London every night for fifty-seven nights. Houses, shops and entire streets are wiped from the map. The underworld is in flux: the Italian criminals who dominated the West End have been interned and now their rivals are fighting to replace them. Meanwhile, hidden in the shadows, the Black-Out Ripper sharpens his knife and sets to his grisly work.

The Imposter

War hero Edward Fabian finds himself drawn into a criminal family's web of vice and soon he is an accomplice to their scheming. But he's not the man they think he is - he's far more dangerous than they could possibly imagine.

In the John Milton Series

One Thousand Yards

In this dip into his case files, John Milton is sent into North Korea. With nothing but a sniper rifle, bad intentions and a very particular target, will Milton be able to take on the secret police of the most dangerous failed state on the planet?

Tarantula

In this further dip into his files, Milton is sent to Italy. A colleague who was investigating a particularly violent Mafiosi has disappeared. Will Milton be able to get to the bottom of the mystery, or will he be the next to fall victim to Tarantula?

The Cleaner

Sharon Warriner is a single mother in the East End of London, fearful that she's lost her young son to a life in the gangs. After John Milton saves her life, he promises to help. But the gang, and the charismatic rapper who leads it, is not about to cooperate with him.

Saint Death

John Milton has been off the grid for six months. He surfaces in Ciudad Juárez, Mexico, and immediately finds himself drawn into a vicious battle with the narco-gangs that control the borderlands.

The Driver

When a girl he drives to a party goes missing, John Milton is worried. Especially when two dead bodies are discovered and the police start treating him as their prime suspect.

Ghosts

John Milton is blackmailed into finding his predecessor as Number One. But she's a ghost, too, and just as dangerous as him. He finds himself in de ep trouble, playing the Russians against the British in a desperate attempt to save the life of his oldest friend.

The Sword of God

On the run from his own demons, John Milton treks through the Michigan wilderness into the town of Truth. He's not looking for trouble, but trouble's looking for him. He finds himself up against a small-town cop who has no idea with whom he is dealing, and no idea how dangerous he is.

Salvation Row

Milton finds himself in New Orleans, returning a favour that saved his life during Katrina. When a lethal adversary from his past takes an interest in his business, there's going to be hell to pay.

Headhunters

Milton barely escaped from Avi Bachman with his life. But when the Mossad's most dangerous renegade agent breaks out of a maximum security prison, their second fight will be to the finish.

The Ninth Step

Milton's attempted good deed becomes a quest to unveil corruption at the highest levels of government and murder at the dark heart of the criminal underworld. Milton is pulled back into the game, and that's going to have serious consequences for everyone who crosses his path.

In the Beatrix Rose Series

In Cold Blood

Beatrix Rose was the most dangerous assassin in an off-the-books government kill squad until her former boss betrayed her. A decade later, she emerges from the Hong Kong underworld with payback on her mind. They gunned down her husband and kidnapped her daughter, and now the debt needs to be repaid. It's a blood feud she didn't start but she is going to finish.

Blood Moon Rising

There were six names on Beatrix's Death List and now there are four. She's going to account for the others, one by one, even if it kills her. She has returned from Somalia with another target in her sights. Bryan Duffy is in Iraq, surrounded by mercenaries, with no easy way to get to him and no easy way to get out. And Beatrix has other issues that need to be addressed. Will Duffy prove to be one kill too far?

Blood and Roses

Beatrix Rose has worked her way through her Kill List. Four are dead, just two are left. But now her foes know she has them in her sights and the hunter has become the hunted.

Hong Kong Stories, Vol. 1

Beatrix Rose flees to Hong Kong after the murder of her husband and the kidnapping of her child. She needs money. The local triads have it. What could possibly go wrong?

In the Isabella Rose Series

The Angel

Isabella Rose is recruited by British intelligence after a terrorist attack on Westminster.

Standalone Novels

The Art of Falling Apart

A story of greed, duplicity and death in the flamboyant, super-ego world of rock and roll. Dystopia have rocketed up the charts in Europe, so now it's time to crack America. The opening concert in Las Vegas is a sell-out success, but secret envy and open animosity have begun to tear the group apart.

Subpoena Colada

Daniel Tate looks like he has it all. A lucrative job as a lawyer and a host of famous names who want him to work for them. But his girlfriend has deserted him for an American film star and his main client has just been implicated in a sensational murder. Can he hold it all together?

Printed in Great Britain
by Amazon